Where Amaranths Bloom

A Novel of Modern Korea

by

Reynold Spector

February 2009

Library of Congress Cataloging-in-Publication Data
Spector, Reynold, 1940-
She Smiled on Constantinople /
Reynold Spector. – First Edition
p. cm.
ISBN 978-0-578-02793-7

Any resemblance to anyone living or dead is purely coincidental.

The characters and incidents in this volume are entirely the product of the author's imagination and have no relation to any person or event in real life.

The reader should note that one US dollar in 1968 was worth about nine US dollars in 2009.

This book is dedicated to Michiko, the two Fredas and Ethel.

"They ask me where I've been,
And what I've done and seen,
And what can I reply
Who knows it wasn't I,
But someone just like me
Who went across the sea
And with my head and hands
Killed men in foreign lands
Though I must bear the blame
Because he bore my name."

"Back," Wilfred W. Gibson

"For the wander-thirst is on me,
and my soul is in Cathay."
"A Sea Gypsy," Richard Hovey

Prologue

Sergeant Brown abruptly ended the tiresome airport wait. With a deep-south accent and a booming basso-profundo voice, echoed by the microphone in the departure lounge, he announced that the flight to Seoul Korea was ready to board. He continued, "Please note once again that today is September 1, 1968. This is special flight 1121 to Seoul, not Vietnam. This is an eighteen hour flight. Only those who have specific orders for this flight can board. No exceptions. This flight is full. The order of boarding will be: first, general officers, then full colonels and other officers; next noncommissioned officers and finally, other enlisted men and civilians. Please have your boarding passes ready."

One hour later, after a seemingly endless ride down the overlong military runway, the Boeing 707, like a giant silver sea bird, quivered and then ascended through the porous clouds toward Korea, a full fifteen years after the armistice that divided Korea in two. Like its ancestors, the steam battleships, which forcibly opened the Orient in the nineteenth century, this mechanical albatross carried the agents of the expansive tendency of western civilization to the East - the American Lebensraum. But unlike the steam battleships, she left not one or two but four, mile-long, black exhaust trails over the Pacific, symbols of impressive power.

Dr. Reginald Houghton, now Captain Houghton, sat on the empty seat beside the general officer, delighted to be beyond the reach of American civil law.

After a few minutes, the one-star general asked, "On your way to Korea, Captain?"

"Yes, General Samet." Dr. Houghton read the name tag.

"What unit will you be with?"

"The Korean Military Advisory Group, K-MAG. I'm assigned to the K-MAG detachment near Chun Chon just below the demilitarized zone, the DMZ. I understand that incidents occur there almost daily due to the stepped-up infiltration rate from North Korea."

"Yes, that's correct," General Samet replied. "In fact, you will be working for me indirectly since I am responsible for all the K-MAG units in Korea."

1

"I understood that I would report to a Colonel in Seoul in the Army Medical Corps."

"Yes, that is correct Dr. Houghton. By the way, I understand you went to Harvard College and Yale Medical, and you did your internal medicine residency at the Brigham in Boston."

"General, how did you know?"

"I read over the backgrounds of the new officers and senior sergeants in my command. Have you ever been in the orient?"

"No, General."

"But I'm sure you read about your medical advisory duties and Korea?"

"I did, extensively." As the conversation lapsed, Dr. Houghton said, "How did you become a General? What does it take?"

"It takes self-discipline, seriousness of purpose. Have you read Conrad?"

"Yes, in college, Lord Jim, Almayer's Folly, Heart of Darkness."

"Good for you. I am now rereading Conrad. As you know, Conrad places his heroes in difficult situations, in places where there is no cop on the corner. His heroes generally start out with ideals. In Heart of Darkness, Kurtz goes into Africa with notions of civilizing the savages *and* extracting ivory, but over time became a savage or worse. To become a general, unlike Kurtz, you must stay true to high principles in adverse circumstances. You must never step off the straight and narrow, not even for a moment, unlike Conrad's Almayer. As you have read, Korea is a place with few controls for the American soldier." General Samet became pensive.

Dr. Houghton would not admit that, as a freshman college student, he secretly admired Kurtz, that it must have been fun to become King of the Savages. It was at least understandable. Moreover, Kurtz procured more ivory than anyone else. But he knew these were "bad thoughts." Clearly, this was not Conrad's point or was it? Was Conrad showing the "real" man coming "out?"

Ironically, Dr. Houghton himself had *allegedly* stepped off the straight and narrow in America, surely no Heart of Darkness. That was one reason for his gladness to be on his way to Korea. The long arms of American women with their sharp legal fingernails did not reach into combat zones. However, after a moment's reflection, he thought he shouldn't talk about the straight and narrow any more, so he changed the subject. "Have you been in Korea before, General? Do you have any advice for me about Korea?"

"Yes, I had four tours in Korea, the first one in 1951 during the Korean war as a fresh lieutenant, just after I graduated from

West Point. Yes, I also have a lot of advice for you. Try to find worthwhile projects to keep you busy, beside your job. The work of garrison soldiers is generally not hard. At five, everyone disappears, too often to pursue the girls or drink too excess. Moreover, drugs are beginning to show up from Vietnam." After a long pause, he said animatedly, "There are other things. As a medical officer you must also do all within your power to prevent venereal disease." Smiling broadly, he continued, "You are a grown man; do not let your lower brain control your behavior. Excessive sex destroys neurons, right; and increases the chance of resistant venereal disease. Finally, do not drink the local wine. If you ever have a chance, visit a mogali factory, go - you will never drink rice wine after seeing how they make it."

"From my reading, I understand Koreans are not honest, they - how should I say it - shade the truth a lot?"

"Yes, Doctor, they have a different view of the truth than you or me. Sometimes they value harmony over truth. Often things are not what they seem. There is also a lot of what we call corruption - people bribe for promotions, entry into schools, even to see physicians. This is the way their society operates. Moreover, you will see Koreans are often emotional, fractious, factionalized. They hate to lose face. They worry about their kibun, their inner feeling. They often stretch the truth to protect it." After a long pause, General Samet continued, "As you also read, the Koreans are hierarchical; they are hard core neo-Confucians. In fact, they are very different from the Chinese in Hong Kong or Taiwan who are natural entrepreneurs, or the Japanese who work so well in teams. You should go to Japan and Hong Kong on your leaves."

The conversation lapsed as time passed increasingly slowly. General Samet dozed off. Dr. Houghton noted that his old unconscious habit of not calling other men, Sir, was exaggerated by the Army. Becoming drowsy, his thoughts were interrupted by a momentary panic, when, for a single instant, Dr. Houghton was not sure with which hand to salute. But within a second, he knew it was his right hand, and in another second, his body relaxed as the correct hand moved. Having resolved this minute crisis, he resumed his observation about this disinclination to call these army officers, Sir.

The planeload of American soldiers knew marvel and enthusiasm as the great bird raced from Seattle, way above the cinereous clouds. They were going to the safety of Korea not Vietnam. Soon after, however, the men grew silent. Their sense of wonder was gradually replaced by fatigue and then a mood of melancholy as they reflected on the thirteen months to come. Yet, this wistful sadness also passed as they approached Korea, perhaps as a result of visions of infinitely alluring slant-eyed women or your name etched on the brassy patina of a North Korean bullet. They would find the former and avoid the latter. For more than a few, the tour in Korea was a welcome escape from unloved wives or girlfriends, from crimes or ethical lapses, or in many cases terminal boredom. In Korea, still considered a war zone, American wives or girlfriends were not allowed to accompany or visit the soldiers.

As the giant aircraft almost imperceptibly began losing its mighty race with the golden disc across the Pacific sky, Dr. Houghton became increasingly disoriented. Watch time appeared twice the length of sun dial time. The sun's andante fortunately did not confuse the great silver bird. She proceeded steadily on the proper course.

As they approached Seoul, weary and confused by time's paradox, the soldiers one-by-one slipped into individual thought patterns. Some thought only of exotic sex, others of savage mayhem against North Korean devils. Many minds were simply empty. The General awoke for a second, bumped by Dr. Houghton who wiped something off his nose as he dreamed of his first spoken word. As a small child, Reggie often watched his father shave. Playfully, his father sometimes dabbed shaving cream on his nose. One morning, soon after learning to walk, after a large dab, the child exclaimed, "Don't," which astounded his father. Moreover, his father would have been surprised to know the depth of the infant's feeling of frustration.

Images came and went. Dr. Houghton's half asleep mind wandered among "lost" memories. Repeatedly, his mother urged him to behave himself. Soon after, his mother's furrowed brow gave way to an image of himself at a costume party. He was ten, dressed in traditional Chinese robes like the eighteenth century Chinese Emperor Qianlong. In a recurrent daydream from that period, he demanded that his second grade teacher Miss Morgan perform the Chinese kowtow. But she refused. So he hissed an order - forty hard lashes - but nothing happened.

As the great bird approached Seoul, Dr. Houghton awoke and thought of the present; he decided he should do several things in Korea beside his job. He would judiciously pursue a Korean girl or two, but he would not be promiscuous; quality, not quantity. He was certain he could find an oriental counterpart to Miss Galt. When this married lady surreptitiously visited him last month during his "basic training" at Fort Sam in San Antonio, they both ascended that magic erotic mountain that the professional soldiers told him only existed in the East. During that tryst, Dr. Houghton had successfully

4

climbed to the top of that mountain for the first time. Miss Galt claimed she rose so high that she saw archangels but he did not see them. He thought the professional soldiers' views were piffle, especially the notion that there were Oriental women who were "doubles," but he was determined to find out. Could they be correct? If the professional soldiers were right about the East, perhaps he too might see angels, conceivably even seraphim or cherubim - but all this was really nonsense. Or was it?

He would also take General Samet's sound advice. He would keep expanding his medical knowledge. He would study the Korean language; it only had 26 letters and should be easy. He would pursue art, possibly jadeite carving collecting; and find other worthwhile activities - perhaps Korean karate. During his Harvard College years, he became intrigued with Chinese jadeite carvings. He would purchase a carving or two if he could find them. After all, in two short years, at age thirty, he would come into his very considerable Trust. Finally and critically, by the end of the year, he must decide what to do with his life. As a bachelor physician with substantial funds, the world was his oyster, but there was still that one unresolved *alleged* transgression in America..... If true, he had been entrapped.

The now thirsty silver bird, running on an empty fuel gauge, unbeknownst to its 250 passengers, began its slow gradual descent into Seoul.

"No wonder can last more than three days."
Italian proverb.

Chapter 1
Introduction

Sergeant Song telephoned Dr. Barnes to announce that his "turtle," Dr. Houghton had arrived at the detachment. One year ago, Dr. Barnes would have been thrilled at Houghton's arrival, but now the coming of his replacement discomposed him. The end had finally and irrevocably come. Dr. Barnes knew he must return to the United States and his wife. What Puritan emptiness Gail was compared to Miss Koo, with her golden, hairless body and perfect white teeth in that magic mouth.

Interrupting Dr. Barnes' reflections, Sergeant Song appeared in the medical jeep to drive him to the dispensary although it was only a minute's walk. In fact, there was droll uncertainty in Dr. Barnes' mind: Was he capable of the walk? He well knew that his nocturnal excesses of chops, rice wine, and sex had sapped him of all vigor. So many times at Miss Koo's, like last night, he had over-indulged in unknown foods, fiery kimchi and cheap rice wine. After an hour or two, he wanted to claw his protuberant belly which burned with belching pain. Finally, paralyzed by this blazing indigestion, he had to stop for an ounce or two of soothing double strength antacid. Then, sitting on the warm obdul floor with what Miss Koo called an antacid mustache, Buddha-like, he would continue his gluttony, finally accepting passive love-making from Miss Koo.

They would repeat this ritual night after night. Each night, not having learned from the night before that passive intemperance enervates the most, a crapulent Dr. Barnes would reach a state of semiconscious oblivion. Unable to rise or move, he observed Miss Koo tilt him to the floor as if she were overturning a sitting statue. Sometimes she said "bad things" thinking him unconscious. The next morning, Dr. Barnes awoke with an aching, malfunctioning mind. He could not feel his body. He was bone dry; he lacked body oil. The scraping touch of one dry hand on the other would send sandpaper shivers of horror up his spine. Only slowly would the sap of life return, hours later. Thus had Dr. Barnes spent the night before; a kind of joy? Was it schadenfreude? Dr. Barnes wondered. No, that was joy in other people's suffering. Then what was it?

On seeing Dr. Houghton at the dispensary Dr. Barnes almost said, "You poor bastard," but instead mumbled, "Good morning. Did you receive my welcoming letter? I hope it was informative."

"No, in fact, I didn't."

Ignoring Dr. Houghton's answer he continued, "Did you have a good trip here?"

"Yes, but you know, the Korean pilot who flew me from Seoul almost killed us. I never flew in a two seater before. He kept turning around, nodding and smiling at me, not watching where he was going. That maniac flew very close to the tree tops on the mountains. I'm surprised I'm still alive."

Dr. Barnes laughed although not very sympathetically. He, of course, had not written that letter. He was sorry in an oblique way, for he knew that Dr. Houghton would have to adapt quickly; would have to learn new Korean tunes, loud ones, to survive in the cacophonous harshness.

Dr. Houghton thought he was dreaming. He suspected he was in the wrong world; first, the lunatic pilot, and now Dr. Barnes, at best, a dilapidated soldier. Dr. Barnes' dusty, unpolished boots, his dirty, baggy-kneed fatigues, his overhanging belly, his unbuttoned shirt, and his greasy, sun-tanned face with great black bags under his sunken eyes – all this Dr. Houghton could accept, but not the intolerable odor, a debauched stink, that emanated from Dr. Barnes' mouth. Dr. Houghton later learned it was called dragon breath, dragon mouth.

In an attempt to complete the transfer of responsibility as expeditiously as possible, Dr. Barnes walked into his office, lit a cigarette and beckoned Dr. Houghton to a seat.

The smoke from Dr. Barnes' self-rolled cigarette had a distinctive odor. Dr. Houghton thought it was hashish.

Dr. Barnes said, "To give you some background, let me till you what I have done here. Did you get a briefing at Headquarters in Seoul?"

"Yes, but it was not specific or definitive. After it was over, I still wasn't sure what I'm supposed to do here."

"You can do as much or as little as you like," answered Dr. Barnes. "You are the boss here. You have an ambulance, two jeeps, Sergeant Morse, and four Korean enlisted men to drive, interpret, and do whatever else you need to have done." Dr. Barnes raised his voice. "Right, Sergeant Song?"

"Yes, Sir," called Sergeant Song from the dispensary proper.

"As you'll see, the dispensary is adequate, and we can get any medicine we need from the Army. You also have access to the helicopter when the weather is good." Dr. Barnes paused, dragged deeply on the joint, and proceeded. "Your title here is 'Senior Medical Advisor.' You're responsible to Colonel Bennet, our compound commander, although that old buzzard Colonel in Seoul is your advisor about technical and medical matters.

"Your prime responsibility is to be advisor to the Korean Medical Corps personnel in the two local Army Corps whose total manpower is about 125,000 men. They defend about one quarter of the DMZ. We here in K-MAG are collocated with Corps Headquarters which is right next door. However, our compound of about 40 GI's and 60 Korean soldiers is independent and self-sufficient. A high fence encloses our compound and is tight. The only entry and exit is through the front gate, unless you have a super-pogo stick or are an Olympic pole-vaulter. The gate is manned around the clock by the Korean army - we call it ROK, Republic of Korea Army. The gate guards will shoot anyone that even looks suspicious. Before you leave the compound, you must get a trip-tik from the motor pool and sign out. Sergeant Song and Morse will explain all this to you later. There is a strict curfew from midnight 'til four AM.

"We have an officer's club for all ten officers, a few Army civilians, and our Korean lady friends. No American wives are allowed in this area. It is far too dangerous. When I leave, you can take over my quarters which aren't bad except for minor irritations like lack of electricity and failure of hot water occassionally. You should buy an electric blanket; in the winter it is really cold. Also beware of carbon monoxide poisoning. It almost got me once."

"What do you mean?" interrupted Dr.Houghton.

Dr. Barnes answered, "The girls' homes, in fact all Korean homes, are heated in the winter by charcoal briquettes in tubes under the concrete obdul floors, which are covered with a kind of thick waxed paper. If the floor is cracked, the fumes can leak into the hooch. One Korean soldier from this detachment died from it last year. Keep the window open a little, and only stay overnight in rooms where you have checked the floor for cracks. Also, these obdul floor heating systems are uneven and can roast your ass."

Dr. Houghton grimaced.

"At any rate," Dr. Barnes said, "we are off the point. Your job is to advise your counterparts, the two Corps surgeons, in any ways you think best and to visit their medical units with them. They are both medical doctors, although staff men. I advise you to read up on typhoid fever, hemorrhagic fever, scabies, tuberculosis, liver flukes, lung flukes and, most of all, venereal diseases. And I advise you to say little, and observe initially; mainly on the job training.

9

Tomorrow, I will introduce you to the two Corps Surgeons, who are both full colonels in the ROK Army Medical Corps."

"Your second responsibility is to advise our detachment commander, Colonel Bennet, about medical matters that are relevant to the health of the approximately one hundred men on our command. Also, you will carry out sanitary inspections of the mess halls and clubs, the main problem now being rats in the noncommissioned officers -NCO club. Make sure the chlorine content of the water is acceptable, and the like. You'll do sick call in the morning for the compound personnel which, with only one hundred men, does not amount to much."

"As far as paper work goes, once a month you must submit a report of your activities to the Commander here and to the medical colonel in Seoul, your titular superior. The format and copies of my old reports are on my desk. The other paper work is done better by the GI sergeant in theory, but in practice by Sergeant Song. You just read it and sign it."

"Finally, I have been seeing indigent civilian patients here with Colonel Bennet's approval – diagnosing them with x-rays, blood tests as necessary, and treating them with our medicines, all free. We have our own X-ray machine and microscope. I read the rays and interpret the tests. There is a vast amount of sickness here, but you must be careful. Some of the patients will try to hustle you for medicine to sell. One bottle of semi-synthetic penicillin is worth a farmer's monthly income. This clinic civic action program, as we call it, you're free to continue, stop, modify, or do whatever you wish."

As Dr. Barnes' finished his advice on where to refer extremely ill patients, Dr. Houghton looked up when the screen door slammed. Through it walked a tall, slender oriental woman dressed in a short black skirt and a sleeveless white cashmere sweater. Her abundant black hair was neatly arranged in a page boy hair style. He guessed her age as 28 although she was 35. She exuded a haughty sensuality.

"Hello, Docs," she said to Dr. Barnes.

"This is Dr. Houghton, Miss Judy."

"Hello, Miss Judy. Good to see you," Dr. Houghton said and rose from his seat.

With an almost imperceptible bow, Miss Judy shook hands with her eyes slightly lowered, subtly fluttering them. She said nothing.

Dr. Barnes explained that he employed Miss Judy from his own pocket for twenty dollars a month to translate and nurse in the indigent civilian clinic three mornings a week.

Dr. Houghton could not take his eyes off her.

Dr. Barnes was interrupted by Miss Judy who, standing up, peered out the Quonset hut office window. "Oh! Some fogs," she exclaimed, excited as if in this land of innumerable small mountains and valleys, fog never occurred. This charming Korean fervor, even about the most mundane and commonplace events, added a new dimension to conversation. Coupled with this fervor was an explosive tendency to laughter or other emotions. Even after twenty years of interacting with blasé Americans, Miss Judy showed this propensity.   Instead of jumping up and participating in her excitement over the fog, Dr. Houghton asked her with a grin, "What did you say?"

"Some fogs," she replied as she continued looking out the window.

Even a jaded, detrital Dr. Barnes, with the familiarity of long association with Miss Judy, sensed the vital saps begin to flow in her presence. He asked, "How about tonight, Miss Judy? How can I leave Korea without......?"

Miss Judy, pretending to be offended, crisply replied, "Nice talk, GI. No can do."

An unrepentant Dr. Barnes patted her gently on her callipygian behind and asked "Are you really a two hundred dollar a month Yo Bo?"

Miss Judy snarled, "Knucklehead," and she pushed him playfully away.

Sergeant Song brought in three cups of tea. After a short silence punctuated only by Dr. Barnes' sipping noises and a jeep rolling by, Dr. Houghton said, "Miss Judy, I'd like you to continue working in the clinic. I'll offer you the same salary. What do you say?"

Miss Judy hesitated. "I don't know, Docs."

Dr. Houghton spoke more forcefully. "I will not take no for an answer. I'll see you on Friday morning. What time do you begin, Dr. Barnes?"

"Eight o'clock."

"OK then; eight o'clock."

Miss Judy left with a "Good-bye, Docs."

Dr. Barnes said, "I suggest the following. Before lunch, I'll show you around the compound and introduce you to the CO, Colonel Bennet, and the other advisors. After lunch, I'll have Sergeant Song show you the local area, the village, and if you wish, our two local tourist attractions, the silk factory and the rice wine factory." Dr. Barnes' broke into peculiar, ironic laughter and then grimaced. "Then tomorrow morning, I'll show you Corps

11

Headquarters and introduce you to your Korean counterparts, the medical colonels. You may know that your job is supposed to be filled by a full colonel but the regular army medical officers are all in Vietnam; the medical draftees, you and me, are staffing places like Korea." After a prolonged pause, Dr. Barnes smiled wistfully, "Tonight they are throwing my going away party, and you must come. I'm leaving the day after tomorrow. Now let's go back to the base officers' quarters, the BOQ. I'll meet you at 11:30 to see the Colonel. That will give you some time to get settled in."

Dr. Barnes turned to Sergeant Song. "Drive me back to my quarters." Dr. Barnes had to sleep.

After lunch Sergeant Song came to collect Dr. Houghton for his tour of the area.

"Do we need to bring guns, Sergeant Song?"

"Yes, Sir. I brought your forty-five."

"Thank you." Dr. Houghton buckled on his forty-five. He realized he must immediately overcome his Janusian attitude. Boston was eleven thousand miles away. Surely he could drink a little rice wine though he would decline the proscribed food.

As the jeep purred along at the maximum allowable speed of 25 MPH, Dr. Houghton asked, "How long have you been in the Army, Sergeant Song?"

"About two years, sir."

"You speak excellent English. You must have studied English for a long time in school."

"Thank you, Sir. I have studied your language at the University as well as Chinese, Japanese, French, Italian and Spanish. I have another year's work to finish my Ph.D. in romance languages. Next year I will resume my studies when I leave the Army."

Dr. Houghton allowed the conversation to lapse as the jeep continued toward the village. Alongside the badly paved road, which purled over the hillsides and through the valleys, the school children had planted flowers. There were no trees. In this linear flower array on both sides of the road, Dr. Houghton recognized an occasional chrysanthemum and dying sunflower, but the most common flower was a many-colored, long stemmed beauty he did not recognize. Now that the fog had lifted, it was sunny, temperate, and pleasant. Dr. Houghton observed that every nook and cranny was cultivated, mainly with rice paddies. The autumn rice was golden and soon would be harvested.

As the jeep bounced along, from a great distance, the happy, smiling children uncannily recognized that an American was coming. They waved with rapid lateral strokes, the older ones shouting "Hel – lo" and laughing gaily. Even the very young strapped on their mother's backs, would wave. Imitating their wave, Dr. Houghton waved back.

On a hill about two miles up the road, Sergeant Song pointed out the one story clay rice wine factory. Dr. Houghton wanted to see why General Samet so stongly suggested he visit. As they approached the factory, Dr. Houghton thought that the pictures and his reading did not convey what the countryside looked like. The factory and the farmers' thatched homes, surrounded by high concrete block walls with sharp shards of colored glass on the tops, were not quaint or appealing. Trying to comprehend what he had seen and heard in his first days in this land, he now knew he must apply himself in a more systematic manner if he hoped to understand the army and this country. This Korean experience wasn't just going to happen to him. He would ease it along, helping to nestle it into his scheme of life. It should prove a fascinating intellectual challenge.

"Do you want to visit Captain?"

"Yes," Sergeant Song.

Sergeant Song, followed by Dr. Houghton, ducked under the open archway into the barrel-strewn courtyard of the factory. Sergeant Song spoke in Korean to the ancient brewer as their sun-blinded eyes accommodated inside the dingy enclosure. Sergeant Song translated. Then, they entered a small room where the rice was initially processed. Next they passed into a warm humid room with the heavy redolence of intense biological activity and, finally into a third larger room where the rice wine was stored in small barrels or large casks. The whole process did not look very sanitary.

After Dr. Houghton peered into an open cask of slow bubbling, milk-white mogali, he said, "Ask the brewer what the alcohol content is, Sergeant Song."

"Three to five percent," Sergeant Song interpreted.

Dr. Houghton made a mental note that this stuff could carry typhoid fever and hepatitis. There wasn't enough alcohol to kill the germs.

"The brewer wishes you to try some of his mogali rice wine and some kimchi – you know, fermented cabbage - with his compliments," said Sergeant Song.

Dr. Houghton hesitated, but he felt he couldn't say no. After removing his boots, he entered a small paper-doored side room. He noted that the honorable brewer, his chin barbate with a few long grey hairs, was delighted. His dark, wrinkled face was only a smile and nose, for when he smiled, his eyes disappeared leaving only residual slits. A young serving girl brought in three porcelain cups, a shiny steel teapot full of warm mogali, and a small bowl of kimchi. The host and his two guests sat on cushions on the floor, cross-legged, facing each other obliquely on the points of triangle around a tiny round foot-high table. The serving girl poured the milky fluid into the cups.

Dr. Houghton said to Sergeant Song, "Tell the brewer we drink to his health." He drank the mogali. An instant later, he almost vomited the vile liquid. "Tell the brewer the mogali is very good." Dr. Houghton attempted to prevent vomiting by swallowing continuously.

Sergeant Song said innocently, "Please taste some kimchi, but be careful, Sir. It is very hot for some Americans, though Dr. Barnes enjoys it greatly."

With his chopsticks, Dr. Houghton tasted a piece of soggy garlic-cabbage which was dotted with innocuous appearing red motes. Ten seconds later, he was on fire and gagging. This he could not conceal.

"Fill my cup!" he commanded.

Sergeant Song filled it with mogali, incompletely suppressing a smirk. Dr. Houghton guzzled it and kept swallowing. Gradually the crisis passed. As Dr. Houghton wiped away the red pepper tears, Sergeant Song ate several more mouthfuls of the soggy fire, smacked his lips with gusto and chased the kimchi down with mogali.

After a few minutes of silent recovery, Dr. Houghton said, "Tell the brewer, thank you very much." Dr. Houghton then bowed low to the brewer, who smiled. As they were leaving, Dr. Houghton hit his head hard on the very low exit, further losing face. Dr. Houghton surmised that, if he were a Korean, his kibun would be broken. But after the oral burning wore off and the tears ceased, Dr. Houghton even laughed at himself. He wondered how Dr.Barnes could eat kimchi and drink mogali? Was that why Barnes looked so bad and had dragon mouth?

As they drove off, Dr. Houghton realized there would be a few customs he would have to circumvent, hopefully not many. But he felt confident. After all, he chuckled, he was a Harvard man. Dr. Barnes' remarks were straightforward. Close observation and common sense should be sufficient. He relaxed.

As they rode toward the village, Dr. Houghton saw a commotion down the road. "What's going on there Sergeant Song? Let's go see."

"Perhaps we shouldn't, Doctor. It is not important."

Dr. Houghton said, "Stop the jeep" and hurried toward the fracas below the shoulder of the raised road. He walked by several Korean adults watching impassively. Coming closer he observed, through a large cloud of dust, seven or eight young children kicking, beating and biting something with sticks. He was horrified as a closer view revealed a child, the object of their violence. As Dr. Houghton began separating the small Korean children one by one, he realized their intent was malignant, indeed murderous. On the ground lay a bloody, badly beaten but still living nine year old boy. With great difficulty, Dr. Houghton induced the last assailant to loosen his bite on the child's thigh.

The small victim had, on cursory examination, a broken arm and broken ribs. He was also bleeding profusely from his nose, mouth, and head. "Let's bring him to the dispensary, Sergeant Song."

As they sped toward the dispensary, Dr. Houghton put pressure on the bleeding points, all the while reflecting on the insane violence of those few moments. Pogroms in Russia, anti-Christian mobs in China, gang fights in America, witch-burning hysteria in Europe – all were swept aside as not relevant. Here, small children in a mob, their behavior sanctioned by adults, would kill one of their own. Or was the child....? This child was different even through the blood and dust.

At the dispensary, Dr. Houghton stopped the bleeding, taped the two broken ribs, cast the fractured arm and gave tetanus toxoid and parenteral penicillin to the child. He noted the child's hair was dark brown, not black; his eyes were not so brown or slanted. It was obvious that this child was a half-breed. Soon a middle-aged Korean woman appeared sobbing wretchedly. "Are you the child's mother?"

Sergeant Song translated. She could only nod.

"Your child was beaten by some other children and has several fractures and some nasty human bites." Dr. Houghton gave her medicine and directions for treating the child. But he had a strong feeling that she wished he had not interceded, that he should have allowed the violence to proceed to its logical denouement.

"Bring the child back in the morning."

"Yes, thank you, Honorable Captain," the weeping mother finally said, bowing deeply, as she left carrying her injured child.

Dr. Houghton glowered at Sergeant Song. "What the hell is going on?"

"I don't know, sir."

"Yes, you do. Out with it."

Sergeant Song hesitated and finally spoke almost inaudibly. "Dr.Houghton, that boy's father was a GI. That woman was a business lady, a GI entertainer, but now, she is too old. Children like that are not too well accepted in Korea."

Dr. Barnes' farewell party began respectably enough. The two doctors, old and new, sat with Colonel Bennet and the Deputy, Colonel Weave, at the head table. Dr. Barnes was as badly dressed as earlier in the day although in a suit and tie. For Dr. Houghton there was no excuse for Barnes' slovenliness. He and now Dr. Houghton had a houseboy who shined boots and pressed fatigues with creases like green knife edges.

As the meal proceeded, there was only minimal conversation, and Dr. Houghton reflected on his new situation. The most vivid images of his first days, the slobby Dr. Barnes and the striking Miss Judy, the fiery kimchi and the nauseating mogali, the beaten child and the loony pilot, involuntarily lingered in his consciousness. Even at this moment, he could look down and almost touch the tree-covered mountain tops floating beneath him.

The after-dinner speaker and master of ceremonies was Lieutenant Kratkowski, a mighty Pole. Kratkowski, Dr. Barnes' closest friend, was also leaving soon. They were an odd pair, the tall muscular Pole, and the short, dumpy doctor. They were both degenerates, the Deputy whispered to Dr. Houghton in one ear. In his other ear, Colonel Bennet, drunk on ten Martinis, his speech slurred almost beyond recognition, mumbled that they had "raised Lucifer" together.

Lieutenant Kratkowski finally rose. He staggered to the head table, glass in hand. "Order, Attention!" Lieutenant Kratkowski slobbered. He banged on the Colonel's glass martini pitcher with a soup spoon. The din quieted. "Dr. Barnes," Lieutenant Kratkowski continued, "is or was, I should say, a fine man. I remember him when he first came. He went to the corps library every night and read his medical journals. For three months, he was a paragon of virtue, scholarship, and dress. Like Cassius he was lean and hungry. Newly married, he was loyal, faithful and true. But fortunately for all," Lieutenant Kratkowski paused, belched, smiled and continued, "he slipped off the straight and narrow track. Miss Koo came into the good doctor's life."

A drunken voice boomed from the rear. "You mean he was pulled off the track by his middle leg."

Lieutenant Kratkowski feigned severity. "Let's not be gross. As the couth officer, the next guy who grosses, I'll take out and shoot. Anyhow," Lieutenant Kratkowski turned to Dr. Barnes, "as

16

Senior Medical Advisor, you Dr. Barnes have been responsible for the health and welfare of the detachment, and you have performed your duties superbly, mainly by example. You brought peace and love to the compound. As deputy transportation officer, you made the ambulance a symbol of…." Here Lieutenant Kratkowski traced in the air the Chinese character for sexual joy. "Who can forget the five AM emergencies? In gratitude, we have a few gifts for you, tokens of our boundless affection and your year in Korea, the world's best kept secret paradise."

"First, we have the only type of woman worth having, a Korean girl for you to bring home. Even your wife will approve of this one."

The other officers clapped and laughed as Lieutenant Kratkowski presented Dr. Barnes with an exquisite traditionally dressed Korean doll.

"Secondly, we have a pair of suspenders to aid your infirm belt."

The Colonel scowled as Dr. Barnes tried on the huge, red suspenders, tripping over his chair in the process.

"Thirdly, some scissors, for your hair. These were graciously approved by the Colonel from the Unit Fund." Lieutenant Kratkowski pulled out a pair of huge, hedge shears, and made minatory snaps at Dr. Barnes' hair covered neck.

"Next, a few ounces of alcohol, to keep you free of the shakes on the trip back." Lieutenant Kratkowski barely raised a five gallon bottle of milky liquid and said, "This is pure mogali."

When the western yelps and mumbling finally ebbed, Lieutenant Kratkowski continued. "Next, some tools for your practice." He lifted a red, one gallon metal syringe with a huge needle attached, almost putting out Dr. Barnes' eye. Pausing for the cachinnation to die out, Lieutenant Kratkowski then raised a one foot long, five inch diameter cigarette. "One large weed – this is a smoke to remember."

Someone yelled, "Where'd you get that Kratkowski?"

"And finally," continued Lieutenant Kratkowski, "the thing you love the most; I mean the thing we love you most for, an ambulance." Lieutenant Kratkowski raised a toy ambulance, labeled "For Legitimate Use Only."

At this point, Dr. Barnes rose, red-faced and shouted, "Kratkowski, I deny that. That's slander. I never smuggled contraband or women on and off the compound in my ambulance. Perhaps the Colonel should look at ……." Dr. Barnes stopped, looked around sheepishly, and slumped into his chair.

Everyone began shouting, "Speech, speech, speech."

Again, Dr. Barnes rose. Sheepishly, he looked at the Colonel and the Deputy, then at Dr. Houghton and finally at Lieutenant Kratkowski. He smiled, too drunk to stand for long, and said, "I have no regrets." His voice grew louder. "I'd certainly do it again." He finally shouted, "Up yours, Kratkowski," and collapsed on his chair with his middle finger raised vertically in a friendly salute.

The audience gave him a standing ovation of comradely affection except the sitting Deputy who would have liked to court-martial Dr. Barnes. He whispered to Dr. Houghton, "Barnes is a caducous leaf."

"What?"

"The tree of life shed him early."

After the dinner, Miss Koo came. Dr. Houghton joined them at the dimly lit officers' club bar. Miss Koo wore a tight white sweater, highlighting her small upright breasts, scarlet red skirt and red pumps. In a hoarse, deep smoker's voice, she barely said two words as she held onto Dr. Barnes' arm. Although she had a svelte body, she was oily and ugly. In his naiveté Dr. Houghton thought her simply a sexual vehicle. At one point, he thought he saw a tear form in Miss Koo's eye – possibly a tear of parting sorrow, but perhaps it was the smoke and heavy air. After Barnes mumbled some incoherent good-nights, he and Miss Koo left for their final debauch.

Dr. Houghton commented to Lieutenant Kratkowski that he didn't figure Dr. Barnes and Miss Koo.

Lieutenant Kratkowski, with an authoritative, experienced twinkle spoke of their eight months of extreme intimacy buttressed by loneliness, danger, and an oriental kind of love based on her service to him of each and every want. Then he winked and guffawed. He banged Dr. Houghton on the back. "You will see," he said.

Dr. Houghton did not understand this; Miss Koo was undeniably ugly. However, he did know that two days later, while Dr. Barnes was presumably in bed with Mrs. Barnes in San Francisco, Miss Koo was in bed with Sergeant Hanley as a "trial" Yo Bo. "After all," Miss Koo said, "business is business."

"Virtue often trips and falls on the sharp-edged rocks of poverty."
Eugene Sue

Chapter II
A Business Lady

"This Seoul traffic is unbelievable, Sir," Sergeant Morse said.

"Perhaps I should spell you?" Dr. Houghton replied.

"I do not think the Captain should drive in this madness."

"I had an excellent nap. I am refreshed. I want to drive." Dr. Houghton thus reopened the conversation that had lapsed since he had dozed off. This ability to sleep any time, any place, in any position, even in the front seat of an open army jeep, bouncing along unpaved roads, he had nurtured as an intern. At that time, naps alone protected him against the peril and paranoia of extreme sleep deprivation. Even a five minute nap could soothe an intern's monstrous fatigue.

Sergeant Morse brought the jeep to a stop. Dr. Houghton climbed into the driver's seat. Palming the steering wheel, he wished he was in his powerful Oldsmobile, its only similarity to the jeep being the "four on the floor." But knowing that if he looked back he'd be defeated, Dr. Houghton forgot the Oldsmobile. He was in Korea. With Sergeant Morse wincing, he cautiously entered the lunatic Seoul traffic. Around them zipped hundreds of Kamikaze mini-taxis. The huge ancient Mitsubishi buses, remnants of the Japanese occupation, lumbered ahead like old arthritic bulls, coughing out vile, black smoke. As they drove along, shrouded in the worsening grey ground smog, Dr. Houghton knew he faced a real challenge with the sound of screeching brakes and out-of-tune engines, complicated by pedestrians and a legal philosophy of "whoever gets there first has the right of way." A safe passage through this obstacle course was a real test of driving skill.

Sharply contrasted with the maniacs around them were the calm, neatly uniformed Korean Military Policemen. On high pedestals, with their bright brass reflecting the hazy sunlight, the MP's performed elaborate, sinuous rituals indicating which way the traffic should flow. But as Dr. Houghton observed, the Korean drivers paid no attention to their directions. Finally, he said to

Sergeant Morse, "This is unbelievable. There is no order here. Why?"

"The Captain read the army background books before coming?"

"Yes."

"The Captain knows these Koreans are neo-Confucians. They owe allegiance only to their superiors – like their father or boss. There is a strong social hierarchy. You see it in the bowing. The junior bows lower. Anyone outside their hierarchy, their circle, especially foreigners, is a nonperson. You know the good Samaritan in the bible?"

"Yes, of course."

"The Koreans do not believe in that. They will walk by anyone down outside their chain, their circle - not their problem. Not only do these aggressive Koreans drive like maniacs - the other drivers are outside their circle; even on the sidewalk they will bump into you as if you weren't there. They look on laws as failures of Confucian social behavior. They laugh at America as a country of laws."

Dr. Houghton wanted to reflect on this more; he changed the subject. "How many patients did we see in the Clinic this morning, Sergeant Morse?"

"Fifty total, Sir, beside the GI sick call of three. The Captain saw twenty Koreans, and I saw thirty."

"I think that our sorting system is working well, Sergeant Morse. I think you should continue to see the trauma, skin, and burn cases, and I'll see the complex internal medicine and pediatric cases as well as oversee your severe cases. Also, let me OK any patients to whom you want to give antibiotics. I'll have Miss Judy translate for me, and Sergeant Song can continue to translate for you." Dr. Houghton paused and said thoughtfully. "I think this kind of civic action is good for all concerned. We see the kinds of illnesses that occur here which is good training for us and helpful in advising the Korean Army doctors – so we know the types of problems they face. We are also providing these indigents with free medical care and drugs they couldn't obtain otherwise. And, we'll keep up our skills and not become rusty, allowing us to take better care of our own compound people." Dr. Houghton paused, "I think these arguments outweigh the principal objections that this program is not self-perpetuating and will fold when we leave, leaving nothing behind. Moreover, Colonel Bennet strongly supports it."

Sergeant Morse nodded. He really didn't care one way or the other. After seventeen years in the Army, being a black man with the rank of Sergeant First Class, he had learned not to question policies, but to carry them out. His salary of five thousand per year didn't pay him to think. The Army fed him well, clothed him and paternalistically cared for him and would do so for life. Sergeant Morse had merely traded the concrete plantation owner of his great-grandfather for a better, but more complex, abstract boss. Moreover, many of the senior officers had treated him extraordinarily well, especially General Samet on his last tour in Korea.

Dr. Houghton continued, "Although it's not authorized, I hope we can get the electrocardiogram machine and the new microscope from the Depot so we can practice more scientific medicine."

"I think we can, Sir, if the Captain raises hell." A few moments later, Sergeant Morse cried out, "Look out for that dog, sir." But it was too late. Dr. Houghton's eye had been on a beautiful Korean girl, and the dog darted under the right front wheel.

"Damn it," Dr. Houghton cursed as he pulled over to the side of the road where a crowd gathered. Someone brought the dead dog over to the jeep. An old man emerged, talking rapidly and angrily.

"Let me handle it, Sir. I speak just enough Korean."

Dr. Houghton did not understand the negotiations between the tall, handsome black Sergeant, dressed in razor sharp fatigues, who towered high above the small Koreans, and the bearded old man, his long beard consisting of fifteen or twenty white hairs. He did note that Morse was extremely well formed. Sergeant Morse would have been a fine model for the great Greek sculptors –Phidias or Praxiteles. However, with the passage of what seemed an interminable amount of arguing, Dr. Houghton grew nettled at what he was certain were excessive demands.

After five more minutes of this unintelligible, but obviously bitter bargaining, Sergeant Morse stuck his head into the jeep. "Sir, I think we should give him 3000 won."

"But that dog ran in front of us."

"Sir, in Korea, if you hit something it is your fault and you must pay. The Status of Forces Agreement makes us subject to their, I hate to say it, law."

"I don't have any Korean money. Do you? Let's pay him ten dollars and leave here before------- damn, here comes a Korean cop!"

After accepting the crisp ten dollar bill, the wizened old man came over to Dr. Houghton with a 180 degree change of expression. Knowing the Captain's rank, the old man bowed deeply and repeated twenty times, "Thank you Honorable Captain" in Korean. He also bowed twenty more times like a Rabbi at the Wall

21

in Jerusalem. Dr. Houghton amazed, climbed out of the jeep, bowed deeply once, and muttered in English, "You swindling old bastard."

On their way again, with Sergeant Morse now driving, Dr. Houghton opened the strained silence. "I think in the future we should let Sergeant Song or the other Korean enlisted men do the driving. What if the dog were a child? That wouldn't be so funny."

Sergeant Morse chuckled and said, "Yes, Sir," but the words sounded like "I told you so."

While Sergeant Morse attempted to avoid the large pot holes in the road, Dr. Houghton said, "Miss Judy is a charming woman. How long has she been working in this area?"

"She has been around for a long time. Miss Judy used to go with the Sergeant I replaced, but Colonel Jones took her over. It's funny, because Colonel Jones was straight until he went to the States on leave. When he returned, the Captain wouldn't believe the change. He began to drink and took up with Miss Judy. Now Colonel Jones is trying to convince her to leave the business, to learn typing so she can work as a secretary. He encouraged her to work in the dispensary. But Miss Judy has been spoiled, very spoiled. She rides around in the Colonel's sedan."

On the return trip to their compound which was adjacent to the village of Tae Bat, they passed through the small city of Chun Chon. Sergeant Morse pointed to his right. "On the hill, the Captain will see where most of the business ladies and prostitutes live. They service Camp Page which is here in Chun Chon."

"I would guess one thousand girls must live up there. That section is huge." Dr. Houghton said. He was astonished at the sheer size of the ghetto. Some of the dilapidated dwellings were barely standing, tilted precariously by past winds. Other cottages were exceptionally tidy inside their walls.

"The captain knows that in Korea we have the female entertainers, all of whom are really outcasts. In the lowest class are the common prostitutes who live in groups of three or four in one small house on the hill. They rarely, if ever, come out in the daytime because the children throw stones at them. Guests go to their houses and pay, maybe fifty cents. Many of these girls have gonorrhea or syphilis, often in advanced stages."

"Have you been there, Sergeant Morse?"

Sergeant Morse feigned shock at the question, but answered good-naturedly. "No, Sir, I don't pay for mine. But I did walk through there once. It was quite an experience. The girls grab you. One grabbed my hat and ran into her establishment. I never did get it back. These girls are desperate. It is the worst thing I have ever seen, and I've been around. The things they are forced to do for fifty

22

cents! The Koreans do not consider them human beings." Sergeant Morse paused. "To kill one is not really a crime."

Dr. Houghton said, "Really?"

"A step up the status ladder is the business lady. They work out of the bars, and they bring their clients to their hooches. Some business ladies go out only with Koreans, while others go out only with GI's. The GI girls like having a steady Yo Bo to support them for anywhere from thirty to eighty dollars a month, and best of all, the GI's give them items from the PX. Since the Americans came, GI business ladies are irregularly checked by the Korean government for venereal diseases, although prostitution is officially illegal. For a while Dr. Barnes worked in a government VD Clinic in Chun Chon. But later he stopped and just took care of our girls near the detachment in Tae Bat. Dr. Barnes felt that it was our responsibility, being medical people, to treat the GI girls since it is from this source that our soldiers catch VD. The commanders have never been able to stop the relations between the GI's and the business ladies although many have tried. They lock the gates, and the GI's build pogo sticks."

Sergeant Morse enjoyed his role of instructor. He continued, "The girls who go out with the Koreans generally work out of the rice wine establishments which vary from very low class places where, if you buy a pot of rice wine, they throw in the serving girl – to expensive geisha-like houses. The Korean geisha are called Kisaeng. The few real ones I've seen are stunning." Sergeant Morse double-clicked his tongue on the roof of his mouth in approval.

"Finally, there are the girls who work in the tea rooms, who border on respectability. A truly decent Korean girl would not work in a Tea House unless desperate for money."

Sergeant Morse thought for a moment and continued with a strange inflection in his voice. "Often, these entertainers are either sold or sent by their parents into the business. They have very little choice. Either the family eats or not. The Tea House girls are the unmarried girls who cannot find work but do not sink totally into the business. Even for college educated women, there is little work." As they approached the detachment, Sergeant Morse warned, "Sir, in my four tours in Korea, I've never met a Captain who didn't ultimately find himself a Yo Bo. I advise the Captain to be careful."

After letting Dr. Houghton off, a proud Sergeant Morse thought about his four tours in Korea in the last nine years. Although the Koreans were even more prejudiced against Blacks than Caucasians, Sergeant Morse had been a real lover. He never paid like the white GI's. What a life – alternating years with his wife in the States and then the girls of Korea. The spring had never been livelier in Sergeant Morse's thirty-four year old calves.

Dr. Houghton arrived at the NCO club party at 8 PM sharp Officers rarely came and only when invited. He looked around the dimness at the shadowy forms distributed around the club. He didn't see Sergeant Morse who had invited him. Some of the GI's stood about the juke box in the corner, laughing loudly, and a few were dancing to the blaring music. At the bar the Sergeant Major and the First Sergeant were having a good-natured row. The First Sergeant, already intoxicated, pointed menacingly at the Sergeant Major. "I run this place, Sergeant Major. You and the Colonel should go out and advise. That's your job. Let me run the god-damned compound."

On the other side of the large room opposite the bar, the stage was set in anticipation of the band. A few couples sat waiting at the small tables near the stage. The women were all Koreans and the men, all GI's. Korean men and American women were not welcome here. Mr. Yim, the bartender, and the band were exceptions.

As his eyes adapted, Dr. Houghton spotted Sergeant Morse seated in a corner with Miss Judy. As he started toward them, a double gin and tonic appeared in his right hand.

The Sergeant Major said, "Good evening, Captain. Welcome."

"Good evening, Sergeant Major. You've got to watch out for the First Sergeant. Don't let him give you a hard time."

In a deep mocking tome, the First Sergeant said, "I would never do that Doctor."

"Hello, Miss Kim."

"Hello, Doctor."

"Why does my Yo Bo, Miss Kim, come over to the dispensary, Doc?" the First Sergeant whispered, after pulling Dr. Houghton aside.

"Oh, nothing serious," Dr. Houghton said. Miss Kim, in fact, suffered from the ravages of pelvic inflammatory disease due to previous inadequately treated VD. For her, relations with men were now a painful unpleasantness, but she did not let this on to the First Sergeant.

"I hope so," said the First Sergeant. "We have been attempting to salvage Miss Kim; get a few more years out of the old gray mare." He walked back over to Miss Kim and affectionately patted her bottom.

Dr. Houghton thought this was an extremely accurate appraisal. Miss Kim was forty, an entertainer of extremely small worth in a buyer's market.

Miss Kim tightly embraced the first Sergeant with real affection, for she knew he would save her for another year. Years ago, she decided that when the day came, she would end it if she could not avoid destitution. Twenty seconals were waiting in a small hidden jar in her hooch.

Excusing himself, Dr. Houghton joined Sergeant Morse and Miss Judy. "Miss Judy, you look lovely tonight."

"Thank you," Miss Judy answered, demurely lowering her eyes. A slender 5 feet 5, she wore a light blue, furbelowed cocktail dress, popular in the States in the mid-fifties. The V-cut of her dress partially exposed a full bosom, an artful décolletage unusual on an oriental woman. Her rich black hair, piled high on her head, was decorated with a scarlet ribbon that matched the color of her lipstick and high-heeled shoes. A thin, scarlet velvet neckband with a solid gold clasp on the side, in the style of the gay 1890's looked slightly out of place. But most striking was her aristocratic, high cheek-boned face and the solid gold jewelry she wore; a charm bracelet, neckband clasp, rings and earrings. The color of the 24 carat Korean gold was very different, yellowier than the dilute gold of the West. From a hidden sachet, a lilac bouquet enveloped her in a fresh, almost virginal aura. In a Chinese costume, she could have posed as an oriental celestial nymph.

However, in an instant, Dr. Houghton knew her innocent black slanted eyes could transmogrify into slits of fiery malevolence and bitter cynicism. A paradox, Miss Judy had been formed in her early twenties by her American boyfriends and magazines. She was an oriental copy of an American woman ten or fifteen years earlier, with the walk and carriage of a charm school graduate. Without a doubt, her mind still lingered on that GI lieutenant, her first love, soon after the Korean War. That boy broke her heart. Even now, when she thought of him, she could feel the irregularity of her heart beats. All the others, well........

"Sit down, Sir, and join us." Sergeant Morse said, interrupting Dr. Houghton's thoughts, which had lingered too long on Miss Judy. She was a Colonel's Yo Bo although Dr. Houghton knew Colonel Jones was temporarily in Japan.

"Thank you, Miss Judy, for helping in the clinic."

"You're welcome, Docs."

"It is a good thing you are doing for your own people, Miss Judy." However, Dr. Houghton recognized that the indigent, uneducated Tae Bat villagers disliked her. Not only was Miss Judy an entertainer but an American business lady. Her translations of Dr. Houghton's advice, often to unwashed peasants who suffered from diseases of poor hygiene, aroused deep but unspoken resentment, particularly in the almost sacred old ones. That this light-skinned business lady with a strikingly perfect complexion, really one of the 'Americans," contrary to the timeless Confucian doctrine of deference to elders, should advise these solid, dark-skinned peasants that they often had diseases of poor hygiene was tolerated only because of the promise of health and free medicine.

Very rapidly, the laughter, music, and gin took possession of Dr. Houghton. Although he had already polished off several double gin and tonics, four more sat ominously in front of him, having magically appeared. He said, "Sergeant Morse, your dancing is legendary around here. Why don't you and Miss Judy show me your expertise?"

"O.K. Docs," Miss Judy replied, "Can do."

She took Sergeant Morse firmly by the hand notwithstanding his false protestations. They began to dance to the loud music; each flashed smiles of perfect white teeth which bobbed about in the dimness. Gradually everyone began to watch them. Sergeant Morse was extremely skillful with rhythmic but controlled movements. Miss Judy was also excellent, improvising an occasional suggestive bump and sinuous grind. As attention gradually focused on Sergeant Morse and Miss Judy, the band increased the tempo and volume of the hard rock music. Sergeant Morse and Miss Judy grew less inhibited, wild atavisms from the past. Dr. Houghton imagined Sergeant Morse's ancestors, millennia before, prancing to the sound of drums in black Africa, and similarly, he saw Miss Judy's forbears on The Steppes of Asia dancing with abandon to the sound of flutes, lyres and lutes. Only rarely did such avatars escape the shackles of modern civilization and reappear intact, but this was one of those moments. The band frothed on, trying to keep up. Dr. Houghton found himself shouting in unison with the others, "Go, go, go."

In a thousand years, he knew he could never dance like these two, but he had in his body a different, more potent energy. Rest, for the first time in ten years, had nourished it. He would ask the Colonel for permission to exercise it when the moment was ripe. These thoughts slipped away as a panting Miss Judy and sweat-beaded Sergeant Morse sat down.

"That was the best example of dancing I've ever seen," Dr. Houghton opined. "Now I understand what the Sergeant Major meant."

"Thank you, Sir."

26

Suddenly, Miss Judy began to laugh outrageously. Unlike her usual custom, she had had three drinks, too much for her. "See that new Sergeant over there," Miss Judy pointed to a very obese Sergeant. "How he make love?" she inquired, holding both hands over her mouth politely to conceal her laughter.

"I don't know," Dr. Houghton imitated Miss Judy.

"He needs two hundred dollars a month Yo Bo."

"How about you, Miss Judy?" Dr. Houghton asked.

"Me? Never happen. No have money, still no can do. I catchy only nice man."

Dr. Houghton pressed on, some old Puritan remnants slipping out. "I understand Mr. Morris offered you two hundred dollars a month. That's a lot of money in Korea."

Anger appeared in her eyes, which blazed and slanted up even more. "Nice talk, Docs; Morris is a number ten man. I only trust" and she pointed to her chest.

Dr. Houghton stopped. "Let me drive you home, Miss Judy."

"No, I walk. You too drunk. Jeep fall off road; we go Happy Mountain."

"OK, let's walk."

After he helped Miss Judy with her thin silk coat, she removed her scarlet, high heeled shoes and put them in a bag. She put on red Korean up-toed rubber shoes.

"Are they comfortable?"

"They are magics."

As they gradually walked away from the lights on the compound, Dr. Houghton was overwhelmed with the spectacular view of the stars in the dark Korean sky. He started whistling as they proceeded to Miss Judy's hooch, a ten minute walk if you walked on top of the high dividers between the rice paddies.

Miss Judy said, "Quiet Docs. You will disturb the Kitchen God who is now resting."

As they came close to the village, they greeted two passing American sergeants who, against regulations, slept in the village with their Yo Bo's. Although sobered up slightly by the cold air, Dr. Houghton held on to Miss Judy's hand to keep from falling off the dividers into the rice paddies below.

Just outside Miss Judy's hooch was a pig pen occupied by a huge oinking pig. Dr. Houghton looked at the pig, and responded, "Sui, sui, sui!"

She laughed as Dr. Houghton almost fell in the mud in front of the pig pen. "Quiet, Docs. You wake up Kitchen God. Let's go inside."

Before entering Miss Judy's hooch, Dr. Houghton said, "Why is almost every house, not matter how poor, surrounded by high walls with glass spikes embedded in the concrete on the top?"

Miss Judy said, "You simple Docs. Everybody must protect property. You not home and slicky boys come and rob you, your problem."

"But isn't it a crime to rob an empty house?"

"No, your problem. You home, slicky boys no come."

Dr. Houghton stepped carefully over the high threshold of the outer door into the courtyard. Miss Judy's room was to the right with two other families living in single rooms straight ahead and to the left. He was curious to see her room. Removing his shoes, he hunched down and stepped through the three foot high, red silk window-door after she had unlocked and opened it. To lock such a door seemed ridiculous to Dr. Houghton. Miss Judy snapped on the indirect re-hued lighting. The comparison with the dirty exterior was overwhelming. The seven by thirteen foot, low ceiling room was decorated in scarlet and black. The rosewood oriental cabinets had mother-of-pearl inlay. The television, stereo, electric blanket cords, exquisite silk bedspread on a queen-size bed, and the books in Korean and Chinese characters along with the Chinese style lamps, paintings, and windows were totally out of keeping with the poverty outside. The cabinets were well stocked from the PX. Her wardrobe was full of expensive Korean silk and western style dresses and shoes. But most impressive to Dr. Houghton in this dusty, dirty country was the neat cleanliness of her room.

Dr. Houghton sat down on a pillow on the heated obdul floor, cross-legged, as Miss Judy prepared some tea. In one sense, she was Tyche's darling, a new American boyfriend every year and this charming hooch. Her modus vivendi certainly beat working in the rice paddies or even marriage to a peasant. On the other hand in this Confucian society, she was a nonperson. Dr. Houghton knew he did not yet understand the nuances of the cultural stones Koreans cast at her. Moreover, as a man who lived in a constant state of inner tension and thrived on it, Dr.Houghton did not understand the oriental goal of inner harmony, the kibun concept. Inner harmony seemed impossible for Miss Judy.

"Who are these pictures on the wall?"

"That man is my first Yo Bo, Lieutenant Weinstein, and the baby is my son."

"The child is very handsome. What happened, Miss Judy?"

"Thank you, Docs. Everybody says baby very handsome. After Korean War, no money. My father dead. What cha goin' to do me? Lieutenant Weinstein come. I love him very much. Baby come. Lieutenant Weinstein married, but he say he bring baby with him. He lie talk. One day, Lieutenant Weinstein gone. What cha goin' to do me?"

"Where is the baby now?"

"I sent the baby to adoption USA. American baby no good here. People no like. Sometimes...." Miss Judy made a slicing motion across neck and then her groin.

With a queasy stomach already, Dr. Houghton almost vomited. "You don't mean they castrate these kids, do you?"

She nodded. "So they won't spoil Korean purity. I had to send him away. Otherwise baby soon slicky boy. No good."

"What exactly is a slicky boy?"

"A thief; a silent thief. So I send him to America."

"Does his father know?"

"No."

"You must be very sad. Does the boy write to you?"

"No. And now I have broken heart again. My Colonel is going soon." Miss Judy started to sob.

"But you have been prudent and saved your money. I see all that gold you have."

"Yes, I have many gold, and I bought my younger brother some rice paddy." Miss Judy was now overwhelmed; she wiped away a sudden onslaught of tears. But in a few moments she composed herself and said with emphasis, "Docs, many GI's bad man. Sergeant Morse bad man too. They promise girl marry and then no can do. They say marry, but no give money; then they go away." Miss Judy paused. "You be careful, Docs. Many girls no good. You see in clinic. They butterfly from man to man, catchy VD. Pretty face OK, but heart no good."

Dr. Houghton smiled at the universal advice of all aging and/or ugly girls to watch out for beautiful girls with bad hearts. His mother also told him the same thing. But in this case, Miss Judy had a point. A dose of the clap or even worse, nonspecific urethritis would not be good.

Dr. Houghton rose. "Miss Judy, it is almost twelve o'clock. I must go back to the detachment before curfew. Thank you for your company. Good night." He kissed her lightly on the cheek.

"Good night, Docs."

Two days later Colonel Jones, Miss Judy's Yo Bo, back from Japan, barged into the dispensary. He walked into Dr. Houghton's office without knocking. He had on his 45 with the clip in place.

Taken aback, Dr. Houghton said, "Good morning, Colonel Jones. What can I do for you?"

"I understand you have been out with my Miss Judy, Captain."

"Well, if you want to call escorting her home...." Dr. Houghton said good-naturedly.

"Don't you at least have the decency to wait until I leave, Captain? I don't mind her working in the clinic, but keep away from her." A red faced Colonel Jones placed his hand on his 45, started to speak, turned and then left slamming the front door.

"The iron entered into his soul."
Psalms Cv 18

Chapter III
Youth

Reg Houghton and Charles Summer agreed the second grade was horrible. "What time 'til the second bell, Charlie?" Reg whispered skillfully with his mouth almost shut like his favorite ventriloquist Edgar Bergen.

"Ten minutes," a whispering Charlie read off his Mickey Mouse watch.

"Let's go down the creek after lunch." As he whispered, Reg kept his head bowed toward his reading workbook, but his eyes never left Miss Morgan's back.

Charlie nodded agreeably.

Charlie and Reg were the two best students in Miss Morgan's class. They had no real intention of playing hooky that afternoon but didn't think about the consequences of going down to the creek.

On the way, Reg commented, "We got penmanship this afternoon."

"Yeah, I know. Last term I got C in penmanship."

"Me, too. Boy was my father mad when I got all A's and two C's. That C in penmanship was bad but it was that C in conduct. I sure got it when he saw I erased the C and substituted a B. I was really lucky he didn't find out about Marie." Charlie and Reg had been caught by Miss Morgan with Marie a few months before behind the school. Miss Morgan had been upset because Marie had taken her off her dress to show the boys "some anatomy." Charlie and Reg considered themselves just interested observers. They were quite innocent, but the "C's" appeared under conduct instead of the usual B's.

"There's not much water in the creek. I betcha I can jump across, Charlie."

"You'll never make it over."

Reg jumped, his two feet landing safely on the other side. "I made it," he screamed. But an instant later, he lost his balance and stepped backwards into the creek drenching his right shoe and sock. "Oh shit; this shoe will never dry."

Meanwhile, Miss Morgan called Charlie's and Reg's mothers who were distraught and had no idea where their children might be. When Charlie and Reg finally showed up an hour late, Miss Morgan made them sit with their heads on the desks. In the blackness of his folded arms, Reg knew his father would be furious and probably beat the hell out of him, but Reg decided it was worth it. They had avoided penmanship.

But Miss Morgan, a forty year old spinster, was Lucifer's child. She knew that both Reg and Charlie's penmanship was initially excellent, but it would deteriorate over the course of the practice session. They knew how to form their letters as evenly as those on the alphabet cards tacked around the room. But, she was determined to have their work high quality at all times. The worse the penmanship became, the more she insisted on repetition which was generally worse than the original. And so the conflicting propensities of Miss Morgan and the children resulted in their penmanship decaying into a scribble. After the final bell, as Charlie and Reg lined up with the others, Miss Morgan spoke in a forced, sugar-toned cadence, used only when suppressing her massive frustration. "I think it would be a good idea for both of you, Reg and Charlie, to stay here and practice your penmanship - some more."

Reg felt an explosive sensation that adults call fury. It blurred his thoughts. As he re-began the repetitive penmanship practice, a grinding whirling inner sound distressed him. His callused fingers tightened hard on his pen. His letters deteriorated even further. His clenched jaw began to hurt and his throat burned. But when Miss Morgan remained a physical presence, after all Miss Morgan was a big, well-muscled woman, Reg suppressed open thoughts of her destruction. However, in the dark of night, she was torn asunder, roasted, toasted and stomped upon. Most often, Reg would pull on one of her legs while Charlie would yank on the other, spread eagle, like what they did to insects. And thus they would finish her off.

"We worried about you, dear," Reg's mother said softly when he arrived home. Where in the world did you go?"

"Me and Charlie went down to the brook."

"You mean 'Charlie and I' don't you? Well, don't do that again."

Reg was amazed that for this major infraction, he was treated gently. At dinner that night Reg's father was home which was unusual, for although financially very well off, he worked constantly. Although he could afford private schools, he believed in the virtues of the high quality, suburban-Boston public schools.

32

As Reg sat down for dinner, he saw the darkened hollows under his father's eyes were worse than usual, and his hands shook. Reg knew his father had trouble sleeping recently. With a cough, Mr. Houghton suddenly looked up. Not a word about the hooky. "Come here, Reg." The awful routine began. "Your finger nails and ears are filthy. You leave the table and wash."

"But I just washed them, Daddy."

"Go wash them again."

After the second scrub with most of the dirt on the towel, Reg did not wish to eat. This rewashing was becoming an unpleasant ritual, but he walked back to the table.

"Let me see them now!"

Out of nowhere, a huge hand rapped Reg's rear. "They are still dirty. Potatoes could grow in there. Go wash again. What kind of example are you setting for Elfreda?"

Reg did not hear any more as he choked on his misery, swallowing to keep from crying out loud. The meal was tense and remained so for years whenever his father was home.

After being excused from the table, Reg sat down at the piano for his second session of the day. His first daily session lased from 6:30 to 7:30 a.m., with the second session an endless half hour after dinner. Reg's father would sometimes stand behind him, keeping time to the music as Reg played precisely and mechanically. Unlike the artist of Plato's Ion, Reg would never have to explain any brilliance. His playing was consummately hollow, each note faultless, computer perfect, but the total an emotional cipher in an absolute vacuum of feeling. One fact that Reg knew that his father did not was that a baboon or a cerebral palsy victim, who practiced nearly two hours a day, would improve.

At the bi-yearly recitals at the Academy of Music, however, Reg played extremely well. His mother said he rose to the occasion consistently. This ephemeral excellence, coupled with exaggerated compliments from loving relatives, reinforced Mr. Houghton's notion that his child was talented. He took Reg's interest for granted. In fact, Reg relished the mild applause under the warm spotlight for several days.

But gradually Reg noted the return of an involuntary daydream. It was true he could barely lift the magic axe in the cellar. But, like the sorcerer's apprentice, since Reg knew the correct malediction, he could activate the ax and slam the baby grand into splinters whenever he wished. Reg would deny complicity. But with time, alas, Reg noted an unpleasant twist in the happy dream; on their own, the splinters would sometimes reassemble into two pianos. His piano lessons continued to torment him.

Reg gradually learned to contain the growth and expression of his evil demon at home whenever the heat of anger or tears of frustration nourished it. But when he closed the front door of his house, he lost that control. Over time, Reg realized that if you earned mainly A's, you studied Latin or Greek and played one sport well, you could commit mayhem with relative impunity. The educators and his father assumed that good behavior was correlated with intellectual and physical distinction. Reg's pranks were generally passed off as just amusing mischief.

In the eighth grade, the last year of middle school, Reg was elected class treasurer. He also became the principal member of the intellectuals, although he was an excellent tennis player. Members of the other major clique were the jocks. The rivalry was good-natured. Reg and the quarterback were friends of a sort, the bond being a mutual addiction to practical jokes.

Elaborating on a suggestion by Sean O'Leary, Reg intended to outdo his pal, the quarterback. Sean suggested they "stink out" Miss Burtis, their elderly history teacher whose favorite words were "cause and effect." They all agreed that the "daffy" Miss Burtis deserved punishment. After all, she daily showered the defenseless pupils in the front row with a fine spit-spray as she made sure her wisdom was projected to those in the back. She spread germs and colds. Here was cause and effect. Here was a justification for retribution.

All the students knew that Miss Burtis' bete noire was odors. In the middle of winter she would open the windows to keep the air fresh and the students alert. Sean had eluded Miss Burtis "cause and effect" analysis for nearly one month with his unique ability to pass gas at will. But she finally grew wise to him. Hence his suggestion, "We gotta stink out Miss Burtis with a new approach."

Reg said, "You know Sean, there's a chemical that smells like rotten eggs. My dad showed it to me once. It is called potassium sulfide I think. It stinks but it won't hurt you. We could put some in the ventilation system."

Sean was supportive of obtaining some and "sampling it."

A few days later, Reg obtained several small "stones" for a "chemistry experiment."

Sean was ecstatic when he whiffed the odor of the greenish-yellow mephitic "stones" in the small container. "They stink beautiful. I couldn't do better myself. They are a stinker's diamonds." In thirty seconds, Reg and Sean agreed on the "diamond plan."

The day before the class picnic, Reg and Sean placed two of the "diamonds" into the forced hot air outlet vent in Miss Burtis' room just before the first class. It was a cool April morning and the heat intermittently flowed. At nine AM, the class was tense and expectant. Everyone knew of the "plan." Halfway through the period, a stout, buxom Miss Burtis, tightly encased in her rigid girdle, suddenly stopped talking. She waddled about, sniffing; her nose was twitching. She asked the children in the front row if they smelled any odor, and they replied in one voice, "No, Miss Burtis." Miss Burtis asseverated, "I definitely smell something; open the windows."

Several students rose to do her bidding. One lost control and laughed momentarily. But opening the windows only exacerbated the odor, for it was chilly outside, and the hot air blew even more forcefully over the diamonds. As expected, in a few minutes Miss Burtis suddenly paused, sniffed, and pointed. "Sean O'Leary, please leave the room immediately."

The class tittered. Reg almost lost his self-control. But Sean's absence made no difference. Quickly Miss Burtis, like a hound dog on a spoor, sniffed right toward the vent. The class watched silently and intently, ready to explode. To the bending of thirty necks, Miss Burtis opened the vent, and with a piece of paper she swept out the two diamonds. Faint and pale, she screamed. "Oh! God!" and wobbled out of the room.

As she left, the class erupted into assorted shrieks, roars, and guffaws. As soon as Miss Burtis was out the door, Reg hurled the two stones out the window.

The laughter abruptly ceased when the vice-principal appeared. An austere, humorless man, he sniffed, attempting to assess the gravity of the situation, but by then the odor had nearly dissipated. He shivered.

"It's cold here. What's going on? Who did it?" The complete silence was impressive. No student moved.

"If no one owns up, I'll cancel the class picnic tomorrow."

Reg realized he and Sean had made a grievous mistake. The class picnic was an expectant occasion. Last year, Mary Lou Jones conceived a baby after beer surreptitiously appeared. This year, Reg's class aspired to a greater brouhaha. Reg now experienced flutters of anxiety. This affair, well conceived and perfectly executed, had been planted in premature soil. They should have waited until *after* the class picnic.

The vice-principal stood on his tip-toes, tight-lipped. He just waited. Reg decided not to confess at that moment; perhaps later if the vice-principal appeared serious. But Reg now worried that someone might tattle. He was very vulnerable.

Cynthia Budd raised her hand. Reg groaned to himself, "No, not Cynthia."

She addressed the vice-principal. "I smelt that same odor this morning in the basement."

"So did I," Pauline Lakin echoed in a most convincing manner.

The vice-principal grimaced, hesitated and walked out.

Reg was amazed and breathed easily again. No one had tattled; the girls had shielded him. Reg stood up, bent over and kissed a very plain Cynthia on the lips. She closed her eyes and said "More." Everyone laughed and applauded.

Pauline Lakin said, "Don't forget me!" Everyone roared with cheers and glee.

Reg never forgot this episode which provided his early sense of optimism about women. Cynthia and Pauline had rescued Reg from expulsion and an even worse fate, his father's wrath.

A moment later, the class began to discuss the pros and cons of a confession by Reg and Sean. They concluded Reg and Sean must not confess. They were confident the vice-principal was bluffing. Moreover, Cynthia's fabrication raised the question of a school-wide odor and thereby clouded the issue. Steeled by this advice, Reg did not confess.

The vice-principal was not bluffing.

The ninth grade saw Reg's intellectual excellence gradually decline, and his previous strength imperceptibly wane. Finally, as a fine tremor developed and his eyes unmistakably protruded, the correct diagnosis became obvious. Reg had Graves disease - hyperthyroidism. Reg was impressed with the physicians who restored his health.

It was during this time of failing health that Reg's interest in certain historical characters developed. First, it was Alexander the Great, but this quickly passed to the Roman Emperor, Diocletian. Reg simply could not comprehend how a Roman emperor, who ruled the world and had himself proclaimed a deity, could give up absolute power to grow cabbages in retirement. Next Reg's curiosity passed to the Chinese emperors of the Qing dynasty. He read a detailed biography of the Qianlong Emperor who ruled China for the last part of the eighteenth century. Reg enjoyed the fact that the Qianlong Emperor prayed to the Kitchen God in the Palace of

Earthly Repose for plentiful food and good reports to Heaven. He thought his mother should pray to the Kitchen God for she was a terrible cook. This Emperor was amazing - he was honest, he worked all the time like Reg's dad, and he expanded China's control over Mongolia, Tibet and Korea. But most interesting to Reg were two matters: the Emperor's infatuation with Xiang Fei, one of his many concubines, and his discovery of the beauty of Chinese carvings fashioned from jadeite mined in Burma. They called Xiang Fei, Fragrant Concubine, because she smelled of the sweetest fragrance of all - jujube tree flowers, whatever they were. However, she rejected the Emperor, even though he gave her a two inch imperial green, translucent jadeite Persian pepper pendant with a tendril, a gift more valuable than diamonds. Persian peppers were long and thin unlike Boston green peppers. In a library book, Reg saw a picture of Xiang Fei with the jadeite pepper pendant around her long white neck. He fell in love with this young oriental woman with pink cheeks on perfect white skin, Cupid's bow lips in a heart shaped face, and mysterious almond-shaped brown eyes. Equally striking to Reg was her shiny black hair, piled high, held up with imperial green jadeite ornaments and yellow gold pins. In this picture, Xiang Fei wore a cream colored Chinese dress over amaranth colored trousers. For months Reg could not erase the Xiang Fei's lineaments from his mind. But gradually, as he improved, he turned his mind to other more mundane thoughts - like sex with Paula.

His parents recognized that his illness, which steadily improved over a six month period, had affected his mind. They were unusually lax in their treatment of the "patient." They humored his notion that he was the Son of Heaven, an Emperor of the Qing dynasty. Contributing to this delusion was the Teutonic meaning of Reginald -strong king. At the time, to Reg, his name intimated a sense of destiny and specialness.

His mother allowed him to redecorate his room in a Chinese motif with dragons and tigers on the walls. He bought a silk "Emperor's outfit" and Qing boots. His younger sister he renamed Black Jade, her friends Bright Design and Musk Moon. He insisted on their kowtowing on entering his "chamber."

At the height of the illness, day and night, Reg was immersed in China, Xiang Fei and jadeite. His high school work suffered for a semester. A little dust in the corner of the room brought threats of skinning and slicing for his humoring mother, although she refused to kowtow. She pointed out that she was the Queen Mother and must not kowtow. Reg accepted this. But fairly suddenly, this Chinese phase passed as he waxed into health. This

37

entire episode became only a dim memory; the tigers and dragons, and the pair of Chinese Qing boots soon gathered dust in the attic.

Throughout the rest of high school, when under stress, Reg frequently succumbed to short periods of a peculiar fantasy, the content being variations of the same theme. Initially, Reg would see an unknown little boy copying an oversized book, perhaps the dictionary. The scene was somehow unpleasant. But suddenly, relieving the gloom, he saw an image of a strange, glorious flower, a bloom that never wilted or died. Try as he could, Reg could never connect the little boy who copied and the everlasting flower. Reg did have vague recollections that as a child his father read the Greek myths to him. Perhaps this was a Greek Myth? He looked into it and found that in Greek mythology there was, in fact, a special flower that grew on Mount Olympus in the abode of the Greek Gods. This flower never died and was called an amaranth flower. When Reg asked his father, he did not remember the myth. But Reg was certain this was not the answer. As the years passed, this peculiar fantasy decreased in frequency, and finally did not recur at all.

Reg's youth was "rounded" out before college. Like all male members of the family, Reg was expected to "estivate" –his father's sad joke- in his great uncle's factory for the summer before college. He must learn about menial work and how the "other half" lived. Being assigned to a machine in his uncle's boiling hot factory and having to perform a repetitive task, he was bored in a few minutes. In an hour, he had ants-in-his-pants restlessness; in two hours, fiery frustration. During that summer, he imagined what Hell must be like. You burn and sweat but the god-damn-clock doesn't tic. His task was to load paper and sipping straws in one end. When the noisy machine stopped and said "500" two minutes later, Reg filled a box with the covered straws, closed it and started again. He soon experienced that same crescendo of mental whirring and grinding that he last felt in grade school, a manifestation of an inner wildness that must never burst forth.

The outcome of that summer's experience was a fierce disinclination to work. He did, however, develop a lasting sympathy for the workers whose minds were slowly ground away by the noise, heat and boredom of factory work. Nature, however, seemed to help these workers by allowing their sensory neurons to be worn down more readily than the motor neurons. The afflicted did not apparently feel their pain or did they? Or perhaps they were less sensitive. Or was this a mere rationalization or was it observations on the already ruined? Perhaps they *had* to work for money, an obvious explanation. Perhaps Marx was correct. Who knew? But there was one experience Reg did enjoy that summer:

several of the female workers brought in the raunchiest pornography imaginable. A sweaty dirty Reg and the "ladies" viewed it during their 30 minute lunch breaks with tremendous good humor. When dreaming after those long days, Reg ofter watched the factory crew dance around huge erect penises - they even danced around his great uncle, the "Big Prick." From the factory workers, Reg learned priceless lessons that summer.

Paradoxically, at summer's end, Reg concluded the reason he reacted so negatively to his "employment" was his own weakness. Moreover, he quickly suppressed the whole experience as best as he could. He would not kill his great uncle, the "Big Prick" after all. He would not become a student of euthenics or a proletarian leader urging revolution. Instead, with a sigh, he went to Harvard.

"Therefore, Prophesy and say unto Gog: When you
come out of the North with your great army against
the land of Israel, I Yahweh will call for a sword
against Gog and I will send a fire on the land of
Magog."
                                                   Ezekiel: 38

Chapter IV
An Open Mind

After Colonel Jones finally left for Viet Nam, Miss Judy
was morose and burdened. Although she worked as efficiently as
ever in Dr. Houghton's crowded and hectic Korean Civic Action
Clinic, her increasingly fragile hold on her senses was slowly
becoming undone. The impressive efficacy of Dr. Houghton's
treatments, like the medical control of the seizure patients, did not
cheer up Miss Judy. In fact, she wondered why Dr. Houghton was
doing this; why should he help strangers?

In an attempt to break Miss Judy into her characteristic,
outrageous mirth, Dr. Houghton said, "You are a quaja cundingio."

"What did you say, Docs? I no understand that talk."

"I spoke in Korean, Miss Judy – translate!"

Miss Judy did as bidden. "Quaja means candy. Cundingio
means – ah – maybe ass?" She turned over candy ass in her mind.
After several moments of quizzical intuition, she exploded into
guffawing glee. This wildly uninhibited social laughter, Dr.
Houghton had never heard before, except once in a psychotic manic
patient. Involuntarily, he echoed her laughter until unbridled tears
and convulsive gasps stopped him. But as suddenly as she began,
she stopped. "What does that mean? Candy ass? Who taught you
that crazy talk? Sergeant Song?"

Sergeant Song had begun to teach him Korean. As an
instructor, he was indeed the obvious choice with his thorough
knowledge of Korean, Chinese and English. After a thoughtful
evaluation, Sergeant Song estimated that with daily half hour
lessons, plus an hour more of study each day, and weekly
examinations, Dr. Houghton should have a fair knowledge of
written and spoken Korean at the end of his thirteen month tour of
duty.

Dr. Houghton had confidence that he could learn the 24
letter Korean alphabet and the Korean conjugations, declensions and

40

polite forms quickly. After all, the enlightened Korean King Sejong in 1443 had created Hangul, the Korean language, so his people could easily learn to read and write. Unlike Chinese with over 50, 000 characters, a language far too complex for the common man, Korean is simple. However, Sergeant Song recommended Dr. Houghton master about 200 Chinese characters since they were sometimes put in parentheses in the newspapers after the Korean words.

After the first few lessons, Dr. Houghton had reservations; was it worth the effort? But he had mastered Latin in high school and college. He reassured himself repeatedly that Korean should be a simple proposition compared to Latin, Chinese or Japanese. He knew that his knowledge of Korean would greatly facilitate his role as an advisor. He also realized that if he wished to associate with these ethnocentric people at any level other than the most superficial, if he wanted to understand the subtleties of the oriental mind, he would have to speak their language. He could not depend on the shaky crutch of possible or purposefully inaccurate translation. Also in his mind was the possibility of access; for example, access to a desirable Korean woman.

For a moment, as Miss Judy played with candy ass, he reflected on what General Samet counseled him. Samet was correct. Each new Korean word he learned brought a queer notion of power. He felt the magic in language he had known as a child when learning English. To name it in this new tongue brought control, particularly over items totally new and strange. Even girls' names turned out to be quaint and powerful. Miss Judy's name was Pervading Fragrance. And when he called her by her Korean name, their relationship seemed slightly altered. Unconsciously, Miss Judy looked upon him as more of a Korean man and assumed a slightly more passive, traditional posture. Moreover, she told him that no American she had known had made a systematic effort to learn Korean. The Koreans themselves discouraged such efforts, for a fluent advisor could be dangerous.

But in Korean, to Miss Judy, candy ass made no sense; she had no idea of its figurative meaning. She was a very concrete person.

Dr. Houghton said in Korean, "Tell Sergeant Morse, he is a candy ass, Pervading Fragrance."

"OK, Docs."

"Morse," Miss Judy called through the open door, "you are a candy ass."

Sergeant Morse with his deep laugh bounded into Dr. Houghton's office. In his playfully severe voice, he asked, "Who taught you that, Miss Judy?" knowing full well who it was.

"Morse, you candy ass," she repeated. Fortunately, she skipped out a moment before a large combat boot could reach her callipygian ass.

"See you Monday, Miss Judy."

"Good-bye, Docs."

A moment after the door slammed behind Miss Judy, Dr. Houghton spoke in a serious, almost dour fashion. Sergeant Morse easily adapted to these rapid, mercurial wills of the Captain. Responding only to the tone, his chin involuntarily stiffened.

"Sergeant Morse, tomorrow I would like to visit the Korean Evacuation Hospital in Chun Chon; the following day, we'll go with Colonel Newton to the DMZ and Nightmare Range. Please lay on the trips. We'll bring Sergeant Song to drive and interpret for you and Lieutenant Ahn, who I understand is our liaison officer, for me. I hear that Ahn speaks English quite well."

"Yes, Sir. He speaks good English."

Impatient to leave for the Korean Evacuation Hospital, Dr. Houghton completed his follow-up patients and GI sick call by 8:10 AM. Lieutenant Ahn and Sergeant Morse clambered into the back of Dr. Houghton's jeep; Sergeant Song drove. The contrast between the slim, muscular Morse and the tiny, yellow Lieutenant Ahn struck Dr. Houghton with unusual force. Hollow cheeked and thin, Ahn continually made sharp rapid motions with his hands, feet, and vulpine eyes. He could be still for only a moment. Moreover, Ahn stank: the odor of sour garlic spired out of his mouth; oozed out of his pores; and could not be washed out of his uniforms. All Koreans ate garlic to excess but Ahn was extraordinarily. He chewed raw garlic bulbs like candy. Dr. Houghton recalled his greatest shock in Korea occurred when a pretty young woman smiled at him the day he arrived. He smiled back, but when she opened her mouth to talk, he almost fell over from her dragon mouth. Then there was Dr. Barnes, equally stinko.

Soon after they left, an old man purposely sprinted in front of the jeep from the side of the road. Fortunately, Sergeant Song was driving slowly. He screeched the jeep to a halt, but lightly tapped the old man to the ground.

"What a screwball! Was he trying to commit suicide?" Dr. Houghton asked as they all jumped out of the jeep. The wizened Korean, all smiles, stood up, brushed the dust off and repeated "I am sorry," a phrase which Dr. Houghton knew. He was clearly not hurt. The old man came over to the senior person, Dr. Houghton, bowed, and said in Korean, "Thank you, Honorable Sir." A mystified Dr. Houghton, with his sense of humor strained but intact, responded with a near kowtow to the ancient one's delight. Lieutenant Ahn and the maniac spoke for a moment before the old man continued his walk along the side of the dusty road.

"I'll give you the poops," Lieutenant Ahn said. "That old man was down in his lucks. Recently his wife and only son went to the Happy Mountain. Now alone, the old man said he was pursued by some demon. He ran in front of the jeep so that the demon, lagging behind, would get killed."

"I see," Dr. Houghton mumbled. "It makes good sense." As his liaison officer, Dr. Houghton thought that Ahn's ability to explain outweighed his stinko odor.

Dr. Houghton bowed slightly to the two Korean Colonels on entering the Commanding Officer's office in the Korean Evacuation Hospital. He did not salute. To Lieutenant Ahn, he said, almost as aside, "I know Colonel Kim, the Corps Surgeon. Dr. Branes introduced us." Shaking hands with Colonel Kim, with a boldness no Korean Captain would dare manifest, Dr. Houghton said, "How are you, Honorable Colonel?" in Korean. Then in English, "It is good to see you again, Colonel Kim. This is Lieutenant Ahn, my liaison officer." Lieutenant Ahn briskly saluted, at attention. Colonel Kim did not acknowledge his presence.

"You know Sergeant Morse." Sergeant Morse saluted, grinning with respectful familiarity. Many a bottle of American whiskey and medicine had passed through Sergeant Morse to Colonel Kim.

"Hello Sergeant Morse," Colonel Kim replied pleasantly. Turning to Colonel Lee, Colonel Kim said, "This is Colonel Lee, the hospital commander."

Dr. Houghton bowed as he shook hands with a nervous Colonel Lee touching his right elbow with his left palm, the polite way to shake hands in Korea.

Colonel Lee did the same. He understood the value of good relations with the American Advisors. His beautiful paramour wished an electric blanket which could not be purchased in Korea at the time. But Dr. Houghton, he knew, within three weeks could obtain one plus many other dear objects. Repeatedly, Colonel Lee's paramour had also commented how profitably Colonel Kim interacted with the Americans. She badly wanted the electric blanket, which for her was a make or break request. Dissemble, she said, like Colonel Kim. But it was difficult for Colonel Lee who did not like the Americans. Finally, he said in his halting English, "I am happy you came to visit our hospital. You please have a seat. Red tea or coffee, Dr. Houghton?"

"Tea please," Dr. Houghton said and at the same time motioned Lieutenant Ahn to sit beside him. Soon a private brought red tea for them all. Sipping the tea, Dr. Houghton noted the white-washed concrete block walls, the dilapidated couch, the rickety chairs, the old desk, and the kerosene stove.

After some probing talk, Colonel Lee asked, "Where did you go to school, Dr. Houghton?"

"Harvard College and Yale Medical School. I trained at the Brigham in Boston."

At this, Colonel Lee looked at Colonel Kim who nodded approval. The Koreans, with their Confucian traditions, were very education conscious. A farmer might "sell" a daughter into the entertainment ranks to finance a bright son's education. Dr. Houghton sensed a propitious beginning.

Colonel Lee stepped up to the charts on the wall to begin his briefing.

He spoke in Korean and Lieutenant Ahn translated quickly. Using his swagger stick as a pointer, Colonel Lee summarized the history, mission and function of his hospital. Then he covered the personnel, equipment, number and types of patients, laboratory services, x-ray and water supply. Then he said the Chief Nurse would continue.

She entered, a very attractive Major, who blushed slightly on introduction to Dr. Houghton. On seeing Sergeant Morse's blackness, the Chief Nurse burst into a scarlet inflorescence - her neck, face and even ears. A myriad of commentary could not recapture this momentary interaction; only a before and after Nikon photograph could. Exceedingly nervous she briefed them on the nursing services and left before Dr. Houghton could ask questions.

Knowing well the oriental proverb about one thousand words and one picture, he said, "Thank you Colonel. May we have a look around?"

"Yes, surely."

As they toured the hospital, Dr. Houghton found the equipment and furnishings were scarce to the point of nonexistent. But most deplorable was the musty appearance of the medical wards. The bed sheets and the concrete floors were plain dirty. The microorganisms could almost be seen in the air. The operating rooms were beyond comment. This was mainly a matter for soap, elbow grease, a few mops and leadership.

Sergeant Morse glanced at the Doctor to observe his reaction to the operating rooms. He saw a slightly pale Captain. In fact, Sergeant Morse could think of no greater contrast between the States and Korea. The polished, gleaming asepsis of operating rooms in the States versus this!

On the ward, Dr. Houghton reviewed some charts and examined a few unwashed patients and their x-rays. Several were extremely ill and were treated cavalierly by the Korean doctors, whereas others were not ill and should have been returned to duty weeks ago. As he toured the wards, he became more and more puzzled by his observations. Colonel Lee had said they had enough beds, but on some wards there appeared to be two patients per cot bed. Also why were there so many non-vehicular accident cases like fractured skulls as well as non-enemy inflicted gunshot wounds?

His silent questioning was interrupted as they paused to observe the debridement of a soldier's hand on a surgical ward. This private soldier had severely damaged his hand and blown off the tips of two fingers in an accident. In profound distress, the wounded man was silently bearing the procedure. Several corpsmen were cleaning and debriding the wound as the patient looked the other way. Dr. Houghton noted tendons and bone exposed. Unable to refrain from comment, he whispered to Colonel Kim, "This should be stopped. This patient has obviously not had enough analgesia or local anesthesia. Moreover, the conditions are septic. A surgeon should do this in the operating room with more sterile technique and adequate anesthesia." Dr. Houghton understated his feelings in the Korean fashion to minimize the Colonel's loss of face.

Colonel Kim understood western men; he spoke angrily in Korean.

The corpsmen stopped and relief appeared on the private's face.

The tour through supply was anticlimactic. As expected, Dr. Houghton mechanically noted that all the drugs and equipment they had were American made. His direct responsibility was to see that these outlays of American wealth were properly used. But this was a difficult, if not an impossible task under the circumstances.

Back in his office, Colonel Lee, nervously but aggressively asked, "What do you think, Dr. Houghton?"

"There are a few problems but I think I need to talk with Colonel Kim first."

"Will you join us for chops?" Colonel Lee asked.

"No thank you. On our next visit, we will join you. We must go back. Thank you again." The staff lined up at the front door to say goodbye as they left. With an irresistible impulse, Dr.

Houghton winked at the Chief Nurse as they walked by. She again blushed, this time in a more patchy way. There were many reds on her face; scarlet, amaranth and even fuchsia. She was a riot of reds. Dr. Houghton was an expert in red and purple colors. He had done his thesis on the synthesis of the dyes mauve, amaranth and imperial purple for high honors in chemistry at Harvard College.

Sergeant Morse, as observant as always, laughed to himself at the Captain's behavior. Houghton was loosening up a little bit. Soon he would be in the village with a business lady!

Dr. Houghton sighed deeply on leaving the Evacuation Hospital.

Sergeant Morse chuckled, "I think the Captain knows how a cherry girl feels now."

"What are you talking about?"

"A cherry girl is a virgin."

"I still don't follow you, Sergeant Morse."

"I think the Captain got raped in there."

Dr. Houghton nodded in understanding. He surely had lost something precious in there.

The next morning, after talking a few minutes with Colonel Newton, Dr. Houghton walked over to his jeep.

"Yes, Sir?" said Sergeant Morse.

"I'll ride with the Colonel. You, Sergeant Song and Lieutenant Ahn follow in my jeep."

As Dr. Houghton climbed into the back seat of the jeep, Colonel Newton said, "Doc, for a potential Black Belt, you are awfully clumsy."

Dr. Houghton laughed.

"Have you asked the Colonel for permission yet?"

"No, I haven't; I will tonight," Dr. Houghton replied.

To the driver, the Colonel said, "Nightmare Range."

Colonel Newton, the engineering advisor to the forward corps in the central sector, looked like a Russian brigadier general or an interior lineman of an American professional football team. The Korean soldiers from private to general, called him in Korean, "Newton the Pig," but this nickname was inaccurate; Colonel Newton, although stout, was as hard as a Korean granite lantern.

A few days previously, Dr. Houghton had asked Colonel Newton to take him on a tour of the northern defenses including the DMZ. Colonel Newton was flattered at this out-of-character request for a medical officer, most of who would rather have stayed in the safe, warm bosom of the U.S. compound. Dr. Houghton had dressed for the occasion in his new fatigues with his 45, M-16 rifle and an eighteen pound bullet - proof vest.

Bumping along the unpaved road, Colonel Newton turned around and opened Dr. Houghton's field jacket. Jokingly he said, "I thought you had it on. What for Doc? It's too heavy." Continuing to rib the Captain, he went on, "Hey Doc, can you shoot that 45?"

"I am not bad, Colonel," Dr. Houghton said casually. In fact, at the practice range two days previously, Dr. Houghton received a near-perfect 9.8.

The conversation lapsed as the jeep slowed to a creep to make way for a long convoy of singing Korean volunteer infantry who were going South, before being shipped to Viet Nam. They would join the two Korean divisions that fought with the Americans in Viet Nam. Soon after, they fell behind a convoy of company after company of infantry going north along the sandy road.

"Colonel, this country is one big armed camp." Dr. Houghton said choking on the dust as they finally passed the convoy.

"Yes, that's especially true here, just below the DMZ."

"Who's that firing over there to the left, Colonel?"

"That's tank practice. Look over there. They are aiming at targets in the side of the hill." Colonel Newton pointed as the shells exploded in small orange flashes. "Doc, never stand near a firing tank. They are very loud; they shoot ultra-fast projectiles."

A moment later, Dr. Houghton asked, "What are those small mounds on the sides of that mountain?"

"Doc, you've got to be kidding."

"No, I really don't know."

"That's where they bury the dead; it's a Happy Mountain."

"So that's the place I've heard so much about." After another short pause, Dr. Houghton continued shooting out the questions. "What exactly is going to happen at Nightmare Range?"

"At about ten, the U.S. Air Force is going to put on a display of close combat support with napalm, rocket, and machine gun fire after an opening artillery barrage. Then a Korean armored brigade will move forward. After the show, we'll head north to the DMZ."

"Sounds interesting."

Shouting to be heard above the noise generated by the jeep as it labored up and down the hills, Colonel Newton appeared ludicrous. His face was now covered by a thin layer of yellowish - tinged road dust, on which someone could scratch his initials or something worse. Colonel Newton said, "What do you think of my Miss Lee?"

"Colonel I think a man of your good looks and social position could find a better looking girl. Besides, Miss Lee wears falsies."

Colonel Newton reddened right through the dust. "How the hell would you know?"

Dr. Smith only laughed, momentarily remembering Mrs. Newton's picture, a beautiful, buxom woman.

Colonel Newton immediately understood, pondered for a moment and continued. "Doc, you know, I think you're right. When I find a new one, I want you to check her out."

"Be glad to, Colonel."

"I mean a medical check up; VD, TB, etc."

"Sure, sure, sure," Dr. Houghton imitated Miss Lee who repeated her replies.

The jeep struggled to climb the hill to the observation post overlooking Nightmare Range, a huge valley with a small hill in its center. The Korean generals and American colonels sat on canvas stools to observe the show. The whooshing of the fall wind, penetrating Houghton's bullet-proof vest, provided the aural background for the loud but invisible crescendo-decrescendo hisses of the artillery projectiles sailing over them on their way to the small hill target. Colonel Newton said they came from positions eight miles distant. With each hiss, Dr. Houghton fought his tendency to duck. He noted the gooseflesh of fear at he thought of one of the shells being anemic, and falling a little short.

After the incredibly accurate artillery barrage, the American-piloted jets roared in two-by-two, just to the left. Dipping dangerously low, they fired their rockets and dropped their napalm into the small white circles on the hill.

Next, as the tanks rolled forward, Colonel Newton pointed out the tall, ominous mountains of North Korea. But Dr. Houghton's attention quickly returned to the tanks. They suddenly stopped; then, he saw brilliant flashes emerge from the tank muzzles which were immediately followed by thunderous reverberations. The whole mountain shook as the tanks rolled back, the projectiles right on target. Now, each time a tank fired, Dr. Houghton involuntarily grasped the stone on which he sat. He was now covered with goose flesh; this was the rawest power.

"What is happening now - Doc?" Colonel Newton asked, after the tanks had rolled into their final forward positions.

"I don't see anything, Colonel."

"Look again, Doc."

Dr. Houghton looked carefully. In the valley, the configuration of the green foliage subtly and miraculously changed.

Then looking to his left, he saw a chaparral of small bushes suddenly move forward thirty meters and stop. "Colonel, the camouflage is excellent. I wouldn't know what to shoot at."

"Yes, very good Doc. That's about it for the show. I think we had better head north. It's growing late."

The country became more mountainous as they drove north. Some areas were not being cultivated. Dr. Houghton was not nervous as they approached the DMZ. He still felt the invincibility of youth.

The Korean Military Police emerged from the final fortified check point.

Lieutenant Ahn and the Military Police spoke quietly. Dr. Houghton grinned as he recognized Lieutenant Ahn say in Korean that the Americans were Colonel Newton the Pig and the Honorable Dr. Houghton. Did Ahn know how much Korean he knew?

Ahn said, "The MP's warn there are North Korean infiltrators, sharp-shooters, in the mountains; be careful."

At company headquarters, just below the DMZ, the Company Commander, a Captain Ro, met them. As they walked up the mountain side to the observation post, about ten meters outside the DMZ, Dr. Houghton was impressed with the nearly complete defoliation inside the southern side of the Zone. Captain Ro showed him the parallel system of trenches, mines and machine guns stretched along the high fence at the southern border of the DMZ. Dr. Houghton wondered how the front line troops in the brutal winter could survive in the trenches. Yet, he well knew the Emperors and Kings of China and Korea had built massive lines and walls across their countries to keep out the feared northern invaders. Although the weapons were different, the strategy and tactics had changed very little through the millennia. In thousands of years, in fact, nothing had really changed except the names of the Northerners. At one time, they were Mongols, at another, Manchu, now North Koreans.

Captain Ro took them through the underground bunkers that housed his infantry company and their mess hall. Dr.Houghton, whose official reason for being there was to observe the sanitation, health, and well-being of the front line Korean troops, rapidly sized up the living situation as abominable. The living space in the bunkers made an old time submarine look roomy. Rats scurried around the kitchen, bedbugs didn't even hide, and the well was below the latrine. All this was in extreme contrast to the ultra-neat Captain Ro. From the razor creases in his fatigues to his crisp, accurate explanations, he inspired confidence. Dr. Houghton knew they chose their best young officers for these difficult front line assignments. Interrupting his thoughts, Lieutenant Ahn spoke. "Do you wish to go inside the DMZ, to the guard post, the Captain wishes to know, sir?"

"Tell the Captain if he wishes to take me, I should be glad to go. I have permission from the Corps Commander. Tell him I have complete confidence in him and would deem it an honor if he would ride in the front seat of our jeep."

"Captain Ro says let's go," Lieutenant Ahn translated. "They probed the ingress road for mines this morning in anticipation of your coming."

Dr. Houghton asked, "Do you want to go, Sergeant Morse, and how about you, Lieutenant Ahn?"

"No, sir," they replied in unison looking at him and Captain Ro as if they were slightly crazy. The two Captains continued a historical discussion through Sergeant Song who added pertinent facts.

As the three of them entered the DMZ, they stopped their discussion of defensive fortifications and modern violence. They rode rapidly across the five hundred meters to the concrete Guard Post. All sane men inside the DMZ became eyes and ears. They assumed a slightly crouched position; they resembled pursued animals. But this was rational behavior in this place, for at any time, a bullet could emerge from the north with your name scratched on the patina.

Dr. Houghton greeted the Guard Post platoon leader, a young lieutenant. He thought to himself, this man has balls, big balls. They made a rapid tour of the living quarters, kitchen, and small mess hall. Dr. Houghton was favorably impressed especially by contrast with the company area. "Sergeant Song, please tell the lieutenant that this place looks sharp. I think he is doing a fine job and taking good care of his men."

The lieutenant blushed at the praise, and said in Korean, "Thank you, Sir."

Sergeant Song went on, "The lieutenant wants to know if you would like to look through the high powered binoculars."

Dr. Houghton's looked at the magnified North Korean Guard Post on the other side. He settled onto a view of a North Korean soldier staring back at him with binoculars. The confusion of Omar Khayyam's puzzled Pot appeared in Dr. Smith's consciousness, "Who is the Potter, Pray and who the Pot?" A moment later, this muddle was punctuated by the crack of a rifle shot.

Suddenly, Dr. Houghton was forgotten as Captain Ro barked orders. Then, Captain Ro picked up the field phone and spoke anxiously.

"What's gong on, Sergeant Song?"

"I don't know, Sir."

After a few minutes, Sergeant Song said, "Captain Ro wants to go."

Dr. Houghton wondered if Sergeant Song read minds since Captain Ro hadn't said a word to them. As they quickly rode out of the DMZ, Dr. Houghton concluded the bullet-proof vest was a good idea, notwithstanding Colonel Newton. He sighed in unison with the others as they passed through the southern gate.

After several minutes of polite talk and hand shaking, Captain Houghton said, "Thank you, Honorable Captain, for the excellent tour."

Captain Ro lit up like a full Korean moon emerging from a cloud. Dr. Houghton knew his father, mother and Latin teacher were correct - there is nothing like good manners, especially with a little exaggeration.

That evening, an already intoxicated Colonel Bennet, in the large mirror behind the bar at the officers'club, saw Dr. Houghton enter. Bennet was drinking with the Deputy, Colonel Weave.

"Double gin and tonic, Mr. Kim," said Dr. Houghton on approaching the bar. In the midst of the many bottles of liquor, beside Dr. Houghton's bottle, sat a steel helmet with a huge colonel's eagle soldered on it.

"I understand you went up to Nightmare Range and the DMZ," said Colonel Weave.

"You are a little dusty yourself, Colonel. You've been out today, too?" Dr. Houghton replied.

Colonel Bennet interrupted, "Have a seat here beside me, Doc, and tell us about your trip."

"OK, Colonel, but let me take off this bullet-proof vest."

"You mean you wore that all day?" the Deputy exclaimed. "What's a doctor doing up in the Zone? It's too dangerous. The North Koreans would love to nail an 'American advisor.'"

"We were inspecting sanitation, Colonel."

"That's part of our mission," Colonel Bennet said, looking over his reading glasses at Weave. "Another martini, Mr. Kim!"

"A double, sir?"

"Yes."

With their fresh drinks on the bar, Dr. Houghton embarked on his strategy, on his first real initiative since coming to Korea. He really wanted this; this was not a velleity. So he started carefully, not wanting a rejection. "Colonel Newton told me, Colonel, that you commanded a tank company here during the Korean War, that you are an expert in tank warfare and camouflage."

"Yes, I was here in 1950 and 1951. Like you, I was a Captain then." Mist welled-up in Colonel Bennet's blue eyes.

"What I don't understand is how the tank crew can stand the noise when the turret gun fires."

"Surprising as it seems, inside the tank it is tolerable," Colonel Bennet paused, "but outside the tank the noise is devastating. Yes, as I'm sure saw today, the Koreans are very good at camouflage. I remember how we carried them dressed as haystacks with their round stones during the war."

"Round stones, Colonel?"

"You see, some Koreans rode into battle on our tanks. They stood on the hot exhaust tubes that came out of the back of our tanks. So as to not burn their feet, they carried thin flat round stones to stand on. Yes, I remember one particular haystack who was a machine gunner. One night under a bright moon, we parked the tank behind a partially destroyed house. This gave us an open view of the road, a wide field where we expected a Chinese advance. Our main haystack got off and set up his machine gun about ten meters in front of us in a small gully. All night long, the Chinese kept coming. Periodically we'd let a big one go from the tank, and our haystack would get whatever we missed. Every time we shot, the haystack jumped two feet in the air. We estimate we killed 250 Chinese that night. We also made a deaf haystack."

Dr. Houghton enjoyed the endless tales of moving haystacks, tanks, and heroes, but not the prodigious killing. After listening for some time, he felt the moment was propitious. "Colonel Bennet, I have a request."

"Yes, shoot Doc."

"I would like to study Hap Gi Do, you know the oriental Karate, if it's OK with you."

The colonel answered thoughtfully, "A little strange for a medial officer, isn't it? But it's fine with me as long as you don't break any bones, any of your bones."

Colonel Weave said, "I think it is a bad idea, Sir. Houghton will never progress; he is a medic. I strongly advise against this. Enlisted men maybe - but not American officers with those dirty Koreans. He'll pick up TB or lice or scabies or worse."

"What's worse?" Colonel Bennet said.

"Leprosy."

Dr. Houghton was enraged but kept his counsel. He knew the deputy was at best a mediocre officer. This was Weave's last tour before separation. He had repeatedly been turned down for promotion. In fact, Weave was sent as a Deputy to Korea because, although the Army was looking for senior colonels in Vietnam, he was considered incompetent for a combat position of any type.

Dr. Houghton responded calmly, "Colonel Bennet, I will do you proud."

There was a very long pause. Dr. Houghton remembered that Weave, reputed to be an expert about trees, called Dr.Barnes - "caduceus." He remembered that word from botany but looked it up anyway. Weave thought Barnes fell off the tree too early. In the process Houghton thought of the related word marcescent. He thought this word applied to Weave - he was withered and dry but just wouldn't fall off the tree.

The Colonel finally said, "Doc good luck. I wanna see a black belt - nothing less." He went back to his stories.

Dr. Houghton didn't pay attention to Colonel Bennet once he received permission.Instead, he thought like a Korean. Why is the Deputy involved in my business? He is upsetting my kibun, my inner harmony; he is outside the decision circle, the SOB. But Dr. Houghton discarded those thoughts and their necessary cultural consequence - revenge. He had obtained what he wanted. After all, he was an existentialist, a follower of Camus. Now he must "do it."

Only Mr. Kim, the bartender, who carefully observed the interaction of Colonel Bennet, the Deputy and Captain Houghton, understood the significance of this request. For over a decade, he had nightly attended the bar at the club. He had watched so many American officers' incomprehensible behavior. In fact, he secretly relished the ruin of many American officers by the three evils; American cigarettes, Scotch whiskey and Korean business ladies. But Dr. Houghton was different. He already knew too much; he asked too many questions; he was studying Korean with Sergeant Song and now Hap Gi Do. Mr. Kim concluded that he should watch Dr. Houghton very carefully.

"For he who lives more lives than one,
More deaths than one must die"
"Ballard of Reading Gaol," Oscar Wilde

Chapter V
Out

Dr. Houghton studied at his desk before supper. He had two small rooms in the company grade Base Officers Quarters, BOQ, sobriqueted the Q. One room he used as a living room/den. It was decorated with a large antinuclear peace poster. The other room, the bedroom, he gradually redid with Chinese motifs, a style he learned at Harvard in his oriental studies class. Initially, he ordered light blue silk curtains from the army PX catalogue. In his travels within Korea, Dr. Houghton also found a matching blue silk bedspread with brocaded red Chinese characters for happy. He also purchased three orange-red paper Chinese lanterns and an excellent copy of a black Chinese brush painting of a Taoist adept walking among the Guilan karst-mountains, deep inside Communist China. Although unlikely, he hoped to visit Guilan some day. But alas, Americans could only travel to Hong Kong.

To Dr. Houghton's surprise, on an inspection tour of the Q, the Deputy disapproved of his "decorations." However, Dr. Houghton pointed out he bought the blue silk curtains from the Army PX catalogue, an admittedly ridiculous response to the Deputy's dumb criticism. In the end, he decided to ignore the Deputy. But the Deputy, Dr. Houghton laughed, did not see the missing *vital element*; a slant-eyed ethereal maiden.

Someone knocked on the door.

"Come in Sergeant Song. It is time for our lesson."

After an hour of letters, words, declensions, and polite Korean forms, Sergeant Song said, "You are making rapid progress. Let us translate together the Korean National Anthem and we will then stop, OK?"

With the dictionary and some help from Song, Dr. Houghton finally came to the words "thousands of miles of mountains, streams and deathless flowers." Dr. Houghton paused, "We call deathless flowers in America - amaranths."

Sergeant Song said, "Do you know Aesop's fable about the Rose talking to the Amaranth?"

"Yes, I remember reading it. When I was at Harvard I synthesized the red dye amaranth- part of my chemistry thesis project. I read about amaranth plants and flowers at that time."

Sergeant Song said, "I know Aesop's Amaranth Fable by heart. Remember in it, Aesop compares the fleeting Rose to the everlasting Amaranth." Sergeant Song recited the fable:

"A Rose and an Amaranth blossomed side by side in a garden, and the Amaranth said to her neighbor,

'How I envy you your beauty and your sweet scent!

No wonder you are such a universal favorite.'

But the rose replied with a shade of sadness in her voice,

'Ah, my dear friend, I bloom but for a time:

my petals soon wither and fall, and then I die.

But your flowers never fade, even if they are cut;

for they are everlasting.'"

Dr. Houghton was astonished by the exact recitation. He knew Aesop was correct; the bright red color which occurred in the amaranth leaves and flowers was fast and did not fade. But how in the world did Sergeant Song know this? He said, choking with emotion, "How do you know this particular fable?"

"I learned this when we discussed the meaning of the phrase 'deathless flower' in the national anthem in high school. I have a good memory. In the west you have the rose; in Korea we have the hibiscus and amaranth."

Soon after, Sergeant Song left – to use a slang expression – a snowed and speechless Dr. Houghton.

A few moments later, someone else knocked. Lieutenant Ahn entered with a broad, nefarious grin.

"And what evil do you have in mind?"

"Not me, Sir."

The more Dr. Houghton looked at Lieutenant Ahn, the more certain he was that this little man was full of worms and flukes, particularly in the liver. As the flukes chewed on his liver, Lieutenant Ahn dwindled, becoming darker and more cadaveric. There was no good treatment for liver flukes. Yet Lieutenant Ahn was extremely active. His movements were darting and unnaturally rapid. Particularly marked, on entering and leaving, was his bent over tip-toed posture, the appearance of stealth.

Contributing to his malignant appearance were his eyes, fox eyes. Moreover, on occasion, Dr. Houghton observed Ahn's eyes darken and become impenetrable, as if some black cloth had been drawn over a portion of his brain. At those times, Dr. Houghton guessed that Lieutenant Ahn concealed the black emotions of anger or hatred.

"I come to twist your ears, Sir," Lieutenant Ahn continued.

"You mean bend my ears, don't you?"

"Yes, Sir."

Lieutenant Ahn studied the American Dictionary of Slang carefully. At night, Dr. Houghton could often hear Ahn, who lived in a small room next door, repeating aloud the American slang he studied. Although Ahn had a good memory, a faulty neuron would occasionally precipitate an egregious solecism.

"You two certainly made a racket last night, Lieutenant Ahn. I don't mind laughter and love noise, but she cried all night. You understand you are not supposed to have women in here after midnight?"

"Yes, Sir."

"I'm the senior occupant of this Q ; I'm supposed to see that no women stay overnight. But that's your business as an officer and gentleman. You know the rules, but if the Deputy catches you, he'll raise hell. He'll eat your balls, fried with eggs on toast. You'll be sent back to the Korean Army. You will have none of the advantages of being with the Americans. By the way, who was the girl? The same one I saw you with the other night?" Dr. Houghton still had difficulty separating some Korean faces. "Why did she cry so much? Did you affiance her and then renege?"

Lieutenant Ahn did not answer. He smiled at Houghton's insight that a simple promise of marriage brought out the most passionate, anything-for-my-lover behavior from normally demure Korean women. Lieutenant Ahn also understood that silence was an admission of guilt.

"Let's go eat, Lieutenant Ahn," Dr. Houghton said as he glanced at the clock. "Then we will to into Chun Chon as we planned."

On arrival at the rice wine house, the Home of Perfumed Flowers, Lieutenant Ahn energetically hopped out of the jeep. As usual he was wearing his combat boots and fatigues. In a blue suit and crimson tie, Dr. Houghton gingerly followed him through the dark muddy alley toward the illuminated flower sign.

After they removed their foot gear, the Madam in the Home of Perfumed Flowers bowed deeply before she led Dr. Houghton and Lieutenant Ahn into a small private rosewood-paneled, paper-doored room. The Madam placed cushions on the obdul floor, put a box of matches and a glass ash tray in the middle of the table, and left.

"This is a middle price joint," Lieutenant Ahn commented

"Order some of the clear, strong rice wine for me, Lieutenant Ahn, not that horrible milky mogali. For yourself, order whatever you want."

Lieutenant Ahn clapped his hands three times. Soon the Madam reappeared and took the orders. Lieutenant Ahn said, "May I smoke, Sir?"

After ten cross-legged minutes, Dr. Houghton regretted his "OK." Lieutenant Ahn's strong cigarette smoke resembled the smog in LA on a hot summer 1968 day. Dr. Houghton began to cough; Ahn put out the cigarette.

Suddenly, the sliding doors opened, and three silk-dressed girls gracefully ducked through the low lintel. Dr. Houghton pointed to the cushions on the floor. Miss Kim, Miss Pak, and Miss Song introduced themselves, batting their long lowered eyelashes in a symphonic harmony.

"Miss Song is very beautiful, don't you agree?" Dr. Houghton whispered to Lieutenant Ahn.

"Yes, sir."

"Tell her to sit here by my right."

Miss Song with an easy, silky grace, moved to Dr. Houghton's right. He admired her closely while her gaze was slightly averted. She had large, almost round eyes, unusual in Korea. Her black glossy hair was gloriously coiffed in that high piled-on style with gold pins deeply inserted. Although no expert, Dr. Houghton noted that her eyes were outlined masterfully with just enough mascara and eye shadow. She wore the traditional silk yellow Korean dress, a hanbok, with the Chinese character for joy repeatedly embroidered in dark gold on the pale background.

Soon the Madam brought in the rice wine in a heated, steel teapot. Two small boys carried in a short, thin table covered with small dishes of squid, oysters, octopus, raw fish, meat and the omnipresent kimchi. On seeing the kimchi, Dr. Houghton leaned over nonchalantly to sniff Miss Song's breath to determine if she had dragon mouth. She misinterpreted the gesture and closed her eyes, only to be disappointed. The dragon mouth, although present, was tolerable and soon became unnoticeable as he drank the rice wine.

Before his first taste, Dr. Houghton worried that the oriental alcohol might dissolve his brain, leaving behind open, raw nerves. He remembered his trip to the mogali factory and the horrible stories of how the Koreans sometimes diluted the rice wine with methanol. Yet here he was and he decided to take a chance. After a few cups, he was feeding Miss Song delicacies with his chopsticks, and in turn she fed him and kept his wine cup full.

After a while the girls began to giggle behind their hands at one of the dishes. They covered their mouths for open laughter was not polite. Finally, Dr. Houghton figured out the mystery; he interpreted Miss Song's Korean as "love medicine." Lieutenant Ahn said it was eryngo, a dubious aphrodisiac. Dr. Houghton ate some and then feigned a huge desire. He pointed at his crotch and made a mime gesture - as if he had a 12 inch erection. This caused raucous hand-shielded laughter and then sudden shrieks of fake panic. The Madam opened the paper door to check that the situation was stable.

Unwound now and already high, Dr. Houghton said, "Lieutenant Ahn! Stop that vulgar display! Get the hell off her!"

Lieutenant Ahn looked up and grinned. "Sir, don't stand on ceremony."

"Lieutenant Ahn, sit up. I have some questions for you." Ahn gradually disentangled himself from the silk and the woman.

"Lieutenant Ahn, why are there so many crooks in Korea, so many slicky boys?" Dr. Houghton thought his curiosity could now be painlessly satisfied as Lieutenant Ahn was too drunk to be offended.

"Sir, in Korea, there are many poor peoples. You must protect your stuffs. If you have stuffs unprotected, and some slicky boys slicky your stuffs, it's your fault. You should never leave your stuffs unprotected or else you invite slicky boys to come. Americans are barbarians and foolish peoples. They leave their stuffs unguarded. They ask for crooks; sometimes Americans murder slicky boys. Slicky boys never violent; they are quiet and invisible; like cats they come, slicky and go." Lieutenant Ahn moved closer to the table. His manner indicated he would now expose some mysterious revelation. "Do you know Province of Thieves?"

"No, I don't."

Lieutenant Ahn continued, "In one province, in south part of South Korea, called Cholla Province, old Choson Kings put all catched slicky boys, all thieves and crooks. They call them knapsack guys. From all over Korea, all knapsack guys put in this province. Anything not nailed down, not screwed down disappears. Never turn your back on one, or he'll steal your pants and money. They are the best crooks in the world, inbred generations of crooks down there."

"Why, knapsack boys, Lieutenant Ahn?"

"Because they put all their slicky work in knapsacks. Even today, people from Cholla Province have trouble getting government jobs. Cholla peoples have their own argot. I can always tell Cholla peoples. I don't trust Cholla peoples."

"No kidding," remarked Dr.Houghton. He almost asked Lieutenant Ahn from which province he came.

"They all live in shacks in Cholla, afraid to show any kinds of wealth for fear it will be slickied."

Dr. Houghton's mind wandered. Long ago, he decided that if ever he had to work in a factory, he would not do it. He would become a thief first. And so Lieutenant Ahn's exposition of the Province of Thieves awakened a dormant tendency. He saw an enormous challenge to go to Cholla Province and steal from the thieves themselves. With some Western common sense, he was certain he could outdo the slicky boys.

Lieutenant Ahn continued, "Another reason is the smashing of Korean society and the Yangban class by the Japanese. We used to have five classes; the hereditary Yangban at the tops. They were scholars, administrators, judges, and military; then there was middle class, next farmers, then polluted chomin and finally slaves at the bottom."

"What are Chomin?"

"Entertainers like Kisaeng girls, shamans, butchers and grave diggers."

"When did slavery end?"

"In 1900; but in 1910, sneaky Japanese came and took over Korea. They forced out Korean King. They were here until 1945 and held Korea tightly under their thumbs. Everyone must speak Japanese and have a Jap name. " At this point, Ahn violently crushed a piece of shell under his thumb. "Every Korean was a slave then."

"Tell me more about the Yangban?"

"They were hereditary, scholar-official class who carried out King's rule. Only Yangban children could take examination for Imperial degree although just before Japanese came, some degrees were sold. If they pass examination, they were appointed by the King to be province governor or salt tax collector or some other big guns. Japanese broke this system.

"Then in 1950, Korean War comes. Seoul and most Korean cities flattened. After the war, many peoples come to cities; children separated from parents. Too little jobs; boys become slicky boys, and girls entertainers to live. No Yangban anymore to hold up Korean Confucian society. All gone. So everybody puts up fences and walls around houses, barbed wires and glass shards to keep out slicky boys. Remember little boy selling gum in the alley?"

"Yes, I do." Dr. Houghton recalled the filthy, emaciated tatterdemalion.

"That boy," continued Lieutenant Ahn, "orphan boy. We have millions in Korea."

"Lieutenant Ahn," Dr. Houghton momentarily hesitated, "do you think I can take Miss Song home with me tonight?"

"Sir, I told you before. Don't stand on ceremony. Why don't you sock it to her?"

"You mean now?"

"Yes, sir."

"Maybe later." Back on course, Dr. Houghton continued. "What was I saying before you interrupted; oh yes. American crooks are different. They buy a submachine gun, enter a bank, and stick it up. Much less sneaky. Sometimes people get shot."

"Barbarians," Lieutenant Ahn mumbled.

"I understand the Turks have no trouble with Korean slicky boys unlike the Americans. I heard three slicky boys once slipped into a Turk compound. The next morning three heads were impaled on stakes at the front gate. No more slicky boys on that compound. Perhaps we should do the same."

"Turks, barbarians."

"Have some more rice wine, Lieutenant Ahn. I think you are drunk."

"No me not drunk. Never happen. I'm a Korean, the son of a tiger." Lieutenant Ahn beat his minimal chest and swallowed another ounce of the 40-proof wine. "Korean peoples think American peoples simple. You give away your national wealth. If everybody took care of their own circles of responsibility, there'd be no sweat. You know the medicine you give away to the village people; they sell it. They laugh at Americans."

At this, Dr. Houghton shuddered. He had seen Koreans walk away from accident victims. No Good Samaritans here. If his indigent patients sold their medicine which was specific and curative for their serious diseases, what fools they were! What possible good would five dollars do for a man wracked with parasitic cramps and bloody diarrhea, or the rusty cough of tuberculosis?

"American peoples are too simple," Lieutenant Ahn repeated. He was so drunk that Miss Kim propped him up to prevent him from slipping. His bloodshot eyes occasionally separated from each other. "American peoples slicky each other wives. No good. Korean peoples think that wife, family very important. Everybody take care of parents, not like Americans. Ask Miss Song where her money go?"

60

"You ask her, Lieutenant Ahn."

He did and translated, "Miss Song says that she graduate high school. No money. Madam give her dresses, food and 8000 won each month. Miss Song says she make 8000 more in perquisite."

"Tips?"

"Yes. She send home 10,000 won every month, maybe thirty dollars. You see? Korean men want good time. They come here. They don't slicky other man's wife. We even have business ladies for GI's. Korean race number one." Lieutenant Ahn held up one finger.

"Excuse me, Lieutenant Ahn, I must go to WC." Dr. Houghton was uncertain where it was in the darkness of the Korean night. So Miss Song, although mildly intoxicated, guided him to the water closet, the WC. Without her support, he worried that he might crash down the fragile structure. In fact, the WC was only a slit in a board inside a one man shack with an odor that would frighten the most malignant Korean Demon. But you had to breathe in there. As his endless stream passed into the black slit, a few momentary waves of stench-induced nausea ended in swallow after swallow. He was grateful for Miss Song's help. Indeed, he felt a certain maudlin love-warmth for her.

She intuited his emotions. She stood ready to serve and minister without complaint or comment. Miss Song knew she was lovely, but penurious and without hope for a decent job. Even the lowest-numbered Turkish Sultan's odalisque was more fortunate. Certainly, she was now and forever unmarriageable. These thoughts shifted into an enormous anger that began in her belly and rose up into her reddening face. Perhaps she could make some arrangement with this handsome Captain. She just could not accept her fate without a try.

As Dr. Houghton staggered back to the Home of Perfumed Flowers with Miss Song's help, he thought of Lieutenant Ahn's unbridled audacity, using a Ciceronian phrase that appeared in his consciousness. These Koreans did not even have reasonable sanitation and plumbing, a WC being, at best, a euphemism for a vile outhouse, the contents of which were saved and treasured. In the spring, he knew that the Koreans emptied its "night soil" onto the fields and rice paddies. The whole country then stank like a giant WC. He would smell it for himself soon enough. He saw pertinent images of hazy effluvia above the rice paddies when suddenly he commented to himself that he was quite drunk. Other images came and went one after another: first a Korean man casually urinating by the side of the road; then a beautiful girl who could knock you down with her breath; next, an outcast orphan, now a slicky boy; then an old, worn entertainer, her money dutifully sent home for years, now in need, rejected by her family, reaching for her final solution, twenty American Seconal tablets; and finally an officer and a gentleman accepting a bribe.

As he reentered the Home of Perfumed Flowers, Dr.Houghton concluded that the Koreans were the barbarians and not the Americans. Moreover, the obnoxious ethnocentricity with its emphasis on the pure Han race was ……. He could not find the right word. Lieutenant Ahn's arrogance angered him most. "We even have business ladies for GI's" was preposterous and beyond belief. The word "even" really upset him.

But gradually, by an act of will, as an old chemist, he dissolved his anger in a cool solution of reason. He had come to this Home of Perfumed Flowers to see, to hear, to observe and mostly to be entertained. If he allowed his mind to close now, he would learn nothing. He would be like the Deputy. He would never grow intellectually or even be entertained. Without doubt, Miss Song was immaculate, sparkling and splendidly costumed. Her somewhat passive savoir-vivre, although alien, soothed him. So he decided to proceed; he firmly grasped her hand and said nothing for a while. Magically, Miss Song's hot hand responded, providing the anodyne to his florid anger of a moment ago. Finally he said, "Miss Song, I came all the way here for you to entertain me; will you begin please? Kaps see da. Let us begin."

"I am sorry," she said, "I no know English."

Dr. Houghton looked for aid from Lieutenant Ahn who lay on his back, his head in Miss Kim's lap. As Dr. Houghton attempted to pry Ahn's eyes open, he shouted, "Get up you bum; that's a direct order." But Lieutenant Ahn was unconscious.

Dr. Houghton concluded he was now on his own. He clapped three times, which brought back the low-bowing Madam. "More girls, sing-song, dancing," he said to the Madam.

Soon two more girls came. The second girl, very attractive said in English, "First, you sing song."

Accommodating, Dr. Houghton broke into a chorus of "You are my sunshine, my only sunshine….." A moment later, this spark kindled a conflagration. Clanging their chopsticks against the glasses and dishes, the girls began to sing loudly in broken English. He realized they did not understand what they sang. When they finished, they all applauded, and he batted his eyelashes which brought endless laughter.

Finally, Dr. Houghton, gasping for breath, said to Miss Song, "You sing song."

In Korean, she replied, "I sing song, love song, OK?"

She began in a lyrical contralto. The song was sad and elegiac. He knew it described a broken love affair between an entertainer and her lover. The other girls now softly beat time with their chopsticks. At appropriate times in harmonic unison, they joined the chorus. Miss Song sang very well. Near the end, apparently identifying with the heroine's tragedy, Dr. Smith saw tears accumulating in Miss Song's eyes. But she sang on with total poise. Embarrassed, he almost stopped breathing at the height of her involvement in the song. For a moment, he didn't know if this was just part of the entertainment or not, but he concluded it was real. Should he applaud or weep? He had never witnessed such a totally open display of emotion, certainly not under such circumstances. He applauded and so did the other girls.

A second girl sang a happy song, and the other girls rhythmically pounded their chopsticks on the table and glasses, creating a raucous din. The third and fourth girls next sang moving tragic songs. To him, the overfeeling of their songs must be the millennial sadness of the entertainers. They were surely very accomplished.

Dr. Houghton rose and mumbled, "Next, mime and salutatory arts." Being very wobbly, he imitated the rapid, shuffling, small-stepped gait of a hobbled, foot-bound Chinese girl. In Korean, he said, "Who am I?"

They looked quizzically at him. In Korean, one said, "Han Guk Saram; American man."

Feigning disappointment, he said in Korean, "No, I middle-kingdom girl."

At this, the girls politely covered their laughter with their hands and turned their heads. However, Miss Song said, "That was very excellent," so that Dr. Houghton would not lose face. Sergeant Song repeatedly told him that public shaming upset the crucial inner harmony of the Korean mind. For example, Sergeant Song finally explained that two men frequently sleep in one small cot in Korean Army hospitals because there aren't sufficient beds. But, Colonel Lee knew Dr. Houghton would be scandalized by the practice, so he lied to save face, to protect his inner harmony and that of the situation as he saw it. Once again, harmony trumped truth.

When he heard this, Dr. Houghton asked Sergeant Song, "Do they sleep head to head?"

"No, head to toe."

Dr. Houghton had to bite his tongue to prevent himself from breaking apart with laughter. Sergeant Song also smiled

Back in the Home of Perfumed Flowers, two little boys began removing the tables and food. Miss Kim stood up while the other

63

girls rolled Lieutenant Ahn into the corner. Another boy brought in an ancient record player. To the scratchy accompaniment of the recorded lutes, flutes and drums, Miss Kim performed the Korean traditional dance. Although she was graceful, Dr. Houghton did not wholly appreciate her expertise nor realize the degree of difficulty of the motions. Still, he knew that this dancing was high culture indeed.

As keenly as he watched them, the girls in return observed his every movement. They were intrigued by their spell-bound guest, never having had an American customer. They intuitively felt that Dr. Houghton came with an open mind to watch and enjoy their performance, not just to carry them off into the dark night to a flophouse. And so they went all out to please.

One of the new girls rose. He did not understand when she placed a full ounce of rice wine in a china tea saucer in front of him on the floor. Dancing in the Chinese fashion, with the sinuous motion of a serpent, without her hands or knees touching the floor, she brought her head closer and closer to the floor with flow and ebb motions. Finally, with Dr. Houghton in a state of disbelief, she grasped the plate carefully between her teeth and with lateral swaying movements rose up slowly and presented the wine to him.

After this extraordinary exhibition, Miss Song left, leaving him to speculate on what she might do next. She returned with a record and was now dressed in a Western gown of the early fifties. She said, "Me stripour." With the scratchy honky-tonk music blaring, he remembered the famous "ecdysiasts" like Peaches and Candy Bar in Boston's Scollay Square when he had been a Harvard freshman. But after the girls dimmed the lights, he concentrated on the oriental Miss Song. Piece by piece, she pranced around like Peaches and Candy Bar and ended in just a G-string. She must have carefully studied the movies of the strippers of the West. She was very good; she could really bump and grind. He cheered wildly at this unexpected performance – unlike his stealthy behavior of ten years before when he felt like a Puritan criminal. But deep inside, he recognized that something was missing; the bumps, the grinds and the wiggles were slightly off. Miss Song had not quite captured the lubricity of Candy Bar or Peaches, women who could stimulate erections on stones.

In contradiction to Dr. Houghton's obvious intense interest, the girls could not understand why at 11 PM Dr. Houghton clapped his hands for the Madam. He seemed to be having such a pleasant time, and yet, suddenly, without reason or explanation, he wished to leave. Miss Song was disappointed. She had decided to accede to any wishes he might have for her.

He perceived the disappointment, but he could not explain to her about American men, the curfew and his drunkenness. He would return. The Madam came, bowed and gave Dr. Smith the check. He looked at the check, and was not certain if it was 3,500 or 35,000 won.

Lieutenant Ahn looked and said 3,500. "This is too much, sir. They think you sucker because you American."

Dr. Houghton figured 10 dollars for an evening's entertainment was reasonable indeed. To each girl and the madam, he gave an extra 1,000 won."

"That is much too much, Sir," protested Lieutenant Ahn.

"Lieutenant Ahn, tell them they were all wonderful, and I enjoyed the evening." Lieutenant Ahn then translated this.

The Madam and the girls all came outside to say good-bye.

Lieutenant Ahn staggered ahead down the alley toward the circle where Sergeant Song and the jeep was to meet them. Suddenly, he stopped to speak to a Korean girl. After a short conversation, he said, "This is Dr. Houghton. This is Miss Ku, Sir."

"Hello, Hiss Ku." Dr. Smith saw a westernized, not unattractive Korean girl.

"Hello," she answered.

"Miss Ku used to go with an Air Force Major who has left," explained Lieutenant Ahn.

"Do you have a Korean girl friend, Dr.Houghton?"

"No, I don't."

"Why don't you come to my house?"

Dr. Houghton approached very close to Miss Ku. She did not have dragon mouth. Moreover, she smelled of gardenia and musk. "O.K.," he replied.

"How about tonight?"

"No, tomorrow at 8:00 o'clock. I'll meet you at the circle."

Unfortunately, the jeep ride back to the Q upset the delicate harmony of Dr. Houghton's stomach; it disquieted the squid and octopus inside. Even the smoothest curve brought them into his throat. Later, in the Q, to avoid a horrible night, he induced a retch and eliminated the beasts. This resulted in a dizzy sleep and only a mild hangover the next day.

Dr. Houghton visited Miss Ku two times. Although her hooch was warm, stereoed and electric blanketed; although Miss Ku never once mentioned money, he "helped out" with expenses. Miss Ku was actually very attractive. She had a body worthy of Aphrodite and was ultra-clean. She was a professional with skills gleaned from a tradition over 3000 years old. She also complimented him wisely.

She called him "Priapus" after their first evening together when she heard he studied Latin.

He did not point out that Priapus was Greek, but appreciated the good intentions.

It was not Miss Ku's minimal requests from the PX or even her previous experiences. He was not sure what it was. Perhaps it was that hard GI slang or the imitation of American movie chic and magazine culture. He was certain that she was as decent as other woman, wanting only protection and even love. After all, she was sold into the business. Dr. Houghton in their short acquaintance treated her like a high society Boston lady. He rewarded her well but he never went back.

"The Superior Man is not one who is good for only one kind of position."
Analects of Confucius

Chapter VI
Harvard

After the wretched drudgery of his great uncle's factory, Reg was certain he did not want to work. So he went to Harvard in a vague quest for a métier. This temperamental disinclination to work had actually extended as far back as he could recall. He vividly remembered an incident one autumn day just before his ninth birthday.

"Hey, Reg," his father called. "Why don't you rake the leaves? I'll be out in an hour or two to see how you are doing." His father placed Reg "in charge of leaves." He asked Mr. Lawler the handyman-gardener not to help. He thought the "leaves" would teach Reg important lessons.

That fall day, in a conscious effort to avoid the raking, Reg sallied forth to collect the neighborhood boys. He suggested a game of touch football in his yard with cookies to follow. The children readily agreed since Reg unquestionably had the best backyard for touch football and excellent chocolate chip cookies. But when all ten finally assembled around the football, Reg said disingenuously, "Nuts, I forgot I have to rake the leaves first." He feigned a deep dejection, but, as if with a sudden glorious insight, said, "But if you help out, I bet that we can finish in fifteen minutes, OK?"

"OK," the ten suckers replied in unison. They scurried off and each soon reappeared with the family rake. Working quickly, the large yard was soon bereft of the brown, wrinkled annoyances.

Reg's mother appeared near the completion of their labors. She found Reg sitting beside his rake while the others were still working away. Initially, she said, "Raking is hard work," with a stony-faced expression. But, on her way into the house, she winked and said, "Cookies after the game?"

It wasn't that Reg had not worked. In fact, at his family's repeated urging, he had worked more than his peers. This seemed ridiculous to Reg, for many of the youths who needed the money did not work. First he delivered newspapers. In high school in the summers, he worked as a construction helper, a brutal, back-breaking job. He learned that the "shit flows downhill." Finally, he labored in his great uncle's factory for a paltry salary. But rather than learning the value of money and thrift, and the more abstract concepts of the nobility of labor and the other plinths of Puritanism and Americanism, he daydreamed of work avoidance. Most important, he became aware of his temperamental disinclination to work. Reg understood that a partial reason for this was his ever-increasing dislike of morning rising. A morning in bed was a great joy. He was most alert at night, a function of his misregulated biologic clock.

Early on, Reg realized that college would be only a temporary manumission from the horrors of work and the pain of early rising, but an obviously worthwhile delay. In high school, he observed that selection of certain subjects such as Latin and chemistry combined with vigorous application was the way to matriculate in the best colleges. As a discrete dividend, the top students had privileges, gained encomia, and walked in the green-eyed glow of the other students. For a prank, for which a lesser student would be punished, Reg only received a mild reprimand, an appeal to his greater reason. Although a member of the aristocracy of achievers, he recognized the injustice of it. But this was the "fact" of high school, and he successfully worked to be "primus inter pares."

As expected, Harvard offered a pleasant freedom. There were only four rules: A tie and jacket had to be worn for all meals; the university buildings must not be burned down; passing grades were necessary; and all bills had to be paid on time. You could study or not, attend classes or not as you saw fit.

Most stimulating was the assemblage of excellent minds, indeed extraordinary minds, in one small community. Bill, Reg's roommate of the first two years, was no exception. Bill and Reg from day one became intellectual pals. On their first meeting, they agreed that modern art, religion, and opera were sham. But Bill, unlike Reg, was a natural for law with his extensive vocabulary and Demosthenian oratorical ability. Bill continuously improved his mind. A dictionary sat beside the bathroom bowl.

The first year, Reg received an A in both chemistry and philosophy, and B+ in math and physics. In philosophy, Reg initially studied Hume and Kant. These two were the smartest philosophers since Aristotle and until Einstein. Reg was particularly fascinated by their views of psychology, how the mind worked. At Eliot house, the residential college where they lived, Reg, Bill and several other students and faculty argued for years over dinner who was correct, Hume or Kant. Reg favored Hume's view, that everything we know comes from our kaleidoscopic, ever shifting experiences not Kant's, that the sensory organs and brain impose notions of space, time, and causality on our experiences. But Kant had a point, Reg realized, when he studied how the eye sees color; nature is not colored. Nature just reflects light off objects. The eye and brain impose color. All the discussion was enormously stimulating but in the end inconclusive.

However, in his sophomore year, Reg discovered Albert Camus. He read the Myth of Sisyphus twice and was converted; he would become a lifelong existentialist. You are what you do. You are born with potential but you must "do." Fruitless talk and lack of action, especially when rationalized with empty excuses, were the only "perversions." Camus taught Reg how to live. Henceforth, Reg spent less and less time on inconclusive discussions; he needed to "do."

He majored in chemistry not only because he enjoyed it, but he was also very good at it. Furthermore, chemistry was a subject where you did things, obviously "true" things. There were many moments when Reg was certain that in the distant past he had mastered chemistry. He told his father that he knew it in a "former life." His now retired father, who was studying Buddhism at the time, smiled and said "samsara." Reg laughed at the notion of the eternal recycling, of continued cycles of birth, death and rebirth. But he somehow really did know chemistry without much study. His competitors accused him falsely of continuous all-night study. Moreover, you just could not deny the facts of chemistry such as mixing hydrogen and oxygen together with a subsequent explosion and the formation of water. He almost blew the lab up with such an experiment in high school. This was clear useful knowledge. Such knowledge proved the second Socratic truth; that knowledge was power.

Reg knew he must take advantage of his skill in chemistry. So at the midpoint of his sophomore year, he visited Harvard's world famous professor of synthetic organic chemistry, a wizard who could make complex molecules from a few simple ones. He did it with a large lab and the many hands of technicians, students, fellows and visiting professors. They were all supported by wheelbarrows full of money from the chemical industry and government.

"Why are you here, Reginald Houghton?"

"I would like to do an Honor's Thesis."

"What are you interested in?"

Reg blurted out, "I like colors, especially reds."

"OK, why don't you synthesize mauve, imperial purple and amaranth which is known as FD& C Red # 2. Mauve as you know was the first dye synthesized 100 years ago. Imperial purple came originally from Italian molluscs, Murex brandaris. The Caesars restricted its use to the Roman imperial family. Amaranth I synthesized when I was a student. Roman Catholic bishops use it to dye their robes. You will learn a lot. There are about 10 steps in each synthesis. I know you are an excellent student; you received an A+ in organic. If you do these three with your own two handles and present me with one gram each, I will give you a magna in chemistry. I will have one of my new fellows, George, supervise you, OK?"

Reg said, "Sold."

"Then we are done."

For Reg it happened that fast. In less than two minutes the die was cast (a terrible pun); he would now have a concrete project with a Master. His adult life finally began.

But on one essential position, Bill and Reg did differ. Bill maintained, "It's the man with special expertise, the specialist that the world needs. The Renaissance man is dead. You just can't even begin to scratch the patina of knowledge today. You must specialize to get ahead of your competition, the earlier the better."

Reg disagreed. "No, Bill. The world more than ever needs the Renaissance man, the man with broad knowledge, wide vision, and the ability to connect means to goals. Someone has to oversee and direct the narrow specialists. Take the mandarins of China...."

This was the essence of their argument for years. Initially, they discussed only the merits of their respective positions. With time they concluded that the actual points of view were secondary. With substantial insight, Bill analyzed Reg's philosophical underpinnings and finally, his psychological make up. Like an archeologist excavating an ancient city often rebuilt, Bill exposed level after level. Reg admitted that Bill was partially correct in suggesting that he, Reg, favorably viewed the generalist in an almost Confucian manner, because he did not wish to specialize. It was true that Reg was interested in almost everything. Bill also suggested that Reg was lazy. It is difficult to do one thing really right, down to the final brushstroke. Bill pejoratively interchanged generalist and dilettante. At the lowest level, however, Bill did not unearth a Freudian artifact, like an all-explaining dildo or a primitive mother goddess.

Reg finally admitted to himself he could not yet tolerate specialization because it would lead to definite fixed labor, like being a lawyer. But Reg hesitated to accept that he was fundamentally a "sloth" as Bill suggested. He needed to find his "métier." Would it be chemistry over the long term?

A consequence of this Socratic "Know Thyself" introspection was Reg's decision to quit the wrestling team. He no longer required this exhausting outlet for his "repressed violent instincts." When he told Bill, Bill derided him. "See I told you; the Renaissance man is dead. You just can't do everything."

"Bill, you are partially correct; wrestling takes up too much time and energy away from my other interests and curiosities." One of these new ones was an excellent course in Oriental Studies focusing on Japan and China's art and history. This was taught by the most famous Chinese Orientalist in America. Reg was enthralled with the reading material and lectures. Moreover, his section instructor Miss Ching was exquisite. With her encouragement, Reg wrote his term paper on his old friend from high school, the eighteenth century Chinese Emperor Qianlong, Xiang Fei and the emperor's imperial jadeite carving workshops. Of course he included a section on the Fragrant Concubine's imperial green jadeite Persian pepper. Miss Ching gave him an A+ on the paper.

After the final class, Miss Ching volunteered, "Leginald Houghton," she said. Like many Orientals, she had trouble with R's. "I will show you the new jadeite carvings in the Fogg Art Museum if you want. They are lelevant to your paper."

"That would be wonderful."

"Would you like me to take you? I know the curators who will also show us several un-displayed pieces."

"I would love it, Miss Ching. I am also studying the solid state chemistry of jadeite in my chemistry course. Jadeite as you know is a pyroxene. I wrote about this in my chemistry term paper. I received an A- for that one."

Miss Ching smiled and Reg melted with desire. When she mispronounced "Conglatulations," he thought he was in love. She really did look like Qianlong's Fragrant Concubine. She had very light skin and Cupid's bow lips.

At the Fogg Museum Miss Ching said, "Here are three translucent jadeite sculptures. They were carved in Qianlong's workshops from jadeite boulders from Burma. See how they give off glow-light as if they are alive. These are loaned from a private collector. This one is 14 inches tall, the Spirit of Longevity. See the Old Spirit's peach of immortality is orange-pink and his staff is brown jadeite. The carver saw the figure in the stone and carved it out. The right colors go with the right objects. Like Michelangelo's and the Greek sculptors' work, this is high art, but on a miclo scale."

Miss Ching had self-conscious trouble with micro; she blushed round-red patches on her perfect cheeks. She continued, "Even back then, in 1800, the imperial carvers used foot pedal diamond drills because jadeite is so hard. That is why they could do this. Look at this tlanslucent Goddess of Mercy carved from impelial green jadeite. This ten inch statue is worth a fortune."

"How much?"

Miss Ching said, "Millions. These were looted from the Imperial City, the Forbidden City, in 1900 when the Western powers and Japan captured Beijing. If you look at the bottom, they have the stamp of the Emperor Qianlong. See."

"Yes."

"That is why I showed them to you."

"I understand. They are fabulous. They have a living glow. When you see these, I can understand why Qianlong was enchanted by jadeite from Burma, carved by his almost miraculous Chinese carvers." At that point, Reg decided in the future he should become a jadeite carving collector. He had never seen anything so enchanting, glowing with life except perhaps Miss Ching. He would have to wait because he didn't come into his Trust until age thirty.

Notwithstanding great efforts to see Miss Ching again, Reg did not succeed. He almost fainted when a Chinese student told Reg that Miss Ching's unusual perfume was from jujube flowers, like the Fragrant Concubine. At this Reg suffered from paroxysms of unfulfilled desire for days. That summer, three weeks later, when he looked up Miss Ching she was no longer at Harvard. However, he wrote to her at her forwarding address.

On the last day of the second semester of the third year, Reg approached Bill with an outlandish smile, and a new vigor. "Bill, I've got the dwindles. You know, I was just twenty, and it's all downhill from here; already I'm missing a tooth and my joints creak. I have bad knees from the wrestling. Damn it, we study too much. We've got to get out more. The solutions are not in the books. After all, the proper study of man is man, not books. That's what the Sophists taught, yes? Let's burn the books; they're full of lies. Let's go out and get looped tonight. It'll do you good; prevent your mind from softening from over-study. If you aren't careful, one morning you'll wake up as a musty book with some exotic title imprinted on your forehead."

Bill said, "Tell me the truth for Christ's sake."

"I am sick of working in the chemistry lab. So far, I only synthesized mauve. I have two more to go and I am bored to tears. It will take the entire senior year to finish imperial purple and

72

amaranth. Moreover, there are no female chemistry majors. Chemists are so boring; sometimes I think they are the living dead."

"Reg, I'm going to hold out for one more semester until I'm accepted at Harvard Law. Then and only then will I take off the rest of the second semester of my senior year. It's too early now. I've work to finish."

"Bill, I'm also going to find a real girl like my Chinese instructor Miss Ching or Amy Band, and then travel straight to hell with her on roller stakes, before medical school."

"And when did you decide on medical school, Reg?" a shocked Bill asked.

"Today. It beats working. At least you do something constructive. It will be a challenge, I hope. It is not boring. It beats loading dynamite into bombs like many people do. Moreover, my dad wants me to do it."

"Gook luck. I'm off to the library."

"Now that I am to be a physician, I will treat the callus on your ass, for free."

Bill raised his middle finger and laughed.

Early in his senior year, decked out in his new tuxedo, Reg entered the exclusive Bat Club, his entrance into Boston's and America's high society. A friend T.B., the president of the Bats whom Reg had helped through basic chemistry, insured his rapid admission into this circle of snobs. The members were the scions of the very wealthy and the "best" families. About eight percent of Harvard undergraduates joined one of these Final Clubs by invitation and election. But just one black ball and you were out. It was not long, however, before Reg realized that his brother Bats were in fact troglodytes in tuxedos. Moreover, the Bats were also the least desirable Final Club.

The high point of Bathood came in the spring of Reg's senior year. On that occasion, each Bat brought as ugly and sublimely wretched a specimen of the "distaff" as he could find. Reg knew he succeeded because when T.B. saw her, he said with an absolutely straight face, "My compliments to you, Reg." In fact, Reg brought an old high school classmate who resembled a witch. She was a consummately perfect hag. Reg crowned his glory and her image by persuading her, with a vile lie, to carry a small besom, a broom of twigs, the standard witch's vehicle.

All twenty Bats arrived dressed in tails and white ties, escorting their "dates." These twenty unmarried Harvard men were knowledgeable, wealthy, and suave; their expertise sparkled that evening. On the other hand, Reg had never seen twenty more frightful women assembled in one place. They were not just homely, plain, or unfavored; they were hideous, repulsive, and offensive. There was scurf on one; another was girdled with roles of fat, boil-pimples on a third, and on and on. Each was dressed as for a ball. Yet, it was a very successful evening. The laughter, gaiety, and general levity amazed Reg. No date discovered the secret. T.B. had quieted Reg's preparty concern with the historical fact of many similar successful parties. Only one Bat acted like a cave men; he had carnal relations with his date on a couch around midnight. As Reg and T.B. watched, T.B.whispered, imitating Churchill, *"This is her finest hour."*

The next evening, the happy Bats selected the "ugliest" date. T.B. proposed Reg's date. She won by a close vote. The clincher, T.B. argued, was the besom. Reg treasured the solid gold watch, the winner's trophy, for years as a symbol - he wasn't sure of what. On the back was carved a besom. But, sometimes, as he grew older, he thought he should throw it away.

However, Reg's first entry into the Bat Clubhouse was not so benign. At the fall initiation ceremony, he said to T.B., "You look as if you were born in a tuxedo. You look real fine."

"You, too Reg. Now don't be nervous; you'll handle the pint of Bat Blood fine."

Reg changed the subject. "T.B., when do they vote at the Hasty Pudding?"

"December."

"I hope I get in and don't get black-balled."

"You'll have no trouble," T.B. reassured him. "I'm looking forward to your joining us over there soon. You'll enjoy the Pudding. It is a great place." T.B. paused, "Let's begin."

The secret ceremony of sophomoric hazing culminated in a blindfolded, wobbly walk down an adit into a small red chamber. Reg's blindfold was removed. He saw a Bat Brother drop dry - ice into water-filled ampullae in the four corners of the room. The containers began gurgling and bubbling, spewing forth cold steam. Red light bulbs behind the curtains indirectly lit the farce. A discontented live bat hovered above. Directly in front of him, Reg saw the spotlighted, bubbling red liquid, the Bat Blood, in a black iron cauldron. T.B. stood on the other side of the cauldron, now costumed as a huge bat. Crowded around the initiate were many fellow tuxedoed Bats.

After the final "quiet," disturbed only by the bubbling of the dry ice in the ampullae and cauldron, T.B. said, "Now Reginald, before you become a True Bat, the final requirement is to drink this pint of Bat Blood." T.B. dipped a black mug into the liquid and handed it to Reg.

Reg accepted the pint calmly, looked deeply into the swirling bloody brew, and said, "To your health, you Batshits." He drank the cold fluid in a trice. Reg figured he could hold down the mixture for one or two minutes before vomiting. He later learned the recipe was nine parts cheap gin to one part pig blood. Reg shook congratulatory hands with his new Brothers. He wore a false smile. Within his estimated two minutes, he slipped into the bathroom, draped a towel over his front, and convulsively but carefully retched the bloody gin into the toilet bowl. After a quick clean up and a brief red-eyed but satisfied view in the mirror, ninety nine seconds after entry, Reg walked out and milled amongst his new Brothers.

One foolish initiate attempted to retain the bat blood. Within an hour, he was unconscious and vomiting in an ambulance on the way to the Mass. General Hospital. T.B. and the other Bats were worried.

At the initiation, Reg knew he was finally an adult for he had lost his youthful sensitivity. As a child, he often wondered how adults could drink gin; even a single sip burned his mouth and gullet. Now he observed the delicious martini in his hand. Adults had no sensitivity. He always thought that adults lacked sympathy for the sick, down-trodden and troubled. But his childhood pantheism and its attendant respect for all had narrowed to an excessive love of self. He noted his own lack of empathy. The gin further dulled his already too hard attitude. He pondered these valid observations; yet as he surveyed the room and its denizens, he saw alcohol and callousness were the adult style. It was purported to be fun.

A few months later, Reg sat down to lunch in Eliot House where T.B. also lived. The previous day, Reg had discovered that T.B. had a personal fortune of five millions, much more than Reg's two million dollar trust which he would control at age thirty. T.B. said, "Congratulations,Reg. You are now a member of the Hasty Pudding."

"T.B., I heard that. I took the liberty of leaving a bottle of your favorite Rothschild claret in your room. I am most grateful to you."

"My great pleasure, Reginald. Consider it a debt repaid. After all, you pulled me through chemistry and I couldn't graduate without that. But now I also have the perfect girl for you." For a pregnant moment, T.B. paused with the confident grin of aristocrats. "Her name is Marsha Greenfield, a third year student as Wellesley. Why don't you date her? She is really beautiful. If you like, you can take her to the Pudding show with us next month, the sixth of Ferurary. I play one of the leads. How does that sound?"

"Thanks T.B. I'll look her up."

"Here is her number; you give her a ring. I already told her about you."

As Reg waited on the corner for Marsha, he concluded that T.P. was right. Marsha was stunning and smart. "Hello Marsha. I can't believe it is Wednesday already."

Every Saturday at noon and Wednesday at four o'clock, the beginning of Eliot House parietal hours, Marsha drove her new Jaguar convertible the forty-five minutes from Wellesley to Cambridge. This was what she wanted and Reg had no objections. Reg slipped into her car. "Where shall we go?"

"Let's go to your room."

After they parked, Reg signed her in the guest book at the main entrance of Eliot House. On the way through the green inner courtyard that the House Master, with Grecian delusions, called "Arcadia," Reg asked, "Did you like the Pudding show?"

"I loved it, Reg. Thanks so much for taking me. I'm sorry you didn't play in it."

Every year the Hasty Pudding Institute put on an elaborate, original, bawdy musical in which all roles were played by the male members. That year's performance, based on the Peace Corps in the Pacific islands, had been a great success. T.B. was fantastic. President Kennedy, an old Pudding alumnus, laughed endlessly the night he attended. So had Reginald. The young hairy legged men with nylon stockings, huge bosoms and clever dialogue showed an expertise that was remarkable for undergraduates.

That night, the vice-president of the Pudding, a man Reg had supported through freshman math, made a very open, flattering pass at Marsha. Reg felt supremely comfortable in his tuxedo, hands in his pockets, as he watched Marsha fend off the would-be-thief. Marsha was indeed a breath-taking, busty beauty with her thin waist, long, shapely legs and flaxen hair.

After the villain beat a chagrined retreat, Reg said, "You know, Marsha, next month the Pudding is going to have a dance to crown a queen. I think you'll win."

"You really think so?" Marsha asked without artifice.

Reg never understood what she saw in her mirror. She wasn't sure of her appearance nor did she know where she ranked in the hierarchy of women. She did not win, but placed second that night, a vision in white.

"A drink, Marsha?"

"Yes, thanks. Where's Walt?" she asked.

His senior year Reg had come to live with Walt, a fellow Bat. Bill had decided to live alone to pursue his studies in peace. Walt and Reg had a small apartment in Eliot House. They had a living room and two bedrooms. Walt had built a small bar in the living room behind which stood a giant faux snowball. A huge crimson Harvard banner hung over the fireplace.

"Oh, Walt took off. He wanted us to be alone."

"Good," Marsha replied. She walked into Reg's bedroom, neatly undressed and adorned herself in Reg's boxing robe, exactly as she had done on their third date. "You are going to get hurt, Reg if you box in the tournament."

Reg did not answer. He thought that she was right, but he was hoping for a fluke. He was strong and reasonably quick. He realized that four of the last five nights he had been intoxicated. First, the Dean Acheson dinner, then the Pudding dance, next the burlesque in Scollay Square with Walt, and now Marsha to sunder any residual vigor. Reg observed that his hand trembled noticeably. What a change, he reflected, from the near all "A" disciplined student with no clear goal or plan, to the tuxedoed sot soon to enter Yale Medical School.

Glancing at Marsha who sat on the edge of the couch in his red satin fighting robe, Reg did not answer but winked. He immediately noted a sudden flushing of her neck and bosom. He well knew his wink alone could excite her silky fluid passion. She stood and dropped the robe on the floor. Lifting her easily, he carried her back into the bedroom and closed the door quietly.

Marsha had become addicted to these sessions. Reg, somewhat less involved, enjoyed her occasional reduction to an exhausted semi-conscious maenad. He sometimes purposely pursued extremes of excess. He could control it and her.

Besides cavorting with Marsha during his senior year, Reg worked hard on finishing his three syntheses. He succeeded relatively easily with mauve and imperial purple. He used small amounts of these two successes to dye several pieces of white silk. These dyes were fast and did not fade. The professor and George were satisfied. With amaranth, however, he repeatedly failed. The toughest decision he ever made was to continue the project. He could have purchased it as FD & C Red No. 2. Who would have known? He actually sweated over the decision but in the end he synthesized it himself. He heard his father's voice quote Polonius in Shakespeare, "to thine own self be true."

While he worked in the lab, he read everything he could about this color. He read Aesop's fable about the Rose and the Amaranth. He read and reread Wordworth's poem Love Lies Bleeding. He pondered Wordworth's explanation - that Venus named the Amaranthus caudatus *love lies bleeding* because the drooping red flowers reminded her of her handsome dying Adonis, bleeding to death after being gored by a huge boar. He read that Catholic bishops and archbishops wear robes and skull caps dyed with amaranth but cardinals wear scarlet. He then read about amaranth plants, all sixty species, especially A. tricolor, Joseph's coat and A. caudatus, the amaranth red *love lies bleeding* – the tassel flower. He obtained seeds and asked his retired father to grow a couple of plants in his gardens. He realized that the different meanings were all tied together; the amaranth plants did not fade because they contained the fast red betalain dyes like the synthetic amaranth. The word amaranth was a contraction of the Greek words -a, without; maran, fading; and anthos, flower. Aesop was perceptive and correct.

Eight weeks before graduation, after desparate prayers to the Chemical God, Reg at last succeeded. After twenty tries over nine days, in which he lived in the lab, ten grams of amaranth crystals finally came out of solution, an unholy miracle. Like a votary of the Chemical God, he danced around his lab bench. He would have danced on the ceiling if he could. He thought this was better than one thousand orgasms, better that diamonds or gold or emeralds. But was it better than Xiang Fei, the Fragrant Concubine, or her translucent green jadeite Persian pepper or jujube perfume? Did the Qianlong emperor know something that Reg didn't understand? Too bad he couldn't find Miss Ching with her perfect complexion and Cupid's bow lips. Finally Reg calmed down; what peculiar thoughts at this moment of personal triumph.

Perhaps he should become a chemist after all. "Forget medical school, you have talent," the Professor's senior fellow George said, when together they dyed a piece of white silk with Reg's amaranth. For comparison, they used commercial FD & C # 2. Both preparations gave the same color; both were fast and did not fade in the sun. For weeks when Reg looked in the mirror, he smiled and said, "Thank you Al Camus. Thank you, Dad."

As mid-second term senior year examinations approached, Reg realized he had probably lost his chance for his magna in chemistry, because his grades in the non-chemistry subjects would not be quite good enough. Marsha, the Bats, the parties, and not

78

least, the knockout at the Intra-Harvard Boxing Tournament had prevented adequate study. He had to reorder his priorities now.

So Reg phoned Marsha. "You know, love, exams begin in two weeks. I'm in bad shape. I'm still slightly dizzy from the knockout. I have to study." As Marsha began talking about some inconsequential nonsense, he touched the lump on his cheek and reviewed for the one hundredth time his last bout in the boxing tournament. He had fought well and gained the finals in the middle-weight class. He invited Marsha and his family to the finals, but his mother prudently declined the invitation. In the first two rounds, he definitely out-boxed and out-pointed his opponent, but in the final third round, a cut oozed blood into his left eye. A perfectly executed right cross came from that blind side. Reg never saw it. The blow knocked him unconscious for several minutes. Even worse, he and Marsha were horrified when his member wouldn't work for several nights, but this problem quickly passed. Yet he was pleased with his respectable showing in the finals.

Marsha implored, "Reg, at least let me come on Saturday night, O.K.?"

"Just that night, Marsha, until all my midterm exams are over. I'll meet you in front of Eliot House at eight. We'll see a French flick at the Brattle."

"Can't we go to the room?"

"No. No sex."

After more rejected begging, a dispirited Marsha said, "Goodbye, Reg."

"Goodbye, Love."

After she hung up, Reg realized that Marsha wanted love and marriage desperately. Both demands worried Reg. The former might detract from his new mistress, medicine, said to be a jealous and demanding lady. The latter was a decision for a thirty not a twenty year old man. He knew her desire for him to go to Harvard Medical School, and not Yale, presaged other demands that would prove stifling. She must follow him if she was interested. Reg dreaded the inevitable confrontation with Marsha.

He suppressed all thoughts of Marsha until after exams. With discipline, he studied for two solid weeks ignoring most meals and much sleep. His tutelary goddess rewarded him with two B+'s and two A's, but this was not good enough for his magna.

Reg and Marsha visited his father and mother every two months. In August after graduation they had their only successful visit. Reg's father showed them the amaranth plants he had grown. The color of the large leaves of the four foot Joseph's coats was striking. A few plants had three colored leaves; amaranth red, bright yellow and chlorophyll green. However, two plants had only bright yellow leaves. The amaranth red tassel flowers, the drooping sprigs of *love lies bleeding*, were also very bright. Reg danced around them and toasted his father with the expensive champagne he brought. His father glowed.

But on a previous visit the week before he graduated, Reg broke the "bad" academic news to his father while Marsha talked to his mother. Reg's father had prematurely basked in the reflected light from his oldest son - of the golden Phi Beta Kappa key and the magna cum laude. For over ten years, he knew that Reg was gifted when Reg scored 157 on an IQ test at age eight. Since then, Reg's father expected great things from Reg. He said angrily, "You were born with brains! How could you discard these honors: for what?"

Reg replied flippantly and he realized later stupidly, "They are idle honors; a Latin phrase and a small piece of gold."

His father was angry. "But I don't understand you, Reg. For three years you worked you head off for that 'small piece of gold' and the magna; now you throw it away for your clubs, a tuxedo, and that girl." His anger swelled and his voice rose. Reg's puritanical father said, "That damn girl is leading you around by your cock!"

Reg almost collapsed. He knew his father did not like Marsha for her lack of deference, although he did admit she was intelligent, cultured and "attractive." But this was a wild, untrue accusation. Or was it? In fact, Reg led Marsha to his boudoir at his whim or so he thought. With a wave of sympathy for his father, he tried to mollify him. "How about this, Dad? I'll earn an AOA Key at Yale Medical. I will also graduate with honors. That is a promise. The AOA Key is much more prestigious. I will do whatever it takes. Then my vest won't be empty."

His father's anger deflated. "I know you can do it. I'm going to hold you to that."

"All right, but if I get the gold Key, you must buy the gold chain." Reg laughed.

His father said, "Why not platinum?"

"Oh Dad, platinum and gold do not match."

A few days later, Reg proved his father wrong. Lying on the bed unclothed and "orgasmed out," Marsha said, "Marry me now; will you Reg? We were made for each other."

Reg scanned her carefully. She had the ideal Western feminine form, with a bosom that stood without help, a thin waist and that glorious Venus mound. She would have been a perfect model for Ingres or Valaquez. If Reg declined her proposal and then lost her, he might never be able to replace her. Yet, he replied as if his father spoke through his mouth. "You know I can't, love."

"Why not? We both have lots of money."

"But neither of us has finished school."

"Don't you love me?"

"You know I do."

"At least go to Harvard Medical School."

"It's too late now. You know that, love."

Reg thought their affair would end when he went off to Yale in September. He thought he might be making a mistake - a bird in the hand is worth two in the bush - but his mind was firm. She certainly was nice. She had taught him lessons about women, love and emptiness - Buddhist emptiness. Increasingly and unfairly, he looked upon Marsha like a female frog he had dissected in freshman biology. That lady frog consisted of some green skin, four legs, two eyes, and a huge belly full of eggs. But this thought was terribly unfair.

So here he stood four years after entering Harvard. At graduation, he was welcomed into the ranks of "educated men." Yes it was true he was a well-trained intellectual knight on a black stallion with a fancy shield of broad general knowledge and a sharp pike of detailed chemistry knowledge. But there was no silver chalice to seek, no damsel to rescue. Reg felt like an unassigned Mandarin. Harvard had prepared him well for something. But what?

Yet somehow, he was on his way to Yale Medical School hoping medicine might contain a suitable challenge. One thing Reg knew for certain *before* he entered Harvard, and when he *left* - he had no intention of working.

"Can the Ethiopian change his skin or the leopard his spots?"
Jeremiah XIII

Chapter VII
The Humble Student

"That was a long, cold ride today to the Mobile Army Surgical Hospital," said Dr. Houghton to Sergeant Song. "We were in that damn jeep five hours. Now I see why the American medical advisors rarely go over there." Dr. Houghton did not mention the most important reason: his ass was sore. He should sit on a pillow from now on.

Dr. Houghton continued as they sat down in the warm dispensary. His speech was now a macaronic mixture of Korean and English. "Honorable Teacher, your Humble Student wishes to begin. Your Humble Student proposes the following ground rules for the examination on Saturday. First, our Honorable Teacher must not fail Humble Student. It would not be fitting for Humble Student to lose face, to have a broken kibun. Second, Honorable Teacher may not beat or flog Humble Student for a performance not up to our Honorable Teacher's standard. Agreed? The Humble Student is not an enlisted man in the Korean army." Sergeant Song had finally confirmed Dr. Houghton's belated surmise; the reason there were so many injuries and fractures in the Korean Army Hospitals was the officers beat the "shit" out of the enlisted men for minor or imagined infractions. The enlisted men did not fight back - neoConfucianism again.

Sergeant Song, alias Honorable Teacher grinned. Dr. Houghton was learning.

"I have a question, Honorable Teacher, before we begin. When you teach me the conjugation of verbs, you always tell me there are polite forms for superiors, other forms for equals or intimates, and impolite forms for inferiors and children. You suggest I only use the polite forms so as not to offend anyone. This is my question; when you meet someone whose social status in relation to yours you do not know, what form do *you* use, Sergeant Song?"

Dr. Houghton knew the answer having seen this type of encounter many times. The ritual behavior was always the same: both Koreans initially employed polite forms, but after an

82

evaluation of each other's position in the social hierarchy, the one with the superior status dropped the polite forms and it was obvious. The superior's speech took on a harsher and less melodic tone. Generally, age, male sex, wealth, birth and employment seemed to delineate social rank in a rigid complex fashion. The old system of Yangban aristocrats on the top and slaves on the bottom was now replaced with a subtler but still very hierachical system.

"Honorable student," Sergeant Song advised, "you should always use the polite form. If you used a child's form to a Korean General, he would grow very angry."

Dr. Houghton did not wish to offend the senior Koreans inadvertently. After all in Rome.....However, the coward's solution would be not to converse in Korean; then there would be no possibility of error. But he was not a coward.

"But, Honorable Teacher, why should I use the polite forms to those obviously of social rank below me? Like today, for instance, you said to that lady selling chewing gum, 'No buy,' using the impolite form. When she asked me, I said the same thing. Yet she was upset when I said that to her."

Sergeant Song replied, "You should always use the polite forms as I advised you."

"Honorable Teacher, you are holding back on me, the Humble Student. Remember, off the job, we are equals as when you are teaching me Korean or when we go out socializing. In fact, Honorable Teacher may be my superior, for I don't speak Chinese nor do I have a second degree Black Belt in Hap Gi Do. But I do want the truth. I cannot properly advise if I don't know what is gong on. So I'm giving you a direct order not to clam up."

Sergeant Song reluctantly answered, "You see, Humble Pupil, in the social classification of human beings, all white men are considered uneducated, very low in the social hierarchy. It's the old barbarian idea. As a Korean, I could use an impolite term to that lady, but you, as an American, should not."

As Sergeant Song explained, Dr. Houghton contained his calescent anger. Although he already knew the answer, he was astonished at the audacity of these ethnocentric people. Because he was white, they lumped him in with Korean thieves, orphans, prostitutes, and butchers. They certainly weren't impressed with Harvard, Yale, the Brigham, the Hasty Pudding Institute of 1770, or his Captaincy or American citizenship.

His irritation quickly diminished as he remembered the uncivilized behavior of the Americans from the gunboat days of the nineteenth century up to the present. And so, he said to Song who was wiping the perspiration off his brow, "I understand." This eased the tension as they began the lesson. After an hour of conjugation, vocabulary and translation, Dr. Houghton sighed. "It is four. Thank you for the lesson. Let's go downtown to Chun Chon, to the exercise hall."

During the chilly, twenty minute ride to Chun Chon , Dr. Houghton pondered the questions of why almost every Korean addressed Sergeant Song as Honorable Sergeant Song. Even Colonel Kim did. Dr. Houghton knew of no one else of similar rank spoken to so politely. It was certainly true that Sergeant Song was multilingual, well educated, and athletic, but there must be another factor involved, perhaps family, he speculated.

As the jeep passed the barren, just harvested rice paddies, Dr. Houghton wistfully remembered the swirling, bright colored leaves of late October in New England. Over there, he imagined the local witches would be polishing their brooms for Halloween. But in Korea there were few trees and no leaves, although there were small pumpkins and many besoms and brooms, for Korea was a very dusty place. These wistful reflections turned into speculation about the future. Before coming to Korea, he had hoped to achieve several goals. First, he planned to learn the Korean language and understand the subtleties of the culture. He had made a good start. He also wanted to study some type of oriental fighting; again he had started. Most of all, he wanted a relationship with an attractive Korean girl. But so far he made no progress; calls to the unmarried nurse major at the field hospital went unanswered. But even in his lonesome moments, he did not think of Marsha or their problem. He was so disappointed in her. Since there was little he could now do, he put Marsha out of his mind until he returned to the States next October.

On the second goal, Sergeant Song had advised him soundly. He had taken him to the Judo Hall, the Tak Wan Do Hall and the Karate Studio. But without question, Hap Gi Do was the superior sport. At that first visit, several Hap Gi Do Black Belts performed an exhibition for Dr. Houghton at Sergeant Song's request. Their quick, chopping hands and twisting, thrusting feet smashed expertly into the targets. Their minutely controlled actions were executed with a ballerina's grace. Even more remarkable was the senior instructor's exhibition of the proper defense against an opponent with a glittering steel knife. Finally, two Black Belts, each armed with a five foot bamboo cudgel, demonstrated the Japanese sport of Kendo. They attacked each other with vicious abandon. Inches and fractions of seconds stood between fractured skulls and harmless wood on wood.

After the Hap Gi Do exhibition, Dr. Houghton concluded this was his sport, with its focus on defense. Surely, this would be worth mastering and bringing home. But he was doubtful if he could succeed in this type of training. The Koreans all assured him that if he was truly determined, he would obtain the wisdom of a Black Belt. But aside of the inherent difficulty in the sport, there were peripheral problems. Dr. Houghton could not imagine how he could practice in the brutal Korean winters since the exercise hall was not heated. Then there was the language barrier although this was diminishing daily.

With these reservations and the Colonel's permission, he bought his uniform. The fee was set at twenty dollars a month for two hours of daily instruction including Sundays. The problem of dealing with an alien race in an atmosphere of explosive, instantaneous violence, Dr. Houghton believed he could overcome. But the major issues in his hesitation were not the external risks, but rather the possibility that he did not possess the self-discipline to practice every day. Could be trust himself not to rationalize using injuries and pain, medical duties, or Korean studies as excuses?

Dr. Houghton was pleased that Captain Chang, the senior liaison officer, had invited him for a few drinks at a local rice wine house that evening. The week prior, he had seen Captain Chang as a patient in the dispensary. Chang had been infected by one of the entertainers with a drug-resistant strain of gonorrhea which the Korean physicians could not treat. Although Dr. Houghton successfully treated him, he advised Captain Chang to have his wife treated, for he had probably infected her. Dr. Houghton gave him a letter for her to be examined and treated if necessary at the Chun Chon Catholic Sisters' Clinic where she could be treated without embarrassment.

After the customary small talk and a large quantity of the strong, pale - yellow rice wine, Dr. Houghton was intensely curious as to what Captain Chang had in mind.

Captain Chang finally arrived at the point. "Doc, I wonder if you can help me."

"Yes, if I can, Captain Chang."

"You know my wife does not seem to become pregnant. We have been married three years. My honorable mother wants me to divorce her and get a new wife. You know, a Korean woman who doesn't have a boy child is looked down upon. Can you help me?"

Houghton had met Mrs. Chang once. She was a graduate of the finest women's college in Korea; she was cultured and had a face like the Buddhist goddess of mercy. She lived in a small room in the village outside of the detachment, on the paltry salary of a Korean Captain. Although they had a small home in Seoul, Captain Chang, a scion of an ancient Yangban family paupered by the Korean War, wished her to stay with him. Dr. Houghton thought that among the entire race of women, Captain Chang could never find a better wife than Mrs. Chang. Her inability to conceive was possibly the result of some venereal infection given to her by Captain Chang. As a childless, divorced woman, she would be ruined in the all-seeing, unforgiving eye of Korean society.

With sincere concern for Mrs. Chang's plight, Dr. Houghton replied, "Yes, I may be able to help. What I'll do is to ask Sister Joan, the Doctor Sister at the Chun Chon Catholic Sisters' Clinic to check your wife, and I'll check you out. Then I'll explain to you the best way to maximize the chances for making your wife pregnant."

"Thank you, Doc."

"One thing, Captain Chang. You should keep away from the entertainers, because gonorrhea can make you sterile."

"Yes, Sir," Captain Chang acknowledged snappily.

After a long pause, Dr. Houghton changed the subject. "Now Captain Chang, I have a question for you. What do you think of my playing Hap Gi Do?"

Captain Chang laughed, though not maliciously, and said, "Good idea." But at the same time, he shook his head from side to side. "I've never known any Americans who successfully played Hap Gi Do. You would be the first and, I am sure, the only one. Hap Gi Do very difficult for an American. I was an instructor in Korean Karate, Tak Wan Do, in Vietnam for one year. Americans cannot bend far enough."

"I didn't know you were in Vietnam, Captain Chang."

"Yes, I was in Korean Tiger division until July 1968. For a while, I was also assigned to interrogate Viet Cong prisoners since I speak a little Vietnamese." Captain Chang was now mixing Korean, Vietnamese and English words

Dr. Houghton had heard reports that the Koreans were inhumanely brutal in Vietnam. They were also the best fighting force there. But he did not ask, "Did you torture the Vietcong for information?" He knew the answer and shivered with a sense of horror at the stories of Koreans throwing the VC out of helicopters and the rest; but paradoxically, he felt safe in Chang's presence.

However, now, as a result of Dr. Houghton's reassurances and the tongue-loosening properties of the rice wine, Captain Chang's hardness and skepticism became open, unwrapped in Korean politeness and kibun-protection. He mumbled, "VC no fuckin'good." He also openly discouraged Dr. Houghton from

86

trying Hap Gi Do, with slurred Korean words like "hopeless" and "lost cause."

But, the more negative he became, the more determined Dr. Houghton was to obtain a black belt.

The Hap Gi Do exercise hall was twenty by thirty with a fifteen foot high leaky ceiling. The floor was matted. Several hanging heavy bags to kick, some rusty knives, and several cudgels were scattered around. All the students placed their uniforms, which they never washed, on nails on the walls. The white belted uniforms hung altogether on one wall, the red belts on another, the blues on a third, and the eight black belts on the fourth. The senior instructor, Mr. Ho, was a sixth degree black belt, but had lost enthusiasm for instruction. Mr. Yun, the 29 year old junior instructor, a third degree black belt, was the principal teacher. The other black belts also acted as instructors; for once you earned your black belt by your skill and dedication, you didn't pay dues to the exercise hall, but rather assumed an obligation to instruct the tyros.

To obtain the black belt, one had to pass through the nine stages of wisdom as well as master the many types of moves including offensive, defensive, flying and rotary kicks. Upon successful completion of the first three stages, mainly self-defense against an unarmed opponent, one received a blue belt. The next three stages, mainly defense against punching and kicking, culminated in a red belt. Mastery of self-defense against an opponent armed with a knife, as well as purely offensive tactics, led to the coveted first degree black belt. At each stage, one had to pass an examination to advance to the next level of wisdom.

In this, his third week, Dr. Houghton, upon entry, bowed to Mr. Yun, the junior instructor, who bowed to Sergeant Song. This inexplicable, almost royal treatment of Sergeant Song, Dr. Houghton still did not understand. Mr. Yun spoke to Sergeant Song in the most polite forms.

Interpreting for Mr. Yun, Sergeant Song said, "Mr. Yun wants you to come for the first examination next Saturday, to go from stage zero to stage one."

"Yes, I believe I can come then. Why don't you observe today, Sergeant Song, and perhaps you can give me some advice."

Mr. Yun and Dr. Houghton bowed to each other, thus formally beginning the day's lesson. Dr. Houghton imitated Mr. Yun as he and the other students, facing Mr. Yun, performed the ritualistic warm up and breathing exercises. Occasionally Mr. Yun stopped to correct or modify some error of Dr. Houghton's posture, or punch him in the abdomen, testing the "hardness". Within twenty minutes Dr. Houghton was exhausted. Although the temperature was 45 degrees, he was wet with perspiration. Next, Dr. Houghton practiced falling forward, to the side, and back. In his first days, he had learned to slap his nearest arm on the mat just before hitting the floor, thus protecting himself even from very high falls. Sometimes Mr. Yun would throw him, now increasingly less gently. The long rapturous flights culminated in smashing but, if properly executed, painless landings. The exercise hall trembled each time his 180 pound, five foot eleven inch frame hit the mat. Mr. Yun then called one of the biggest students, a blue belt, for demonstrating various defenses against an opponent attempting to strangle you. Using the student as an offensive dummy, Mr. Yun patiently showed Dr. Houghton the proper defenses.

The final portion of each lesson was free fighting. After the ritual bow, Dr. Houghton stood before the day's opponent, a fifteen year old red belt who with a horrid shriek, attacked. Fast and skillful, he kicked Dr. Houghton in the ribs and buttocks. Dr. Houghton realized he was properly blocking only fifty percent of his opponent's moves. Each unblocked blow left a welt or bruise which he didn't feel until hours later. A low swing kick that Dr. Houghton had never seen, knocked him off his feet and high into the air, but he recovered in mid-air and landed as he had been taught. He jumped up grinning, for although he missed the defense, he had rescued himself from potential catastrophe. If he had the guts to persevere, he just might beat them at their own game. Moreover, before ending the free fighting, he saw a weakness in his small opponent's defenses. He masterfully placed a punishing elbow on the little fellow's chest. He remembered something useful from his unsuccessful Harvard boxing days.

Being overcome by a small oriental boy did not chagrin Dr. Houghton, for he was learning. This attitudinal volte-face had occurred gradually over a decade. In college and medical school, he had steadily narrowed his previous too broad abhorrence of authority. He had now come to, if not revere, at least respect authority when combined with genuine knowledge or skills. His synthetic organic chemistry professor, an authentic magician, and a prima donna ballerina he knew were worthy of respect, indeed great respect. The oriental notion of the Honorable Teacher was in him before he came to Korea. But arrogant authority without knowledge, excellence or accomplishment, particularly the modern Western hierophants and their Eastern cousins, the neo-Confucians and Hindu Brahmins, he profoundly detested.

"What do you think, Sergeant Song?" Dr. Houghton asked, hoping for an honest answer and not oriental ambiguity and flattery.

Sergeant Song complied. "You did well, Sir, and are improving rapidly. But you make one very big mistake."

"What is that?"

"You take your eyes off your opponent's eyes. Don't do that! You must at all times, as Mr. Yun and I have repeatedly told you, keep your eyes on your opponent's eyes. Your peripheral vision is adequate to watch your opponent's hand and feet."

"You're right, Honorable Teacher," Dr. Houghton said in Korean, as his mind flashed back to Mr. Yun's eyes on his second day of training. On introducing Hap Gi Do, Mr. Yun said that they were about to teach him dangerous skills, refined over two thousand years. There was one condition.

"What is that?"

Mr. Yun paused and looked into Dr. Houghton's eyes as if he could see into his soul. He finally said that they only taught those who would employ these skills wisely and in self-defense. He also said, "Always watch the eyes."

Dr. Houghton assured him that he would do both. He hoped he would; he hoped he could.

Almost two hours later, as he ducked low under the gate and walked across the small courtyard, Dr. Houghton spoke in Korean, "I'm sorry to be late, Miss Judy."

"That's O.K., Docs."

Dr. Houghton noted that Miss Judy appeared much more appealing in her fifties cocktail dress than she had twelve hours earlier in the clinic. Now she visibly throbbed with vitality. The moon enveloped her in a magic glowing suffusion which disappeared in the sun's revealing beams. Of course, the daylight also brought out wrinkles and freckles. But he did not believe the difference was only due to the light. He also did not believe the difference was in the evening eye of the observer. Dr. Houghton believed that Miss Judy was different at night. He saw the skin of her face was better hydrated at night.

Miss Judy interrupted Dr. Houghton's prolonged gaze. "There's a good show tonight at the NCO Club. I am so happy you come with me tonight. I am full of sads. Let's go, Docs."

As they walked across the moonlit rice paddies toward the American detachment, he asked, "I understand there has been trouble in the village?"

"Yes, Docs."

"Sergeant Morse told me about it."

That morning, Sergeant Morse had asked Dr. Houghton's advice before they left for the Korean Mobile Army Surgical Hospital. To Sergeant Peters who was with them, Sergeant Morse said, "Tell the Captain what you told me."

"Well," Sergeant Peters began, "did you know the girls in the village have a little protective association?"

"You mean the GI business ladies?"

"Yes, Sir. Miss Kim, now the Sergeant Major's girl, the most senior girl, is the president. They have occasional meetings to keep out competition and to discuss other matters of common interest. Every month each girl gives the president money to pay off the mayor and the police to keep their hands off them. Once in a while, the bribery system breaks down. The police round up the girls and throw them in jail until they cough up more money. The cops often sock it to the girls. Last night, they tossed my Miss Lee in the jug. She denies that anyone socked it to her, but I know better. I'd like to kill the bastard who did it. Miss Lee and I have been going together for thirteen months; our relation is sacred. I'm due to go home soon; I don't want to get VD from her and then give it to my wife."

Dr. Houghton advised the Sergeant what to do, thinking of General Samet's strictures. General Samet, a Puritan by reputation, berated his colonels for any VD in the command. For this and other more basic reasons, Dr. Houghton also did not want VD in the command. Similarly, Colonel Bennet fumed when Dr. Houghton refused to inform him who had contracted VD. After Dr. Houghton's repeated requests, the Colonel finally dumped the problem into his hands, including guidance and discipline as well as diagnosis and treatment. Dr. Houghton and the First Sergeant then worked out a reasonable détente, a compromise tacitly accepted by the Colonel.

Dr. Houghton, in his orientation lectures, advised either continence or a *steady* business lady. Everyone now understood that an "incontinent" soldier could employ a steady business lady who must live in the village outside of the compound, and no questions would be asked. She would be checked for infection by Dr. Houghton. The soldier could also sleep off the compound in the village if he so wished. The Colonel unofficially sanctioned this for several reasons. During an alert, the troops demonstrated that they could all be back on the compound in a few minutes in a simulated emergency. They scurried out of their hooches and across the rice fields like paddy rats. Second, the Colonel could make no reply to the First Sergeant's retort, "Colonel, we got a 'superior' on the inspection. Let's bend the rules a little." A 'superior' on the inspection made a bird Colonel's year. So, for reasons of morale and other obscure motives, the Colonel looked the other way, although he made it clear he disapproved.

The compromise worked reasonably well. The only troops who contracted VD did not follow the policy and butterflied from entertainer to entertainer outside the local village. They regretted it. They were only treated by Dr. Houghton after tales of "rare strains resistant to all treatment" that would "turn your penis black" which would then "have to be cut off." Dr. Houghton often said, as part of the treatment, "You see this spot; it's already turning black." One soldier wept as he observed the imagined black spot.

Dr. Houghton asked Miss Judy, "Did they throw you in jail?"

"No, Docs. The bastards."

"That's good," he commented.

A few minutes later, as they entered the NCO Club, Sergeant Morse and the First Sergeant greeted Dr. Houghton. "Good evening, Sir. We are glad to see you."

"Thank you for the invitation."

"Miss Judy," the First Sergeant said, "I'm going to steal you from the Doc."

"Miss Judy and I are only friends. I'm her boss, not her Yo Bo." The Sergeant looked skeptical as Dr. Houghton continued. "If you have an extra $200 a month, Miss Judy might, and I say 'might' advisedly, consider you."

"$200! Do you think I'm a millionaire? I never heard of a $200 Yo Bo, and I've been in Korea on seven tours in the last eighteen years."

"Knucklehead," she said. Miss Judy laughed and walked toward an empty table.

The first sergeant sent over a gin and tonic as well as a coke for Miss Judy. After an hour of raucous laughter and great cheer, the first sargeant's co-conspirators - expensive gin, excessive celibacy and exotic candle beams glimmering off Miss Judy gradually weakened Dr. Houghton's previous resolve.

He said, "Let's dance, Miss Judy."

"In a moment."

After a brief disappearance, Miss Judy returned smelling of osmanthus perfume, one of Dr. Houghton's favorites, and phermonal lust.

As they danced, he decided that he would take her to the Q for a sample of what the First Sergeant suggested was the most expensive entertainment in Korea. But a well-timed wink from a Korean girl dancing lubriciously with a laughing Sergeant Morse momentarily diverted him. Dr. Houghton had never seen this girl and he carefully watched her. "Who is that girl?"

Miss Judy said, "That's Miss Moon. She's rotten." Suddenly, Miss Judy transmogrified from a lusty civilized business lady to an outraged big cat in the presence of a competitor.

"Wow!" Dr. Houghton involuntarily commented at one of Miss Moon's wild sexual thrusts.

Miss Judy frowned. There was jealous fire in her eyes.

"And who is Miss Moon?"

"She has a bad heart."

Dr. Houghton assumed she might be a rival, a contestant for the crown of village queen which Miss Judy now possessed. "Why do you say that?" he asked.

"I know, Docs. You ever take out Miss Moon, I no longer speak you."

"Tell me why." Dr. Houghton prepared himself for the malicious gossip of an angry competitor.

After a theatrical pause, Miss Judy drew him closer as they danced. She rubbed her generous bosom and motile pelvis against him as she began her story in a rapid, husky voice. Her cold hatred spewed forth in tiny, evanescent clove-scented particles. "Miss Moon about one year ago, Yo Bo of some Sergeant, but she butterfly. He hear and he say to her 'no more.' He get another Yo Bo. Miss Moon angry, jealousy. She write letter to Sergeant's wife in the States. She say Sergeant have Yo Bo. Wife begin divorce. Sergeant figure Miss Moon write letter. One time, she came to NCO club. He try kill her with a knife, but she ran away and leave village. Soon Sergeant hear his only baby has cancer. Sergeant many drink. One night, he come back from DMZ, drink too much, and drive off mountain. He Happy Mountain go." Miss Judy paused and then said, "Miss Moon then go east coast to Air Force Seven Compound. Over there, she became Colonel's Yo Bo. Then Miss Moon make big trouble at Air Force Seven. She tell Colonel that GI's buy too much stuffs in PX for girls." Miss Judy paused, out of breath.

Dr. Houghton understood that Miss Moon was not a solid member of the business community. After all, any Yo Bo of a GI should have illegal PX privileges, not just the Colonel's Yo Bo. Americans are egalitarian.

"Colonel much pissed off," Miss Judy continued. "All Yo Bo's in village over there try to kill Miss Moon, but she move over here. Also, now big GI trouble at Air Force Seven. Miss Moon say girls stay on compound overnight." Finally, to hammer in the peg of evil all the way, Miss Judy concluded with a theatrical flourish, "Miss Moon, when she Colonel's Yo Bo, she sleep with some GI private in daytime. Miss Moon rotten: she no fucking good!"

After this wild tale, to preserve harmony, Dr. Houghton whispered in Miss Judy's ear, "Miss Moon no good." But Miss Moon was very pretty, perhaps the most attractive woman he had yet seen in Korea. Dr. Houghton imagined the puffed chest of the private who cuckolded the Air Force Colonel with the beautiful Miss Moon.

But alas, Miss Judy's tale, in truth a catalogue of horrors, loosened the tight spell she had cast on him with the rubbing, the perfume, the smiles, the pheromones and jokes. And so he slept alone that evening once again. But he did think of Miss Moon.

The next day, Sergeant Morse said, "General Samet on the phone, Sir."

Dr. Houghton picked up, "General Samet?"

"Yes, Doctor. General Lee, the Korean Corps commander, has a medical problem and I recommended he see you."

"The three star Lee."

"Yes."

"I would be happy to see him. What's the problem?"

"He will tell you. By the way, I hear you are studying Hap Gi Do."

"Yes, General."

"Good luck. Stick with it. Let me know how you make out with General Lee."

"I will."

"Thank you. Goodbye."

Sergeant Morse said, "The captain should know that I see General Lee's jeep coming up the hill."

Dr. Houghton saluted and in Korean welcomed General Lee at the door. The Korean enlisted men shook with anxiety at the sight of General Lee.

"General Lee, please come into my office." His staff Captain waited outside.

General Lee said, "I speak good English but I appreciate your making the effort to learn Korean."

"General Lee, General Samet just called and told me you were coming. What is the problem? How can I help?"

General Lee paused and finally said, "My penis drips pus and it won't stop. It burns when I urinate like the fires of Buddhist Hells. The Korean physicians tried massive doses of penicillin and then tetracycline. My penis still drips. I talked to General Samet and he suggested you - a Harvard and Yale trained physician. Can you help me?"

Dr. Houghton said, "First, we must make a diagnosis. Then we can initiate proper therapy." Dr. Houghton, although slightly nervous, went into his automatic "good medicine" mode. "Take off your pants. First, we must take a sample of the pus and stain it and look at it under the microscope." Dr. Houghton took three samples and gave them to Sergeant Morse to stain. While Sergeant Morse stained them, he said, "General I must feel your prostate gland. Bend over and assume the position."

General Lee was not accustomed to anyone talking to him like this but he was now desperate. His penis had been dripping for almost two months. He finally complied.

To relieve the tension, Dr. Houghton said, "You are not the highest ranking man on whom I did a rectal. When the King of Saudi Arabia came to the Brigham with his four wives, I was the designated to do his rectal since I have such good technique."

General Lee did not laugh but he also did not flinch during the procedure.

Dr. Houghton said, "Some good news. Your prostate is firm, nontender and normal. Let us look at the slides now." Sergeant Morse brought them in and bowed out. "General, I was able to obtain a really good microscope from the US army depot in Seoul. Let me look at the slides." As he looked Dr. Houghton said, "I see no gonococci, only inflammatory cells. General, please sit down. I think I can help you."

"Good; will you have to instill silver up my penis?"

"No. First, I think you have nonspecific urethritis, NSU, an infection caused by an unknown germ. We had cases like this at the Brigham that responded to very high dose erythromycin, but the pills, called Big Red Bombs, are very hard on the stomach. Are you tough?"

General Lee said, "I eat nails and sergeants with my kimchi for breakfast."

Before answering, Dr. Houghton knew his diagnosis by exclusion was probably correct, but he had no data on whether Korean NSU would respond to erythromycin. But this was a rational plan. If it didn't work, would General Lee take him out and shoot him? Dr. Houghton finally said, "Good, you must take 6 grams the first day and four grams per day for 7 more days. I heard you do not have erythromycin tablets in Korea but we do and I will give them to you."

"Where did I get this?"

"Possibly from an-"

"Continue!" General Lee boomed.

"An entertainer."

An angry General Lee left with his erythromycin.

Four days later, Sergeant Morse said, "General Lee on the field phone."

"Good morning General."

"Dr. Houghton, my penis no longer drips or burns, but my stomach is going to explode!"

"General I told you they are Big Red Bombs but you need to finish all eight days or the infection may come back. The stomach pain will go away when you finish them. Remember no alcohol. Be tough."

General Lee hung up, still angry.

Six days later, General Lee called. "I finished and my penis is well and works. What do you want?"

With a rehearsed response to this not unexpected request, Dr. Houghton said, "A promotion." But this was not Dr. Houghton's first choice request: in order, they would be a suitable Korean beauty, jadeite sculptures and finally a promotion. But he was not yet ready to say this to General Lee. "But General Lee, you must be careful in the future. Next time I may not be able to help you, you understand?"

"Captain, I want to talk to you soon. I will tell you when."

An hour later, Sergeant Morse said, "General Samet on the phone."

"Hello, Captain. General Lee told me you almost killed him but he is cured. Thank you. Good luck with the Hap Gi Do. Also General Lee told me you speak Korean."

"I'm learning."

"Captain, you are on the right track. I shall keep my eye on you."

Three days later, Sergeant Morse interrupted Dr. Houghton and Sergeant Song during the Korean lesson.

"Colonel Bennet wants to see you right now," said Sergeant Morse.

Dr. Houghton, two by two, took the long flight of steps to the Colonel's office.

"Good afternoon, Colonel," said Dr. Houghton after knocking and walking in unbidden.

"Afternoon, Doc. Have a seat." The Colonel lit up a Camel long.

Dr. Houghton hoped Colonel Bennet was the last of the "tanker" breed, a man who ruthlessly killed hundreds of Koreans and Chinese, but in an oblique way, admired him.

"Doc, they have a requirement over at Air Force Seven near the east coast for a doctor. Their doctor is leaving soon, and his replacement isn't due in for a week."

"Why do they need me over there?" Dr. Houghton asked a little too loud.

"Well, General Samet gave several reasons. First, about one hundred infiltrators landed on the east coast. You will be responsible for Korean helicopter medical evacuations. We must be sure the Koreans use our choppers and pilots only for serious patients, not cases of champagne. There has also been trouble in that command. At any rate, the General says they need you over there, and he will personally talk with you later. You should plan to go tomorrow morning."

Dr. Houghton did not argue. He was presented with an accomplished fact.

Colonel Bennet graciously concluded, "It'll only be a week, Doc."

"All right, Colonel. Good-bye." He saluted crisply and walked out angry.

Dr. Houghton understood that Colonel Bennet realized he had labored diligently to upgrade the dispensary. Moreover, he and the First Sergeant had removed all medical and paramedical problems from the Colonel's back. They handled VD, broken hearts, and bastardy as well as broken bones and other medical problems so the Colonel and the Sergeant Major could "advise." Moreover, the medical civic action program kept the villagers and politicians grateful, cooperative, and friendly.

But to Dr. Houghton, the advisory effort depended on continuity. He was just beginning to understand the situation and know his counterparts. He hoped it would only be a week. As he entered the dispensary, he immediately called Colonel Bennet. "May I take Sergeant Song, my interpreter and driver with me?"

"Yes, Doc. I see no reason why not."

"Thank you, Colonel."

"Sergeant Song," Dr. Houghton called as he hung up.

"Yes, Sir."

"You and I are going to the east coast for a holiday. Sergeant Morse will stay here."

"Where, Sir?"

"The Air Force Seven Detachment. By the way, where is that exactly?"

"It's about seven miles from Soochow, the seaside fishing resort."

"It's not a dull place?"

"No, Sir." Sergeant Song displayed more enthusiasm than ever before. "They have many beautiful entertainers there, true Kisaeng. There are almost no Americans."

"General Samet is on the phone, Sir," Sergeant Morse called out.

"I'll take it here." The connection was bad and crackling. "Good afternoon, General."

"Good afternoon, Doc. We need you over at Air Force Seven to control the med-evacs of the Koreans who are using our choppers and pilots. Make sure they don't abuse the service. They are trying to pin down some infiltrators who landed on the coast. There appears to be many more than the initial estimate of one hundred. And there has been trouble in the command. I want you to keep an eye on the Colonel over there, Colonel Murray. I'll brief you about this when you get there. We will talk tomorrow afternoon. Doc, you should only be there about one week until the new doctor arrives. Be sure and call me if anything comes up, anytime day or night. I'm relying on you to handle a difficult situation."

"Thank you for your call, General."

"Good-bye, Doctor," General Samet clicked out.

"Sergeant Song, one more thing; get a note to the Hap Gi Do instructor, Mr. Yun, explaining that I will be gone for about a week and will have to miss training, but that you will take over as my instructor in the interim."

"Yes, Sir."

"Meanwhile I will call Colonel Kim and postpone our plans, damn."

That night, Dr. Houghton thought the Korean moon was extra-bright. Viewing it, he almost drove his jeep off the unlit road into the fallow rice paddies below. Slowly proceeding up the narrow village alley toward Miss Judy's hooch, he noted a taupe light in her paper window. Good, Miss Judy is in, he figured, as he hopped out of the jeep. He heard soft music but he was prevented from ducking under her wall gate by a cool, gentle hand.

"Hello, Miss Judy."

"Hello, Docs. I knows. Sergeant Morse told me."

"Let's go in."

"No, I have a friend for some drinks. You wait here."

Dr. Houghton immediately realized that she was back in the business. But what else could she do? Cast out by her own society, she could still enjoy the company and money of American Colonels, Captains or Sergeants. Why not? After all, he had tacitly rejected her.

Miss Judy returned with unspoken thoughts of real respect and unrequited love for Dr. Houghton. She almost felt the same way about him as her first love, Lieutenant Weinstein, the father of her baby. But even though she tried, she could not suppress the tears which fell on the big box she carried.

Dr. Houghton opened it in the bright moonlight. Wrapped in protective paper, he found an exquisite doll in a traditional Korean blue silk hanbok dress.

"Thank you so much, Miss Judy," Dr. Houghton said with real gratitude. "How did you know I would come down tonight?"

She smiled. "I knows. I love you; be careful."

"Miss Judy, come here." He kissed her passionately on the lips and wiped away her tears with his big silk handkerchief. "When I come back, Miss Judy, we will reopen the Clinic. I hope you will continue to translate for me."

She said, "Good-bye, Docs. Be careful; the infiltrators are big plicks." She had known too many Americans either shot dead or effectively dead, living in America.

Dr. Houghton suppressed an impulse to make a rejoinder about how tough he was. Instead, he said, "I will see you soon. Do not worry. Good bye, Miss Judy."

"A fool always finds one still
more foolish to admire him."
Baileau

Chapter VIII
The Air Force on the Ground

Dr. Houghton wondered why Sergeant Song and the gate MP for the Air Force Seven Compound were talking so long. "What's the trouble, Sergeant Song? Why won't that runt let us through? I see his rifle is loaded, Sergeant Song; the clip is in. Tell him not to point the gun at me. Damn it, let's not dilly dally. It's been a six hour ride."

Sergeant Song continued in Korean. But the MP was still resistant to their entry.

Finally, Dr. Houghton eased himself out of the jeep. Every bone of his body was badly shaken by the rough roads. Moreover, several bone heads felt out of joint. For sure, he needed to fly more on the helicopter from now on. Focusing on the present problem he counseled himself: Patience, this MP is a microman but his rifle is loaded. We haven't studied rifle bullet deflection in the exercise hall, yet. Finally at his wit's end, he said, "Tell the MP to come here, Sergeant Song."

Dr. Houghton, towering over the little man who was too small for his rifle and U.S. Army forty-five, which was as long as his femur, said, "Tell him, I said to stand at attention." The MP snapped to attention as this was translated to him. "Tell him I'm Captain Houghton and we are going to see the Colonel. Do I look like a North Korean infiltrator? Tell him to use his head."

Sergeant Song translated and the MP finally allowed them to enter. After waving them through the entrance, he picked up the telephone.

Sergeant Song explained. "He has his orders, Sir."

"Let's go to the dispensary first. I see the Red Cross over there."

Entering the dispensary, Dr. Houghton said, "Hello?"

A sergeant with the name of Dawson on his fatigues appeared.

"Hello, Sergeant Dawson, I am Captain Houghton."

"We've been expecting you, Sir. Quite a ride from Chun Chon! I bet you're petered out."

99

"Yes, we are. This is Sergeant Song who will be with us."
Sergeants Song and Dawson shook hands. "Where is the Doctor,
Major Tierney?"

"Oh, he left for the day. He asked me to show you around."
As Sergeant Dawson showed them the small, shiny dispensary with
its highly polished stainless steel fixtures, he said, "We have, as you
see, a small dispensary where we do sick call for our people and the
Koreans assigned to us. We also see a few indigent civilians and act
as the Air Force Liaison Medical Section to the Korean Army East
Coast Defense Force, mainly overseeing their use of our choppers
and pilots. We are very isolated, and not too busy, generally."
Turning to some Korean soldiers, he went on, "These men are
Sergeants Chang and Min, and this is Corporal Heme. They are
assigned to us, and you'll see that they are great men." In unison,
the three saluted sharply.

"Good to meet you," Dr. Houghton said.

Sergeant Song began to speak with them in Korean.

Sergeant Dawson continued. "I'll show you to your
quarters. You can meet Major Tierney and Colonel Murray
tomorrow morning or perhaps tonight at the Officers' Club where
you will eat. Major Tierney leaves tomorrow. Here is the key to
your room."

"Thank you, Sergeant Dawson."

"It is very isolated here, Sergeant Song. We shall not be
able to do much in this place," Dr. Houghton said as Sergeants
Chang and Min carried his bags down the narrow corridor to his
room.

"No, Sir, but I hope you can go to Soochow to see the
Kisaeng," Sergeant Song smiled. Then he whispered soberly.
"Something very strange here, dispensary soldiers say."

Dr. Houghton opened the door to a small chilly room where
there was barely space for a cot and an unfinished pine chest of
drawers. "Please proceed, Sergeant Song."

"Sergeant Min says there is big GI trouble here."

"What kind of trouble?"

"He didn't say. He also said ......," Sergeant Song stopped
abruptly.

"Don't clam up, Sergeant Song."

"He also said that Dr. Tierney left just before we came
wearing a papa-san suit."

"A what?"

"A papa-san suit, you know, the costume Korean men wear
after they reach age sixty two."

"Yes, I know." Dr. Houghton recalled the white suited elders, the papa-sans, with their off-white baggy pants, white jacket, black felt stove pipe hat with a narrow rim, white rubber shoes with up-going toes, and the long thin pipe. "I wonder why? It's dangerous around here after dark. Where did he go?"

"I don't know."

"Thank you Sergeant Song. I'll see you tomorrow." After Sergeant Song left, Dr. Houghton wondered how a man of *his* position, a member of the social and intellectual elite, could end up in a cold room like this, but, in a few minutes, dancing visions of the fabled Kisaeng provided a balm and banished his discontent. Also, he could have ended up hot but dead in Vietnam.

After shivering through a cold shower, he climbed into his cot to momentarily warm himself before supper. A whirring noise in the background, a noise like he sometimes heard in his childhood brain, puzzled him, until he realized it was the generators that supplied his electric blanket, his most valuable possession. The Americans brought their civilization everywhere in huge crates.

A few moments later he awoke, but his watch said four a.m. The cold deterred any potential trip to the water closet. Before falling asleep again, he wondered if an electric blanket or a ninety-nine degree girl friend was preferable in the present circumstance. The conclusion seemed obvious, for the electric blanket did not talk back, was uniformly warm, stayed put, never had cold feet or gave you a hard time. But, this also sounded like the fabled description of a Korean girl. Once committed, they were supposed to be the most passionate and supportive of women. He needed one, and soon.

Dr. Houghton overslept that frigid morning. He quickly put his winter fatigues over his red silk pajamas and rushed to the dispensary. Major Tierney was there.

"Good morning, Major Tierney."

"Morning, Houghton. Welcome to Air Force Seven. I'm sorry to leave without the chance to give you a briefing, but my flight to Seoul leaves in two hours. I must go right now. Sergeant Dawson knows the ropes. I wish you the best of luck."

"Good-bye Major, have a good trip to the States."

"Thanks," a very thin Major Tierney said and entered the waiting jeep.

"Dr. Houghton," Sergeant Song said, "Major Kennedy is here and would like a word with you."

"Send him in."

"Good morning, Doc. I'm Major Kennedy. Call me Mike."

"Have a seat, Major. I didn't know the US Air Force did much flying in the Land of the Morning Calm."

Mike wore his shiny grey flying jump suit. He was big, balding, steel-eyed and hairy. He looked like an Irish rapparee. He said, "You're right, Doc.; here in Korea we're mainly liaison and it's pretty tough for a pilot like me to sit on my ass for thirteen months. I was flying steady in Vietnam for almost two years, but the Air Force insisted I take a break for thirteen months before I return to Nam." Mike paused and then continued, "Here, we advise the Koreans on all aspects of Air Force techniques. Now I am demonstrating forward air control from our radio jeeps. We select mock targets and bring in Korean and American jet fighters on these targets. Tomorrow, it'll be for real against the infiltrators."

Sergeant Min brought in coffee.

Mike continued, "I came over to ask you a question. I couldn't find Dr. Tierney for the last two days."

"Shoot."

"One of my drivers was exposed to a girl with hepatitis. Should I insist he come in for globulin shots? He doesn't want to."

Dr.Houghton explained that he should. "Before you go, Mike, I have a question. What the hell is going on in this compound? How come Tierney went off the compound in, of all things, a papa-san suit?"

Mike laughed. "Hasn't anyone filled you in?"

"No."

"Look, I'll meet you at the club tonight at six. I'll give you the lowdown."

The morning was dragging on with Dr. Houghton attending to mundane administrative duties. Before noon, Colonel Murray's office called and said the colonel was out but "might be in the club tonight." At noon Houghton heard peals of laughter outside hsis office. He walked into the patients' waiting room to investigate. "Who are these girls?"

Sergeants Dawson, Song, Min, Chang and Corporal Heme smiled and came to attention but none answered. Four well dressed Korean girls in Western skirts and white silk blouses politely muffled their risibility with their hands - at an apparently droll Dr. Houghton. He wondered if his fly was open. It wasn't.

Sergeant Dawson finally answered with obvious strain, "These are some of Dr. Tierney's friends who came too late, too late to say good-bye."

"Where do they come from?"

"They work across the river."

One girl, the spokeswoman, perhaps eighteen or nineteen, addressed Dr. Houghton in polite Korean. As she spoke, she battered her eyes and gazed at him with a forwardness unusual in a proper Korean lady. Even Miss Judy could not tolerate direct eye to eye confrontation for long. "What did she say, Sergeant Song?" Dr. Houghton asked although he really understood.

"She invited you to come and visit them like Dr. Tierney did."

This sounded like an interesting caper in this dull place, but to what purpose? "Tell them I'd be happy to," Dr. Houghton replied without understanding the obvious. He bowed politely but too deeply.

This response was, to them, wildly inappropriate - Korean buffoonery. It drew more mirth from the girls, their laughter covered behind their open hands. Sergeant Song also smiled, wryly.

Dr. Houghton knew he must have stepped in it, deeply. A few minutes later, safely ensconced in the solitude of his office, he called out, "Sergeant Song, please come here."

A straight-faced, indeed dour, Sergeant Song appeared. "Yes, Doctor." He surmised the upcoming line of inquiry.

"Who are these four girls? Enough riddles."

"They are friends of Dr. Tierney."

"Yes, I realize that. What do they do?"

"They work across the river."

"What kind of work?"

"I'm not sure, Sir." Sergeant Song hedged.

"Call Sergeant Min in here."

"Sergeant Min, come in here now," Sergeant Song said in Korean. "Dr. Houghton wants to know why these girls are here."

"They came here for their penicillin injections."

"Penicillin injections!?" Dr. Houghton was incredulous. He was certain they were tweaking him.

Sergeant Min continued without expression. "Yes, every month, Dr. Tierney, ah, well, actually I give each girl 4.8 million units of benzathine penicillin, 2.4 million units in each buttock."

"What for," Dr. Houghton asked?

"The Captain can see they aren't sick because they get the penicillin injections."

"But what in Satan's name was Dr. Tierney trying to prevent with those huge doses of penicillin?" Dr. Houghton now knew the answer.

"I don't know the English for this," Sergeant Min said, his bag of deception now empty.

"Well tell Sergeant Song, and he will translate for you."

Punctuating his exposition with sly grins, Sergeant Min spoke for several minutes.

Finally Dr. Houghton interrupted, "OK, Sergeant Song, let me have it."

Sergeant Song summarized. "These girls are entertainers, and Dr. Tierney was trying to prevent them from getting VD."

Dr. Houghton knew that Min said a lot more but Dr. Houghton stopped the inquiry. Later, he would try to learn the details. At present, however, they had to leave to finish up the polio program. He only said, "No more shots for the girls. That is an order!"

Dr. Houghton asked, "Sergeant Dawson, when was the polio program initiated?"

"About a year ago," he said. "Dr. Tierney saw about ten serious polio cases here in one month last year. Five died; no respirators. The Korean government in this isolated rural area had no vaccine. So we ordered it from the States, and our pilots bring it here frozen in dry ice. After it thaws, we have to use it in three days or it spoils."

"Why do we have to administer it? Why not give it to the local officials?"

Sergeant Dawson smiled condescendingly, as if talking to a simpleton. "Dr. Tierney felt they might sell it or misuse it as they so often do. To be sure, we go around to all the schools we can reach by jeep, in a radius of about one and half hours, and pass out the oral vaccine. Soon we'll have completely stamped out polio here."

"How much does it cost, and how many kids have you done?"

"It costs eight dollars per hundred kids for the two doses. We plan to do five thousand. We have finished three thousand, and we have to give a second dose to two thousand to complete the project. We have eight bottles and plan to do eight hundred children today."

Bouncing along in the jeep with Sergeants Dawson, Min and Song, Dr. Houghton considered this project worthwhile, if they didn't become icicles first. "This heater doesn't work well, does it, Sergeant Min?"

"No, Sir."

"Let fix it."

"Yes, Sir."

"It certainly is cold for early November," Dr. Houghton observed as he carefully studied the brown, sleeping rice paddies. They occupied every possible nook and cranny, even terracing there way up small mountains. Without them, the Korean people could not exist. While the rice paddies slumbered through those long, wintry days, there were few signs of life in the countryside, except the vermicular smoke emanating silently from the flues in the under-the-floor heating systems of the farmer's homes. Now Dr. Houghton better understood the original Confucian ethic; in the natural hierarchy of human kind, Confucius placed the farmer only below the scholar-official-aristocrat class, the Yangban in Korea and the Mandarins of China. It was the rice of the farmers' tedious labor that sustained everyone. The city folk provided only embellishment, riot and corruption. After driving about an hour, Dr. Houghton, lost in metaphysical thoughts of cycles and the eternal recurrence of all events, arrived at the school.

As he stepped out of the jeep, Dr. Houghton wondered if the Koreans really approved of this new magic from the West. Only a fool would deny the value of overcoming polio, a great victory of Harvard science over disease. Dr. Houghton once shook Dr. Enders' hand. That self-effacing little man discovered how to culture polio virus in tissue culture and opened the door to the vaccine, a Nobel Prize achievement.

The school principal gestured that they sit down and partake of the inevitable cup of tea and polite conversation. Within a moment, Dr. Houghton saw that the unctuous principal bowed too deeply and behaved too politely. He wondered if the principal considered him a barbarian, or worse, a fool for distributing America's wealth without expectation of return. Dr. Houghton also wrestled with Malthusian pessimism and with the conviction that the Koreans should be doing this for themselves. They were not strengthened by Americans doing their work for them. But, as he had long since realized, such rational considerations have minimal influence on action. One small Korean child, in an instant, resolved all Dr. Houghton's doubts.

After they entered the first classroom of seventy children, two at a desk, Sergeant Min gave a delightful high pitched talk to which the children gave their rapt attention. They knew what polio did to their brothers and sisters. The three Sergeants then quickly placed two drops of the pink vaccine in each child's upturned, expectant mouth. As Dr. Houghton watched, it seemed impossible that he once thought they all looked alike. Obviously some of the little girls and boys were beautiful, and some were not. When they were finished, at the teachers cue, they all rose together, bowed, and in one clarion voice said, "Thank you, Sir," in English and then applauded.

Dr. Houghton bowed ever so slightly in response and applauded with the children. As they left, he waved and said good-bye in Korean using the polite form which was incorrect for the children. This elicited a pleasant, "Good-bye, Honorable Teacher."

When they finished the last class of the eldest pupils, the sixth grade, one small girl rose and limped to the front of the class, an obvious polio case. She had an exquisite face with perfectly clear white skin and larger than usual glowing eyes. After bowing, she addressed Dr. Houghton in English. Resisting an impulse to pick up the child, he fumbled with his forty-five, which he now prudently wore off the compound.

She said with excellent pronunciation, "We want to thank you for your good deed, Honorable Teacher." She, then, in an American gesture extended her hand to Dr. Houghton. For an instant he hesitated with intense emotion, on the verge of tears. But then he shook her small hand as the children applauded and laughed.

Answering in Korean, Dr. Houghton said, "You are welcome, little one," and waved good-bye. The children concluded with more applause, lateral waves and many rowdy good-byes in English.

That evening, he greeted Mike at the bar at the officers' club. "Hello, Mike."

"Hi, Doc."

"Doc, this is Mr. Koo, the bartender."

"Hello, Mr. Koo."

"What you'll drink, Doc," Mr. Koo said.

"Gin and tonic, please. Give Major Kennedy another, too. Mike, I had an interesting afternoon. We passed out polio vaccine. I wonder if the Koreans realize how much we are doing for them."

"I think you and Dr. Tierney are wasting your time!"

Dr. Houghton strongly disagreed, remembering the crippled child, but to avoid unnecessary friction, he said, "What's Mr. Koo doing, Mike?" Mr. Koo was dismantling a small box that contained a red bulb and a green one.

"Oh, that was the safety box; when the light was green, it meant everything was fine; when red, it meant caution."

"I see," said Dr. Houghton still wondering at the mysteries at Air Force Seven.

"You play shuffle board, Doc?"

"Just a little," Dr. Houghton understated his skill.

106

"I'm also not very good," Mike said, his eye-twinkle revealing all. "I just started playing last week." In truth, Mike had played for seventeen years.

"I'll play you a game for a drink," Dr. Houghton proposed, figuring he would have no bar bill.

Mike laughed. He thought of P.T. Barnum's apothegm about "suckers and takers." They flipped. Mike lost.

"What are you doing, Mike?" Dr. Houghton asked as Mike raised and lowered his 210 pound frame into a squatting position four times.

"Just warming up," Mike said. He then pushed a perfect slide for a three.

"I thought you never played much, Mike."

"Just beginner's luck," Mike laughingly replied.

Mike was astonished when Dr. Houghton slid a three, knocking his shot off in the process."

"Mike, what's going on around here? What was with Dr. Tierney? I can't find out. No one wants to talk about him and his behavior. Why did he leave the compound in a papa-son suit? Why do young girls come over to the clinic for huge penicillin shots?"

"Didn't you meet Dr. Tierney?"

"Yes, I met him for a few minutes before he left."

"Doc Tierney was out of his mind," Mike chuckled. "He had only two off duty uniforms, a tuxedo and a papa-son suit, both of which he wore off the compound. Every third or fourth night, he'd get shaky; easy to happen here in this rotten, isolated place with the same old faces every day. At any rate, Dr. Tierney would dress up in his tuxedo or papa-son suit and sneak off the compound. Of course, this was impossible because he had to go out the gate.

"When the river wasn't frozen, he'd have to go across the bridge. He generally walked. I couldn't figure him. He tied to sneak around and would deny everything, but he wore those outlandish costumes and didn't take the jeep. Why he never was shot, I'll never know." Mike paused and drained his glass. "The gate and bridge guards would stand at attention as he walked by. They saluted him in his disguise as a papa-son with his extra tall stovepipe hat. Tierney would throw off a furtive salute with his right or left hand. Tierney also had a funny gait, even when sober. He called it a titubation. Anyhow, as soon as he was out of sight, the gate guards and the bridge guards would imitate him, his titubation, and his wrong-handed salute. They'd be wracked with laughter. They knew, of course, who he was and exactly where he was going. The jokes about Tierney were good anti-depressants for the troops."

Mike related this story with relish, charging it with his deep Irish sense of absurdity. His words conjured up a clear and distinct mental image of Tierney. Although Dr. Houghton was spellbound by Mike's storytelling, he remained skeptical.

Mike continued. "In his last month here, he drove Colonel Murray frantic. Colonel Murray forbade him to wear his papa-son suit off the compound, so Doc Tierney took to wearing his tuxedo. Then Colonel Murray forbade him to wear the tuxedo off the compound.

"What am I going to wear, Colonel?" Dr. Tierney asked.

"Colonel Murray got so red in the face, he almost stroked."

"Where was he going, Mike?" Dr. Houghton interjected.

"He went over to that little shack with the thatched roof directly across the river; you've probably seen it."

Showing exasperation, Dr. Houghton asked, "Who lives there?"

"It's a whorehouse. Tierney's trouble was that he was so cheap. He was too cheap to employ a regular business lady although he did for a short time. What he would do was convert five dollars into won before he went and rent the whole house for one and half hours. No other customers when he was there. Of course, the girls got fringe benefits from him, medical care and so forth. But what was so strange was that Doc Tierney spoke absolutely no Korean. One time when he was drunk, he told me that when he went over there, he would have one cup of rice wine, and then each of the four girls, one after another. Afterwards, they would sing to him, bathe his penis, dress him, and he'd leave. Tierney also demanded they come over to the dispensary for showers, *before* he went across the river. Apparently, the girls really loved him; they'd do anything for him, and he certainly took advantage of it."

Dr. Houghton interrupted. "They also came over for penicillin injections."

"Yet he got gonorrhea two times," Mike laughed. "Doc Tierney would generally sneak over on late Wednesday afternoon, which is physical training afternoon, after four o'clock. One Wednesday, we decided to call a practice strike, right over the whorehouse - at five." At this point in his narrative, Mike convulsed with mirth. Tiny particle of dancing spittle fell before him.

Dr. Houghton was dumbfounded at this irresponsible use of jet fighters for practical jokes. Misuse of penicillin for VD prophylaxis was bad enough.

Mike finally contained himself. "We took the radio jeep up the hill behind the whorehouse. I called the jets in right over the thatched shack using it as the mock target. We knew Doc Tierney was in there because we watched him sneak in. I brought my Nikon telephoto. The first jet flew about forty feet above the tip of the roof and blew some of the thatch off. About one minute later, Doc Tierney ran out of the house in his tuxedo pants and suspenders. No shoes, no shirt. You could hear him for miles. He was wild with fury. 'You sons of bitches; you dirty rats,' he screamed. Soon, the girls piled out and dragged him back in. A minute later, the second jet passed over. Again, Doc Tierney ran out screaming. 'You bastards, you big pricks.' Bastards and big pricks echoed in the valley. Being prepared, I snapped high quality telephoto pictures of the whole scene. The best one shows Doc Tierney with his middle finger raised high with the four girls dragging him back into the shack. I'll have to show them to you." After Mike wiped the tears of glee from his eyes, he continued, "When Tierney returned that night, I asked him if he had a good time. He said, 'Yes, thank you, you bastards.' He would not talk to us for days."

Dr. Houghton thought that if Mike had pictures, the whole fantastic story might really be true.

Mike went on. "Colonel Murray and Doc Tierney despised each other. The Colonel was concerned about Doc Tierney's behavior. It all came to a head about three weeks ago. Murray was drinking at the bar when Doc came in with a quart of cheap rice wine. When Tierney tried to open the bottle, a little spilled. He said, 'Oh, shit!' Colonel Murray looked up and said, 'Doc, that's not English. You are a company grade officer!' Doc Tierney said nothing.

"Colonel Murray went on. 'You know, Doc, I am concerned about you, not just your English.' Again, Tierney did not reply, but just continued drinking the rice wine. Attempting to get some response, Colonel Murray provoked him. 'That rice wine is no good for you. It will ruin your liver.'

"Tierney finally took the gudgeon. 'You know Colonel, that expensive scotch you drink? I once put a drop on a turtle's tongue, and it immediately dropped dead.'" Mike laughed, "The Colonel went on, 'Doc, I am not a turtle. But it is really not your English that concerns me, but your health and your image. I just don't think it's healthy for you to leave the compound in costumes. I've heard you even break the curfew. Someone's going to put a bullet in you. You have gained, how should I say it - a certain kind of notoriety.'"

Dr. Houghton asked, "What did Colonel Murray mean?"

Mike launched into an explanation. "Colonel Murray referred to another of Tierney's habits. Dr. Tierney thought all Koreans look the same. He just couldn't distinguish one from another, nor could he tell the Korean ranks. He'd be introduced to one; five minutes later, he'd come over to that individual, rap him on the back and say, 'Long time, no see.' Well, he did that to General Lee after being introduced three minutes before. He was very lucky General Lee didn't shoot him."

"Well, by this time, Doc Tierney had polished off the quart of rice wine. Colonel Murray said, 'Why don't you find yourself a business lady and bring her on the compound. It would be much safer, much better than those prostitutes you frequent. God, you are awful pedestrian. Any Korean farmer with fifty cents, they'll take him on.'"

"At this, Doc Tierney totally lost his temper. 'Who the hell do you think your Miss Moon is, the Queen of Sheba? She's the lowest of the low, that slut. Colonel, you're being cuckholded by your driver, a god-damned private. At least my girls are not hypocrites.'"

"'What are you talking about, Doc?' Colonel Murray asked threateningly. But Doc Tierney was in clear distress. He said, 'Excuse me, I have to go to the men's room,' and staggered off. He didn't return. With that accusation ringing in his ears, Colonel Murray hurried to the men's room to find him. A minute later, there was a crash in the men's room. Colonel Murray screamed, 'That god-damned doctor.'"

"Doc Tierney had vomited all over the bathroom, the sink, the toilet and the floor. Colonel Murray had skidded and fallen in it."

Mr. Koo, the bartender, interrupted. "Dr. Houghton, there's a call for you; it's Sergeant Song."

"Yes, Sergeant Song."

"Captain, there is a man in the dispensary who's been shot in the arm."

"I'll be right over." Dr. Houghton hung up. "Excuse me, Mike. I've must go over to the dispensary. Someone is shot. Before I go, I thought I would meet Colonel Murray here tonight. Where is he?"

Mike replied, "I hope God knows."

The following evening, Dr. Houghton walked into the officer's club bar. Mike was grunting and snorting and making pseudo- Hap Gi Do moves.

"What are you doing, Mike?"

"Imitating you, Doc. I saw you working out today. Why so much grunting Doc?"

"The shouts and grunts are meant to frighten your opponent."

With a laugh, Mike signified he understood. "How about some shuffle board?"

"I'd rather play with a woman, but OK, Mike."

110

"Doc, you've got to give me odds."

"Horsefeathers, Mike. I bet you've been playing for your entire seventeen years in the Air Force."

"Bullshit, Doc. How much?"

"We'll play for drinks."

An hour later, after Mike won three games to two, Dr. Houghton asked, "Where's the Colonel?"

"He's probably at the NCO Club, since Miss Moon left."

"Let's go over there, Mike. I must talk to him."

Colonel Murray stood at the bar at the NCO club drinking very expensive Scotch, his left arm around an older Korean business lady. Her rasping, bronchial, broken English tones emerged from her gold toothed mouth on a cloud of cigarette smoke.

Mike walked over to the Colonel and opened the conversation. "This is the new Doc, Dr. Houghton; this is our Colonel."

"Nice to see you. Welcome to Seven."

"Good evening, Colonel."

"I made Koo take the light off the bar," Colonel Murray said to Mike.

"What was it for?" Dr. Houghton asked.

"When the light was green, you could keep the girls on the compound; when red, you had to get them off by eleven," Mike answered.

The Colonel said to Mike. "I lost my Legion of Merit today. I told General Samet the whole truth." Turning to Dr. Houghton, presumably a man with an open mind, Colonel Murray explained. "Doc, this is my last overseas tour. For four months, I played it straight. But this compound is isolated; it is the end of the road. We had to make a change. Since the change, we've had minimal VD here, no morale problems. I know where our troops are at all times except for that damned Tierney who used to visit the whorehouses. My troops are right here on the compound, in the clubs or their quarters having a good time. They are not out chasing tail all over the countryside, getting into trouble with the Koreans." Colonel Murray banged his hand on the bar. "When I need them, they are right here!" He pointed to the floor. "We had very good morale. I told the troops their private lives were their own business as long as they did their work. They did. We got 'superior' on all three inspections. We have the best compound in Korea. Right, Mike?"

"Yes, Sir," Mike answered.

With the near empty Scotch bottle in his left hand, the Colonel gesticulated with his glass-holding right hand, splashing

111

Scotch all over the floor. "Somebody blew the whistle on us. The General called me to Seoul. I told him the truth. He disagrees. I lost three medals. The General ordered the gate closed to the girls, after ten. I will also receive a letter of reprimand. I just don't think the General is being a realist. What do you think, Doc?" But before Dr. Houghton could answer, Colonel Murray continued, "I begged Samet to give me another chance but he would not relent. I'm finished. I will be discharged soon." He placed his hand on Captain Houghton's shoulder, "What do you think, Doc?"

On seven ounces of gin, Dr. Houghton was high. He just could not comprehend how the Colonel lived, how he could stand up. He had observed this man swallow at least half the fifth of Scotch in fifteen minutes. "I think you are definitely right on one point Colonel. It is better to have the men on the compound at night in this dangerous area. The South Korean soldiers are trigger happy, not to mention the infiltrators; too many accidents after dark." In reality, he thought that Colonel Murray was fortunate he hadn't been immediately relieved and court-martialed. In the Korean army he might be shot.

Dr. Houghton's tongue was now loose. He said, "Colonel, I met a friend of yours in Chun Chon, Miss Moon."

"Yes, Miss Moon and I had a good time. She was very beautiful." The Colonel displayed a peculiar, contented smile like a heroin addict on a high. "Before she left, I gave her eight hundred dollars for her sick brother."

Dr. Houghton wondered why the Colonel didn't see Miss Moon had flimflammed him. While they were playing shuffle board earlier, Mike told him how Miss Moon would come over to the bar, interrupt, stand beside the Colonel and insinuate her hand into his pants. She would then lead him off by his member. She nicknamed him "Lollipop." But what "bugged" Mike most was that Colonel Murray borrowed money to give to Miss Moon.

Dr. Houghton, slightly unhinged by the gin, the tales, the company and the place, almost said "Lollipop," but instead said, "Colonel, you know, Errol Flynn could piss a quart. Mike says it is impossible. What do you think?"

Colonel Murray didn't answer immediately. Instead he finished the last two ounces of Scotch in the fifth. He then unzipped his fly and discharged a slow but endless stream of colorless urine into the bottle until it overflowed. "Here's your answer, Doc."

Dr. Houghton was speechless, devoid of words, as he accepted the steaming, overflowing fifth. Finally, he looked at Mike, and said, "It's only a fifth, not a quart."

112

A few minutes later, Colonel Murray and the gold-toothed business lady sashayed out the side door. Mike and Dr. Houghton followed. After pausing for some uproarious laughter, Colonel Murray and the "girl" staggered gaily toward his quarters in marked contrast to General Samet's ideal of life after dark at Air Force Seven.

Dr. Houghton summed up. "Mike, this goddamned place is the end of the road; even the business ladies here are worn out. Good night, Mike." Dr. Houghton stumbled toward his small room, sadly alone.

Mike called out, "Doc, come back for a minute. Don't be discouraged. Come with me on leave to Japan, Hong Kong and Thailand. I can arrange flights for us on the Air Force Mac command. Since I'm in the Force I know who to ask. You will see a different East. The girls in Japan, Hong Kong and Thailand are different and fascinating. There are also nice gardens and, for an intellectual like you, art and museums. I will show you a great time even though you are a babe in the woods. You can do me a favor in return!"

Dr. Houghton said, "Sounds like fun. Let's do it. Ask me anything and I'll do it."

Mike said, "Tomorrow."

That night, Dr. Houghton's dreams were very unpleasant. They were filled with bad sex with gold-toothed Korean business ladies. He woke up many times, once sweating profusely. At that moment, he was entrapped by a gold-toothed vagina dentata – a vagina with gold teeth.

"Full many a flower is born to blush unseen,
and waste its sweetness on the desert air."
"Elegy written in a Country Churchyard,"
Thomas Gray

Chapter IX
A Sing - Song Girl

"Major Kennedy is here."

"Send him in."

"Doc, I am sorry to bother you but my twin sister was just diagnosed with acute leukemia. I hope to visit her next month. I hear they have experts at the Brigham in Boston where you trained. Can you help me?"

"Mike, I can definitely help. I know the Professor of Hematology there quite well. He is the world's expert on the therapy of acute leukemia. I spent one month on his service. With the new therapies, leukemia is not always hopeless. I will write a letter to him right now. Your role will be to send it to him through the Air Force system. I am sure the moment he receives it, he will take your sister under his wing. The Professor is the nicest caring physician I ever met and he is Irish too."

Mike said, "Doc, God bless you" as he wiped away a few tears.

What Dr. Houghton did not tell him was the nightmarish complexity and brick-wrinkling side effects of the new chemotherapy for acute leukemia. That would be for another day - hope first. But it was true that, for the first time, some patients "went into remission," a near miracle.

"What time do you think we'll get to Soochow, Sergeant Song? Before eight o'clock, I hope."

"Yes, sir. It should be very soon. The road is now getting better. I think we're approaching the outskirts. Sergeant Min says it takes only forty minutes."

Dr. Houghton was impatient. He had won two Beefeater double gin and tonics from Mike in shuffleboard after supper. These, coupled with the expectation of finally visiting the fabled Soochow, exhilarated him. The vague reports of North Korean infiltrator landings added a dimension of danger. Based on these reports, he should have remained on the compound under the

114

circumstances. He was also very sore from the beating he was taking in Hap Gi Do practice. His shins looked like knotty tree trunks. Yet they were almost in Soochow.

But the winter chill and his slow progress in both the Korean language and the Hap Gi Do training gradually tempered his exhilaration. He looked over at Sergeant Song who drove with intense concentration. "Sergeant Song, I'm not pleased with my progress in my Korean language training. I almost failed your examination. And in Hap Gi Do, I just can't seem to master the swing kick."

"But you passed, Sir, and it was not easy. You are really making good progress in Hap Gi Do. You must have patience."

"Sergeant Song, remember what I told you. In the dispensary I'm the Captain, but tonight we're two guys out on the town. Let's cut out the 'Sir' and the saluting until tomorrow."

"Yes, Doctor."

The streets of Soochow were empty. The stores were closed. The dark city appeared deserted. Dr. Houghton suddenly warmed as a surge of adrenalin circulated through him. He slipped his hand over the pistol butt. "Where is everybody?"

"I don't know," Sergeant Song replied.

Suddenly they were momentarily blinded by a bright light in front of them. Two shots cracked the eldritch silence. As Sergeant Song slowed the jeep, Dr. Houghton, still blinded by the intense glare of the beam, pulled out his forty-five, felt the clip in place, and cocked it. He was ready. He was an excellent shot.

As they slowed to a halt, an armed mob, silhouetted in the glare, surrounded the jeep. Dr. Houghton heard the Korean word for American amidst their noisy babble.

Through the open window, Sergeant Song began talking to a Korean officer in full field outfit, grenades hanging from his jacket. As Dr. Houghton's eyes accommodated to the brilliant light, he prepared to flee if necessary.

As the moments passed he saw that the silhouettes were a motley group of Korean soldiers, dressed in many different types and colors of uniforms. As they milled around the jeep, he chuckled: a few carried wooden rifles. Dr. Houghton gingerly uncocked his pistol and slid it back into its holster. The soldier with the grenades finally waved them on.

"What's the story, Sergeant Song?"

"Tonight there is a local seven-thirty curfew. These men are in the Homeland Defense, like the U.S. National Guards. More infiltrators landed on the coast today."

Escorted by the Homeland Defense Jeep, Sergeant Song drove to the Kisaeng House that Colonel Murray recommended.

That morning Dr. Houghton had entered Colonel Murray's office to report that, while the Colonel enjoyed the lady with the gold teeth, a jittery Korean guard had shot a Korean soldier returning from across the river, in violation of the midnight curfew. Before seeing Murray, Dr. Houghton expected to see a hung over, barely alive, still drunken Colonel if he showed up at all. The evening before, he observed Colonel Murray consume enough alcohol to kill a giant, according to the textbooks. Even eight hours later, Murray should be in an alcoholic coma. But when he saw Colonel Murray, he gasped in disbelief. At eight a.m., the Colonel sat cheerfully behind his desk.

Dr. Houghton could not resist. "Do you have a headache, Colonel?"

"Why should I have a headache, Doctor?" Colonel Murray asked ingenuously.

Dr. Houghton was envious of the man's resiliency but he came to the point. "Colonel, I came over to tell you we removed the bullet from the soft tissues in the Korean's calf. He will be fine."

Excellent."

"One other thing, Colonel; I'd like to go to Soochow tonight, if it's all right with you. I'll be back before the twelve o'clock curfew."

"OK, Doc." It was at that time that the Colonel advised him where to go. Walking back to this office, Dr. Houghton became aware of a partially conscious and intense undefined longing. His days in Korea were irretrievably slipping way. He was conscientiously reading his medical journals; he was right up-to-date. He was learning Korean and Hap Gi Do. He was doing his duty to his country - being in the army defending "Freedom's Frontier." But how could he practice Virgil's advice, which hung on the wall of his high school Latin teacher's school room: "Faman extendere factis / hoc virtutis opus – broaden fame with actions, this is the task of virtue." He reluctantly admitted to himself: in Korea, he still did not know which end was up.

Sergeant Song parked the jeep near the concrete block exterior of the Kisaeng House with its black, iron-barred windows. After they removed their boots, they were ushered into a yellow hued room as serving girls placed magnificent blue silk pillows on the floor. A peacock motif in deep blue and gold was embroidered on the pillows and walls. A Korean lute, flute and hourglass-shaped

116

drum sat waiting in a corner. The serving girls and the Madam disappeared quietly, sliding the door shut.

"Sit down, please," Sergeant Song said with a polite gesture.

"Thank you."

Dr. Houghton eased down into a cross-legged posture. The warm floor was inviting after the frigid ride. "May I take your forty-five, Sergeant Song," Dr. Houghton said as he stood to hang both weapons on wall pegs.

After several months of intimate contact with Captain Houghton, Sergeant Song at last seemed at ease. He knew the Captain's interests. "Do you know how the Kisaeng originated, Doctor?"

"No, not well. Tell me please."

"For two thousands years off and on, Korea, although independent and with her own King, had to send tribute to the Chinese Emperor, the Son of Heaven. This tribute consisted of gold and silver bars, fine jewels, embroidered silk and beautiful virgins.

"In return, every two years, the Chinese Emperor sent his envoys. The Korean King, wishing to please these foreign ambassadors, provided entertainers for them. The king hoped to intoxicate the envoys with their charm and talent so he could drive a less onerous bargain. The entertainers had to be virginal, beautiful and intelligent. They had to sing and dance and speak Chinese and write poetry in Chinese. Although often distasteful, they must please the envoys at night. These girls were considered patriots for helping keep the unacknowledged Chinese yoke light. These girls were termed Kisaeng which means sing-song girls. There are very few true Kisaeng left now, but the girls in this place are real."

"Excellent," Dr. Houghton replied.

"Many girls from Yangban families were trained patriotically to be Kisaeng. After being deflowered by the Chinese envoys, they sometimes committed suicide when the Chinese mission left, since the loss of their maidenhood precluded any chance of marriage - which is still true today. A few lived as outcasts. Only very rich men and foreigners can afford Kisaeng now."

Dr. Houghton pondered this paradox of Korean society. These girls were patriots, yet, once "wrinkled", they were cast out.

Changing the subject, Sergeant Song said, "The Madam says that because of the curfew, we are the only patrons tonight. Miss Han, the most accomplished Kisaeng, will be for you, Doctor."

At the mention of Miss Han's name, two Kisaeng, Miss Han and Miss Lee, seemed to float through the paper doors, thus creating a fabulous illusion. Miss Han laughed gaily at Dr. Houghton's "How are you?" in Korean. Involuntarily he stood up at their entrance as Sergeant Song explained in Korean who they were. Only then, Miss Han, eyes averted, bowed very deeply and politely said in Korean, "How are you, Honorable Doctor, Captain Houghton?" After a short pause, she said blithesomely, "You are most handsome."

Dr. Houghton imagined that Miss Han had talked with his father. He repeatedly counseled Reg to adorn the ugly women with elegant flattery and caparison the pretty ones with blandishments of high intelligence and wit. To this day, such premeditated dishonesty grated his overgrown childhood sense of honesty. Just the recollection of his father saying to some Gorgon-ugly hag, "Why you look lovely tonight," nauseated him. But incomprehensible to him, the hag welcomed the obvious falsehood. But now, like that hag, Dr. Houghton found delectation in her words. After all, to her, he knew he was just a barbarian, comparable to his father's hag, but with money.

In reply he said in Korean, "You too are beautiful." But this was not prevarication for she was the image of perfectly disciplined elegance. At this, in the traditional stylized manner, Miss Han blushed, averted her eyes, lowered her lashes and raised her left hand over her eyes, palm out, in proper feigned embarrassment.

Dr. Houghton understood he sat in the presence of high refinement, now fading away in the modern world. The contrast between Air Force Seven, with the alcoholic Colonel and his gold-toothed lady, and this ethereal enchanting vision in her yellow silk dress reminded him of the difference between a popular New York trash artist called Andy Warhol, who painted Cambell soup cans, and Michelangelo.

Dr. Houghton and Miss Han shared small cups of rice wine passing the cup back and forth. Miss Han, in one graceful sip, would swallow the pale yellow liquid, with her left hand politely covering the cup and her mouth. He imitated her.They communicated in his humorous error-laden Korean which fractured her composure. He knew that Korean men never buffooned, for they lost face when laughed at, but Dr. Houghton purposely made comic errors and puns just to discompose her into unrestrained laughter.

As he watched her, he imagined the hours of preparation just to adjust and position her abundant, perfectly coiffured black hair, piled high and held in place not with glairy chemicals but with long, jade-tipped gold hairpins. The odor of East Indian and Chinese oils enveloped her. An imperial green jadeite charm with a Chinese character for double happy hung around her neck on a thin gold chain. Her skin appeared perfect under her makeup. Only the very fine wrinkles around her almond eyes gave away her age as thirty two.

"Let me take over, Doctor," Sergeant Song said. "I will compose a verse in Chinese to which Miss Han must answer." Dr. Houghton observed. Miss Han wrote faster than Sergeant Song, especially poems that dealt with nature and love. Her calligraphy was exquisite. The English translations of this Chinese poetry by Sergeant Song were obscure or ambiguous, although Miss Han's innuendoes about "the Captain" pervaded this poetic dialectic.

The entrance of the inevitable alien delicacies interrupted these clever exchanges. Miss Han ate with relish and served a reluctant Dr. Houghton unknown foods. Eaten from her chopsticks he almost enjoyed the worms, crabs, and octopus arm.

At the end of the feast, she clapped three times. Three female musicians entered and picked up the lute, flute, and drum from the corner. Sergeant Song explained that Miss Han would now dance a Chinese dance called "Butterfly." Indeed, to the eerie almost primitive music of the lute and the flute, Miss Han transformed into a large, yellow butterfly flitting about the room. The illusion was complete. She next performed a Korean traditional dance. Her sinuous movements and exquisite refinement, polished over two thousand years, reduced Dr. Houghton to silence. He applauded with real admiration. About this performance, a magic he had not felt since he saw Rudolf Serkin play Beethoven's Emperor Piano Concerto in Boston's Symphony Hall years before, he could only say, "She is really very good, Sergeant Song."

"Yes, she is really good," Sergeant Song echoed.

She returned a few minutes later in another silk traditional dress, this time, bright white with the large Chinese character for Good Fortune embroidered in gold. She would sing now. Sergeant Song explained the contents before she sang. "This song is about a young Yangban girl separated from her fiancée and family. She had volunteered to be a Kisaeng at a time when the Chinese threatened to overrun Korea. She laments her having to deal with the foreigners, but she knows it is her patriotic duty. She sings of the dilemma of her inevitable demise: Suicide now or after her patriotic deed is done."

As Miss Han sang, the primitive, rather harsh background of the lute, drum and flute added a desperate flavor to this highly emotional music. Moreover, she sang these haunting, ancient strains with a terrible involvement.

She, too, Dr. Houghton thought, like the Kisaeng entertainers of old, placated the barbarians: him. "Miss Han, that was beautiful," he said in Korean at a loss for a more expressive word. "Do you know any English songs?"

"Yes," she said in Korean. "I know several, but I don't understand the words." She knelt in front of Dr. Houghton and took his hands in her gentle warm palms. She peered straight and deep into his eyes. With a nod, she signaled to the band which started. "Oh, I wish I were in the land of cotton......."

Dr. Houghton was tickled by her oriental English. "Well, I'll be .....Dixie, with an unusual band."

Miss Han observed a definite fullness in Dr. Houghton's formerly limpid eyes. When she finished singing, the evening was gone.

Dr. Houghton slipped out and paid the Madam the five thousand won bill - twelve dollars. He gave Miss Han and Miss Lee two thousand won each and each musician one thousand. "Thank you very much, Miss Han. I shall see you soon."

Miss Han smiled respectfully. "That would make us very happy. I am glad you enjoyed our humble entertainment."

As they laced their boots, Dr. Houghton said, "It's eleven. Do you feel up to driving back?"

"Yes, sir. I did not drink much rice wine."

In the darkness of the bouncing jeep, Sergeant Song said, "Miss Han told me she is in big trouble. She owes the Madam 30,000 won. Business is very bad because of the infiltrator problem. Daily she slips deeper into debt."

"Do you know how she got to be a Kisaeng, Sergeant Song?"

"No, she didn't tell me. I don't like to ask. It saddens me so much."

The following Sunday, as dusk spread over the lifeless countryside, Dr. Houghton was exhausted. "This ride is a killer, Sergeant Song, even with a pillow. Let's stop for a cup of tea and a little warmth before we enter Chun Chon. This is a hell of a way to spend a Sunday afternoon."

They entered the Voluptuous Flower Tea House. One of the girls came over. "May I serve you, Sir?"

"Ah," Dr. Houghton said, studying her closely, "a girl who speaks English. Yes, we'd like to have two cups of red tea." He noted she wore a black skirt with an amaranth colored silk blouse. This immediately stirred memories of Harvard, Yale and Miss Ching. But most of all, he remembered that triumphant day at Harvard when he and George dyed a piece of white silk with the amaranth dye he synthesized.

Soon she returned with the oriental treatment for shivering.

"Won't you please sit down?" Dr. Houghton asked in Korean using the polite forms. The girl looked at Sergeant Song who echoed, "Sit down."

"Thank you, Sir," she said as she sat down opposite Dr. Houghton. Lara's theme - music from Dr. Zhivago - played softly in the background

"My name is Dr. Houghton. This is Sergeant Song. You speak English well."

"I don't know English."

"What is your name?"

"My name is Miss Pak." She enunciated each monosyllable clearly, but lingered too long on each sound.

Dr. Houghton guessed she learned her English at school, not from Americans. "Did you learn English in college?" he asked her. She did not understand the question, and he repeated it slowly.

She understood. "Yes, Honorable Doctor."

Dr. Houghton wished to ask more questions, but contained his curiosity. He realized it was very difficult for women, if they had to work, to find jobs. If they did not marry, were jilted or unmarriageable for other reasons, they had little choice, if they wished to sustain themselves but to drift into the entertainment business. As he now knew, the Koreans disdained the Tea House girls least, but he did not wish to embarrass her. So he drank the tea in silence. As they stood to leave, he said to her in Korean, "Goodbye, Beautiful."

She flushed and lightly grasped, by her standards, his big right arm. She said in English, "How did you know my name?"

Dr. Houghton did not understand. "What?"

"My name is Yong Me which means Beautiful Flower; Yong means flower."

"I am a magic man," he improvised in Korean by way of explanation. "Good-bye, Beautiful Flower." He restudied her. By classical oriental standards, she was very attractive although she did not have Cupid's bow lips. She did have plump lips, a type Dr. Houghton also preferred. Moreover, she had a perfect unblemished complexion and a light skin color.

"Good-bye, Sir. See you again, soon." She waved at the jeep from the Tea House door.

Dr. Houghton, who rarely looked back, did so. "Stop the jeep, Sergeant Song." He capered out and walked over to the florist stand they just passed. For years, Marsha had accused him of not having a romantic bone. Now he bought a solitary red rose and walked back to the Tea House. Miss Pak did not see him enter. He tapped her on the shoulder and she turned around. He said in Korean to her, "I bought a beautiful flower for you, Beautiful Flower."

She accepted the rose with a dazzling smile of perfect white teeth; her cheeks reddened in two round circles and then she bowed.

He winked, turned about, entered the jeep and, this time, he did not look back.

The following morning he said to Sergeant Song, "I am mixed up about the Korean word for flower. Yong Mi, the teahouse girl, said the word for flower was yong, but in the Kisaeng house you told me flower was hoa."

Sergeant Song said, "It is complex."

"Yes."

"In Chinese hoa means flower but we use that term for the entertainers, not real flowers so much. We Koreans use the Korean word yong for flower. However, the Korean entertainers like to call themselves yong - flower. Thus yong in Korean is ambiguous in its connotation."

"I think I understand."

What Sergeant Song did not mention was that Pak Yong Mi was not the teahouse girl's real name, but why add further ambiguity?

At 9:15 AM, Sergeant Song interrupted Dr. Houghton who was treating the executive officer for arthritis.

"The General is on the phone, Sir."

Dr. Houghton picked up the phone. "Good morning, General."

"Good morning, Doctor. What are you doing over there? You're supposed to be at Air force Seven."

"I have sick patients over here. Colonel Murray said it was all right if I came over this morning."

"I've sent a chopper for you. Colonel Murray has apparently been hurt in an accident. As soon as you can, call me as to his condition. Keep a close eye on the old devil. I want him to return to the States in one piece. I promised his wife to keep an eye on him. If she only knew, ….."

"I'll call you as soon as I can, General Samet." He hung up. "Sergeant Song, we need to return to Seven. I'll meet you at the helipad in ten minutes. We are going back right now."

Thirty minutes later, they landed in back of the dispensary at Air Force Seven. Sergeant Dawson was there to greet them.

"How's the Colonel; where is he?"

"He's fine now. Here are his skull x-rays."

"They look normal," Dr. Houghton said as he examined them. "Nothing broken; no shift. I can see his pineal right in the midline."

Sergeant Dawson said, "Colonel Murray was brought in here last night, smashed out of his mind, with two large lacerations on his scalp. There was a lot of bleeding, but I finally got it stopped, and sewed it up. This morning he is fine although a little pale from the loss of blood."

"Sergeant Song, bring my bag, and we'll go see him. By the way, how did the General find out?"

"I don't know, Sir."

"Good morning, Colonel," Dr. Houghton grinned on entering the Colonel's bedroom. "I hear you have a little headache."

"Morning, Doc."

"What happened, Colonel?"

"I tripped and fell through some glass after leaving the Kisaeng House last night. Some of the Korean officers and I went down for a farewell party. You know, I go home next week."

"How about the curfew?"

The Colonel didn't answer.

"Let me examine you."

Dr. Houghton concluded that the Colonel was fine except for the sutured lacerations and mild anemia due to the blood loss. He also discovered that Colonel Murray had spindle legs. He could not resist, "The only thing the alcohol has affected, Colonel, is your legs; they seem to have dissolved."

Colonel Murray grimaced.

Dr. Houghton cut the jokes. "You don't mind if I call General Samet from your phone? He asked me to call back." He knew that Murray was in big trouble, and if the General became cognizant of the Colonel's escapade downtown, he would court-martial him. After all, this bit of zany behavior had come after the formal warning and reprimand. "Operator, get me General Samet in Seoul, would you please."

"General, this is Dr. Houghton. I called to reassure you that Colonel Murray is fine. He fell down and banged his head, but it is sutured. He's doing just fine."

"How did it happen, Doctor?"

Dr. Houghton did not hesitate at the critical question. "He tripped and banged his head."

"Doc, keep a close eye on him, would you, even if you have to nail him down....." the General paused. "Have Murray call me himself, would you?"

Later that afternoon, with the cold sun slipping toward the horizon, Dr. Houghton said, "Sergeant Song, it is four now. I'd like to see Miss Han. If we leave now, we will be there in forty minutes, and we can be back by the seven o'clock curfew."

On the ride over, as they passed a Buddhist temple, Dr. Houghton thought of his Harvard days; then of the Buddha and the Scottish philosopher David Hume. Both the Buddha and Hume taught that life was a series of brief perceptions, one after another, often unrelated, rarely retained. They both wondered what is real. Moreover, the Buddha explicitly asked; what is the self since we are ever changing? All this distressed Dr. Houghton: he was searching for permanence like jadeite carvings or women with everlasting white skin, hard thighs, callipygian buttocks, and plump lips or if possible Cupid's bow lips. He wanted these and a beautiful mind. Was it possible to find such women? Or was the Buddha correct: in the end, is it all change, illusion and emptiness? Does it all end only with disappointment, decay and death, then recyling? Perhaps, but Dr. Houghton still thought Camus was right. He went into the Kisaeng house expectantly.

"Hel-lo," Miss Han greeted them. She was dressed in black slacks and a white buttoned-in-front cashmere sweater although her hair was all done up for the evening. Her head now appeared too large for her small, wispy body. Like a child, she took Dr.Houghton's right hand in hers and guided them to a small back room.

"Sergeant Song, see if you can find out what happened to Colonel Murray here last night." Sergeant Song talked to Miss Han and Miss Lee. As Dr. Houghton listened, he wondered at the intensity with which Miss Han clung to him. Either she cherished him with a fierce affection or she desperately required succor. He said in English, "Sergeant Song, tell me also what is wrong with Miss Han."

Sergeant Song talked with her at great length.

Miss Han started to cry. Then she wept, wiping away rivers of tears punctuated with sobs of anguish. Dr. Houghton was cut by the depth of her emotion. For only a moment did he question this scene as deception, but if she was acting, he concluded she deserved an academy award.

At length, Sergeant Song began in English. "Business is terrible. Miss Han is desperate. Her father is dying of tuberculosis. The Madam is insistent she pay at least some of her debts. Miss Han has no money, nothing to sell. Consequently, she is unable to send

124

money home to her penurious father who needs medicine. She hopes that perhaps you can help her, Honorable Teacher. If you would, she would be extremely grateful; forever at your service. She would do anything you ask, she says. She would commit suicide if her father were not sick and in need. Since no Korean will help her, she hopes maybe you will. She also thinks you are not wicked, and is happy you like her singing and dancing."

"Tell her everything will be fine, that we can help her." As Sargeant Song translated, Dr. Houghton was concerned about her slender body. He wanted to ask her if she coughed or spit up blood. He would later. He shuddered as thought of her suicide. "Tell her we have lots of excellent TB medicine for her father in clinic. Tomorrow she can collect it at the clinic." He paused, "Ask her now much she will take for that jadeite pendant around her neck."

"She says it's worth 5,000 won, if she sells it. It's her only valuable possession."

"In the States, it is worth at least 15,000 won. I will give her 15,000 won –almost 40 dollars." When they entertained him before, he had examined it. It was a finely carved piece of translucent apple green jadeite. Of that he was absolutely certain.

Tears of joy flowed down her cheeks as she put the beautiful jadeite pendant around his neck.

"I am very happy to have it," he said in Korean with the polite forms. "It has the Chinese character for Double Happy."

He counted out purposely 15,500 won, but Miss Han returned the extra 500.

In Korean, Dr. Houghton whispered in her ear, "I have love sickness. Do you have the medicine?"

She understood, laughed, and squeezed his hand. "I know number one medicine," she replied in Korean and pointed to herself.

Dr. Houghton was now warm with a combination of sympathy and lust. He also could not refrain from caressing his new jadeite pendant, but he said, "We must go because of the curfew. I'll come back as soon as I can."

She physically tried to prevent him from leaving. "Please don't go. I beg of you. I have medicine for your health," she said in Korean.

Dr. Houghton rose, lifted her body into the air and then put her down gently.

She playfully banged on his chest. He only understood, "Like a rock."

"I will come here soon. Good-bye."

"Good-bye Honorable Doctor. I am waiting for you."

On the return trip, he thought of a story his mother read to him when he was a child: Miss Goodie Two Shoes. He did not remember the details except that Miss Goodie was poor and only had one shoe. But when she was given an old pair, she was so happy she told everyone she had "two shoes." Hence, her name. She became a model of cheerful, happy optimism. Later Miss Goodie became wealthy and a do-gooder. Reg's mother told him that Miss Goodie was "too good to be true." The implication was that in life there must be balance.

Reg frequently studied his jadeite pendant; in bright light and from many angles. He loved his new pendant. Miss Ching at Harvard and the Emperor Qianlong were correct: there was something magic about translucent jadeite - it was alive. He had achieved the correct balance with Miss Han when he bought it from her.

"What did you find out, Sergeant Song?" Dr. Houghton asked during the jeep ride back.

"I found out what happened, confirming Private Lee's story."

"You mean Colonel Murray's driver knew?"

"Yes, Sir. General Lee and his men took Colonel Murray to the Kisaeng House for a farewell party. Everybody got too drunk. Colonel Murray took a fancy to a MissYun, the Kisaeng, but she is the mistress of a Major Kim, one of General Lee's aids. She ran away from Colonel Murray who chased her down the alley. Major Kim in turn chased the Colonel. They had some conversation, and as Colonel Murray lurched off to continue pursuing MissYun, Major Kim pushed him and his head went through the window."

"That old lecher! Drop me off at the Officers' club, would you please, Sergeant Song."

"Good evening, Mike," Dr. Houghton said as he approached the figure at the bar.

"Hey, Doc. What do you think about the Colonel?"

"A few big scratches, Mike. He'll be fine."

"Do you know what happened, and how it happened?"

"Yes, I do. I just found out from the Kisaeng."

"I'd like to kill the Korean who did that to our Colonel. If you know his name, tell me, and I'll get him. Did you know Murray was an Ace pilot during the Korean War? He shot down eight MIGs although he no longer flies. He is a legend. I will kill the bastard."

126

"Mike, you're drunk. Don't be crazy. You'll get killed. It won't do any good."

"Damn it, Doc. Tell me now." Mike pushed Dr. Houghton back with his right hand.

Dr. Houghton was outraged at Mike's aggressive behavior. For a moment, he was blind with black anger. He was about to act. But he contained his nearly irresistible impulse to break the offending wrist, although he had practiced this move for weeks. Stepping back, he said, "Mike, don't be a fool. I heard the whole story. Colonel Murray was partially at fault."

"Don't give me that crap, Doc," Mike raged as he towered over him. But Mike, noting the fire-burst from Dr. Houghton's eyes, also stepped back. "These little bastards can't go around beating our Commanding Officer."

"Mike, be reasonable."

"Doc, I wanna know." The ferocity was suddenly gone.

"Mike, I'll tell you in the morning when you're sober, and that is that."

Mike shrugged his shoulders, shook his head and sat down.

Dr. Houghton saw a shadowy figure in the corner of the club. "Mike, who is that?"

"I don't know. Some Korean. He's been asking for you."

"Why Lieutenant Ahn," Dr. Houghton said as he walked over to the corner. "What the hell are you doing here?"

"I'm in whopping, king-bed trouble, Sir. I need 6,000 won right now."

"What for?"

"Well," Lieutenant Ahn said with a dark smile, "I need some abortions."

"Who's the girl?"

"A Chun Chon girl. She is the one who comes to the Q - the noisy one. She threatened to tell General Lee. Big trouble if she does. She claims that I affianced."

"Did you?

Lieutenant Ahn did not reply. "She's respectable. I want to help her out."

"Garbage, Lieutenant Ahn. The General would throttle you if he found out."

Lieutenant Ahn meekly agreed.

"You should be ashamed of yourself. If you don't marry her now; she's not a cherry girl. No one will ever marry her now that she's not a cherry girl. You ought to only screw the entertainers."

Lieutenant Ahn rebutted, "Too much VD. Cherry girl, no VD. You say so yourself."

127

"Lieutenant Ahn, you are an incorrigible louse. Here's the money."

"Thank you, Sir."

"Where are you going?"

"Chun Chon."

"What about the curfew?"

"No problem."

Like a small rat in a land with only a handful of trees and hence few owls, Lieutenant Ahn disappeared confidently into the black night.

Chapter X
Yale Medical School

Student Doctor Houghton averted his gaze from the approaching Dr. Foo, the intern responsible for the care of Henry. Like Reg Houghton and Henry, Dr. Foo had been an undergraduate Harvard student. However, Reg always felt shame when he saw this handsome and brilliant young physician with a golden personality. Six years previously when a Harvard senior, Dr. Foo, nominated for the Hasty Pudding Institute at Harvard was rejected by the Pudding Council when a single anonymous black ball rolled onto the table. His name, not his qualities or appearance, which resembled his Caucasian mother not his Chinese father, motivated one trogdolyte to insure his rejection.

"How's the patient?" Reg asked.

"He's doing as well as can be expected," Dr. Foo replied.

Reg knocked and entered Henry's hospital room. Henry was a fellow third year student and friend, "Good evening, Henry boy. This is no way to spend a Sunday night."

"Good evening, old man, how good of you to drop by."

"Henry, why the ear-to-ear grin?"

Henry did not answer, but the grin, like a frozen Greek mask of comedy, remained.

"I drove back from Boston about an hour ago. It looks like Marsha and I are through. Anyhow, I was eating with Jim and he told me you were here. He said you were a patient. He said you fractured it. That's a new diagnosis to me. Jim was laughing so loud, he couldn't get control of himself. He finally told me what happened."

Henry said, "What did the prick tell you?"

"Jim said, 'Saturday night, last night, I was doing a little studying in the dorm when I heard this horrible shriek from Henry's room. I ran over, knocked on the door, opened it, and there stood Henry, skinny as a pole, wearing only his shoes and a short T-shirt. He held his extended organ in obvious agony.'

"'Why?' I asked Jim.

"Jim continued, 'The Chief Nurse from the Emergency Room, June, was there. She stood with her back against the wall, holding a slip in front of her. She looked like Caravaggio's Gorgon. I was afraid to look at her – I might turn into a stone.'

Reg said, "I told him to stop the literary allusions and tell me the story."

"Jim said, 'I asked, "What's the matter, Henry? What is going on June?"'"

Henry said, "What did he say?"

"Jim said, 'Henry, like a Shakespearean actor grimacing in pain, with his left hand on his organ, imperiously raised his right arm pointing at June, like Cicero pointing at some wicked Catiline in the Roman Senate, and made the accusation. "She broke it; she beaked me. I heard it snap. Get me to the hospital quick!'

"'Then what happened,' I asked Jim?

"Jim said they took you to the Emergency Room, and they admitted you. He's telling everyone you fractured your penis." Reg paused. "I can't believe that. What really happened Henry?" Reg waited patiently for his friend's explanation.

Henry Leary and Reg had attended Harvard together, but at Yale their friendship flowered. Reg was the better student but Henry the more protean man. Henry had a very distinctive appearance, a lineament one could not forget. Henry's head resembled a triangle placed upside down on top of a broomstick, his forehead too large and out of proportion to his thin frame. Moreover, when he spoke, he emanated a jerky, nervous vitality. He moved as if he had just avoided being struck by a fast train. Reg thought Henry was not handsome or desirable but women obviously disagreed.

Although an excellent student, Henry overindulged in most things, especially women and gin, "Irish water." Born with a massive reserve of energy, his vigor was legendary. After a standard, exhausting day of medical study, Henry would rush to his laboratory to study the urine of autistic children. Then, off to the library for a few hours hidden in a corner. Often at eleven, he would then rendezvous with some nurse or other young lovely, enter the dormitory by the back door and take the elevator up to his room. Reg lived in the room next door; he wore ear plugs to avoid the prurient distractions. Henry would always ask the young lady the same initial question, "A martini, my sweet?" This was Henry's main source of nutrition for he ate few formal meals.

Occasionally, his "sweet" would say "Oh, no thanks, but I'd like a beer."

Henry would gingerly tip-toe into Reg's unlocked room, quietly removed a beer from the refrigerator and say, "Hope, I didn't wake you up."

The answer was generally the same. "Henry, tonight be nimble, be quick and please be quiet. We have to get up and draw blood at six in the morning. You have to come."

Henry answered with mock outrage. "Take it easy, man. I'll be there."

Reg could estimate how much gin Henry drank by the bottles in the trash cans. He averaged three fifths each week. Reg knew how much gin should destroy him but Henry, notwithstanding his cadaverous appearance, thrived on it. Equally remarkable were Henry's often tumultuous sexual escapades. He managed to destroy two beds in three years.

Occasionally Reg and Henry, with his omnipresent late evening martini, would sit down and talk at midnight having finished their work for the day. Henry would occasionally admit to a little fatigue as he twitched under a huge picture of a megathere, the Pleistocene sloth. This black humor hung on his wall.

"Yes," Henry would say, "the dwindles are certainly getting worse."

"Henry boy," Reg answered, "you look just like you did in college." Henry hadn't changed in six years. He looked equally cadaverous then as now. But Reg always warned, "Each man is born with a certain fixed amount of energy and a limited number of heart beats. Some men have more, some less. At the rate you are going, you'll use all yours up soon."

Looking at his sloth on the wall, Henry would gesticulate with a cigarette in his left hand, the martini in the right, enveloped in a smoky cloud, "You're right." Then he continued. "I'm near the end. I just don't have the energy anymore." In the next breath, he would launch into grand plans for a challenging seduction or further work on his autism project. To Henry, rest, relaxation, and escape were just words, not needs.

Finally, Henry launched into his explanation of the catastrophe. "I had a date with June, you know her, the Chief Nurse at the Emergency Ward."

"Yes, I know her. You were asking for trouble with her. She's a big, tough girl."

"Anyhow," Henry said, "just before dinner, I figured what the hell. She was mildly stiff from a couple of martinis. She resisted a little, but I was finally able to undress her. I pushed her up against the door...."

"Standing up? You couldn't wait to take her over to the bed, huh?"

131

"Anyhow, she finally accepted me. She threw her arms around my neck and her legs around my waist, heaving and moaning. 'It's good,' she says. Suddenly she moved. I hear a tear. I thought she had torn it off. The next second, Jim's in my room laughing while I'm in excruciating pain. They have been giving me high-dose morphine for it." Henry paused, tacitly explaining his peculiar grin, "You ought to see it."

Reg pulled the white sheet back to reveal the black, swollen suffering organ. "Will it heal O.K.?"

"It's only blood under there. The urologist says it will heal, but possibly somewhat bent," Henry replied sadly.

"Jim's diagnosis of fracture wasn't far off, was it, Henry?"

"The prick." The irony didn't elude grimly grinning Henry.

Reg and Henry disliked their humble stature during their last two years in medical school, the clinical years. Moreover, in the outside world, vast changes were occurring and they were not part of them; the Vietnam War, birth control, student protests, and woman's liberation. Most shocking to both Reg and Henry, some women did not wear underpants. But Reg and Henry had both made a serious commitment to medicine. "To hell with the outside world, for now," Henry said. Both Reg and Henry knew that for the well motivated, very smart Yale medical students who wanted to learn basic medical science, clinical medicine and something about medical research, Yale was unsurpassed. The only requirements for graduation were passing the second and fourth year national medical boards and writing an original research thesis under the supervision of a faculty advisor. They were there to learn and grow.

But there was one big issue for them: the other side of the scholarly Yale medical system. Since there were no examinations and grades, the students depended on the evaluations of harried interns, busy residents and attending physicians. These evaluations, critical for internship placement, were often inaccurate and subjective. Some fortunate and some scheming students found a deus ex machina in a patron from the professorial ranks.

Unlike most of the students, Reg and Henry avoided unctuous, guileful behavior; they were intellectually hyper-honest. Any intercourse with a superior, beyond a polite greeting, elicited wild accusations of, as Henry called it, "ass osculating." They were determined to advance only on merit. So they accepted their status on the lowest rung. Before sunrise, they drew the blood and performed the unpleasant "scut work." In time, they could, like warlocks, draw blood from stones.

Reg reluctantly admitted that it was proper to begin at the bottom. Reg realized that, although he was second in his class, the interns and residents knew more than he. They had a certain justification for their arrogance. He understood, although he profoundly disliked, their lack of patience and understanding for the students. "Jesus," Henry moaned, "they were students last year; how quickly they forget." Moreover, exhausted and overworked, the house-staff were very poorly paid.

Like fledgeings, the medical students were tossed out of their nests of book learning and mental ease at the start of the third year. Many plummeted without a solitary flap and splattered on the pebbles below. These "birds" often went into non-clinical fields. But for Reg, the most difficult aspect of the transition was the development of absolute control over ordinary needs and drives, like holding your urine for hours after you had to go. These inner demands one had to ignore. Besides this purposeful loss of inner sensitivity, one had to develop a shield against outer catastrophes, against the unfairness and brutality of Disease and Death. But consciously, no matter what the circumstances, Reg always tried to be pleasant and understanding with the patients. They must not suffer indirectly from his tribulations. Reg knew all these adjustments were mandatory to be a good physician. Fatigue, sleep deprivation, and ignorance were never good excuses.

On a typical third year morning, on the surgery rotation, Reg awoke at 5:30 A.M. He hated the early rising. He sat on the edge of the bed in blurred confusion, a state of near paralysis, for five minutes. The tumultuous events of the night before in the Surgical Recovery Room ended in a desperate sleep at two AM. In a flurry, Reg washed, brushed his teeth, gagged, and spat through a cotton batten, dehydrated mouth. Too late for breakfast, he ran to the hospital. Completing the blood drawing by seven, he scrubbed ten full minutes for his first case in the operating room. One of his patients, a teenager he had worked up three days before, would undergo open heart surgery. Reg knew the senior surgeon was slow and meticulous. Sleepy and dry, Reg braced himself.

The nurses wheeled the sleeping child into the operating room. At eight, the senior surgeon came, after the anesthesiologist had gassed him into a deep, painless sleep and the residents had placed many tubes in the patient.

"Dr. Houghton," the chief surgical resident said, "today we want you to guard the femoral catheter. You stand here." The position he pointed out was near the end of the table where he could not see the operating field. Two hours later, Reg stood in exactly the same spot, both hands guarding the femoral catheter. He ignored the

133

persistent itch on his nose created by the mask. One hour later, he tightened his calves ten times, prophylaxis against syncope, although he never once had fainted. In a slight daze, Reg vaguely heard the first words spoken to him in three hours.

"Is there a student here?" the surgeon, a full professor, asked.

"Yes," the resident replied.

"What nerves innervate the heart?" the senior surgeon asked.

Reg replied correctly, hoping for more instruction, but the next question did not come until noon.

"What's the Finkelstein approach?"

Reg did not know, and the surgeon did not explain. They finished at three, the heart repaired. Thesurgeon and residents had a unique advantage. They worked while he stood there useless and mindless; really only a pulsating, urine-filled blob.

The following month Henry and Reg both had their rotation through the Emergency Room. One evening they were on together.

"Henry, come here quick," Reg called, "This man is complaining of chest pain and shortness of breath." The old man, just brought in by ambulance was sweating profusely and ashen gray. "Henry, his pulse is 180. Would you put in an intravenous?" Henry slipped in the man's life line with the ease of long practice as Reg examined the man's chest. Reg said excitedly, "I never heard them before; listen Henry, I think this man has cannon sounds. I bet he's in ventricular tachycardia. We need an E KG." A moment later, Henry said to the Emergency Room nurse, "June, bring down the defibrillator after you tell the resident that we think we have a man in ventricular tachycardia here. Quick."

"What's your name?" Reg asked the patient as they worked.

"Ludwig," the frightened man replied.

"Mr. Ludwig," Reg assured the old man, "you came just in time. Everything's going to be fine."

With prescient anticipation of approaching doom, the horrified old man was still able to mumble, "Thank you, Doctor."

Like a genie, Dr. Kline, the resident, appeared at the critical time.

Reg said, "Dr. Kline, the EKG confirms this man is in ventricular tachycardia."

"Good boys," Dr. Kline said in praise, looking around. "Real pros. You've got an IV started, the EKG, drugs, and defibrillator."

At that moment, the EKG changed from a rapid regular beat to ventricular fibrillation. "Damn!" Reg said. "He's going."

"Reg, you pump his heart, and I'll put in an endotracheal tube." Dr. Kline ordered. Reg knew that left alone, this man was dead, but with Reg, Henry, June and Dr. Kline working, he would have a fair chance.

Reg began pumping on the dead man's chest. Simultaneously, in motions so expert, almost invisible, Dr. Kline slipped the tube into Mr. Ludwig's lungs and handed the bag to Henry. "You breathe him, Henry."

A muffled crack occurred. "Damn it!" Reg cursed again, "I broke a rib."

"Don't worry," Dr. Kline said, "keep pumping."

"Let's shock him," Reg almost shouted. He was very excited.

"Wait a minute," Dr. Kline said. "Let's prepare him for the shock."

In thirty seconds, Dr. Kline had injected the medicines. Then he ordered, "Everybody away from the bed."

Reg took a deep breath as Dr. Kline pressed the button, sending a searing 500 watt-second pulse slamming through Mr. Ludwig's chest. At this, the body jerked.

"The EKG is flat-line," Dr. Kline observed. "June, intra-cardiac epinephrine, please; now!"

June had anticipated this request. She handed Dr. Kline the syringe with the six inch needle which he shoved into Mr. Ludwig's heart. A few seconds later, Mr. Ludwig's heart beat returned – eighty and regular. Then his blood pressure slowly normalized. An hour later the Intensive Care Unit intern wheeled Mr. Ludwig upstairs.

"How long do you figure he was dead?" Reg asked.

"Exactly two minutes and twelve seconds," Henry calculated from the EKG tracings.

"Do you think he was conscious?" Henry asked.

"Yes, partially so," Dr. Kline replied. "The cardiac message sent some blood to his head.

Reg imagined the terror Mr. Ludwig must have experienced; the thumping on his chest after the broken rib, the tube rammed down his throat, and the fierce electric shock. But these two minutes of unrelieved horror ended in the rebirth of his life, instant samsara. June, Henry, Reg and Dr. Kline all agreed the price was small indeed.

Dr. Kline announced with a sigh, "God rests," and sat down.

Henry whispered, in an aside to Reg, "Kline knows when to move, doesn't he?"

But the two assistant gods and June, God's buxom aid, did not rest. Another patient was wheeled in.

Four weeks later, Reg did not recognize Mr. Ludwig, but Mr. Ludwig had not forgotten his brief sojourn in the Emergency Room.

"Are you student Dr. Houghton?"

"Yes, I am."

"I ought to punch you in the nose," Mr. Ludwig assumed a boxer's stance.

"Why?" Reg stepped back.

"You broke my ribs."

Reg remembered and said, "Mr. Ludwig!"

"But thanks anyway." Mr. Ludwig extended his hand to a smiling, pale, imperfect god. He then said, "This is my wife, Sarah Ludwig."

A smiling Sarah Ludwig said, "Thank you. I hear you raised Mr. Ludwig from the dead." She kissed him on the cheek. "This is for you, Student Doctor Houghton." She passed Reg a bottle of neatly wrapped Dom Perignon champagne.

Before he could say more than "Thank you," they were gone.

The following evening at dinner, Henry commanded, "Reg, tonight, you must take the evening off. You study too much."

"No, Henry, I can't. I must study."

"Reg, you got the second highest mark in the class on the National Boards last year."

"You're trying to ruin me. Bloom won't take the night off. He scored highest in the country."

"Bloom is queer."

"But, he'll get further ahead of me," Reg protested. "I wasted enough time at Harvard in my senior year. My father is still annoyed about that."

"I have a date for you, a friend of June's. She works at the Veterans Hospital."

"Henry boy, you must be mad, going out with that girl after she did that to you, after she bent it."

"I'll knock on the door when the girls come," Henry concluded.

Reg locked his door, hoping by this maneuver to exclude some addle-headed female. Soon, he was deeply immersed in his cardiology text. But at ten, he was interrupted by knocking and then thrashing against his door.

Henry yelled with speech slurred by gin. "I know you're in there. Open the damn door!"

Reg replied, "I'm out."

"Open the door, you worm."

Reg opened the door, and Henry staggered in spilling his martini over the rug. Like some ancient Dionysius, he was followed by two large maenads, June and Sally.

Reg was sweating and dressed only in undershorts. When he studied, he always perspired since studying for him was a tremendous physical effort. Only by severe discipline could he keep his restless body in one place. This lack of movement paradoxically required work.

Knowing he was impressively muscular, Reg puffed his chest and scrutinized Sally. Silently, Reg walked behind this black haired, busty nurse wearing a scarlet silk blouse, pumps to match, and a short white skirt. She had a thin waist and very good legs. Her appearance punctured his bookish intentions. So, with feigned ire, he threw his cardiology text on the floor, an action wholly uncharacteristic, while Henry, June and Sally watched in disbelief. Finally, he breached the silence. "Make yourselves at home. Let me shower and dress. Then we'll start with proper introductions."

Reg showered. He was happy he lifted weights. Somehow, he credited the physical exercise with the preservation of his sanity. Did they not prescribe physical training for the psychotics in lunatic asylums? The Greeks also taught the notion of a sound mind in a sound body. Moreover, the exertion itself provided a certain pleasure. So every Monday, Wednesday and Friday, if possible, Reg and four or five other students congregated in the weight room in the basement of the brand new ten story medical dormitory at five PM for good-natured, but rough, comraderie and macho exercise. By six PM, most of the day's tension and anxiety had indeed floated out of the weight room.

Paul, one of the senior students, was the weight-group leader by virtue of his unquestioned physical superiority. At 190 pounds, he could military press 250 pounds. To his fellow students, Paul was smart, aggressive, and obnoxious, but Reg, who was not threatened by Paul, could "put him down" easily." A spirited competition arose between the two when Reg questioned Paul's superiority in the bench press. "I will beat your ass on the bench," Reg touted. For some reason, Paul was only moderately proficient at this particular exercise. The contest, the "agon," was on. The loser would have to pose for a photograph lying on the floor with the winner's foot on his chest.

The day of the bench press agon, a group of thirty students piled in to watch the test of strength and will. Without exception, they all came hoping to observe Paul's defeat although they knew that Paul was grossly superior except possibly in this one exercise. They started at two hundred and Paul quickly shot the weight up to three hundred and forty pounds which he did with a prodigious vein-popping effort.

"That's ten more than I ever did before," Reg pronounced pessimistically. "Let's have three hundred and forty-one." Reg mumbled. He then looked over at Henry and the others for encouragement. Henry said only, "Get tough." Paul meanwhile admired his right arm.

Reg slid under the crushing weight, as the three safety men stood ready to lift it off his chest if necessary. This is sheer lunacy, Reg thought. But with peculiar confidence, like that of the Greek wrestler Antaeus who was invincible as long as his feet touched the earth, Reg was optimistic. And so with a deep breath and his feet flat on the ground, Reg lowered the massive weight onto his chest. He then gradually pushed it up as Henry shouted, "Let's go, big boy." He knew his eyes were red and protruding with the strain. He hoped he wouldn't blow anything out. After the weight finally reached the apogee of his physical excellence, Reg slowly rose from the bench, and in dizzy incoherence, screamed, "I'm King of the Bench!"

Paul laughed and said, "A little premature, my boy." But Paul failed twice at three hundred and forty-five and once at three hundred and forty-one. With an unexpected graciousness, Paul extended his hand, "Congratulations, Reg – I mean King."

"I'll only shake your hand Paul if you don't squeeze mine."

Henceforth, Paul called Reg "King" and so did everyone else. Paul eventually consented to the humiliating photograph.

Reg returned from the shower to his room. Henry and June sat on his bed waiting, and Sally on the desk chair in the corner of the dormitory room. "Now look the other way," Reg instructed as he quickly dressed. Although facing away, Reg in the mirror observed all three watching him closely as he dressed. After combing his hair, and adjusting his tie, Reg finally said, "I'm ready for introductions, Henry."

Henry convulsed with laughter. "You candy ass."

Sally stood at near attention uncertain how to respond to Reg's playful formality.

Henry said, "Sally, this is Dr. Reginald Houghton, the local King."

"How good to see you," Reg said.

Sally didn't understand the behavior of these two apparently deranged Harvard men. June told her that they were very bright – and unmarried. But on observing Reg, Sally had an auspicious intuition about him. Sally, from a wealthy and respectable family, except when her father was in the throes of the manic phase of his manic-depressive psychosis, entered nursing school for idealistic reasons. Easily the most attractive student in her class, she was seduced and abandoned by a married senior resident during her third year. He was a handsome and very accomplished physician. But in her vulnerable heart, notwithstanding the advice of her friends to go with the flow, this experience dimmed her idealism considerably. Sally just could not accept that scoundrels could be great physicians. But she gradually and steadily regained her verve. A year later, Sally and her classmate June graduated. After graduation, still idealistic about nursing, they both worked initially at the Veterans' Hospital.

"May I get you a drink, Sally?"

"I have one, thank you."

Henry suddenly shouted, "Shock him, shock him!"

"What are you talking about, Henry?"

"Don't you remember yesterday?" Henry queried. "Mr. Ludwig."

"Oh, yes, I remember."

"You're trigger happy, Reg." Henry paused. "Kline and the other residents are certainly cool under pressure, cucumber cool. He placed that endotracheal tube in less than ten seconds."

"Yes, it's certainly a pleasure to work with experts like Kline," Reg agreed.

Sally was looking at the large sign on the wall which said in large Gothic letters, Illegitime non triturundum. She finally asked, "What's that sign say?"

"Oh, that's vulgar Latin. It means, 'Don't let the bastards grind you down.'"

"Where'd you get it? I like that."

"From an old friend." Marsha, a now very infrequent guest, gave it to him years before.

Mildly anesthetized after several drinks, Reg said, "You know, June, I bet you're happy that Henry recovered from his – ah, well, accident. Henry should sue you for assault with a deadly weapon."

June crimsoned in all visible parts but in a few seconds regained her composure with a huge sigh. She was somewhat relieved that someone had finally broached this delicate subject. For weeks, she had avoided contact with Henry, the students and her friends. She was humiliated and chagrined by the "accident." She wondered who knew what? Perhaps at last she could resolve her doubts.

When Henry started to laugh, June said, "Shut up, Henry." She leaned forward anxiously looking at Reg, "What did Jim say?" She remembered with hot shame Jim's sudden appearance the night of the calamity. She thought she was naked. And even worse, Henry pointed an accusatory finger at her. After all, she was the innocent seducee. She had intended no evil. But over the next days June had observed several medical and nursing students' smiles and smirks; she wondered who knew what. She interpreted many of these expressions as silent derision. June said, "Did he implicate me?"

Reg reassured her with a rare falsehood. "No, only Henry, Jim and I know who the girl was."

With a hissing sigh, as her taut muscles deflated, June relaxed. "That's super."

Reg twisted about and focused on Sally, "Sally, please walk back and forth."

Sally missed the point. "I'm not drunk, not yet, at any rate."

"Let's see."

Sally performed as instructed.

Henry interrupted the momentary silence after Sally's rather incendiary walk. "Excuse me."

"Me too," Reg echoed as they retired to the men's room. Henry again mentioned Sally's painful seduction and abandonment in nursing school. But Reg thought that adult women should easily recognize the sweet lies. Reg imagined that they chose their subsequent sorrow. Alternatively, perhaps, they were overcome by nature's burning fluids. As a scientist, Reg thought he should analyze blood drawn from these women at the moment of the "I'll divorce my wife for you," line. The rise in the hormone levels and the cessation of chalone activity, he suspected, produced a fire hot enough to melt any reasonable resolve. It would be fun to study.

"Be kind and gentle with her, not a big prick," Henry concluded with a verbal tweak.

"Look who's talking! You are the devil incarnate, Henry. You seduced more girls than I care to count, and then you counsel me with such baloney. You know I've been a man of the book since we came to Yale."

140

"Yes," Henry said, thinking of Marsha's infrequent visits to Reg, "that's true. But it is not good for you, Reg, all this study. Why don't you take up with Sally for a while? She's really stunning and it will do you both good. We can have some orgies."

"Yes," Reg nodded negatively, "another fracture."

At eleven, Reg checked his watch. "Henry, we have to draw blood tomorrow morning. I'm taking Sally home; you two coming?"

"No," Henry replied with a smile. "We'll stay here tonight." June blushed.

"Be careful!" Reg cautioned.

In the privacy of the car, Reg said to Sally, "I'm glad you came. Tonight was my bright spot this week, this month; you know what I mean." Five minutes later, Reg, very tempted, said, "Goodnight," but he had no intention of dating her again for he had a new mistress.

She was his Yale thesis. At Harvard he had synthesized amaranth dye, FD & C Red # 2. It was a synthetic azo dye that the Food and Drug administration considered safe even for coloring foods and medication. But Reg had his suspicions. He thought that if amaranth could penetrate living cells it might be gene toxic and hence carcinogenic. So he found a pathology professor who agreed to sponsor his thesis. With the great work of Watson and Crick, and Arthur Kornberg and others, a lot was now understood about DNA, toxic gene mutations, and cancer. So with help from the pathologists at Yale, Reg worked for two years on the project in every moment of his spare time. His results were very suggestive but inconclusive, enough for a thesis and graduation but not for a publication. He wrote to the FDA with his data and concerns but received only a polite acknowledgement. Unfortunately, in retrospect, Reg's methods were not sufficiently sensitive or reproducible. However, ten years later, in 1976, the FDA banned the use of amaranth dye, FD& C Red # 2 because it was a probable carcinogen. Reg was correct in his hypothesis but failed in the execution. However, he learned a hard positivist lesson: do not waste time on questions you can not answer definitively.

The following month at the alpha omega alpha honor society banquet, Reg, with the three other top junior medical students, would formally be presented with their AOA gold keys. But when he telephoned his father to inform him of his selection, his partial atonement for the missed Phi Beta Kappa key, his father damned him with Shakespearean faint praise. But more distressing,

Reg saw the award as another idle honor. The award in one student's case was due to consummate "ass osculation" and thus tainted. Moreover, Reg viewed himself as ignorant. He had mastered only a small fraction of the known medical corpus. So, for these reasons, in all humility and honesty, Reg thought he should have declined the award but in the end did not.

But even more grievous was the gradual transmogrification of his fellow medical students. With few exceptions, they subtly and gradually became bereft of graciousness and idealism. So often they turned into ungenerous, over-striving, hyper-individualistic men and women in their intercourse with their peers and in their personal lives. They were often shallow, jealous, and insensitive hypocrites. They bent the rules and norms to "get ahead." Technically and intellectually proficient, many students grew around themselves a callus which began on their heels from standing around so much. The irritation of the constant daily stresses of medical school and its financing produced a reactive waxing of this callus so that it gradually surrounded the entire body and then their "soul." After a few years, in some cases, there was no definite flesh underneath, just callous covering bone. Reg knew that morality and kindness is not generally "innate."

Reg, too, changed and hardened. But Reg knew he was the most honest of the bunch, a small comfort at best. Like the child's who pointed out the Emperor wore no clothes, Reg found little praise for truthful observations or criticism; surprisingly more frequent were hostile, defensive reactions. Still, he resisted his father's advice to 'flatter' and when necessary 'bend with the wind.'

Marsha arrived for the formal Saturday night AOA award dinner in her brand new Jaguar. She was completing her last year of graduate schooling in art history. "I'm here," Marsha called, lightly opening the door.

Reg awakened from the spring nap's warm embrace and, on seeing Marsha, was angry. Reg should have been happy to see her, for although she did not provide Henry's prescription for mental health, weekly sex, her rare visits prevented sexual psychosis, like an occasional lemon prevents scurvy. "What have you done to your hair, Marsha?" Reg asked. Marsha had bleached it, and wore it straight down. "Marsha, you know I like your hair up. That color is not becoming."

"But I like it better like this. I love the color. I hate mousy brown."

"You'll wear it up at the AOA dinner tonight, I hope."

"No, I won't," Marsha replied sullenly.

"I want you to."

Marsha wore it up.

That summer Marsha went to Europe. His senior year she came to New Haven less frequently and then did not come at all.

Several months later, sweating at his desk, rereading the hematology text, word by word, sentence by sentence, Reg attempted to reduce it to assimilated knowledge once and for all. Someone opened the door. "Henry," Reg said his eyes still on the book, "It's too early. I'll join you at eleven; I must finish this."

A female voice answered, "It's not Henry. It's me, Sally." Reg knocked his chair over, as he stood. "Come in, Sally."

"I'm sorry to bother you, but I had to talk to someone. I'm …." Sally dissolved into tears.

"Sit down, Sally." Reg closed the door, walked to the chest of drawers and extracted a huge red handkerchief. "Here's a Kleenex."

Sally laughed at this joke through her tears. "I'm sorry. I'll go."

Reg said, "Stay!" But thinking like a medical student, accustomed to suicidal, pregnant girls, he asked, "Are you pregnant, Sally?"

"No," she sobbed. "It's my father. He's manic again. I'm so afraid that I'll go crazy too, and then I'll have to be hospitalized. It runs in families."

"Oh, Sally! Don't worry." In his most professional tone Reg tried to reassure her, "Everything is going to be fine." After a short pause, he said, "How about a game of casino?"

"OK," Sally replied. After an hour of play, Sally said, "I'm cold. I want to stay here tonight in this little bed." She motioned to Marsha's old cot.

"Are you sure, Sally?"

She nodded.

"How about some pajamas?"

"No, I'll sleep in my slip."

"Don't be ridiculous. I've perfect ones for you." Reg showed her his red silk devil pajamas.

Over the next eight months, Sally occasionally appeared at eleven o'clock at night. She'd quietly enter; change into the devil's pajamas, which now had a large Sally written in gold across the front and took out the cards.

Reg attempted to discover her motives. "Sally, why do you come?"

"I want to play casino."

143

"No, seriously, why?
"Do you want a baby?"
"No, God no. I take birth control pills. You know that."
"What do you want?"
"To play with you."
"I'm glad to have you. You are considerate. You always come when I've finished my work."

A few months before graduation, Henry commented on Sally's unusual behavior. "Reg, your Sally is nuts. Yesterday, she told me incredible stories. And, at night, sometimes the sound of her laughter shakes the whole dormitory."

"I know what you mean," Reg replied seriously. "I do not understand her at all. She's a mystery to me. And the things she suggests we do. It's fortunate I'm strong."

"Yes, like......," Henry described in detail their activity behind the locked opaque wood door.

"I don't understand what's going on. Does she tell you what we do?"

"No," but Henry attempted to lead Reg astray, "but after all, I live next door. You know, Reg, you're the envy of every medical student. Everyone would give his eye tooth for such a girl, a girl who comes at eleven and is gone before sunrise, who asks for nothing. Probably half the class has made a pass or proposition including money, but she won't listen."

One day at dinner, Reg heard just a whisper pass between Henry and Jim. The overheard word was "periscope." He now understood their detailed knowledge. He immediately went to his room and rearranged his breached curtains

More concerned, two weeks later, Reg said to Henry. "You know, I'm really worried about Sally. I've had the time of my life with her. Our nocturnal "communications" are exquisite. She makes no demands of any kind. She's never a daytime nuisance, only a night time joy. But now I think she's gone off the deep end. You've seen how she comes dressed to see me in velvets and silks. Those clothes cost a fortune. I bet that black velvet dress cost a thousand dollars. And every time she wears a new dress, she says, 'for the King.' I think she visualizes herself as a Queen or a King's paramour, which is a delusion that I, the local King, perhaps have fostered. Last week, the tiara; you saw it. This really was too much. Yet, she won't talk to me of her thoughts, family, or anything. What do you think? I need some counsel. She's too good to be true."

"Reg," a dour Henry interrupted three days later. "Can I talk to you in private?"

"Sure, shoot."

"Some bad news. Sally wants to see you."

"Where is she now?"

"June says she's in the Connecticut Psychiatry Institute in Medbrook."

"What happened?"

"As far as June could find out, Sally grew excited over the last few weeks at work. The VA nursing supervisor said she developed regal pretensions as well as delusions of great healing power the last few days. She told patients she could heal them by the 'laying on of hands' – on their genitals. Imagine that, at the VA! They hospitalized her with a diagnosis of manic - depressive psychosis."

Like a man hit with a hammer, Reg slumped into a chair. "Oh, no! So that's it. I should have known. Her father has it too. I should have known."

The next day, Henry said, "June says Sally wants to see you."

The following day, a glorious spring day, Reg entered Sally's room with a nurse. "Hello, Sally."

"Hello, King." Sally had picked up the name from Paul and Henry, but Reg now understood its real significance to her.

"I've missed you. There's no one to play with here."

"I've missed you, too."

"How about a game of casino?"

"No, I don't think so, Sally. I'll come back soon, and see you again." But the psychiatrist advised against it until she was normal. After all, he was the King in her delusional system.

The outdoor medical school graduation occurred on an overcast humid June day. Reg sat with his father and mother. She repeatedly said, "I'm very proud of you."

Reg, however, was sad as the graduation ceremony proceeded. Marsha had slipped away. The pitiful error with Sally should have been obvious from her first visits. She certainly was not real. She was a young woman without questions, complaints, tantrums or perversity. Instead, she only knew play, pleasure, and the deep joy of sex. She made him laugh. Such a woman does not exist. Even the emperor Qianlong could not find such a woman; correction, he found the fragrant Xiang Fei but she was not compliant.

Reg was also sad because he had not completed his studies. He had made an excellent start as his honors testified that

145

graduation day; but was he adequate for the two years of great responsibility ahead? How would he perform as a medical intern and junior resident at the Brigham in Boston?

Knowing military service was inevitable because of the physicians' draft, a consequence of the Vietnam War, Reg had chosen not to enter the Public Health Service, which was open to him, but the Army. He was deferred for two years but would have to enter active service in July 1968. After a lot of thought, Reg had decided to volunteer for military assignment in Korea or Japan. He hoped to find something new and exciting there, but he was not sure exactly what. Perhaps exotic women, fantastic art, possibly even jadeite carvings. Who knew? But this was two years away.

The Dean interrupted his thoughts and mentioned his name, then AOA and finally graduation with honors, cum laude. He made many complimentary statements about Reginald Houghton. He even joked that Reginald Houghton could walk on water on Tuesday nights. He concluded by saying that Yale had the "highest expectations for Reginald Houghton."

With flashbulbs popping, Reg walked up to the stage to collect his medical diploma and awards. When he returned to his seat with the polite applause still echoing in his ears, he whispered to his father, "I told you, Dad, I'd graduate with honors and a gold key. Even the mean Dean likes me."

"Excellent, Dr. Houghton, very good; but what are you going to do for me over the next few years?"

"We'll see, Dad."

"Not good enough, Professor."

"Is that a hint?"

146

"Though this may be play to you,
'tis death to us."
Aesop's Fables

Chapter XI
The Field

Standing at the Air Force Seven officer's club bar after supper, Mike and Dr. Houghton discussed the day's events. "What did you think of the briefing, Mike?"

"The new Colonel is a candy ass," Mike replied. "He's a Miss Goodie Two Shoes."

"The military certainly goes to extremes. First Colonel Murray ran a …."

"A whore house," Mike interrupted.

Dr. Houghton continued, "And now this new guy. What did he say? Women only in the movie theatre and the NCO club; and under no circumstances could the officers go to the NCO club, even if invited?"

Mike moaned, "You know, he also said no recreational jeep after duty hours. This is what's called in the Air Force a lock-in, Doc. We're all going to end up like ol' Doc Tierney, walking across the frozen river to the fifty cent whore houses." Mike stopped and thought. "He's what we call a hanging Colonel."

"You can always take the Korean bus. It runs once an hour in the daytime."

"You must think I'm a lunatic," Mike exclaimed, with that blotchy, Irish erythrism appearing. "That bus was built by Mitsubishi before the Second World War; it is totally unreliable. It can't go ten miles without a wheel falling off or an axle breaking. Besides, the stench of garlic and Kimchi would asphyxiate you. I rode it one time and ….Yuk!"

"I never rode on it."

Mike said, "By the way, Doc. I received a letter from my sister last night. She started chemo and she wants me to thank you. She has been treated real well by everyone at the Brigham. I owe you one, for sure." Mike stopped and looked in the mirror behind the bar. He saw the new Colonel coming toward them. He hissed, "Here cometh the candy ass."

"Evening, Colonel," Dr. Houghton said.

"Good evening, Doc., Mike. It's real cold." The Colonel shivered and rubbed his hands together.

Dr. Houghton thought, but did not say, "Yes, you're cold, you desiccated old bastard. But I'm on fire. Miss Han waits for me in Soochow, and we're locked in this wretched compound like common prisoners, by your orders."

However, notwithstanding the new Colonel's directives, Dr. Houghton had decided on a course of action. Like Colonel Bennet often said, sometimes you have to bend the rules. Tomorrow at four-thirty, Dr. Houghton and Sergeant Song would visit the Home of Supreme Happiness, the Kisaeng House at Soochow. He and Miss Han would then proceed to a small, local Korean hotel for several private hours. But without fail he and Sergeant Song must still return before the seven PM curfew. For an excuse, he'd tell the cold Colonel, if he inquired, that he had been on a "house call." The new Colonel was very enthusiastic about civic action.

After a prolonged silence, the Colonel, said, "I'm a little concerned that we may have a morale problem here with the curfew and the infiltrators."

You jerk, Dr. Houghton thought: You naïve dessicated fogey. It's not the curfew or the infiltrators that depress the troops. It is your interdictions. Since you came, the troops have quickly succumbed to an almost catatonic depression. The troops won't perform for you.

Mike replied, "Yes, sir."

Dr. Houghton imagined practicing today's new jump kick on this Colonel. Houghton was finally making real progress in both his Hap Gi Do and Korean lessons; at long last.

The Colonel continued in a deliberate, confidential manner. "You know, General Samet gave me explicit orders about indigenous guests on the compound, after what happened with Colonel Murray...."

As the Colonel rambled on, Dr. Houghton recalled that, after the morning's briefing on his new policies, the Colonel said, "Doctor, would you stay for a moment, please."

"Yes, Colonel."

The Colonel paused. "Before he left, Colonel Murray would not speak to me. The General advised me to speak to you about what happened before I came."

Dr. Houghton wondered if the Colonel thought of him as a tattler. He would not implicate anyone in misfeasance. In fact, he would rationalize Colonel Murray's excesses. He responded, "Basically, Colonel Murray was very concerned about the troops leaving the compound after dark due to the danger in this area which you know is considerable. Like last night, a Korean Captain was accidentally shot and killed in his own jeep no less."

"It wouldn't have happened if that Captain had not been out after curfew," the Colonel commented.

"At any rate, Colonel Murray pursued a policy of liberal entry of the known, and I emphasize known, entertainers onto the compound with suitable precautions of course. He liked to know where *all* the troops were at *all* times, kind of like a mother hen. He also tried to prevent VD by prohibiting butterflying."

The Colonel interrupted, "What do *you* mean by butterflying?"

"Going from girl to girl. I agree that things got slightly out of hand." Dr. Houghton grinned at this understatement.

The Colonel coughed stiffly. "Well, I see no reasons for this sort of thing. These men are seasoned troopers, mainly married men. They'll have to adjust to the situation. We had the same problem in Vietnam. I just don't understand the new generation. Why, my own daughter enters college this year. I wouldn't let her apply to Vassar or Sarah Lawrence or those Eastern schools. Did you know that some of the girls in those places don't wear underpants?"

Dr. Houghton swallowed his almost irresistible riposte. His sister had just graduated from Vassar. As a compromise, he proposed, "How about a Saturday evening party, on the compound?"

The Colonel replied with a resounding "No!"

He's a hopeless squib, with a broken brain, Dr. Houghton thought. He predicted that Air force Seven would quickly fall from its superior inspection status. There'll be accidents and deaths. The village where the GI entertainers lived was twenty minutes by jeep from Air Force Seven. It was dangerous there, a squalid village. If the GIs went there instead of bringing the girls to the compound, they'd contract typhoid fever and hepatitis from the non-potable water. They'd be poisoned by the carbon monoxide from the faulty under-the-floor heating systems. They'd degenerate into drunken violence with the hostile Koreans of the village. It would be much better to bring the Buddha to the compound than visit the Buddha; he knew this was a flagrant but wise misuse of an old saw.

In his heart, Dr. Houghton knew Colonel Murray was right. No one on the well-guarded compound, under the Sergeant Major's watchful, law-giving eye, would sicken or die except perhaps from excessive lovemaking. Colonel Murray was very proud that only three cases of VD occurred on the compound in ten months, two of which occurred in the solitary butterfly, Dr. Tierney, notwithstanding all of his antibiotic precautions.

Mike finally ended Dr. Houghton's thoughts. He mercifully broke the strained silence with "Shuffleboard, Doc?

"Sure, Mike."

The Colonel followed, watched for a while, said nothing and left.

The following evening, Dr. Houghton limped into the Officer's Club as the cuckoo clock struck ten. Miss Han had renewed his spirits, big time. Dr. Houghton actually enjoyed the ache in his groin as Miss Han had been merciless. Sergeant Song had also been merciless earlier in the day at their Hap Gi Do lesson. His shins were swollen with chestnut welts. But that was what he had wanted from Sergeant Song. He learned most quickly from painful mistakes. He didn't often make such errors twice.

"Doc," the Colonel said, "we missed you at dinner."

"Yes, I missed dinner. I was tied up."

"It's not good to miss meals," the Colonel paternalistically offered.

"No, it's not," Dr. Houghton said. There was no further inquisition.

They had arrived at the Home of Supreme Happiness at four-fifteen. "I hope Miss Han received your message, Sergeant Song. Why don't you park and lock the jeep at the police station where it'll be safe from slicky boys. I'll pick up Miss Han and meet you at the hotel. I hope she got the chest x-ray. I'll take the electric blanket."

"Yes, Doctor."

Miss Han stood inside, with natural red cheeks, ready, surrounded by chattering maids and two other Kisaeng girls. Dr. Houghton slipped the Madam 10,000 won unnoticed. Dr. Smith removed his Captain's cap, and then bowed deeply to an exquisitely costumed Miss Han. He said in Korean, "How do you do, how are you?"

Five left hands politely covered their smiling mouths at Dr. Houghton's droll Korean. Miss Han bowed deeply and smiled. "How are you, Honorable Captain?"

Dr. Houghton replied with conviction. "You look most beautiful." He had just studied superlatives with Sergeant Song. This statement elicited more good-natured laughter from the other Kisaeng and maids. Miss Han enjoyed the flattery and badinage at which she was expert. She carried her rolled up x-ray wrapped in an elastic band. In polite Korean, he said, "Let's go."

Miss Han walked ahead, Western style, as he waved a smiling good-bye to her fluttery friends. He followed her rapidly down the frozen mud alley. She was to him at that moment of lust, woman as goddess. In her traditional scarlet Korean costume, her thinness was not apparent. The intoxicating scent of unknown Chinese perfume filled the air as she glided along.

Dr. Houghton wondered if he were taking advantage of her. After all, he was a barbarian. But on the other hand, she was a beautiful sing-song girl, and he possessed the gold, the ancient arrangement. Hopefully, gratitude sown in the soil of joy would bud into affection and fond memories. But they only had two hours.

Dr. Houghton gave the micro-hotel manager the four hundred won. The manager bowed and with a lubricous smile said to Dr. Houghton, "Have a good time, Honorable Captain."

He winked in reply.

Dr. Houghton pulled his boots off his numb feet before stepping in the room; Miss Han hung the forty-five on the wall. He plugged the electric blanket into the wall socket, and hung it Indian style around Miss Han who tried to conceal her impolite shivering. She had never seen an electric blanket and did not understand.

"This is hot," he tried to explain in Korean.

"Hot?" she questioned. "Is it a magic blanket? I heard the Beautiful Country Persons – Americans - have these. Feeling the relaxing enveloping warmth of the blanket, she was enraptured.She smiled with joy, showing her perfect white teeth.

Dr. Houghton, enchanted by the obvious genuineness of her reponse, carefully studied her x-ray. "Your x-ray shows only old, inactive tuberculosis," he said in Korean. He thought her thinness was probably due to intestinal parasites, almost universally present in Koreans. That probable problem would need attention in the near future.

Sergeant Song appeared and said, "May I talk with you for a moment?" He conversed with Miss Han for a short time; Dr. Houghton only partially understood them.

Sergeant Song finally said, "Miss Han thanks you for the medicine and needles for her father, Sir. I have several things I must tell you."

"Yes, Sergeant Song."

"I asked Miss Han, whom I like very much, how she was able to leave the Kisaeng House at this time. She said she owes the Madam two thousand won to leave because the Madam loses business and the Madam is greedy. I promised not to so inform you. She says she came out on a Western style date with you."

Dr. Houghton said. "Thank you, Sergeant Song. I already gave the Madam a large sum so Miss Han need not worry; she is *my* date. Ask her if she feels the heat now."

"She says it's wonderfully warm."

"Tell her it's hers."

Miss Han, on hearing this, showed the genuine joy of someone who really had known extreme cold. A thirteen year old Miss Han, during the Korean War, had almost frozen to death. She leaned over and kissed him on the cheek.

Sergeant Song stood up. "I'll leave you now. I'll be back at six thirty; it's almost five now."

"Sergeant Song, buy a good snack because we won't be back until seven." Dr. Houghton chuckled to himself. He did not mention that he did understand one part of Miss Han's untranslated Korean badinage to Sergeant Song. "Bring an ambulance for Houghton when you pick him up." The pick-up was a triple pun in Korean.

"Please sing a song," Dr. Houghton asked in Korean holding her hands under the electric blanket as the dusk swallowed the small room. She sang a sad Korean threnody. He was re-enchanted by her sad singing, by her obvious emotional involvement

Miss Han unbuttoned the fatigue shirt, laughing outrageously at the hairy chest, Korean men being hairless. She mumbled many things, but only "monkey" did he understand. She felt the hard, large muscles of his neck, arms, chest and thighs. She knew her anatomy. She said in Korean, "Beautiful Country Man; first time I see." She then pointed toward his belly, widely opening her slanted eyes and continued talking and laughing, feigning many emotions, but mainly fear. Dr. Houghton understood her repetitious "too big" in several different guises. He was sorry he did not understand all of her charming chatter even though he asked her to speak slowly. Even without complete verbal ken, her entire performance, a hodge-podge of badinage and flattery, was delightful. He absorbed it all good-naturedly as she intended and did not comment on her thinness, cautious not to harm or hurt in any way.

But unexpectedly, she became extremely serious when he gingerly held her fragility. Being an expert and a doctor, he well understood women. She knew he was a medical doctor; he knew she was a professional entertainer. He knew the Korean custom of male pleasure with the entertainers, but he was not a Korean. Miss Han, treated like a princess, not an entertainer, responded with wanton exuberance as the involuntary impulses of the human sexual response possessed her. Reg was delighted at her sexual color changes, spasms, contractions, and carnal joy. In days past, she might well have become a senior concubine, even a first concubine, some Emperor's favorite.

As Miss Han had predicted, at six-thirty Sergeant Song found a drowsy, glazed Dr. Houghton, gazing at her in a slightly confused state. With a similar expression, Miss Han none too nimbly finished buttoning Houghton's fatigue shirt. He had cast a spell on her, a shocked Sergeant Song surmised. This was not supposed to happen; but the fragile spell was shattered when he asked her some questions.

She replied in Korean "big," and held her hands two feet apart.

Dr. Houghton looked at her in wonder, and thought, "a nation of liars." Then he slumped to the floor holding his belly. He laughed until he could only gasp for breath. Miss Han and Sergeant Song joined in the laughter.

Finally, he recovered.

Miss Han also calmed down, wiping away her tears of laughter.

He quickly buckled on the forty-five. He gently kissed her forehead. "Tell her we'll come back as soon as we can. We'll try to leave a message for her as to what day."

Miss Han started to weep.

He reassured her in Korean, "Do not cry, beautiful one. I'll be back very soon."

Clutching the neatly folded electric blanket to her sparse body, Miss Han stood in the hotel entrance with happy tears still streaming down her cheeks. She waved as the jeep roared off.

Dr. Houghton looked back at the hotel as they hurried to beat the curfew. His abdominal ache eased as Sergeant Song drove through the black cold of early Korean winter. During the bumpy ride back, Dr. Houghton worried that this brief time with Miss Han was the apogee, the pinnacle of his sexual life. No, it was not just an intuition; it was based on his readings in physiology, sexual response and most of all his experience in the urology clinic in his last year in medical school. For ninety minutes he was a phallic god - perhaps Shiva or Priapus. He remembered jack-hammer lust; continuous contractions, his and hers; and a river of semen. He knew that he precipitated status orgasmus in Miss Han. That phenomenon could not be faked. He remembered a similar response in Miss Galt, a girlfriend of his internship days but Miss Han was more extreme; her spasms lasted 30 or 40 seconds before the contractions began. The books said it never lasted longer than 4 or 5 seconds; the books were wrong. He thought he would never, ever beat this afternoon, like he would never ever bench press 341 pounds again. But he had one idle thought; Mike had told him in Japan they had images of phallic deities that could perpetuate youthful vigor. Perhaps there was still hope. He would buy one as a memento when he visited Japan with Mike.

They arrived at the compound just as the curfew went into force, having passed the last check point just as the military police began to seal the barrier. As they approached Seven, Sergeant Song said, "I obtained a new grammar book for you today in Soochow. We'll have the Korean lesson in the morning."

Honorable Teacher; don't be easy with me because I was out with Miss Han."

Sergeant Song smiled, "No, Sir. I will not."

Dr. Houghton limped into the Officers' Club an hour later, a spiritually revitalized being, ready for the cold, dessicated "new" Colonel.

The following morning, Dr. Houghton, obviously annoyed, returned from a briefing with the Colonel. "Sergeant Dawson, please come in here with Sergeant Song and Lieutenant Ahn. I want to hold a brief meeting.

After everyone sat down, he began. "Sergeant Dawson, have you met Lieutenant Ahn?"

"Yes, Sir."

"Lieutenant Ahn is from K-MAG at Chun Chon. He has been sent over here to help out as my liaison officer." He paused, "Anyhow, the Colonel informed me that the North Koreans have landed an estimated two hundred more infiltrators about fifty miles down the coast from here. These men are elite troops, specially trained for this sort of hell-raising. Unfortunately, we have to move out in the field, about thirty miles from here. We'll be collocated with the Korean Mobile Army Surgical Hospital. Our job will be to provide advice to the hospital doctors in all aspects of patient care. I'd guess that in killing those two hundred plus infiltrators, there will be, maybe, one thousand South Korean casualties. Wouldn't you agree, Sergeant Dawson?"

"Yes, Sir."

"We're also responsible for okaying all helicopter and fixed wing requests for medical evacuations since they'll be using United States planes, helicopters and pilots. We don't want to jeopardize our pilots' lives on silly missions." At this point, the muscles of Dr.

154

Houghton's face tightened. "The Colonel informed me that this will be my mission until the new doctor arrives. This operation should take two weeks they estimate. There will also be other K-MAG advisors in the field area. At all times I want Sergeant Dawson and/or me physically present there. I'll go down there for the first five days and set up the policy and other details. Then, Sergeant Dawson can reprieve me for a day, and I'll come back here. Whoever is here will do the sick call, civilian and Army, as best as he can, Sergeant Dawson. Now the same for you, Lieutenant Ahn and Sergeant Song, but I will make out the schedule so that lieutenant Ahn will not take advantage of you, Sergeant Song. I want one of you there at all times."

At this, Lieutenant Ahn displayed that malignant expression that some interpreted as a smile. Sergeant Song remained expressionless.

Dr. Houghton continued, "Now, tomorrow after breakfast, we'll all go down there to set up tents, stoves, weapons, field phones and other vital details." Suddenly overwhelmed by an irresistible urge to see Miss Han, he said in a quiet voice, "It's going to be chilly out there and dangerous."

"A question, Sir."

"Yes, Sergeant Dawson?"

"Where exactly is this place?"

"It's twenty miles south of Soochow on the coast about two hours from here by jeep. Any other questions?"

"No, Sir," Sergeant Dawson said, "but I have a correction. It's not going to be chilly as you say. It's going to be colder than a witch's tit."

Lieutenant Ahn, the voracious student of American slang, said, "What does that mean?"

The next morning shortly before noon, Dr. Houghton and Lieutenant Ahn, with the Korean Commanding Officer, walked through the large well camouflaged tent that the Koreans had positioned as their mobile Army Surgical Hospital. Lieutenant Colonel Lee explained to Dr. Houghton, with Lieutenant Ahn interpreting when necessary, that their intention was to provide emergency, life-saving treatment, and evacuate the seriously wounded for definitive care.

The Koreans had sent their best doctors for service here and were well supplied with drugs and blood. Three small generators provided adequate electricity for emergency surgery. The few patients on hand seemed to be receiving adequate care. "Tell the

Colonel that I think everything is well planned. I have only two suggestions."

Lieutenant Ahn translated and replied, "The Colonel agrees and thanks you."

"Ask the Colonel if he'll join us for a C-ration supper tonight."

"He says he will," translated Lieutenant Ahn.

Dr. Houghton stepped out on a limb. "Ask the Colonel to bring over the beautiful Kisaeng that I hear shares his tent."

The Colonel laughed at Lieutenant Ahn's skewed translation. He, in fact, spoke excellent English. He said to Dr. Houghton in English. "I only wish it were true."

After lunch, Dr. Houghton rode the one mile from the field hospital to Colonel Newton's tent. "Colonel Newton, good to see you. I heard they sent you over here too. At least you are collocated with Headquarters."

"Doc, have I got the shaft. I already paid my Miss Lee, my Mary for this month – in advance."

"Those are the breaks."

Colonel Newton scowled. The Army had promoted Colonel Newton quickly to full Colonel in fifteen years. In Viet Nam, Colonel Newton had performed extremely well, a fact corroborated by the silent testimony of his many medals. He did things his "way." Unlike his generally dim view of "medics," Colonel Newton respected Dr. Houghton since their trip to the DMZ soon after Dr. Houghton arrived. At "no charge," Colonel Newton also seeded Houghton's "army path" with the fast growing weeds *and* flowers of army wisdom. An example: soon after they first met, he said, "Doc, I learned a little ditty when I was a second lieutenant fifteen years ago. It's held me in good stead. If you live by it, you'll be successful. It goes like this:

'If you have a buddy who is fine and true,
screw that buddy before he screws you.'

On that occasion, Colonel Newton also emphatically maintained that good army commanders don't get involved with the local girls. "You can't command the troops if they don't respect you, if they think you're a whore-hound."

A naïve Dr. Houghton disagreed. He hadn't yet heard about the true Newton. "Thirteen months is a longtime alone. I don't think that if one of the Colonels, in a moment of weakness, had a discreet bounce with one of the girls, verified by me as VD free.... There's no harm in that. An occasional bounce is better than

156

standing at the bar all night, night after night, drinking yourself to death or, at best, non-effectiveness."

"Doc, you're wrong."

"Look at Gaius Julius Caesar. Surely an outstanding commander, you'll agree. He was an incredible whore-hound. There is no harm in it, especially if you know me." Dr. Houghton thought he had tweaked this putative lily-pure Colonel enough but couldn't resist, "Colonel, I can cure any VD you contract, well almost any, and then teach your tricks for Colonels only."

Colonel Newton smiled quizzically. "Doc, drop by my room tonight at seven."

That evening after returning from an advisory visit, Dr. Houghton hurried to the Colonel's Q. He knocked on the door. There was no answer, so he walked in. On the couch sat a Korean woman dressed in a flimsy pink nightgown. He could see her body right through it. A tiny movie screen was set up in the corner. Dr. Houghton stepped back to recheck the name on the door. It had not changed; it said Colonel Newton."

Colonel Newton appeared.

"Good evening, Colonel."

"Don't call me Colonel; call me Gaius Julius," he guffawed.

Dr. Houghton realized he had "been had." With a near instant recovery, he asked, "What's playing at the movies tonight?"

"Have a seat, and you'll see. By the way, this is my Miss Lee, Mary Lee. I purchased her for a month."

Dr. Houghton greeted her in Korean.

She whispered to Dr. Houghton in Korean. "Colonel Newton too big! How about you and me?"

"No thank you. I have no money."

"You lie," she replied, with a haughty pout.

Colonel Newton interrupted. "What did she say?"

"She said I'm a handsome man."

"Here we go," Colonel Newton laughed. Miss Lee cuddled up against Dr. Houghton when the lights were turned out. The movie began harmlessly enough but rapidly degenerated into XXXX pornography. Dr. Houghton watched and said nothing. He had been humbled. No, he had been brain-raped. What a simpleton!

Colonel Newton pointed and roared at the inanity of the Chinese pornography. Later he told Dr. Houghton that his wife had said "anything goes overseas"- she "understood." But in America she would castrate and then kill him if he ever so much as looked at another woman. He was genuinely afraid of her, the old "battleaxe."

Several nights later, Colonel Newton knocked and entered Dr. Houghton's unlocked room. He called out in the darkness. "Doc, get up."

Recognizing the voice, Dr. Houghton said, "Sock it to me, Miss Lee." In the next seconds, he switched on the light, not completely awake. When he saw the stricken expression on Newton's face, he asked, "infiltrators?"

"No, Doc. It's Mary Lee. She's dying."

He momentarily studied the pleasure-seeking Colonel, who now stood there ashen and agitated, uncertain what to do. Only guilt or fear could bring about such a metamorphosis.

"What's the matter?"

"Well, I went down to her hooch in the village tonight. She was sick, she mumbled. She said her lower belly hurt. I felt her face and she was very hot. As the night wore on, she got delirious. When I left, I couldn't feel her pulse."

"Let me get my stuff in the dispensary and we will pick up Miss Judy. It's almost eleven. We'll take my jeep. I hope we can get back before the twelve o'clock curfew or Colonel Bennet will be furious."

"Right, Doc."

On the way, Dr. Houghton beeped in from of Miss Judy's. She came out partially dressed. "Miss Judy, come quick. We need you. Just get your coat."

In a second she returned. Colonel Newton clambered into the back seat of the jeep, and Miss Judy sat in front.

"What's up, Docs?"

"You know Miss Lee, Colonel Newton's Mary Lee. She's very sick. We need your help." Dr. Houghton had grave reservations about Miss Judy's help, for he knew she disliked Mary Lee for some past insult. The Koreans never forgot.

On entering her hooch, Dr. Houghton observed, "God, Colonel, this is a hovel." One look at Miss Lee ended such trite observations. She was comatose. Her temperature was 105. Her blood pressure was 50 over nothing. Her neck was not stiff and her chest seemed clear but she seemed to have right low back tenderness. Miss Judy inserted a urinary catheter and obtained pus not urine, as Dr. Smith started a large intravenous. "OK, Miss Judy, we have the diagnosis. Colonel, she has a urinary tract infection. Miss Judy, save the sample and we'll culture it at the dispensary. Take two blood cultures and a couple of other tubes for studies."

He then poured a liter of intravenous saline containing two grams of ampicillin into Mary. This raised her blood pressure to 80 and slowed her pulse. He next injected a gram of kanamycin into her buttock.

After they stabilized Mary, he explained to Miss Judy how to give the ampicillin intravenously, every six hours, until Mary could swallow fluids and pills. The other standard procedures Miss Judy knew. Finally, he said to Colonel Newton, "She's a sick cookie, but I am sure of the diagnosis. I don't think it would be wise to bring her to the Korean Hospital. It is almost twelve; it's too late anyhow. They really can't do as much as we can because they don't have our medicines. And she's a business lady and not too popular. They might just let her die. You now owe Miss Judy a big one."

Dr. Houghton turned to Miss Judy.

Colonel Newton observed the strange interplay between the independent Miss Judy, the most expensive business lady around, able to choose her boy friends, and Dr. Houghton.

Initially, Dr. Houghton said nothing but took her face in his hands and looked at her intently. He said, "Miss Judy, I know you hate Miss Lee. I know she did you wrong a long time ago, but Colonel Newton and I want her to live. I do not want you to kill her. Do you understand?"

Miss Judy answered, "Yes, she will live!" Dr. Houghton kissed her and so did Colonel Newton with a sigh of relief. Then they left, as two old village ladies magically appeared to aid Miss Judy.

On the way back to the icy jeep, Dr. Smith said, "Colonel Newton, you've abused her, haven't you?"

"Yes, Doc," Colonel Newton admitted.

Dr. Houghton caught himself. He was not the military police; he was a physician although he knew it was not right. "She'll be all right, I'm sure, but we didn't begin the treatment any too soon."

"Good, that's a relief. She really had made me scared."

Dr. Houghton probed, "Why do you feel this responsibility for her? After all, she's in the business. She's a salaried employee. You don't provide health insurance."

Colonel Newton mumbled, "You know, Doc."

Dr. Houghton heard what he wanted. "Yes, I know. She's a human being like the rest of us, notwithstanding what the Koreans think of her."

"Yes, all men are brothers," Colonel Newton, the great whore-hound echoed. For a month, he was the great expiator and restored Dr. Houghton's faith in him and mankind.

With these sharp recollections of Colonel Newton that awful night, bent way out of shape, almost broken, he said to this now straight and confident officer in front of him, "Colonel Newton, please brief me on the situation here."

"Doc, about two hundred infiltrators from North Korea landed on the East coast two days ago and went up into the hills. The idea is to have three brigades, one division, surround them and gradually close the circle in on them."

"Why did they come?"

"To raise hell, I guess. The South Koreans have already captured one and have killed twenty already. They're all second lieutenants, well trained and very big for Koreans. They are well armed and very, very dangerous. There is a large reward for capturing them alive. Do you want to see a couple of their bodies?"

Dr. Houghton was curious to see these fanatics. He followed Newton to a small hut where the bodies lay. He examined the corpses. "They are badly shot up. These men were also seriously frost-bitten."

"Yes, they are. It's cold in those hills at night without an electric blanket."

"I wonder why they came, what they hoped to achieve. The South Koreans will kill them one by one if they don't freeze to death first. The farmers won't help them. These fanatics have been misled."

"Yes," Colonel Newton said.

During the two weeks in the field, Dr. Houghton saw that the Korean doctors practiced reasonable medicine on the wounded. Only twice did he have to check overzealous demands for U.S. Army air transportation. His job was cold, easy and boring except once.

On that occasion, when he and the hospital commander were riding over to inspect a battalion aid station, a bullet caromed off his jeep. Another blew out a tire. To reach their destination, they had had to pass through the outer portion of the division's contracting circle. As usual, a jeep full of heavily armed escorts led the way, one hundred yards in front. Sergeant Song immediately stopped the wounded jeep. Dr. Houghton jumped out of his seat the moment the tire blew. He saw exactly where the infiltrator was hiding on the hill. As he crouched behind the jeep, he grabbed his M-16 rifle and eyed the infiltrator in the telescopic sight. In the second before he squeezed the trigger on the easy target, he experienced a disjointed series of incomplete impulses and thoughts, before slightly lowering his rifle's aim. Initially, he considered the infiltrator an ill-mannered man, and he aimed at his head. "Doesn't he know that I am a Hasty Pudding member? On the other hand, he thought 'Thou shalt not kill.' Finally he concluded it would be better to incapacitate the man, and if they catch him alive, buy Miss Han something splendid with the reward. As he pulled the trigger, he imagined General Samet and President Park presenting him with a nice round gold medal, a huge medal covering his entire right chest. He counted his chickens.

After he pulled the trigger, he felt like a big game hunter, seeking a live, fleeting, rare animal for the zoo. He hit the North Korean infiltrator in the thigh. The man fell over, incapacitated. Ten seconds later, however, Captain Houghton's tardy escorts charged up the hill, and placed thirty bullets in the frost-bitten second lieutenant, thus shooting away Miss Han's present and Dr. Houghton's gold medal. From start to finish it was over in two minutes.

The following week in late December, the temperature sank below the thermometer's ability to register. The extreme cold was depressing. There was no generator, no electricity. The Korean kerosene stove was inadequate and occasionally went out. It was too cold for Dr. Houghton to read his medical journals or even novels. Initially, happy thoughts of Miss Han were displaced by images of warm cavities and electric blankets. But as the days slowly passed, Dr. Houghton noted his thinking slowed as if the lubrication for thought was freezing. Again and again, he saw the frozen hands, feet, noses, and ears of the dead infiltrators. Sometimes, he thought his own hands and feet were becoming cold damaged, especially during the windy nights. Finally, his testicles became icy. He worried that his semen would freeze. Then he stopped shivering.

Maybe, Dr. Houghton surmised, it was the result of the emptiness of the days, each day seeming longer than the preceding. He began to worry when the hands on his watch slowed to a largo. Would they soon freeze to a halt? He thought that perhaps the infiltrators put some hallucinogen in the water. He was becoming unglued. Or was it the constant sight of the wounded, the mutilated, and the dead that tipped him over? He did not know.

But he was convinced that something was wrong, dreadfully so. On one occasion, he emptied his pistol into a thicket having thought he saw a man with a gun. Several times he heard infiltrator footsteps outside the tent, but he never saw anyone except the interior guards.Other times, though, he thought it was Lieutenant Ahn who often would disappear into the day or night, only to reappear, like a magus. But worse than the visual and auditory illusions was the real question that he might be losing his mind.

161

Lieutenant Ahn, who had been a source of black humor, was now testing Dr. Houghton's diminishing patience. One evening at two AM, Lieutenant Ahn appeared and climbed into the cot beside the stove.

"Is that you, Lieutenant Ahn?"

"Yes, Sir."

"Where the hell have you been?"

"I had chops at a farmer's house tonight."

"You'll get killed being out at this time of the night. I want you to cut it out. Did he have a daughter?"

"Yes, Sir."

"A cherry girl?"

"Yes, Sir."

"Lieutenant Ahn, you are rotten. After that last girl you impregnated, you know, the one I gave you money for, you should be more careful. You ruin these girls if you deflower them. You know that."

"Yes, Sir. But it wasn't easy. This farmer, about one mile from here, invited Sergeant Song and me for chops. Sergeant Song didn't go. I brought C-rations. We ate them, some rice and rice wine. Farmer's daughter served the table, but she held her eyes down. I could not get her attention. The farmer wants to talk about the army. I think how I can get her attentions. I say I go to WC outside, but I sneak in kitchen. I knock on the door. She won't come out. No lucks."

Dr. Houghton did not hear the denouement of the seduction for the field phone rang. Lieutenant Ahn spoke rapidly in Korean.

"What's up, Lieutenant Ahn?"

"One critical infiltrator, Sir. They want a chopper for him."

"We'll go right over."

The Korean doctors were correct. The transfusions poured into both arms of a wounded North Korean Lieutenant. Dr. Houghton called for the helicopter immediately.

Dr. Houghton visited Miss Han in Soochow twice in the two weeks he spent in the field. Both times, Sergeant Song drove him across the dangerous icy mountain roads, arriving in Soochow at three o'clock after the wild ninety minute flirtation with extinction. With Miss Han's ministrations, he was transformed from a pale, lifeless body into an ardent paramour, oddly enough passing through a stage of severe shivering. During this brief period, she bathed him in hot water and scrubbed him with a towel, the only time he removed his clothing while in the field. Her attentions were lavish, but delicate, a human nepenthe.

In a period of less than three hours, she soothed a near desperate, illusion-ridden man. No physician or drugs could have effected such regeneration. He was well aware of this. Deeply grateful at that moment, he would have given her anything he possessed had she asked. He discarded the idea of giving her money, as this clashed with the romantic notions he had about her, although he realized she needed money above all things. A vague, indefinite plan for her should wait until he returned from the field.

At five-thirty, he thought of a thin Sergeant Song, for whom the weeks of cold had also caused severe, though unspoken, anguish. On their arrival, Dr. Houghton and Miss Han had wrapped Sergeant Song in her electric blanket, fully dressed, and rolled him into a corner in the next room where he slept in the glorious warmth. He had been too fatigued to remove his boots, contrary to the Korean custom. Miss Han and Dr. Houghton almost forgot him.They woke him at five-thirty. Each time, after a mad drive back, they arrived out of the black darkness at the field tent at seven, just before the death-dealing curfew.

The day before the field operation ended, Sergeant Song appeared after lunch. "Sir, Miss Han has come to see you."
"Where is she?"
"At Ahn's farmer."
They drove the one mile to Lieutenant Ahn's farmer's house. How Miss Han managed to travel to that house, he never knew, for Sergeant Song arranged the rendezvous. He now trusted Sergeant Song implicitly.

As he removed his boots, Miss Han came to the threshold to help. He held her hands. "How are you?" he asked in Korean. Before he could continue, she lapsed into tears. "What's wrong, Miss Han, Sergeant Song?"

As Sergeant Song and Miss Han conversed, Dr. Houghton observed the farmer and his older daughter. He felt sympathy for this girl whom Lieutenant Ahn, probably with outrageous deceit, may have seduced and ruined in society's eyes, in her father's, and worst of all, in her own. But he could not help them. He was too late.

Sergeant Song summarized. "Miss Han comes to say good-bye. She is being sent by the Madam to another Kisaeng establishment, The Home of Stolen Pleasures. Because of the curfew and the lack of customers, Miss Han has gotten further into debt to the Madam. So the Madam decided to transfer her and her debts to a Kisaeng House in Cholla Province, the Province of Thieves, where the customers, although they have money, are notoriously bad men. She goes tomorrow. She is stuck on you, Dr. Houghton."

Dr. Houghton said, "Tell her, I am very sorry to see her go." On an impulse, he continued, "I will give her my gold ring. It will bring her good luck." He took off a two ounce solid gold Korean ring he had purchased with Miss Judy's aid in Chun Chon. He placed it in her cold hand. He also took his lucky platinum rabbit out of this pocket and placed it in her other hand. "If she needs money, the ring and lucky rabbit will help pay off her debts."

Miss Han accepted them. "Thank you, Honorable Doctor. Please stay with me." She spoke with dignity, but her eyes were begging. She bowed and touched her forehead to the floor.

For the first time in his adult life, he did not know what or how to respond. Sergeant Song and Miss Han, the farmer and his daughter were all waiting anxiously for a nuance of behavior or word that would reveal some intention. Should he buy her or let her go?

He slowly raised her up from the kowtow bow. "Tell Miss Han to write to me at Chun Chon. When we arrive there, probably next week, we'll work out some plan, but we must go back now."

Miss Han, with an air of resignation, stopped crying. With her head high again, and her delightful smile, she accompanied them to the jeep. He kissed her, repeating that the gold ring and platinum rabbit would bring her good fortune. He said, "I'm sorry."

Later, after an hour of agitation in his tent and recurrent visions of her white- toothed enchanting smile, he thought he may have made an error in letting her leave, but he was not sure what to do. She would always remind him of Reginald as the Apotheosis of the Penis, a living Shiva or Priapus. He suddenly thought of his Harvard days, of his visit to the Fogg museum with Miss Ching to see the jadeite carvings. As they walked through the museum, he had seen a Hindu lingam, the phallic manifestation of Shiva. He asked, "Miss Ching, what is that?" Annoyed, she said, "You should know, Hindu paganism!" Next he thought of Miss Galt who accused him of trying to "kill" her after he precipitated multiple episodes of status orgasmus in her; death by exhaustion.

Dr. Houghton caught himself; his thinking was diffuse and off the subject of Miss Han. He had been in the field too long. He continued to waffle. Was he rationalizing when he blamed the Koreans for forcing her, a fine, indeed magnificent creature, into this estate, necessitating potential rescue by a foreigner? Indentured into the profession for years, she was now unable to leave it, in a sense prevented by her own people, by the system. But he felt warm, indeed happy, that he had given her the gold ring and lucky

164

platinum rabbit. With them, she could pay off much of her debt and perhaps be free. He finally decided he would contact her soon.

Two weeks later, Miss Han wrote them in Chun Chon. Sergeant Song translated. "She says that business is bad, the customers are not gentlemen, and she says, she broke her wrist." Dr. Houghton guessed that one of the drunken guests probably broke her wrist in either lust or rage.

"Sergeant Song, I want to write her a letter. Please help me. I want her to come here to Chun Chon as soon as possible. I will pay her expenses including housing when she comes."

But Miss Han never came. One week later she sent a letter and the gold ring back. Inside the ring, she had inscribed in Korean "For Reginald, with love, 1969," and her full name in Korean. It meant "Miss Attentive-to-Etiquette Han." The letter in Korean read:

"I'm sorry, I cannot come. I will be happy. Do not forget my face.

With love,
Han Miss."
"Why can't she come, Sergeant Song?"
"I don't know, Sir."

Several weeks passed without a word from her. At the finish of a brutal Hap Gi Do exercise session in mid-January, Sergeant Song spoke quietly. "Miss Han is dead."

"How did it happen?"
"I don't know, Sir."

Dr. Houghton accepted some responsibility for her presumed suicide, a weight he shouldered for his entire life. He now knew he should not become involved with these queer people although he was already intrigued with Beautiful Flower.

Before he left Korea, eight months later, he discovered that Miss Han had left a final letter. In it she explained her father had died, that even if she could pay off her debts, what could she do as an older "worn-out" Kisaeng? She used the pejorative Korean word for worn out – a kind of detritus. Dr. Houghton could only shake his head and say, "too horrible for words."

He never forgot his brief time with Miss Han. He wore the inscribed gold ring for years, almost like the Ancient Mariner. In a sense, Miss Han was his Albatross. He never forgot her face.

"Sleep, rest of nature; sleep, most gentle of the
divinities,
Peace of the soul, at whose presence care
disappears,
who soothest hearts wearied with daily
employments,
and makest them strong again for labor."
                    Metamorphoses of Ovid

Chapter XII
At the Beach

Reg lay on his back baking in the late June 1968 sun,
dressed in sunglasses and a skimpy, blue bathing suit. Jan had
insisted they "hit" the beach this Sunday, his first day at the beach
in two years. For a few minutes, he read the Boston Globe. He
scanned the continuous bad news from Vietnam since the Tet
offensive. He read the commentary about the closure of Columbia
College by the protesting students. He also knew Harvard was
having trouble with the undergraduates. Clearly Kennedy and
Johnson had involved America in a morass. With their Harvard
advisors, these two ignoramuses didn't seem to know that the
Vietnamese hated the Chinese since Kublai Khan invaded and
devastated Vietnam in the thirteenth century. It was plain stupid to
push the Vietnamese into China's arms. Unfortunately Reg was
caught up in this disaster because of the physician's draft. Soon he
too would know the reality of the US Army. He threw the paper
down in disgust.

Unaccustomed to the sun, he was quickly enveloped by its
warm embrace. His mind floated dizzily over the past. Occasional
glances at Jan, whose richly tanned body lay beside him on the
blanket, conjured up vivid images of pleasant days and nights
together. Inexplicably, he saw his first vision of her well-shaped calf
at a party six months ago, soon replaced by a view of that same calf,
shadowed in candlelight, in a motel bed on Martha's Vineyard three
weeks previously. Now a one-eyed glance at the same calf beside
him disappeared in the overwhelming eye-closing glare of the red
sun.

"Feel OK, Reg?" she queried, her voice coming from a
seeming great distance after the long period of silence.

"Yes, how about you?"

"Yes, I feel wonderful, Reg," Jan answered, as she lovingly placed her hot hand on his shoulder.

This caress, like a small child lighting a thin wick on a huge string of firecrackers, set off kaleidoscopic memories of their past joys. He knew that Jan and the sun and the rest would soon arouse him to a desperate turgid state. But the notion that they would slake their ardencies in a few hours relaxed him as he drifted back into warm reveries.

During the pleasant hour's ride to the beach, with Jan driving her new powerful Pontiac GTO, Reg decided that this day at the beach would be an excellent time to think about the future. For the past two years, he knew that his chronically fatigued, hopelessly clouded sensorium was incapable of reasonable decisions. Fortunately his trustees and his father took care of all financial matters. But all personal decisions of importance he consciously postponed as, for example, what to do about Jan, if anything. The decisions he had made in medical school would take him through his two years in the army and one year final post-army residency training back at the Brigham. Yes, the Army, on 30 July 1968, would induct him at Fort Sam in Texas. In one month, they would mold him, a volunteer draftee, into a Captain. Then in early September send him to Korea for 13 months as a "senior" medical advisor.

However, the chronic fatigue and the broiling sun conspired against his rational plan. Like a pack of wild horses, memories and thoughts ran up and down the hills and valleys of his cerebrum in an undisciplined fashion, Occasionally, the pack would pause for a momentary glimpse of Jan or some passing beach girl.

Finally, with a major effort, Reg initiated his review with the first day of internship two years ago. The Chief Resident assigned him to replace his old weight lifting pal, Paul, who was the intern on the coronary care unit. Paul showed him around that first morning, explaining his duties as well as certain unique subtleties of internship. Paul introduced him to his inherited patients as a "superb clinician," flattery Reg enjoyed. But at the final moment of passage, when Paul transferred his walky-talky and emergency alarm, Paul's monstrous ear-to-ear grin shocked him. Reluctantly, Reg accepted these symbols of responsibility. Reg thought that Paul stood taller after the transfer of these two small weights.

As Paul walked away a "free man," Reg reflected on the change in Paul. In just one year, pale flabbiness had replaced his once rock-solid muscle. A sheepish, almost sly grin, substituted for the arrogant smile of a year ago. Deep lines and furrows clouded his pale but still handsome face. But most distressing, Paul slouched like an old man, so unlike a year ago when Paul hoisted huge weights with a straight back and grunting grace.

After thirty-six hours with no pillow's caress, Reg tossed his clothes, brushes, and electric shaver into his suitcase, and slowly walked the fifteen minutes back to his apartment across from the park, which he shared with his Yale friend, Henry, now an intern at another Boston hospital. After he showered and drank a coke, he fell on his bed and slept. At midnight and four, he woke, staggered to the bathroom, urinated a river, drank another coke, and returned to bed. Up at six, he arrived at work at six fifty-five un-refreshed. Every other night, and every other weekend, this imposed madness continued for two years. They called themselves "iron men," but this proud eponym only helped for a while. This two year lunacy made six week marine boot camp seem a first grade picnic.

But the weekends in the hospital were particularly agonizing. They began Saturday at eight am and ended in bitter enfeeblement Monday evening. Reg averaged two hours sleep per night with rare daytime naps. Days and nights merged. Time lost its cyclic pattern, replaced by a steady electric consistency. On each shift, sleep, initially a velleity became an irresistible impulse. He became preoccupied with this unsatisfied horrid lust. Yet he could not lie down when patients needed him, when they were about to "croak". On nights off, the nine prone hours passed moments after crawling into bed, clean-showered.

Second only to slumber-lust was the hot, soothing shower and its attendant cleanliness. After endless hours of furious activity, Reg removed stess-soaked T-shirts and dirty uniforms that smelled of uncertainty, sickness and death. But time and again, when under the hot shower in the hospital, the walkie-talkie or pager would squeak its urgent demand. In time, the only pleasant showers were apartment showers, where no interruptions were possible. Fatigue often prompted him to sit too long on a small plastic chair Miss Galt bought him; passively and illusively hoping for an infusion of strength from the water.

Jan turned over on her back, thrusting her large, well formed bikinied breasts at the sun. He resisted the temptation to remove the halter, but instead placed a hand on her right breast, only to have it gently shoved aside.

"Don't," Jan said.

"Don't," Miss Galt echoed, almost two years previously, as an exhausted Reg placed a fresh hand on Miss Galt's crisp, white uniform. Miss Galt, the Chief Nurse on one of the private wards,

168

took the offending hand off, and said, "Reg, you don't look well. You are out of control."

He had lost ten pounds in that first month. In response, he once composed a letter of resignation to the Chief of Medicine protesting the inhuman hours and the inadequate working conditions. But he finally tossed this bitter letter into a drawer, never to-be-sent.

Miss Galt volunteered. "I'm coming over to cook you a decent meal tonight." She was in her early thirties, attractive and unmarried. An excellent nurse, she was too domineering for most men whom she tried to control in the same fashion as she managed her ward – with an iron hand. Reg knew that her patients were excellently cared for. He admired her expertise. He accepted her offer. "Here's the key to my apartment. I'll try to get back by seven-thirty tonight."

When Reg returned at eight, he noticed her thorough job of dusting and cleaning his entire sloppy apartment. The bathroom now gleamed, even the toilet, polished by her efficient hands. A pink candle sat on the table and new sheets were on the bed. After a warm shower, he enjoyed an excellent meal by candlelight, his first hearty meal in a month. He recalled Miss Galt awakening him in the shower in a deep sleep under the spray. She dried him with a large towel and helped him dress. Normally he behaved very modestly, but he was not embarrassed in the least by her maternal ministrations.

After dinner, mildly intoxicated from four ounces of red wine, Reg, who usually drank well, embraced her. The candle light made her very desirable. She was warm and very alive. She had wonderful firm breasts. But, alas, he experienced a total nothing. When she coyly suggested leaving, he said, "Please don't go." He hoped she could reawaken him. "Henry and I work every other night, but alternating. He's not here tonight."

Miss Galt stayed. He enjoyed her warmth and pleasant domination, but she could not help him find his body. She left at 6 am. At work that morning, she smiled and winked at him, a signal that she understood.

Herman, one of the married, senior residents, had a brief affair with one of Miss Galt's friends. When he heard Reg dated Miss Galt, he maintained, "The nurses are sexual toys for us to play with."

Reg retorted, "That's unfair, unscrupulous."

A superb, indefatigable doctor that Reg greatly admired, Herman said, "But what do you think you're doing with Miss Galt? You'll never marry her. She is seven years older that you are!"

Herman's analysis was accurate. So as far as Miss Galt was concerned, Reg drifted from one day to the next. Although he knew she knew marriage was not in his mind, she continued to visit for six months. Reg treated her extremely well, because she was a very decent woman. He bought her an expensive Japanese triple-stranded 8 mm. cultured Akoya pearl necklace with pink overtones. She loved it. He sent her flowers, chocolates, and did not ruffle her weaknesses.

His roommate, whose peregrine ways never changed, chided him for his fidelity. "Herman warned you; rotate the girls," Henry said. "Miss Galt will get the wrong idea."

Gradually, over the course of months, Reg noted his strength and enthusiasm return, almost imperceptibly. He started lifting weights and running around the track again. Unlike some heroes of literature, especially Conrad's, whose crises lasted only a moment or a short time, Reg realized good physicians must resolve crisis after crisis indefinitely.

Accompanying his transformation, he began, at first subtly, but later openly to dominate Miss Galt. Their early relationship of desperate intern and motherly lover disappeared. In the hospital, Reg and Miss Galt also assumed their expected roles where he, the confident intern, wrote the orders and she effected them.

In the hospital only the intern could write orders, not the attending doctors or anyone else. The intern was the final common pathway through which all the patients' care filtered. Residents, consultants, attending doctors, experimentalists, and other could suggest, inveigle, or command, but the intern must finally decide what to do and when to act. The intern always attempted to keep his patients' best interest in the forefront of all decisions. The more senior physicians must persuade, teach, refer to the literature, and/or point out physical findings to the skeptical intern. If unconvinced of the wisdom of a certain course of action, the intern could refuse to write the orders. This occasionally did happen. The chief resident or the physician-in-chief then had to arbitrate.

Being advised by older and generally wiser men, Reg and his fellow interns learned very quickly because, in the end, the responsibility for a successful outcome of the plan was theirs. Others helped decide but they executed.

A consultant might argue, "Let's let Mr. Bloom go. He's riddled with terminal cancer; his pneumonia will carry him off painlessly and quickly."

"No," Reg argued, "I disagree. Let's treat his pneumonia. I do agree it's the end of the road, but you know, Mr. Bloom told me he had one more wish, to see his grandson confirmed. He told me,

170

before he went into the stupor, that as an old Jew, he's not yet ready to die. Let me treat his pneumonia with penicillin. He'll wake up and have his last wish."

The consultant argued persuasively. "But he'll suffer so much. The family will be burdened emotionally and bleed financially. Can they afford it?"

But Reg knew the old man well. He was wealthy. Moreover, Reg remembered the old man's plea, as if Mr. Bloom intuitively understood that only Dr. Houghton could grant his final wish. Reg had promised. So after a substantial effort by Dr. Houghton and Miss Galt, old Bloom attended his grandson's confirmation and then died a week later. The last person with whom Bloom spoke was Dr. Houghton. He called at four am his last night alive.

"Yes, Mr. Bloom, what can I do for you?" Reg was in the hospital working when the operator transferred the call.

"I want to thank you for what you did for me. I mentioned you in my will. I'll say a few words for you upstairs. Good-bye." Mr. Bloom then lapsed into unintelligible Yiddish.

"Thank you, Mr. Bloom."

Two hours later, Mr. Bloom died.

Reg was certain he acted wisely in keeping Mr. Bloom alive for ten more days. The attending physician was wrong. Moreover, two weeks later, he received a solid gold watch inscribed on the back, "Dr. Houghton, Thank you. Bloom. 1967." Reg loved it. Miss Galt received a long string of 9 millimeter pink Japanese Akoya pearls.

It was unfortunate that he could not discuss many of his most difficult questions with anyone, except occasionally with his father. It was especially sad since Miss Galt yawned and even fell asleep when he started to talk of Kant or Hume or the Buddha or morality. Hence, their conversations remained superficial - about dinner, wine, sex, movies and the like, with never mention of plans or philosophy, as if by tacit agreement. He continued to treat her well, and also satisfied her intense, obvious need to be dominated. He realized she was attaching herself to him like a hungry octopus.

Miss Galt, who had never submitted to anyone before, increasingly enjoyed her affair with Reg. She was satisfied in every way. She loved the pearls and the sex; she had never experienced an orgasm before. Now, she could not stop the overwhelming spasms, contractions and suction noises he brought out of her. In fact, she did not really understand what was happening to her. So one day she purchased the recently published Masters and Johnson's book on the

Human Sexual Response. She read that some women occasionally have a climax initiated with a lower vaginal spasm, a so-called barrel contraction that lasts up to 4 seconds. Miss Galt was different; her spasm sometimes lasted 20 seconds, before the releasing contractions began. The book was wrong. But the result was great joy, awesome joy that ended in the most severe exhaustion. Was Reg trying to kill her? Afterwards she could hardly arise from the bed. Once her eyes were crossed for five minutes after her most intense climax but they came back to normal, Thank God. On balance she was very happy.

But one evening, a complication occurred. She walked to her mirror naked and observed her legs which she knew men considered attractive. She saw a single small varicose vein. She suddenly imagined all the veins were becoming too prominent. Was this a nurse's reward at 32? For years, she took the walk from her bath to her body-sized mirror in joy. The refreshing feeling of the bath along with the bounce in her step, which she cultivated, always ended in that vision of herself as truly desirable, with her large firm breasts and long shapely legs, until now. But today, feelings of aging, bordering on horror, crept into her ritual of the bath and the inspection. Although she could not yet see it in the mirror, Miss Galt also felt that her breasts were shriveling, her face was wrinkling, and her secretions were drying.

The following evening, his white suit covered with blood, Reg arrived at his apartment after a particularly gruesome thirty-six hours on duty. Three terminal patients had died. "Hello, Miss Galt."

"Hello, Reg." Miss Galt wore a black, sheer low-cut evening dress. Her cheeks flushed on his entry, indication the growing need he brought out of her.

"Why are you doing that?" she asked, as Reg, now in his sweaty T-shirt and shorts began push-ups on the floor.

"I used to be a fair athlete, and weight lifter of sorts. As part of my new leaf, I've decided to do fifty push-ups, ten chin-ups, and fifty sit-ups every night I come home, so I don't go to complete ruin."

"You're too exhausted for that; don't do that! Save your energy."

"You mean for you?"

She crimsoned but did not answer.

"Don't worry! Are you ever left unfulfilled?"

"No, not now."

The end began that night. After maneuvering Miss Galt with his still powerful arms and shoulders, dangling her here and there like some immense toy, she finally fell back exhausted. Reg

172

realized that the sleeping gorilla had reawakened. So instead of whining about the aggravations of work, he savagely began to beat his sweaty chest.

"What are you doing, Reg? Stop!"

He roared in uncharacteristic laughter.

She insinuated her arm through his, and with no warning, she said, "Marry me."

Reg swallowed hard and noted two dropped beats. "Let me think it over, and I'll tell you within a week."

The following week, she took the polite but firm "No" calmly. Within two months, she moved to New York. Two months later she married. For a wedding gift, Reg sent her a very expensive pearl bracelet to match the choker necklace he gave her. He wished her well. She was a nice lady but not for him. He now knew he must be able to talk to his lovers and potential wives. She inadvertently taught him that.

Henry did not calm down after medical school. In fact, his antics multiplied. After Miss Galt left, notwithstanding Henry's encouragement, Reg did not date for the last four months of his internship. On nights off, he exercised and then studied his medicine books and journals intensively. Some of these same evenings, Henry was off. Although they had a large apartment, Reg overheard Henry at play since Henry often brought nurses or other lady friends from the hospital. Occasionally, one young woman would arrive at seven and leave by ten, only to be replaced by another young lovely. By contrast, in the hospital, Henry was extremely serious. He would, without doubt, become Chief Resident if he didn't succumb to his excesses.

One evening Henry and a lady friend arrived after work, carrying huge sacks of plaster of Paris. Henry had become fascinated with fertility rites and sympathetic magic a la Sir James Frazer. Intoxicated within an hour, Henry came into Reg's room costumed in amaranth red shorts. Henry was now very hairy. With his Martini splashing, Henry broached the plan. "Reg, we're going to build a Maypole right here in the living room for the May Day orgy."

Reg laughed, but a few weeks later, when the monstrosity grew into a huge phallus, like a Hindu lingam or a manifestation of Priapus, Reg could only frown in wonder. He was more discomfited when, on May Day, two of Henry's nurses attached long, red ribbons to the Thing. Then they threw off their clothes and pranced around It with flapping breasts. They were "liberated." Henry asked Reg to take pictures of them dancing around the phallus - a request

173

Reg thought the height of folly. Afterwards they disappeared to "service" Henry. Henry argued that that these particular nurses, who cared all day or night for the infirm and moribund in their neat, white uniforms, required occasional release. Henry maintained it was harmless "fun," that these women could "handle" it but Reg was not so sure. Reg thought they were wasting their youth, their ripeness on nonsense.

Henry, with a "noble intention," invaded Reg's sanctuary one fall evening. "Reg, you study too much. You'll saturate your few remaining neurons. I rest my single synapse at night. You should do the same. You work a 120 hour work week; isn't that enough?"

"Enough advice, Henry! What are all the tomato plants for?"

Before Henry answered, in pranced Gail, Henry's "lovely" of the moment. She wore white shorts only. "Hello Scholar," she giggled. "You like what you see?" She turned around slowly. She pointed at her naked breasts and said, "Skyhooks hold them up."

Henry ignored her. He said, "It's sympathetic magic. The more I make love to Gail, the bigger the tomatoes grow. The tomatoes are in sympathy with me. I'm the fertility god."

Reg answered, "Goodbye Gail and Henry."

Gail scowled.

Two nights later an intoxicated Henry knocked over the Thing which shattered. "A bad omen," Henry declared. Henry was correct, for two nights later he limped into Reg's room. "I'm sick."

"What's the trouble?"

"I've got bad pain between my legs."

"Henry, you have a fever of 103 degrees," Reg said after taking his temperature.

Henry had "red hot prostatitis" but would only go to the hospital for cultures. He ingested ampicillin capsules by the tens, but remarkably missed no work despite the pain. The infection cleared over two weeks during which Henry slept alone.

A few days after the diagnosis, late one night, Gail popped in.

Reg said in a whisper, "Look Gail, Henry is sick. He is sleeping. Don't bother him."

Gail tiptoed, followed Reg to his room and shut the door. She undressed and faced Reg.

"What do you think you are doing?"

"I've undressed."

Reg laughed. "You're very well-built, Gail. You are built like a brick shithouse."

"What does that mean? Is that good or bad?"

"Good. Very good! I'm tempted, Gail, I admit, but I'm not Henry."

"You're too aloof. Henry says that all that studying is softening your brain. I'm going to soothe you. Do you want the tomato plants to stop growing?" Gail approached a retreating Reg. She correctly observed a momentary vacillation, but she over-interpreted it; so, like a viper, she prepared to pounce on her prey.

"Look, Gail. I want you to go. I'm telling you I'm not Henry. The fertility of those tomatoes is not my concern; it's Henry's. Please leave."

Gail left unwillingly after several extremely lewd moves. "I'll have you yet," she pouted.

Reg thought but did not say, "I do not need prostatitis."

Except in rare moments when he laughed at them, Reg did not like "liberated" women. The grasping, open aggression annoyed or even repulsed him. But far worse than the saucy, unsubtle Gail, were the nylon-scraping, perfumed bitches that calculated and caballed. These man-traps plotted day and night, creating new deceptions for unwary, seducible men. Man-traps, however, were not a threat to Reg. Rather, he worried about a woman without an obvious motive, particularly after Sally went mad.

One evening in the hospital, Marsha, Reg's girlfriend from college and medical school, called when he was on duty. "I must see you."

Reg knew he should have rejected her request. Their relationship was over; he hadn't seen or heard from her for over a year, but he was curious. She sounded desperate. Against his better judgment, he said, "Come to my place tomorrow at eight."

She came, dressed in an evening gown similar to the one she wore when she was runner up to the Hasty Pudding Queen. She was a comely woman, a pun Reg's Jewish friends would relish. She also had princess overtones. Perhaps he should have married her. At nine-thirty, after they devoured the ice cream and champagne she brought, she changed into Reg's silk robe without a word. At midnight, apparently satisfied, she kissed him passionately, a sweet, tearful good-bye, and never returned.

He twice tried to call her but she would not return his phone calls. He wondered if she was making a comparison or if she, for the barest moment, had attempted to recapture the past. But he missed the obvious motive.

In the broiling sun, he felt Jan's hand reposition itself on his sun baked belly. "You there, Reg?"

"No, I'm in Korea. What are you dong, Jan?"

"I am dreaming about the future."

"I'm dreaming about the past."

"I love the sun as much as I love you," Jan said, lapsing into silence, the waves roaring in the background.

Reg realized that he had forgotten what the sun and beach looked like. For two years in the hospital, he had not "seen" the sun or even a tree. It was true that he had passed trees and been outside in daylight, but until today, he had not scrutinized these once familiar objects. They appeared vaguely strange and not quite as he remembered them. Since dryads no longer inhabited trees, and since the polytheism of his childhood was only a pleasant memory, he concluded his lack of interest in trees and the sun was not unreasonable. Nature was unessential, whereas people were. One gaze at Jan in dishabille was worth many nights of star-gazing or strolls through verdant forests. Surely in off-duty hours the proper study for man is woman.

But, if you were interested, the ultimate place to study mankind and medicine was in a Boston hospital, not in nature, not in a psychology laboratory. The hospital education was, at times, excruciating; at other times grimly competitive, but Reg did very well continuing his upward medical trajectory. Persistence in sound study habits, not innate brilliance, was Reg's explanation for his success. Moreover, it was a pleasure to be surrounded by associates, students and professors as smart and ambitious as he was. What could be finer than to be one of the chosen, to work in an environment suffused with excellence? Beginning at the hierarchy's top with the professor, it spread throughout the senior physicians and down into the resident and intern staff, finally reaching the not-so-humble Harvard medical students. Excuses or ignorance were just not tolerated. Sloth, stupidity and ineptitude were absolute evils. Moreover, those who did not possess integrity and physical toughness, beside superior intelligence, disappeared.

Because of the well know innovation and results at the Brigham, patients came from far and wide. The King of Saudi Arabia and Howard Hughes came. So did Meyer Lanski, the alleged Mob Banker, who like Mr. Bloom gave Dr. Houghton a gold watch. He now had four. During Reg's internship, he participated in ground breaking dialysis and transplantation, the first coronary care unit

176

and many other spectacular advances in medicine. Reg realized that he was present at a medical revolution - that Nobel prizes and other great honors would accrue to the faculty. What a joy to be part of this - although Reg was very low on the totem pole.

But Reg learned the two qualities necessary above all others were intellectual honesty and good judgment. When you didn't know, you must admit it and then seek the facts. Speculation, good guesses, and probability were inadequate. The bluffers and guessers often beached themselves and their patients on the sharp rocks of disaster.

With time and continued training, Reg observed that some physicians acquired judgment, the critical intangible factor, and others did not, but he did not know why. Judgment came or it didn't. It was very hard to teach. Smart patients sought physicians with good judgment along with factual knowledge, and intelligence and integrity.

However, the great corrupter, Pride, always lurked in the background, ready to ruin everything. The ancient Greeks wrote about this, about hubris, thousands of years ago. But they were only qualitatively correct. In the hospital one had to discard *all* ego and personal feelings to the point of self-abnegation. Rather than being resentful about being shown some recondite fact, Reg knew he should be grateful to the "teacher," even a lowly medical student or nurse. Although the physicians were ultimately responsible for prolonging life and improving health, everyone in the hospital aided in this worthy effort, even the maintenance workers who cleaned the dust off the corridor floors. A physician should not puff his chest, but it was hard to be humble and responsive to criticism.

The proper behavior on rounds the next morning, after being up all night with sick patients, was the true test of equanimity and judgment, of intelligence and humility, and of honesty and results. Sometimes Reg bit his tongue as the rested professor, incisive and relentless, a Monday morning quarterback, reconstructed the ideal progression of the events of the night before. In the smoke and fire of those past moments, with only partial information at hand, Reg and the team had to act. Their interpretation and treatment of the patient occasionally appeared imprudent when the facts were clear and the outcome known. Frequently Reg thought the professorial judgments were harsh or carping, sometimes definitely wrong. Reg and his team in fact had a remarkable record. But Reg realized the professor was only trying to teach. When Reg did err, he never made the same error twice.

.Reg reflected on good judgment one day when Michael, the new intern, and he, now a junior resident, stood on opposite sides of a critical patient's bed. The patient had arrived moments before with excruciating chest pain. The diagnosis of heart attack was immediately established by the electrocardiogram. Now this man's life depended on correct decisions during the upcoming two minute crisis. Reg remembered similar cases when he was a student.

""Michael, start the intravenous now and give him 5 milligrams morphine through the line," Dr. Houghton ordered.

Michael said, "Look at that pattern on the monitor, it's chaotic. I think the patient is in some kind of peculiar multifocal ventricular tachycardia. Let's shock him now."

"No, not yet, Michael. Start the IV."

Michael started the intravenous expertly and gave the morphine. He said, "Why not?"

"Although the monitor looks bad, the patient looks OK. I can feel a basic steady, slow rhythm of about thirty-five or forty in his pulse. The crazy ventricular activity comes in between. He has a severe sinus bradycardia with worthless escape beats." Dr. Houghton kept his fingers on the patient's pulse. "Now inject one milligram of atropine, Michael. That will speed up his heart"

Michael did so as the sweat dropped off his brow and splattered on the patient's belly.

Dr. Houghton comforted the patient. "We're not going to shock you. You're going to be fine."

Ten seconds later, Michael implored, "Let's shock him, now. He's not responding on the monitor."

Dr. Houghton slowly felt the essential beats beginning to accelerate toward normal. The good was crowding out the bad. With a reassuring smile, he said to the horrified grimacing patient. "The crisis is passing. You're doing fine. Your pain will also slowly resolve as the morphine takes hold. Do not worry."

Michael was exasperated by Dr. Houghton's egregious arrogance, or was it confidence? Michael wondered if he or the patient would collapse first; Michael's head pounded crazily.

"Michael, now inject five milliliters of lidocaine by push!"

A minute later, Michael ordered the equally pale nurse, "Tape this IV in, please!" He watched intently as the monitor ever so slowly assumed a regular beat of eighty and the extra beats gradually disappeared.

Dr. Houghton put his firm, muscular hand on the patient's shoulder, the touch of life. "That's it. The crisis is over. You hear the monitor? Your heart is now beating at eighty and regular.

You're going to be fine except you will have a very dry mouth. By the way, how is the pain now?"

"You're right, the pain is resolving and I feel much better. Is that the morphine?" The patient then started smacking his parched lips. He relaxed with a loud sigh of life.

"The nurses will give you some ice chips," Michael added.

"Michael, let's go outside and discuss this. I'll show you what happened."

As Dr. Houghton reviewed the rapid series of events recorded on the many feet of EKG paper, Michael wiped away the sweat from his forehead. Even his crotch was soaked with sweat.

"Are you warm?" Dr. Houghton could not resist.

Michael refrained from asking Dr. Houghton if he was human.

"See you later, Michael. He's a great case." Dr. Houghton pointed to the lip smacking patient. "Give your patient more ice chips."

Michael marveled before going back in with the patient. He and Dr. Houghton had worked all night. Michael felt ready for the grave, yet Dr. Houghton appeared his usual cucumber cool, slightly mean self. But Michael knew Dr. Houghton must be human. After all he dated that big-titted nurse Jan for obvious reasons.

The next day on rounds, Dr. Houghton gave Michael all the credit for the "save." The professor agreed and said to Michael, 'Takes a lot of courage to wait, not to act."

Michael swallowed and looked at Dr. Houghton who winked.

Dr. Houghton had not forgotten. As a student, he too had yelled "Shock him" prematurely. He also used to sweat.

In the first six months of his internship, Reg developed mechanisms to prevent the total disintegration of his personality. There was little question that Miss Galt, in those first few months, helped him greatly. She patiently listened to his whining complaints and then ordered him, like some addle-headed drill sergeant, to "shape up." Others "had done it and so could he." After three months, Dr. Houghton did not need such advice.

He found that an almost uncaring attitude was optimum. Detached, in an observer mode, he could overview situations. Extraneous noise, like carping relatives, he ignored. Rather, he would calmly do what was necessary based on facts and scientific medicine. If a patient vomited blood, he would side step the stream, not run off in horror, and labor over the patient. As long as his personal integrity was not menaced, he acted without hesitation.

179

Some would interpret this attitude as a loss of sensitivity which in a narrow sense was correct. But in another sense, it was maturity.

How did he arrive at this state? As a child, he empathized with wounded ants, trees, and animals, hoping to find harmony and consilience in nature. This was a false hope. Nature was grim and mean. A female mantis would eat a male after sex! Later, when he looked inward, he also found destructive impulses. But he learned to control these. It was not difficult. Now he looked out once again, with a ruthless objectivity, almost like a Martian of science fiction. At work, he let none of his prejudices interfere with his patients' best interests. With glinting hardness, he looked right in the eyes of horror, while many others looked askance. With the hard-won facts, he acted rationally and honestly; his patients benefited enormously. Reg let nothing human repel him. He let nothing upset him except illness in himself or immediate family. He knew it was not his fault that people suffered, withered and died.

In a moment of serious reflection, Reg remembered his Harvard college professor's description of the three stages of the historical Buddha's journey toward enlightenment. First, the Buddha moved out of the realm of suffering into the realm of insight in order to see through the illusions of conventional experience; then the Buddha began to understand the world for what it REALLY was and temporarily reengaged himself in the world. But finally having found Nirvana, Nothingness, he died and was gone forever. However, many of the Buddhist faithful were not satisfied with this type of drop-out philosophy. So the Mahayana Buddhist's of Southeast Asia, China and Japan developed the concept of the Bodhisattva - a person who had attained Buddha-like wisdom - but did not drop out and leave the world. Miss Ching had shown him several jadeite statues of Bodhisattvas. He especially remembered a translucent imperial green one of the Chinese Kwan Yin, She Who Listens, the Goddess of Mercy. He ached to own one - the symbolism was perfect and now six years older, he understood the concept better. He also thought professionally he should emulate the philosophy of the deeply engaged Bodhisattvas.

This remarkable change in Dr. Houghton was summed up in a new enthusiasm. Instead of "I hope no more patients come in tonight because I'm exhausted," came statements like 'Whatever comes in, we'll handle somehow." Perhaps this attitude was possible because Dr. Houghton also acquired the Buddha-like ability to ignore inner demands for rest, quiet and amusement. This lack of sensitivity to inner demands grew extreme. What a change from the child who had chronic "ants in his pants."

Of course, outside the hospital, the suppressed demands, like unshackled demons, burst out. With Jan he was an olio of sex, laughter and aggression; he was a sensualist. Jan often commented that the hospital personnel, who saw him as an aloof, competent physician would never believe what a "nice bum" he could be.

Near the end of the residency, Reg did develop one new hobby - jokes, especially with the Jewish physicians who were masters of jokes. He tried to have one new one each day to share with them. The chief-of-medicine also told occasional jokes and expected the residents to antiphonally reply with a superior joke. Although not a natural, with practice, Reg improved and enjoyed the wit and repartee.

Toward the end of the two years of internship and junior residency, he recognized an ancient theory of behavior was correct, the theory that mood depended on the physical state of the body. If the body was well rested and well nourished without disease, the mood would be positive and optimistic, the philosophy – meliorism. On the other hand, if there was lack of sleep or nutrition, or disease, the mood would be negative and depressed. And it was surely true. When Reg was rested, the world was a great place. He was absolutely certain that, when this period of sleep-deprived stress ended, he would be consistently happy, indeed gay, if he could but sleep. It was almost as simple as that.

"Hey, Reg," Jan mumbled. "Let's go. The sun is too hot."
"Soon, Jan."
"Let me have your T-shirt, then."
Reg passed it to her. Through the titian eyes of one exposed to the sun too long, he said, "You are right, I've been in the sun too long but I have one more thing to think about before we go."
"What?"
"You."

One late winter day, six months ago, in a neutral condition of mind, Dr. Houghton observed Jan attending one of his patients. He noted she was built "like a brick shit house" and had a pretty face as well. His father's rule of thumb suggested her cranial vault contained sawdust or air.

That evening Henry said, "Reg, you look like a hungry owl without a mouse."

"Henry, boy, you're right. I haven't been able to study efficiently lately."

"You need a woman. Since Miss Galt left, I've told you a million times: Celibacy is harmful to your genital tract; too much back pressure. Reg, you are so full of semen you may blow up." Henry laughed at his folk-wisdom.

"You're right, Henry. I saw a nurse at work. I'll think I will ask her for a date."

For their first date, Dr. Houghton, now a teaching assistant in medicine, a courtesy appointment, took Jan to the Harvard Faculty Club. She casually mentioned that she didn't want to marry. "I'm just twenty-two and I want to look around."

Reg thought he should take her at her word. He would not assume any obligation.

Jan was perfect for the time. She was willfully childish and, as she herself said, a "drifter" at heart. They dated perhaps once a week at first, then, twice, and finally, she even visited Reg in the hospital some nights when he was on duty, for a "quickie." She dabbled in painting and liked to cook for him. Her painting was horrid and she was a poor cook. But, shaped like Aphrodite, she was sexually indefatigable.

Reg now arrived at his decision about Jan. He leaned over, marveling at the golden-hued woman beside him, "Jan, you want to go to California, don't you?"

"You know I do."

"You can drive me from Fort Sam in Texas to Seattle after I finish basic training. I'll have ten days. It'll be a nice excursion before I go to Korea. Good idea?"

"Yes," Jan whispered. "We'll go to Denver, Salt Lake, Vegas and California."

"I'll pay for the trip, but we well use your car, OK?"

"OK," Jan agreed, placing her boiling mouth on his.

But at the mention of Korea, even with the anticipation of the upcoming trip with Jan, his mind turned to the East. He had now read extensively about Korean history, culture and society, and one of Korea's fabled attractions, the Kisaeng, the legendary sing-song girls similar to Geisha. With the enthusiasm of a pubescent teenager, he pictured these beautiful women in their exquisite silk costumes; these females who were trained to sing and dance, to indite and recite poems, to discuss philosophy, to please and be consummate lovers. Was it true? Did such women exist? Or was it just hyperbole? But, without doubt, the Kisaeng did not have shapes like Jan. Once again, Reg gazed at her marvelous figure. If only she could sing or dance or paint or recite poetry or discuss philosophy or….. but she couldn't. During the dizzying walk across the burning sand, he wondered if Korean or American girls were superior lovers.

"And here abideth faith, hope and charity, these three;
but the greatest of these is charity."
I Corinthians XIII: 13

Chapter XIII
The Clinic

"It's good to be back at Chun Chon. It was brutal out there in the field," Dr. Houghton pointed to the east, "colder than a witch's tit."

"I'll bet," Sergeant Morse replied with his mellow, good-natured laugh.

"Let's keep the clinic to only thirty Koreans this morning, especially since Miss Judy isn't here."

"Yes, Sir."

"I have a question for you? Why are we doing this? Why should we do civic action when we know the Koreans really don't like Americans and don't respect us for doing this?"

"The Captain knows it is the right thing for us to do; the bible puts charity first."

"Sergeant Morse, I guess you are correct," Dr. Houghton replied with a sigh. "Tell me what happened while I was away in the field. Exactly how did that agent Noback die? Colonel Newton told me he was involved in a jeep accident."

"Yes, Sir! It happened on Christmas Eve. Noback got polluted at the Officers' Club with Miss Ha, his steady Yo Bo. Just before midnight, he received a phone call. He and Miss Ha jumped in his jeep and drove out the front gate. About one hundred yards down the road he drove the jeep into the rice paddies. It tipped over. The MP's saw it happen. We raced down there. Noback was pinned under the capsized jeep with a broken neck. I pronounced him. Miss Ha died in Seoul twelve hours later."

Dr. Houghton recalled seeing Noback and Miss Ha around the club. Although nineteen, Miss Ha acted like a spoiled eight year old, even in public. Such behavior was unusual in a Korean woman. On one occasion Colonel Bennet banned her from the NCO club for throwing a glass at Noback.

But Dr. Houghton remembered her best the morning she created a scene in the dispensary. Noback brought Miss Ha in for the results of her syphilis blood test, a follow up of her pelvic exam.

"Noback," he said to them both, "your Yo Bo has a positive blood test for syphilis and should be treated with penicillin."

Miss Ha, with a rabid ferocity, interrupted, "You lie! I golden girl here." She pointed to her pelvis.

Noback flushed in anger. "Don't talk to the doctor like that." He slapped her face with a light blow.

Miss Ha responded with angry Korean curses and then whacked Noback with a closed back hand. His left check immediately turned bright red.

Dr. Houghton stood. "Miss Ha, if you don't wish treatment, please leave."

She finally relented. When she lowered her underpants, he smelled frangipani perfume. Dr. Houghton then personally administered two syringes full of penicillin; one in each firm buttock.

She said, "I nice smell."

He said, "You do, very nice." But after the shots he gave her a sound smack on her behind. "Now you may leave; wait outside."

After looking at him with a malevolent stare, she walked out with her head high, each cheek smarting. At the door she presented Dr. Houghton with her thanks, a new sign for his repertoire. It was the Korean equivalent of "Screw you" and then she winked.

Dr. Houghton knew that he and Miss Ha understood each other.

"Noback, come in and shut the door. Look, your blood test is negative but...." Dr. Houghton explained to him what he had to do. As he left, Dr. Houghton advised, "Noback, for you, Miss Ha is trouble. Aren't you afraid she could compromise your work in the criminal investigative division? In a country of mainly obedient, passive women, you chose a violent one."

"No," Noback said. "She's dumb and young. But she has the best body I've ever seen in a Korean, or American woman for that matter. I mean, you're only young and, in Korea, once. You must also admit she has a stunning face too. I can not walk away from her. "

Dr. Houghton said, "I agree she has a fine body, a perfect complexion, and a classic oriental face." He did not say she had pelvic organs, labia and buttocks that most women would kill for, what the Greeks called callipygian.

Upon reflection Dr. Houghton conjectured that Miss Ha was partially responsible for Noback's demise. He should have been stronger with Noback.

Sergeant Morse continued, "Because of that accident and the resulting furor, we're not allowed to have Korean nationals in our jeeps at all, except you, Doc; patients, of course. By the way, Sir, the Colonel wants to see the Captain in ten minutes in his office."

"Come into my office, Doc." Colonel Bennet directed an already present Dr. Houghton to a chair. "Have a seat beside Colonel Newton."

"Hi, Colonel Newton."

"Hi, Doc."

Colonel Bennet began. "Doc, we're glad to have you back safely."

"I am glad to be back. Colonel Newton and I nearly froze to death." Colonel Newton, with a nod of agreement, visibly shivered at the recollection. "You know Colonel, it's a peculiar thing, but I am a little nervous. I see a shadow or a branch move, and I'm ready to shoot."

"Doc," Colonel Bennet replied, "welcome to the club! We're all like that. By the way, I heard you shot an infiltrator. Congratulations, Doc. I mentioned it to General Samet and placed it in your personnel record."

"Thank you Colonel."

After more small talk, Colonel Bennet finally came to the point. "Colonel Newton and I have been discussing Major Norman, who is not doing well. I know he's having trouble with his wife at home."

Colonel Newton interjected. "Norman often isn't at work in the afternoon. I'm sure he's down in the village. He seems out of it, as if he's on dope or marijuana. Are you giving him anything?"

"No, I'm not."

Colonel Bennet said, "What I want you to do is talk to him. I think he's sick. Then if you have any recommendations, let me know. If you can handle it yourself, please do so. But, we must put his head on straight." A short silence intervened. "One other matter, Doc." Colonel Bennet frowned parlously. "Doc, there were two cases of VD here last month. You know that I have delegated responsibility for VD control to you. I don't want anymore VD here, period. Use whatever methods of propaganda, fear or punishment you deem necessary. I'll support you."

"But, Colonel, I wasn't here last month."

"That doesn't matter, Doc. Any more cases and I'll order Colonel Newton to take you out and shoot you."

"That's a bit extreme, Colonel. How about a dunce cap and a short stay in the corner first?" But, before Colonel Bennet could reply, Dr. Houghton preempted him. "I'll have some classes with mandatory attendance for all personnel on the compound. You don't mind if I show some horror pictures, do you?"

"No."

"I'll also talk to Major Norman, this afternoon."

"Thanks, Doc."

"So long, Colonels"

Dr. Houghton pondered the irony as he walked back to the dispensary. Colonel Newton was a woman chasing goat, and Colonel Bennet, an off-duty drunkard. They were two very dark pots calling the kettle black. But, perhaps, they understood the secret of the army – they knew just when to call it quits. They knew the geography of the army pale. Colonel Murray at Air Force Seven and Major Norman did not; they willfully walked over the line into minefields. Every day, Colonel Bennet and Colonel Newton appeared for work on time. To a casual observer, they were effective. But, in his unique position as their physician, Dr. Houghton know that Colonel Bennet often suffered the throes of daytime liquor sickness, a painful abstinence syndrome that only ceased with the five o'clock whiskey. And Colonel Newton, a truly energetic man, with a pathological lust, also required the work-day to recover his vigor, in time to renew the sexual combat with his "shrewd" employee, Mary Lee, an invincible opponent.

Fortunately for them, the Colonels could delegate responsibility. They only needed to guide and counsel. If they could lead, they could accomplish the mission. Of course, they had to be told what the mission was, but in the army, this was not difficult. And this was Major Norman's problem. He must be effective, for he was not a Colonel or the leader.

"Let's begin to see the patients, Sergeant Morse," Dr. Houghton said when he returned.

"Right, Sir. I have about ten patients which I'd like the Doctor to see. The rest of the patients have scabies, lice or skin trouble which I can handle. The first patient I'd like the Captain to see is a lady who was bitten by a snake in the rice paddies. She's in the treatment room with Sergeant Song and Corporal Kang. Corporal Kang will also help you with translation since Miss Judy is not here today."

Dr. Houghton walked in. "What happened, Corporal Kang?"

"This lady got leg bit by a snake in the rice paddy. She brought snake."

"It's a poisonous viper." Dr. Houghton observed the snake's triangular head with the two frightful fangs.

"Yes, Sir, it is."

Dr. Houghton examined the peasant lady. "She has low blood pressure, chest pains, and huge swelling of the leg."

Sergeant Song said, "She knows she is going to die, Sir. She says if there's anything you can do for her, she'd be grateful. She has much pain."

"Tell her we have viper anti-venom, and anti-coagulants, and other medicines. We can save her life and probably her leg."

Dr. Houghton leaned over the lady and whispered in Korean. "Everything will be OK. I'm a magic devil." He thought he said magic doctor and did not understand why the Korean lady smiled and Sergeant Song laughed.

But Dr. Houghton's bungled reassurance gave this forlorn lady hope. The anti-venom, penicillin, saline, and anti-coagulants saved her body. After the initial eight hour treatment, two farmers carried her on a stretcher back and forth from the village at eight AM and eight PM daily for four days. Then for another week, they brought her once daily. One eye turned in; one toe blackened and fell off. But the eye recovered slowly. The last time Dr. Houghton saw her, she walked on a crutch, carrying rice-cakes in gratitude. She attempted to kowtow, but Dr. Houghton forced her to remain standing.

"You see, Corporal Kang, I am a magic devil," Dr. Houghton commented in Korean. They all laughed, but no one would correct his catachresis. He proceeded in blithe ignorance. "She doesn't have to return anymore."

"She has one question, Sir." Corporal Kang manufactured the question for his own purposes. "She wants her toe back. She thought you were a magic doctor."

To Corporal Kang, the Christian skeptic, Dr. Houghton said with a feigned gravity. "There will be no problem. We'll just transplant one of your toes."

"No, Sir!" Corporal Kang replied, beaten.

"Bring the next patient into my office, Corporal Kang."

"Yes, Sir!"

A Korean woman and her son entered and bowed deeply.

"What's the trouble?"

Corporal Kang spoke to the boy's mother in very rapid slangy Korean for a long time. Dr. Houghton, who understood the gist of her problem, gradually lost patience. "What did she say?"

"Little boy has some devils," Corporal Kang said. At this moment, the mother collapsed on the floor and imitated a grand mal seizure.

"Ask her how long and how often."

"Five years, about one time a day," Corporal Kang translated.

"Do you think this boy has devils, Corporal Kang?"

"Yes, Sir."

"Do you believe in devils? You're supposed to be a Christian."

"Yes, Sir. I does. Jesus Christ cast out devils into swines. It says so in the bible."

"I'm greater than Jesus; I'll cast the devil out of the child into the air."

"I don't believe you, Sir."

Dr. Houghton examined the child and asked, "What are these four burns on the child's head?"

"Chinese medicine, but the burns did not help, the mother said. The boy's mother brought her every place in Korea, but nobody can help."

"Corporal Kang, you mean him." Dr. Houghton corrected.

"Yes, Sir."

Dr. Houghton reflected momentarily about this peculiarity of the Korean language; it didn't distinguish him from her. "Corporal Kang, I'll touch him two times, and you tell him to take one of these capsules two times a day. He is to return in two weeks with x-rays of his head."

Two weeks later, Corporal Kang with open awe, translated, "No more devils, Sir, Her mother is very happy."

"You mean his mother. The x-rays are normal," Dr. Houghton said, as he scrutinized them in the view-box. "Tell her to continue to give the boy one capsule two times a day and return in six weeks. Also, I do not want her to kowtow," Dr. Houghton said as the woman began her descent. "I'm a magic devil," Dr. Houghton ho-hummed in Korean to Corporal Kang as the patient and his mother left. The patients always laughed or smiled at this. Much later to his chagrin, Dr. Houghton understood why. On a South Korean propaganda poster, Mr. Kim, the dictator of North Korea, was also termed a "magic devil" with obvious pejorative intent.

After lunch, Sergeant Morse walked into the office. "Sir, that's it for the civilian clinic, but Lieutenant Herlong and Major Norman are here to see the Captain."

"Send in Lieutenant Herlong first."

"Jeff, come on in; have a seat here." A youthful, six foot botany major, Lieutenant Herlong flopped in the chair, obviously distraught.

"You know, Doc, I'm the signal advisor and that's fun. But I am also responsible for communications on this compound. The Colonel is really pissed because most of the time, you can't call five miles down the road."

"Me too, Jeff; I'm pissed. Half the time, the phones don't work or if they do, you have to shout to be heard." One of Dr. Houghton's first impressions in Korea was a red-faced Colonel shrieking into the phone. At the time, he did not understand such behavior, but he too was soon screaming into phones.

"The trouble is, Doc, that as soon as we string up the wires, a slicky boy steals one or two hundred meters of the lines. You know the story of the Hydra."

"Yes."

"It's like that. Sometimes I catch whoever's doing it and ...." Jeff executed a karate chop. "Some nights I can't sleep. Every five minutes I try the phone. If it goes out, I know someone has cut the wire. Some nights, I go out and patrol the lines, hoping and praying...."

Dr. Houghton did know that some nights Jeff Herlong left the compound to check the lines on foot, a dangerous practice. One evening the national police arrested him for breaking the curfew, after Jeff and the police exchanged several rounds in confusion. They thought Jeff was the wire thief.

"Jeff, I'm going to give you a nighttime tranquilizer and a direct order. You are not to go off the compound after curfew to check the lines unless the Colonel gives you a countermanding order to do so. Just don't sweat it. You know, it used to be worse in this country. You'd leave your jeep for ten minutes and on return – no motor, no tires, no battery. At least that's let up. Unfortunately, they still go for your copper wire. OK, Jeff?"

"OK, Doc. Thanks." Jeff left with relief in a bottle.

"Come on in, Major Norman."

"Call me Bob."

"Have a seat, Bob."

"Thanks."

190

"You probably know why I called you over here," Dr. Houghton paused. "The Colonels think you are not as effective as you should be. Colonel Bennet wants us to handle it here. So I want to hear from you what the trouble is."

A thoughtful and liquid-eyed Major Norman spoke with a thick southern accent. "The main trouble, Doc, is my wife. You see, we were married when I was 16. I'm 33 now, and have four kids." He spoke in a monotonic drawl, weak and passive, in fact pitiful. "I went to college for one year and then to OCS. I am not a good officer, but the army has pushed me along. Just before I came over here, after my 'Nam tour, my wife and I were discussing a divorce. At any rate, I was assigned here. I was bored to tears until I met Miss Chang." A slight glow in his eyes, combined with the minimal movement of the slouch forward at the mention of Miss Chang, hinted at a buried, smoldering low intensity fire. "I want to bring her home with me. I wrote to my mother who is encouraging me; maybe she can be my mother's house-girl."

Dr. Houghton interjected. "I understand your wife came over here to visit for one week while I was in the field. Colonel Newton mentioned that there was a commotion one night."

"Yes, she came for one week."

"Against army regulations?"

"Yes. She somehow got a visa. It was horrible. She came to patch things up, but I couldn't even perform a husband's duty with her. Instead, I drank all the time. One night, my wife and I got very drunk, and I took her down to the village to meet Miss Chang, Sally Chang."

You must be joking, Dr. Houghton thought.

"It was awful. My wife was so drunk she didn't realize who Miss Chang was. The next day, though, she asked me. Then, the night before she left, we had a big fight. My wife says I only want unnatural acts with a woman, that I am not normal."

Dr. Houghton understood the problem. "I see. But why doesn't your mother like your wife?"

"She never has. She really hates her. I don't know why."

Colonel Newton told Dr. Houghton that Mrs. Norman was a kind, quiet, in fact, not unattractive woman.

Dr. Houghton realized he could not resolve Norman's sexual and marriage dilemma now. So he turned to the two other potentially soluble problems. "Colonel Bennet feels you are intoxicated with drugs. Is that true?"

"Yes, I smoke marihuana and opium. I picked up opium smoking in Vietnam."

"That, as you well know, is a severe offense in the army, especially in Korea where we have all the nukes."

"Yes, but is it any worse than booze, Doc?"

"Not really, I must admit." Dr. Houghton ignored the slash at Colonel Bennet.

"Doc, I really don't think you can understand unless you see. Tomorrow night we have a cock fight in the village, my cock against the village champion. Will you come?"

"Yes, I'll come. What time?" Dr. Houghton thought that if he could see Norman and Sally Chang in their habitat, he might be more helpful.

"Eight o'clock."

"But there are two things, Bob. First, can you stop the opium smoking?"

"Yes, I think I can."

"Good. I want you to stop that. Second, I want you to be physically on duty during the day. The Colonel thinks you've been in the village during duty hours."

"He's never caught me in the village," Major Norman rebutted.

"Now you are talking like the Koreans, Bob. Reality is only that which somebody saw. Nobody saw, not true, huh? Is it true?"

"Yes, Doc," Major Norman admitted hesitantly.

"OK. I want you to cut out the opium completely, and I want you to stop going to the village during duty hours. That is all I want. If you do that, I'll keep you off the Colonel's hook. Your word?"

"I promise but don't ask me to stop seeing Sally Chang."

"I'm not asking you that. I'll see you tomorrow night at Miss Chang's." Dr. Houghton stood. "Bob, I have to deliver the VD lecture now. Let's go over.

Dr. Houghton walked through the small movie theatre up to the lectern. He shivered. "Somebody forgot to put on the stove, First Sergeant!" The audience of forty Americans chuckled. "Is everybody here, First Sergeant?"

"Yes, Sir! Everybody is accounted for but Colonel Bennet. He's not coming."

Major Norman proclaimed, "He needs Alcoholics Anonymous!"

The room became silent.

Dr. Houghton began, "Gentlemen. The topic of this lecture is VD. Last month we had two cases of VD among us forty. The Colonel, like Moses, has said, 'There will not be anymore VD,

192

Doctor.' I say there will not be anymore VD troops." Dr. Houghton paused for effect. "Colonel Newton, are you here?"

"Yes, Doc." All thirty-nine heads turned toward Colonel Newton who, in his winter outfit, looked like a Colonel General in the Soviet Army. "I'm here in the back row. Why do you ask?"

"Because this, this could happen to you."

On cue, Sergeant Morse projected a color slide of the front view of a stout, naked, white man with a swollen, black penis. The audience gasped in unison, then broke into raucous laughter. Dr. Smith wondered how Colonel Newton would tolerate the ridicule.

"Sergeant Morse, are you here?"

"Certainly Sir, I'm showing the slides," Sergeant Morse said in his velvet basso-profundo voice.

"This could happen to you."

Sergeant Morse flicked on a slide of a large, muscular, black man with a miniscule penis. The laughter again rippled through the troops.

"Dr. Houghton, are you here?"

"Yes, I'm giving the lecture." Dr. Houghton answered his own question. "This could happen to you."

Sergeant Morse flicked up a slide of an old, unshaven, unkempt, obviously demented man. The audience did not laugh.

"Enough jokes, gentlemen. VD is serious. Today, I will not speak of morals, ethics, conscience or religion. I'm here only to give you the facts. Each one of you is a grown man. Each one must decide for himself his conduct. But I want you to have at hand the facts to aid in any decisions. It is up to the Colonel and the Chaplain to lecture you on army regulations and morality. I also want to deny the rumor that it was the Chaplain, one of the two, who contracted VD this month." The audience guffawed.

"Now this talk is aimed mainly at those of you who think variety is the spice of life. I will tell you that continent men do not get VD. Also, men like the First Sergeant, who has a steady girl in our village, a girl who loves only him and henpecks him if he so much as looks at another girl - men like him do not catchy VD. The First Sergeant will not butterfly, will you First Sergeant?

"No, Sir!"

"So, there are the two solutions to the VD problem – continence or a steady girl.
For any potential butterflies, let me make several comments about the VD rate among the entertainers. The girls in our village are VD free. I have examined them all and I certify them. I, of course, deny they have bribed me."

The audience chuckled at this. To them, it was a real possibility, for there was little in Korea that wasn't venal.

"Seriously, you all know that Sergeant Morse and I check all the girls in our village. If any girl does not cooperate, we have the National Police throw her in the can, but all the girls cooperate, and there is no problem. In fact, there is a village Association of Business Ladies. But outside our village, among the Korean entertainers who mainly date Koreans, during any given month, 20% have gonorrhea and 5% syphilis. Many have nonspecific urethritis, NSU, and other syndromes, but we do not know the exact numbers. Among the girls who entertain mainly GI's the figures are 10% and 4% respectively. Those, gentlemen, are the facts, and I'd say the facts are horrible." Dr. Houghton stopped for a moment. "There is one other fact of note: our village girls will not get pregnant, and that is another obvious advantage."

After these introductory remarks, Dr. Houghton discussed in common language the manifestations of VD as well as its early diagnosis and treatment. The audience gave him their undivided attention. By the questions, he knew everyone understood. One question concerned him. "Doc, will you check out girls who don't live in the village for us?"

Dr. Houghton, like Colonel Bennet, did not want "straying sex" outside the compound or village if at all possible. He said, "I strongly urge and advise you not to fraternize with women outside of our village for the reasons I gave earlier, plus many others. But if you find a girl you must have outside our village, I will check her for you. I advise you then to move her here so that you can be sure she doesn't butterfly on you. The eyes of the village are all-seeing and all-knowing, and its tongue uninhibited."

At the end of the lecture, there was raucous applause.

Colonel Newton said, "Doc, I'd like to speak with you outside." They walked up to the club. "Good talk, Doc. Very enlightening. I think everybody will think twice before plunging in." He laughed.

Dr. Houghton nodded.

"If I understand you correctly, you can reliably treat every venereal disease except non-specific urethritis."

"Yes, that's correct."

"I'm tired of Miss Lee, my Mary Lee," Colonel Newton said. "I need fresh meat."

Dr. Houghton made no comment.

194

When he entered his room, the phone rang. "Sergeant Morse here, Sir. Lieutenant General Lee wants to see you now. I will bring the jeep and we can be there in five minutes."

"Do you know why?"

"No, Sir."

General Lee's adjutant said, "Enter, Captain."

Dr. Houghton saluted crisply and said in polite Korean, "How are you Lieutenant General Lee?"

"Excellent since you almost killed me with your big red bombs."

"I was happy to help."

"Sit down here. My son has a problem; he goes to University in Seoul. Can you help him?"

"Of course; what is the problem?"

"He will call you when he needs help."

"Excellent."

"I hear you are making rapid progress in your Hap Gi Do, that you have good ability. I see you are also rapidly learning the Korean language."

"Yes, I enjoy the Hap Gi Do but my shins are damaged." Dr. Houghton raised his fatigue pants to show the welts and blue-black marks. "I will never be as good the Korean black belts."

"Do not quit. I hear you are very good. You will be happy when you receive your back belt." General Lee paused, "I also asked you to come because I spoke to Abbot Kim."

"Abbot Kim?"

"Remember you asked about jadeite carvings in Korea."

"Yes."

"He told me in Korea there are very few. But in his monastery, the Golden Buddhist Monastery outside Taegu, they have a few very fine jadeite carvings. What happened was that a Japanese lieutenant who was involved in the sack of the Forbidden City in Beijing by the Europeans and Japanese in 1900 came to Korea in 1905. He was sent by the Japanese government to help administer Korea after the Japanese took over Korea in 1905. He ultimately became de facto governor of the Taegu area and stayed until he died. Anyhow he brought with him the looted Forbidden City jadeite pieces he smuggled out of China in his personnel effects. He later married a young Yangban Korean lady. After he died, she donated them to the Golden Monastery during the Korean War just before she died. Abbot Kim said she gave them five looted imperial pieces including those from the Qianlong Emperor and the last Empress Cixi." General Lee unfolded a paper. "They have a

195

jadeite carving of Chinese-style Apsarases, you know, celestial angels; they also have an imperial green Kwan Yin, a translucent pale green Buddha's Hand citron, a field of red and yellow amaranths, and the moon goddess, Chang`e. He says they are of the highest quality."

Dr. Houghton felt an almost sexual lust. "How can I see them?"

"I told Abbot Kim you would come. You should have a Korean take you to visit. By the way, the monastery is decrepit, is falling apart. The Abbot told me he hoped you would make a contribution. They are desperate for money. Perhaps he might even sell you carvings if you paid enough."

Dr. Houghton started drooling mentally. He heard little of the remainder of the conversation. He *must* see these carvings. Since childhood, he had dreamed of the Qianlong Emperor and the Fragrant Concubine, Xiang Fei; of jujube perfume and jadeite peppers and citrons; and the goddess of mercy, Kwan Yin; the moon goddess, Chang'e; and the spirit of longevity. Now, he could see the imperial jadeite carvings here in this place - in Korea. What good fortune! He must. He must.

After returning from the Hap Gi Do practice that evening, Dr. Houghton entered the Q. He heard a string of Korean curses and violent thuds from Lieutenant Ahn's room. He entered the partially open door. Captain Chang was pulverizing an unresisting, frail Lieutenant Ahn.

"What's going on here?" he asked as Captain Chang gave Lieutenant Ahn a final wallop in the gut.

Captain Chang replied with the authority of a righteous indignation, "Lieutenant Ahn has disobeyed orders."

"But Captain Chang," Dr. Houghton remonstrated, his sense of justice outraged. "You're big, a Karate expert. He's just a tiny guy."

"That is true," Captain Chang replied, "but in the Korean Army, they'd kill him. We must maintain discipline. He's no good, a number ten officer."

"Please leave, Captain Chang. I want to talk with you later." Dr. Houghton said in Korean.

After examining Lieutenant Ahn, he called Sergeant Morse on the phone. "Look Sergeant Morse, Lieutenant Ahn had a slight, ah, accident." This type of "accident," Dr. Houghton observed over and over again in the Korean Army Hospitals, sometimes even with fractured skulls or ruptured viscera. Colonel Kim rationalized that these beatings maintained discipline and outweighed the obvious drawbacks of hospitalization. In a society where, outside of the immediate circle of the Confucian family, shame, not notions such as honesty or conscience, motivated behavior, Colonel Kim argued forcefully that making examples was necessary. This was how they did it in Korea for centuries. He concluded, "Your Puritans used the pillory."

Dr. Houghton continued, "Sergeant Morse, I want you to bring Ahn to the American Evacuation Hospital right now to see my old friend, Dr. Riley. Explain to Dr. Riley that he should make sure Lieutenant Ahn is not broken, but also check the uncooperative little bastard for flukes and other intestinal parasites. Maybe we can see why he's so skinny and dark-skinned. I still think he is full of liver flukes."

"Yes, Sir."

Dr. Houghton returned to a prone Lieutenant Ahn, "Lieutenant Ahn, we're going to send you to the GI Hospital. One of my friends, Dr. Riley, will care for you."

"I won't go," a recusant Lieutenant Ahn groaned.

"That's an order."

After Lieutenant Ahn left for the hospital, Dr. Smith knocked on Captain Chang's BOQ door. "Captain Chang, tonight, I want to go downtown with you. Let's leave at eight o'clock. Is that convenient?"

"Yes, Doc," Captain Chang replied.

Captain Chang, a Karate instructor, extended his Army tour once to avenge the deaths of his Yangban family by the Northern Devils during the Korean conflict. But at heart he was a would-be scholar. Soon he would be a teacher, a "book man." The K-MAG liaison officer assignment was his last. The Koreans considered Captain Chang an honest man, a real compliment in a society of thieves and venality. But Dr. Houghton knew he must persuade Chang that Americans do not sanction direct physical violence for discipline.

At eight they left for Chun Chon. Dr. Houghton and Captain Chang did not converse much during the twenty minute journey, both deeply occupied in thought. Dr. Houghton said in Korean to the driver, "We are going to the Morning Glory Tea House. It used to be called the Voluptuous Flower Tea House but they changed the name. Pick us up at ten-thirty, please."

"Yes, Sir"

Dr. Houghton and Captain Chang, equals in rank and age, sat in a dim corner of the Tea House. In one matter, however, they were not equal. Quite openly, Dr. Houghton envied Captain Chang his wife. Dr. Houghton fervently hoped she would become pregnant and thus retrieve her tenuous position in life.

A single ash tray, and a large box of inferior matches, which generally shattered on being struck, sat on a battered rectangular table. Captain Chang lit his cigarette on the third attempt.

A waitress appeared with two cups of steaming rice water. Dr. Houghton asked in Korean, "Where is Miss Pak?"

The waitress answered in Korean, "Wait a minute please."

Soon Beautiful Flower came. "How are you, Honorable Doctor?" Beautiful Flower bowed slightly and lowered her eyes politely.

Captain Chang looked briefly at Dr. Houghton, who smiled. He then surveyed Beautiful Flower. Captain Chang disapproved. This girl was a real Korean girl, not a business lady, and not for Americans. But gratitude welled-up into Captain Chang's heart. With Dr. Houghton's advice and treatment, his wife had missed a period. And so his mother would not require him to divorce his lovely childless wife. Captain Chang was desperately hoping the child would be a son. "Do you know her?"

"Yes, I have seen her several times."

"Do you like her?"

"Yes, I do, very much." But involuntarily, Dr. Houghton thought of Miss Han whose final words, "Do not forget my face," echoed in his mind. His vast debt to Miss Han seemed still outstanding; she demonstrated conclusively that supernal joy with a woman was possible. He could not believe she had really died, but like a child, he thought she had just gone away. Moreover, immediately after her death, he resolved not to become involved anymore with enchanting Korean women who were untouched by the West. They were too strange, too full of tragedy.

Moreover, Miss Han had broken through long-buried layers of emotion in Dr. Houghton, feelings of undefined danger. In moments of doubt, he thought that Korean women were like witches or demons or jinns of story books, who enveloped one in spells of jeopardy and risk. He was not yet ready for these women. Who knew what they might do? And yet, by some unknown tropism, he was irresistibly drawn toward Beautiful Flower even though he knew she presented real risks, different from those of the entertainers. For years he contained many impulses behind walls of oppugned rationality. He knew that the walls were now cracked. Where was his father when he needed him?

Captain Chang motioned to Beautiful Flower to sit beside him. He conversed with her in rapid, colloquial Korean that Dr. Houghton understood reasonably well. Finally Captain Chang said,

198

"She knows Major Kennedy, the new Air Force Major, who transferred from Air Force Seven. He come here many times and wishes to take her out."

Dr. Houghton was shocked that Mike was also interested in Beautiful Flower but he understood her charm and magnetism. He was pleased to have Mike at Chun Chon. Indeed, he thought Mike was fortunate to escape the prison that Air Force Seven had become, but Mike was not serious competition for Miss Pak...Mike was not her type.

Miss Pak said in English, "Major Mike, over here, hair no have." She pointed to her scalp. She pointed to her chest, "Over here, too much." She laughed and flashed thirty-two pearl-white teeth untouched by the dental drill. "Him monkey, I think so."

"How do you know?" Dr. Houghton asked.

She blushed and looked down.

Dr. Houghton restrained an alien impulse to grab her. Such impulses, however, were not alien to the forward Korean men. Instead he said in Korean, "Captain Chang and I would like two cups of Chinese red tea, hon cha, and one white flower..."

She then disappeared to fill the order.

Dr. Houghton observed the energy of Miss Pak's stride. Dressed in her short, white, high-necked Western dress, her gait approached that of a caper. One expected a skip at any moment. This contrasted with the floating, even, small-stepped, rubber-shoed ambulation of a woman in a traditional Korean dress. Simple mechanics probably dictated the difference, but it seemed that in Western dress, Beautiful Flower was a carefree, liberated woman in contrast to the passive, obedient distaff in the traditional outfit.

In her temporary absence, Dr. Houghton asked Captain Chang, "Why did you beat up Lieutenant Ahn?"

Captain Chang rejoined. "He disobeyed orders. You must watch out."

Dr. Houghton continued, attempting to hammer the point home. "You know, Captain Chang, my Colonel absolutely forbids assaults on our compound. We Americans feel that a beating of that sort is not proper. I know as a Korean you disagree, but you are now assigned to us. Your people must not do it. Besides it makes too much work for me as a Doctor."

"I will try to do as you wish," Captain Chang replied, "but you must watch out for Ahn. He is a number ten man."

"Why?"

Captain Chang remained impenetrable, thus closing the discussion. But suddenly he brightened. "You know, Doc, I think my wife full of baby."

199

"Congratulations," Dr. Houghton almost shouted and pumped his hand with enthusiasm. "You must have followed my advice."

"My wife is very happy. She thanks you."

"Your wife is very beautiful. I would say that most beautiful face I have seen in Korea."

"Thank you, Doc."

"You are very lucky, Captain Chang."

But Captain Chang viewed it from another angle. His wife was very lucky to avoid a divorce.

Two weeks later at the K-MAG officers' club, Captain Chang succumbed to a mixed intoxication of joy and alcohol. He was so inebriated that he was now no longer Colonel Bennet's liaison officer, but Colonel Bennet, the Commander. Everyone bought him drinks when Dr. Houghton announced that his wife's pregnancy test was positive. Now Captain Chang, in the ancient Confucian tradition, would have a son to perpetuate the sacred continuity of the generations.

Dr. Houghton also uncharacteristically guzzled gin to excess, partly sharing Capt. Chang's success, but also to assuage an intense pain in his right chest from an inadequately defended Hap Gi Do smash.

After thirty minutes of loud badinage with Mike, Dr. Houghton experienced a whirling intoxication. He stood on the bar, after demanding complete attention. He paraphrased the moon-man, "This is a great leap forward for womankind," and then jumped into Mike's great arms.

Mike said, "Bullshit, Doc. That bastard Chang would divorce her if she didn't get pregnant."

Captain Chang either did not hear or understand Mike. Caricaturing Colonel Bennet, he said, "Let's eat." Chang walked brashly into the bright white table-clothed officer's dining room and instructed everyone where to sit. He slumped into Colonel Bennet's chair at the head of the table. Colonel Bennet, gracious and also fall-down drunk, allowed Captain Chang his brief delusion.

Mike commented on this unusual departure from protocol, "Doc, Bennet is not a candy ass."

In total concurrence, Dr. Houghton arose and wavered, "A toast to the Colonel; an Army Colonel who's not a candy ass according to Air Force Major Mike." An hour later, deeply anesthetized, Dr. Houghton staggered to his room, unable to feel the heel mark on his right chest, but even so he berated himself for his defensive tardiness. Captain Chang had shown him how to avoid that particular high kick. There was no excuse.

As he fell asleep, Dr. Houghton replayed their conversation in the Tea House about Beautiful Flower.

"What do you think of Miss Pak, Beautiful Flower?" Dr. Houghton asked in Korean, hoping for a favorable comment.

Captain Chang smiled, acknowledging approval.

"I would like to take her out."

"I will see to it," Captain Chang replied as if he possessed some power over her.

Miss Pak finally returned from the kitchen with the red teas and one small white carnation.

"Miss Pak, I wanted a white rose."

"I'm sorry. Very cold. Rose no have." She switched into Korean. "They only had a carnation."

"Miss Pak, I want you to put the flower in your hair."

She did not completely understand his Korean, so Dr. Houghton mimed his thought, and she obliged. The white flower, in marked contrast, stressed the beauty of her jet black hair. Before she went off, Dr. Houghton slowly asked in polite Korean, "Miss Pak, I very much hope you will be my guest at K-MAG one day."

Not committing herself, she replied, "Maybe," and left to serve another teahouse patron.

The jeep came at ten-thirty as instructed. Miss Pak waved good-bye to the two Captains. During the icy ride back, Captain Chang passed on the requested information. He said Miss Pak had left Seoul after three years in college because she had no more money. Her interest was in Chinese studies and botany, and she was an excellent student. The following two years, she tutored, but her income was so meager that she began the disreputable work in the Tea House. She worked daily from nine AM to eleven PM with three days off a month for fifty dollars per month plus board.

"Can you tell me anything else about her?"

"No."

"Did she have a broken love affair?"

"I don't know." Captain Chang stated this is such a way as to end further discussion.

The following evening, Sergeant Song took him to Sally Chang's hooch in the village. In the darkness of the frozen alley, he saw a figure too large for a Korean.

"Hi, Doc."

"Hi, Bob."

"Glad you came, Doc. This is Miss Chang, Sally, and here is my cock."

Dr. Houghton bowed and said, "How are you?" in Korean. He couldn't see her face in the darkness or the fluttering cock in its wooden cage. He followed Major Norman down the alley as emaciated dogs barked. He jumped when several huge pigs oinked. He choked on noxious smoke spewing forth from several flues. In the bitter cold, he inhaled strange odors of previously unimagined foods. This sobering walk through the dirty alleys explained why the farmers and village people where so physically dirty, and suffered the agonies of poor hygiene – scabies and all the rest. In their defense, the prohibitive winter temperature militated against bathing; the nearest community shower or bath was in Chun Chon forty-five minutes by bus.

Major Norman led them to a barn-like structure with a crowd of Koreans inside, a few of whom Dr. Houghton recognized. Several Korean enlisted men from the compound greeted him politely. In the dim interior, Dr. Houghton glanced at Miss Chang and was repelled. She was distinctly unattractive with severe acne. She had the grin of subnormal intelligence.

After some wagering and boisterous chatter, the farmers and village folk formed a large circle. Dr. Houghton anticipated two resplendent game cocks with arched, orange necks. He waited expectantly for saucy, flamboyant killers. Instead, two scraggly, undernourished birds emerged from the cages and circled each other with a few weak flaps. Major Norman said in a whisper, as if he had cheated, "I gave my cock vitamins and tetracycline. It should make the difference." After some initial wing-beating, the village cock lunged for Major Norman's cock, grabbing it by the throat, and the contest was over. Dr. Houghton wondered if that was all there was to a cock-fight, as he began to shiver.

Major Norman, showing as much disgust as his emotional state permitted, said, "Let's go Doc." He closed his cage's door.

"Aren't you going to take your cock?"

"No. He was a lemon. He was too old."

Dr. Houghton followed Major Norman to Miss Chang's thatched, mud-walled, one room hut. Parts of the wall had crumbled. Coke and beer cans were heaped in a conspicuous pile beside a large pig pen. Dr. Houghton, who did not demand his father's absolutely crystal clear drinking glasses although he preferred such an immaculate standard, wasn't anxious to enter. His intuition was confirmed as he crawled through the solitary door-window into the squalid love nest. Major Norman snapped on a single overhead light bulb as several cockroaches scurried into their nooks. The furniture inside the small room consisted of an old bare mattress, a tattered chest of drawers, a battered table littered with cosmetics, and one plastic bag full of laundry, mainly Western style women's clothes. He heard rats scurrying on the corrugated iron roof.

"You've been smoking marihuana?" Dr. Smith asked.

Major Norman nodded, and added "but not opium. I promised." Then he placed one arm around Miss Chang and said, "Doc, this is my love," and kissed her on the cheek. Dr. Houghton tried to be charitable, but in the harsh light of the eighty watt bulb, Miss Chang was hellishly repulsive. He thought he detected a certain craft in her smile.

After a few minutes, she brought in a steaming bowl of rice and some vile- smelling winter kimchi from outside.

"You want some rice wine or chops, Doc?"

"No thanks, Bob."

Major Norman started deftly eating the rice with wooden chopsticks. So did Sally Chang. In the lip-smacking silence, Dr. Smith realized that Major Norman was oblivious to the situation. But in fairness to Miss Chang, no one could deny that she waited on him attentively, knowing the nuances of his every wish. Her motives and inner feelings, unknown and unknowable to Major Norman, were seemingly of no consequence. Whether she despised him, as Lieutenant Ahn said, seeking his money, only she knew. Did it really matter to Major Norman? Like Harvard's Professor Skinner, Norman was a behaviorist; her deeds not her thoughts or motivation were what counted.

But from Dr. Houghton's personal perspective, Major Norman had descended into a kind of hell; not Dante's or Sartre's Hells. This was a different and un-American Hell. Dr. Houghton had to escape; he was slightly nauseous. Like a deus ex machina, Sergeant Song appeared. "I'm sorry, Doctor, Major Norman, but there is a patient in the dispensary."

"I'm sorry, Bob, I must go."

"If you get through early, Doc, come on back."

"So long, Miss Chang, Sally Chang," Dr. Houghton slipped out and clambered into his jeep with a vast sigh of relief. To Sergeant Song, he said, "Only the point of a loaded cocked gun would entice me into that hut again."

Sergeant Song understood.

"What's the trouble?"

"Lieutenant Chae beat up Private Kim."

"Badly?"

"Yes, sir."

Four minutes later, Dr. Houghton entered the dispensary. Private Kim lay in his blood on the examining table. Mike towered over him.

"Hi, Mike."

"Hi, Doc." Mike was ashen.

"What happened, Mike?"

"I was duty officer tonight. I heard a commotion behind the dispensary. I went to look, and there was Lieutenant Chae pounding Private Kim who stood at attention. Finally, Chae knocked him to the ground and started kicking him in the head and chest. I almost shot him."

"Did Kim resist?"

"No."

Dr. Houghton examined the bloody Private Kim as Mike muttered in a fury. "We ought to take that little bastard Chae out and shoot him. These Koreans! I just don't understand. They are so damn primitive."

"What did Private Kim do? Do you know Sergeant Song?"

"No, Sir."

"Well," Dr. Houghton said concluding his examination, "I think Kim has one or two broken ribs, four missing teeth, but I don't think he has a skull fracture." After telling Sergeant Song what to do, Dr. Houghton turned to Mike. "You know, Mike, I just spoke to Captain Chang about this kind of violence here. I told him it must stop! But have you ever peeked in the Korean MP compound down the road?"

"No, I haven't, Doc."

"You should if you want to see real violence. They have a monkey house, a stockade down there. I went to visit it. You wouldn't believe it. They couldn't wash the blood stains out of the wood. This is the orient, Mike. Violence is a tradition."

Mike mused. "We should get out of this country. What are we doing here? Defending freedom's frontier; balls I say!"

Dr. Houghton called Colonel Bennet for an update report. "Colonel, you've got to sack Chae. This was not just a pat on the butt but a malignant beating, one that could easily have resulted in a stiff."

"All right, Doc. Have Chae in my office at eight tomorrow."

"Thanks, Colonel."

Mike said, "We will see."

"Hey, Mike," Dr. Houghton said, "I hear you're chasing Miss Pak – my Miss Pak."

"Who?" Mike asked.

"Miss Pak at the Morning Glory Tea House."

Mike lit up like a Roman candle. "She's nice and pretty and speaks some English. She's educated. She's well built, too."

"I thought you didn't like Orientals, Mike. Miss Pak is mine!"

Mike grinned. "I hope you have a big pocketbook."

"Men and women who know each other
easily are cheap lovers."
Chinese proverb

Chapter XIV
Preparation

Reg completed the first two years of his internal medicine training on July 1, 1968 at noon. That same evening, an orgiastic party with Henry, Jan, and several others climaxed in slow motion clowning and finally a drunken stupor. Reg only remembered exaltation and rapture. He was a newly manumitted slave. At seven AM he awoke with a bone-dry mouth. He wondered how Jan had been able to function on only three hours of alcoholic sleep, but the radio revealed it was July third. He had slumbered twenty-seven hours, a new personal record but still inferior to Henry's twenty-nine hours.

This "new" beginning suited him well. For three weeks he intended to do little except read about Korea and Korean diseases. Although he worked at keeping the vacuum in his head, he could not prevent past hospital events leaking into his awareness. As a consequence he read pertinent medical texts, reviewed the treatment of certain complex diseases and finished one academic paper that he and Henry submitted for publication. He also called a few patients to see how they were doing.

Inevitably, he thought of the Army and his future tour in Korea. He somehow must not waste two years in the army. These were his best years but like all young physicians he was screwed by the exigencies of this ill advised war. The saving "grace" was that he would not be sent to Vietnam. However, it was not "grace;" he had wisely volunteered for Korea or Japan in medical school. With romantic intuitions of Korea and Japan, he hoped to encounter some unique adventure or perhaps a lovely maiden.

On July 10, he received a letter from a General welcoming him to Korea and The Korean Army Military Advisory Group, K-MAG. The General said he was leaving, but an extremely "sophisticated" General, General Samet, was replacing him when General Samet finished his tour in Vietnam. This general recommended he read about Korean history and culture, and the medical problems of Korea *and* the medical problems in the American army in Korea – especially venereal diseases, alcoholism and depression. The problem of boredom was especially acute in Korea. The general noted that the army job Reg would fill was a Colonel's billet. But because of the Vietnam War and Reg's "extraordinary qualifications," Reg was asked to fill this particular slot. The general ended his helpful letter with "All good wishes."

Almost every sunny day, Reg drove to the beach for a few hours with Jan or his youngest brother. The hot July sun, the long runs on the beach and eight hours of uninterrupted sleep restored his vigor. The vacation abruptly ended in late July when the Army movers came. They crated and sealed his belongings, shipping them to Korea. No one would tamper with his belongings including customs – Reg would unseal them in Korea.

Reg and Jan decided to meet in Chicago when he finished "basic training" in Texas. They would then drive from Chicago to San Francisco sight-seeing along the way. She then planned to work as a nurse in California. She already had a job lined up.

When he arrived at Fort Sam in San Antonio, he found the base had no on-post officers' quarters available, so at the Army's expense, Reg moved into a gaudy motel with a large swimming pool. He was now an Army Captain. Classes were held from seven to four PM five days a week for four weeks with a three day field trip. After the initial days of lectures, Reg cut many of the formal classes, but read over the mimeographed class notes. However, he was compelled to appear for the morning and afternoon formations. During this time he memorized the necessities like where the brass was positioned and how to read maps. He also read more about Korean medical diseases as well as Korean culture, since the Fort Sam orientation was heavily slanted toward Vietnam.

Some of the time Reg spent at the motel swimming pool in the hot, summer sun of southern Texas. After a week, deeply tanned, he accepted with pleasure the daily infusion of vigor from the sun. Only his blues eyes, penis and scrotum were not tanned. Reg attempted to capture and store as many of the precious beams as possible before his descent into Korean dimness, fog, cold and snow. There apparently was also a big frostbite problem in Korea.

Early one evening, Reg enjoyed a double gin and tonic as he watched the nubile, young women dive into the motel pool. Through his green sunglasses, he watched these ripe specimens flaunt their charms, their golden-tanned wet bodies alive with animal quickness. Tempted, Reg sat in the exact same chair each afternoon and observed. But immobile and unsmiling, he invited no dalliance. He was dedicated only to the sun and his thoughts. A motel clerk temporarily interrupted when Jan called. They finalized their arrangements for the rendezvous in Chicago. She had a new car. But Jan, with her typical lack of savoir-faire, nettled him with her "good news." She and her date had won at the dogs.

Back at the pool he reflected on his and Jan's infrequent excursions to the dog track near Revere Beach in Boston. He always lost. His dogs fell, were bumped, suddenly limped, or just ran an inexplicable last. And yet, knowing he was deluding himself, he continued to bet his two dollars on each race along with the motley crowd of rich and poor suckers.

By mutual consent, Reg and Jan remained uncommitted. However, older and "wiser" counselors continuously urged Reg to marry. But he resisted such advice, unlike the majority of his peers. Reg did not want to leave a wife "alone" while he worked. Over and over again, but particularly in the confessional of the doctor's office, he had observed the hackneyed saw "out of sight, out of mind" was generally true. Although he recoiled from this harsh reality, he realized that the mythic Penelope was a rarity. Already Jan went to the dog track with another, after a brief three weeks. He anticipated her complimentary closings while he was in Korea; "All my love, Jan." Then, "With love, Jan." Next, "Love, Jan" and finally no more letters. Thirteen months was a long time to leave a normal, childless, beautiful woman alone. Moreover, Jan was not for him; she was not close to the right girl. Of course, there were exceptions, and Reg had seen such dedication in his medical experience. But he saw the reality of Fort Sam: the extremely causal liaisons of the overseas service-men's wives. These women abounded at the bars, the clubs, and PX, primed and ready. Women's liberation was definitely here.

In the past, particularly with Marsha in college, Reg suffered from occasional violent paroxysms of jealousy. Often when Marsha noticed a handsome man, he would be nearly overcome by murderous impulses, although he manifested only sullen ill temper or attempts at dominance. He now laughed at his unreasonable demands such as how Marsha should wear her hair. Perhaps he should have wed that beautiful girl, but he wondered now, as then, if he could satisfy Marsha's entirely reasonable demands for love and affection, *and* the rigors of medical training. Moreover, he was now off on a thirteen month tour in Korea. Would it have been fair to Marsha, during her most glorious years, to be married to a near invisible, always exhausted crumb? Suddenly, Reg laughed at the crumb-image. Several girls glanced over to see what might be funny. Finally Reg decided he was filling his cranium with trash. He was thinking too much. Let Jan do what she wanted, let the morrow bring what it would. He would enjoy the sun and wait.

208

One of the other recruits, Dr. Trout, a boyish looking mid-westerner, walked out to the pool with his wife. She was bawling. Mrs. Trout lived at the motel with her husband and lounged endlessly in the sun, while he conscientiously attended all the military classes.

"What's wrong?" Reg asked.

"They're sending me to Vietnam."

Reg wasn't surprised. He said, "I am sorry to hear that."

The personnel officer, a true bastard, had informed Dr. Trout that he would have to volunteer for a third year if he wished to bring his wife to Japan with him, or else he would be sent to Vietnam. Dr. Trout excused himself saying he had to move his bowels and never went back. He avoided numerous messages to call back. Instead, he called the Army Surgeon General's office where he received a vague verbal reassurance.

"I got orders for Vietnam today," Dr. Trout repeated.

Mrs. Trout vigorously clutched Reg's arm, hypertrophied by the hundred push-ups and thirty chin-ups he did every day. She kneeled beside his chair, her bikinied bosom now against his arm, her head against his neck, sobbing violently. "What are we going to do?" she cried.

Reg gently placed his arm around her for a moment and then gingerly disengaged. He sought deep within himself the sympathy and advice she requested. He was flattered by her emotional appeal. But it was too late. He had urged Dr. Trout to sign his extension and fight it later. Now he was empathetic but not sympathetic. Dr. Trout made his choice.

Mrs. Trout's tears of intuition left a salty, brackish taste in Reg's mouth. She wept and writhed, although she was not a hysterical woman. "He has a solitary ticket to hell," she moaned.

The next day Dr. Trout attempted to extend. He begged; he pleaded; he called his congressman but his request was denied. Unfortunately, Mrs. Trout's intuition was correct. Dr. Trout lost his right arm and his hearing in a rocket attack in Vietnam.

In the early afternoon, Reg received a call from Miss Galt. "Where are you?"

"At the airport in San Antonio."

"Why?"

"I came to see you."

"But you are married."

"I must see you."

"I have army formation now but come to my motel at five and we can talk."

Reg was flabbergasted by the sudden appearance of Miss Galt. He had not seen or talked with her for over a year. He was intensely curious. What did she want? He speculated continuously through formation and a quick shower.

He just finished dressing in yellow shorts and an amaranth colored tank top when he heard a knock on the door. Miss Galt wore a light white sheath dress with black high heeled shoes. She looked unchanged by marriage; she still had long, fine legs and an hourglass figure. She said nothing, walked over and kissed him passionately. She smelled of rose perfume and clove breath. She said, "May I use your shower; it is hot here."

"Of course."

Suddenly, tears welled up in her eyes. She said, "I loved the wedding present you sent. The pearls were so large and plump. Thank you so much. It was so thoughtful."

After her shower, they sat in the noisy air-conditioned room. Reg said, "I made two strong gin and tonics. Here is yours." He waited.

She said, "You look extraordinary well, Reg. Only your blue eyes are not tanned. You have grown more muscular too."

Reg said, "My scrotum and penis are not tanned - baby white still."

"I will soon check."

Reg waited for her explanation. Finally, out of patience, he said, "As my Jewish friends say, 'Neu?' Why are you here?"

"I had to see you. I love my husband – he is the nicest man. I am so lucky to have found him. He is in Europe for a few days so I came to see you before you went to Korea."

"Why?"

"You know."

"No, why?"

"You did something to me. You don't know?"

Reg now knew.

"How did I let you slip through my fingers, Reg?"

Reg did not respond.

"I came for one last treat. I will not come again. Next month I stop my birth control pills. Please, once more. I beg you." She fell on her knees.

That afternoon Reg and Miss Galt re-established that Masters and Johnson's laboratory observations on the human female sexual response were incomplete at best. Miss Galt's involuntary barrel spasms, contractions, and suctions lasted much longer and

210

were more powerful than they reported. Her pelvic organs doubled in size. Afterwards, her uterine contractions continued as Miss Galt lay on the bed exhausted. She saw double. She could only moan.

In turn, after almost two hours of intermittent, conversation-less Herculean efforts, Reg finally said, "I have no skin on my member; I hope it will grow back. You squeezed the life out of it."

She did not laugh or respond except to grunt.

He looked carefully at Miss Galt whose eyes were crossed. "Are you OK?"

"Don't worry, Reg. It happened before," she mumbled.

"Can I buy you a royal dinner?"

"Yes. But I need an hour to recover, for the swellings to go down and the contractions to stop." She then smiled weakly and said, "You need to let the sun shine on your penis and scrotum; it looks funny, a white member on a black man."

Reg and Miss Galt had a sumptious candle light dinner at the most expensive restaurant in San Antonio. He ordered the best champagne, caviar and two small fillet steaks. Lucullus would have approved.

Miss Galt said, "Although I feel like overcooked spaghetti, I want to be serious, very serious, for one minute. This afternoon I was al dente; it was glorious, Reg. At the last climax, I heard archangels singing. I thought I would ascend to heaven." Miss Galt paused; she looked directly into his eyes, "I also want to say one other thing. I know that you have a large trust. I know you do not need the money but I admire you and the others for working so hard to learn medicine and care for the sick. I saw you perform miracles."

Reg said, "We learned from you. You set the standard."

Tears welled up in Miss Galt's glittering eyes. She caressed Reg's hand. "That is so kind of you, Reg. I will never forget you and this afternoon and this candle light dinner. You have given me things I will eternally cherish. I love the pearls too."

The next morning at 6 AM Miss Galt left for her flight to New York. Reg was sorry to see her leave. For two days Reg felt like a puffed toad or better, like Shiva or Pan or Priapus or even better, like Zeus, the night Zeus stopped the sun so the night would last three days. Reg forgot the name of Zeus' lady-friend that particular session. Was it Danae or Semele? But over the next several days, Reg decompressed. He knew it was only two hours, not three continuous nights. But he was very happy with Miss Galt's appreciation. After all, Reg's mother was correct: good manners and being "nice," although not a Miss Goody Two Shoes, was the best way to "be." He also admitted that he learned the actual techniques from watching his father with women. However, Reg's father overdid it; he prevaricated. Reg's approach was different. He employed gentle flattery, real empathy, appropriate kindness, and well chosen gifts. But most important, he listened carefully. The rewards were truly magnificent for her and him. Of course you had to perform but Reg was quite capable - especially when rested. He would never forget Miss Galt's involuntary responses, nor would she. He did wonder why he never heard angels, never mind archangels, sing?

At seven AM, four hundred physicians and dentists, including Reg and Dr. Trout, filed into the theatre to "meet the Commandant." This was their next-to-last day of "basic." In the balcony of the theater, a twenty piece brass band butchered John Philip Sousa. To a man, these draftee physicians and dentists were angry and upset. They experienced horror and disbelief as the Commandant waxed "poetic" about the importance of the Vietnam War and the value of their service to the nation. They were not stupid; they watched the nightly news from Vietnam. They knew lies when they heard them. After the commandant departed, Reg heard only bitter, cynical and vile expletives that poured off four hundred tongues. His peers were correct.

Following this cacophonous debacle, Reg went to his platoon's fourth and final hour of drill instruction. In a southern drawl, the drill instructor, an enthusiastic obese Major, commanded the troops to look "sharp." The flashing hostility of this mainly Vietnam-bound physician platoon would have withered a more sensitive soul. They guffawed at the Major when he stated that, "Even the Dentists marched better." Under their breath, several physicians intermittently said, "Quack, Quack." After all, the Major walked like a goose.

At the half-hour break, this clueless Major asked for a light for his cigarette. Without exception, the entire platoon walked away as if he carried pneumonic plague. His eyes clouded over. After the break the troops wimbled him as they chomped on chimerical gum. The Major ignored the provocation.

Reg did learn one thing at Fort Sam, how to shoot. He became an Expert Marksman, and wore a rifle badge on his uniform. He also became an expert with a pistol.

Captain Houghton found Jan waiting at the airport. Their discover-America, parting "honeymoon" soon became a regressive dream. Reg and Jan spent every moment together, a man and his shadow. There was never any disagreement, not a harsh word. They stayed in sumptuous hotels in each city, from Chicago to the cattle

212

city of Omaha, to the high city of Denver, and then to the desert city, Salt Lake City. Approaching Cameron Gulch, Arizona, Jan wished to visit a Navaho hut.

"I've some reservations," Reg said.

Jan replied, "Another bad pun, smart boy."

After walking ten minutes in the shimmering, sandy candescence, Jan knocked on the only door within miles. A short, vile-smelling Navaho emerged with a shot gun, distinctly hostile.

"Jan, let's get out of here," Reg said.

When they got back to the boiling car, Jan fainted. Using the ice from the cooler, he revived her quickly. As she came to, he said with a groan, "Jan, do you think you could pull the arrow out of my back?"

"Oh, my God, no!"

Reg won four hundred dollars in Las Vegas, but almost lost Jan that early September day driving across the Nevada desert to Los Angeles. Jan's car was not air-conditioned. Halfway across the desert, Jan started to speak incoherently.

"Drink the coke, Jan, and eat the bacon," he ordered.

She tried to rest her head on his shoulder as they sped onto LA. She inexplicably wouldn't drink. He finally stopped the car, and felt her neck and her breasts. They were very hot and dry. He removed her shirt and bra, and rubbed her with ice. She again refused the coke. He slapped her but she only moaned. Finally, in desperation, he pinched her right nipple.

"Stop!"

"Drink the coke."

"No! Stop!" Jan finally drank the icy coke although gradually.

As they sped away from the desert, Jan recovered and forgave him the pinch, although her breast was discolored from it. She, as a nurse, understood the danger of heat injury.

As they passed through the San Bernardino Valley, an ugly brown haze appeared which obscured the sun. Jan commented, "Who would want to live here?" The choking vile smog extended into Los Angeles, so they spent the evening in Ventura. Then, they enjoyed a balmy day in Monterey and finally on to San Francisco.

Reg expected the excesses of love making along with the eight hours in the car each day might arouse hostility, but the reverse occurred. He, as well as Jan, became more solicitous of the other. Of course, in the evenings, they dined in the most expensive restaurants, in the most conventionally romantic settings, with candles, flowers, champagne and caviar. These artifacts lubricated any potential friction. Further aiding the harmony was the realization of the approaching end of their idle and a small amount of hypocrisy. Deep down, they both knew that they were not "right" for each other.

The journey abruptly ended in San Francisco when Jan saw him off to Seattle. Just before he boarded, Jan volunteered a dark comment, "An affair around every corner." Reg could not remember the context, but he thought she meant this to comfort him.

In Seattle he learned of a one day delay. There were also two letters waiting for him. One from his Dad who wished him luck and suggested that Reg consider a professorial career. His Dad noted that being a professor of medicine would nicely employ Reg's skills and experience in medicine, chemistry and education. He asked Reg to consider this possibility carefully.

The next letter was from Marsha. He intuited this was not good news. Except for her one visit to him several months ago, he had not seen her for over two years. He opened it reluctantly. It read:

"Dearest Reg,

You are the most handsome and greatest lover I could ever imagine. I am now pregnant with your baby, from our visit several months ago. I am sorry to have done it this way but I had to have you, for life. I will now have a beautiful child with blue eyes, light brown hair, a Phidias' body, and a great intellect. You know this is not a money question, for like you I come into my grandfather's trust in two years. When you return in thirteen months time, we will marry.

With good luck and all our love,

Marsha and Junior."

For several hours a furious Reg was at a loss for a plan. Should he call his father? Should he call his lawyer? Should he call Marsha? Was it true? Was the baby his? Was she really pregnant? He had read Thomas Hardy after all. All possible plans had significant downsides. So when he calmed down, Reg decided to do nothing. He could do nothing definitive now. He had his army orders. They were written in stone. The army was rigid - adamantine. After he returned from Korea he would deal with this and his future. Moreover, when he was in Korea she could do nothing.

Two days later, Reg boarded a big jet that flew him to Korea via Alaska. He was comfortable with his plan. What else could he do?

214

"O wild dark flower of woman,
deep rose of my desire
an Eastern wizard made you,
of earth and stars and fire."
          "The Rose of my Desire,"
          Charles G.D. Roberts

Chapter XV
The Chase

Dr. Houghton had been in Korea almost six months. Except for two visits with a business lady and the several happy/sad times with Miss Han, he had spent his time doing his army advisory work, seeing civic action patients, learning the language, practicing Hap Gi Do and reading his medical books and journals. He also gradually became Koreanified. He ate red hot kimchi occasionally and sometimes had dragon mouth. Like the Koreans he enjoyed a bowl of sticky rice with a fried egg on top and a side of kimchi, all for 100 won, 25 cents.

But in his life he was missing two very important experiences - awe and the sublime. It was true that on several occasions he came close, like that day at Harvard College when he finally synthesized amaranth dye and saw the crystals come out of solution. He was so glad he did not purchase the amaranth. Had he done so he would never be able to look at himself in the mirror! But it was also true that during his life there were three times he did feel true awe. Two of them occurred in the last year: the sexual episodes with Miss Galt and Miss Han, although he confessed he did not hear angels sing. The other time was ten years ago when his Harvard instructor, Miss Ching, showed him the jadeite carvings in Cambridge. He often thought of her descriptions of the Qianlong Emperor and the Fragrant Concubine, Xiang Fei. He now understood what the Emperor was seeking: Awe and the Sublime. He should continue to seek them too. But how and where?

After days of reflection about Awe and the Sublime, he decided he must act now, before he succumbed to tea poisoning. Almost daily, after Hap Gi Do practice, exhausted and often in pain, he would purchase a solitary flower, walk to the Morning Glory Tea House and drink a cup of red tea. At seven, his driver would pick him up for the ride back to the K-MAG detachment for a quick shower and dinner before the dinning hall closed. On this, the first day of spring, he entered the Tea House determined. He would succeed or fail today. He bowed to the Madam. He took his customary seat in a dimly lit corner.

Miss Pak sat down in a rickety chair opposite him. She wore intoxicating jasmine perfume.

He immediately felt heady. "Yong Mi, Beautiful Flower, how are you?" he asked in Korean, handing her the red rose.

"How are you, Honorable Doctor? Thank you for the rose. Every day I am so happy you come to see me. By the way, what is in the school bag today?"

Miss Pak and every Korean expressed grave disapproval whenDr. Houghton carried a green U.S. Army cloth bag with his Hap Gi Do uniform in it. Only school boys and thieves in Korea carried large bags. To the Koreans, in his dark green fatigues, shiny combat boots, and holstered forty-five, Captain Dr. Houghton appeared harmonious, even handsome, but with the large green bag, ludicrous. He spoiled the necessary harmony of things. He wasn't a school boy or thief. How could he carry such an object of scorn? Did he not know shame? Yet, after all, Dr. Houghton was no fool. Miss Pak thought there must be some highly significant mystery associated with the green bag. Like all Koreans, she felt she must peek inside the blackness of the bag to fathom its enigma.

Miss Pak did not know that Dr. Houghton had read extensively about the Buddha-of-the-Future. In China and Korea they called him Maitreya and in Japan, Hotei. Maitreya was a Being that had attained enlightenment, a Bodhisattva, but he decided to stay on earth and help mankind. He was generally portrayed as a fat, happy man who carried a large cloth bag full of Goods: gold, jewels and rice cakes. Dr. Houghton thought the green bag might conjure up images or memories of Maitreya.

Miss Pak reached into the bag. She saw the uniform and a small box wrapped in white paper with blue ribbon. She gleamed when she read the characters for her name on the white paper. She shook and then sniffed the box. "This is what?"

In korean, he said, "It's for you, if you come to K-MAG on Saturday night." He vacillated. Should he abandon the plan and give it to her now, just to observe her joy? The pleasure of just watching her eagerly scrutinize the unopened box presaged some fantastic response. One might expect the box contained the world's finest emerald or some other equally valuable object. But Dr. Houghton resisted his impulse. For three weeks he had invited her out, without success, and so, the rather mundane ploy.

She replied, "Maybe."

He knew, for both Mike and she had told him, that Mike had also asked her for a date. But Miss Pak said, "No thank you."

She said to Dr. Houghton, "Mike, he married. Also, he have no hair over here." This baldness in so young a man never ceased to amuse her. "He has hair," she lapsed into Korean, "on his chest, arms and legs, but not on his head. Only the head is necessary to have hair."

Dr. Houghton replied in Korean. "His mother is also bald."

Beautiful Flower said, "It is very bad for woman have no hair. I am sad for her."

Dr. Houghton laughed. "Many false fairs, she has." He didn't know the Korean word for wig.

"You mean wig?" She brightened when she realized what he meant.

"Yes."

"You are liar," Miss Pak said with her irresistible sloe-eyed twinkle.

"Will you come?"

"Maybe."

"Yes or no?"

She spoke softly. "I will come."

"Do you promise?" he asked.

"I will come," she repeated.

Dr. Houghton realized that this decision was not easy for Beautiful Flower. The Americans had to pay Korean women a bonus just to work on American compounds, for the Koreans frowned on any contact with Americans. Far worse was the dating of an American man, particularly a soldier. The Koreans felt that such an association, no matter how innocent, placed the woman in the dubious status of a business lady or worse. In this land of paper doors and watchful neighbors, any encounter was impossible to conceal. The gossip of the omnipresent Korean quidnunc and the collective view of Korean society, with its immense power of shame, were very difficult to ignore. This, in part, was the reason that virtuous Korean girls did not seek employment in a Tea House, for the Tea House girls must serve and converse with any paying guest, including Americans and even worse Japanese.

On the other hand, Dr. Houghton surmised that Miss Pak's status was already compromised. She may have succumbed to some unscrupulous seducer, like Lieutenant Ahn. She must also be in desperate need of funds to withstand the shame, and to work the unconscionable hours.

Dr. Houghton promised himself that he would not repeat the serious errors he made with Miss Han. He now knew the Koreans' queer customs better with their emphasis on preserving face and the necessity of appearances. He would be certain that Miss Pak would not suffer in any way from her association with him. In fact, she would benefit.

He anticipated Miss Pak's request as she sat opposite him with the red rose pressed to her body. "Do not tell that I go to the GI compound." With her head she indicated the Tea House personnel. "I will come Saturday before seven."

"I am very happy you will come. We will have a big chicken for you, and then we will go to the American movies at the base theatre." Dr. Houghton knew of the Koreans' inexplicable delectation for juicy American chicken.

Miss Pak brightened further. She attempted to catch him with a loose tongue, hoping he might blurt out the answer. "What in little box?"

"You will see." He was overjoyed at her heightened skin glow. This cutaneous emotion he had read about in old novels. He also saw it in American children and in mature women; the sexual flushs of Miss Han and Miss Galt. Perhaps Beautiful Flower would be his Xiang Fei, his Fragrant Concubine.

When Dr. Houghton returned to the Detachment there was a Special Delivery letter from Marsha. Dr. Houghton was reluctant to open it. He thought that the "shit would hit the fan." He read:

"Dear Reginald,

I am so sorry I sent you that erroneous letter last September. I am happy to tell you that you are not the father of my new baby boy; I have married the father. I beg you to destroy that letter and this one. Also, do not attempt to contact me. Please send me a telegram to the address below stating you destroyed the letters and will not attempt to contact me, ever.

Thank you in advance. With all good wishes for your service in Korea,

I remain.

Marsha"

Dr. Houghton reread the letter twice. He immediately decided not to destroy the letters. He wired her that he received her letter and he would not attempt to contact her. He wished her luck but he was silent on what he would do with the two letters.

Later that evening he enjoyed a Martini. He was now determined to pursue Beautiful Flower vigorously. But for a brief moment he remembered the psychiatric patients he saw in medical school: the nympholepts. They pursued young women with the hope of finding a kind of ecstasy but never succeeded. Their objective

218

was unobtainable. They ended up in mental institutions. Reg was not a nympholept. Finally, he once again remembered what Albert Camus said: there is only one "perversion"- thinking too much. He threw aside all reservations once and for all. He savored a second Martini.

Dr. Houghton waited in his office for the Corps Surgeon, Colonel Kim. Colonel Kim had entered the Korean Army just out of medical school. He had studied radiology in the Korean army and the United States. He was a cosmopolitan man. He detested the North Korean regime whose soldiers had killed his elderly mother for no apparent reason during the Korean War. For Dr. Houghton's considerable aid and advice, Colonel Kim was genuinely grateful. He enthusiastically encouraged Dr. Houghton in his Hap Gi Do and Korean language studies. Unlike most Americans, who either stayed on the U.S. compounds drinking an alcoholic hole in their livers or pursued the easy, inexpensive business ladies, he saw Dr. Houghton as almost dangerously curious. Colonel Kim often gasped at his questions, obviously based on information that Westerners should not know.

Dr. Houghton knew that Colonel Kim was a humane and enlightened man by Korean standards. He even treated his low ranking subordinates well. Unlike the other Korean Colonels, he brought his drivers lunch as they waited in his freezing jeep to prevent its theft.

Sergeant Song announced, "Colonel Kim is here, Sir."

Dr. Houghton went outside and opened the door of the older man's jeep. "Good morning, Colonel."

"Good morning, Doctor."

They walked into Dr. Houghton's office. Sergeant Song brought in steaming coffee, sweetened precisely to the Colonel's taste. In the polite, inevitable, pre-business conversation, Dr. Houghton almost mentioned Miss Pak. He wanted the Colonel to meet her and hopefully favor a liaison; for he knew that all the other Koreans would disapprove. It was virtually impossible for an American soldier to date a respectable Korean girl. The Colonels and Generals always took him to Tea Houses or Kisaeng Establishments - to be sure their wives and daughters were not exposed to him. But he decided not to broach the subject at this time.

To preclude any loss of face, Dr. Houghton anticipated the Colonel's request. "I'm sure you require some medicine for special patients. Why don't you tell me what you need? While we are finishing our coffee, Sergeant Morse can gather them up."

219

"That would be fine. The Corps Commander's wife is ill. She needs......"

"Colonel, that's all right. Give me the list and Sergeant Morse will assemble it."

The list had about fifty dollars worth of medicine that the Koreans could not obtain.

"We have all these medicine the Colonel needs," said Sergeant Morse.

"Colonel, I would like you to look at my shins." Dr. Houghton rolled up his fatigues. His shins, discolored and lumpy were ridged with welts. In one place there was an escarpment of new bone. "Any suggestions on how to avoid this?"

Without any sympathy whatsoever, Colonel Kim said, "You have to improve your defenses. You must not wear shin guards; you will lose face. As I learned in America, you are screwed until you improve."

Dr. Houghton laughed. He said, "In two months, I'll have my red belt. Pretty good?" Dr. Houghton wanted the Colonel's approval and encouragement.

After some reflection, Colonel Kim replied, "In my nineteen years in the Army, I have never known any other American officer who got his Black Belt in his tour of duty here."

"I hope I'll be the first," Dr. Houghton smiled wryly. Finally turning to business, he asked, "Where do you want to visit today, Colonel?"

"The 47th Division Medical Company."

"Good, I haven't been there yet."

"Tonight also," Colonel Kim continued, "we must go to a Kisaeng House where they have the best dancer of Korean traditional dancing. I know you are interested in Korean culture. You must be my guest." Colonel Kim stood. He said, "Kaps shi da-let's go."

Since it was foggy, they could not go by helicopter. Carefully placing his precious donut, Colonel Kim settled in the front seat of Dr. Houghton's jeep. Dr. Houghton and Sergeant Morse, who carried the bag of drugs, clambered into the back seats. Sergeant Morse also meticulously arranged his donut. As they prepared their seats, Dr. Houghton thought of the K-MAG Deputy, who also suffered from horrible hemorrhoids. Dr. Houghton had also procured him a donut. As part of their discussion, the Deputy complained how frequently the helicopters did not fly because of the fog, so he had to travel in the "God-damn jeep." As an aside, he derided Dr. Houghton for not sitting in the front seat. This was the position of comfort as well as authority. "After all," the Deputy said, "it's your jeep."

Initially Dr. Houghton argued with him – suggesting the importance of good will and savoir faire. The Deputy laughed at that. He also gratuitously added, "You will not get your black belt even if you try to butter them up."

Dr. Houghton almost assaulted the SOB but kept his fists in his pockets, his feet on the ground and his mouth closed. He did not brag that he did not have hemorrhoids, that he had buns of iron. Perhaps he should slicky the Deputy's donut.

That evening at exactly eight o'clock, Dr. Houghton entered the Morning Glory Tea House to meet Colonel Kim. In the corner, he noticed Miss Pak perched opposite Colonel Kim. Dr. Houghton sat beside her and ritually presented her with a white carnation.

"How are you, Miss Pak?" Dr. Houghton asked in Korean.

Miss Pak flushed - a reaction the Colonel noted. "You two know each other?"

"Yes, I have had tea here many times. I think Miss Pak is a beautiful girl."

"Yes, she is a beautiful girl."

Miss Pak excused herself.

Dr. Houghton again hesitated in revealing his feelings toward her. Miss Pak brought two cups of red tea but did not join them.

Colonel Kim, unsuspecting of the potential future liaison, began to discuss one of his favorite subjects, the Kisaeng, with an apt and interested pupil. "Come," he concluded, "let's go and watch the dancing. To see it is worth thousands of words."

Dr. Houghton bowed good-bye to Miss Pak, now absolutely sure of his own mind. He also did not mention to Colonel Kim his previous visits to Kaeseng Houses or Miss Han.

The Red Gate Kisaeng House was surrounded by a seven foot cinder block concrete wall topped with threatening pieces of jagged broken glass and barbed wire to discourage potential slicky boys. After removing their boots, they were directed to a medium sized room with a gay scarlet motif. On the walls and ceiling were huge gold Chinese characters for good fortune, joy, peace, and harmony. Dr. Houghton read them aloud as Colonel Kim chuckled. The Madam disappeared closing the sliding paper doors as the hot floor transmitted a feeling of warm expectation.

Dr. Houghton sat cross-legged on the floor on a magnificent scarlet pillow opposite the Colonel. Sergeant Song, whom Dr. Houghton asked to join them, sat down in a corner. "Join us,

Sergeant Song. What are you doing off in the corner? Sit here." Dr. Houghton indicated the third point of an equilateral triangle. "I'm sure the Colonel doesn't mind."

"Surely," Colonel Kim concurred as Sergeant Song assumed his new position. Dr. Houghton knew Colonel Kim greatly admired Sergeant Song but was still not sure exactly why.

Suddenly the Madam entered with a group of seven Kisaeng caparisoned in different colored traditional silk dresses. Colonel Kim conversed rapidly with the Madam in colloquial Korean that Dr. Smith did not fully understand. Finally, Colonel Kim commanded, "Doc, I want you to choose two Kisaeng, but one must be Miss Ra."

. All the girls were exquisitely costumed in their traditional bright silks of yellow or mauve or amaranth or crimson. Here and there among them was amethyst, topaz, jade and solid gold jewelry. Several wore matching flowers in their hair. Another was festooned with a periwinkle garland. Augmenting this profusion of brilliant colors was a nearly overwhelming olfactory experience, a mixture of oriental perfumes. Dizzied by this aesthetic excess, Dr. Houghton contained an impulse to leave. In the next instant, he restrained the antipodal notion - I want them all. He finally said, "I'll choose this one and that one."

The un-chosen girls left quickly. The dejected expression on one parting Kisaeng's face brought a sudden wave of depression over Dr. Houghton. This necessity of selecting two from the many was more than just awkward. He now understood how an un-chosen entertainer must feel; not only wall flower pangs now, but hunger pangs tomorrow. He hoped that the variety of tastes in the customers would equalize who was chosen and who was not. But on reflection, he knew that, in this homogenous society with a shared concept of beauty, some would be chosen more frequently than others. The ultimate fate of the unselected entertainers was distressing. He now knew that, with no paying pleasure seekers to thaw the Madam and shower the girls with gifts of gold or money, these charming and talented, often strikingly accomplished, young women would be consigned to lower and lower class establishments, like the multitude of places on that awful hill in Chun Chon. These hill "businesses" had four or five girls, and catered to the harsh demands of Korean society. Dr. Houghton now knew that the health of these girls was often ravaged by fevers and the pain of untreated venereal and other diseases. Over time if they did not attract many customers, they were lucky to have a small corner of a tiny, cold room shared with four others. They rarely ate well and were uniformly skinny and remarkably bosom-less, although there was always enough rice wine to consume with the customers. These "businesses", really only vile shacks, were virtual daytime prisons, for the street urchins possessed the uncanny ability to recognize these girls whom they bombarded with rocks and epithets. The police looked the other way except when the girls struck back. Then the Police moved in expeditiously.

When such a "soulless" creature reached the last house at the hill's bottom, she might survive there for a final few months of night work. Then the Madam would eject her, the un-chosen, if she did not have clients. Finally, in one desperate attempt, she would knock on family doors, but she often found that a parent or sister would not speak to such a being. Her final fate was suicide, or death from the wasting diseases of syphilis or tuberculosis, or for those with an iron will to survive, the intolerable travail of the road gangs, each with a tale more horrible than the next. Several patients in his clinic were such women. Early in his tour, Dr. Houghton forced Sergeant Song to translate one such woman's tale. It was summarized in a photograph taken seven years before. The photograph showed a beautiful, thirty year old Kisaeng in her costume. Now she sat before him, a wrinkled walking skeleton. That morning, Dr. Houghton almost vomited his coffee.

In an attempt to do something about this situation and other difficult issues common to the US Army and the local Korean government, in early March, with Colonel Bennet's encouragement, Dr. Houghton visited the governor of the province. Once the governor realized he spoke Korean, the governor treated him graciously and thanked him profusely for his civic action program for indigent Koreans. The governor confided that they were just beginning to implement a plan to retrain some of the "Business Ladies" at state expense to become taxi drivers.

Dr. Houghton was somewhat buoyed by this progressive and humane action.

The Colonel laughed. "You have correctly chosen Miss Ra and Miss Na."

Dr. Houghton resumed the cross-legged posture and allowed the warm rice wine to erase his social conscience. He listened instead to Colonel Kim's lecture about Korean traditional dancing. With a booming voice seeming to come from a distance, an odd illusion, Colonel Kim explained that Miss Ra had danced with the Korean National Dance Company, but as a result of a scandal was forced to resign. Without work, she drifted into the Kisaeng.

Miss Ra danced. The Madam played the Korean flute. Miss Na played the hour-glass shaped drum. Miss Ra's motions were smooth and continuous. Her delicate, almost boyish form swayed and turned. Muscles quivered when she moved, agonist in perfect harmony with antagonist. Her sinuous elegance concealed a central mechanism with perfect peripheral feedback. That she could possess such absolute control over her musculature seemed impossible.

Colonel Kim, now intoxicated, continued his lecture in jumbled phrases saying that the Korean dancing was the "ultimate" with its graceful, civilized artistry. It was superior to the primitive black dancing with its bumps and grinds and jerks; it was better than the polka of Poland, the kizatski of Russia, or the national dances of the United States, the burlesque and go-go-dancing. Colonel Kim had seen these in the US. He rose and did several bumps and grinds before sinking into a drunken heap. He concluded that only Western ballet even distantly approached the Korean Dance for "grace, elegance and skill." Moreover, in Korea, only women performed this art, thus emphasizing the beauty, grace and femininity of women.

Dr. Houghton nodded at the Colonel's confused lecturing but did not reply. He watched Miss Ra carefully, but for inexplicable reasons he recalled images of Peaches, Rose, Bubbles and Candy Bar belting out their rhythmic dances at the Old Howard burlesque when he was Harvard student. The white carnation, which had airily freed itself from Miss Ra's hair while she performed, corresponded, in a sense, to the rose that Bubbles plucked from between her legs and tossed into the cheering boisterous crowd. But Dr. Houghton knew that this comparison was gross and unfair.

Perhaps it was Miss Ra's artistry or perhaps the rice wine, but suddenly as Miss Ra finished, Dr. Houghton became gayer, as if a mental belch relieved some invisible pressure. He no longer felt he had consigned the un-chosen to poor fates. He was not responsible for this. He had after all spoken to the governor.

He reached over, gently took Miss Ra by the hand, and placed her, like some exquisite doll, on his lap. He said to her in Korean, "You are very beautiful. Your dance was excellent. I'd like to bring you to America to show your wonderful dancing to my friends."

At this, Miss Ra overflowed with tears and ran from the room. Like many Korean women, particularly those compromised by ill fate, Miss Ra had often dreamed about embarking for America to dance or even to work, if necessary as a house-girl. The freedom of occidental women she had read about or seen in the movies. But she had no money and did not speak English.

But Miss Ra dried her eyes and soon returned. Dr. Houghton soothed her low spirits with an imperfect mime of her dancing after placing a flower in his hair. Colonel Kim and Sergeant Song, both helplessly drunk after their repeated toasts to women, sex, Hap Gi Do, and the Colonel's upcoming promotion to General, applauded Dr. Houghton's pathetic efforts. But as he danced, Dr. Houghton developed a plan.

So one evening three days later, Dr. Houghton hatched it. He paid the Madam to allow Miss Ra to perform for them at the Officers' Club. Mike had never seen the Korean traditional dancing and, skeptical about all things Korean, mocked Dr. Houghton and his enthusiasm. He waxed eloquently about the Japanese and Chinese dancers and acrobats. His mind was almost closed.

But Miss Ra, on the small spot-lit stage, danced gracefully to the accompaniment of a small band of traditional Korean instruments. As she performed, Dr. Houghton observed that Colonels Bennet and Newton, and even Mike, became entranced with her.

"What do you think of her, Mike?" Dr. Houghton whispered, as she danced.

"She's real good, real fine," Mike conceded.

"Real good," Colonel Newton, the great goat, agreed.

After her performance, Colonel Newton, Mike and Dr. Houghton enjoyed having dinner with her, all three treating her with varying degrees of respect. She was truly accomplished. While they ate and complimented her, the slender Miss Ra focused on her meal and greedily devoured every bit of her chicken.

Mike commented, "She obviously doesn't get enough to eat."

"I guess not," Dr. Houghton agreed.

But the Colonel, Mike and Dr. Houghton were stunned by the burping crudity of her dining habits, in such marked contrast to the refinement of her dancing and costume. When she spat some un-digestible food on the floor, Dr. Houghton, with face saving periphrasis, quietly cautioned her in Korean that Americans did not do that. Mike laughed at her table manners which confirmed his tendentious view that in the end, the Koreans were brutal and uncivilized. Dr. Houghton realized he made a mistake: he should have advised her of western table manners in advance. He was a failure as an impresario.

Soon after, Dr. Houghton escorted her back to Chun Chon, to the Morning Glory Tea House with gratitude. He gave her a large sum of money which he insisted she accept. She indicated that she was at his disposal. He hired her twice more for special dance exhibitions before he left Korea.

He wondered if she was coming. Dr. Houghton had almost given her up as a liar, but a phone call turned his anger into tense excitement when the gate guard announced her arrival. She was fifteen minutes late. He hurried down to the gate to sign her onto the compound. After he scribbled her name, Miss Pak hesitated before she entered, realizing that this step through the gate would irrevocably transform her life. But then with confidence, she strode through.

"How are you?" he asked. "You are late."

"I am very sorry, very sorry."

"But you look beautiful. Your white dress is beautiful." In fact, she had outdone herself.

"Thank you, Honorable Doctor."

Dr. Houghton and Beautiful Flower walked up the hill to the BOQ. She held her head high, almost too high. This haughtiness, alternating unpredictably with the more passive traditional Korean manner, was difficult to explain.

He brought her to his quarters, an act now forbidden except on weekends. The Colonel had bent to the pressure of the Deputy. They had instituted a "squeeze" on the personal lives of the command over the objections of the First Sergeant and Sergeant Major. Mainly intended for the married men, it affected all alike.

Miss Pak inspected his room. She made no comments.

"I have the present for you," he said. He wondered if it was the decisive factor in her coming.

"Let's see, let's see," she implored in Korean, now another person, a greedy little girl. "Hurry, hurry!"

She tore the ribbons and paper off the box with her perfectly manicured, richly polished crimson nails. As she opened the red velvet jewelry box and beheld the solid gold Korean "Happy Bag," she bounced with unfeigned joy – no piker Dr. Houghton.

"Thank you," she said, spinning around so that he could fasten the solid gold chain around her neck. Then, with her characteristic compete lack of restraint, she whirled around, capered forward and kissed him. Unlike Western women, the Korean emotions of joy and anger existed on the surface, quite obvious and real.

Dr. Houghton, as happy as she, said, "Let's go eat, Yong Mi. I am very hungry."

She paused, uncertain.

"After you, Yong Mi. You are a lady, and in America, ladies always go first." As they walked he explained to her about Western table manners.

226

She said she understood as they gingerly walked into the small K-MAG Officers' Club. Inside her courage thinned, and she grasped his hand for safety. In the dim, mirrored bar, she saw five giant silhouettes, standing with their backs to her. One of these was black, and one Major Mike. She saw his face in the mirror.

In traditional fashion, eyes down on introduction, she bowed deeply to Colonel Bennet who responded with an equally deep bow. He was a gentleman.

Recognizing her, Mike roared, "Hello, Miss Pak. What a pleasant surprise. And how are you?"

Miss Pak replied in English as Dr. Houghton had taught her. "I am very fine, thank you." Then she added her own, "Very many fines."

Mike grinned. "So you finally scored, Doctor. You know she's the only one in six months I've seen that I like."

"Me, too," Dr. Houghton echoed, not quite honestly, for there had been Miss Han.

Miss Pak blushed.

Mr. Cameron, one of the Department of the Army civilians and his girl friend, an older Korean business lady, entered the club.

"Mr. Cameron, this is my Miss Pak. Miss Pak meet Miss Pak." The two girls conversed in Korean.

Mr. Cameron, about fifty years old, was silver haired, of medium build, and had an extremely distinguished appearance. His ebony pipe spewed forth aromatic clouds. Through the pleasant smoke, Mr. Cameron had one day confided in Dr. Houghton his reasons for coming to Korea. "Doc, you know, I never served in the army although I've worked closely with the armed services since the Second World War. When my father passed on, he left me very well off. I really didn't need to continue working, but I've always felt uneasy about not serving directly. So I volunteered and asked to be sent here. I am here for one year."

Dr. Houghton imagined this explanation might be a fraction of the true motive. Away from his wife, he knew Cameron sought venery in this "ancient and enchanted land" before his dotage. He and his Miss Pak, who claimed to be thirty, were inseparable. Mr. Cameron had purchased a home for her in the village, and when he left Korea, she should be comfortable for life. For obvious reasons, his Miss Pak cosseted him.

"Mr. Cameron, may we join you for dinner tonight?"

"Certainly, Doc. It would be our pleasure. Mike, you too?"

The waiter overheard and prepared a table for five. After they were seated, Dr. Houghton observed Beautiful Flower imitate Mr. Cameron's Miss Pak, as to where to position the large white linen napkin, and how to hold her fork, knife and the rest. Beautiful Flower performed well with the chicken dinner, the first time she handled Western utensils for an entire meal.

Mr. Cameron commented, "That Deputy, that bastard, is tightening the screws too tight. I understand this is the last weekend they'll allow women in our quarters."

"Yes, so I've heard," Dr. Houghton replied.

"That SOB. My private life is none of his business."

Dr. Houghton asked in Korean, "Do you have enough chicken to eat, Yong Mi?"

"Yes, Honorable Doctor."

"Beautiful Flower, call me by my name, Reginald."

"Reh-ji-no-da," she enunciated slowly her four syllables.

"You know," Mike opened with his usual gusto, a manner indicating he would impart some outrageous fact, "I was down the dispensary this morning at seven thirty to get some peroxide from Sergeant Morse, and I looked up the hill. The Deputy was up there with binoculars watching the front gate, seeing who came in from the village. He's checking to see who is staying off the compound at night."

Dr. Houghton added, "I heard last night that Major Norman and that broad of his were holding hands in the movies. In front of everyone the Deputy chewed him out for a vulgar display."

"Doctor, you're treating the SOB. Why don't you slip him a little cyanide," Mr. Cameron suggested.

As was inevitable, the Deputy arrived for dinner and approached their table. Dr. Houghton rose to introduce Beautiful Flower but Mike, who detested the Deputy, pre-empted.

"Colonel, I'd like you to meet the Governor's daughter, Miss Pak." By no great coincidence, the Provincial Governor's name was Pak, as was twenty percent of the population. Another twenty percent was named Kim.

"Who is she with?" the Deputy inquired, impressed.

"The Doc." Mike answered.

The Deputy bowed and in Korean asked "How are you?"

In the Confucian style, Miss Pak executed the traditional bow and greeting of inferior to superior, answering politely in Korean.

In English, the Deputy continued. "Doc, how'd you do it? She's very beautiful and well dressed."

As if planned by Mike, the flickering candles cooperated with his canard. The beams reflected off Beautiful Flower's glowing eyes, her perfect complexion and her gold Happy Bag, her only valuable possession. The unique yellow color of the Korean solid gold suggested wealth.

The Deputy continued. "Doc, first the Hap Gi Do," the Deputy assumed a fighting stance, as Beautiful Flower politely covered her smile with her hand, "and now this beautiful girl, the Governor's daughter. Will you marry her?" His tone, however, unlike his words, intimated a subtle hostility and conservative condescension.

Dr. Houghton mumbled an incoherent statement, the necessary double talk required in such a situation.

The Deputy cast a final eye on Beautiful Flower. He concluded in ultra-polite Korean, "Have a good time." He walked off to the bar.

Miss Pak did not reply to his Korean solecism; she only looked down.

"That Tartuffe, that bastard," Mr. Cameron concluded.

Mr. Cameron's Miss Pak explained the hoax to Yong Mi who gasped at the deception. She screened her laughter and scorn behind her hand. To Yong Mi, Mike and even Dr. Houghton, it was patently ridiculous that any American man would know, never mind date, the Governor's daughter.

When he arrived in Korea, the first thing Colonel Newton told him was that the Korean people have little else to be proud of except the homogeneity and purity of the Korean race. The Chinese and then the Japanese held them in thrall for centuries. He was clearly right.

On the way to his quarters, under the cold, star-filled sky, he asked, "What happened to your mother, Yong Mi?"

"She die, when I was fifteen; she catch cancer and die in two months. I am very sorry. But I have a new mother who has pimples." She lapsed into Korean. Dr. Houghton did not understand "pimples" in Korean.

She gesticulated and said "Small, white hills on face."

"Oh, pimples, I'll give you no-pimples-medicine for your new mother."

With a wistful sigh, Miss Pak said in Korean, "I have fleckles."

Again Dr. Houghton did not understand.

She pointed to the five small freckles on the bridge of her nose, her only blemish.

He laughed and said, "Fleckles?"

"Do you have no-fleckles-medishein?" Beautiful Flower stumbled over the words.

"Yes, I shall give you some."

"Oh, thank you." With near violence, she threw her arms around his neck and shoulders and with fiery gratitude kissed him on the mouth, "Fleckles in Korea very bad." She had wintergreen breath, not dragon mouth.

When they arrived at the Q he approached her obliquely, his naïve goal direct answers. "How did you get the name Pak and Yong Mi?"

She evaded the question. "Silla Dynasty, you know two thousand years ago. On east coast Korea, old village wise men find big egg. Egg baby strong and number one soldier. He make country one. Last one thousand years. His name Pak, my name Miss Pak." And so in her limited English, Miss Pak, groping for words, told him the initial tale of hundreds with which she would amuse him. With her strong background in Korean and Chinese literature and mythology, she knew hundreds of stories and myths- of Chang'e, the moon goddess, of Zhong-kui, the purifier, and Kwan Yin, the goddess of mercy and on and on. She knew what she was taught and what she read; she had a prodigious memory. She knew 50,000 Chinese characters. In six months he now knew 150. But like most Koreans, notwithstanding their focus on education, she knew "facts" but did not understand analysis well – the core of enlightened Western civilization. That was what they taught in Korean Universities- "facts"- which were not to be questioned or analyzed. If the Professor said it, it must be true.

As her fluency in English and his knowledge of Korean improved, each story became more sophisticated and more charming than the previous one. She entertained him like Scheherazade amused the Sultan. In time, he almost believed, if she said it, that certain stones contained voices, and certain idols housed spirits. But at that moment, he sought, unsuccessfully, occidental facts, not Korean amusement or inner harmony.

"But, Lieutenant Ahn says your name is Yi, not Pak."

She hesitated, so Dr. Houghton bluffed, "You're ID card says Yi. I saw it."

She confessed. "It's true." As a Tea House girl, she had not informed her father of her employment for he might beat or kill her. She employed a false name as Korean entertainers have done for millennia.

Dr. Houghton, at that time, realized this deception was only the first hint of a cover of lies in which she wrapped herself. He also knew that the name Yi was an aristocratic or Yangban name – the name of Korean Emperors and prime ministers. So, if her name was really Yi, were her family Korean aristocrats until 1905 when the

230

Japanese occupation abolished the Yangban? Perhaps her heredity explained her natural dignity and fine looks as well as her very superior intelligence.

Her only flaw, like most Koreans, was slightly bowed legs. A very careful observer could see this, maybe. He guessed she had had mild rickets during the Korean War. He said in Korean, "Do you remember the war, Beautiful Flower?"

"Yes, I remember the soldiers, the shooting, and our beautiful house – all gone. There was big fire." She shivered.

"Did you get enough to eat?"

"I no think so. I vely skinny and belly vely swollen. Vely hungry, I remember."

Dr. Houghton's eyes clouded with sorrow at this obvious description of malnutrition. This presumably explained her slightly bowed legs.

"I must go," Beautiful Flower announced gathering her coat.

"When will you come again, tomorrow?"

"Two weeks, I come again."

"That's too long."

"I'm sorry, but you know I work in Tea House."

"I'll see you in the Tea House soon. I have a plan, a secret."

"Tell me."

"Not yet."

"Tell me now." She pounded his chest with both fists.

"Soon I will tell you, Yong Mi." Dr. Houghton exulted in her response. He relished the thumping. She was opening up a new vista. Finally he knew he must let her go. He said, "Good-bye" employing the most polite forms.

With strict attention to Korean custom and etiquette, she bowed, thanked him demurely, and glided back to the Tea House.

That evening in bed, pondering a Nikon portrait of Beautiful Flower who photographed extremely well, he said, "Come in," to a rap on the door. Lieutenant Humbert, the Headquarters Commandant, otherwise fondly known as the Headquarters Comedian entered. "Humby, it's you. What's up?"

"I came to take a vote. You know the Deputy, without consulting anyone, moved the tube at the club out of the common room into a side room. I'm opposed. I've taken a poll. Everyone so far wants it back."

"I really don't care, but I don't like the Deputy's high-handed tactics. So I, too, vote to move it back."

"Doc, I like your girl; she's outstanding."

"Humby, I've told you many times that there is an equally attractive girl for you. After all, you're West Point, handsome, single and young. Moreover, your noodle will atrophy."

"You know I tried once, Doc, but I couldn't stand the dragon mouth. I'll stick to the tube until I leave."

"Humby, I've got a question for you. When are these restrictions going to stop? No girls in the jeep since Noback died. Soon I hear no girls in the Q., only the Officers' Club on Saturday nights. Is the Deputy still blowing smoke up the Colonel's ass?"

"Yes, he is. You're right. Starting Monday, even on weekends, I am directed to allow no girls in the Q – only in the club where the Deputy can leer, the prurient SOB."

"He's crazy. He's driving everyone off the compound, at least those of us not enamored of the tube."

"Thanks, Doc."

Humby, an excellent student at West Point, didn't drink, smoke, read, or play cards or sports. After duty, he ate and reclined on the sofa before his innamorata, the television, which appeared to satisfy his total needs. But even more aggravating to the Deputy, a regular army officer, but not a West Pointer, was Humby's tolerant, liberal outlook.

One evening a month before, the Deputy, frustrated by his role as Deputy, a full senior Colonel without real authority, drank too much Scotch. Approaching Humby, sprawled out on the sofa in front of the tube, the Deputy exploded, "Is that what they taught you at West Point, Lieutenant?"

"What, Sir?" Humby asked quizzically.

"Sit up like a man!"

Humby sat up slowly, his eyes saturated with hatred. Henceforth, Humby whispered froward thoughts into the Colonel's ear to counter the "smoke the Deputy blew up the Colonel's ass."

When Humby closed the door, Dr. Houghton lay back. He ignored the steady ache in his right shin. Unconsciously cradling that sick member, Dr. Houghton formulated a tentative strategy for himself and Beautiful Flower. Since the Deputy would soon lock the gate to Korean national females, Reg would require a house outside the detachment. Perhaps, like Mr. Cameron, he too should purchase or rent a tile-roofed cottage in the village for the next seven months - a paper house.

As he drifted toward sleep, Reg was determined to construct a pleasure-dome like Kublai Khan, a Xanadu......Coursing under Tae Bat, the village at the bottom of the hillock on which the high-fenced American K-MAG detachment sat, he saw a sacred stream burst into a mighty fountain. Like Alph, this sacred rill meandered away from the village ending somewhere in a sunless sea. His pleasure-dome would rest beside the fountain. Soon the imagery changed and the Emperor Qianlong, in Tae Bat, sat in front of Xiang Fei, the Fragrant Concubine, pleading with her and offering her an imperial green jadeite Persian pepper. Next he observed Beautiful Flower sitting unseen inside an amaranth chamber. She resembled Xiang Fei, the fragrant concubine.

Suddenly this blissful scene was disturbed by Captain Chang beating the "Christ" out of Lieutenant Ahn. He kicked him in the shin repeatedly. It was still not clear why. Next, Dr. Houghton watched his right shin swell to watermelon size. Then they placed him on a steel table in an operating room.

Sweating and exhausted, Dr. Houghton awoke for a few minutes as painful impulse after impulse flowed from his right shin. He took two codeine tabs and finally fell into a very deep sleep.

A jolly Miss Pak arrived late, once again, that early April afternoon, carrying a red carnation. She wore amaranth leather pumps to match her miniskirt and a white silk festooned tuxedo shirt; her black hair sheened in the mild sun of early spring. The gold Happy Bag around her neck nestled conspicuously among the silk ruffles on her shirt. The sun, the true critic of beauty, revealed Beautiful Flower to be flawlessly complexioned except for the five tiny freckles which, already, the non-freckles medicine had partially erased. Moreover, in the mini-skirt, Dr. Houghton thought her legs now looked quite straight. After Beautiful Flower changed from her Western pumps into her Korean rubber shoes, they strolled along the road to Mr. Cameron's home in the village instead of taking the short cut across the rice paddies.

Mr. Cameron was watching the Deputy, who in turn observed the front gate with his powerful binoculars from his position on the hill in front of his quarters. "The bastard sits there all day and watches, but I watch him."

"As long as he doesn't get a telescopic camera, what difference does it make?"

As yet, Dr. Houghton did not fully understand the Deputy's motive. Was it curiosity or prurience; or like Dickens' knitter, did he possess a small black book prefaced with the Ten Commandments? But what was clear was that, by the venerable Puritan ethic, the Deputy thought they were all adulterers or worse.

"You are right, Doc. Pictures could be dangerous."

"Let's just ignore him." But Dr. Houghton was concerned. In a rare moment of confession, the Deputy confided that if he were the Commanding Officer, he would court-martial all the married men who had Korean girl friends.

Dr. Houghton rejoined, "But that's ninety percent of our personnel." He hoped that as long as there were no arrant scandals, Colonel Bennet would hold the Deputy in check.

Cameron's Miss Pak and Beautiful Flower walked hand in hand, Korean style, as the "elder sister" explained more about the peculiar habits of American men.

Dr. Houghton observed the sun-darkened, elder Miss Pak, nearing menopause, and contrasted her with the nonage of Beautiful Flower. Korean girls reached menarche about seventeen, rather than twelve or thirteen as in the Occident, so a twenty-three old Beautiful Flower was biologically comparable to a nineteen year old western sister. Certainly the elder Miss Pak could advise her, for in her last twenty years, she had known a multitude of Americans. But Dr. Houghton was not sure the advice was suitable.

Cameron's Miss Pak was very fortunate that she found Mr. Cameron at the final moments of her business career. The day before she met him, she spent her last few won on a fortune teller who predicted "good luck." She had no dinner that night, having spent all her money. All this, Dr. Houghton knew, for he cared for her at the Clinic. Miss Pak was another Korean with chronic gynecologic problems.

On the outside, Mr. Cameron's tile-roofed home resembled the peasants' habitations except for the towering TV antenna. Inside the main room, a bed, sliding screens against the hungry spring mosquitoes, a television, tiny refrigerator and a portable record player all made this electrified room livable and sanitary, but not fancy. Many small items from the PX lay about. The house seemed to be a small scale imitation of America, totally different inside from the villagers' humble abodes.

"Sit down, Doctor."

Miss Pak served coffee and boiled white rice with kimchi and a few side dishes with pieces of raw garlic. They ate the sparse fare with chopsticks. After a polite length of time, Dr. Houghton suggested they "visit" the "house for rent" near the "sacred fountain."

They walked the ribbon-thin road to the un-rented house, out of view of the Deputy's spy glass.

The elder Miss Pak said, "This house for rent for ten months. You give Papason fifty thousand won. At the end of ten months, Papason gives you back the fifty thousand won. They call it key money. For two hundred and fifty thousand won, 625 dollars, you can buy the house."

Dr. Houghton and Mr. Cameron inspected the house.

Mr. Cameron, now a country squire, commented as they poked around. "It has a good cinder-block fence around it, and a tile roof. The beams seem solid. It's well constructed, electrified, and there's extra land for further building if you wish."

"There's no bath," Dr. Houghton mumbled. "It also needs a new porch."

"The fence will keep out most rodents."

The house itself consisted of one large room and one small room beside the outdoor kitchen. The small room was intended for a house-girl who was a necessity to protect against slicky boys as well as to aid in the domestic chores. Dr. Houghton realized that a small bathroom could easily be constructed adjacent to the main house. For a minute investment, he could transform this small edifice into his pleasure-dome, with Beautiful Flower the mistress. The larger room could be decorated in the Korean or Chinese style in crimson and gold silk with Korean furniture. Now he must convince Beautiful Flower.

Beautiful Flower suddenly spoke out. "I must return to the Tea House before the Madam too angry." She had lied to leave that afternoon.

"Please don't go yet."

"I am sorry. What you going to do me if no can work in the Tea House? I must goes."

Dr. Houghton walked her to the dilapidated bus that went to Chun Chon. He insisted she take money for her transportation and "expenses." He guessed correctly she had spent all her money on clothing for their three dates.

A perceptive Beautiful Flower noticed hope in his eyes. She sought the look of love, which is difficult to differentiate from desire, and thought it was probably there. She waved and laughed, still uncommitted, as the ancient bus bellowed and spewed a blast of brown smoke at the tall muscular American.

The following evening, Dr. Houghton and Lieutenant Ahn met her at the circle where they had arranged a rendezvous. She had slipped out of the Tea House at the appointed time. The three of them walked in the darkness toward their destination, a Chinese restaurant. As they passed a fortune teller's shop, he suggested they enter. "Why don't you have your fortune told, Beautiful Flower?" Dr. Houghton suggested not-so-innocently.

Dr. Houghton and Lieutenant Ahn waited outside, having pre-arranged this strategy with the venal hag. A few minutes later, an excited Beautiful Flower emerged, "She say my fortune soon very, very good."

Dr. Houghton sighed in relief. The ploy had worked. He now regretted bringing Lieutenant Ahn, since he no longer trusted him, but he still hoped that Ahn could, if necessary, help persuade her. He was not sure that alone, he could convince her.

Lieutenant Ahn was also not optimistic. "I don't know. Miss Pak is not a business lady. You cannot buy her. She's a Korean girl. It's a great shame for her to date Americans, Korean peoples think."

In the restaurant, Miss Pak and Lieutenant Ahn ordered Chinese noodles with small fishes and three types of kimchi. Dr. Houghton ordered rice with an egg on top.   With fast clicking chopsticks, Miss Pak and Lieutenant Ahn devoured their food with much slurping and smacking of their lips. They both spit small bones and other indigestible odds and ends onto the dirty Chinese restaurant floor. In the Officers' Club, Rome to him, Lieutenant Ahn could eat American food with a fork and knife politely and quietly. But he obviously enjoyed the noodles and kimchi and chopsticks much more.

When they finished, Dr. Houghton asked Lieutenant Ahn to translate fully his plan. Dr. Houghton wanted her to leave the Tea House, move to Tae Bat and be mistress of their new house. If she accepted, he would assure her well being. In the daytime while he worked, she could re-enter and finish college. She could then open a shop when he left. If all worked out, like Mr. Cameron's Miss Pak, she would be set for life.

Lieutenant Ahn translated, interrupted by her many questions. Dr. Houghton understood most of her concerns; Ahn's translation was unnecessary.   As the conversation proceeded, like another Captain from Boston three hundred years ago, Dr. Houghton greatly regretted Lieutenant Ahn's presence. He no longer had confidence in him. Henceforward, he decided not to involve Ahn in his affairs.

In translating her responses, Lieutenant Ahn summarized her unanswerable objections, most of which Dr. Houghton well understood. "First, she says village water no good and hot sun would turn her skin black color. Then she not beautiful, then what's she goin' to do? Second, she might fall in love with you, and then what she goin' to do? A man in America and a dead man are to her 'same, same!'"

After a long pause, Lieutenant Ahn whispered in his ear, "However, although she's very interested, she wants me to help extract money from you. She's very greedy."

236

Miss Pak understood the betrayal. She stared at Lieutenant Ahn in disbelief, then in open hatred, before she lowered her head in misery - having lost face.

Dr. Houghton recognized the opportunity. He raised her head gently, looked into her eyes and said in Korean, "Beautiful Flower, do not cry. I understand, and I do not blame you. I, too, would do the same."

This soothed her. She wiped her eyes, and said, "Tonight, I many think. Tomorrow, I meet you at the Red Door Tea House at seven." She then said something in impolite Korean to Lieutenant Ahn that included the words "bastard" and "traitor." Finally she stood, smiled at Dr. Houghton, bowed, fluttered her eyes and with head high, strolled out of the restaurant.

As she walked out, Dr. Houghton saw a new glow in her sloe-eyed face and heard the scrooping sound of her nylons rubbing aginst her inner thighs. In that instant, he exploded with lust. He must have her. She was the promise-of-joy; possibly even awe.

"Good counsel has no price."
Mazzini

Chapter XVI
The Advisor

The morning of Miss Pak's decision, Dr. Houghton anticipated Colonel Kim's imminent arrival at his office. They had pre-arranged a follow-up visit to a small Korean Army Surgical Hospital in the far north. They had planned to go by helicopter but once again it was foggy; so they hoped to leave promptly at eight because the trip was a three hour jeep ride each way.

Colonel Kim arrived at five minutes past eight. "Good morning, Colonel."

"Good morning, Doc."

"Shall we go now, Colonel? It's a long ride up there."

"Yes, let's go."

"Sergeants Song and Morse have brought hot coffee and sandwiches for us. They also brought chains so as not to get stuck in the snow like last time."

Following Dr. Houghton, a scowling Sergeant Morse clambered into the back seat of the jeep. Sergeant Morse was distraught. These long dangerous jeep trips exacerbated his hemorrhoids. In fact, hemorrhoids were his bete noire, his wood cross, his living hell; no one could fix his hemorrhoids. He found this out the "hard way" after two worthless operations by two army "rear admirals." Without his donut and lidocaine on such a trip, Sergeant Morse believed he would die.

"Is there something wrong, Colonel?" Dr. Houghton asked at the Colonel's delay. Colonel Kim stood by the open jeep door, until his driver scurried over with his donut, transferring it to the front seat of Dr. Houghton's jeep.

Inwardly, Dr. Houghton almost chuckled but he knew hemorrhoids were not "funny." Dr. Houghton was surprised that accidents, especially jeep accidents, and hemorrhoids were the principal occupational hazards of American advisors, not North Korean bullets or dread diseases. So two months ago, he had presented Sergeants Morse and Song, and Colonel Kim with new expensive hemorrhoid donuts to assuage their suffering. The six and seven hour advisory excursions over unpaved rocky roads brought evenings of terrible travail to the sufferers, particularly to Sergeant Morse.

Dr. Houghton understood why Koreans' would have difficulty in prolonged sitting but could not understand why Sergeant Morse, a muscular black man, should have this affliction. Unlike the Koreans with their small flat buttocks, Sergeant Morse possessed two protuberant, fleshy cheeks that should behave as magnificent cushions. Instead, after a long trip, Sergeant Morse was barely able to climb out of the cruel vehicle, and he could hardly walk. At the visited units, the Koreans would imitate Sergeant Morse's gait the instant he was out of sight. Some of the Korean enlisted men assumed that all black men hobbled about with their thighs apart and buttocks raised high.

On the return trips, knowing the donut was now marginally effective, Sergeant Morse would apply the local anesthetic lidocaine to his "rrhoids." Sometimes the lidocaine was not that effective; so he would end up half standing in the rear of the jeep. Once, Dr. Houghton observed an envious Korean driver pick up and fondle Morse's "golden" donut. A normally pacific Sergeant Morse flew into a rage and threatened to shoot the potential thief. Unfortunately for poor Morse, Dr. Houghton required Morse's experience to evaluate fully the Koreans' field medical capabilities and their enlisted training programs. So Sergeant Morse "had" to go. Fortunately, Dr. Houghton had buns of tempered steel; after these long jeep trips, he only experienced a buzzing in his ears and vibrations in his bones.

In an attempt to mitigate his suffering, Sergeant Morse often argued, "The Doctor takes too many trips. The Captain is working too hard. Why doesn't the Captain let them come here?"

"You know as well as I, Sergeant Morse, that the only way to find out what is going on in their units is to observe them. Their briefings are misleading or sometimes damn lies. The only way we can check is to see if they've actually implemented our suggestions. Today we'll find out if they did anything at this hospital over the last two months. What a deplorable situation. We, you and I, have the responsibility to make sure that the drugs and equipment we provide the Koreans are actually helping the patients."

Dr. Houghton paused before the final thrust. "On top of that, I have good rapport with our Colonel and even the Deputy. They allow me to bend the rules, like using my jeep for personal use. They also permit me to practice Hap Gi Do which has become my great privilege. They don't subject me to the usual Army nonsense, particularly since I cured the Deputy's bronchitis. In return for the special status, I feel even more of an obligation to do our job well. You too benefit greatly, Sergeant Morse!"

Bouncing along in the rear of the bone-rattling jeep, Dr. Houghton thought of the Inspector General's team that inspected the entire K-MAG Detachment the previous week. The team leader, a Lieutenant Colonel, was a sophisticated, surprisingly sensitive infantry officer. He spent considerable time with Dr. Houghton who in turn impressed him with his Korean language skill, the frequency of his field trips, the civic action clinic, and his intimate knowledge of the situation. But most of all, the Lieutenant Colonel appreciated his detailed monthly reports. As expected, the Inspector General's report singled out Dr. Houghton for high praise.

However, during their interviews, the inspector had placed Dr. Houghton in a precarious position. "Doctor, as you well know, in Korea, strange things occur. More particularly, older men lose their consciences and their sense of balance. The Korean girls seem to be irresistible. Moreover, the senior officers often drink too much. As the Doctor, you know the situation here, better than anyone."

If Dr. Houghton were to report the cold, unvarnished truth, with the Puritan ethic or even Army Regulations as the canon, he would have to admit the Colonel was a nice sot, the Deputy was a prurient spy and Major Norman was a troubled drug addict, etc.,etc. However, Dr. Houghton doubted that the truth would yield any practical benefits. Moreover, the truth would engender a punitive investigation. This would ruin morale as well as eliminate any chance for a "superior" on the inspection. Furthermore, Dr. Houghton would probably have to forfeit all his privileges. Finally there was the issue of doctor-patient confidentiality. He concluded that pragmatism was vital, although in retrospect, he termed it rationalization. At that critical moment, he also saw a vision of Beautiful Flower in a pleasure dome in Tae Bat.

However, he would not lie. He had promised himself that when he was at Harvard - no lying except under the direst circumstances. He responded truthfully, "No officer has contracted VD since I arrived. No officer drinks on duty. I would be lying if I said there were not a few problems, but I feel I can handle them here in my office."

That evening the Detachment received a "superior" on the inspection. In a festive mood, the Colonel and the Deputy drank to their usual excesses. Colonel Newton was not present to celebrate; he was temporarily in the arms of his "new girl," a big busted business lady, unlike Mary Lee. What would happen, Dr. Houghton

240

wondered, if there a sudden attack or catastrophe with the Colonels drunk or gone? Who would be in charge? The always sober, ever present Lieutenant Humbert could hopefully make the necessary decisions.

"Doc," Colonel Bennet glowed. "You really snowed the Inspector General."

The Deputy interrupted, "If the Inspector General knew you were a KILLER..." The Deputy assumed a fighting stance and attempted to kick Dr. Houghton in the shin. At the last moment Dr. Houghton skipped away from the Deputy who felled a bar stool with a loud crash. Dr. Houghton raised his hand and initiated a power chop, indicating with a flourish where it would land, resulting in a broken collar bone. The Deputy understood.

The Deputy continued, placing an accusatory finger on Dr. Houghton's chest. He exhaled a vile Scotch-laden miasma. "You, Sir, are a liar!" His speech was very slurred, almost incomprehensible. "I saw Miss Pak, the Governor's daughter in the Morning Glory Tea House, and what's worse, she turned me down for a date even though I'm a full colonel." The Deputy puffed his chest and raised his head high.

"Colonel," Dr. Houghton replied with a finger on the Deputy's chest, "You must withdraw your accusation. Mike said she was the Governor's daughter. Not me. Second, I will tattle. I will tell your wife that you are chasing the local girls. You should be ashamed. I never figured you for an adulterer."

The Deputy said, now serious, "I'm glad that you are chasing someone, rather than just putting down the money." He then added, "You won't mention this to my wife?"

Colonel Bennet belched; then roared with glee. He muttered, "Wife, ha!"

Dr. Houghton now faced Colonel Bennet. He was very happy on the Colonel's gin and tonics. "Colonel, you know the Inspector General asked me if any of the officers drank to excess, particularly the Commanding Officer."

"What did you say, Doc?" The Colonel asked, eyes a twinkle. After all this was his terminal assignment; he had little to lose.

"I said, 'No, during the day, the Colonel never gets drunk and falls down.'"

At this, the Deputy frowned.

"The Inspector General also asked if any of the married officers chase the girls. I answered that only the Deputy chases the Tea House girls."

The Deputy scowled.

Colonel Bennet concluded, "Doc, you're outstanding! Give the Doctor another drink." He smacked Dr. Houghton hard on his "hard ass."

As they headed north toward the hospital, there was some April snow on the mountains. The so-called roads were in post-winter wretched condition. As he peered down the mountainside at the descending narrow road-ribbon, Dr. Houghton realized the slightest driving error by Sergeant Song would plunge them all to an instant death. Often the road abruptly ceased to exist, as if designed by a North Korean. Moreover, gullies and arroyos alternated with the thick spring mud. Complicating the situation were the maniacal Korean military drivers. To forestall disaster, Dr. Houghton insisted on proper and frequent jeep maintenance. He rotated drivers at ninety minutes. After Sergeant Song, Sergeant Morse drove if he could tolerate the driver's seat; otherwise he drove. During these trips he knew that his life could end at any moment. This fostered a "why worry" attitude. Who knew what the morrow would bring? Yet, in only six months he would be returning to the United States. The seeds of parting were about to bloom even before he possessed Beautiful Flower.

They arrived at eleven and were ushered into the hospital commander's chilly, whitewashed office. The Commander, a Major, a pediatrician by training, was discouraged by the lack of drugs and equipment. Apathetic, he delegated his responsibilities. Two months previously, they had visited this hospital, which they agreed was in a sorry condition. At that time, Dr. Houghton and Colonel Kim had discovered that almost every post-operative patient had developed a wound infection. After an objurgation and a terrific slap on the executive officer's cheek, Colonel Kim had outlined the necessary changes.

The executive officer again presented them with a rather flimsy briefing. Sergeant Song whispered occasional translations into his right ear. But Dr. Houghton recognized the deception in the briefing and awaited the inspection.

With the briefing concluded, they walked over to the jeep and gobbled Sergeant Morse's superb Virginia ham and mountain Swiss sandwiches on fresh dark rye. Both Colonel Kim and Sergeant Song relished them and smacked their lips in appreciation.

Dr. Houghton was delighted that Colonel Kim was now all business, unlike his former self when he conspired with the hospital commanders to conceal deficiencies. Dr. Houghton was especially pleased with the sandwich lunch, which contrasted with the previous two-hour banquets in which the Koreans attempted to

242

intoxicate him and compromise his critical faculties with rice wine. Today Dr. Houghton only tagged along, providing encouragement and support for Colonel Kim's new attitude. Recently, Dr. Houghton mentioned the quality of Colonel Kim's work to General Lee who then praised Kim publicly. The praise was legit but the two of them began to sound like a mutual admiration society. Dr. Houghton thought he better not overdo it.

Colonel Kim wished to examine the wards first. The ward physician presented the first case to Colonel Kim as Dr. Houghton observed rats scurrying across the floor. The ward physician concluded that the patient, dirty and lying in filthy sheets, was a case of bronchitis. Even from the foot of the bed, Dr. Houghton observed the patient was yellowier than a Korean should be.

"Don't you think he's jaundiced, Colonel?" Dr. Houghton asked in Korean. "I'd also like to see his chest x-rays."

The ward doctor said the x-ray was lost and did not think that patient was jaundiced. He looked at Dr. Houghton condescendingly, suggesting that the patient was "mongoloid" and hence yellow.

"What do you think, Colonel?"

"He's jaundiced; there is no question about it." In harsh, impolite Korean, the Colonel asked the ward physician if he were color blind.

The next patient, a twenty five year old soldier, had been in the hospital for one month and carried a diagnosis of angina pectoris. Colonel Kim interrogated the patient for two minutes. A gentle pressure on the anterior chest reproduced the pain that started after blunt trauma to the patient's chest. The patient reluctantly revealed to Colonel Kim that an irate lieutenant had provided the force for the blunt trauma. Dr. Houghton concurred with Colonel Kim that if an x-ray of the patient's chest was negative, the patient should be discharged with a bottle of aspirin.

Colonel Kim then told the ward physician that the diagnosis of angina pectoris was ludicrous. The ward doctor, in desperation, now quoted a passage about angina pectoris from Dr. Beeson's Textbook of Medicine.

In Korean, a disgusted Dr. Houghton said, "Dr. Beeson was my professor at Yale, and what you say is untrue." The ward doctor skulked to a far corner, now publicly humiliated, without kibun, without face.

As they reviewed several other patients, it was obvious that many patients carried the wrong diagnosis, whereas others had received incorrect, not just inadequate, therapy. Some of the patients were not ill; their presence in the hospital suggested bribery or worse. All the doctors rapidly lost face, particularly the commander whose responsibility was to oversee patient care. "So far," Colonel Kim summarized, "no progress, the situation is even worse."

They went on to inspect the laboratory. The tiny room was cold and very dusty. While the Colonel questioned the technician, Dr. Houghton attempted to use the U.S. Army monocular microscope, but could not focus the instrument. The only conclusion was that the technician must be manufacturing laboratory results.

The pharmacy was nearly empty. Drugs such as penicillin, which should be readily available, were either absent or present only in small quantity. The only possible conclusion was that either the medicines were not ordered or were being stolen.

But at the generator shack Colonel Kim lost his temper. The generators were critical to the hospital since there was no commercial power. On the last visit, only one of the two generators worked. Colonel Kim instructed them to repair the other one. The x-ray, operating room, and the lights now all depended on this one generator. As they approached the generator shack, an ominous expression clouded Colonel Kim's face as he observed the shack's roof was partially blown away and had not been repaired. As a result, the brutal winter had further damaged the only working generator.

Dr. Houghton retired to a distance. He guessed that the mixture of Colonel Kim's inflamed hemorrhoids and the Commander's gross malfeasance would be explosive.

Colonel Kim was now in a towering rage. He grabbed the executive officer by the throat and started shouting in Korean. "You son of a dog......" As he screamed, the Colonel spat saliva which also driveled from the corners of his mouth. With a solid back hand, he drew blood from the Captain's lower lip. The Captain stood at attention as the Colonel continued cursing. Then Colonel Kim was suddenly quiet. He thumped the Captain on the chest, kicked him in the shin, and pushed him over. The unresisting Captain rose slowly to a position of attention. Colonel Kim then hit him with a deft right cross to the chin which knocked him down again. Dr. Houghton could hear the crunch of a shattered jaw. Finally Colonel Kim kicked him in the groin aiming at his undefended scrotum with the statement "you son of a dog, you are no better than a traitor."

Dr. Houghton understood it all. His Korean was improving.

Colonel Kim then turned to the Major and said, "I'll be back in two weeks. If this place is not fixed by then, I'll court-martial you and him." He pointed to the downed Captain.

Colonel Kim called to Dr. Houghton, "Let's go." In the jeep, he rubbed his right fist. "That's the only way to get action."

Three hours later passing through Chun Chon, Dr. Houghton said, "Colonel, I'm going to go to my Hap Gi Do class. Sergeant Song will take you back. I'll call you tomorrow."

Dr. Houghton entered the exercise hall mentally exhausted. But when he saw his fellow pupils and the smiling instructor, to whom Dr. Houghton bowed, he called up some "piss and vinegar." After all he only sat in the jeep; he didn't do anything. "Get over it" he told his rattled bones.

The instructor rapidly put him through the warm-up exercises and the moves for his Red Belt examination the next day.

Finally, Dr. Houghton prepared for the day's free fighting. Instead of conserving energy for tomorrow's examination, he called on his adrenal reserve. Free fighting intrigued him. He was learning how to look in his opponents eyes, and anticipate their moves. Like boxing, he enjoyed the controlled violence, the clash of two trained wills. But unlike boxing, the degree of skill was potentially much greater. His opponents were generally the three second degree Black Belts or Mr. Yun, recently promoted to fourth degree Black Belt. They rotated off Dr. Houghton until he called for a stop. Now in excellent physical condition, Dr. Houghton often continued for twenty minutes unless he was kicked in the right shin which would paralyze the leg and force him to stop. The sensory nerve had been damaged.

In recent days, he had studied two fancy rotary kicks for an emergent attack on his head. His favorite was the low swing-kick. At the instant before his opponent's high kick made head contact, he would spin around, lowering his body, and bring his right heel around four inches from the ground in a 300 degree arc, making hard contact with his opponent's ankle. If done properly his opponent would fall. He had practiced this kick hundred's of times.

His first opponent was Mr. Ro, a second degree Black Belt, who, although only 5' 4" could jump over small mountains. After five minutes of inconclusive sparing, Mr. Ro achieved only a small advantage. Then Mr. Ro smiled and leaped high into the air. The moving foot was only inches from Dr. Houghton's skull when he ducked under it into his swing kick. Mr. Ro, when he landed, was upended by a vicious heel to his ankle. He fell hard on his butt. Dr .Houghton towered over him, hand raised, ready to destroy a shocked Mr. Ro with a chop. As he glanced at Mr. Yun, Dr. Houghton received a smiling nod of approval.

Mr. Bak, the next opponent, also a second degree Black Belt, was only an inch shorter than Dr. Houghton. Generally at will, he could clobber Dr. Houghton. However, in the last week, Dr.

Houghton had performed more adequately. As usual, Mr. Bak overcame Dr. Houghton's best moves.

But flushed with his success against Mr. Ro, Dr. Houghton formulated a similar fate for Mr. Bak. As he backed away slightly, he could not exactly remember the apothegm about lightening striking in the same place twice. As with Mr. Ro, he waited for Mr. Bak to assault his head. Of course, in a real fight, this strategy would be useless if not fatal, but here in the exercise hall...... As anticipated, Mr. Bak did finally aim at his head. Again at the last moment, Dr. Houghton spun below Mr. Bak's raised foot and, with his own foot gaining a terrible momentum in the wide circular arc, hit Mr. Bak square in the ankle and upended him. Mr. Bak fell very hard and did not rise like a "rubber ball." Dr. Houghton glanced at Mr. Yun who scowled.

Then Mr. Yun himself came forward. Mr. Yun bowed and assumed his stance. Without a conscious plan, a tired Dr. Houghton in a daring opening, jumped high. Twisting to the side, he thrust out his right foot in a side kick. To gasps of surprise, the blow landed high on Mr. Yun's chest and knocked him completely across the room into the open arms of the other students. Mr. Yun, however, with total control, bounced high like a kangaroo and performed the exact same maneuver. He caught Dr. Houghton in the chest. The years of weight lifting and more recently the Hap Gi Do training allowed Dr. Houghton to absorb the blow with only two backward steps, thus avoiding a catastrophe.

Dr. Houghton was now exhausted. On just "instinct," he tried a high chop to Mr. Yun's neck which Mr. Yun easily blocked. Mr. Yun responded with a rapid series of low kicks, the first three of which, Dr. Houghton brilliantly blocked, but the fourth struck squarely on his injured right shin. He tried to conceal the pain. He immediately backed up and bowed, indicating he wished to stop. The pain was excruciating, and he could not bear weight on his right foot.

The final series of finishing exercises were a searing horror to Dr. Houghton who tried to mask his agony. Bowing to Mr. Yun, he limped out, after saying thank you to each opponent. Hobbling along the road, in a lot of pain, he was not unhappy.

He limped into the Red Door Tea House that night. The aspirin and codeine, or perhaps the decision to ignore the painful shin, helped. When Beautiful Flower walked toward him, he recalled that Lieutenant Ahn generally employed polite language forms with her but not to the business ladies or even some married Korean women. He thought this was very significant unless they were in cahoots and were extremely subtle. He rose as Beautiful Flower sat down and smiled.

"What did you find out about college in Chun Chon?"

"No can do. Government quota."

"Did you offer a bribe?"

"Yes; then college poo-bah say can do this year; part time can do. He say one course with fifty dollars bribe. Next year, full time."

"Too bad not full time," Dr. Houghton said, somewhat disappointed. After a moment he gently grasped her warm hand. "What is your answer, Beautiful Flower?"

"Maybe. But I stay in Chun Chon."

"No," he said. "You must live in the village, in Tae Bat."

She pouted and repeated her previous litany, "Village no good! Water no good. Soon face black. Then what you do? Maybe new girl comes. Then, what you going to do me?" Beautiful Flower continued to list her arguments in English but her tone was softening. "Also, no bath in village. No movies. I like Kendo movies very much."

"Beautiful flower, you come. We'll build a bath house for you. We can go to the American movies on the Compound."

"If I come, you must buy me a TV or I shall be very bored."

"There is no problem," he replied in Korean. The rest of the conversation was mainly in Korean

"If I come, I'll quit the Tea House in one week and move to Tae Bat the next week."

"That's fine and in the interval, we can make arrangements to rent the house and begin to decorate it."

"If I say yes, what will you give me now?" She needed a token of sincerity, a demonstration of good faith.

Dr. Houghton anticipated this and pulled out an envelope that contained fifty thousand won, a sum well over two months salary in the Tea House.

When she saw the money, she glowed with an expression of happy greed. She took the won. In Korean she said, "It's a bargain, but you must remember that I am a young Korean girl. I don't know American habits. I don't know sex. You must be gentle."

In the darkness, she led him through back alleys to an old house in which she and two friends shared a room. He removed his muddy shoes and entered the six by seven foot room, lit by a forty watt bulb. There were three quilts stacked in one corner and a small lacquered Korean chest of drawers. A dozen dresses hung on a wall.

Her two roommates were there. He knew Miss Chang who also worked in the Morning Glory Tea House. Little Miss Kim, he liked on first sight. She was a small, young, innocent girl, considered very plain by the Koreans. She was a skillful dress maker and supported herself by sewing in a small dress shop. Her family was poor and at age twenty-four she was rapidly passing the age of marriage.

Miss Chang was an unmarried mother of a little boy. The father, a farmer, wished to marry her, but Miss Chang's father was ill with tuberculosis. She needed her salary in the Tea House which she gave to her father. On several occasions, to pay her father's creditors, Miss Chang sold herself in filial piety. As a consequence, she viewed herself as an evil woman, a damned harlot and could never look anyone square in the eye.

With little Miss Kim smiling innocently, really embarrassed at Beautiful Flower's huge barbarian, and a melancholy Miss Chang, he sat cross-legged and waited. Beautiful Flower poured two tiny Chinese cups of rice wine and proposed a toast in Korean. She pulled out a small velvet box and opened it. She placed one thin gold ring on his second finger and the other one on her own. She closed her eyes.

Overcome, he kissed her gently. "I am very happy." Inside his ring was written in Korean, "With all my love, Beautiful Flower," and the date.

Little Miss Kim wept as did Beautiful Flower. Then Little Miss Kim applauded.

Soon Beautiful Flower and Miss Chang entered into a rapid, animated conversation in colloquial Korean. They talked of future plans and good fortune. Dr. Houghton, now ignored, turned to little Kim and showed her his black swollen right shin.

She examined the injury with grave concern and then said in Korean, "Take off your trousers."

"Beautiful Flower, Miss Kim wants me to take off my trousers."

"There's no problem," she answered.

Though embarrassed, he took off his trousers. At first she gazed on his legs with horror. "Monkey," she pointed and broke into laughter.

"No," he replied in Korean, "mink." His legs were really not that hairy - average.

Then Little Kim began the first of her many shin massages. Her small hands were expert. In a short time, he felt the pain dissipate as she continued her soothing magic. He decided he would ask her to be his house girl – to assist Beautiful Flower.

.   .   .

248

Lieutenant Ahn sat on the edge of the chair. He made frequent non-purposive motions of his head and arms. His beady eyes also darted about, revealing his crafty intelligence. But he still looked chronically ill with his thin, dark-skinned, hollow-cheeked face. Dr. Houghton had ordered Lieutenant Ahn to the American Hospital after Captain Chang beat him. He was diagnosed as having round worms, whip worms, and liver flukes. Dr. Houghton easily rid Lieutenant Ahn of the round and whip worms, and he treated the liver flukes. But, unfortunately, the flukes had already caused considerable scarring in his liver. Dr. Houghton estimated that Lieutenant Ahn's prognosis was between five and ten years, but had not advised him of this, only the facts as to the types of parasites and the damage they had done to the liver.

Dr. Houghton had called Lieutenant Ahn into the office because he heard persistent gossip and undying, indeed flourishing rumors about him. He surmised this babble often contained bits and fragments of truth. The tattlers whispered that Lieutenant Ahn participated in various forms of malfeasance, black marketing in particular. In fact, Dr. Houghton often wondered how Lieutenant Ahn could afford so many expensive items, like a Nikon camera and a powerful short wave radio, on his miniscule salary.

"Lieutenant Ahn," he began, "I understand you were rifling through the safe in the Command Post last weekend. Is that true?"

"No, Sir. I just happened to notice it was open, and I was closing it."

"But, Sergeant Morse, who was on duty last weekend, found you present with the safe open. What were you doing in the Command Post at all?" Dr. Houghton was angry now. The safe contained secret documents. He had checked with the clerk-specialist who swore he locked the safe. Colonel Newton confirmed this. Yet, apparently, Lieutenant Ahn had somehow opened it.

Sergeant Morse immediately advised the military intelligence people – MI - of the event. He suggested they interrogate the clerk-specialist's Korean girl friend who was also a friend of Lieutenant Ahn. They, rumor whispered, were involved in a cabal. At that time, however, the MI personnel were involved in an internal scandal of their own. They only performed a cursory examination after which they exonerated Lieutenant Ahn, mainly for lack of proof. The enigma of the breached safe was never resolved.

Lieutenant Ahn, in constant motion, nervously anticipated further questions, but Dr. Houghton was silent, pondering Colonel Kim's relevant admission about misfeasance in the Korean Army. While under the influence of excessive rice wine, he explained how

Korean Army Commanders supplemented their paltry salaries. The Korean Army gave the various Commanders large sums of money for food, equipment and all other expenses for the troops in their commands. A "typical" division commander with ten thousand troops might appropriate ten percent for his own pocket. An "honest" commander might take 7 percent; a "virtuous" commander less; a saint, nothing. However, egregious theft if discovered, led to charges of corruption, removal from command with loss of face, public censure, and total disgrace. A commander must, therefore, thieve delicately and in accordance with the principle of Aristotle's golden mean. Too much could cause disgrace whereas too little engendered familial destitution. Dr. Houghton wondered with a smile if anyone had published guidelines. If not, he should write a pamphlet entitled Defalcation – a Primer. It would sell well in Korea.

And yet, most Koreans agreed that the Korean Army, with its ten or fifteen percent "corruption," was near ideal. Civilian businesses in Korea also depended on intricate, balanced venality. So, Dr. Houghton was not too concerned about reasonable Korean black marketing. This was the "norm."

Moreover, many of the American soldiers bought Scotch, watches, and cameras at the PX and resold them through their girl friends to the black market with a large profit. The U.S. Army, consequently, rationed such items. The Army ignored the petty black marketing which was impossible to eradicate. But had Lieutenant Ahn done more? That was the question.

A gentle tapping at the door interrupted them. Colonel Kim poked his head through the door.

"Come in, Colonel," Dr. Houghton said.

Lieutenant Ahn snapped a brisk salute.

"Lieutenant Ahn, I'll talk with you later. You may go."

An agitated Colonel Kim sat in the proffered chair. Sergeant Song brought in coffee. With a quiver in his voice, Colonel Kim said in polite Korean , "Big trouble at the Evacuation Hospital. The Corps Commander, General Lee blew up." Colonel Kim rose, and flicked an x-ray in the view box. "What do you think?"

"It looks like far advanced tuberculosis to me."

"This soldier died yesterday," Colonel Kim said in despair. He wrung his hands. "He was in the Evacuation Hospital for three weeks before anyone took an x-ray. Also, remember that evacuation two nights ago?"

Dr. Houghton remembered because he had approved the transport by a U.S. Army helicopter of a South Korean soldier wounded by an infiltrator. "Yes. How did he do?"

"He also died. He arrived at midnight, but they did not operate on him until nine the next morning." Colonel Kim threw up another x-ray which showed a rifle bullet in the dead man's abdomen. "General Lee found out because he heard the helicopter, and he is very angry. He has all the doctors and nurses in the hospital confined. He is going to court-martial them all." Colonel Kim slumped back in his chair.

"I think that is unreasonable. In General Lee's defense, I agree that the hospital is not well run. The Commander is no good. He should be punished and perhaps the doctor on duty that night, but to court-martial everyone seems too harsh." Dr. Houghton observed time and again that the commanders would allow situations to decline gradually. Then they would respond ferociously when something peccant finally happened.

"Colonel, why don't you pacify the General? Tell him you'll conduct an investigation. Assume responsibilities for the hospital for a few days. Find out what is wrong, and then make a report to General Lee."

"Yes, you're right. I'll do just that. There is no sense in court-martialing the nurses." Colonel Kim, relieved with the new plan, said, "I'll see you later. I've got a meeting with General Lee. I hope to come out of the meeting with both testicles."

"Good luck!"

Colonel Kim scurried off. On seeing General Lee, Dr. Houghton knew that Colonel Kim would tremble like a leaf on a windy day. Unlike Americans, Koreans shook more than they sweated. They had sound reasons for being afraid of the generals.

That night, dreaming of the upcoming Hap Gi Do exhibition match in about three weeks, he heard a thunderous pounding. As he staggered toward the door, partially asleep, he continued dreaming of missed blocks and punishing blows. Dr. Houghton had a queer habit of reviewing his errors time and again. He then reconsidered all the alternatives through the retro-spectroscope and arrived at a better course of action for the future. He did this while both awake and asleep.

At length, after considerable violence was done to his door, he opened it a crack. Not certain where he was and exhausted from the day, he slowly departed from the dream world to observe a hand insinuate its way toward his light switch. The light snapped on. First Mike, then Colonels Bennet and Newton, Major Norman, and Mr. Cameron charged into his bedroom like angry bulls. They were plastered. Soon Lieutenant Humbert appeared in his shorts, awakened by the uproar. Lieutenant Ahn and Captain Chang arrived

251

in Korean long johns. Only the Deputy was missing. Mike wore only jockey shorts; the Colonel, boxer shorts, boots and a cowboy hat. Major Norman wore a far-away look. Mike said, sharp and aggressive, "We were at the club; we even brought Mr. Kim."

"Why are you wearing binoculars, Mike?"

"I'm the Deputy."

Colonel Bennet laughed. He knew everyone detested the Deputy's spying and yet he continued to tighten the detachment restrictions. The Officers' Club was now a tomb, populated by an occasional intoxicated "cowboy," or a sober Lieutenant Humbert in front of the television.

The Officer's Club bartender, Mr. Kim, dragged along unwillingly, recalled the crazy American laughter, gaiety, and irresponsibility in the Officers' Club over the years. Tonight's episode was really nothing much. Mr. Kim compared tonight to the time five years ago when Major Lester, bragging about its size, pulled his huge erection out of his pants and Miss Koo grabbed it. When Mr. Kim saw the monstrosity he almost fainted. Without letting go, Miss Koo pulled him out of the club to a standing ovation. Before she departed, she bowed. Another time a different Miss Koo shot ping pong balls out of her vagina to raucous cheering of the crowd. Mr. Kim did not believe it was possible but he also saw this with his two eyes. However, Mr. Kim realized that K-MAG gradually, like any good advisory effort, must work itself into oblivion. Dr. Houghton was the last Medical Advisor at the detachment. Soon Mr. Kim would need a new job.

Mike said, "We are celebrating. We came to toast you, our fine Medical Advisor."

But Dr. Houghton was in no mood for the revelers, the final gasps of a once wild, amoral detachment. He did not even know what they were celebrating. Moreover, they spilled whiskey and flicked ashes all over his room. He had his sleep to finish, and no matter how he tried, he never learned how to sleep "quick" as his father advised. And what was worse, for all the laughter and openness, the next morning, Colonel Bennet still thought Colonel Newton was a lazy whore-hound. The Deputy still chewed on Lieutenant Humbert. Mr. Cameron once again raised the finger to the Deputy. Mike still had no plane to fly. Also, the next day, Lieutenant Humbert enunciated further restrictions, by order of Colonel Bennet. K-MAG center was no longer an Army unit but a monastery.

The next morning at ten, Sergeant Morse said, "Major Mike is here to see the Captain."

"Come in Mike."

"Doc, I am sorry about last night. But I have good news for you on two fronts. First, I heard my sister is in complete remission from her leukemia. The Brigham folks worked a medical miracle for her. We want to thank you for introducing her into the system. We - my father, my sister and I - want to do something for you." At this point Mike started to cry.

Dr. Houghton said, "That is great news." He waited patiently.

Mike finally said, now composed, "We had given her up for dead. That is what our local physicians told us. Anyhow, that brings me to the second piece of good news. I have asked the Headquarters Comedian to cut orders for you and me for six days of R and R, beginning in three days. You and I will first fly to Bangkok for one day to see the imperial palace and the Emerald Buddha, then on to Hong Kong for two days to see the jadeite shops, Chinese gardens and all the other things on your list, and finally the best part, three days in Japan, to see the Japanese gardens, the Buddhas, Kamakura, Kyoto, Nara, Geisha and the other things on your list. I have arranged all the flights for us on Air Force planes; after all I have some pull. I have also arranged for guides for us, and we will stay at the best hotels. My family insists on treating you. Moreover, I will provide you with a couple of forbidden treats. Finally, my wife is coming from the states during your last day in Japan to spend a week with me there. You will meet her; she is a doll. By the way she is one-quarter Japanese."

Dr. Houghton also became teary-eyed. Finally, at last, at long last, he would see Hong Kong and Japan and the jadeite Emerald Buddha, the symbol of Thailand. Almost unable to speak, he said, "Mike, the trip sounds good. I will be ready."

Observing Dr. Houghton's emotional response, Mike added, "I talked to Colonel Bennet and General Samet about this. They thought this was an excellent idea. They think you have done an excellent job for us, and you deserve it."

That night in the Tea House, Dr. Houghton told Beautiful Flower he would be gone for six days but be back in time for her move into Tae Bat. He also said that he must rest his shin from the Hap Gi Do punishment; he could now barely walk. She scowled, but before she could inquire as to the nature of the trip, he said, "I hear from little Miss Kim your real name is Yi Non'gae."

After a very long pause, she said, "That is true."

"I know who Non'gae was."

Beautiful Flower looked slightly worried.

"She was an assassin. She killed the Japanese General Keyamura Rokusuke in 1593. True?"

In sophisticated Korean, she replied, "Non'gae was an accomplished and patriotic Kisaeng whom the Japanese General could not resist. Remember, Captain Houghton, the Japanese Shogun Hideyoshi was an aggressive, very wicked man who many times tried to conquer Korea. He killed many Koreans. Anyhow, one day Non'gae and Keyamura Rokusuke were gazing at the sea from the top of a cliff near Chinju. She grabbed the bastard and toppled them both to their deaths on the shore below. She is a Korean heroine. Some day I will take you to Chinju to see her bronze statue and the memorial to Non'gae. Will you come?"

"I would love to go to Chinju. I also want you to take me to the Golden Buddhist Monastery outside Taegu."

"I know that place. They have a famous amulet of the Buddha there."

"They do?"

"The amulet is a small jadeite Buddha - a symbol of the Buddha and an instrument of the power of the Buddha at the same time. The Buddha is present and absent at the same time."

"What?"

"This is very hard for Western people to understand. I will explain to you better soon."

"We will have fun on our trips, yes, Non'gae?"

"Yes," she paused for a long time. "You are not worried my name is Non'gae?"

He smiled, "Not too much."

Beautiful Flower smiled in return, flashing her perfect white teeth and plump lips.

Dr. Houghton's heart skipped two beats. He thought he had made an excellent choice. He also suspected there might be some unknown danger here but he was ready. Very soon they would consummate their relationship. Would he see apsarases, Chinese angels, or Western archangels a la Miss Galt? He thought of the Qianlong Emperor and Xiang Fei. He said to himself: Eat your heart out, Qianlong.

Mohammad said,
"Seek learning though it be in China."
Hadith

Chapter XVII
Bangkok, Hong Kong and Japan

Reg Hougton and Mike Kennedy landed at the secret U.S. Air Force base in Northern Thailand after a long flight from Yokota in Japan. Reg said, "Mike, there are so many B-52 bombers, here! Wow!"

Mike said, "Remember, the only reason you could fly here is because, as a member of K-MAG, you have secret clearance."

Reg said, "We must be bombing North Vietnam into the Stone Age."

Mike laughed, "That will be my job beginning next year when I return to 'Nam. But remember, you must not talk to anyone about this base. The U.S. and Thai governments have a secret arrangement."

"Mike, with this much bombing, why is the Vietnam War still so hot?"

"That is a good question."

At that point, a B-52 slowly lumbered down the runway, obviously heavily loaded with ordinance. The screaming noise from its four powerful engines made conversation impossible. At the very last moment, it lifted off the end of the runway, leaving behind four trails of brown-black exhaust fumes. Another B-52 lined up on the runway ready to roll.

Twenty minutes later, sandwiched between the B-52's, a small jet took Reg and Mike to Bangkok. On the way, Mike said, "We have a guide to take us on a tour of the Grand Palace Complex, which is closed to the public today. One of my Air Force friends is going to tag along. We'll go to the hotel first and then to the Complex."

At the hotel, Mike introduced Reg to Colonel Casey.

Colonel Casey said, "I heard you went to Harvard."

"Yes, Harvard College, '62."

"I went to the Business School, '52, but I came today because in my spare time I've been reading about Buddhism."

"Me, too."

Colonel Casey said, "I finally understand what the Indian Buddha, the historical Buddha, taught: Life is suffering, in part due to the passions. You need to understand that to see reality for what it truly is and escape into nothingness, Nirvana. The Buddha did not believe in gods. Yet here in Thailand they have protector demons, gaudy demons, lucky golden bird ladies and all the rest including the Bodhisattvas."

Reg laughed, "Great Vehicle, Mahayana Buddhism is much more fun – look at all the fabulous art it fostered."

"But is it true? They turned the Buddha's austere philosophy on its head, into paganism. How can the Thai nation call itself Buddhists?"

Miss Chulalongbang, the guide, bowed deeply to Mike, Reg and Colonel Casey with her hands palm-to-palm in front of her chest. She was ultra-polite and spoke fair English. She first showed them the sealed 180-foot high gold-covered Siritana Stupa which contained a few Buddha's relics, and then the rest of the complex including various gaudy demons and scary protectors. For some reason, Reg enjoyed the kinnari, the half-bird, half-women most. These six foot, gold-covered Beings apparently brought good fortune. Reg knew he must come back; he needed more time. There was too much to see and savor in a half day.

Mike said, "In Thailand, everyone is so polite. The Thai people hate waves – completely different than the hell-raising Koreans."

Reg said, "Or the Irish!"

Mike and Colonel Casey laughed.

Miss C. said, "I received special permission for us to enter the Emerald Buddha Temple."

As they entered, shoeless, they barely noticed the strong odor of sandalwood incense because right in front of them on a 20-foot raised platform was the four-foot sitting Emerald Buddha – made of solid green translucent jadeite. Surrounding and adorning the Buddha, there was finely crafted, glittering gold filigree in the under-platform, frame, and over the large hanging crown. A series of well placed spotlights illuminated this masterpiece of sculpture.

Miss C. recited the history and then discussed the meaning of the Emerald Buddha to the Thai nation. As he listened and watched her closely, Reg became choked with emotion. He understood the notion that the Emerald Buddha was both a symbol and had "power" to protect the nation, a fact that all "Thais believed." Reg reflected that Beautiful Flower said something similar: in the

256

Buddhist Golden Monastery in Korea, there was a small jadeite Buddha image that also had that "power."

"Would you like to go up close, Captain?" Miss C. asked.

"I can't fly," Reg said.

"But I received permission for you Captain Houghton to climb the scaffold; you can also take pictures if you wish."

Reg whispered, "Thank you Mike."

Two workmen wheeled in a tall scaffold which Reg climbed. When he sat down on the top and saw the masterpiece closely – comparable to a Michelangelo or a Canova or a Praxiteles or Phidias sculpture – he understood the Thai fascination. After all, the Western sculptors produced their masterpieces out of a soft common easily carved stone; marble. The Emerald Buddha, a single piece of jadeite, was extremely hard – only diamonds, rubies and sapphires were harder. You needed diamond drills to carve it. How in fact did they carve it hundreds of years ago?

Reg asked, "Where did they find such a huge stone?"

Miss C. said, "Probably in Burma, but we believe it was carved in Sri Lanka."

For a few minutes Reg gazed at the Emerald Buddha's serene face. Then, he studied the hypnotic eyes: Suddenly, he saw the right eye wink. He was absolutely certain. But he said, "Did the lights flicker?"

Mike said, "I don't think so."

Colonel Casey said, "Maybe, for an instant."

Reg continued to gaze at the Buddha's face. If the Buddha winked at him again, he would be ready. He would wink back. But after several minutes, nothing happened.

Mike finally said, "Doc, we have monkey business tonight."

Reg gave Miss C. a ten dollar tip and whispered in her ear. "You have shown me one of the great wonders of the world. Thank you."

Miss C. accepted the tip, sighed, smiled, and bowed deeply – hands in front in the polite deferential Thai style. The tip was equal to a month's pay.

That evening Reg, Mike and Colonel Casey had a wonderful Thai meal in the "best restaurant" in Bangkok. The waitresses were lovely and polite; there was a cornucopia of orchids, hibiscus and bougainvillea, and every imaginable fruit. The fragrances of jasmine, osmanthus, angel's trumpets and moon flowers were everywhere.

Mike said, "The ambience begs for romance."

Reg said, "I agree."

Mike continued. "Shall I take you to the entertainment district? You will see things that are not possible," Mike guffawed, "like the girls who can shoot ping pong balls."

Reg said, "I don't think so. I thought the Thai's were good Buddhists?"

Colonel Casey said, "No, I don't think so, either."

Then Mike said to Reg, "You will receive a special gift tonight."

Reg did not respond. He was not certain what Mike meant. He said "We leave for Hong Kong at ten tomorrow. I'll meet you at 8:00 AM for breakfast.

That evening Reginald Houghton pondered the days' events; he thought most of the spoliating B-52's and the pacific Emerald Buddha, both masterpieces of human skill and ingenuity. Moreover, the Buddha winked at him or was it just a light-flicker, an illusion?

Then, there was a soft knock on the door.

Reg opened it. There stood a thin but quite attractive Thai girl. She stepped in the room and shut the door.

"I am Miss Krathong."

Reg knew that word – it meant a nighttime micro-boat loaded with flowers and candles sent down the river to appease the river goddess for polluting the river. "Do you float?"

Miss Krathong said, "I am your gift for tonight. I have a magical body." She undid two buttons and her dress fell to the floor. She was naked underneath.

Reg thought she was too thin. Also, he was in a spiritual mode. This was the first day in months he did not exercise to exhaustion. Moreover, he was still wondering where they found the jadeite bolder and how they carved the Emerald Buddha over 200 years before. Reluctantly, he finally said, "No, not tonight."

"But, I show you Thai Magic Mountain sex, only in Thailand."

"What?"

"I will take you to top of Magic Mountain! I can also shoot ping pong balls."

"You must go."

Twenty minutes after a rejected Miss Krathong left and for the rest of his life, Reg wondered what Magic Mountain Thai sex was. He should have tried it.

At breakfast and on the flight to Hong Kong, Mike did not mention the rejected Thai gift. But he did say, "I received a wire from my sister. She is pregnant with her second child. A few months ago, we thought she was dead, but now she's pregnant. Again, we all thank you." Mike wiped his eyes.

Reg said, "I really appreciate your taking me on this tour. I needed to escape from Korea for a while." But Reg already missed the Hap Gi Do practice and Beautiful Flower.

The Hong Kong tour guide met them at the Peninsula Hotel in Kowloon. She presented a history of Hong Kong, the "Beautiful Harbor," as they rode on the Star Ferry across Hong Kong Harbor from Kowloon to Hong Kong proper. Then they rode up the cable car up to Victoria Peak. Reg enjoyed the impressive view of Hong Kong below and Kowloon on the other side of the Harbor.

Next, she accompanied Reg to the jadeite shops while Mike attended to personal business. As Reg walked through the shops on the Hong Kong and then on the Kowloon sides, he began to perspire; there were too many choices. But fortunately on careful inspection and evaluation, there were only a few truly excellent pieces. Well prepared, Reg had a jeweler's loupe which magnified 10 to 20 times, a Chelsea filter, a portable spectrometer and battery-powered 254 and 280 ultraviolet micro-lamps. He was quite confident he could tell jadeite from nephrite jade and the many counterfeits including dyed pieces. Majoring in chemistry with a focus on dyes was now "paying off."

After four hours of looking, he finally found two carvings in the Arts and Crafts store between the Star Ferry and Peninsula Hotel on the Kowloon side. One was a 12-inch tall jadeite basket of fruits carved from a single translucent jadeite boulder. The jadeite fruits had four natural colors: imperial green peppers, yellow lemons and citrons, red apples and purple grapes in a white jadeite basket. The carving was intricate, seemingly beyond human skill. The other piece was a 12-inch tall spirit of longevity, a happy old man, in translucent green jadeite with a brown staff, deep green double gourd and a large red-orange peach of immortality.

In excellent British English, the Chinese general manager agreed with Dr. Houghton that these were "lovely" carvings. Every piece was different since the carver never knew what was inside the stone until he "opened it." The general manager opined that jadeite carvings with three or four natural colors were especially valuable. The Chinese carvers were comparable to "Michelangelo, just on a smaller scale. Would you not agree Dr. Houghton?"

"I agree." Reg said. He and the general manager then had a wonderful conversation; they discussed solid-state jadeite chemistry and, after a few minutes, bantered English persiflage and puns back and forth like a game of badminton. Reg wondered where this man mastered his English; the general manager finally told Reg he received his master's degree in "English Lit" from Cambridge in the UK. Reg missed such interactions in Korea.

The manager asked for forty thousand dollars for both, but Reg bargained him down to ten. This was more than his annual salary as a U. S. Army Captain but Reg and his father had agreed he could spend up to twenty thousand on objects of art. Fully insured, they would be air mailed to his father in Boston. When Reg left the store, the General Manager thanked him profusely for his business. Then he said, "In Hong Kong we have the finest Objects of Art anywhere; you made two marvelous choices. We also have the most beautiful and accomplished women in Hong Kong. I know you like both."

Reg laughed, "You are correct." He winked salaciously.

In fact, the general manager was correct. Reg did love these jadeite carvings. He was hooked. They were valuable, difficult to craft, colorful, and would last forever, like diamonds. Many had associated Chinese mythology. Moreover, if properly displayed and lighted, they glowed, as if alive. Miss Ching at Harvard was correct. Moreover, Reg knew his father would appreciate the carvings, especially the "spirit of longevity." He strongly encouraged Reg to make "worthwhile art investments" while in the East. At that moment, Reg decided to become a jadeite collector.

Later that afternoon, Reg visited a classical Chinese garden with Mike and the guide. Reg enjoyed the round windows and doors, the zigzagged granite bridges over the streams and small ponds, and the colorful pavilions. But he had many questions. "There is something that puzzles me," he said to the guide. "Why are these bridges all zigzagged?"

She looked at him as if he were a moron. She said, "Evil spirits can only run after you in straight lines. Understand?"

Notwithstanding his ignorance of spirit behavior and other Chinese superstition, Reg greatly admired the omnipresent stone dragons, roaring lions and Chinese protector dogs. But, there was something aesthetically wrong with these gardens: Perhaps it was the concrete and granite manmade miniature mountains or the slight lack of neatness or perfection, unlike the jadeite carvings.

Mike said, "Before dinner, let me take you to the Bottoms-Up bar. You wanted to go there, to see James Bond."

Reg was profoundly disappointed at the gaudy interior, the very aggressive bar girls and the large number of noisy drunken U.S. servicemen on R and R from Vietnam. But you couldn't blame the soldiers. Everyone now knew that the war was goingly badly; moreover, no one knew the reason for continuing the war.

A Chinese banquet at the Peninsula Hotel improved his mood. Without doubt, this was one of the best meals Reg ever enjoyed. But food was not Reg's interest. He would never be a gourmet. He did not understand the Roman and Chinese Emperors who enjoyed "delicacies" like roasted Peacock's balls.

After dinner Reg also enjoyed the Chinese opera which he saw once before at Harvard as a student. In fact, he wanted to ask the female lead out on a date.

Mike started to laugh, to roar.

"Mike, you don't think she is accomplished and exquisite?"

Mike controlled himself just long enough to say, "Doc, the female parts are played by men in Chinese opera." At that, he totally lost control.

They returned to the hotel at 10:30 PM. After a quick shower Reg was incredibly energized. He was extremely pleased with his jadeite carving purchases. He pulsated with vigor. His shin no longer hurt.

Then, he heard a soft knock on the door. He was not surprised. He tied his robe and opened the black hotel door. There stood a stiking young Chinese woman with light make-up that reminded him slightly of the Chinese female opera singer. She also had gold pins and jade combs in her glistening black hair. Was she a Tang dynasty princess?

"Yes?" Reg said.

She stepped in. "I gift for tonight."

She then unbuttoned her red silk coat and dropped it. She was naked underneath. This young Chinese woman was his ideal of the perfect female shape. Reg guessed her measurements at 35-23-35, five-foot three; she was firm and well toned. She had no body hair except on her head and eyebrows. She had a perfect light complexion and not a single freckle or blemish, anywhere.

Reg vacillated.

She noticed and said, "Tight, very tight," and pointed to her lower abdomen.

Reg understood.

She spoke little English. He knew only four Cantonese words; please, thank you, good day and bathroom. But Reg had learned over 200 Chinese characters as part of his Korean studies so they could communicate somewhat.

Reg gave her the second bathrobe. When she was in the bathroom, Reg decided to slow down and savor this night.

261

Moreover, he would be an ingrate if he turned down Mike's "gift" again. So he "talked" with her in written Chinese characters for a while.

Her name was Miss Han. To Reg's surprise she worked in the silk section in the Chinese Arts and Crafts store, where he bought the jadeite carvings. She was twenty three. He asked for her identification card and she showed him. She was honest about her age; she was born in 1946. She also had a store identification card. What he could not find out was whether she was a "gift" from Mike or somehow related to the store. However, she did know he purchased two very expensive jadeite carvings in the store. He began to think she was a "gift" from the general manager. He would clarify this tomorrow.

He changed the topic. When they were discussing the Chinese opera, he mentioned that he enjoyed it, using the double happy Chinese character. He said he especially enjoyed the "climax."

At the Chinese character for climax, she looked intently at him and said in English, "No can do; too tired me. Next day, must work."

To Reg, there were suddenly overtones of adventure and of irony here: Was she a Chinese version of his Korean "Miss Han?" He paused for just a moment but Reg saw no danger. She was a legitimately employed healthy adult. Finally, he asked her to disrobe, so he could admire her face and figure again. He asked her to stand on a chair and slowly turn around. She complied. What a shame he had absolutely no artistic skills: how he envied Goya and Titian and Praxiteles and the other great capturers of the female form.

That night he again wondered if he was a magician for he brought out of *this* Miss Han, a very tight lady indeed, barrel spasms, contractions, suctions and other female sexual responses, repeatedly. He would never misuse the Chinese character for climax again. He now knew what it meant.

At three AM, before sleeping, Reg made a tactical mistake. He decided to tell Miss Han a joke; the joke about the three annoying house flies and the three martial arts experts; a Korean, Japanese and Chinese. It was very difficult with their limited common language skills, but he persevered. First, he told her the Korean was so fast he knocked one fly out; then the Japanese was so fast with this right hand chop, he cut the second fly in half. Finally, the Chinese expert moved his hands but the third fly kept flying.

Miss Han said, "What? Chinese number ten?"

"No, Miss Han. That fly, no more babies."

For a long minute, Miss Han pondered the joke and Reg Houghton. Then, she broke into loud, outrageous laughter. "Han Chinese number one," she screamed.

Reg told her to be quiet.

She banged on his chest. She started to bite him and, in the dim light, blossomed again into red-skinned lust. Somehow, she swallowed his weary sex organ with hers, and initiated another round of ultra-aggressive sex.

Reg was actually slightly worried. Although he was in superb physical condition, she undoubtedly maxed out her cardiovascular responses during her final status orgasmus. He did not want another catastrophe.

Finally slaked, she stopped. At four AM, they both slept.

At the seven wake-up call, Reg was exhausted, unlike anything he ever experienced in his years of wrestling, boxing or Hap Gi Do. He remembered hearing angels sing but when was that? He was bone dry; his hands felt like sandpaper, his mouth refused to make saliva and his penis was damaged and shriveled! Now, he knew what the Romans meant by "vagina dentata – vagina with teeth."

Lying in bed, he had his second epiphanous moment in Honk Kong. He decided that perhaps he did not want to be Shiva or Zeus, Pan or Priapus after all. Perhaps Aristotle was correct: moderation in all things. For about ten minutes, he worried that he might need intravenous fluids but after he drank the superb Peninsula Hotel coffee, he slowly emerged from his torpid state.

He gently re-awakened Miss Han, who slept quietly, like an angel. She now emanated a delicious fragrance, a subtle, enchanting aroma he never smelled before. When she awoke, she smiled and wrote in Chinese characters, "You, bad man; you climaxed me too much."

Reg laughed. He looked in his Korean dictionary for Chinese characters. He wrote, "What kind of perfume?" She did not understand. He wrote "You hear angels?"

She smiled and wrote, "Many Celestial Nymphs – Chinese angels - at climax."

Reg then wrote, "I give you tip."

She sat up and said, "No, thank you. I no Business Lady! I show you store card!"

Reg flushed, recovered and quickly said, "Tonight, come to Peninsula Hotel for dinner with me. I pay."

She smiled, "I come. Time?"

Reg sighed with relief, "Seven," pointing to the seven on the clock.

That evening, Reg, Mike and Miss Han dined at the splendid restaurant on top of the hotel. They looked over Hong Kong Harbor at Hong Kong, a spectacular view. A full moon lit up the city. Again Miss Han was surrounded by her unknown, enchanting perfume.

When he saw her, Mike said, "Doc, where did you find her? She is gorgeous."

"I thought you sent her, Mike, your gift?"

"No, I did not."

After another perfect eight course dinner, Reg said good night to Miss Han who wished to return home. Before she left, Miss Han smiled and gave him an envelope. Inside was a golden paper with red Chinese characters. It said, "Come store soon. I want see Celestial Nymphs - again; with you."

Reg glowed with pleasure. Fortunately, he had almost recovered, but he was not ready for another conjugation - a terrible pun.

When he returned to Korea, Reg found a wire from his Dad. "Reg: Jadeite carvings arrived safely. Your Mom loves them, too. Love, Dad."

Reg immediately wrote a letter to the Hong Kong general manager. He thanked him for the quality carvings and excellent service. He specifically told him how much he enjoyed the conversation, how much he enjoyed the food at the Peninsula hotel, and how he already treasured the jadeite carvings. And not least he thanked him for the "extraordinary gift" of Miss Han. He sent a copy to Miss Han who in the decades ahead became his contact in Hong Kong for buying jadeite carvings. In Chinese, he enclosed a personal thank-you note to Miss Han with two puns on the word climax. But it was only twenty years later that Reg found out the name of Miss Han's perfume; it was the aroma of the Japanese witch hazel flower. He subsequently grew a Japanese witch hazel tree in his back yard. Every March when he inhaled the tree's subtle flower fumes he thought wistfully of his brief enchanted time with Hong Kong Miss Han – of the jadeite, the climaxes, the Chinese angels and most of all, her rollicking response to his joke.

When they landed at Yokota in Japan, Reg said, "Mike, I can not believe the amount of U.S. Air Force traffic here."

"Reg, you seem to forget there is a war going on in Vietnam with five hundred thousand U.S. soldiers."

"I hope President Nixon's Vietnamization program works so we can leave Vietnam."

Mike did not respond; he did not want an argument. He thought we should play to win; we must bomb North Vietnam into the Stone Age.

The Japanese guide, a middle-aged lady, Mrs. Suzuki, in a conservative black and pale green silk kimono, greeted them at the Imperial Hotel. She was neat; every black hair, jade hair pin, and item of clothing was perfect. She seemed to float along with small steps. She bowed frequently and was incredibly polite. In fact, in Japan, every one was polite and helpful. There were no screaming Koreans or rude Americans except near the noisy bar-lined American military bases. The hotel lobby, although busy, was hushed.

Since she spoke excellent English, Reg said, "What type of perfume are you wearing? It is very nice."

She flushed slightly, "Japanese ladies do not tell secrets, but it is jasmine."

Mike echoed, "Very nice."

She added, "Japanese ladies use perfume, but just a little – to be, I think, subtle."

"Very nice," Mike repeated.

She said, "I heard you wish to visit Japanese gardens. So we will first go to Kouraku-en Garden and then Rikugi-en Garden in Tokyo, two of the ichiban – number one – gardens in Kanto area and also around the Imperial Palace where there are many very nicely shaped pine trees."

"Excellent," Reg said.

"But first I must change into guide clothes."

Both Japanese gardens were in many ways similar, Reg observed, with perfectly trimmed grass and moss, stepping stones, ponds, streams, small bridges and stone lanterns. Everything was arranged and organized to perfection. Unlike the Chinese gardens, the bridges did not zigzag and there were no dragons, lions or miniature stone mountains.

But what stunned Reg were the trees, especially the black pine trees. The trees were bent, curlicued and transformed into other unnatural forms. Some pine branches extended laterally for twenty feet or more, held up by wooden poles. "How did they do that?" he asked Mrs. Suzuki.

Mrs. Suzuki said, "With wooden poles and copper wires – starting when the trees are young. Some they also graft."

Mike said, "Like the Catholics. Start when they are young and flexible, shape them and they will be twisted forever."

265

Reg bent down and felt the moss and then carefully observed the huge colored carp in the pond; red, yellow, orange, gold, black, and variegated, all opening their mouths, begging for food. He said to Mike "I wish there was such a park in Boston. These Japanese gardeners have improved nature; they are in a sense like the great Western sculptors and painters."

Mike said, "I told you, Doc. Now you know what I mean." Mike added, "But unlike the Westerners, these guys are really creating – not just copying. They are the Einsteins of gardening." Mike smiled; he liked this comparison.

Mrs. Suzuki said, "Over there, we now go to the Tea House to see Tea Ceremony."

Reg did not appreciate the Tea Ceremony too much. The green tea was too thick and not pleasant. The ceremony was too long, too artificial for just a cup of tea. But the Tea House itself was intriguing.

In the next pavilion, Mrs. Suzuki said, "In there, we have the prize winning flower arrangements. Shall we see them?"

After a careful inspection, Reg said, "They are nice but slightly austere."

Mike retorted, "Doc, the British and we westerners just stuff a zillion flowers in a vase. That is not 'flower arranging.' This is." He pointed to the arrangements. "Moreover, as you have seen when you buy anything in Japan, they wrap or package it in the most artful way. They know how to present objects to bring out their characteristics or beauty. In Korea you are lucky to get a soggy sack."

"I agree."

For two hours, Reg visited an Ai Ki Do training facility, the Japanese equivalent of Korean Hap Gi Do. Like the Koreans, the Japanese black belts were very skillful.

As he watched the exhibition, Reg reaffirmed his determination to obtain his black belt. General Samet and his father encouraged him not to waste time. His father's motto was "Make Hay While the Sun Shines." But was it worthwhile to do this, to risk potential damage? Yes, it was. If he kept it up, he would have several "achievements" to show his father: the jadeite carvings, a black belt and there was still six months to go. He turned his attention back to the exhibition.

On the way to the Zentsu-ji Buddhist temple and the Kotohira shrine in Kagawa, they stopped at the Yo-Ko Museum in Saga which had a fine jadeite carving collection and a splendid azalea

266

garden extending over several acres on a hillside. Although they just missed the cherry blossoms, the azaleas were in full bloom – reds, yellows, and pinks. This was an overwhelming flower show.

The jadeite carvings in the Yo-Ko Museum were of the highest quality. Reg asked, "How did the museum acquire them?"

There was no clear answer by Mrs. Suzuki or the Museum spokesperson. Reg wondered if they were looted from the Forbidden City in 1900. If they were, he understood why the provenance could not be discussed.

In Kagawa, they first walked up the 785 steps to the Kotohira Shinto shrine; then in the afternoon to the Zentsu-ji Buddhist temple. Inside the dim shrine, Reg inhaled the sandalwood incense, washed his hands in the sacred water and enjoyed the environment, the ambience. Men, not women, especially sailors, came to the shrine and afterwards walked to the many inns and entertainment establishments in this area. They came for sexual stimulation before they went to sea or in other cases for rebirth and retooling. Mike, not the guide, told Reg that the finest "specialists" for these purposes were here.

In both the Kotohira shrine and Buddhist temple, Reg observed many middle aged men praying for sexual awakening or reawakening, or for celestial nymphs for themselves. Reg loved the ideas, the concepts. After praying, the supplicants donated money to the priests to lubricate the flow of messages to the correct spirits.

During his medical training, Reg saw many middle-aged men, impotent or uninterested, bored with their wives, unable to find a lover, demoralized, depressed and generally down. He would have recommended they come here, first to pray, then to donate - and finally to use the "specialists" in the local establishments. If anyone could help, according to Mike, it was these ladies.

Moreover, Mike argued, "Once you get your confidence back, you have a real chance at success."

Reg said, "Great idea."

In the shops outside the temple and shrine, there were many types of potency amulets. Mrs. Suzuki declined to enter these establishments. In one shop, Reg purchased a masterfully carved ten-inch Hinoki Cypress happy old man carrying a tall staff. The wood was stained with many coats of antique red varnish that brought out the old man's smile and the grain of the wood. Somewhat shocking, the head extended up in the shape of an erect penis with an anatomically correct glans on top. Reg thought this carving was probably one of the Eight Immortals, Japanese style, or possibly another aspect of the Spirit of Longevity. When Mike asked the little old Japanese sales lady who it was, she only laughed as if that was the dumbest question ever. But she did explain how to care for carving with special oil once a year. She then said it was "very important for a man to rub it once daily;" to forget to rub it would bring the "droops."

Reg laughed but, as he grew older, he remembered her advice and periodically did rub the glans.

She continued with Mike translating, "I will give you a special deal if you buy two more; I'll give you one free."

Reg declined, but when he looked back, he knew he was too often a "Scared-y Cat" or "Miss Goodie Two Shoes." He was worried that, if he mailed them back, the postal service would confiscate them. He should have just placed them in his sealed "household goods" when he returned from Korea. He was a fool for not buying these masterpieces of wood sculpture for a "song."

That evening they attended a dinner in Kyoto with two Geishas and a novice, a Maiko. Reg enjoyed their artistry but they were aloof and he could not communicate with them. The next day, Miss Suzuki explained, "They are not used to Americans, and if you pardon my frankness, the Americans sometimes behave not so good."

Reg said, "I understand."

The last day in Japan, Mike introduced "Doc" to his charming wife. She also expressed her personal thanks for steering Mike's sister to Harvard and the Brigham. She said, "We all love Mike's sister. She is an angel. God bless you."

Reg said, "Thank you for arranging the tour with Mrs. Suzuki. She was excellent."

After a pleasant lunch, Mike took Reg aside.

He said, "I hope you enjoyed our trip."

"Yes, I loved it. Thank you so much."

"But, you missed the best part of the East, here in Japan."

"What was that?"

"Japanese women! Remember what Lafcadio Hearn said, 'The best of Japan is its women.'"

"Perhaps another time," Reg said.

"If you ever have a chance, ask General Samet about this."

"I will, Mike. Thanks."

On the return trip to Seoul, Reg reviewed the trip. He was still awed by the jadeite Emerald Buddha in Thailand. He was overjoyed with his purchase of the two jadeite carvings in Hong Kong and the manager's gift, Miss Han, although she almost killed him after the joke. Telling jokes in the East was potentially a dangerous activity.

In Japan, he didn't know where to begin his reflections. Having just visited a number of Shinto and Buddhist temples, he started with the Buddhist notion that the Self is just a series of quickly passing images and events and illusions, one separated from another. Underneath is the hard reality of suffering and impermanence and samsara. This trip, especially in Japan, was an example of evanescent images and events; he experienced the haunting temples, glorious gardens, polite Japanese and aloof Geisha. He involuntarily contrasted these with the B-52s lumbering down the long Thai runways on their way to North Vietnam. Although Reg had sidestepped the war, he too, like the students in America, questioned what we were accomplishing in Vietnam.

But Reg regreted the one "miss": that he had no real contact with Japanese women. He saw them on the streets and in the shops: neat, well dressed and polite. The Japanese certainly understood how to interact with each other - so different from the pushy, aggressive Koreans. But he did not understand what Mike was talking about. He would talk with the sophisticated General Samet when he had the chance.

At the end of the two hour flight, he saw Korea emerging from the clouds. He remembered what his Aunt Freda often told him, "Gird your loins, Kiddo." Tomorrow, he would be back in the Hap Gi Do Hall. He knew a Black Belt would be a clear accomplishment. What else could take from Korea?

"To love her is a liberal education."
Of Lady Elizabeth Hastings,
Sir Richard Steele

Chapter XVIII
The Paper House

With newly promoted Colonel Kim, now General Kim, Dr. Houghton returned from another long advisory trip north, this time by helicopter. General Samet had repeatedly told him, "Doc, you have a colonel's billet; you should travel as much as possible on the choppers." Henceforth, Dr. Houghton scheduled his trips whenever feasible to avoid the dangerous and unpleasant jeep journeys. By doing so he could return to Chun Chon before three. That particular June evening, after a long practice session at the exercise hall and a short but salubrious nap, he met Mr. Cameron at seven-thirty for dinner. Mr. Cameron waited at the bar of the officer's club.

"Hello, Doc," Mr. Cameron saluted as Dr. Houghton's eyes adjusted to the dim interior.

"Hello, Mr. Cameron. Hey Mike." Dr. Houghton returned the salute.

"Gin and tonic," Dr. Houghton said to Mr. Kim.

"Mr. Cameron tells me you're going to have a home in downtown Tae Bat," Mike initiated the teasing.

"Yes, Mr. Cameron and I are going to the village tonight to make the final arrangements. Let's go eat, Mr. Cameron, Mike, before they close up."

Everyone else had finished eating when they walked to the officers' dining room. In the corridor between the bar and dining hall, Mike surveyed the village of Tae Bat in the valley below the fenced-in detachment. "Not downtown Toyko!"

"Mike, let's be honest," Dr. Houghton said. "I am not a monk. On July 1, 1970 I return to the Brigham to finish my last year of residency training where I will become a monk. I now have a chance for some fun. You told me you think Beautiful Flower is my best hope. I can not live alone; but I do not want to hire a Business Lady. You understand I hope?"

"I do," Mike taunted, "but I never figured you for a villager, Doc. I wouldn't mind, but you won't play shuffle-board with me anymore."

Dr. Houghton laughed. "You SOB; you won enough to put your son through college." This was an exaggeration; in recent months Mike often lost.

"No," Mike said. "You wouldn't catch me in the village in the spring. Why the odor alone...." Mike referred to the use of night soil, human excrement, to fertilize the fields and rice paddies. In Korea in the winter, the Koreans "saved" all the human excrement in the "shit holes" in their outhouses. In the spring and summer the "honey truck" drivers collected it and the peasants spread it out over the fields and rice paddies. As the strengthening sun heated the ground, a smelly, visible miasma rose off the fields. To the Koreans this was a necessary part of the cycle of life. How else would the rice grow? In fact, the children laughed and clapped when the honey truck drivers came. Alas, if your jeep ended up behind a honey truck, you were in for a sickening ride. However, like dragon mouth you gradually learned to ignore the pervasive odor of human ordure in the spring and summer. What else could you do? Put a "clothespin" on your nose?

"But Mike," Dr. Houghton said, "one of nicest flowers of all, the lotus comes out of the muck at the bottom of the pond."

"Yes," Mike retorted, "but the pond doesn't stink."

In Japan, Colonel Casey echoed Mike's dim view of Korea. He opined, "Korea is known for a few things; venereal diseases, lying, pigs, frogs, lice and scabies, and most of all shit."

It was hard to argue with such sentiments so Dr. Houghton retreated. "But Mike, Miss Yo is bragging that you spent an evening or two down there - in the village."

Mike ignored the comment. He continued, "Those paper houses down there in the village are awful, beyond belief, with the paddy rats, the snakes, the bugs, and soon the mosquitoes and frogs."

Dr. Houghton realized the conversation was spinning out of control. He said, "In some cases you're right, Mike." He remembered vividly Major Norman's hovel. "But some are nice. Look at Mr. Cameron's and Miss Judy's. I'll invite you down to mine, when and if I get it fixed up."

Mike said, "By the way, Doc, whatever happened between you and Miss Judy? The Colonel said you were constant companions before you went out into the field, but now she doesn't work in the clinic. What happened?"

"Her Yo Bo, Sergeant Lewis, disapproved of her working in the clinic, so she stopped. Miss Judy and I are friends and co-workers, not lovers. There was no monkey business between us."

"She is a good looking woman," Mike said, almost wistfully, totally inconsistently. "Doc, you should have...." Here he echoed Colonel Newton's advice.

Dr. Houghton pondered this. He said, "Perhaps I should have." After a longer pause in which he thought of her son in the United States, he said, "She certainly is a splendid woman."

"Doc, all jokes aside, I have reservations about the village, but I must say if I had to choose anyone, it would be Beautiful Flower."

"Thanks Mike." Dr. Houghton deflated with relief. "One thing, Mike, if you would; I don't want the Deputy to know of my activity in the village. His binoculars do not reach my house from the compound."

"Good luck, Doc."

"General Samet is on the phone, Sir."

"Hello, General."

"Doc, I have sent my helicopter for you. I want you to come down here to Seoul with your medical bag, now."

"But I....."

"No buts!"

"I will brief you on the problem when you come. This matter is absolutely confidential; do you understand?"

"Yes, General."

General Samet met him at the helipad in Seoul forty five minutes later. He was clearly distraught. "Doc we have a problem and I want your help."

"Certainly."

"You must not talk about this to anyone."

"I will not."

"A senior Korean army officer has a health problem." Dr. Houghton later found out this man had been selected to be the new Korean Army Chief of staff - the second most powerful man in Korea after President Park. "I want you to see him and decide about appropriate therapy if you can."

General Samet's driver drove them the two miles to a hotel next to the Korean Army headquarters. Surprisingly General Samet said nothing more. They entered the hotel and rode the elevator up to the top floor, Suite 1002. General Samet knocked and a wiry middle aged man in civilian clothes answered the door. General Samet said, "This is Doctor Houghton, our best. He was trained at Harvard, Yale and the Brigham in Boston."

The un-introduced man said in fair English. "I have a problem."

General Samet said, "I will wait here while you two go into the bedroom."

Dr. Houghton and the Korean officer went into the bedroom. In a corner sat an attractive young woman who looked out the window at Seoul. She was not introduced and said nothing.

The Korean officer said, "Let me show you." He lowered his trousers and removed his boxer under-shorts very carefully.

Dr. Houghton was shocked. The man's penis, scrotum, and groin, all the way around to the area around his anus were red, inflamed, macerated and seeping serum. His pubic hair was also absent. It looked like a terrible case of localized poison ivy.

Dr. Houghton said, "Where did you contact this rash?"

"I don't know."

Dr. Houghton thought this was contact dermatitis. "Did you or anyone rub anything on this area?"

The Korean officer said, after a long look at the young woman, "I went to the House of Penis-I don't know the translation." He mentioned a Korean word.

Dr. Houghton looked it up in his dictionary – refreshment, refurbishment. He said, "So you went to the House of Penis Refurbishment."

"Yes."

Dr. Houghton almost began to laugh. He remembered his father often talked about old cars that required work - he said they needed "body and fender work." In later years his father applied this expression to anything that needed work. Did this Korean officer really need penis refurbishment? His father would convulse with laughter at this. But Dr. Houghton bit his tongue, trying not to go off on a tangent. Moreover, laughter might get him shot. "When did you go and what did they do at the House?"

"They gave me a message with special oils and refurbished my penis. Two days later the rash began and all the pubic hair fell off. I'm now bald. I have a bald penis and scrotum." He scowled.

Dr. Houghton saw the young woman smirk. He said, "I am almost certain you have what we call contact dermatitis. Someone put something on your penis and scrotum which caused an immunologic reaction. It looks like poison ivy."

"What?"

Dr. Houghton looked up poison ivy in his dictionary and showed the Korean word to the officer.

On a guess, Dr. Houghton said quizzically, "Would anyone wish to harm you? Could this have been done on purpose with a sensitizer?"

273

The Korean officer looked knowingly at the young woman who clearly understood the question. Dr. Houghton had raised a real possibility in their minds. But with focus the officer said, "How shall we treat this?"

Dr. Houghton outlined a course of oral steroid therapy with prednisone over fourteen days. He then said, guessing, "General, you must be careful not to re-expose yourself to the contact agent. I would never go back to the House of Penis Refurbishment if I were you. Use a shower and ivory soap on your penis; that's all. In fact, "Why did you go in the first place?" Dr. Houghton was growing confident and bold.

The General said in Korean "I had a mild case of the droops, the softs, the dwindles. So I went. I will go never again except to punish....." He abruptly stopped.

Dr. Houghton understood the threat.

Soon after, without a thank you or an acknowledgement from the Korean General, General Samet and Dr. Houghton rode back to the helipad. General Samet said, as Dr. Houghton boarded, "Thank you. Remember we will never talk about this again since it never happened."

However, two weeks later, General Samet mentioned in passing that the steroid therapy worked like a "charm" and that the "evildoers" were caught and punished. He would say no more. However, many years later he mentioned to Dr. Houghton that "two Korean angels had looked out for him when he was in Korea - Lieutanant General Lee and the Army Chief of Staff - in repayment for his 'medical magic.'"

Mr. Cameron and Dr. Houghton walked leisurely across the rice paddies to the village. Mr. Cameron, with his silver-gray hair, possessed a natural dignity. This was buttressed by the certitude of wealth; he had recently inherited several million dollars from his father. As they climbed over the rice paddy dikes and levees in the moonlight, Mr. Cameron seemed grotesquely out of place.

"You know, Mr. Cameron," Dr. Houghton always addressed him formally, "the contrast between the lighted K-MAG detachment and the dark moonlit countryside seems more marked tonight, sort of a small piece of America floating in a rice paddy sea."

"I know what you mean," Mr. Cameron replied.

Although of two different generations, Mr. Cameron felt a peculiar bond existed between them, perhaps related to their both being financially independent. After a sprightly caper across a small stream, Mr. Cameron said, "I don't like Mike's taunts and barbs. Doc, as I said before, I have a commitment to the village. You're the only one who understands. My Miss Pak is a human being in spite of her past. I owe her a lot. I have never been happier."

Dr. Houghton understood these sentiments somewhat. He knew Mr. Cameron was not a sentimental fool. What Mr. Cameron did not approve, he made clear to his Miss Pak and everyone else. In return for his generous support, she was loyal and "serviced" him as the Koreans termed her behavior - an uncomplaining attention to his physical and mental needs. Such "service" did not exist in the occident. Moreover, Dr. Houghton knew Mr. Cameron was genuinely fond of the Koreans. The villagers and their senior elder, the Mayor, also sensed Mr. Cameron's attitude and came to rely on his counsel and judgment in certain technical village matters. Furthermore, there were times when Mr. Cameron permitted detachment trucks to help the villagers with construction projects. The only other person to do such civic action was Dr. Houghton with his civilian medical clinic. So when they walked into the moon-lit village, without exception, the villagers all bowed, saying "How are you, Honorable Mr. Cameron, and Honorable Teacher Doctor Houghton?"

Both Mr. Cameron and Dr. Houghton bowed lightly in reply.

But Dr. Houghton's motives were different from Mr. Cameron's. He hoped to catch a glimpse of the workings of the mind of a beautiful, intelligent female of another race, whose civilization extended back millennia. After all, she was a Yangban. He longed to observe her habits, play her games, enjoy her amusements, as well as confirm certain whispered imputations. Younger, and perhaps less mature, he thought that Mr. Cameron was not correct in his assumption that all men were essentially similar and potentially brothers. Dr. Houghton suspected and hoped that Beautiful Flower was really different.

As a child, though, Dr. Houghton assumed that all men were similar, that everyone would worship the truth. He now knew that men often dealt with each other dishonestly. So many diddled and cheated. A glorious exception was the practice of Western science and medicine where the standards of honesty were the rule. However, in Korea, the truth was not a priority – so there is, in a peculiar sense, less hypocrisy and serious prevarication in Korea since everyone knows the rules of the "dishonest" game.

With age, Dr. Houghton also recognized more and more human diversity. How could one deny the gulf between Einstein and the idiots he saw in the Neurology clinic? These were apodictic facts. Into adolescence, all sorts of weird and wonderful phenomena became possible; spirits, magics and wish fulfillment. But college and maturity crushed the unreal promises, particularly physics, chemistry and most of all philosophy, which were eschatological zeroes. Camus, Marx, Darwin, Freud and Nietzsche taught him the universe was not enchanted. A brief trial of mind expanders in medical school ended the notion of "consciousness expansion." Perhaps in the village in Tae Bat, though, he might discover some new mystery or, almost as good, a worthy challenge.

Mr. Cameron and Dr. Houghton found their respective Miss Paks with the owner of the cottage and a Chinese-writing notary. They removed their shoes and walked into the unpainted, paper-windowed home. After the ritual exchange of greetings and formal introductions, the elder Miss Pak said, "The agreement remains the same – fifty thousand won, key money for eight months. After eight months, the owner will return the fifty thousand won, about one hundred twenty five dollars."

"That's reasonable," Dr. Houghton said and pulled out the money as the notary concluded the written agreement in Chinese. Beautiful Flower translated it into Korean out loud.

"I didn't know you knew Chinese so well," Dr. Houghton said. Her skill was comparable to a running translation of Latin into English.

"I went to college for three years. I was an excellent student. Did you forget?" Beautiful Flower asked with an arrogant twinkle. Then, as if she were the captain and he the corporal, she said in not-so-polite Korean, "Please be quiet."

Beautiful Flower finished translating the agreement. The notary stamped it with his chop seal. Beautiful Flower and the owner signed it with their seals. The owner counted the money and left. Then the notary to whom Beautiful Flower passed some money, bowed and left.

As Dr. Houghton relaxed, Mr. Cameron pre-empted. "Doc, you'll need some screens for the mosquitoes. That's the number one priority. You'll also need my carpenter to put up a low porch up under the middle roof, so you can sit outside. And you want a bathhouse. I think it'll be more practical to build it of concrete with a Japanese style tile bathtub. You can heat the water like the Koreans do."

"Sounds good, Mr. Cameron."

"I will handle those construction projects for you. The final thing you will need is someone to stay in the small room all the time. My Miss Pak knows a deserted woman and her daughter, Sugi, who can come here when everyone is away. They can also perform household chores to help Beautiful Flower. If you don't have someone around all the time, the slicky boys will rob you of

276

everything." Mr. Cameron paused, "I'll speak to the Mayor and the village policeman and advise them of your presence here."

Dr. Houghton said, "Miss Kim, a seamstress is going to work and live here with Beautiful Flower some of the time. She will stay in the small room. Sugi will only be necessary when the two of them are not here."

Beautiful Flower said in English, "Tomorrow morning I move my stuffs here."

Mr. Cameron concluded. "I'll send my Miss Pak's Papason over. These things can probably be taken care of in two days."

Mr. Cameron and Miss Pak rose to leave for pleasures that within less than a year would be impossible. He was really "too old even now."

"Thank you very much, Mr. Cameron."

"You are very welcome, Doc. See you tomorrow."

Soon after, Beautiful Flower said in Korean, "Thank you very much." She kissed Dr. Houghton like a sister.

"I must go back to Chun Chon now."

"Why not stay awhile?"

"No, I must go. It is late."

"I have a lock here, one key for you and one key for me."

Dr. Houghton walked her to the main road. After about ten minutes, they waved down a mini-taxi. "Good night, Beautiful Flower. I'll meet you tomorrow in Chun Chon after Hap Gi Do."

The following evening they shopped for furnishings and decorations for the house and bathhouse. In the sprawling outdoor market, they purchased some rich silk embroidered with red and gold poppies and the Chinese characters for Double Happy. She chose a Japanese scroll of a geisha girl and several blue mother-of - pearl inlay vases. Dr. Houghton bought a magnificent yellow silk robe for himself with the Chinese characters for Wisdom all over it. The emperor Qianlong wore such a robe. Again, Beautiful flower wished to remain in Chun Chon. She was clearly putting him off. But on parting she said, "Come to the village in two days. We will have the House Blessing Ceremony and inspect the construction."

Two evenings later, he was hot and annoyed, screaming-angry after the day's advisory visit. The mobile unit was worse than the month before. Once again, General Kim beat another Captain, this time with an elbow to the nose. He broke the wretched Captain's nose. Dr. Houghton again told General Kim that he disapproved of such violence. But General Kim insisted that he must do it "to insure compliance."

Futhermore, at the exercise hall, Black Belt Yun expected an excellence in rotary kicks Dr. Houghton did not quite possess; the "play" that day was very rough and exhausting. For the first time in months, he was discouraged.

After showering in the detachment, he headed to the village to meet Beautiful Flower for the Ceremony. Beautiful Flower, Miss Chang and little Miss Kim awaited him at the door. The prospect of being surrounded by women after the constant interaction with men improved his spirits. To his amazement the bathhouse and other carpentry work was indeed finished and dry. But Beautiful Flower commanded graciously in Korean, "Please do not come in. We will have the ceremony outside." Beautiful Flower had hired a Korean witch, a mudang, to purify the "new" house of evil spirits and pernicious ghosts. The old wizened lady performed a few unintelligible chants, danced around helter-skelter, drank a lot of rice wine and then went into a trance. On emergence, she made salacious comments and performed a lewd dance, pointing and laughing at Dr. Houghton and Beautiful Flower. Her comments and dancing were gross exaggerations of the male and female sexual response, especially of barrel contractions. What did that have to do with ridding the house of ghosts and evil spirits?

Dr. Houghton finally said, "Enough, pay her and get rid of her!"

After the mudang left, Beautiful Flower said in Korean, "Go directly to the Blue Chamber." This was her name for the bathhouse. The small concrete structure was most unimpressive from the outside, but as he ducked through the low door, he marveled at the quick construction and the girls' decorating skill. The place was rich with the aroma of freshly plucked flowers. The geisha girl scroll was tastefully placed. The powder, bath oils, and soap that Dr. Houghton had purchased at the PX were arranged on a small, blue-lacquered mother-of-pearl inlay table. Clear hot water shimmered in the deep rectangular blue-tile Japanese style tub.

He heard someone enter. It was little Miss Kim, all smiles; she flushed when Dr. Houghton winked at her. In turn, at her chaste blush, he felt himself redden. Little Miss Kim's emotions were infectious. When she smiled, he did. When she blushed, he did. When she wept, everyone who knew her wept.

Miss Kim entered with a definite task in mind. She first disarmed Dr. Houghton of his forty-five and then expertly unbuttoned his fatigues. He decided that passive acceptance would be the only gracious way to handle this situation. Soon down to his shorts, and finally naked, she ordered him into the scalding water. She sang a plaintive, gentle Korean song as she scrubbed him as his mother did when he was an infant. She was thorough, scrubbing behind his ears and in every possible location. She paused at one place for a gratuitous comment; "big," and some words that he did not understand.

Dr. Houghton, with a supreme effort, contained a wild impulse to laugh. She was excruciatingly funny, but dignity was crucial here. He did not wish to taint this pleasant ritual with occidental prurience or immature modesty or Harvard Puritanism.

After the hot bath, she commanded, "Please, Honorable Doctor, sit down." She motioned to a small three-legged wooden stool.

He sat, as directed, completely relaxed by the heat of the bath. But from behind and without warning, little Miss Kim poured a bucket of ice cold water on him to wash off the bath residue. He almost fell off the stool from the violent shock of the water. He jumped up. Miss Kim, with a gentle hand on his shoulders, forced him back down onto the low stool. Again, from behind, she belted him with a second bucket.

He spun around, hands up, in a posture of self-defense, "No more, Miss Kim. Damn, you'll kill me."

She answered in innocent soft Korean, "I am sorry Honorable Doctor. I don't know English."

No matter how he tried in the future, even with offers of money, he could not persuade Beautiful Flower, little Miss Kim or Sugi, the daughter of the deserted woman, to stop the cold water. It was essential, they maintained.

After Miss Kim finished wiping him with a large Turkish towel, she said, "Lie down, Honorable Doctor." She covered his mid-section with a small towel. She massaged him from face to toes. At the vital area, he said in Korean, "Don't bother there." He tried to speak casually.

Miss Kim persisted. In Korean, she laughed, "I will not harm you, Honorable Doctor." Next she turned him over, jumped on his back and walked around on him, using her prehensile toes with a dexterity Dr. Houghton did not believe possible. Finally, she commanded him to return to the stool. With open cupped hands and then machine gun chops, she pounded his back, arms and chest with a strength and vigor that little Kim could not possess. The small bathhouse reverberated with hollow echoes. He turned about to see if such sustained ferocity really came from her. It did. Before he left, she helped him into his embroidered silk robe.

On other nights, Sugi or occasionally Beautiful Flower would bathe him, but Dr. Houghton preferred Miss Kim.

All did not proceed smoothly at first. The following Saturday evening, the elder Miss Pak and Mr. Cameron planned to dine with

279

them. Beautiful Flower was due at five at the Officers' Club. Dr. Houghton had instructed the cook to have a juicy chicken for the girls, their favorite dish.

Mr. Cameron and Dr. Houghton waited at the gate as the senior Miss Pak arrived alone. "How are you? Where is Beautiful Flower?"

"I don't know. This morning she and her friends went to Chun Chon. She was not at your house when I stopped there."

"Doc," Mr. Cameron smiled empathically, "we'll meet at the club." Dr. Houghton walked halfway down the hill and sat down to watch the route from the village to the front gate. As the moments ticked by ever so slowly, he worked himself into a rage. The emotion increased minute by minute as wild notions appeared. Perhaps she had taken the money and left town. In Korea there are so many hustlers and thieves around. Why, in her whole life, she probably never saw a lump sum of fifty thousand won. Or perhaps she had a Korean boyfriend.

He ridiculed himself for his foolish jealousy. Surely she had some excuse or else it was simply tardiness. The occident and the orient certainly differed in their view of time.

But by the time he spied her an hour late, hurrying across the rice paddies, he pushed aside all attempts at reason. As she approached the main gate, he almost suffered a stroke when he noticed her slow to a stroll and then a purse-swinging loll. He walked quickly down the hill to the gate. She had not done her hair.

With a disarming, gracious smile, she said, "How are you, Reginald?" with her eyes lowered.

"Where have you been?" he sputtered in Korean, attempting to contain the anger. "Do you know what time it is?"

She did not reply but stood there with her eyes lowered. The gate guard watched and grinned.

"What time were you supposed to come?"

"At five," she answered correctly.

"What time is it now?"

She did not answer. She only looked toward the village.

"I am angry," he understated. "I think perhaps you should go home. You are too late."

To this, she inexplicably replied, "I am angry, too!" Without further explanation, she turned and walked toward the village with her head cocked high, casually swinging her new shiny-black leather pocketbook.

Dr. Houghton was stunned for a moment. Suddenly, he became aware of the grinning gate guard. "Wipe that smile off your face!"

The gate guard did not understand this colloquialism, but he snapped to attention and saluted.

He walked glumly up to the club and explained what had happened to Mr. Cameron and Miss Pak.

"Doc, don't be hot-headed, Doc. After all, she's a Korean girl. She really doesn't know the American style."

"You're right," Dr. Houghton answered.

"I'll speak to her," Miss Pak said.

But an angry Dr. Houghton did not enter the village for two days. The next afternoon, at the conclusion of the Hap Gi Do practice, Mr. Yun reported that two young "women" were awaiting him outside the exercise hall. Dr. Houghton wondered what Mr. Yun thought since Hap Gi Do training was supposed to involve a pure mind in a disciplined body. Sex and relations with women were discouraged.

Moreover, Dr. Houghton knew that Mr. Yun did not appreciate Americans enjoying the company of respectable women of the superior Korean race. Business ladies were specifically for the barbarians. Dr. Houghton dissembled, "Koreans or Americans?"

Mr. Yun replied, "Koreans, one very beautiful."

Dr. Houghton dressed, buckled on his forty-five, and dripping with sweat, laced on his boots. The residual anger dissolved when he saw Beautiful Flower magnificently caparisoned in a tight amaranth colored silk skirt and white silk blouse with a red hibiscus flower in her hair. A smiling little Miss Kim stood by.

Dr. Houghton bowed.

Mr. Yun smiled at the inexpert deception. Who was the American trying to deceive?

Dr. Houghton whispered, "What are you doing here?"

"We want you to come tonight."

"OK. I'll come at eight. Have the bath ready!"

Dr. Houghton scurried away. He was self-conscious in the public street, an unkempt, unshaven soldier with sweat staining the arms and back of his wrinkled fatigues.

Beautiful Flower bathed him expertly that night, sometimes cantillating ancient Chinese poems; other times singing and humming the wistful, Korean love songs. Miss Kim accompanied her playing a Korean lute. They soothed him quickly. In fact, he was not certain that this was happening to him.

He returned to reality only when the two of them by force, denied his protestations. Miss Kim grabbed both ear lobes from behind, and Beautiful Flower pushed against his shoulders until he sat down on the three-legged stool. Then they poured the ice cold water on him, twice. It was "necessary." They were providing the barbarian with an elementary education.

Overcome and finally dry, he slipped into his silk robe and went into the house proper. Inside, Sugi served them individual stainless steel bowls of steaming white rice. Beautiful Flower and he had compromised the issue of diet and sanitation. He had explained that only well-boiled or iodine treated water could be used for drinking; all food must be adequately cooked. On these points, he was firm. He did compromise on the kimchi issue. He understood the Koreans intense, even passionate love of the noxious garlicky, red-peppered dish. So he did not interdict kimchi, but asked them not to put too much garlic in it. The girls "agreed." The cooking and eating utensils would be Korean style. They ate cross-legged on the floor around a small low table except when guests came, and then Beautiful Flower assumed the polite knee-up position. He also demanded no spitting on the floor. Satisfied, he enjoyed the rice as the girls also ate huge bites of the low garlic Kimchi from the common bowl. There was much smacking of lips. No question, they were fire eaters who occasionally morphed into fire balls.

"Beautiful Flower," he said. "I enjoyed the bath. You are almost as expert as Miss Kim." Realizing that Miss Kim did not understand, he switched to Korean.

Miss Kim understood and laughed, holding her hand in front of her mouth. She thought he was a funny man unlike Korean men, who at home were severe and tyrannical. Korean men only laughed and clowned in the entertainment districts. But Captain Houghton made her collapse with inner laughter. He made one social mistake after another. The Honorable Doctor was not harmonious and just not proper. He committed the gravest "sins." He was a buffoon. His kibun was missing.

Miss Kim's simple, shy laughter echoed through Dr. Houghton's brain for the rest of his life. He never truly understood why she laughed so much or was unmarriageable. She was well shaped, neat, industrious, and certainly a virgin. As a seamstress she was an artist. Her silk brocade mythological figures were "alive." He paid her generously for a silk brocaded Moon Lady for his sister and a Celestial Angel for his mother using gold and silver thread. Although poor, she was of the race of children, innocent, good-humored, and sensitive. Dr. Houghton treated her with great respect. With time, he knew she would do anything for him, and on one violent occasion, she confirmed this. She was always welcome in his heart.

"Beautiful Flower," he said as he turned his attention to her, "why were you so late the other night?"

282

She replied in Korean, "I went to the Chinese movie. I forgot the time. I have no watch."

He accepted this. "I will buy you a watch and you'll have no further excuse."

The next day he bought her a Japanese self-winding, calendar watch. After the no-freckles medicine, the gold Happy Bag and the TV, this was her most valued possession.

Still sitting at the table, she became very serious. She said "I am very angry at you, Reginald. When you see me, you should say 'How are you?' politely in Korean, the traditional Korean greeting. I lost face in front of the gate guard. He tells everybody about the scene, and everybody laugh. If there is a problem, tell me privately. My kibun is terrible."

He understood immediately. "I am sorry. You are right. I shall do as you say." He knew he must not add to the considerable social pressure on her. He also knew many Koreans said to her, "Shame on you. You are no better than a business lady." But a proud Beautiful Flower would rejoin "It is not your business. You are Viet Cong."

Having resolved the crisis, he and Beautiful Flower began to play Chinese chess for money. To her, the sums were enormous, and she employed her considerable skill with unrelenting initiative. On that particular night, after winning eight of ten games, she said, "Honorable Doctor, perhaps we should call you Honorable Mr. Simple; what is your IQ?"

Dr. Houghton, whose mother blessed him with an IQ of 152, replied in Korean, "Pig and me – same, same."

This remark reduced Miss Kim to unstoppable belly-holding, face-shielding laughter. No adult Korean male would ever make such a self-derogatory statement.

With time and contact, he figured Beautiful Flower's IQ was comparable to his. Her excellent mind was reflected not only in games but in her language ability. She taught him Korean in return for nightly English lessons, but unlike him, she never required the same instruction twice. His retention was excellent, but hers was superior. Although he mastered Korean relatively easily, he only learned about 250 Chinese characters in three months. Chinese characters had to be memorized by brute force; there was no language instinct for Chinese and he could not find a persuasive motive to learn it.

Two matters, however, disturbed him. Beautiful Flower was extremely pale. Only after considerable threats and urging would she come to the clinic. On arrival she met Miss Ku, the nurse who replaced Miss Judy. There was instant hatred between them, each resenting the other's role in his life. Time and again, he resisted Beautiful Flower's demand to work in the clinic as nurse interpreter in place of Miss Ku. On the other hand, he resisted Miss Ku's florid-faced attempts at seduction. After several weeks of this he insisted that Beautiful Flower not visit the dispensary except for an emergency.

Without much effort, he diagnosed her iron deficiency anemia and its cause. She suffered from a common Korean problem - chronic GI bleeding from hook worms and roundworms. In a few days he eliminated the parasites, and gradually, with iron tablets, cured her anemia. With the resolution of her anemia, he saw that Beautiful Flower now glowed with vitality, a wonderful transformation. He had created a dynamo. Moreover, he thought her slightly bowed legs had straightened; was this possible? She was a knockout in a short skirt.

Perhaps obliquely related to her anemia was Beautiful Flower's obvious fear of being alone with him. A third person was always in their presence. After what he considered a reasonable period of several weeks, he asked Mr. Cameron's Miss Pak for aid and counsel. She arrived the following evening, her first act being to eject little Miss Kim. The elder Miss Pak was outraged. Dr. Houghton counseled patience, but she launched into Beautiful Flower in rapid Korean. He heard, "You little fool....money....you'll end up in the rice paddy....Dr. Houghton is a gentleman....you are very lucky....Dr. Houghton and your father are your responsibility, not your friends." The elder Miss Pak worked herself into a frothing rage which culminated in two sharp slaps across Beautiful Flower's face.

Dr. Houghton finally interceded as Beautiful Flower made no effort to protect her face, an oriental admission of guilt.

"Let's compromise," he said. "Between ten and midnight when I am here, your friends, if here, must go next door to the small room. They can return when I leave or when midnight comes. I have no objections to your friends. I like them very much."

"Particularly Miss Chang," Beautiful Flower forced out between sobs.

He laughed and said, "No, I only want you."

However, this intervention by the elder Miss Pak did not stop the resistance, for like a hydra, another perverse stratagem popped out the next night.

Beautiful Flower said, "My father is ill in Seoul. I must go and see him tomorrow, yes?"

He was certain she lied. "Yes, but I hope you will return in a few days. Let me know if I can help him like with medicines?"

284

The following evening, now armed with oriental intuition, he visited his old haunt, the Morning Glory Tea House. Miss Chang, still employed there, brought him red tea at the dimly lit corner table where Beautiful Flower previously served him. "Has Beautiful Flower been here?" he asked in Korean.

"No," she replied turning her head evasively. Dr. Houghton suspected she lied so he reached across the table and gingerly turned her face toward him. He looked far inside her defenseless eyes, and as expected, they became two rippling pools. A blink sent two tears down her high cheek bones. In Korean he said, "I understand. You are only trying to protect your friend."

"I am sorry," Miss Chang intoned. "I should not lie to you; you've done so much for me and my old father." She averted her eyes and wiped away the tears.

He saw a chance to resolve a lingering concern. "Does she have a boyfriend?"

"No, only you," Miss Chang answered placidly.

If she is lying, he thought, she is either a superb actress or else she doesn't know. "Where is she then?"

"She went to Chinese movies."

Fifteen minutes later, Beautiful Flower bounced through the Tea House door. She started to speak to Miss Chang, but Miss Chang indicated by a glance - the corner. Beautiful Flower, after a glimpse into the dark nook, walked over and sat down. "Why did you come here?"

"To find you. How was the movie?"

"I have lost face."

"Yes, you have. Your face is gone."

With a sly look, with her head slightly bent to the side, she said, "Maybe you came here for Miss Chang since I went to Seoul?"

"Beautiful Flower, don't be ridiculous. But if you persist, I'll take her back with me. She'll not resist so strenuously."

Beautiful Flower grasped his hand firmly. After a very long pause, she said, "Let's go home."

"Be happy," Miss Chang commanded as she lowered her eyes in understanding.

As he gazed at Miss Chang, for the barest moment, he wondered if he had the right girl. At the thought "right girl," he recalled a bitter quarrel between his mother and sister, just after his sister's marriage. His mother had said, "I wish Reggie would marry. He's no youngster anymore."

His sister answered, "Apparently he has never found the right girl."

That night there was considerable doubt if the virginal Beautiful Flower was the right girl. She was not Miss Galt or the Korean Miss Han or the Chinese Miss Han. But as she gradually recovered from her anemia, he realized that, even by the canons of venery, she was valuable. Although she was not a perfectly cut, clear sparkling blue diamond or an orange-red, three caret Padparadschah sapphire, she was not just a dusty, greenish stone. She was, in fact, a rather rough emerald. She required careful cutting and gentle polishing before being positioned in a proper platinum setting.

Dr. Houghton knew this because he had expertise that was unavailable to most other men; he had an in depth understanding of the physiology of the male and female sexual responses. Like the Buddha, he could both participate, being a causal agent, and observe. He could not be fooled easily. He had a huge advantage over Masters and Johnson's artificial observations of humans in their physiology laboratory. Humans are like rats in the sense that rats in cages are totally different than rats in the "field." He was *both* participating *and* observing in the "field." He could measure times and count responses. Moreover, Dr. Houghton's subjects were not prostitutes or other overused women or men. But who would believe him? Some day he would investigate such matters thoroughly and write them up.

Most nights after work and the exercise hall, he went into the village. He and Beautiful Flower decorated what she now called the "crimson chamber." They purchased bright decorated silks for the walls, the pillows and the floor puffs. He bought soft pillows; she preferred the hard rectangular Korean pillows. For himself, he bought a solid gold Emperor's medallion, the Chinese character for Double Happy, which he wore around his neck on a solid gold chain with his dog tag. After hard bargaining, they also bought Korean red lacquered furniture and Chinese porcelain vases which Beautiful Flower filled with fresh flowers daily. When mildly intoxicated he thought of himself as the Qianlong Emperor and Beautiful Flower as the Fragrant Concubine. He even found for her what was reputed to be jujube flower perfume.

When Mr. Kim, the bartender at the club, a former wireman in the Korean Army, installed a field phone under Mr. Cameron's watchful eyes, Dr. Houghton could sleep in the village. With the secret telephone connected to a jack on the back of the detachment switchboard, be could be at the dispensary within five minutes. In the event of an emergency, Colonel Newton, Lieutenant Humbert, Sergeant Morse, as well as Sergeant Song knew where to find him.

Of course, if the deputy discovered this illicit use of the Army Field phone, he would demand its return.

Dr. Houghton also moved his Japanese stereo equipment to the crimson chamber. Beautiful Flower adored Beethoven. Several times, he had to phone her from the Q to turn down the volume. This occurred for the first time as he and Mike walked to the club one evening for dinner.

Mike asked, "Am I cracking up or do I hear the Beethoven's Emperor Concerto rising out of the village?"

"I hear it too." Dr. Houghton guessed that Beautiful Flower had turned up the volume. For some strange acoustical reason, the sound waves, emanating from the village in the valley, reverberated around the surrounding hills.

Dr. Houghton said, "I'll turn it down."

Mike said, "Sure, Doc, sure."

Pretending to empty his bladder, he called Beautiful Flower and instructed her to turn it off in exactly three minutes. When he informed Mike that the music would end in thirty seconds, Mike said mockingly, "You're pretty cocky, Doc. You really do think you are a magic man." When the music stopped, he scratched his head, "Only in Korea."

Dr. Houghton grew accustomed to having the girls sleep in the crimson chamber with him on their raised sleeping pads. This was a Korean custom. Occasionally he would awaken in the middle of the night to find little Miss Kim in his left arm and Beautiful Flower in his right.

But all was not mirror smooth in this pool of love, friendship and compromise. Occasional ripples were caused by the splash of strange customs jumping into the pool. One late spring evening, he and Beautiful Flower sat hand-in-hand on the screened, inner portion of the house. The tile roof extended over them. A few minutes earlier, Beautiful Flower had experienced the ultimate joy of Aphrodite for the first time. The after glow in her cheeks confirmed it was so.

As they sat in happy tranquility, he noted the contrast between their silken robes and satin pillows and the wild world on the other side of the protective screen. Facing Mother Nature at dusk, one could hear the mosquitoes that slammed into the screens. They were intoxicated with blood lust for him and Beautiful Flower. Larger and more ferocious than American mosquitoes, the Korean variety pursued one in an insatiable, suicidal fashion. A Korean mosquito bite left one with a swollen, painful wound; two bites left you miserable. Mosquitoes spawned by the millions in the stagnant water of the rice paddies.

Neither could the frogs be ignored. They also spawned in the rice paddies, emerging in the spring to hop around everywhere. The rains brought them out. The first day Dr. Houghton saw them in force, he looked out his rear view mirror at the jeep track of run-over-frogs left on the wet road, a gruesome sight, especially for a Buddhist. But even worse, the frogs crawled under doors and through cracks, so that some corridors in the BOQ were full of tiny green frogs. After the first mid-spring rain storm, when they emerged in force, he wondered if the Colonels had brought the seventh plague down on the detachment. Unlike the vicious mosquitoes which he loathed, Dr. Houghton found the frogs a sad race and he grew to dislike the silent jeep rides on rainy days. After a while he stopped looking in the rear view mirror at the pancaked track of frogs. Was he a closet Buddhist?

The chirping of the jay birds interrupted his reveries of frogs and mosquitoes. The jay birds made their nests under a corner of the roof, a sign of good luck. The birds often perched on the electric inlet wires, and he feared they would be electrocuted. With a shudder he remembered one week ago, that he had joked that he was hungry for a bird egg. Making a vague motion to steal an egg, Beautiful Flower revealed her impulsive, mercurial Korean nature. In an instant, she had his forty-five and ominously clicked the clip into place. "Do not touch the eggs. Are you a savage?" She pointed the gun at him.

Afraid of no man, he trembled with fear as this emotional Korean woman pointed his forty-five at him. "I was only joking. Please put that gun away." As she placed the gun into the holster, his courage returned. "I want you never, but never, to play with that." A forty-five at two feet was a canon, and he had too often seen the bloody consequences of Korean hot tempers.

"I would not shoot you." She ran into his arms and sobbed with grief at the thought.

A few days later they observed the parent jay birds push the surviving three fledglings out of the nest. One plummeted to the ground, unable to fly. Dr. Houghton repaired the wing which had been torn by the fall. Beautiful flower cared for the bird with intense Buddhist devotion. When the fledgling finally flew off, she wept for joy.

Her volatile emotional makeup was again demonstrated the next night, when he reached high with his toes, with his ever increasing flexibility and skill, and purposely gently tapped her on the cheek with his right big toe. To his total surprise, this slender woman upended him with a vicious counter. He fell hard on the obdul floor.

"You wretched barbarian," she screamed in Korean. "You put your dusty foot on my face!" She was fireball-red, a much higher temperature than his mother's hot potatoes.

From his position on the floor, he said, "I am sorry." He wondered where she had acquired such skill. She denied the study of oriental fighting, but he thought that as a child and adult, particularly with her craving for Kendo movies, she had probably observed the counter. He knew she must be handled gently.

Looking down at him, she finally said. "I am sorry. I hope I did not hurt you." With her now twinkling eyes and condescending words, she accused him of being a number ten athlete.

One slight complication arose with the Tea House Miss Chang. Alone with her one afternoon, she put his hand down her dress on her large firm breast. She wished to "sleep with him, just once. Please, Honorable Captain." She wore a captivating fruity perfume; she was a very ripe peach – sure to be juicy and delicious.

Although tempted, he rejected the idea. He did not know her motivation although he unsuccessfully tried to find out from little Miss Kim. He did not mention it to Beautiful Flower who would probably explode. Miss Chang, however, did not easily accept a polite rejection. Beautiful Flower was correct to worry about Miss Chang; for several weeks, he asked Miss Chang not to visit their Tae Bat house.

The following days and weeks, Reg and Beautiful Flower enjoyed each other in the crimson chamber after dinner. They laughed and played. They planned excursions to places in South Korea on his upcoming weekend passes. One great pleasure for him was her endless tales. Like a Korean Scheherazade performing for the Sultan, she told him Korean and Chinese myths. She loved spirits - some resembling sylphs, salamanders, and gnomes as well as more malignant beings like the evil fox-women. But he enjoyed the Taoism tales most – especially those of men seeking the secret of Everlasting Life. Taoists were the first alchemists and crude chemists. She told him he must take her to Western China where every thousand years, on a high mountain, a certain peach tree produces special peaches. If you eat one, you will live forever.

Dr. Houghton said, "Let's go tomorrow!"

She laughed.

The animism and shamanism of central Asia lingered in her fictions, mainly in the guises of the recent, often grateful dead. But often Beautiful Flower did not know the correct English or Korean word for a Chinese character. But by stratagem, mime, mimicry or the dictionary, she was able to portray her meaning. .

In turn he told her American fairy tales such as the Legend of Sleepy Hollow and the Cinderella story. He didn't know the Korean word for pumpkin. He did not look it up at the moment but he described its color, size, and what happened to it in the story.

She understood a pumpkin to be some kind of a magic American device. At the end of the story she said, "Will you buy me a pumpkin?"

"Yes, I will, in the fall."

Cocking her head to the side and with definite uncertainty in her voice, she softly asked, "How about two?"

"You're too greedy, but I'll buy you two."

"Oh, good," she replied, expecting two things as wonderful as two televisions. "You know me, greedy girl."

Two months later he brought her two small young pumpkins.

"You meant pumpkins," she said in Korean, pointing disdainfully at the green- turning – orange fruits. He explained the story to her more carefully. Henceforth, she never again asked for an item without a careful check.

One evening she gently lifted her head off his chest, which she was using as a pillow. She cautiously broached a potentially troublesome subject. "Why Sergeant Morse have too many fingers?" He had six fingers on each hand.

Dr. Houghton succumbed to uncontrolled laughter at the delicate manner in which she approached this subject. In turn, she too laughed. For some reason Sergeant Morse's physical anomaly amused her and her friends enormously. Finally, he said, "All black men have twelve fingers."

"You lie," she thumped him on the chest.

He fabricated one falsehood after another about how they arrived there and what Sergeant Morse employed them for, each time maintaining that at last he would tell the truth. Moreover, he told her Sergeant Morse had six toes on each foot.

"I want to see six toes. I do not believe you, Honorable Liar."

Dr. Houghton received permission from the Headquarters Comedian to take the second weekend in June "off." Dr. Houghton wanted to visit the Golden Buddhist Monastery outside Taegu to see the jadeite carvings. Lieutenant General Lee kindly informed the Abbot of his upcoming visit. General Lee reminded him of the importance of a "donation," for the Abbott was desperate for money.

On that Saturday they took the early train from Seoul to Taegu, a three hour ride. Under the hot sun, he saw a shimmering effluvium, a horrid fog arise from the night-soil covered paddies. The earth stank and Beautiful Flower had unusually strong dragon mouth. But Dr. Houghton ignored these distractions. He was very excited about seeing the jadeite carvings looted from the Forbidden City in 1900. They took a mini-taxi from Taegu to the monastery, a one hour ride on the dusty unpaved roads. Beautiful Flower kept repeating mongi, mongi – too dusty, too dusty.

But first, they went to the Inn of the Amaranth Flower to check in and clean off the mongi. Dust had sneaked into everything, even his under-shorts. Beautiful Flower changed into a very conservative Korean dress and, after a long hot shower Reginald Houghton wore a green tie and dark jacket. At one sharp, they walked up the winding dusty path to the front door of the Golden Monastery. Dr. Houghton thought the name was a terrible misnomer; the unpainted building was not golden. It was rotting wood and might collapse at any moment, like the house of Usher.

Beautiful Flower banged the gong. The bent-over, head-shaved Abbot Kim himself came. "Pardon our humble monastery," he said. He used a gnarled wooden cane and wore a saffron robe.

Dr. Houghton said in Korean, "I am Dr. Houghton and this is Miss Yi who will translate for me." He bowed deeply.

The ancient Abbot said in polite Korean, "I know. You went to Harvard and Yale like President Kennedy. Please come in and have a cup of tea. As you see, we are in very bad condition."

Reginald Houghton looked at Beautiful Flower who occasionally translated a word. He said, "Perhaps I can help."

The Abbot continued, "The Christians and the Christian missionaries in Korea are snouting and snorting money." The pig metaphor was very strong. "No one cares about us, about Buddhism any more." He sighed deeply as Buddhist chanting began in the Great Hall in the rear. "But we make due. We are Pure Land Buddhists; we believe in the Amida Buddha of the Western Region."

"I know. I studied Buddhism at Harvard."

"I know you know. I too studied Buddhism as a young man. I went to China almost fifty years ago. In one of the caves in Western China in Dunhuong, I saw the Indian Buddha Shakyamuni's shadow on the wall."

Dr. Houghton did not challenge this although he was taught that the Buddha's shadow only lasted 500 years. So how could the Abbot observe it? He often told Beautiful Flower he too could leave his shadow on the wall, but it only lasted a minute.

Her response was a not so polite term for "night soil."

After more polite small talk, Dr. Houghton said, "Can we see the carvings?"

As if by magic, a monk carried several boxes from cabinets in the rear. He unpacked the four carvings and carefully placed them on the table.

"May I pick them up, Honorable Abbot Kim?"

"Yes."

Reg did not discuss the provenance or that they were very dusty and covered with grime. But even so, he saw immediately they were worthy of the Chinese Emperors. "May I have a damp towel, honorable Abbott?"

"Certainly."

After a little cleaning, Dr. Houghton was certain they were jadeite carvings. There was a six inch yellow translucent Buddha's Hand citron with six "fingers;" a five inch imperial green pepper; a twelve inch translucent reddish Chinese celestial nymph, an oriental angel, floating on white translucent clouds; and a translucent apple green Kwan Yin, She Who Listens - the spirit of mercy. Each was a masterpiece of carving in a rare jadeite stone. The Japanese lieutenant who looted these carvings knew what he was doing.

Dr. Houghton said, "They are very fine." His heart was racing. In fact, he would do anything he could to obtain them; he would certainly buy them if possible.

The Abbot nodded but said nothing.

Dr. Houghton passed him an envelope containing one hundred dollars, more than twice what General Lee suggested. He said, "Thank you Honorable Abbot Kim." After a short pause, he said, "Do you have any more jadeite carvings, large or small?" He knew they had the small green Buddha pendant. He took out a second envelope that contained another fifty dollars but he did not hand it to the Abbot.

The Abbot said, "Yes." The same monk appeared with a big black box and a small jewel box. "Here is our jadeite Buddha that has the power." He passed the jewel box politely to Dr. Houghton who, after carefully inspecting it, passed the imperial green two-inch, Buddha-pendant to Beautiful Flower.

Holding it up to the dim light, she said, "The stone is translucent and the Buddha is carved with such a serene face." She switched to English and smiled, "I want it."

Next the monk unwrapped a twelve inch square flat, half inch thick brown jadeite field. Out of it were growing four jadeite amaranth plants - all about nine inches tall; two yellow, one red and yellow and green - a Joseph's coat amaranth, and one amaranth red. Dr. Houghton had never seen or heard of such a jadeite carving or

292

such colors. Could it be dyed? Without asking he examined it with his equipment. It was jadeite and not dyed as far as he could tell. The stone was homogenous and quite translucent throughout. This jadeite would be considered Grade A, of the highest quality. It was jewelry or bangle quality. Because the stone had five colors it was very valuable for that reason alone. He passed the second envelope to the Abbott.

The Abbot smiled and said, "These are all real, from China."

"I know. General Lee told me the story. Would you consider selling these?"

The old Abbot paused for a long time. "They will be very expensive. I will let you know."

Dr. Houghton had one final question. "Why do they call the inn, 'The Inn of the Amaranth Flower?"

The Abbot said, "Because they grow amaranth plants here for salads and seeds for nourishment, we have fields of colorful amaranths in the fall. Amaranth seeds are excellent in soup. Amaranth seeds are also complete protein. You understand?"

"I see."

After they left the monastery, he took Beautiful Flower out for a Korean beef dinner cooked over a wood charcoal fire. She also indulged in the finest high-garlic red pepper kimchi. Why not satisfy her kimchi lust? During the dinner, they discussed the jadeite Buddha pendant and its power. He teased, "If the little Buddha is so powerful, how come the Monastery is broke, is about to fall down?"

She said, "I do not know."

Back at the Inn of the Amaranth Flower, as he undressed, she said, "Reginald, you have a body like a Western statue I studied in college."

"Which one?"

"The Farnese Hercules in Naples, Greece."

"No, the Farnese Hercules is in Naples Italy. He is much more muscular than I." Notwithstanding her mistake, Reginald Houghton was exceptionally pleased at her observation. He knew he was now an excellent physical specimen; he ought to be with all the Hap Gi Do exercise.

He then jumped on her, "Ready?"

She laughed, "I ready but are you?"

He made love to her with abandon. She was now willing and able. She even manifested the full repertoire of female sexual responses but at a much lower intensity than Miss Galt or the Misses Han. But that particular night he was honest with himself; he knew his lust was for both Beautiful Flower *and* the jadeite carvings.

But in one matter, he was thwarted. He was intensely curious about her past. He was puzzled by certain intimations that she must have some tragic or unspeakable event in her life. All he knew was that she suffered as a little girl during the Korean War. Notwithstanding all his tricks, she answered his persistent questioning with renitent silence or she would say, "You say the past makes no difference. If so, why do you ask so many questions? There are certain matters you should not know."

.During this time he once or twice wondered if he should stay in the Orient forever. He was very happy. He was doing a good job as an Advisor and civic action clinic physician. His Hap Gi Do was progressing; he now had a chance to buy really precious jadeite carvings. He would enlist General Lee's help. Almost daily his attachment to Beautiful Flower strengthened. Although he did not condone their behavior, he now understood Dr. Tierney and Dr. Barnes better. He realized he too was, in a sense, schizoid, two men; one the rational American physician, the other, the near oriental denizen of the crimson chamber. The former behaved in terms of truth; the latter in terms of inner harmony and beauty. But deep down, he knew that the truth was more valuable to him. In the end, nothing would beat the joy of that day at Harvard College when he saw his amaranth dye crystals coming out of solution. Chemistry not Taoism was true magic. Chemicals could cure TB and control leukemia. Chemicals could kill parasites, worms, and scabies. Chemicals could control seizures. What could an orgasm do; even status orgasmus? What could a jadeite statue do? What could the priests do? They could pray and shrive souls; they could chant and beg. But in the end, everyone, everywhere, understood that priestly commerce was ineffective and nonsense. The Koreans knew; they came from all over to his civic action clinic - a big problem for Dr. Houghton. He could not begin to handle the demand.

"That for ways that are dark
And for tricks that are vain
The heathen Chinese is peculiar."
                "Plain language from Truthful James,"
                Francis Bret Harte

Chapter XIX
Extortion

Dr. Houghton and Mr. Cameron were at the club by six, attired in tuxedos. The bartender, Mr. Kim said he had never seen such suits in all his years at the detachment. Soon after, Colonel Bennet, the Deputy and Mike arrived.

"Where are you two going?" the Deputy asked.

"We've been invited to a formal dinner," Dr. Houghton replied, enjoying the gin and persiflage.

"Where - in Chun Chon?" The Deputy continued, "Who in this part of the country would give a formal dinner? Are you sure you are not going to marry the Governor's daughter?"

"No," Dr. Houghton grinned. "No marriage tonight."

The Deputy, who always took liberties, unbuttoned the tuxedo jacket and saw the forty-five in Dr. Houghton's shoulder holster. "What are you bringing that for?"

"You know, Colonel, with all the crooks and infiltrators running around….."

In his off duty cowboy costume of Texas boots and ten gallon hat, Colonel Bennet interceded, "I think the Doc has a point there."

"You know, I have seen your Miss Pak at Mr. Cameron's house several times," the Deputy said.

Mike laughed in his martini glass.

By the question Dr. Houghton realized that the Deputy did not know of his paper house in the village. "Oh," he replied. Fortunately, the Deputy's binoculars did not see around corners.

"I'd like to go," the Deputy said.

"If you have a tuxedo, you can come."

Mr. Cameron kicked Dr. Houghton in the ankle.

"I don't have a tux, Doc," the Deputy replied, crestfallen, generally disappointed.

Dr. Houghton swallowed his gin and said, "Mr. Kim, two sacks of ice to go."

"Yes, Sir!" Mr. Kim placed the ice in two bags.

The Deputy said in familiar Korean, "Have a good time."

A moment later the duty jeep beeped. Dr. Houghton and Mr. Cameron rose to leave.

The Deputy said, "Next time let's have an invite for me."

Mike laughed again.

Like Sean O'Leary so many years before, Mr. Cameron passed gas.

Dr. Houghton said, "So long."

Within five minutes the jeep left them and their two sacks of ice at the crimson chamber. Adorned in their Korean traditional dresses, Beautiful Flower and Miss Pak greeted them at the gate. The girls buzzed about like young hummingbirds.

Mr. Cameron remarked, "The girls look stunning. I bet this is the first formal dinner party in this village in one thousand years."

Dr. Houghton nodded. Even Sugi was well dressed in the silk gown he had bought her for the occasion. But his eyes settled on Beautiful Flower. She glowed in the layers of rich silk. In her lush black hair with thick braids behind her ears, rising up to the crown of her head, in the ancient Korean style, she had placed the recently purchased solid gold, jade-tipped hair pins perfectly. She seemed to float, not walk, in her up-toed red shoes. Her serene, now perfectly complexioned face with her black almond-shaped eyes and large mouth enchanted him. She did not have the Cupid's bow mouth of the Fragrant Concubine but she was equally attractive. He knew many hundreds of years ago there were identical women in appearance, dress, and language in King Yi's court.

Dr. Houghton and Mr. Cameron sat cross-legged in the outside, but screened, middle portion of the house, sipping gin and tonic as the girls supervised the preparation of the dinner. Soon the two girls joined them, but declined the offer of liquor. To them even the bouquet of gin, never mind the taste, was nauseating.

Sugi served the rice, salad, kimchi and steak strips which were cooked over red hot charcoal brickets. With gold chopsticks, they ate with Korean gusto, not just to please the girls. They drank small amounts of rice wine to be social.

After dinner they entered the crimson chamber for entertainment. Mr. Cameron scanned the room quickly. "Doc, you've really done wonders here. This is as nice a place as I have seen anywhere in Korea; to think it is here in the village." After a moment, he continued, "Take my advice; never, ever, invite the Deputy down here. If he saw the field phone here, he'd court martial you."

Dr. Houghton chuckled, "You're right. I was only bluffing at the club. I knew he didn't have a tux."

"He is really malevolent bastard. If he became a commander, we'd all have to watch out."

Dr. Houghton disagreed, although he wasn't certain that his analysis of the Deputy was correct. He saw the Deputy as a very curious, if not prurient, man who wanted to abide by Army Regulations. But Dr. Houghton was the only one who had this notion.

Dr. Houghton was pleased that little Miss Kim, although late, was able to come. When she finished her bowl of rice and a small fish, having refused to eat any animal flesh, she played the Korean lute and sang. Beautiful Flower then played the Korean flute for them. After a short intermission, Beautiful Flower performed the Korean traditional dance with Dr. Houghton thumping a large hour-glass traditional drum, little Miss Kim on a small flute, and the voices of Miss Kim and Mr. Cameron's Miss Pak.

Next, the three girls, with contrasting soprano and contralto tones, trolled the melancholy Korean songs. Mr. Cameron, deep in thought behind the smoke screen of his pipe, tapped out the rhythm. Dr. Houghton, the drummer, was affected with pathos as he listened to a song the departed Kisaeng Miss Han sang so well. To him, it was now a threnody for her. At he end, he had to stand up and leave the room. Outside, he wiped away his tears. He could still hear her parting words, "Do not forget my face." She, in fact, had gained a temporary immortality in him; she was not forgotten. Although he realized he was not to blame, he upbraided himself time and again for her suicide.

When he returned, he noted tears streaming down Mr. Cameron's cheeks. The girls also noticed but continued their sad melodies.

"Are you all right?" he whispered.

"Yes. I was thinking that in two more months, I have to leave all this." Mr. Cameron wiped his eyes. "I have to go."

As a now somber Mr. Cameron rose to leave, he said, "Doc, there are two things I'd like you to look into. First, my driver says Lieutenant Ahn has been extorting money from the enlisted men. Second, Miss Pak tells me that your Sergeant Kim has been extorting money from one of the village farmers whose son you had operated upon."

Miss Pak informed him of the details.

"Thank you very much, Honorable Doctor," the elder Miss Pak said.

Saddened by Mr. Cameron's talk of extortion, and the recollection of Miss Han, he gently kissed Beautiful Flower and now spoke in confident Korean. "You looked really beautiful tonight. I have my Nikon. We must take pictures. Miss Kim, I am very glad you also came tonight. You also look lovely. Beautiful Flower, please call in Sugi."

"Than you very much for your help," he said to Sugi when she appeared.

"Thank you for the beautiful dress, Honorable Captain," she replied with a deep bow. "I have never had such a pretty dress."

"You're welcome, Sugi."

He took pictures of the girls and Mr. Cameron who left after the pictures. At ten minutes to twelve, Dr. Houghton hurried to leave before the curfew.

"Do not go, Reginald. You should stay here tonight!"

"No, Beautiful Flower, or should I say Non'gae, I must be on the compound tonight. I had a wonderful evening." Dr. Houghton could barely contain the emotions which welled up in his eyes. He kissed her gently. "I will stay over tomorrow night."

Miss Kim asked "May I walk you back?" She did not understand Mr. Cameron's tears or now, Captain Houghton's obvious emotions.

"Yes," Beautiful Flower answered.

Dr. Houghton and little Miss Kim, hand-in-hand, walked along the road, the long way around. He was the only one in her entire acquaintance that treated her as a lady. Everyone, even her family, took advantage of her cheerful but passive temperament. In this society of emotional and aggressive people, a little Miss Kim was lost. And so, a walk with the kind, blue-eyed white giant, their funny barbarian, was a joy to her.

At the half-way point he gave her the flashlight and said, "Now you take the flashlight and go back."

"But Honorable Doctor, you must take the flashlight."

"I am the Captain. This is an order, Corporal Kim."

"Yes, Sir," Miss Kim saluted.

He kissed her forehead. "Good night."

"Good night, Honorable Doctor," she whispered and started back.

For a minute he watched her feminine silhouette and then the flashlight beam diminish in the night. At two minutes to twelve, he turned and hurried toward the detachment gate.

Lieutenant Ahn bounded into Dr. Smith's office at eight o'clock. "Good morning, Sir." Lieutenant Ahn plunked himself down in the chair. His tendency to perpetual motion grew steadily worse. He constantly shifted the position of arms and legs. His eyes darted about observing every detail.

"Shut the door, Lieutenant Ahn," Dr. Houghton said. "I have heard serious accusations made against you."

Lieutenant Ahn looked worse every month. His eyes popped, his cheeks were hollower and his skin was blacker. His prognosis was poor, perhaps several years. As usual, he carried occidental reading material including comic books and the American Dictionary of Slang.

"Lieutenant Ahn, it has been alleged that you have been extorting money from the Korean enlisted men."

"No, Sir," Lieutenant Ahn protested. "That is a viscous lie!"

"Now I have reasons to believe it is true. This is your final chance. If you are involved in any more hanky-panky, and that includes black marketing, you'll be in big trouble. You know, Captain Chang said he would cut off your penis with a rusty knife if you cause more trouble." Dr. Houghton shuddered; he knew Chang might really do it. "Now, Lieutenant Ahn, I consider this the end of it. I'll keep this to myself if you keep your nose clean. Do I have you have your word?"

"Yes, Sir. I will keep my nose extra clean."

Dr. Houghton said, "You know what I mean!" He realized that asking Ahn to promise was like asking a Korean pig to stop oinking, but he hoped for the best. He was tempered in his judgment by Lieutenant Ahn's obviously failing health. But since Dr. Houghton now knew that Ahn's performatives were worthless, he stopped associating with Ahn after duty hours. Moreover, Beautiful Flower distrusted Lieutenant Ahn. She said he was "Viet Cong" a Korean epithet for the dregs of the earth.

"Now, Lieutenant Ahn, you may leave, but I want you to wait outside. Please tell Sergeant Kim to come in."

Dr. Houghton recalled how Sergeant Kim came to the dispensary. Four weeks ago, Sergeant Song, his valuable interpreter, was discharged from the Korean Army, having completed his tour of duty. Before he left the detachment, Dr. Houghton and several male Korean friends held a farewell party at the best Chun Chon Kisaeng House. The Koreans drank heavily of "golden" rice wine.

As the Koreans grew increasingly drunk, Dr. Houghton observed the great respect ex-Sergeant Song commanded from the Koreans. Although slender, his physical excellence was amply demonstrated during several detachment Black Belt exhibitions. He not only knew eight languages, but he also understood the literature and customs of the respective countries. Sergeant Song, without question, emanated dignity except for an occasional tic-like rising of his right shoulder. But what puzzled Dr. Houghton most was the fact that even Korean Generals called him "Honorable Sergeant Song." And during the party, as expected, Dr. Houghton watched the emotional Koreans weep unrestrained tears of regret at Sergeant Song's departure for Seoul.

He, too, would miss Sergeant Song's counsel, teaching and presence. He recently discovered that Sergeant Song respected him. At first Sergeant Song saw him as another large, uncivilized GI but with the flow of time, as the "Doctor" gained command of the Korean language and customs, and manifested genuine good feeling toward the Korean people, Sergeant Song moderated his impression. Sergeant Song also greatly admired his dogged pursuit of the Red and then Black Hap Gi Do Belts.

Near the evening's end, Dr. Houghton said, "Sergeant Song, do you remember the many discussions we held in the jeep about philosophy?"

"Yes, I remember."

"Well, I have come to realize that you are the Korean version of the Nietzschean Obermench, the Overman." He continued, "Now Sergeant Song, when you obtain your PhD next year - that will be a great day for all of us. Remember, if you ever wish to come to the United States, I shall be happy to sponsor you. I've told you many times, if there is anything you need or want, just ask." In fact, Sergeant Song was the only Korean who had never requested anything from the PX. He proposed a final toast, "May Sergeant Song have many sons, a happy life, and of course, a beautiful wife."

After the toast, everyone applauded and continued drinking. Dr. Houghton looked at his watch. "It's time for me to go now."

Dr. Houghton's Kisaeng of the evening, Miss Hu, the lead sing-song girl, another charming, talented attractive young woman whispered into his ear in polite Korean, "I need to talk with you."

"I must go because of the curfew."

"I knew Miss Han. I must talk with you."

Dr. Houghton said in Korean, "I will meet you at the Red Door Tea House tomorrow night at six, after my Hap Gi Do practice, for a short time." He corrected himself, "for a few minutes." "Short time" in Korean meant a brief sexual tryst.

The next evening Miss Hu arrived at the tea house five minutes late. When he looked at her carefully, he understood why she was the lead Kisaeng in the best house in Chun Chon. But he was surprised that she wore an amaranth-red silk skirt, a white silk tuxedo shirt with a red jade pendant, and an elaborate piled-high hair style. Her black hair gleamed with reddish overtones. Her lipstick and high heeled shoes matched her skirt.

He guessed, "Why did you wear that outfit, Miss Hu?"

"I knew you would like it, Honorable Doctor; I heard from from Miss Han."

"Please speak slowly; my Korean is not too good. What else do you know about me?"

"I know you run a free clinic for the Korean peoples. I know you are a Hap Gi Do player. I know you are very handsome." After a pause, she looked directly into his eyes. Korean woman did not do this; it was not polite. She said, "Miss Han told me you made her happier than anyone before. She said you made her body ….." Miss Hu used an unknown word.

Dr. Houghton said, "I don't know that word."

Miss Han said, "You made her hear celestial angels."

Dr. Houghton interrupted, "Miss Hu, I am certain I met you before."

"Yes, Honorable Doctor. I brought my mother to your clinic. She had TB and we could not obtain isoniazid medicine for her in Korea. You gave it to her and you saved her. We are so grateful to you Honorable Doctor. You are a savior."

"What else did Miss Han say?"

Miss Hu blushed, as the late afternoon sun intermittently suffused her face with yellow-orange light. Suddenly, after a dark cloud passed, a bright chiaroscuro beam spotlighted her face like in the great Italian paintings of the Annunciation, when Gabriel told Mary the news.

But Miss Han shattered his memory of Mary when she stood up and walked back and forth. "Am I beautiful?"

"Yes, you are a doll. You have an hour glass figure."

"Is that good?"

"You are the best."

"I wish to date you. I also wish to hear celestial angels at least once in my life." She slipped onto one knee before him, and took his hand, a suppliant.

He said, "Please sit down." He took her well manicured smooth hands in his. They were very hot. Up close, she had a perfect complexion, Cupid's bow lips, not just a lipstick artifact, and was the image of the Fragrant Concubine. He did not know what to do or say. He felt like the Christian saints in the desert being tempted by the devil or the devil's female associates. Or in the East, like the Buddha being tempted by Mara's three daughters, Discontent, Craving and Lust. Capping the temptation, he

301

remembered his time with Miss Han; he intuitively believed Miss Hu was another Miss Han. He just could not say no. But he finally said, as an unknown inner force resisted her, "Hu means fox in Chinese character, Yes?" He suddenly remembered the Taoist tales Beautiful Flower told him. He drew the Chinese character, somewhat clumsily.

"Yes," she said, suddenly worried that Captain Houghton might be setting a trap for her. How would he know though?

He said, "I know a fifty year old fox, a Hu, can change into a ravishingly beautiful girl temptress. She can pursue a scholar or physician and make love to him, every night. She would have a goal: to suck him dry, to imbibe the essence of immortality from him. Consequently, each time they make love he would become weaker and weaker."

Dr. Houghton watched her expression transmogrify from politely concealed foxy lust to shock. However, she quickly said, "I am not a fox. Remember Hu's have one or more tails. Come with me and I will show you that I have no tails. I will show you I have other things, good things."

He laughed to himself - she is fast. "No, there is only way to be sure: fox-temptresses never change their clothes - their clothes never become wrinkled or soiled."

At that Miss Hu smiled broadly. "Last night I wore a Korean traditional dress. Yes?"

Dr. Houghton said to himself, checkmate. He finally said softly, "I will be honest with you."

She waited.

He took her hot hand in his and inhaled her aroma-osmanthus perfume. He was slightly dizzy. "I have a Hap Gi Do exhibition coming up in the Chun Chon arena soon.'"

"I know."

"I must be strong for the exhibition. My Honorable Teachers will kill me if I do not do well, because of a fox temptress."

She waited.

"Please come to the exhibition. After the exhibition, I promise I will take you out on a real date."

"I can not wait. I want to hear angels sing soon," she laughed. "But if you promise I will wait. In the mean time I will cut off my tails." She leaned over and kissed him on his cheek. "I will see you at the exhibition, Honorable Captain."

As she walked out he recalled her looks. She had dimples when she smiled, perfect white teeth, a hint of a cleft chin, muscular but perfectly shaped feminine calves, and a complexion and lips that were the promise of joy. Perhaps, though, she was a little pale.

302

Finally he said to himself - What would his father do? His father believed that he who hesitates is lost. He would probably go with her; his father believed you must seize the day - make hay while the sun shines. His father would point out that Paris left his wife, the nymph Oenone, for Helen of Troy. Who could pass up the most beautiful woman in the world? But Reg always argued that the theft of Helen led to a disaster.

But enough theory: he vividly remembered his time with the Miss Hans. They had weakened him, especially the Hong Kong Miss Han. He needed days to recover from his one night with her. He should have checked her for a tail. He liked his plan. He would decide what to do with Miss Hu after the exhibition.

During the short bumpy jeep ride back to the detachment, he also thought of Beautiful Flower and his continued questions about her. He realized he would probably never understand Sergeant Song's unspoken dislike of Beautiful Flower. At the army discharge party he had asked him one final time, and received no answer.

As a replacement for Sergeant Song, General Kim recommended Sergeant Kim, who had been in the Army seven years. With American funds the Korean Army had sent Sergeant Kim to the States to study for six months. He spoke English well; he translated accurately and performed all his duties in an exemplary fashion. In return, with Captain Chang's aid, Dr. Houghton had secured Sergeant Kim a room in the village for his wife and child. He also arranged for his pregnant wife to be delivered in the American Hospital in Seoul against regulations. Sergeant Kim was very grateful. Even in retrospect, Dr. Houghton's only intimation of potential corruption was Sergeant Kim's repeated complaints that the Korean Army did not pay enough for a married man to support a family.

Sergeant Kim knocked and walked in.

"Sit down, Sergeant Kim." Dr. Houghton pulled out the clinical record of the injured boy and reviewed it as Sergeant Kim waited anxiously.

The nine year old boy, whose family lived near Mr. Cameron's Miss Pak in the village, presented two months before with a hot swollen arm and high fever. Blood cultures, x-rays, and orthopedic consultation confirmed Dr. Houghton's impression that this boy had osteomyelitis. The child required large amounts of expensive antibiotics *and* surgical intervention. As a favor to Dr. Houghton General Kim instructed the new Commanding Officer at the Korean Army Hospital to admit the child to his hospital. The Commander provided the surgeon and the hospital bed; Dr.

Houghton donated the necessary medicine which cost about two hundred dollars. They saved the child's arm and life. The father, who could never afford such treatment, had brought the boy to Dr. Houghton as a last resort.

"Sergeant Kim," said Dr. Houghton, "it has been alleged you extorted money from this boy's father. I heard that in the ambulance on the way to the hospital, you took eight thousand won from the father, having threatened him with denial of treatment. Is that true?"

"No, Sir. That is not true."

"Did you take any money from the father at any time?"

"No, Sir."

"I'll look further into this matter. Let me warn you that if you are lying, I'll toast your ass over red hot coals." He had seen this in a Chinese movie the other night with Beautiful Flower. "This is the last chance to tell the truth – now."

Sergeant Kim looked at the floor.

"You may go now, Sergeant Kim. Send in Lieutenant Ahn."

Lieutenant Ahn bounced in, obviously anticipating some request.

"Sit down, Lieutenant Ahn," he said to an already seated Lieutenant Ahn. He explained to him that the boy's father had complained to the elder Miss Pak. The father had the notion that Americans, unlike the Koreans, did not extort money for good deeds. "Lieutenant Ahn, I want you to find out the facts. I want you report to me tomorrow. At zero nine hundred, have any witnesses here in the office. Sergeant Kim has denied everything. If you do a good job on this case, we'll call you 'Ahn, private dick.'"

"Yes, Sir." Lieutenant Ahn smiled and scurried off.

Dr. Houghton realized he was taking a risk. But no American officer could ever discover the true story. Captain Chang was on leave, and so Lieutenant Ahn, by default, was the only choice. The old saw about it takes a thief to catch a thief was a further, although thin, consideration.

"These are the poops," Lieutenant Ahn said the next morning with rapid, excited gesticulation. "Papason says he gave Sergeant Kim eight thousand won in the ambulance. He also says that he also gave an envelope to Sergeant Morse's houseboy that contained five thousand won. Papason say that when he threatened to inform you, Sergeant Kim returned the five thousand won. Last night, Sergeant Kim threatened Papason and told him not to talk. There is big commotion in the village about this scandal."

Angry, Dr. Houghton said, "Damn! One such episode can ruin our whole civic action program. This is serious. Please bring in Sergeant Kim."

Sergeant Kim entered.

"Sergeant Kim! Lieutenant Ahn says the boy's father states that you extorted eight thousand won and then five thousand more, but you returned five thousand won. What do you have to say?"

Sergeant Kim said very softly, "The doctors in the evacuation hospital mentioned that it would be nice if Papason gave a party for them - for fixing his son. Papason agreed and gave me the eight thousand won in the ambulance which I gave to the doctors."

"How about the five thousand won?"

"I don't know anything about that."

"Bring in Papason and the houseboy." While waiting, Dr. Houghton was troubled. He could not easily investigate Sergeant Kim's allegation that the Korean doctors at the hospital asked for the money and Kim only passively transferred the money.

Papason was an ancient appearing farmer, although only fifty. The houseboy, the thirty-eight year old man, worked for Sergeant Morse and the Sergeant Major. In tears, Papason first asked Dr. Houghton to be lenient with the culprits. Dr. Houghton was amused by this device of the ancient Greek rhetoricians.

Facing the two culprits, Papason confirmed Lieutenant Ahn's account.

Dr. Houghton asked the houseboy if he possessed any knowledge of the situation.

The houseboy remained silent.

With a raised voice, Dr. Houghton said, "If you don't tell us the facts, I am going to fire you." This was an effective threat; the only other work available to the houseboy would be the agonizing drudgery of the rice paddies or worse. Although he was not paid much by the Sergeants, he supplemented his income by a factor of two or three by PX "gifts" from the Sergeants which he sold for huge premiums on the black market.

The houseboy glanced at Sergeant Kim, at Papason, and said, "Yes, I gave the envelope to Sergeant Kim, but I didn't know what was in it."

"What have you got to say, Sergeant Kim?"

"I never received such an envelope."

Dr. Houghton pondered the situation for a few minutes. He said to the houseboy, "I can't believe you transferred the envelope without knowing its contents." To Sergeant Kim, he said, "Both the houseboy and Papason say you are lying to me. Sergeant Kim, I am very upset. This conduct of yours is not just a Korean affair. You have damaged our civic action program. We have worked hard to keep good relations with the people of our village. The village people have been very cooperative, but now you, by your one act, have hurt our effort. Lieutenant Ahn says the village people are very disturbed. I will return you to your Unit with a letter of explanation."

Dr. Houghton turned to the houseboy. "I think you were in league with Sergeant Kim. You're fired. I will tell Lieutenant Humbert to remove your gate pass."

At this the houseboy glowered with rage. He advanced toward Sergeant Kim.

"There will be no violence here," Dr. Houghton said as he stood up. "Lieutenant Ahn, take the houseboy to the gate guard. Take his gate pass; inform the guards not to allow him on this compound. I'll call Lieutenant Humbert."

To the old man, Dr. Houghton said in slow polite Korean. "I am very sorry that you were threatened. It will not happen again."

The Papason bowed. With tears in his eyes, he said, "Thank you for saving the life of my only son, Honorable Doctor."

Dr. Houghton bowed deeply.

The next morning the village Mayor visited. Although Dr. Houghton understood his request reasonably well, Lieutenant Ahn translated. "Sir, the Mayor feels that the houseboy was unfairly treated. He says that Sergeant Kim has more to say that will exonerate the houseboy."

.   Sergeant Kim said, "Yes, it is true that I received the envelope from the houseboy, but he knew nothing of the contents."

"I find that difficult to believe. Even if he didn't, he used very poor judgment. But your statement leaves me very little choice but to reinstate him."

The Mayor bowed politely and left, having accomplished his purpose.

Sergeant Kim then spoke up. "You know, Sir, that if you give a bad report to General Kim, not only will my army career be ruined, but he may even kill me for deceiving you. He recommended me; he will lose face. My family, my old mother, my wife, my children will be ruined. Even my sister will die." Sergeant Kim sobbed.

Sergeant Kim would never know that it was his very ill sister who softened Dr. Houghton. The day Sergeant Kim reported to the Detachment, she came for her first visit. She could barely walk into the office. She was twenty-five and, at one time was, without doubt, a beautiful young woman. Dr. Houghton remembered her vividly; a pale, breastless, breathless girl full of tuberculosis. Her marriage had been postponed indefinitely. As she tottered near death, Dr. Houghton provided her with daily injections of streptomycin, and isoniazid and PAS pills. After four weeks of this intensive triple therapy, she stopped coughing blood. Her appetite returned. She would survive.

She said he had altered her "karma." She implied only "Buddhas or Bhodhisattvas" could do that. She was very gracious.

"Can you make restitution, Sergeant Kim?"

"What, sir?"

"Can you give back the money now?"

"No, Sir. I have no money."

"Sergeant Kim, I plan to send you back to your Unit. However, I will state you adequately performed your duties here, which is true. However, I do expect you to repay Papason. I'll verbally tell General Kim, who will be surprised when I send you back, that you became involved in a scandal, but I will not say what kind. I'm going to tell him that you have a debt of 8000 won. He will make certain you pay it." After a long silence, he concluded, "Sergeant Kim, in all honesty, you have been an excellent soldier. I do not wish your sister or wife to suffer. I still want your sister to come here for her treatments. She will die if she doesn't continue."

"Thank you, Sir, for your kindness. I am sorry I let you down, but I am a Korean."

"But this is not just a Korean affair. I hope you will not do this again. General Kim might kill you if he found out."

"I will go back tomorrow. Good-bye and thank you, Sir." Sergeant Kim knew he was a lucky man.

The next evening before he entered the blue chamber for his bath, Dr. Houghton saw the deserted woman signaling him. In a whispered, toothless voice, she said, "Lieutenant Ahn was here today. It is bad."

The deserted lady and her daughter, the house girl, Sugi, depended on Dr. Houghton. In return they spied for him and did other useful tasks. He didn't ask for the spying, but he did not decline their information.

After he bathed and Beautiful Flower told him several jokes, a new passion of hers, he causally asked, "What was Lieutenant Ahn doing here today?"

"He is Viet Cong."

"What did he want?"

She did not reply.

Dr. Houghton grasped her hand. "What did he want, Non'gae?"

"I cannot tell you. I'll tell you when I'm ready. Lieutenant Ahn is Viet Cong."

"But you must tell me."

"You must trust me. Do you think I don't love you? You are everything to me. I am very lucky girl. I knows."

Mollified, Dr. Houghton still wished to know, but when Beautiful Flower made up her mind, she was stubborn. Tricks or bribes would fail. He needed a better strategy. Moreover, he must be careful. She demanded civilized treatment quite properly, and for this, he respected her. When in the wrong by her cannons, she would silently absorb punishment from a superior or elder as she did when Mr. Cameron's Miss Pak thrashed her for deceit. But, when unjustified aggression or even playful roughness confronted her, she would strike back with abandon as he well knew. Within moments she could transform from a passive, obedient woman to a wild inexpugnable opponent. She had the temperament of quicksilver. She was a paradox, at least on the surface, until you understood her beliefs. Some of her blacks were his whites.

He finally said, "I don't want Lieutenant Ahn here anymore. Do you understand?"

"I already told him that. Him Viet Cong." She handed Dr. Houghton a cup of Ceylon tea and said, "I have a Kisaeng joke for you."

Dr. Houghton sat up straight. He thought she could not possibly know about Miss Hu. He was not even guilty yet. He waited expectantly. Fortunately, the joke was excellent and not about Miss Hu. He relaxed as he rolled in laughter. But there was something ironic here. Non'gae was named after the famous Korean Kisaeng who killed the Japanese general; yet, she was telling him a Korean Kisaeng joke in Korean slang. Moreover, here he sat, another barbarian, who also had an eye for Kisaeng girls. When he stopped laughing, he said, "I loved your Kisaeng joke; tell me another."

> "What we obtain too cheaply we esteem too lightly;
> It is dearness only that gives everything its value."
> "The Crisis," Thomas Paine

Chapter XX
Violence

On that sultry Sunday afternoon, Dr. Houghton's eyes swept across the vast concrete gymnasium. He observed the capacity crowd of thirteen thousand nine hundred rabid slant-eyed fans. Only fourteen round eyes were bunched in a cluster near the Governor of the Province. They belonged to General Samet, Colonel Bennet, the Deputy, Colonel Newton, Mike, Mr. Cameron and the Sargeant Major. Beside the Governor sat the Corps Commander, General Lee. The Governor, a retired three star general, and General Lee, an active three star general, like the despotic Korean Kings of old, possessed absolute power in this province. The Koreans regarded them with extreme respect and sometimes fear and trembling. Scanning further, Dr. Houghton saw Beautiful Flower and Mr. Cameron's Miss Pak. On the other side of the gymnasium, in a white silk shirt he saw Miss Hu. She carried a small red balloon, a prearranged signal.

Along with the rest of the crowd, the round eyes had come to see this annual exhibition of Korean Karate, Hap Gi Do. The teachers of this ancient sport, unlike judo, wrestling or boxing, taught the student how to defend oneself against an aggressor with a knife or a stick, or just hands or feet. They also taught the student how to maim or even kill the aggressor. In practice sessions, however, just before the final dispatching blow, or the snapping of an opponent's limb, they taught the student how to stop. Or after jumping high to kick your opponent in the temple, they taught the student how to pull the blow. The Japanese and the Chinese had their own versions of this sport. Well-trained experts, the Black Belts with these skills, were very dangerous. In recognition of this, the Korean National Government registered all Black Belts. Moreover, in a fight, the law was clear; a Black Belt was automatically guilty of an assault no matter what the circumstances, unless he could "prove" that he acted in self-defense.

From the start, compared to the Koreans, Dr. Houghton recognized he had to compensate for his inferior ability to kick high and react instantaneously. He did this with his greater size and strength, and with his determined, near-crazed repetitious practice. One month previously, he obtained his Red Belt, and if all went well, in three months he would reach his goal, a first degree Black Belt. Although this exhibition was somewhere between sciamachy and a real defense against a murderous opponent, it was crucial to perform well, a milestone on his road to the Black Belt.

As he thought of milestones, he remembered vividly that warm June day in 1962 when the President of Harvard awarded college degrees. President Pusey welcomed him into the ranks of educated men. Then on graduation from Yale Medical School, Dean Lippard personally welcomed him into the society of healers and physicians. Soon, Dr. Houghton would join the company of oriental men who had educated their bodies. In his now flexible body, he possessed a new strength and vitality. He was also quite fast. Through the centuries, he knew that very few white men had mastered these Korean skills. Some of these were seventeenth century Dutch sailors, ship-wrecked off Korea. They joined the Korean Army, married Seoul women, and mastered Hap Gi Do. He recently read about them in a Korean history book with Beautiful Flower. Now he knew it could be done. He imagined how these ancient occidental seamen must have felt. He, too, an outsider, was about to compete in controlled violence. As he again surveyed the murmuring crowd, each of whom from a distance closely resembled his neighbor, he was reassured; for he was a little less alien than the sailors. Unlike the Dutchmen in the history book, his hair was light brown not blond.

Since the seventeenth century, however, a change, a forced democratization, had occurred in Korea. In the past, only the sons of the hereditary scholar-official class, the Yangban, participated in this sport. However, the Japanese, during their forty years of occupation in Korea, extinguished the Yangban. The Japanese also forbade instruction in Hap Gi Do and, finally, the Korean language itself. After the Japanese expulsion at the end of the Second World War and at the start of the American occupation, the Koreans opened small gymnasiums in the large cities, sanctioned by the parent Hap Gi Do association in Seoul. Now, the criterion for entry was not Yangban status, but whether one could afford the instruction fee.

Suddenly, over a crackling loud speaker, the announcer silenced the crowd with his introductory remarks. The senior and junior instructors, seven Black Belts in their heavy off-white fighting uniforms, and Dr. Houghton, conspicuous in his Red Belt, ran to the middle of the gymnasium. They climbed through the

310

ropes of the spot-lit boxing ring where the action would take place. Dr. Houghton realized that the area inside the boxing ring was slighter smaller than the normal practice area. He remembered he had been knocked out at Harvard in such a boxing ring. This time, however, he knew he must not fail for he would never be able to look in the mirror again. When he looked up into the crowd at Colonel Bennet who had given Dr. Houghton permission to learn Hap Gi Do, he read the Colonel's mind; "You had better not screw up, Doc. We came to see you, and we don't want to lose face." He also looked at the Deputy's scowling face. He read the Deputy's thought. "Colonel, I told you this was a bad idea. The Doc is going to humiliate us." After all, he represented America, white men, and the occident. But, he soon discarded these worries as ridiculous. He represented only himself.

A glance at the senior instructor, Mr. Ho, finally suggested an answer to an unsolved riddle. Dr. Houghton had questioned Mr. Ho's motives in having him, who was the least skilled, perform in this exhibition. Mr. Ho's answer was incoherent. Now Dr. Houghton understood Mr. Ho's rationale; he realized that if he showed himself to advantage, Mr. Ho could say, "See, we can even teach a barbarian this art." If he failed, Mr. Ho would say, "He, after all, is a barbarian." Mr. Ho could not lose.

After entering the ring, the senior instructor called out each name. At the Korean words, "Houghton, Captain," he stepped forward, and bowed deeply and politely to the Governor. The Governor nodded, General Lee smiled but General Samet was poker faced.

For the initial demonstration, they were all expected to kick a three-quarter inch plywood board and break it. Each man performed the same kick with Dr. Houghton last, as befitted his humble rank. On the first kick, a jump side kick, one man, a second degree Black Belt, failed to break his board. When Dr. Houghton's turn finally came he hesitated briefly, then jumped high and, at the apogee of his leap, threw out his right foot shattering the board. On this kick, he did not possess that ballerina grace or the feline facility of the Koreans, but the board burst no less forcefully. As the cameras flashed at the moment of contact, he wore an appropriately vicious expression. A small ripple of applause encouraged him.

He was last again in the next kick in which the same man failed to break the board. Almost involuntarily, Dr. Houghton, with tremendous force, spun around like a leaping top, his eye fixed on the target as his right heel smashed the board into smithereens. He thought his crack sounded louder than the others, although the kick was an inch or two too high. He almost touched Mr. Yun's upper hand which held the board but Mr. Yun did not flinch.

The others then demonstrated more difficult kicks, sometimes shattering two or even three boards during one high leap - crack, crack, crack. For his individual stunt, Dr. Houghton shattered a stack of ten tiles with a single chop of his hand. To applause, they all left the ring.

While the audience watched spellbound, two second degree Black Belts, agonist and antagonist, demonstrated the proper defenses against various punches and chops. Twice, the defender tossed the wingless attacker in incredible high arcs through the air. The crowd applauded enthusiastically. As the program proceeded, Dr. Houghton watched but did not see the excellent performances. Instead, he mentally reviewed his routine.

Finally, he heard the crackling loud speaker announce his name. He wiped his palms on his uniform and winked at Mr. Kim. He and this particular Mr. Kim, a second degree Black Belt, had practiced their performance for two weeks. He was now confident. Entering the ring, holding Mr. Kim's right hand in his left hand, Dr. Houghton bowed to the Governor who did not acknowledge the bow.

Mr. Yun, the junior instructor, entered the ring, bowed, and ceremoniously passed Mr. Kim a Korean stiletto. The shimmering six inch steel blade reflected the overhead spotlights into the expectant crowd. Mr. Yun left the ring with parting advice in Korean. He said, "Red belt, remember to follow through. Remember to bow at the end to the governor."

Dr. Houghton and Mr. Kim went to the opposite ends of the ring and bowed to each other politely. Then, as planned, Mr. Kim became "vicious." He approached Dr. Houghton, the stiletto low in his right hand, his right foot forward. He plunged the steel toward Dr. Smith's abdomen. With his eyes trained directly on Mr. Kim's eyes rather than the knife, the hardest lesson of all, Dr. Houghton grasped Mr. Kim's right wrist with both hands as he stepped to the right. Then he slithered under Mr. Kim's compromised knife-holding arm as Mr. Kim sailed through the air to avoid a broken elbow. He pinioned the fallen Mr. Kim's right elbow with his knee and removed the knife from the prostrate, immobilized Mr. Kim; he then indicated he could plunge the blade into Mr. Kim's if he wanted. Dr. Houghton then rose like a bounced ball and bowed to Mr. Kim as he returned the knife politely with both hands, handle first. The crowd applauded politely.

Mr. Kim again attempted to stab him in the stomach, but Dr. Houghton this time executed a defense to the left, went under, and brought the knife around with his two hands on Mr. Kim's right wrist, so that Mr. Kim would plunge the stiletto into his own stomach. Just before entry, Dr. Houghton held Mr. Kim's knife-holding wrist taut. They held this pose, gradually rotating so the entire audience would see the denouement of this defense. The crowd applauded enthusiastically.

Eight more times Mr. Kim tried to thrust the knife into Dr. Houghton, several times high, and several times from the left or right sides. Dr. Houghton performed the defenses skillfully except perhaps the ninth maneuver when, without feeling any pain, he noticed a short slice in his forearm. Fortunately, the wound did not bleed. He was relieved when the first ten moves were complete. The knife was sharp and dangerous, but Mr. Yun over- ruled his objections to its use, even in practice. He maintained a wooden knife would not do since wood was "meaningless."

The final ten of the twenty maneuvers were defenses against an opponent who grasps your wrist, shoulder, collar or lapels in a threatening way. Dr. Houghton hoped, with the dangerous stiletto aside, they could now perform with violent abandon. He and Mr. Kim paced about the ring like two mortal enemies. He imitated Mr. Kim's malignant expression. Mr. Kim approached, screamed and grabbed Dr. Houghton's right wrist. With an echoing shriek, Dr. Houghton flipped Mr. Kim over his right hip.

Mr. Kim, as he slowly rose, whispered some unknown Korean phrase. They continued with defenses 12, 13, 14 and 15. Dr. Houghton ignored the camera flashes or the applause at the moment of each throw. He did note, however, that his fifteenth scream was a little weak.

Before number sixteen, Dr. Houghton was anxious. The ring was too small for the requisite long throw. He whispered to Mr. Kim to skip sixteen, but Mr. Kim was already viciously bearing down on him. A short throw would not allow Mr. Kim adequate time to spin around in mid-air and land properly. An adequate long throw would propel him out of the ring. Mr. Kim attacked, and Dr. Houghton perfectly executed the defense with an excellent scream that would congeal the hottest blood. Mr. Kim sailed across the ring, thrown as far as Dr. Houghton dared. But Mr. Kim expecting to be thrown a little further as in practice, had not turned far enough, and he landed on his head. Mr. Kim fell in a heap and did not move.

Dr. Houghton mumbled in English, "Mr. Kim, no jokes now, get up! Please get up! They will lynch me." He started to sweat profusely.

In the oppressive silence after the entire crowd rose to their feet, the senior instructor jumped into in the ring and sat Mr. Kim up. He banged Mr. Kim with a reverberating slap on the back. Mr. Kim opened his eyes. Then, he struck Mr. Kim on the head with the heel of his hand.

Strangely detached, Dr. Houghton rubbed the potential rope track around his neck. He mumbled in English, "Outstanding treatment for a broken neck." He almost collapsed.

But in about a minute, Mr. Kim recovered enough to complete the final four demonstration maneuvers. They then bowed deeply to each other as the crowd applauded enthusiastically. Dr. Houghton remembered they were supposed to bow to the Governor before leaving the ring, but he wasn't sure in which direction to bow. He was mixed up; Mr. Kim had a confused glassy-eyed expression and was of no help. He figured there was a one in four chance that he would be correct, so he took the still dazed Mr. Kim's hand and, side by side, he whispered, "Bow!" They bowed deeply together.

A deafening uproar followed. The crowd screamed in unison, "No, over there!" and pointed to the right. Embarrassed, Dr. Houghton smiled and with Mr. Kim, hand-in-hand, turned to the right and bowed. The crowd then burst into tumultuous laughter and vigorous applause. Bathed in the glare of the bright lights, Dr. Houghton and Mr. Kim trotted from the ring. As he left the floor, Dr. Houghton noted the power grin of the Corps Commander, General Lee, who flashed the V-sign.

Mr. Yun said to Dr. Houghton as he dressed, "That was nice," and then succumbed to nervous laughter. He concluded, "Very close!"

As he left the dressing area, Dr. Houghton saw Miss Hu with her little red balloon. As Reg's mother said, she was dressed "to kill." She was the irresistible fox temptress. Her eyes glowed in the dimness. He winked at her.

She came up close, her breath wintergreen. She said, "I must hear angels and soon."

He inhaled her fragrance and said, "I will come to see you very soon. I promise."

"Hurry, hurry. I can not wait much longer or my tail will grow back."

As prearranged, Dr. Houghton met Colonel Newton, Mr. Cameron and the Sargeant Major outside to ride back with them. General Samet, Colonel Bennet and the Deputy had departed in the General's sedan.

"Very good, Doc. That was outstanding," commented Colonel Newton.

Mr. Cameron agreed. "Except for the confusion at the end, Doc, you were the best of the bunch. I snapped excellent pictures with my Nikon. I will develop them for you."

Colonel Newton immediately turned the conversation to women, for in his mind only women were worth discussing. At Dr. Houghton's urging, Colonel Newton was now back with the chestless Mary Lee. After a prolonged discussion of the relative merits of large versus small women, Dr. Houghton said, "Colonel Newton, I'd like to invite you to my house for dinner. I want to show you what we have been doing."

Mr. Cameron chuckled.

"What night?" Colonel Newton asked. "I am free every night," he laughed.

That evening, after Sugi bathed him, he joined Beautiful Flower for Korean cards and Chinese chess. He waited patiently for a comment on the day's exhibition, but it was not forthcoming. Finally he said in Korean, "What did you think of the exhibition?"

"You play very well, very fierce," she said. She smiled, and then in an instant change of mood, typical of children and Korean women, she launched into a blazing critique. He understood, "You're a big man.....small opponent.....too rough ...... kill..... crazy .... very crazy ....Governor ...everybody said ...."

Dr. Houghton interjected, "Slow down. I don't understand."

Beautiful Flower said in simple Korean, "You were too rough."

"But it was all an act."

She shrugged and allowed the subject to rest.

He changed the subject. "In three days, I must go to the DMZ."

"Be careful. You die. What I going to do?"

"How about Colonel Newton or Mike?"

She retorted, "Nice talk, GI! You think me business lady?"

"I am sorry," he replied, kowtowing. "Forgive me, Noble One."

"Why you give me hard time? You die; I go to Happy Mountain."

Dr. Houghton took hold of her wrists forcefully with one hand, "Non'gae, don't you ever say that! That's not funny. Promise me that never will you even think that!" He knew all too well the high incidence of suicide among the Koreans. He had treated several of the business ladies who had made serious attempts, and most recently a Korean virgin who was seduced by his dispensary Corporal Kang on a detachment picnic. She overdosed with sleeping tablets, went into a deep coma and required artificial respiration. Unfortunately, one week later, she succeeded with the aid of a pistol. And, of course, there was the suicide of Miss Han.

The next evening Dr. Houghton met General Samet at seven for a "nice one-on-one dinner at Camp Page in Chun Chon."

General Samet said, "I have not seen enough of you!"

Dr. Houghton replied, "Anytime."

General Samet laughed. "General Lee and I were very impressed with your exhibition last Sunday. But you were a little rough."

"General, Hap Gi Do is not Tiddly Winks. You can imagine how rough they are with me." He then said in Korean, "I am a humble student."

General Samet roared with laughter. "Have another gin and tonic with me." He then became serious. "I am impressed with your efforts to learn Korean, your Hap Gi Do and most of all with your civic action program. I know of your many medical achievements, including your treatment of the Chief of Staff's and General Lee's problem. I also read your reports and they are models of Advisory Reports. I hear you have even Americanized General Kim who now calls it like it is and doesn't cover up. In short, I hear high praise from everyone, especially Lieutenant General Lee. I myself may come to see you since I am not completely happy with my physicians."

"Thank you for the kind words. Come anytime!"

"But there is one matter I must delicately mention. I know you have a Korean girlfriend in the village, a Miss Flower."

Dr. Houghton almost fainted. How would he know this? Even the Deputy did not know.

"The CID reports to me and I know. I have no problem with that; it is better than the business ladies but I want you to know she has family in North Korea."

"Do you think she is a spy?"

"No I do not, but I am just advising you to be careful."

"Do you have any other advice for me?"

"One of the dividends of being in the military is you see the great things all over the world; you are now being expanded while here in Korea, learning things that you and I could not learn at Harvard." He rotated his gin and tonic glass, "Why did McGeorge Bundy not know the Vietnamese have hated the Chinese since Kublai Khan? He was a Harvard professor but obviously hadn't traveled; in the end he is just just another ignoramus with power! But, enough of that!"

"Tell me the great things in the world, especially those that show one how to lead your life."

General Samet said, "There are four, four perfections."

"Only four?"

"As a given, I assume you will find a worthwhile vocation - in your case as a physician or professor of medicine or medical scientist. I do not recommend a career as a Hap Gi Do instructor or a proprietor of a Kisaeng House." General Samet smiled, "Understood?"

"Yes." Dr. Houghton reddened slightly. Did the General know of the Miss Hans or potentially Miss Hu?

"You must pursue your vocation with relentless enthusiasm, so choose well! Then there are the Four Perfections I mentioned: A Japanese wife, German culture and music, a Chinese amah who cooks Chinese food, and an American house."

Dr. Houghton listened closely as General Samet explained why he believed in these "Four." Then, as General Samet wished, they discussed Hume and Kant's epistemological theories and then Schopenhauer's dim view of women for almost an hour.

Suddenly, General Samet said, "I truly enjoyed our dinner tonight. Is there anything I can do for you? I want to keep in touch especially after you return to the Brigham."

"Yes. I have a question and a request."

"Shoot."

"I hope to be promoted to Major."

"You will. I will accelerate the process. Your question?"

"I had a Sergeant Song who worked for me for over six months. Do you know why he was so highly respected? I could not find out."

"I do know. In his last year in college, he represented Korea against China and Japan in a contest dealing with reading and understanding archaic Chinese poetry. He won and was a national hero. He was a symbol of Korean pride. You well know that after the long occupation by the Japanese and then the Korean conflict, there was a national feeling of worthlessness. Sergeant Song helped to improve the Korean self image. For that, he is a hero, but as I hear it, a very humble hero. Also his father was a hero in the resistance against Japan."

The night after he met with General Samet, the Deputy called. "Doc, I am appalled by the abysmal sanitation and living conditions at the Korean intra-zonal C guard posts. I want you, Sergeant Morse and General Kim to inspect them. I want you to advise the commanders and fix the problem. Capish?"

317

Due to the marked increase of incidents in the DMZ, the Corps Commander General Lee, had to approve any trips inside the DMZ to the guard posts. General Lee gave his permission although reluctantly. He told Dr. Houghton that, aside of the frequent fire fights, the North Koreans were suddenly mining the roads with plastic bombs that could not be easily found with conventional mine detectors. Hence, the Korean army probed the intra-zonal roads with long pikes before vehicles could drive over them. General Lee advised "caution."

As he became "short," his tour of duty in Korea approaching the three-quarter point, Dr. Houghton became less enthusiastic about such arduous and potentially dangerous trips, like to the DMZ. And so he gradually decreased the numbers and distances of advisory visits. He had already evaluated most of the units in his monthly reports. As a consequence, he spent more time studying medicine, practicing his Hap Gi Do, seeing indigent Korean patients and discussing problems with the Koreans at the Corps headquarters, although he knew that field visits were much more productive.

Pondering these matters, Dr. Houghton bounced along in the back of the jeep on the way to the DMZ, the only occupant without a donut. That day, at the last minute, the helicopter "pooped out" and was deemed unsafe, but they were committed to go. In place of the others' rectal pain as they came close to the DMZ, he experienced a subtle fatigue, a creeping exhaustion. The daily rigor of the exercise hall and the love making with Beautiful Flower were tiring but there was also a new psychological fatigue. He suddenly knew what marriage might be like. Was he ready? He realized she controlled his libido; this was not by ruse or stratagem but by her own inner magic. But he knew the solution; all he needed was a little more rest. Each day he must find fifteen minutes for a daytime nap but not in jeeps. Jeep naps in the heat of summer days were now unsatisfactory. . But perhaps equally important, he decided to severely limit distant trips even more.

On this trip, the ceaseless bounding along, like on the back of an intoxicated two-humped camel, was expected. But the summer heat and dust almost overwhelmed him. There was sweaty "mongi" in every crack in his body, covered or not. Even though he wore a cloth face mask, vile dusty fluid emerged when he sneezed. Moreover, the lush viridity of the endless rice paddies did not just bore him; they stank to "high heaven." Moreover, the night soil bubbled in the paddies it was so hot. You could just not ignore it. As they approached the DMZ after three hours in the jeep, he

318

developed a violent throbbing headache. Even an iced tea and aspirin break was of no use.

Sickened by the pounding headache and filthy dirty, he accompanied General Kim into the DMZ. He wondered how many Americans would survive in these bunkers for uninterrupted rotations of six months. He estimated very few. He knew he could not. The stench, rats, bugs, and the stifling horror of the sultry Korean summer were reminiscent of the lowest circles of Dante's Hell, much worse than the Greek Hades. But equally bad, in a different way, was the four month winter rotation without a single shower or bath. The very souls of the troops froze. He remembered suffering through the field for just a few winter weeks not months; he often thought of his Savioress, Miss Han. Even with her, he almost did not make it. The Koreans thought that hatred of the North Koreans and Korean discipline would sustain the soldiers. But Dr. Houghton did not agree.

When it was time to proceed, Dr. Houghton dourly insisted that the Korean infantry Captain, the company commander, accompany them. He still retained the near mystical notion that these captains provided safety. The Captain reluctantly agreed only when General Kim insisted. Dr. Houghton had the clear impression the Captain was afraid which was unusual in these tough men.

Their jeep was followed by a supply truck with a machine-gun toting guard. The Captain reassured them for the third time that the roads had been probed several hours earlier. A machine gunner opened the gate into the DMZ. For reassurance, Dr. Houghton unconsciously patted his bullet proof vest.

They made a quick dash along the raised sandy-ribbon road. The one mile ride to the guard post normally took about two minutes. Everyone crouched forward as the jeep hit thirty miles per hour. About halfway there, Dr. Houghton heard an explosion rip the air behind them. Fragments smashed into the jeep. As Dr. Houghton jumped out, he saw the flaming truck behind them waver and tumble off the road into the gully six feet below. Dr. Houghton and the Captain ran toward the truck. They saw that the supplies and four men had dropped out of the back of the truck. One of the men, apparently disoriented, walked away from the road about ten paces. The infantry Captain screamed "Come back!" but the soldier continued walking away from the road. The Captain ordered Dr. Houghton to lie down on the road. They put their fingers in their ears. An instant later the dazed soldier stepped on a South Korean mine meant to deter infiltrators. The poor bastard sailed toward the sky in small bits and pieces.

Eyes closed, Dr. Houghton heard the shrapnel and pebbles zoom over their heads. Then they stood up and looked at the three remaining soldiers in the gulley. One of them had squirting arterial bleeding from his neck. Dr. Houghton was poised to jump down when the Captain cried, "No! That area of the road is mined. Didn't you notice?"

Of course he had just "noticed." But this soldier in the gully was bleeding to death.

General Kim ordered one of the other soldiers in the gully to stop the bleeding. The soldier, in slow motion, removed his fatigue shirt and pressed it on the wounded man's neck. General Kim ordered, "Let's go back. Send another jeep to pick them up."

As they drove back Dr. Houghton knew they must have rolled over the mine, but the heavier truck behind them had detonated it. Three men died, two were slightly hurt, but the soldier with the arterial bleeding was moribund when they retrieved him. Dr. Houghton started saline infusions intravenously but he knew whole blood was necessary. Sergeant Morse noted the soldier had no detectable pulse or blood pressure, although Dr. Houghton heard heart sounds. "General Kim," Dr. Houghton said, "the saline will only keep him alive for a few minutes. He will never survive the forty minute trip to the hospital. He needs whole blood, now. Get two volunteers with the same blood type."

A few minutes later, General Kim said, "No one volunteered."

Dr. Houghton was stunned. He understood the Koreans dislike of blood donations, but this unfortunate soldier might survive if.... "Choose two volunteers, General!"

Two minutes later after a near mutiny, General Kim selected two volunteers with the correct blood type, the Captain and a very unwilling private – at gun point. Dr. Houghton first connected the private to the wounded soldier and transfused an estimated one pint. This produced a palpable pulse. The Captain's blood then produced a clear blood pressure. In the interim, Sergeant Morse had arrested the neck bleeding. At that point, they loaded the soldier into an ambulance. Dr. Houghton later learned that he survived when the soldier sent a "thank you for my life" letter."

As if nothing unusual had happened, Dr. Houghton went to the Hap Gi Do lesson as usual. The sight of his exercise hall friends raised his spirits; the exercise itself cured his headache, leaving him lucid and pleasantly fatigued. Later that evening, during the ritual bath in the blue chamber, little Miss Kim interrupted the physical alembic of her magic hands; she pointed to a previously unnoticed hole and linear welt on his right shoulder. "What is that, Honorable Doctor?" She knew right away.

320

Dr. Houghton glanced at the wound in the mirror. It suddenly started to hurt. He remarked, "Oh, it's probably a lost or misguided worm."

Miss Kim did not laugh. She forced Dr. Houghton face down on the pillow to continue her gentle back massage. She and Beautiful Flower, by exaggerated reports, knew of the day's events. And Miss Kim was not as simple as everybody suspected. She knew it was not a burrowing worm but a shrapnel injury. She also knew he needed to attend to it. Several of her tears fell silently on his back, but she continued without interruption.

At dinner, Beautiful Flower could not conceal the fact that she too knew about the DMZ episode. In Korea, such incidents spread faster than the plague. After little Miss Kim whispered in her ear, Beautiful Flower burst into inconsolable weeping.

Not certain of the reason, he tried to sooth her. "If you stop crying, I'll give you one chocolate bar."

"I want two," she said as she wiped the tears away. Then more subdued than usual, she said, "You funny man, also brave man, I think so."

Dr. Houghton shuddered involuntarily. Without doubt they had heard an exaggerated version of the story. This may be excellent for my image, he thought, but he was certainly not a brave man; to be precise, he was now a lucky man to have Beautiful Flower in his arms. For his jeep must have rolled over that mine. As she dried her tears, he flipped his most lecherous wink at Miss Kim.

Beautiful Flower laughed at this in the midst of her bubbling emotions. She said, "Can do. I can do. Miss Kim no."

Dr. Houghton sighed. He wished he had taken his "essential" daytime nap.

Exactly four weeks after his exhibition, Sergeant Morse knocked. "Yes, Sergeant Morse?"

"A Miss Hu is here to see the Captain. She says you know her."

"Please bring her in."

Dr. Houghton rose from his neurology textbook and observed an obviously sick Miss Hu. He said in polite Korean, "Please have a seat." Gentle tears slowly flowed down her fever-flushed cheeks. He observed she had lost weight and had dark rings under her eyes. He involuntarily thought of Japanese cherry blossoms, and their evanescence. "What is the matter Miss Hu?"

"I am sick. Can you help me?"

"I will try. But you must tell me the whole story, the truth. Will you? Speak slowly in Korean so I do not need a translator."

"Yes, Honorable Captain."

"Well?"

"About four weeks ago, after a Kisaeng party, a drunken customer, a rich bad man tried to force me. I told him I am not a business lady. One of his servants grabbed me. They ripped off my pants and this rich man tried to mount me. I fought him and he stuck it in me once partially, but I fought him off in a few seconds. I bit him on the neck, hard, until he bled. Unfortunately, the next week I developed uterus pain and went to the Korean Hospital. The said I had VD from this dirty man. They gave me penicillin for two weeks and then tetracycline for ten days. I am worse. I have fevers every day; I can not eat; I still have pain." She pointed to her right lower abdomen. "I can not work. My money all gone. I am desperate. I thought of you. Maybe you have better medicine; you can help - me?"

"I must examine you."

"Of course."

Dr. Houghton called for the nurse and performed abdominal, pelvic and rectal examinations. It was difficult to believe that four weeks ago she was an ideal specimen. Moreover, she smelled bad. Sergeant Morse took blood tests, stained the smears and placed several cultures. They looked at the smears together. "No gonos. Agree?"

"Agree," Sergeant Morse said. "Will the Captain try high dose erythromycin?"

"Yes." He also asked Sergeant Morse on her next visit to take stool samples. Almost everyone in Korea had parasites from the night soil they spread on the fields. Intestinal worms can cause abdominal pain.

After she dressed, he said, "Miss Hu, we think you have pelvic inflammatory disease. Your right ovary is very swollen and inflamed. We do not think you have gonorrhea or syphilis but we have cultures and blood tests to be sure. We think you should be treated with high dose erythromycin."

Miss Hu took out a piece of paper that said erythromycin on it. She said, "My Korean doctor say the same thing but they no have in Chun Chon pharmacy."

"We have it and we shall give it to you."

Over a period of two weeks, on erythromycin, Miss Hu gradually improved. She came twice weekly. On her fourth visit, she was clearly better. She no longer had fever, but she had some residual abdominal pain.

Dr. Houghton said, "You have several other problems. You have hookworms and round worms and are also anemic. Your worms may contribute to your abdominal pain and anemia."

She said, "Will you help me? Can you help me?"

"Yes." Dr. Houghton said. He treated her round worms first and then her hookworms. He gave her iron and vitamins for her anemia.

At a follow up visit the following week, she said, "I passed a huge number of worms. Now I am free of abdominal pain. I can work but I am now going to be a Kisaeng nun, and boil my water and vegetables as you told me. I feel wonderful!"

Dr. Houghton was delighted. In a sense, when he first saw her so sick he thought he had lost a soul-shaking carnal opportunity; now he saw a different and richer opportunity for bonding and possibly friendship with Miss Hu. He might need a Korean woman to help him with certain vague future plans that were floating in his head. Beautiful Flower could not, especially after General Samet's subtle warning. Moreover, he did not have confidence in the venal Business Ladies. He wanted someone who he could trust implicitly. Although he did not treat her initially with ulterior motives, he now thought he might be able to use her gratitude and intelligence. Moreover, he was not planning to use her *only* as what Kant would call a "means." He would be certain that she obtained something of real value to her - not just a gold happy-bag or ring.

So when she said, "You promised me before; I still want to hear angels. Now I am well," Dr. Houghton was intellectually committed. He said, "In a few more weeks when you are all better, when you anemia is better, I promise."

Miss Hu winked at him. "I know Honorable Captain honorable. What song will angels sing?"

Although unprofessional, Dr. Houghton patted her on her buttocks and said, "Don't be greedy! Moreover, maybe one day you can help me."

She smiled broadly with her perfect white teeth and dimples. "Yes. Anything you want!"

In a medical sense, he was overjoyed she was cured, for, in fact, he did not know what venereal disease he treated. He did know, however, that some patients like General Lee and Miss Hu responded. Operationally, did it matter? There was no alternative. In an aesthetic sense, he was also overjoyed; with an antibiotic and worm medicine, he saw the fragrant concubine reborn, with her Cupid's bow lips, dimples and promise of celestial angels' smiles. He also noted the return of the spring in her shapely muscular legs. In a practical sense, he now had a potential colleague.

323

At the BOQ, Dr. Houghton stepped into the shower after returning from the exercise hall. He pondered his plan for Miss Hu. It was not ethical of him to have any real relationship with her if he were her physician. It was not ethical to take advantage of patient gratitude. He remembered Drs. Barnes and Tierney. He would find her a physician at Camp Page in Chun Chon. Second, he knew that his mother was correct: virtue was its own reward. But why should he not obtain a few small rewards for his many "good works?" Isn't that how the world works? Practically, he reminded himself that he must give the operator of Miss Hu's Kisaeng house money, so he could take her any time he needed her and be certain the operator did not move her.

As he emerged from the shower, Lieutenant Ahn walked in. He flailed his arms about and his eyes darted around with great excitement. Dr. Houghton thought Neil Armstrong must have landed on the moon.

"Captain," he asked, "did you get the latest poops?"

"No, I didn't. What's up?"

"We're locked on the compound until further notice."

"Can guests come on the compound?"

"Yes, Sir, to the movies and club, only."

"What's the reason? For how long?"

"Nobody knows, Sir."

Dr. Houghton picked up the phone and spoke ----- operator. "Zero, zero, zero, one; three rings, please."

A hesitant female voice answered in Korean with a shy, "Pak, Beautiful Flower, here."

He spoke in Korean, "Hello, Beautiful Flower. How are you?"

"Is that you Reginald?"

"Yes, Humble Student here."

"I will come to the movies tonight with Mr. Cameron's Miss Pak."

Dr. Houghton was not surprised that the girls already were aware of the lock-in. "Is Miss Kim there, Beautiful Flower?"

"No, Reginald. She will come later."

"Why don't you bring Sugi along?"

"OK, I'll see you at eight. Good-bye, Reginald."

"Good-bye, Non'gae."

"Hi, Mike, Mr. Cameron," Dr. Houghton said as he entered the bar at the officers' club. "What's up?"

"I guess you heard. We're locked in by order of Colonel Bennet, and he won't say why."

"Yes, I know. Things are getting pretty grim."

324

"Don't see much of you these days," said Mike. "Most of your time is spent making house calls and ....." Mike shrieked and assumed a fighting stance. "Doc, I really enjoyed the exhibition. I'd really like to come for the Black Belt examination, where it's for real, not pre-arranged stuff."

"Mike, I'd really like to have you come. I'd be honored, but they don't allow visitors. It gets pretty rough. You have to fight with the instructors, and sometimes the instructor dismantles the candidates. I've seen several really brutal beatings. One time, I thought Mr. Yun, the instructor, went too far. I tried to stop it. What a commotion I caused! I was threatened with the bamboo stick for overstepping the bounds of a student."

"They're savages, Doc," said Mike. "I've told you time and again." In a different tone, Mike asked, "How are things with Miss Pak?" Mike continued, counseled by his Irish demon. "Are you having as much fun as with Miss Han in Hong Kong?"

Dr. Houghton ignored Mike's leer. "Things are going well. I'm having an excellent time."

"Why don't you marry her?" asked Mr. Cameron. "You're single. She's a beautiful girl, smart, educated. What do you want?"

As he approached the bar, Colonel Newton said, "Don't Doc. In the States it wouldn't work. Take my word for it. I've been in the Army for a long time. I've seen too many of these interracial marriages." Colonel Newton shook his head in categorical disapproval.

Dr. Houghton answered, "Colonel, I want you to withhold judgment until after you visit our house. Maybe you'll have a different view then." He laughed.

With Non'gae, Miss Chang and Miss Kim, he planned to blow poor Colonel Newton's mind into quivering fragments, as soon as the crazy lock-in ended. They would tease Newton mercilessly; he had a fiendish plan. After a pause, Dr. Houghton borrowed the rapier from Mike. "Colonel, in the States, I bet you never chase girls. I bet you're a pillar of the WASP community, a complete hypocrite."

The Colonel admitted, "Even in Germany, I never seriously thought of philandering. I have done it only on my two tours here in Korea. I am a different man here."

Colonel Newton turned to Major Norman, who sat at the bar, depressed, teary-eyed, and silent. He said, "Norman do not fret; the lock-in will soon end."

"I hope so," Major Norman replied in a monotone.

Mike said, "Norman. I'll lend you my Po-go stick or my wire cutters."

Dr. Houghton cautioned Major Norman, "Watch out, the Deputy is keeping an evil eye on you. Don't let him catch you in the village."

"I won't, Doc," Major Norman answered.

Dr. Houghton enjoyed the movie and, even more, Beautiful Flower's deep involvement with the emotional heroine. For more than an hour she identified with an occidental girl, her knots of desire, and even her destiny. She cried but loved the movie.

At eleven thirty, the phone rang rousing him from dreams of the Kisaeng Non'gae and the Japanese general, then of Non'gae as Beautiful Flower. He was mixed up. Was he on call at the Brigham? He finally reached for the phone, "Yes?"

"Doc, this Miss Judy," she whispered. "Come down to NCO Club now. Major Norman, him crazy man! Him have gun. Big trouble, here. Quick come!"

Dr. Houghton dressed quickly and ran down to the club. As he approached, he heard very loud juke box music. He entered cautiously. As his eyes accommodated to the dimness, he saw Miss Judy rush toward him. She put her hand in his, "Norman, he going to shoot someone."

There were six NCOs including Sergeant Morse and several Korean girls cowering near the bar. They were scared "shitless." Major Norman disheveled and drunk, waved his forty-five at them.

"Shut off the juke box," Dr. Houghton whispered to Miss Judy.

At the sudden cessation of the screaming Beatles, a menacing silence enveloped the club. Major Norman flinched when the music stopped.

Dr. Houghton approached him with Miss Judy at his side. He said, "What's the trouble?"

"You come close, Doc, and I'll shoot you."

Sergeant Morse said, "Doc, the clip is in place."

Dr. Houghton paused and noted the look on Norman's face. He was mad, berserk; he had run amuck. Dr. Houghton had promised Colonel Bennet he would keep an eye on Major Norman. He had clearly failed. He should have seen this coming.

The clink of a glass to his left momentarily captured Major Norman's attention. With the focus of a hungry hawk, Dr. Houghton watched Major Norman's unsteady eyes turn slightly to the left. For nine months now, he had learned to watch his opponent's eyes for intention; open eyes do not conceal information, and so, as if in the exercise hall, he kicked. The pistol flew out of Major Norman's hand and discharged when it hit the floor. A shot harmlessly sailed

326

over Miss Judy's shoulder into a wall. Twenty hands grabbed a shocked Major Norman.

That evening, Dr. Houghton put Major Norman in restraints and a deep sleep. He planned to send him to Seoul in the morning for psychiatric hospitalization. He reported the episode to Colonel Bennet. That night, after midnight, on the way back to the BOQ to resume his slumbers, Dr. Houghton became aware of Miss Judy's hand in his. He remembered she wished to speak with him. "Come in, Miss Judy," he said, as she entered the BOQ which was now forbidden to Korean women.

Miss Judy fumbled with her hands as she prepared to speak.

A slightly dazed Dr. Houghton observed her soigné appearance, especially her high cheek bones and her dimples. He recalled the two middle-aged American Colonels, her former boy friends, who had traveled to Korea to see her recently. He had dined with one of them, Colonel Blue, a former detachment Commander who had returned hoping to recapture a long gone past. Colonel Blue said that Miss Judy was one of the sexual "magic ladies." He was obviously in love with her, five years after he left Korea. But Miss Judy would not even see him. Colonel Jones was the other one. Before he left Korea, he had threatened an innocent Dr. Houghton. But Miss Judy would not see Jones again either. He understood the feelings of Colonels Blue and Jones about Miss Judy. They were not simpletons; but sophisticated men of the world, hoping for more, trying to recapture awe and the sublime. As Dr. Houghton waited for her to start, he also remembered Colonel Newton words, "Doc, you are crazy not to enjoy her."

Miss Judy finally spoke with a contorted face in her broken English. "Doc, you nice man; not chicken or knucklehead. You help many Koreans. I love only two men, my baby's father and you. Please!"

Dr. Houghton felt sweat form on his forehead and in his armpits. Why did she say this? Did she feel guilty for no longer working in the clinic?

Miss Judy stood and removed her sweater and her bra.

He stood.

She took his hand and placed it over her breast which was that of a twenty five year old. He thought again of Colonel Blue's sexual "magic lady".

"I want you to make love to me, now! I boil!"

He kissed her on the lips. "Miss Judy, I think I love you too, but tonight is not the right time. Another night. I want to make love to you. Please dress, Miss Judy. I'll come right back."

He walked to the bathroom and observed a white face with red eyes in the mirror. He was now shaky, afraid, but of what he was not certain.

At the gate, she said, "I want you to say, 'Can do. I love you.'"

Again he said, "Another night," but he lied.

Before finding sleep, he trembled in bed for a few minutes before calming down. He thought of Major Norman, a very close call, and of Miss Judy's recent Sergeant, with whom rumor said she no longer associated. Then he reflected that a sampling of Miss Judy would not spoil his splendid affair with Beautiful Flower. Who would know except him? He could find no reasonable motive not to possess her. Colonel Newton's advice pounded in his ears. "Doc, you are crazy ..... Doc, you're nuts. You will never have such an opportunity again!" He also ruminated over Colonel Blue's description. What exactly did Blue mean? But finally, a vision of the youthful teary eyed Non'gae at the movies calmed him down. She would come again tomorrow for the new movie. He checked the alarm and fell into a deep sleep.

Tossing and turning later, half-sleep, he perceived some danger in a vague way. This had happened several times before. Previously, he awoke reluctantly, looked about, and found no cause for alarm. But this night, he turned his head, opened one eye and saw the hall light disappear as the door to the living room quietly closed. But he heard only his heart beat and cricket chirpings. But he could smell the odor of Lieutenant Ahn's Korean cigarette smoke. In an instant he jumped up and opened his door. The corridor was empty. There was no one outside the door. But as he walked toward his bed, he heard a door click and then a cricket chirp in the silence. The click and the cigarette smoke make him quite sure that it was Lieutenant Ahn who visited his room that night.

Dr. Houghton checked his possessions and papers carefully, but nothing was missing. Certain that this had happened at least several times before, he decided to lock his door even when present. Although he always locked his door and even the windows when he went out because of the problem with slicky boys, he did not secure the door when he slept there.

The next night, during the movie Dr. Houghton received a message from Colonel Newton to come to the dispensary. At the dispensary, Colonel Newton explained, "The Korean MP's brought Lieutenant Ahn here a few minutes ago. I'm duty officer tonight. It looks to me like he has been badly beaten. The MPs say they found him in an alley in Chun Chon. He wasn't supposed to be off the detachment because of the lock-in."

"I'm all right, Sir. It's nothing," Lieutenant Ahn mumbled.

"Lie down, Lieutenant Ahn," Dr. Houghton ordered, noting Ahn's broken nose and several broken ribs. He was covered with bruises and bumps.

"I think we had better send him to the Korean Evacuation Hospital now," Dr. Houghton said to Colonel Newton.

"I'll call Colonel Bennet," said Colonel Newton, "and inform him ----- because of the lock-in."

"What were you doing in Chun Chon?"

Lieutenant Ahn said nothing.

"Who beat you up?"

Lieutenant Ahn maintained his silence.

Colonel Newton replaced the phone in the receiver. "The boss says OK."

Three days later Dr. Houghton's houseboy said Lieutenant Ahn had returned to the detachment and packed his few possessions after leaving the hospital. After seven days, he was considered AWOL. After two weeks, the Deputy called the Korean Army personnel section to inquire about Lieutenant Ahn. They knew nothing. A replacement was requested by the Deputy, and Lieutenant Ahn was transferred on paper back to the Korean Army.

"The little Road says, Go;
The little House says, Stay;
And oh, it's bonny here at home,
But I must go away."
                "The House and the Road,"
                Josephine P. Peabody

Chapter XXI
Sentiments of Love

"Reginald, I wish to go to Maitreya's birthday celebration next week. My favorite Bodhisattva is Maitreya, the Buddha of the Future. When I was a child, I loved Maitreya with his huge happy bag; I always wanted to know what was in it for me. Alas, generally nothing. The Buddhist monks also taught me Maitreya was a shape-shifter but how could such a fat man shift his shape? As I grew older, I could not believe that Maitreya passed through the ten stages of wisdom and achieved sartori. But the monks claimed he did. The monks also said he could alter reality and everyone prayed to him. I did too but nothing ever happened. However, I still have some hope.

"What are you praying for now?"

"You knows."

"My favorite is the Kwan Yin, the Goddess of Mercy, She Who Listens," Reginald said. "I hope to buy the jadeite carving of the Kwan Yin from the Golden Monastery."

"Will you take me?"

"Of course, Non'gae; who else would I take, Miss Chang?"

"You are Viet Cong!" She jumped on him with a hot fragrant kiss.

Lovely in a white silk brocade Western style dress they had bought in Chun Chon, after a long climb up a high hill, Non'gae arrived at the local middle school at dusk to celebrate Bodhisattva Maitreya's birthday. Reginald met her there in a suit and tie. A throng of Korean women in bright traditional dresses carried candle-lighted, white waxed-paper lanterns. They milled around and intermingled with the tonsured Buddhist priests and nuns dressed in special grey garments. The priests carried huge signs on sticks.

The white signs were covered with large scarlet Chinese characters. As daylight ebbed with fading pink streaks in the sky, a

330

pale red suffusion overspread the celebrants and observers. Gradually Dr. Houghton was infected with the spiritual ambience. He too hoped the Maitreya was about, hopefully with his happy bag.

The chaos of the crowd suddenly began to assume an order, a hierarchy. At the head of the coming procession, eight Buddhist monks would carry a twelve foot white lantern. Dr. Houghton watched the monks light the large inner candles. As they did so the translucent lantern came alive, coruscating and showing off the huge scarlet Chinese characters on all four sides. Next musicians with hour-glass shaped drums, huge cymbals, and giant triangles assembled. They were followed by a multitude of women with individual lanterns, also inscribed with scarlet Chinese characters. As the candles were lit, these lanterns also shimmered with pink overtones. Interspaced were schoolboy bands and other musical groups.

The partially ordered crowd now hushed as the senior Buddhist monk, high on a platform, spoke a few words in Chinese and then Korean. When he finished, hundreds of ringing bells, accompanied by the throbbing of drums and the discordant crash of cymbals, indicated the start of the procession. Walking at the head of the throng, two by two, were the tonsured Buddhist priests with the giant lantern and then the tall white posters. They were followed by the well dressed women laity with their smaller lanterns, also two by two. Dr. Houghton estimated the endless numbers of celebrants with their swaying lanterns: thousands. After the three bands passed by, there was another multitude of young girls with even smaller candle-powered lanterns.

Enthusiastically, Dr. Houghton observed the procession which now seemed to float in front of him. He watched it snake its way down the high hill and into the valley, and then like a lit serpent wind its way up the next high hill. The two by two procession ultimatlely extended several miles.

When he finished his small flask of Scotch, he carefully observed Non'gae who looked eerie in the whitish-reddish glow of the lanterns. For a moment, he needed reassurance that this red-tinted girl actually stood there, that this was not just a dream from his schooldays. Even the touch of her hand did not completely convince him of her reality. He could not remove his eyes from her while she watched the procession pass. She was unaware of his gaze.

Out of nowhere, a huge pinkish eidolon walked toward them. It was Colonel Newton. Initially, the Colonel watched the preoccupied Beautiful Flower, not the procession.

He whispered, "I see what you mean, Doc. She is something."

331

"We'll see you tomorrow at eight."

Colonel Newton walked on followed by Miss Lee, Mary Lee. She, too, paused to look at Beautiful Flower who was entranced by the procession.

Dr. Houghton nodded to Miss Lee, stepped back and whispered, "This is my girl."

"Doc, she is very beautiful," Miss Lee said in polite Korean.

As the individual instants flowed by, Dr. Houghton wondered exactly what was happening to Non'gae. She was possessed, as if by Maitreya or the Pure Land Buddha.

He asked again, "Are you a Buddhist?"

"Yes and no," she replied in Korean.

"Are you feeling all-right?"

She answered in Korean, "I am well, thank you."

As he continued to watch her, he did not understand the slight contractions of her face; he did not recognize her strange expression, a mask of some kind, not horrid, but...... That exact facies he had observed somewhere. Anxious for a moment, he vaguely recollected the pictures of Michelangelo's Cumae Sybil; the drug intoxicated priestess of Apollo at Delphi; the drunken followers of Sabazius, the beer god; the maenads of Dionysius; and the Gorgon, Medusa. He also thought of his psychotic patients in the hospital. But none of these occidental visages were actually what he sought. What he had forgotten was a small picture in his Chinese culture textbook; a visage of an enchanted shaman lady from the delicate wastes of Siberia three thousand years ago. Had he remembered, he would have observed the identity of expression; Non'gae was a perfect avatar. He asked, "What is happening, Beautiful Flower?"

She smiled. "You do not know?" She said innocently without condescension, "I will tell you one day."

She crushed him. He weakly made another unsuccessful attempt. He incorrectly guessed she was thinking of her lost past, what she might have been, a royal Yi, a Yangban, an aristocrat. Only she and, possibly, the Maitreya understood.

As the procession continued, she said, "Please wait here. I'll be back in a few minutes. Then we must return home."

He waited.

Ten minutes later, she returned, different now, with three white Chinese roses. Later she was "primrose gay."

The next evening Dr. Houghton and Colonel Newton walked into the village, then toward the red-tiled paper-house. Colonel Newton said, "The Orient is a strange place. If my Miss Lee knew

332

that I was going with you tonight, she'd be furious. The girls are really possessive. By the way, Doc, what was the matter with Beautiful Flower last night?"

Dr. Houghton said, "You noticed too. I have no idea; I thought I'd seen it all in my medical studies – assorted gods, nuts full of Christ, madmen, epileptics, the intoxicated, the poisoned. I've never seen that before; I guess a kind of spell." After a short silence, he said, "Colonel, I've scheduled a special program for you tonight, similar to what I experience when I go into the village. First --- but you'll see."

"I'm in your capable, but dangerous hands." Colonel Newton postured with a Hap Gi Do imitation, with obvious anticipatory relish.

They arrived at the paper house and Colonel Newton inquired, "Doc, what's first?"

"You see the small building beside the house? First go in there. It's called the blue chamber. You must do as you are told."

Colonel Newton walked in, and Sugi, the housegirl, followed. She had volunteered to bathe the mighty Colonel. Somehow he managed to indicate to Sugi, although she spoke little English, that he was huge because in America he ate small women for breakfast. For weeks, Sugi trembled at the thought of the huge Colonel.

Reginald and Beautiful Flower along with Miss Chang and little Miss Kim had planned the evening with extraordinary care. Beautiful Flower and Miss Chang had renewed their friendship from their Teahouse days after Miss Chang promised not "to poach Dr. Houghton." She also promised to call Non'gae Beautiful Flower to minimize confusion.

Beautiful Flower wore her most expensive, canary-yellow hanbok, the traditional Korean dress. She looked like an exotic butterfly. Exhilarated with anticipation for the upcoming evening, Miss Chang also looked more sensual than ever in a short navy blue skirt and tight white sweater. Her breasts, large for a Korean woman, quivered when she moved. Moreover, tonight, as planned, she was confident that she could arouse lust in a stone. Little Miss Kim was bedecked in a sleek, floor length, blue silk Chinese cheongsam with a single slit on the right side.

Fifteen minutes after he entered the blue chamber, Colonel Newton screamed as the ice water hit him. The girls and Dr. Houghton contained their laughter. Finally, the Colonel joined the four conspirators. He wore a blue silk Chinese robe with a wide yellow band. There was nothing underneath except shiny red silk shorts and massive black hirsuteness. As he observed the crimson chamber, and then the three girls, his eyes opened wide, like the doltish white men, painted as Negroes, in the cartoons. "Wow, Doc, this is really something!"

"Colonel, you know Beautiful Flower, and you have seen Miss Chang at the Morning Glory Tea House. This is little Miss Kim."

Like most Americans Colonel Newton misused the bow. He bowed in awe, gratitude, or respect rather than according to the rules. He made deep bows to Beautiful Flower and then to Miss Chang and Miss Kim.

The girls bowed back. Miss Chang smiled broadly revealing her perfect white teeth.

"Colonel, look at those teeth," Dr. Houghton commented. He pointed to Miss Chang. "It's a pleasure to look in her mouth, at her clear glistening tongue and clean white teeth. There is no gold, silver or porcelain." The Korean girls were always brushing their teeth, Miss Chang no exception.

A little later Colonel Newton peered inside Miss Chang's mouth. He said, "You're right, Doc."

"And here, Colonel, is little Miss Kim. She speaks no English."

Colonel Newton bowed deeply again and in Korean said, "How are you, Kim?"

Little Miss Kim blushed scarlet at Colonel Newton. Dr. Houghton was large, but this stout, hairy giant .... She bowed and lowered her eyes.

As the evening proceeded, Colonel Newton did not conceal his lust for Miss Chang. He could not keep his eyes off her or her bosom. He compared her with his flat Mary Lee.

Miss Chang repeatedly glanced at Dr. Houghton for reassurance. He winked back. The plan was working, clearly and already.

He asked, "Did you enjoy the bath and massage?"

"Outstanding. You know, Sugi ran all over me, my back and chest; her feet and toes are incredible. Do you do this every night?"

"Most nights," he smiled and clapped three times. The deserted lady and Sugi brought in the meal in gold bowls.

"Because you are a guest, Colonel, you must have these chopsticks as a token of tonight."

"They are solid gold, aren't they?"

"Yes, but remember gold is 32 dollars an ounce here."

Colonel Newton asked, "Do you think Nixon will take us off the gold standard?"

"I don't know."

The Colonel ate the boiled rice, broiled steak strips and kimchi ravenously, with much lip smacking and several excellent belches. He reclined on the silk pillows and puffs, too stout to sit cross-legged for long. He drank an enormous quantity of high quality rice wine, encouraged by Miss Chang.

"The meal was excellent," Colonel Newton bowed to the hostess. He touched his forehead to the floor. "Thank you very much, Beautiful Flower." All three girls politely placed their left hands over their smiles at this egregious solecism.

The Colonel is all charm tonight, Dr. Houghton thought. Even the belches outdid the Koreans by an order of magnitude.

"Now, Colonel, I want you to take this tablet. It's a mild mind-expander and will help you to enjoy the entertainment." He handed the Colonel a sugar coated placebo pill. "Now sit back here with me and enjoy the entertainment. Beautiful Flower will first perform the Korean traditional dance. We'll accompany her."

Following the girls' instructions, Dr. Houghton began tapping on both sides of the large, hour-glass shaped drum. Little Miss Kim played the Korean lute and Miss Chang sang as Beautiful Flower danced.

Colonel Newton watched her sinuous grace with rapt attention. She danced a butterfly dance; to him that evening, she was a butterfly. To Dr. Houghton he whispered, "Doc, I retract my advice about marriage. She is without doubt a charming accomplished woman."

Miss Kim was featured next, playing the lute and singing Miss Han's favorite song.

Holding back his tears, Dr. Houghton explained to Colonel Newton that it concerned a Korean Kisaeng whose lover had abandoned her. She was about to commit suicide. Dr. Houghton did not expect Colonel Newton's reaction. Tears glistened in his eyes. With their eldritch songs, the girls of this tragic country consistently caused American men to cry or even weep; men who had previously been emotional stones. And yet, Dr. Houghton did not believe his own eyes. He could not imagine that this tough, cynical Colonel, the "employer" of Mary Lee, would be so touched by alien feelings. When Miss Kim finished, they applauded boisterously.

Dr. Houghton said in Korean, "Little Miss Kim. That was wonderful; I have purchased a present for you." He placed a solid gold bracelet encrusted with several smoky topazes around her tiny wrist.

She was overcome with gratitude. She could not speak for several minutes.

While the girls busied themselves with the trivia related to the comfort of their large guest, Dr. Houghton arranged the red spotlight and turned on the stereo. The brassy strip tease music surprised Colonel Newton.

"Miss Chang is an ecdysiast," Dr. Houghton explained.

As part of the plan, Miss Chang had watched the illicit movies of Bubbles, Peaches and Candy Bar carefully and practiced diligently. Fortunately the "G" string and tassels had just arrived from the States. He told his shocked mother he would explain when he came home. Fortunately, she was a "good sport." Miss Chang was now ready for a bold attempt. For a minute, she left the chamber, put on her costume and high-heeled red pumps.

Glowing in the direct and indirect red light, she performed well. First she removed the scarlet ribbon from her ebony black hair, and it tumbled down over her shoulders; Colonel Newton grunted. Next she removed her sweater and kicked off her skirt revealing long legs, a thin waist and ample bosom. Then her bra came off, and she tossed and then rotated the tassels; Colonel Newton groaned. Finally, she took off her scarlet panties, bumped and ground. When the music suddenly stopped, she stood still and rippled the "G" string. Dr. Houghton wondered how she did it. Colonel Newton moaned. After her final gratuitous bump, he attempted to grab her, as she tapped him on the head with her hip, and was gone.

A red-eyed Colonel Newton, as the lights came on, said, "Now what, Doc?"

"It is ten-thirty, Colonel. Soon we must go."

"What?" he whispered. "Doc, I want you to let me have Miss Chang."

"No, that's impossible."

"Well then, I am giving you a direct order."

"That's an illegal order. I'll tell you why when we leave. There's a good reason."

Miss Chang returned in a silk robe. She adored the adoration. Her life would be different when and if she married her suitor farmer; a life of passive acquiescence and hard labor for her and her son.

Dr. Houghton wondered if perhaps she might desire Colonel Newton. He, after all, was a remarkable specimen of manhood. Virile, big and powerful, perhaps he would please her, but Dr. Houghton knew how she had reacted to her previous liaisons, motivated by filial piety. "Miss Chang," he said to her in Korean, "Beautiful Flower and I have bought this for you." He placed a gold Happy-Bag around her neck.

As she turned and lowered the front of her gown to receive the gift, Colonel Newton saw the cleavage of her recently exposed ample bosom. "Doctor, she's mine, please." He leered and pleaded; finally he begged.

Miss Chang understood and winked at Colonel Newton but threw her arms about Dr. Houghton and kissed him. She thanked Beautiful Flower and then touched Colonel Newton on the cheek with a hen peck.

With hoarse lust, Colonel Newton mumbled, "How about one for me like the Doc?"

"I'm truly sorry," she said in English and smiled.

Then, Dr. Houghton produced the surprise of the evening; five small diamonds framed in a white gold heart. He hung it around Beautiful Flower's swan neck. With Korean abandon, she overwhelmed him with kisses.

"We have to go, girls," Dr. Houghton said in Korean. "Thank you very much. Tomorrow at noon, Beautiful Flower and I fly to Taegu. I have a four day pass. I'll be here at ten. Be packed and ready Beautiful Flower."

Both pleasantly high, Dr. Houghton and Colonel Newton walked back to the detachment.

"Doc, why not?" The deep rasp of lust lingered in his throat.

Dr. Houghton explained Miss Chang's predicament with her father, son and unhappy past and her possible marriage to the farmer.

"Do me a favor, Doc; at least ask her if she'd be interested."

"I will Colonel, I will. But, you see, I don't want her to do it out of any obligation to me. You know, we arranged to blow your mind tonight. Did we succeed?"

"You succeeded, you scoundrel! One other thing, Doc; that all must be expensive."

"A secret, Colonel. It costs very little. You may not know that Chinese jade, nephrite, not the more valuable jadeite, is inexpensive in China. Here in Korea nephrite jade is very valuable. I obtain it from Hong Kong and give it to Beautiful Flower. She keeps some and sells the rest for ten times what it cost. Understand?"

"How do you get it?"

"I have a contact in Hong Kong that mails it to me at the U.S.Army Post Office."

"How did you make the contact?"

"I arranged it when I was in Hong Kong with Mike." Dr. Houghton did not explain that Miss Han from the Arts and Crafts shop was helping. In return, he owed her more nights of "angels'

337

singing" *and* more expensive purchases at the shop. He would keep his promises.

"Ah, so," Colonel Newton said.

The next day, Dr. Houghton and Non'gae strapped on their seat belts inside the small propeller-driven airplane of the fledgling Korean Air Lines. She had never flown before. He observed her childlike wonder as she surveyed her country from the air with its low mountains, rugged hills and omnipresent rice paddies.

Dr. Houghton interrupted her thoughts. "Non'gae," he said. Recently he began to call her Non'gae, her real name, and they spoke mainly in Korean although slowly, "I have a surprise for you. After we go to Kyongu, I wish to see the amaranth fields around the Golden Monastery and then go to the Golden Monastery. I have an appointment with Abbot Kim."

"Why?"

"I want to purchase the jadeite carvings if I can. I spoke to General Lee who spoke to the Abbot. The monastery desperately needs the money and I want the carvings. After all, they were stolen." He decided not to proceed further down that road. It was hard to explain that these carvings were, in reality, stolen Chinese Imperial goods that he wished to buy. He would then bring them to America "legally" with a "bill of sale." The European and American collectors and museums did this but, to Dr. Houghton, these practices although legal, seemed not quite "kosher." But he had decided to do it if he could. He had four million won in ten thousand won notes with him.

After a few minutes Non'gae seized the role of instructor. As the propellers noisily spun, she said loudly, "I must tell you about flowers, especially amaranth flowers so you do not lose face."

"Go ahead," he sighed in resignation.

"Korean people think Americans barbarians. They do not understand flowers. You too! It is very bad. I will tell you about colored amaranths, Joseph's Coat I think, and amaranth mop heads, red and purple mop heads. "

"Great."

"You know inflorescence?"

He flipped through his pocket dictionary and found the English word inflorescence. In freshman biology, he vaguely recollected a few lines about the general arrangement and disposition of flowers on their axis. At the time he ignored the section. He also recalled how, during his early youth, he did not understand his father's passion for flowers. Dr. Houghton thought his father wasted time tending potted plants in the house, especially orchids and night blooming cereuses in the winter. Admittedly, Reginald did like the roses in the summer garden. But he thought his father should employ his time more productively. Now he was being lectured in the same condescending tone by a woman of another race. She continued, "Flowers of all growing stuffs most beautiful. You think so?"

"No. I think women are more beautiful. Flowers make many people sneeze."

An annoyed Non'gae replied, "Why you funny man all the time? You listen to me. I knows. You learn or I punch your nose." She limned soft flowing pictures as she explained the types of inflorescence. He copied her pictures and wrote down the eleven types, with one sample of each. Initially, he was confused but soon he could draw all the types.

She said, "Now, you and Korean baby same – same," she indicated the height of a child of seven or eight.

"That's a gracious concession," he laughed. At least he was no longer a barbarian. Her next lecture, he thought would be on butterflies or the art of paper folding. But she relaxed and enjoyed the view from the plane.

Non'gae now thought of Reginald as a fine lover, a rough but skillfill martial arts-man and most of all a medical magician; he was no longer just a barbarous Westerner. After his easy cure of her parasites and anemia, she was convinced of his skill. She was now a new person. But he lacked face. He must have either a terrible kibun or else he did not have one, like a child born with no hands. Westerners were peculiar indeed. One day about a month ago she remembered him walking down the village road like a duck.

Reginald remembered that episode too. He had suddenly turned and observed Mr. Cameron's Miss Pak imitating his duck-toed saunter. He was well aware of his peculiar gait; his father, uncle and grandfather walked that same way. He wondered if the gait was learned or hereditary. Turning again, he saw Non'gae, her hand over her laughing mouth, watching the interplay between Reginald and Miss Pak.

At that point, Reginald exaggerated the peculiarity of his gait and grotesquely ambled toward his village house. Another rapid turn revealed several children and two peasant women miming his gait. He guessed that the entire village made fun of him. Now that they saw he wasn't angry, they openly duck walked. For weeks the villagers walked as he did with unconcealed, unbridled pleasure. Sometimes a dozen children, all infected by him as if he were a pied piper, walked behind him in a line, ducks in a row.

That evening, Non'gae told him the Korean soldiers on the compound also mimicked his gait, although he never saw this. The Koreans held to the traditional neo-Confucian view that you must never ridicule a man to his face, particularly one at a higher social or power position. If you did, you caused him to lose face, and he must then retaliate – often viciously. Even in their wildest fancies, no Korean woman would openly shame a Korean man. At best, she would receive a severe beating. Clowning and buffoonery, which invite mimicry, were alien as well. In public, Korean men always tried to preserve their dignity and inner harmony. To Non'gae, then, Reginald's lack of interest in inner feelings and harmony was very puzzling. And so, she occasionally called him "funny man," but for serious matters or favors she hedged to the traditional polite "Honorable Reginald."

When they landed in Taegu, a city that was spared the leveling of the Korean War, they hailed a mini-taxi to Kyongu. At the resort hotel, they checked into the best suite. Dr. Houghton had read that this Buddhist compound was the best one outside China. This was an exaggeration, he soon saw, based on his visits to Japan and Thailand. But even so he and Non'gae wiled away happy hours in the shabby ancient temples amidst the various Buddhas, scrolls, and general wonder of Buddhism. A small contribution secured the service of a tonsured monk as a guide. From the silent lilies, not lotuses, on the infusorial ponds to the deep, dark richness of the Buddhist ceremonies, he was impressed. Timelessness hung in the air; for well over one thousand years flux was absent. There was no interest in social upheaval, reforms, or politics here, only complex chanting for the Indian Buddha Shakyamuni, or the repetitious chanting for the Buddha of the Pure Land, Amida. In Japan, he heard the repetitious chanting, "Namu Amida Butsu" over and over again. If you repeated that phrase endlessly and believed in Amida, the Japanese Buddhist priest said you could go to the Pure Land in the West after death. Dr. Houghton queried whether the Pure Land in the West was America, a comment that flew like a lead balloon. But surely, if worldly burdens became too heavy, you could drop them for the largo existence of a Buddhist monk; and then gently drift to Nirvana, Nothingness. Schopenhauer encouraged that. Would they consider his application for admission if he ever grew discouraged? The brush of Beautiful Flower's hot hand ended those thoughts.

To Dr. Houghton, the Korean style resort hotel right beside the shrine seemed ironic, but similar to the Kotohira Shrine in Kawagawa Japan. Korean men and their lady friends, not wives, came here for relaxation and sensual amusement. That evening,

340

when they entered the Korean style nightclub, Dr. Houghton noted the maitre d' furnished elegant hostesses for those men who did not bring their own women. As the nightclub show proceeded, Reginald, the only Caucasian, was not impressed with the continuous succession of performers; first there was the inevitable dancing, not superior to Beautiful Flower's; then an atonal trio of flautist, cymbalist, and drummer. Not only did the music possess the shrieking, goose-flesh inducing quality of long fingernails scraped on a blackboard, but the flute player eerily resembled the Korean Miss Han. This unsettled him. Next "two funny people," an obese man and a tawdry woman, did an obscene routine. But Dr. Houghton did not understand their punning. Non'gae would not or, perhaps, could not translate. She did however occasionally smile at their clowning.

At the end of the show, a solitary female dancer performed a sensual, ritualistic dance based on an ancient fertility rite. She showed Dr. Houghton a glimpse of Korea's feral past. Armed with an immense dildo, she awoke any resting tigers hiding among the males of the audience. She was the most interesting and skillful performer.

The audience did not applaud much for any of these performers.

As they rose to leave, Dr. Houghton asked, "Did you enjoy the entertainment Non'gae?" He should have known that an affirmative was not polite.

"Let's go," she said.

He said, "You and Miss Chang dance very well. Maybe if you need extra money ....."

"Funny man," she whispered.

That evening, he fully recognized that Beautiful flower was unusual sexually. There had been a gradual evolution. To be sure, her anatomy was subtly different from occidental women, but this could not explain her physiology; the function was different. For comparison, he remembered his exquisite experiences with Miss Galt and the Miss Hans. They responded with superb repeating climaxes- an initial vaginal spasm, then vaginal and continuous uterine contractions and suction – status orgasmus. But Non'gae was different. She satisfied the man in an extraordinary way. One must postulate a third internal hand or vaginal prehensility, but that was patently silly. Dr. Houghton searched for tricks or devices.

"No like?" She blushed and laughed.

"How do you do that? Who taught you?" He took nothing for granted in this country.

341

"I don't know. Is there a problem?"

"No. Did you have a good time?"

"Yes," she replied, although it was not polite to admit erotic pleasure. Then, she volunteered a mysterious comment. "I hear my mother, same – same," and she laughed.

"Who said?"

But she would explain nothing further. This functional mystery he could not understand. He searched through Korean anatomy and physiology textbooks: nothing. The only oblique references were oral, whispered ones; those of the experienced American soldiers who valued certain of the Korean girls as "magic ladies." Colonel Blue said that Miss Judy was one. Miss Judy apparently knew this; now Dr. Houghton understood her confidence, her arrogance, and her high price.

After a while Dr. Houghton stopped wondering. Initially he thought he should take scientific measurements and submit the findings to a medical journal. But they would never publish such findings even if true with their conservative skepticism. Even his old friend, Henry, who was in vague pursuit of such a woman, wouldn't believe him. Although it all seemed impossible, he enjoyed himself as she did. He decided to be a Taoist, and go with the natural flow of life. However, he now saw Non'gae through a different glass, a tinted glass. Together, they had started in a valley and now were approaching some heaven - perhaps the portico of the Buddhist Pure Land.

When they were about to leave, Non'gae suddenly sat down. "No go," she said with a pout. She stamped her foot. "I am too sad. We stay here, forever."

Dr. Houghton said. "Non'gae we are going to see the amaranth fields and then to the Golden Monastery tomorrow. In two weeks, I will take you to the old Paekche capital, Puyo."

"Really, no lie?"

"No joke."

She ran toward him and embraced him with a force that almost knocked him over.

Dr. Houghton and Non'gae gazed at the bright fields of Joseph's coat plants and the related species, the tassel – *loves lies bleeding* - amaranth flowers. She gleamed with pride at her knowledge of the botany, "This is the best time to see the amaranth plants. The Joseph's coats are at their peak color with bright yellow-edged leaves with amaranth red bases.The red drooping tassel flowers on their sprigs - I like those best."

342

The September sun was hot, but the enervating summer sun was past. He said, "When I was in college I synthesized a dye like the red color in the leaves and flowers. It is called FD & C Red No. 2; amaranth red. It doesn't fade and is used to color food and clothes."

"If it doesn't fade, can I put it on my lips so I do not need lipstick?"

"Good idea," he said as remembered that triumphal college day; tears rose in his eyes as he remembered that he had almost given up and bought the dye crystals.

Nongae said, "Are you OK, Reginald?"

"Yes, let's go see the fields over there."

At the one acre *love lies bleeding* flower field, Non'gae said, "They are very strange with their red mop heads. Why are they here?"

"Some one planted them for food. You can eat the seeds and leaves; you know that."

She hit him, "Why do they exist? I call them mop heads. They look like mop heads!"

"Ask the the Maitreya. He might know. I certainly don't."

She said, "I am going to squeeze you tonight into a pancake."

"Me or my.....?"

She laughed. "Tell my why you call them - *love lies bleeding* - flowers! Be serious!"

He explained to her Wordworth's explanation that Venus named them after the dripping blood of her boar-gored dying paramour Adonis.

She was noncommittal in acceping this seemingly farfetched explanation but Reg was serious when he said it. If correct, this was another of those queer Greek myths. Venus was a goddess. How could she let her handsome lover die? Too sad; much too sad!

At dusk, they checked into the Inn of the Amaranth Flower. He didn't ignore her but focused his thoughts on how to bargain with the Abbott. He must succeed. He would ask his father to wire more money if necessary.

But after dinner, he screwed in his courage for one question that he had postponed for weeks. "Non'gae, I hear you have relatives in North Korea?"

"Who said?"

"CID."

After a long pause, she said, "I do, but I never see them."

"Do you write to them?"

"Yes, I send letters to a cousin in Japan first, and then she sends them to North Korea, like for Buddha's birthday and New Year."

"Like an American Christmas card?"

"Yes."

He took a deep breath, "You are not a spy?"

She jumped on him and laughed, "Never happen."

That night he could not sleep well. As he looked at this enchanting woman who slept quietly beside him, he thought of Moses Mendelssohn who centuries ago thought there was a "Beauty Center" in the brain. That is why all humans recognize beauty. On the other hand, Locke thought that a "Beauty Center" was boloney; what is beautiful is learned. Reg thought Locke was correct. He did not think a tattooed, muti-ringed, expanded-lipped cannibal lady was beautiful but her husband did. Yet why did he find these oriental girls so alluring? Was it because there were no Western women around? He grew up on Western women like Marsha and the incomparable Miss Galt, not cannibals or Orientals. Moreover, both he and Miss Galt loved pepperoni pizza after sex, not human flesh or kimchi. He fell asleep without any answers.

The next morning the old edentulous Abbot was gracious. Dr. Houghton sensed he wanted to make a sale. After a prolonged amount of polite small talk, Dr. Houghton said, "I would like to see the jadeite carvings."

The Abbot said, "Come with me."

They walked to a back room just opposite a back entrance. Dr. Houghton noted the doors were not locked; there were several scruffy cats but no guard dogs. The Abbot clapped and two monks appeared in saffron robes and opened two locked cabinets with the jadeite carvings. They took out the amaranth forest carving first. In the bright light it was magnificent; they had cleaned it. It gleamed; it was alive. Dr. Houghton drooled.

The Abbot said harshly, "Put it back. That one is not for sale."

They then placed the four smaller jadeite carvings on the table; the yellow Buddha's Hand citron, the imperial green pepper, the apple green translucent Kwan Yin, the Goddess of Mercy, and the translucent white celestial angel flying above aqua waves. They had cleaned them all. In the bright sunlight, they sparkled and glimmered and shimmered, depending on the light angle, as if alive. Dr. Houghton could barely contain himself. He understood the Chinese imperial family's enthusiasm for these carvings.

The Abbot said, "Let us sit down."

They walked back and sat. Immediately, the Abbott said in English, "Forty thousand American dollars for four.

Dr. Houghton pretended incredulousness and horror. General Lee had told him the Abbot would settle for ten thousand dollars but Dr. Houghton thought it was for all five carvings. Dr. Houghton said in Korean, "I will give you four million won in cash now for the four carvings. That is all I have. I will also make a pledge to give you an annual donation." He understood the extreme poverty of the monastery. Even a one hundred dollar donation would go a long way.

Non'gae was astonished by these sums. She had no idea of the value of these carvings.

The Abbot made faces but he finally said in Korean, "Sold. We desperately need the money."

Dr. Houghton had Non'gae pull out the Bill of Sale in English and Korean they had together prepared and typed the week before. He lightly scratched out the fifth carving, the jadeite amaranth forest, with a pencil, filled in the price ($10,000 - four million won) and date in ink, and signed both copies. The Abbott did not read them, signed them and stamped his Chop with traditional red ink. Dr. Houghton passed one to the uninterested Abbot and kept a copy for himself. However, he intended to ship the carvings home in his army baggage, crated and sealed in Korea, thus hopefully avoiding customs. He then politely passed the small leather case with the money to the Abbott who clapped. A monk took the leather case and disappeared, returning with the carvings individually wrapped in a shabby wooden box.

Dr. Houghton said, "Most Honorable Abbot Kim, are you sure you will not sell the amaranth forest carving if I obtain more money?"

"No," the Abbott said firmly. "We will not sell it."

Dr. Houghton stood and then almost kowtowed to the Abbott. Non'gae did the same. He said, "Thank you, Most Honorable Abbot."

In less than a minute they were out the door. To Dr. Houghton this moment almost equaled the day the amaranth crystals came out of solution. He now had four Chinese imperial jadeite carvings. He whispered to Qianlong's ghost; Eat you heart out. He said to Non'gae, "Tonight you will be Xiang Fei, the Fragrant Concubine."

She said, "You know Xiang Fei was an inferior lover! I am Non'gae a Korean. I am a much better lover."

He didn't argue. But like Xiang Fei, Non'gae also wore jujube perfume. That night at dinner, he felt Taoist power running through his body; for a few hours he would be Priapus or even Shiva *and* then dance on the ceiling.

After the trip to Kyongu, Dr. Houghton changed his life. He knew he must focus. He would be in Korea for only a few more months. "Non'gae, Chinese is too hard for me. I quit. I've studied a long time, and I sill know only two hundred and fifty characters. There are forty thousand to go. This is hopeless. How in the world do you remember this crazy language?" Instead he focused on his productive Korean lessons, the Hap Gi Do, and his medical reading.

A few times at Non'gae's urging, they visited local fortune tellers. Her favorite fortune teller, whom Dr. Houghton and Lieutenant Ahn had previously bribed, was an emaciated, toothless hag. On several visits, she made frightening prognostications. Once she predicted his death in a town near the DMZ. Non'gae made him swear never to enter the town. He denied any concern with the old woman's words, but as promised, he did not enter that town.

A shaman lady was more accurate. She somehow knew of Beautiful Flower's sexual uniqueness. Beautiful Flower denied any complicity or deception in this. He wondered how the old woman knew; but did not appreciate the salacious suggestion that he liked her for that reason alone. On another visit, Non'gae had several conversations with ancestor spirits. Although not certain, Dr. Houghton felt that she staged this for his benefit and amusement.

As promised, he took her to Puyo, the old capital of the ancient kingdom of Paekche, celebrated in song and literature. But the decision to ride the train and bus from Seoul to Puyo was unwise. They did not arrive until eight that Saturday night after leaving Seoul at noon. Even more discouraging was the inferior hotel and drizzle. This combination of adverse circumstances annoyed him, but she retained her cheerful temperament.

At dinner, even the rice was inedible, so he ate a little kimchi and drank a local variety of rice wine. Non'gae sensed his unspoken irritation, knowing that he generally attempted to accommodate the miserable conditions.

She said, "Do not be sad. I will provide you with excellent guide service. Let's go to the Rock of Falling Flowers. I will tell you all about Puyo."

"But it is raining."

"It stopped; tonight it will be a full moon."

"You're a number one girlfriend. I feel better already." As they left the hotel, he realized that he was intoxicated although he had not imbibed much rice wine. He feigned sobriety. Suddenly, the moon passed from behind the clouds to light the way as they

346

strolled to the Rock of the Falling Flowers. When the rain stopped, a sultry ambience had enveloped Puyo. As she talked, he started to see vivid images of her descriptions.

She said, "At this time, Korea was divided into three Kingdoms, Silla, Kogura, and Paekche. Puyo was the capital of Paekche. In 660 A.D. the Chinese attacked Paekche from the sea, from the West, landing on the coast. From the East, the Koreans of Silla attacked. Gradually, the Chinese and the Silla armies converged on Puyo."

Dr. Houghton saw the Chinese horde burning, looting, and raping as they marched toward the fortified city of Puyo. He could smell the destruction and hear the screams.

"The old King and his army fled north where they were defeated and the King captured."

Dr. Houghton watched the bearded old King, bound and humiliated, being prepared for his trip to China and a lingering death. He wondered how the old King felt, leaving his Queen and friends in the undefended Puyo, waiting for the Chinese to come. At this point in her narrative, Non'gae and Dr. Houghton reached the escarpment above the river below. He peered over the side as the full moon, like a perverse child, momentarily went behind the clouds. They sat down on a damp stone bench beside a monument inscribed in Chinese.

She continued, "During the night, as the Chinese horde approached the city, the Queen and all the court ladies, one thousand in all, dressed in their finest regal silks, jumped off this cliff to avoid capture by the Chinese."

Dr. Houghton knew he was more than plain drunk when, as the moon obligingly re-illuminated the mise-en-scene, he could hear the screams of the court ladies in their brightly colored, silk hanbok dresses as they jumped, to their deaths.

"They call this the Rock of the Falling Flowers."

Dr. Houghton observed Non'gae. Like those brave court ladies of old, she pulsated with the same Yangban blood. In a traditional Korean dress and with her regally coiffured hair, with her thick braid over the top, she could have been one of them.

Suddenly, Dr. Houghton intuited danger. We must go away from this place before she jumps. In the midst of his rapid, crazed stream of thoughts, he saw silent tears falling from her cheeks. "What's wrong, Non'gae?"

"I am very sad. Soon you will go, and what am I going to do?"

She made a motion that he, incorrectly, interpreted as an intention to fling herself over the side of the cliff. He grasped her. "I

347

shan't allow you to throw yourself over the cliff. You're too valuable." Then, he hiccupped.

In the midst of her tears, she purposefully hiccupped.

He said, "Do not worry. I'll take care of you even if I go."

"Tonight I will not jump over the cliff. When you go, I jump."

He suddenly saw her jump. Gradually, in slow motion, like a yellow rose on a small parachute, she fell into the river. "I want you to promise me that you will never jump even if I go." He knew he was becoming confused now. Was this 600 AD? Were the Chinese coming? Where was his gun? He grasped her for protection.

Non'gae thought he was drunk, the only time she had seen him in such a pitiful state. She did not know that the rice wine had been adulterated, diluted with the cheap poison, methanol. Fortunately for him, as well as her, she had not drunk more than one ounce of the vile wine.

Dr.Houghton, more disciplined than most men, did his best even when his vision dimmed. The methanol turned his blood acid and nauseated him, but he did not vomit. He was weak, and his abdomen was hard as a board. Every step became painful; he was surrounded by hallucinations.

She led him back to the hotel. She moved her hands in front of his eyes, but he responded inconsistently. She wondered at the strange odor on him; it was formaldehyde, not alcohol.

Dr. Houghton did not remember the Korean doctor whom she called; he pronounced Dr. Houghton drunk without even a cursory physical examination. Dr. Houghton did not remember but he asked for his sodium bicarbonate tablets. He carried lots of them to relieve kimchi-induced heartburn. By a queer aleatory stroke, these pills were excellent treatment for the acid blood of methanol poisoning. During the night, he swallowed numerous tablets. His only recollection of the entire night was Non'gae's hand in his or her head on his chest.

The boiling sun rays woke him at nine. He finally retched. He experienced his worst hangover ever. Non'gae was indistinct and blurred. "Where are we, Non'gae?"

"Puyo."

"Where?"

"Puyo."

"I cannot see you well. What happened?"

"I don't knows."

He swallowed more sodium bicarbonate and woke again at noon. He attempted to stand but couldn't, even with Non'gae's aid. Finally, she slept in his arms. The following morning, although unsteady, he could walk. Now fully conscious, on the way to Chun

Chon, he suffered on the train and then the dilapidated, fume filled bus. Non'gae was also sick on the bus and she vomited.

Back in Tae Bat, she called Sergeant Morse who came at once. After an examination, he said, "The Captain is like a prune, very dehydrated. The Captain must have really tied one on." Sergeant Morse decided that two liters of intravenous fluid was the proper treatment.

The next morning at six Dr. Houghton's only residual symptom was a profound fatigue. She bathed him. Before leaving for the short jeep ride to the detachment, he said, "Non'gae, thank you." In retrospect, he vaguely recollected the intensity of her devotion. He guessed that the hotel had served him cheap adulterated rice wine. He should have been more careful; on the plane coming to Korea almost a year ago, General Samet had warned him about Korean rice wine.

Their final trip that summer was to the Walker High Hill resort in Seoul for the weekend. He had received more jade from Miss Han which Beautiful Flower sold at almost twenty times the cost. With some of the money she went on a shopping spree in Seoul and returned with gold jewelry and silks. While she shopped, Dr. Houghton rented a small villa at Walker Hill resort for that weekend. The view of Seoul was magnificent.

"You buy me house like this?" Non'gae asked as she opened the empty western-style cabinets and drawers. "You know, I am a greedy girl."

Dr. Houghton watched as she investigated every nook and cranny. When finished, she banged on his chest. Then she showed him her power of love and laughter and wisdom. He relaxed, then deliquesced.

When she fell asleep, he thought it was now time to "think." The issue was what to do about her when he left Korea. But he could not formulate a plan; there was a knot, a block in his stream of thoughts. But he did feel committed. For sure he would care for her as long as necessary, in perpetuity if need be. For with her, he had realized the wild dreams of youth. She gave him intellectual and sensual pleasures he never dreamed possible. Although somehow tarnished when he first met her in the Tea House, or so he thought, he provided her with robust health and polished her to a high gloss. But he had irrevocably spoiled her in many senses. She was no longer a cherry girl. Although he treated her as an equal, no Korean man would tolerate her now, with her expectations of reasonable treatment. But a more definite decision would have to wait.

She woke up. He now braced himself to receive her weight as she leaned over him.

The potential tragedy of his affair with Non'gae became transparent to Dr. Houghton when Mr. Cameron departed in August. In a lovely early evening ceremony, the village Mayor presented Mr. Cameron with a letter of appreciation. Dr. Houghton and Captain Chang also spoke on this occasion. Then Captain Chang, with his back to the bright orange setting sun, translated the framed letter into English. Mr. Cameron was moved by their formal recognition and appreciation of his aid to their village. In reality, now an old man, he wept and could not speak coherently.

Mr. Cameron was gone forever two days later, back to his wife in America. As Miss Judy pointed out, in a sense he was dead. Miss Pak was inconsolable. She could not eat or sleep. Dr. Houghton gave her soporifics and she finally rested. "I have known many Americans," she confided to Dr. Houghton, "but Mr. Cameron was number one. Now, I am no longer in the business. Mr. Cameron gave me enough money forever. You know I hate Korean men. I am tooooo…old for GI's; now all alone. I soon die."

Dr. Houghton said, "But you have your own house, and you can…."

She began to cry again.

Non'gae listened and almost nonchalantly said, "Soon me same – same."

Dr. Houghton shuddered. "Never happen." In Korean he mumbled obscure non-sequiturs, the ancient Korean double-speak. But he still prorogued a decision.

Chapter XXII
Death

Dr. Houghton and Non'gae discussed the Tang dynasty of ancient China. Although directed toward the art work in the book which she held in her lap, his eyes were out of focus. His mildly intoxicated mind was occupied by fantasies of former years, not quite outgrown. Six months ago, the descriptions and pictorial representations of the Tang, one of the high moments of human civilization, had influenced him in his choice of decorations for his paper house and his off-duty behavior. Like the ancient Tang emperors, after the violence of his Hap Gi Do exercise, his boots and fatigues were removed, he was bathed and massaged with sweet oil, and then clothed. Today, he admired his bright imperial yellow silk pants and long flowing Chinese gown, open in the oppressive warmth of the late September night. Miss Kim had enbroidered a large single Chinese character in gold thread into the silk of this costume. A fabulous character, it meant all at once, good luck, welfare, and happy. Feigning attention to Non'gae's explanations and comments, he looked at the Chinese chess board near his left hand, with the strange, wonderfully carved black onyx and white ivory pieces.

But his gaze ultimately rested on Non'gae, without whom, the entire house was meaningless. She was attempting to demonstrate an error in the inflorescence of one of the flower paintings. "This arrangement doesn't exist in nature."

"Perhaps it is a thrysus," he said, not in real knowledge, but to show interest, momentarily attending to the subject.

She explained in detail why it was not.

He imagined the Chinese emperors of the Tang, 1400 years ago, enjoying evenings like this with their favorite concubine, surrounded by a chessboard and Chinese primroses. However, two differences existed. He did not resemble the emperor, and second, the moment he ventured outside, the absence of extreme deference and the shortage of several hundred million subjects would belie any regal pretensions. Undismayed, he said in Korean, with eyes aglow, "Do you think I would be an effective Honorable Tang Emperor?"

351

Without showing much emotion, she closed the book. "You are either crazy or an un-funny funny man - a Lussian buffoon?"

"You mean Russian? That is no way to address your Honorable Lord."

Beautiful Flower demurred. Then abandoning ridicule for excessive Korean laughter, hand over her mouth, she finally gasped and said, "I'm sorry," and kowtowed.

"That's better," he said. "Non'gae, you are lovelier every day. Your health is so much better, now that your anemia is completely gone. I think that has something to do with it. Your breasts are now very full. Your legs were a little too skinny, but now they are very pretty."

"Yes, I think so," she answered.

He was pleased with her new confidence. She no longer accused him of flattery. With the success of his no-freckles medicine and the resolution of her anemia, she now had a perfect complexion on top of classical aristocratic Korean features. She looked like the Yi queens of old. These days, she never mentioned rounding her eyes.

The phone rang first one time, then two more times and stopped - their number. Non'gae answered, talked for a moment and said, "It's many fingers. He wants to talk to you."

"Dr. Houghton – here."

"Sergeant Morse, Sir. I've sent the jeep for the Captain. There's a man here stabbed in the chest. Come quick!" Sergeant Morse clicked out.

"I'm sorry, but I must go."

He slipped into his boots and put on his green fatigue shirt but not his fatigue trousers. There wasn't time as the the jeep approached and beeped. Within three minutes he entered the dispensary.

Sergeant Morse, whose blackness was exaggerated by a blood splattered bright orange shirt, worked over a near naked white man covered with dried blood. The wounded man's mauve jockey shorts, his only article of clothing, were soaked with sticky drying blood. "What's the story?" he asked Sergeant Morse. Dr. Houghton noted a stiletto hole in the man's chest and answered his own question, "Stabbed in the heart. Any heart beats or blood pressure since he's been here?"

"No, Sir. But he breathed one time."

Dr. Houghton listened to his chest; he heard no sound and said "Keep the intravenous saline pouring in!" Sergeant Morse had started an intravenous line. "Get the ECG machine. Cardiac massage, Sergeant Morse. I'll put a tube in the windpipe."

With the expertise of professionals, Dr. Houghton slipped in the endotrachial tube, Sergeant Morse messaged his heart, and one of the Koreans ventilated the dead man with a breathing bag. The ECG showed a straight line, so Dr. Houghton injected intracardiac epinephrine and intravenous sodium bicarbonate.

The Deputy and Colonel Newton entered the dispensary. They watched the resuscitation effort with discomforture.

"Stop, Sergeant Morse. He has a heart beat now. See the ECG!" Dr. Smith palpated the carotid pulses, "But no blood pressure." Despite these measures, the beats on the ECG machine gradually slowed, and finally ceased altogether. "He's dead. We did what we could Sergeant Morse. Thank you."

Said the Deputy, "You medics! What kind of costume is that, Doc? Sergeant Morse looks like a ......"

Dr. Houghton interrupted the Deputy. He realized the resuscitation attempt probably appeared ludicrous with him in his yellow pants and Sergeant Morse in his wild orange shirt. So what! "Can someone tell me what happened?"

Sergeant Morse said, "Captain Chang can probably tell the Captain. They brought this man here, and I came from the NCO club just before the Captain came."

Captain Chang, two Korean national police, and a distraught Korean girl sat in the waiting room.

"What happened, Captain Chang? Who is this man?"

Captain Chang stood and replied in English, "This girl lives in the next village. Long time ago - this man a GI in Korea. He came back to the village yesterday to find her. They go to her room. That man on the floor bleeding. They brought him over here."

"Did she stab him?"

"I don't know."

"Ask her."

Captain Chang questioned her in Korean.

She succumbed to fits of gasping sobs.

One of the policemen produced a long, bloody knife. He said in Korean, "Yes, she stabbed him."

"Why?"

"He did not give her money."

The policeman produced the victim's clothes and wallet.

"Not an active soldier," Dr.Houghton said, as he went through the wallet. The man's wife and children smiled up at him from a laminated photo.

"Captain Chang, thank you."

Dr. Houghton filled out the medical paper work and gave a copy of the death certificate to the Korean police with the cause of death as "Stab wound of the heart." Sergeant Morse completed the rest of the paper work. The next day the Deputy instructed them to turn the body over to the United States Civilian Authority in Seoul.

Dr. Houghton called Colonel Bennet who was drunk. He briefed him fully.

Colonel Bennet asked, "Why did she stab him?"

"Captain Chang said they argued over five dollars."

"What was he doing here?"

"Captain Chang said he had returned to recapture the past."

Although it was nearly eleven o'clock, Dr. Houghton hurried back to the village to say good-night to Non'gae. He decided to sleep at the detachment that night. He told her, "Big trouble."

"I knows," Beautiful Flower replied. The legs of Korean rumor were skinny but Olympic swift.

"I also heard from Sergeant Morse that Lieutenant Ahn was seen in Chun Chon?"

"I did not hear that."

"You know, Non'gae, that the Korean army considers Ahn AWOL."

"I knows."

He continued, "You told me you would tell me about Lieutenant Ahn one day. Now that he's gone, please tell me."

"Before, I told you Lieutenant Ahn and Viet Cong same-same."

"Yes, I know. But why do you say he is Viet Cong?"

"He try ..." She placed her palm on his chest.

He was not surprised that Lieutenant Ahn had attempted to seduce her.

"One time," she continued, "him very Viet Cong."

"You mean that he tried violence?"

"But him small, weak man ..... Viet Cong."

Now Dr. Houghton thought he understood why Lieutenant Ahn acclaimed her virtue. "Did he offer you money?"

"Yes."

"How much?"

"No say!" she laughed and then blushed.

"A little?" Dr. Houghton asked in Korean.

With an outraged look, she indicated a stack of money. "A lot!"

After a short pause, he asked, "What was he doing down here later?"

She demurred.

"Don't be shy, Non'gae."

354

She snswered in Korean, "Last month, Lieutenant Ahn came here one day. I had the deserted woman listen at the window. He said to me to give him money."

"Why?"

"He say he tell you everything...." She hesitated.

"Go on."

She continued in rapid slang-filled Korean. "He would tell you bad things. I say, 'Go away. I will tell Dr.Houghton. He will punch you in the nose.' He gave me a hard time, but he went. He is a flagitious man – Viet Cong."

"What does flagitious mean?" He looked it up in his Korean dictionary. "What was Ahn going to tell me?" He was certain it concerned her past. This solitary cul-de-sac of ignorance about her continued to infuriate him. She just would not illuminate that particular space. He was certain that she was not sexually promiscuous. Miss Chang confirmed that around the time she made the pass at him. He waited.

But Non'gae only smiled demurely. This great-granddaughter of aristocrats had sealed her past to him. That was how he interpreted her silence. He almost contained his frustration; but he did momentarily place his hands on her slender neck as if to wring the past out of her. She was feminine and vulnerable, he thought, as he withdrew his hands.

She noticed a fleeting, almost horrid, contortion of his face as the struggle passed through him. He finally said in crude Korean, "You should have told me. I would have boiled his balls in hot oil. When I finished with him he would have left you alone."

She said in polite Korean, "You are right. I had nothing to hide."

At her admission, he was relieved and said with a salacious wink, "Next weekend I will take you to Chinju to see the statue of Non'gae. I have a weekend pass. We can fly down there; but this time, I am bringing my own sandwiches and whiskey."

She jumped on him and pleaded, "Do not go! Stay here tonight; please!"

"I must go but I have more surprises for you."

"Tell me."

"Soon."

That night, just before midnight when he returned to the Q, Sergeant Morse called. "I have a message from Miss Hu. I believe she is the Kisaeng we treated for pelvic inflammatory disease."

"What is the message?"

"She said to call her about an important matter."

"Thank you Sergeant Morse." He called her and said he would meet her next Monday night.

That weekend, at Chinju, Non'gae explained, "In 1593, the Japanese Shogun Hideyoshi's army and his favorite swordmaster, General Keyamura Rokusuke, attacked Korea and there was a great battle here. The Japanese won and killed sixty thousand Koreans." She choked with patriotic emotion as they walked up to the cliff above the river.

"There is the statue of Non'gae," she said as they reached the top. "The statue is not in good condition. I never came here before."

They looked over the cliff. He could almost imagine Non'gae embracing Keyamura and then toppling them both over the cliff; a Korean Judith or Esther.

She looked at Dr. Houghton. "Let us go back to the hotel. I am hungry for a nice sandwhich with a side of kimchi." She was watching the American movies a lot.

At the hotel, Dr. Houghton enjoyed the sandwich, the very old Scotch and an emotional Non'gae. Like all Koreans, Non'gae was temporarily saddened by the massive loss of Korean life at this place and the heroic action of her namesake.

But that night, buoyed by thoughts of her namesake, Non'gae slowly became enraptured with knowledge of the safety of her secret - now Ahn had disappeared - and Reginald's powerful lovemaking. Moreover, there was a perfect Chinese character combination for this feeling; she taught it to Reginald. She was now very confident.

After she fell asleep, Reginald could not sleep. He was preoccupied with his up-coming Black Belt examination. He was torn between making it strictly on his own merits and "greasing the skids" with a large donation *before* the examination. It was like the dilemma he faced in college; whether to buy the amaranth dye crystals or not. Once again, he decided that he must do the right thing: he must make it on his own merits. He could do it. A nice gift could *follow*. Finally he settled this in his mind.

But he just could not decide what to do about Miss Hu. Without doubt she was another professional enchantress - now tuned up and repaired with his what his father would call "body and fender work." He now required her help though, if his plan was to succeed.

He met Miss Hu at the Greenish Dragon Tea House after his Hap Gi Do practice. They sat in a back corner. Initially he did not recognize her. When he did, he thought he was in the the Buddhist

Pure Land of the Western Paradise and she was a celestial angel. What a difference eliminating her pelvic infection and gastrointestinal parasites, and treating her anemia made. For just a moment he thought of Miss Galt, the Miss Hans, Non'gae and now Miss Hu; all in one year. He wanted to freeze these moments but alas, Hume and the Buddha were correct about impermanence. He said in Korean, "You look splendid. You are the most beautiful woman I ever saw." He had trouble finding the correct superlatives in Korean. "Please stand up and walk back and forth."

She did. She had worn her best Western outfit over her hourglass figure; a tight black short skirt, an off white silk blouse, and black high heel shoes to accentuate her shapely legs – long for a Korean. She smiled showing her perfect white teeth framed by her scarlet Cupid's bow lips.

He said, "How are you feeling?"

"I will tell you the truth, yes?" she said in Korean.

"Yes, I want the truth. We do not have time for games."

"I am excellent - thanks to your skill. Two weeks ago, Dr. Dawes in Camp Page started me on American birth control pills since my periods were irregular; he said I may have damaged my right ovary but Tincture of Time will fix it."

Dr. Houghton appreciated her honesty. This straightforwardness was rare in Koreans. He was also happy he was no longer her physician. He owed Dr. Dawes one. He said, "I am so pleased you are doing so well. Why did you call me? "

"I must see you soon for a 'date.'" She used the English word. He said, "I have a plan."

Over the small coffee table, she grasped his hands in hers after the waitress brought two green teas. She wiped away two incipient tears. "Can I tell you the truth? Can I tell you what I want? I think American men like the truth?"

"Yes of course." Her hands were warm and soft. She smelled of osmanthus flowers.

She said, "I am now twenty six. I was born in 1942. My father fought againt the Japanese in the underground. He was caught and executed in 1945. During the Korean War we were very poor. My mother almost died of malnutrition in 1955 when I was thirteen. Since I was thought beautiful, I was apprenticed as a Kisaeng. I was lucky - with food and a place to live. I studied very hard - dance, music, jokes, persiflage, and poetry; both Korean and classical Chinese. I can make stones laugh or cry, like the Greek man; his name was Orpheus I think. I am again the number one Kisaeng in Chun Chon, thanks to you." Her eyes teared.

Dr. Houghton loved the story of Orpheus, a story his father repeatedly read him when he was a child. He remembered the two morals: finish the job, don't look back until you are done and do not spurn women in love with you. Orpheus did; then, the Maenads tore him to pieces and threw his still singing head in the river. The fate of Orpheus was a timely lesson, for a Korean maenad sat in front of him. He would not spurn her.

She continued, "I also exercise a lot because of the long sitting at the Kisaeng parties."

He said, "That is why your body is so shapely, so firm, so nice!" He was having trouble with the correct Korean words.

She smiled and came closer, whispering, "I have never had a real love affair with a man although I have been attacked several times by bad men as you know. I smile and entertain almost every night but it is just Kisaeng business." She wiped her eyes. "So when Miss Han told me about you I thought it would be excellent to meet you. When she told me you made her hear Celestial Angels sing - involuntarily - I had to meet you. I did at the Kisaeng party for Mr. Song, but then I was raped by that flagitious man."

"What do you want?"

"I told you a 'date' as soon as possible. I am afraid they will ship you to Vietnam like so many of the Americans."

He said, "I don't think so but, you are correct, the situation in Vietnam is a mess."

She said, "You will be happy. I am a professional entertainer. I know how to make men happy." She then made a face and sound like a tiger; she pawed the air with her right hand. "We will both hear Celestial Angels, Yes?"

He said, "Let me tell you my plan."

She interrupted, "Do you know moonflowers and night blooming Cereus and jasmine?"

"Yes."

"They all open at night and smell of love, yes? I am a night flower." She wrote the Chinese character. "Do you understand?"

"Yes, I do." Sergeant Song had explained the Chinese word for flower was applied to the entertainers by society, and the Korean word to real flowers. However, the entertainers sometimes used the Korean word for flower for themselves. He was delighted he understood the nuances of the words. She had used the Korean character.

He said, "Please listen to my plan. You will be pleased. Next weekend, I want you to fly on an airplane to Taegu and rent villa 202 at the Inn of the Amaranth Flower near the Buddhist Golden Monastery outside Taegu. I will meet you at the the Golden

358

Happiness Chinese restraurant at five o'clock, about four miles south of the Inn - on Saturday. Here is an envelope with you tickets and money for the room. Pay in cash when you arrive. We will stay at the Inn and return to Chun Chon on Sunday afternoon together."

"But I have to work on Saturaday."

"I spoke to Mr. Ku and you have all day Saturday and Sunday off."

In response, he saw her eyes gleam. She sent high energy vibrations out of her eyes into his. She placed his hand on her breast. She could not speak.

He said, "I have a few other requests."

She said, "I am at your command," a Chinese statement that retainers made to the Emperor. "I will do anything you say. I will be a moonflower and more that night."

"Please do not eat kimchi or garlic for two days before we meet. Second, please wear the same osmanthus perfume; it is lovely."

She broke into laughter, but quickly covered her mouth with her hand. "That is all?"

"Yes."

After she left, Dr. Houghton once again thought of Moses Mendelssohn and the Beauty Center in the brain. Maybe Moses was correct after all. Or was he deceiving himself? Were these beautiful women and objects on this happy Korean sojourn just the terminal intoxication of youth, the final flowering of lust, of freedom, of a carefree existence? Were they spillovers of his pride in learning Korean and excelling in Hap Gi Do? After the deepest thought possible and a serious attempt to avoid self-deception, he decided that Miss Galt, the Miss Hans, Non'gae and now probably Miss Hu were very rare. He was a lucky man to know them. Moreover, they also all emitted various enchanting vibrations and unknown pheromonal chemicals. Some day he should study these phenonena to understand the mechanisms since he was one of the few who appreciated such subtleties. He wanted them all, perhaps in a seraglio, but that could not be. Soon he would be back in the Brigham, a senior resident, a slave to the sick and dying. But that must be. He concluded he must seize this rare opportunity, now.

But just as he rose to pay and leave, he felt his mother's heavy arm on his shoulder. She said, Reginald! You are on the horns of the eternal male dilemma. Do you want the temporary thrill of the professional entertainer who in the end can only harm you, or the wholesome, unspoiled and loyal virginal woman? You are a fool to jeopardize your relation ship with Non'gae for a few moments with Miss Hu. Remember St. Augustine!

Reginald answered, I hear you mother. But, remember, St. Augustine ended up with Jesus not Miss Hu. Moreover, Miss Hu is also going to help me. I need her and she needs me. This is both business *and* pleasure.

His mother did not answer. Like Aeneas, she did not say no.

An intoxicated Captain Chang and Dr. Houghton walked to Captain Chang's room in the village. They walked hand-in-hand, as Korean friends do. "My wife wishes to say good-bye to you," said Captain Chang. "Tomorrow she goes to Seoul in anticipation of her delivery. She is very happy. Soon, a boy, I hope. I thank you very much for making her pregnant.

Dr. Houghton roared with laughter, "Not me. I just told you what to do. You did the work."

Mrs. Chang was radiant. The pregnancy heightened her beauty. Dr. Houghton still thought she was one of the most attractive women he had seen in Korea, although now, both Non'gae and Miss Hu with their health restored had comparable faces. "How are you, Mrs. Chang?" He spoke to her in Korean, bowing low.

"I am very happy you came. I want to say good-bye."

Dr. Houghton said in Korean. "I think you will have a boy. I am not usually wrong."

Mrs. Chang clapped her hands together, like a Korean child, delighted at the prediction.

He swallowed the catch in his throat. "You are a very fortunate man, Captain Chang, to have such a wife."

Mrs. Chang served some rice wine.

In the midst of the conversation, Dr. Houghton queried Captain Chang, "Have you seen Lieutenant Ahn?"

"No, he's number ten man – Viet Cong! He AWOL, I hope forever," Captain Chang replied.

"Why do you say that?"

"You over there; he say bad things. You over here; he only smile. You know Shakespeare – Iago. I am sorry Lieutenant Ahn Korean man."

But Captain Chang would say no more. Before leaving, Dr. Houghton wished Mrs. Chang good luck. He wrote the Chinese character for good luck. An expert at Chinese calligraphy, Mrs. Chang was not impressed but pleased.

Dr. Houghton pondered Lieutenant Ahn's behavior as he walked across the rice paddies to his village house. Lieutenant Ahn was a bad man without a doubt. He made disparaging remarks about everyone, behind their back. He extorted money from Korean enlisted men. He seduced innumerable Korean cherry girls. He dealt in the black market. Dr. Houghton wondered if he trafficked in secret documents, for Sergeant Morse had caught him in the detachment safe. But these evils somehow disturbed Dr. Houghton less that his unproven notion that Lieutenant Ahn, silently, at night, had entered his room on several occasions. He was certain of this. A subliminal, gnawing anxiety was the residue.

These thoughts temporarily disappeared as Dr. Houghton recounted to Non'gae Mrs. Chang's joy. Non'gae laughed when he mentioned that Captain Chang had thanked Dr. Houghton for the pregnancy. Non'gae shared in Mrs. Chang's joy although Mrs. Chang was no more than civil toward her.

After another exhausting advisory visit, Dr. Houghton replied sharply to the Korean driver, "Don't tell me I have to go to my Hap Gi Do lesson!"

"But, Sir, I only meant that if you are to get your Black Belt, you must not skip lessons."

"Just drive me to the detachment." Annoyed, Dr. Houghton had to soak his bottom and medicate his newly developed hemorrhoids. His buns of iron had finally cracked; he had joined the donut club with Sergeant Morse and General Kim.

At dinner, he sat with Mike and Lieutenant Humbert. Major Mike, the heavily decorated Air Force pilot, now a Lieutenant Colonel, poured venom onto the undecorated Humbert and the army for its "venal sins" in Vietnam. Mike was reacting badly, inconsolably frustrated by his prolonged "ground duty." The Deputy, sitting alone at the next table, heard it all and fumed in silence.

Dr. Houghton also ate in sullen silence. He was annoyed at the sudden appearance of his -rhhoids. He also disliked Mike's negativism although Mike's critical analysis of the Vietnam War was correct.

Mike suddenly paused. He turned to Dr. Houghton, "You sick, Doc?"

"Yes, I don't feel well. Please excuse me."

Dr. Houghton walked rapidly to the village and his house much earlier than usual. Both Mike and his new hemorrhoids had discouraged him, but he knew that Non'gae would cheer him. Pushing open the squeaky iron-gate, he was puzzled. In the light of the early dusk, he saw the locks fastened on both the deserted woman's room and the crimson chamber. He said in Korean, "Is anyone here?" He listened, and after his echo passed, he thought he

361

heard a rustling inside. He removed his boots. This was the first time no one had been present in his house when he came.

As he inserted the key, he discovered that the waxed paper-door had been forced open. This made him furious. The whole point of having the deserted woman and Sugi was prophylactic – to prevent the entrance of thieves, of slicky boys. He ducked through the low door into the chamber. Within several seconds, as his eyes adapted, he saw a figure near the light switch. In the dimness, he could not recognize the face. With the light of dusk penetrating the low translucent door, the bottom portion of the room was clearer. He saw a man's trousered legs and a right hand holding a stiletto.

He was certain the figure was a slicky boy. Still he said, "Is that you, Non'gae?"

The alien did not move.

Dr. Houghton swallowed his hatred. That theft and possibly violence should contaminate his house angered him. That the guardians, the deserted lady and her daughter, whom he maintained for the explicit purpose of being thief scarecrows, were inexplicably absent infuriated him. He had worked hard to build this chamber of joy, music, and art; of friendship; of love. But now, the thieving hands of evil could ruin everything in seconds; just for a few pieces of gold, jade or small diamonds.

Dr. Houghton reached for his pistol to shoot the scoundrel full of holes. But, the icy realities prevented him. Killing a trespasser and thief in Korea was considered murder. The U.S. and Korean authorities would investigate. There would be a terrible scandal.

The figure remained immobile with the menacing knife. Slicky boys were supposed to run when the owner noted their presence. But this thief did not run. The Koreans had somehow ensnared the American, notwithstanding all his precautions. However, he was ready even for this. In fact, his present predicament was familiar to him. In the Hap Gi Do exercise hall and even in his dreams, he often confronted a "faceless" man with a knife. He had learned multiple defenses against such an attack, including a few which he demonstrated at the exhibition in Chun Chon. This was just another repetition. The outcome was certain. Even the choice of defense was neat, settled and narrowed to two. Dr. Houghton proceeded with confidence. The defense to the right, however, the thief precluded as he moved to his left. Hence, the defense to the left. At that moment, Dr. Houghton screamed, "Lieutenant Ahn!"

In the dimness, the startled thief paused for the briefest moment. Dr. Houghton grasped Lieutenant Ahn's right arm, the stiletto arm, at the wrist with both hands. He stepped sharply to his

362

left. Then, Dr. Houghton went low and, with his right foot forward under Ahn's right arm, he twisted Lieutenant Ahn's knife hand around toward his unprotected abdomen. Dr. Houghton sensed his assailant was much weaker than his friends in the exercise hall. The stiletto blade, which possessed a great momentum as it approached Ahn's abdomen, was difficult to stop. Then at the moment of impact, Lieutenant Ahn inexplicably lunged forward. The long stiletto did not just cut into the surface but plunged in deep, up to its handle.

Lieutenant Ahn groaned and slowly buckled to the floor.

Dr. Houghton flicked on the light switch. Lieutenant Ahn was on the floor, obviously gravely injured. A gold chain hung from his pocket. He turned over onto his back, gripped his belly and grimaced. There was no external bleeding.

Dr. Houghton picked up the phone; it was dead. He said, "I'll go get the jeep. I'll be back in five minutes to take you to the hospital. Just lie there."

Dr. Houghton knew the penetration was very serious, so he ran across the rice paddies, climbed in the jeep and was back at the paper house within seven minutes. He kept asking himself over and over, "Why did Lieutenant Ahn lunge forward on the knife like that?"

As he re-entered the house, he wanted to ask "Why were you trying to blackmail Non'gae?" But Lieutenant Ahn could not answer. He was dead.

Dr. Houghton had suddenly dropped into an unexpected hell; not Dante's or Sartre's; or even Hades. But if he were smart, he would immediately climb out. He knew he should not go to the Korean authorities. In Korea, killing a slicky boy when you had a red belt was a serious crime although in America, his action was clearly self defense. As a physician he was trained not to panic, not to vacillate but to act. He was now his own judge and jury: he pronounced himself not guilty under American law.

With that verdict, he acted decisively. He took a few deep breaths and his heart pounded less. He took the jewelry from Lieutenant Ahn's pocket and put it back into Non'gae's teakwood box. Then he tied a thick rope around Lieutanant Ahn's waist. He securely attached a ten pound stone from the yard to the rope. There was no blood on the floor. He apparently had bled out internally. In the dark, he carried Lieutenant Ahn to the jeep. He locked the door.

After he placed Lieutanant Ahn in the back seat of the jeep, little Miss Kim walked toward the gate. She bowed.

"This man is very sick," he said in Korean. "I shall be back soon. Promise me that you will not tell Non'gae or anyone else about this. Do you promise?"

"I promise," she said. "Lieutenant Ahn?"

"Yes, it is."

Dr. Houghton drove ten minutes and parked the jeep on the old Japanese bridge over the river. It was a very dark night. When he was certain there were no cars or jeeps about, he threw the weighted body and the knife over the side. Lieutenant Ahn was now AWOL for good. He was certain no one would find the body in the twenty five foot deep river; it would decompose fast to unidentifiable bones.

He drove slowly back to the detachment and walked to his paper house.

Non'gae demanded, "Where were you?"

"I don't understand."

She handed him a letter in handwriting that resembled his own. The letter asked Non'gae, the deserted lady and Sugi to meet him in Chun Chon. He pocketed the letter. He told her that he was sorry he could not meet her in Chun Chon.

She then told him about the damage to the front door.

He said perhaps a slicky boy tried to rob them.

She thought nothing was missing.

As quickly and casually as possible, he twisted the conversation to other matters.

That evening, he watched Non'gae and Miss Kim play cards after he declined a bath. At an appropriate time, he pleaded paper work. Nothing seemed different. He kissed Non'gae goodbye with a sad passion. It was a long kiss; he wondered if an unspoken message passed between them.

Little Miss Kim accompanied him back to the detachment gate. She took his hand and said, "I worry about you."

After a long pause, he said in Korean, "Remember your promise."

She replied, "I saw nothing tonight."

At the halfway point, they sat down on two flat roadside stones side by side. "Before I go, I'm going to arrange for you to have something that Non'gae does not have." He paused. "You cherry girl?"

Little Miss Kim demurred.

He repeated the question.

She sighed softly, "Yes."

"That's good. I'm sure we can do it."

"What?"

"Soon, I'll tell you."

He lifted her on his lap. He kissed her on the forehead.

Little Miss Kim felt water on his cheeks. She did know her future depended on him. She had overheard what he had in mind and she was thrilled. Like Captain Houghton, she too would walk on ceilings.

After a short silence, he gave her the flashlight. She disappeared into the moonless night; the light the only evidence of her continued existence. As he watched the beam, he was determined to present this small exquisite doll, with a heart of gold, the only thing she truly wanted. Moreover, he now had another strong reason to do it.

"A hero may be willing to lose the world,
but not his concubine or his horse."
Chinese Proverb

Chapter XXIII
Parting

Dr. Houghton had spent the previous five days in a relentless review of the nine levels of Hap Gi Do expertise recorded in his notebook. To obtain the Black Belt, the examinee had to exhibit skill at each level. He must then conclude with a free fight with the senior instructor, all performed before the exercise hall members. No outside guests were allowed. Dr. Houghton was confident with the exception of several high jumps. He had completed his homework and conscientiously attended the practice sessions. He was prepared. On his almost six foot frame, he had no fat; only 178 pounds of muscle. He now lusted for the Black Belt, the ancient symbol of physical attainment.

In recent days, he had suffered from intense feelings of inadequacy, particularly when he watched the second and third degree black belts lollop and jump high. At the apogee, they would thrust out a smashing kick and then descend to the floor with a quiet feline grace. Their jumps were as natural as those of frogs and hares. Moreover, their execution of the basic levels of self-defense was seemingly effortless. He wondered how he looked when he performed these same moves. He tried to observe himself in the body length mirrors, but this ruined his concentration. A few snapshots arrested him in correct postures, but uniformly, he wore a strained expression in the pictures. He was not a "natural." Neither the hard evidence of the photographs nor the warm compliments in the exercise hall convinced him of his skill.

On that early fall afternoon, with an unseasonal Solano-like wind oppressing the air, Dr. Houghton entered the sweltering exercise hall. He continued to have mixed feelings of confidence and inadequacy. A drop of distracting moisture fell on him from above as he changed into this red-belted uniform, he hoped, for the last time. He thought of Colonel Newton's advice to start with his best play first, a strategy reminiscent of Liddell Hart and Hitler, an individual blitzkrieg around the senior instructor's defense. He would again employ his finely honed, circular swing kick as his first offensive move. He had a plan, although it was not a new plan.

366

The junior instructor, Mr. Yun entered and walked to the front. As if by magic, everyone formed into perfect lines facing Mr. Yun. Dr. Houghton was the first man in the red belt line. They all bowed in unison to Mr. Yun, who uttered a few words of encouragement. Then the senior instructor strutted to the front of the class. Everyone bowed deeply. After a short speech, Mr. Ho ordered everyone to perform well.

Dr. Houghton did not completely understand Mr. Ho's Korean slang, although he did know that Mr. Ho employed the impolite form to his "inferiors" in either age or skill. Somehow this annoyed Dr. Houghton more than usual. He knew he would not have to put up with such behavior much longer. His resumption of American values would occur very soon. But Dr. Houghton, at that moment, was still angry. He also knew this was his last opportunity to show his mettle in front of his assembled "brothers." Moreover, in the free fight with Mr. Ho, if all went according to plan, he would upend Mr. Ho. He hoped to gaze down at the toppled instructor; he would then say in the most polite Korean, "I am sorry."

En masse, they all warmed up, controlled by a common mind, a third degree Black Belt. Then the students drifted to the edges of the exercise hall to watch the examinations.

Dr. Houghton observed the uneven, and at times, ludicrous performances of the tyros, a few of whom fell or forgot their lessons. The Blue and Red Belts were better. However, Mr. Ho angrily responded to an outburst of laughter at a truly comic blunder. He halted the examination and summoned the offenders to the center of the hall. Dr. Houghton, guilty of laughter, also arose. Like the other laughers, he knew laughter was interdicted in the exercise hall for obvious reasons.

Mr. Ho, however, cast a treatening eye on him. With an impolite command, he said, "Sit down, Red Belt." Without doubt, Dr. Houghton had upset Mr. Ho's inner harmony. Mr. Ho then proceeded to flail the laughers with thin bamboo. They would not laugh in the future.

When his name was called, Dr. Houghton stood and bowed to Mr. Ho and then Mr. Yun. He was the only candidate for the first degree Black Belt. Mr. Yun then walked on the floor and instructed him to perform certain kicks. Then, as aggressor, Mr. Yun attempted to punch, kick, throw, and stab Dr. Houghton who defended himself well, often reducing Mr. Yun to a "helpless" suppliant. Finally, Dr. Houghton assumed the offensive. On the last move, he sent an apterous Mr. Yun sailing toward the far corner of the hall. Mr. Yun was not hurt. In fact, they had practiced this many times. Dr. Houghton bowed to a sweaty Mr. Yun.

367

Although Mr. Yun didn't show great pleasure, his most determined pupil had defended himself very well. He wondered what Mr. Ho might do with Houghton.

After an almost theatrical delay, Mr. Ho rose from his chair. He limbered his thirty-seven year old bones. His status as a seventh degree Black Belt, by itself, was menacing. He scowled at Dr. Houghton.

Dr. Houghton knew that Mr. Ho could dispatch three opponents in twenty seconds or less if he so wished. But Dr. Houghton was warm and ready. Suddenly, Mr. Ho was ready, too. They bowed and assumed the fighting stance. Mr. Ho uttered a piercing screech. But, Dr. Houghton, accustomed to this mad yell, responded only with a blink. As the shriek echoed and reechoed in the exercise hall, Dr. Houghton feinted with his right hand. Mr. Ho countered with a foot kick toward his temple. At the last possible instant, according to his prearranged strategy, Dr. Houghton swung down and around under Mr. Ho's raised foot. He watched his heel travel in a wide arc and, after a seeming eon, bash Mr. Ho on his left ankle. Mr. Ho, whose right foot was only inches from the safety of the mat, was upended as Dr.Houghton's heel knocked his left limb from under him. As the upended Mr. Ho fell toward the mat, he slapped his right arm on the mat, and like a rubber ball, was up again in a fighting stance in an instant. Surprised, Dr. Houghton knew that his plan that had worked perfectly and yet failed utterly. Never had he observed anyone similarly upended recover so quickly. But by the force of the impact, he knew he hurt Mr. Ho, so he bowed and in the most polite form said, "I'm sorry."

Dr. Ho said impolitely, as if talking to a dog, "Go."

Dr. Houghton was now afraid. His best move, the fruition of a year's work, had succeeded yet misfired. However, Mr. Ho did not attack him immediately, so Dr. Houghton cautiously attacked Ho. Mr. Ho easily and expertly defended himself. Suddenly, Mr. Ho bowed. It was over.

The whole test seemed extremely inconclusive. Unlike the usual examination where Mr. Ho punished the examinee - those "passing" suffering the least humiliation - this contest was unusual. Dr. Houghton looked at Mr. Yun for guidance but Mr. Yun was poker faced. He also noticed that Mr. Ho limped back to the chair.

Dr. Houghton sat down and watched the final candidate for the second degree Black Belt. He absorbed a pitiful beating from Mr. Yun. This man did not pass. During the slaughter, Dr. Houghton, still excited from his own combat, wondered if Mr. Ho was gentle with him because he was an American; or because Mr. Ho was temporarily disabled. With the passage of time, he decided that a middle position appeared valid; he had injured Mr. Ho, but Mr. Ho had not really tried. Because of these lingering questions, Dr. Houghton always doubted if he really deserved the Black Belt. Somehow, the award was slightly tainted, no matter how vigorously Mr. Yun and the others reassured him.

Yet, when Mr. Yun removed the Red Belt and tied the gold-lettered Black Belt around him, Dr. Houghton was gloriously happy. He suppressed tears of joy. His name was spelled phonetically in large Korean letters and correctly in small English letters. He scrutinized the certificate and identification card that indicated his new rank. However, the fact that these were prepared in advance reinforced his belief that they had intended to award him the Black Belt irrespective of his performance. Dr. Houghton politely shook hands with his friends in violence; they congratulated him with unmistakable sincerity. He profusely thanked the second degree Black Belt who taught him the defense against an opponent with a knife. Unseen, he placed a small envelope with twenty thousand won in the man's hand; that poor man and his scrawny children were starving. For a moment, as he thought of the many defenses against an aggressor with a knife, he was lightheaded. Finally, Dr. Houghton bowed deeply to Mr. Ho.

Mr. Ho said with an inscrutable, Oriental grin, "It is good."

During the jeep ride back to the detachment, Dr. Houghton realized that, although he had made an excellent beginning in Hap Gi Do, he was only a tyro. He had not finished. Within two weeks he would leave Korea. Almost morose, he thought of his Black Belt gathering dust in a closet as a layer of fat enveloped him.

Mike and the Deputy, at opposite ends of the bar at the Officers' Club, were waiting for him. Mike stood up and asked eagerly, "How did it go, Doc?"

"I passed." He showed them the Black Belt, the identification card, and the diploma, which the Deputy read in his halting Korean. Again, Dr. Houghton wondered aloud if he really deserved the "Belt."

Mike answered, "Doc, you're crazy. I saw the exhibition months ago. You were awesome; you were better than the Koreans. I'm really sorry we couldn't go today."

The Deputy added, "I saw your jeep, against the regulations, bring you back from Chun Chon every day, from your lessons. For just your persistence, I'd give it to you."

Dr. Houghton rebutted, "The Colonel gave me permission."

The Deputy replied, "I would not have."

"Then, I am glad you were not the Commander here."

The Deputy ignored the bitter tone. He graciously extended his hand and shook Dr. Houghton's hand vigorously. "Doc, Congratulations. I never thought you would succeed. I'd say that's quite an achievement. Along with Miss Pak, you've picked up two experiences you'll never forget." The Deputy grinned salaciously.

Dr. Houghton thought to himself, "There were interactions with two Koreans you missed Colonel, the departed Miss Han and Lieutenant Ahn."

He hurried over to see Colonel Newton who was not at the bar. He entered the Colonel's unlocked door immediately after knocking. He recoiled when he saw the huge naked Colonel making love to Mary Lee. "Sorry, Colonel, I'll see you later."

"Doc, damn it. Sit down in the corner. Shut and lock the door.Let me finish her. I am almost done!"

Dr. Houghton did as he was told. He turned the chair away from the lovers. After another minute of very hard pumping, groans and a huge Ah, Colonel Newton finally disengaged himself. Still facing away from the lovers Dr. Houghton said, "Colonel, you're taking a big chance with the Deputy nosing around all the time. You are aweful noisy."

"Yes, I know, Doc, but you understand. Screw the Deputy."

"I know when the blood runs hot, to quote the venerable Colonel Newton..."

Colonel Newton roared at hearing himself quoted; the image of himself as a respectable sage was too much to bear. He knew what he was, and he was not a wise man. He knew he suffered from terminal lust. In two months, he would go home for his final tour at Fort Benning. In those two months, he better purge his system of lust once and for all. Finally, he emerged in shorts.

"Mary Lee, come here," called the Colonel.

She emerged in the Colonel's T-shirt which extended below her knees. She was now completely flat chested, unlike her usual big-breasted self. She smiled sheepishly.

Since Dr. Houghton and Miss Judy cared for her in the clinic, he knew she was flat chested. But he couldn't resist. He observed in Korean, "Your breasts are sleeping?"

Mary Lee said, "What'd you say, Doc?"

"Oh, nothing much." He knew that this was a really stupid remark.

She pouted and pointed at him, "Number ten man."

Dr. Houghton showed Colonel Newton and Mary Lee the Black Belt, the diploma, and the identification card.

"Congratulations, Doc. That's real fine. I'm proud of you."

The encomium of the day came from Mary Lee. In polite Korean, she said, "Honorable Doctor, if all Korean peoples like you, the world would be a better place. I owe you my worthless life."

Dr. Houghton answered her in Korean. "Miss Lee, you life is not worthless; you make the Colonel happy. In fact, every time I see you, you make me happy."

Her eyes clouded over.

"Colonel, excuse me. I want you to complete your operations here, so that you can move her out before the Deputy gets wise."

"Right, Doc; I'll see you later. I want to make Mary Lee happy one more time but I need thirty minutes." He winked salaciously, roared and grabbed a resilient Mary Lee.

By ten o'clock, a drained Dr. Houghton slipped into a troubled sleep. He held Non'gae in his arms much of the night because he was pursued without mercy by three viper-haired Korean beldams. At about four, she awoke him gently. He was perspiring and it wasn't hot.

He woke confused. "Hey, Mom, they're still chasing me," he muttered. However, as he awoke, he was comforted by Non'gae beside him.

"Reginald, *what* is the matter?"

"If you hold me tight, I'll be O.K."

"I worry much about you. What is the trouble? You are now a first degree. Congratulations again. Why do you worry?"

"I worry about you. What am I going to do when I leave? No Non'gae, no Korean house, no Korean games, no Hap Gi Do; only hard work and mountains of aggravation. I'll be very sad."

"What am *I* going to do? No Reginald. But I think you must go to the States."

"I am very sad."

"I am very sad, too."

"But Non'gae, before I go, we'll spend four days in Seoul. You can show me King Yi's palace. Good idea?"

"Yes, number one idea," she sighed.

"In Seoul we must talk about the future. I'll tell you my plan. Do not worry!"

"I will not worry, until then," she said hopefully.

"Now hold me tight so that those old ladies don't harm me."

"What ladies?"

"Oh, some old ladies. Good night, Non'gae."

"Good night, Reginald."

Dr. Houghton knew she thought him strange. As he drifted back into early stage sleep, he felt stronger. When the three Korean

371

beldams reappeared, he pointed accusingly at them. He said the Furies are supposed to be Greek arbiters of justice, not Korean. He looked closely and they were now Greek. After a prolonged discussion in Greek, they said they would not bother him any more. They had made a mistake. He was not guilty.

After a few mnutes, Dr. Houghton finally fell into a restful stage-four sleep.

General Kim arrived early the next morning. They drove to the Provincial Government building. Dr. Houghton was anxious. They waited for the Governor in an anteroom for about ten minutes. Finally, a small Korean man announced, "The Governor is ready."

General Kim and Dr. Houghton entered the western style office. The Governor, a former three star General, was slightly round bellied, a sign of good health and good fortune in Korea. They bowed politely.

"Sit down, please," the Governor of the Province said in poor English.

"Thank you."

"Please have some coffee."

The Governor's aid poured the coffee.

The Governor continued, "I saw your exhibition."

"Yes, I know. I subsequently earned my Black Belt," Dr. Houghton said in Korean.

"That is good," the Governor replied.

"I've also learned the Korean language."

"What else?"

"I am also a number one Korean card and Chinese chess player," he continued in Korean.

The Governor laughed. "Who taught you, the Kisaeng?"

Dr. Houghton smiled.

"Do you have a Korean girl friend?"

General Kim answered to prevent any potential embarrassment. While Dr. Houghton did not understand the entire reply, he did hear that, "Dr. Houghton does not employ a business lady."

Dr. Houghton added in his most polite, honorific Korean, "I am sorry to leave Korea. I have many friends here, like the Honorable General Kim. I hope you will help General Kim be reassigned soon for he is a good man."

General Kim crimsoned at this boldness, but Dr. Houghton knew what Dr. Kim wanted.

With a sudden change of expression, as a camera man entered the room, the Governor stood and said in English, "I wish to thank you for the many good deeds you performed for the people of our province."

General Kim indicated that Dr. Houghton should stand. They listened as the Governor haltingly read a formal letter of appreciation in English, framed under glass in a heavy teak wood frame. The letter documented Captain Houghton's civic action programs including the polio vaccinations and the indigent out-patient clinic with characteristic Oriental exaggeration.

Dr. Houghton smiled as the flash bulbs popped when he shook hands with the Governor. Then it was over.

Next they rode over to the Corps Headquarters. First, Dr. Houghton visited Lieutenant General Lee. He had been reassigned to Army Headquarters in Seoul. He was leaving tomorrow. Dr. Houghton saluted.

General Lee pointed to a chair and said, "Congratulations on your Black Belt."

"Thank you."

General Lee said, "I am now well." He pointed at his groin. "It works better than ever. Thank you." He paused, "Did you purchase the jadeite from the Abbot?"

"Yes, four pieces for four million won."

"Not five?"

"No, General."

"The Abbott told me five. He swindled you."

Dr. Houghton did not answer.

General Lee said in polite Korean, "You have done an excellent job here. But I have one final piece of advice for you." He whispered, "My replacement, General Ku is, how do you say it in English? a 'plick.' Be careful of him. Let me take you to his office. He will present you with the Certificate of Appreciation since he is now the Corps Commander. Good luck."

Dr. Houghton saluted the new Corps Commander, General Ku, who flashed a wide power grin. Coffee was served by the General's adjutant. General Lee did not stay for the ceremony which greatly disappointed Dr. Houghton.

General Ku said in Korean, "I hear you graduated from Harvard and Yale."

"Yes, General Ku."

My twelve year old son would like to go to Harvard like President Kennedy."

Dr. Houghton did not comment.

"Congratulations, now you and I are both first degree Hap Gi Do Black Belts."

"Thank you," replied Dr. Houghton. For some reason, he was intimidated by this solid little man.

General Ku read a Letter of Appreciation to Captain Houghton for his excellent advisory work and then pinned two Korean medals on him. For the only time in his life, Dr. Houghton stood at rigid attention. The only other person in the room was the adjutant; no photographer. The adjutant passed him a fancy envelope with the Letter.

After the brief ceremony, General Ku continued in Korean, "Colonel Newton says you have a nice house in the village."

"Thank you," Dr. Houghton replied. Dr. Houghton then said, "If you wish, I'd be glad to have you visit my house." He immediately knew he blundered.

When he returned to the Detachment, Sergeant Morse said, "The Deputy called the Captain twice. He is on the phone again."

"Good morning, Colonel. I just saw the Governor and General Ku."

The Deputy said, "Be careful of Ku. He is a prick. But that is not why I called. I wanted to let you know that Sergeant Clooney was killed in Vietnam. I know you and he were friends. Did you know he was investigated for jewelry theft while on leave in Hong Kong, but CID, the Army Criminal Investigative Division, could never prove anything? I liked him. He was full of fun. I hear he has no family."

"Yes, he was not married," Dr. Houghton paused. "Was the reason he was suddenly sent to Vietnam because of the jewelry investigation?"

The Deputy did not answer right away. He said unconvincingly, "They needed motor pool sergeants badly in 'Nam.' We recommended him highly. He was excellent."

Dr. Houghton understood the Deputy's "recommendation" was literally "the kiss of death."

Dr. Houghton remembered Clooney well. Master Sergeant Clooney helped him with jeep and helicopter access all the time. In return, he helped Clooney with his amorous adventures. Clooney was the only one who employed two business ladies; a senior and junior. He was an indefatigable lover and superb motor pool sergeant. When Dr. Houghton first came, Clooney educated him in the ways of the Army. He maintained Dr. Houghton was "too curious." Clooney often said, "I do not want to know." If you don't know, he said, you do not have to worry or tattle or gossip. He was the antithesis of Dr. Houghton who believed in Aristotelian curiosity. At Clooney's request, Dr. Houghton treated his two

374

"employees" for parasites, questionable TB in one and anemia in the other. After his ministrations, Clooney's girls were in tip-top shape. But most of all, Dr. Houghton remembered Clooney's inexhaustible supply of Irish and Jewish jokes.

After a few minutes of refecting about poor Clonney, another victim of the madness of Vietnam, he remembered Clooney had asked him to keep a small package in the narcotics safe in the office. He asked Clooney, "What's in it?" It was about two months ago.

"Don't ask, Doc. Please do me that favor. You know you owe me one," Clooney paused. "No one else has access to that safe. Right?"

Dr. Houghton did owe him, for Clooney had broken the regs for him many, many times. Dr. Houghton said, "I will do as you say." When Clooney went to Vietnam, he asked Dr. Houghton to hold the package until further notice.

Dr. Houghton closed his office door, opened the safe and untied the small box. Inside were two pendants on platinum chains-possibly a ruby and an orange sapphire, both about three carets or more he guessed. He almost collapsed. Here was the product of the Hong Kong theft. Both stones looked perfect to the naked eye. He attempted to scratch his drinking glass. They both made deep cuts. They were very hard, probably real.

He said to Sergeant Morse on the way out. "I have to go up to my quarters for few minutes. I will be back in an hour. By the way, did you hear Clooney died in Vietnam?"

"Yes, I just heard. Does the Captain know Clooney was screwed; tragic?" He shook his head in disgust. "He helped us and the Captain helped him with his girls."

In his room Dr. Houghton locked the door and pulled out his jadeite indentification equipment. He did the tests he could with his loupe, fluorescent lamps, Chelsea filter and his slit spectroscope. He couldn't make a definitive identification but he was sure that the red stone was a perfect ruby and the orange stone a Padparadscha sapphire from Ceylon. He wrote down the spectral lines for both stones; he did not have a book that contained the lines for ruby and sapphire but he could find out in Seoul. Then he would be absolutely sure that the stones were real. If real, each was worth more than his annual US Captain's salary with his M.D. premium, or twenty years of Tea House work. What should he do with them? After all, they were pelf as his father would say. They were also very beautiful, especially the Padparadscha sapphire, but not worth a man's life.

When he returned to the dispensary, Sergeant Morse said, "It is one. I am off to lunch."

"Please bring me a ham and swiss sandwich, and a coke."

Sargeant Morse nodded and closed the door.

The phone rang, "Yes?"

"It is Miss Hu. Is this Captain Houghton?"

"Yes."

In polite Korean, she said, "I called to congratulate the Honorable Captain on the Black Belt. I also heard the Captain saw the Governor. I know him too; he visits our Kisaeng House. As the Honorable Captain asked, I have set up the trip to the Inn of Amaranth Flowers although it is quite far away."

He interrupted and said, "Maybe we shouldn't go. An army friend of mine just died in Vietnam."

She said, "I am sorry but you (the most polite form) promised me. Also I have most excellent news for you."

"Tell me!"

"I will tell you at the Golden Happiness Chinese Restraurant."

"I will see you on Saturday."

She said, "Many Celestial Angels have also made reservations at the Inn." She laughed.

He said, "Goodbye Miss Hu."

"Goodbye, Honorable Captain."

That evening Dr. Houghton invited the Morning Glory Tea House Miss Chang to visit. He wished to say good-bye before leaving for Seoul. Little Miss Kim came also. Miss Chang wore a tight yellow sweater and black skirt. Like Non'gae, she had also been anemic and responded to iron pills. With the anemia cured, her downtrodden appearance, gloomy moods and low spirits improved. Now Miss Chang could return his gaze directly for a few minutes. She was even proud of her impressive bosom. Dr. Houghton cosseted her. He savored the victory of "iron" confidence over Korean shame.

Dr. Houghton wore a saffron silk mandarin's costume with scarlet borders, an unknown Chinese combination. They all laughed at the gauche mixture of bright colors and the funny man who wore them. But soon the talk sobered as they discussed whether Miss Chang should accept an offer from another farmer, a fifty year old widower who could adequately support her. Dr. Houghton argued for acceptance. She would be respectable and be able to provide a home for her son. But the three girls, with romantic notions, unrealistic in Korea, voted no. Although a humble offer, he knew that Miss Chang might never receive another.

He almost collapsed when Non'gae, the shy, fluttering, cherry girl of only eight months before, crowned her argument and warned, "With that old man, there will be no fulfillment for you. Sex is important...."

At nine, Dr. Houghton heard a jeep cut its motor outside. Who could it be? He walked into the moonless courtyard after putting the forty-five in his Chinese girdle. He opened the gate.

A Korean man emerged from a jeep. When General Ku approached, Dr. Houghton recognized him. He was dressed in dark slacks and an open white shirt. He said to his driver, "Wait here."

Dr. Houghton saluted and against all good sense said, "Won't you please come in."

After removing his shoes, the General ducked inside the chamber and was visibly impressed. He whispered in Korean, "Do not say who I am."

The General sat on the proffered silk pillows and carefully observed the stereo, TV, field phone, and art work.

"This is Mr. Pak, my friend," Dr. Houghton said.

The girls, although they had seen him from a distance, could not imagine, even in their wildest fantasy, General Ku here. Complicating matters was Non'gae's categorical interdiction against Korean male guests in the chamber unless cleared by her in advance.

The General scowled for an instant at the "Mr. Pak." He pointed impolitely at the tight-sweatered Miss Chang, "Your girl friend?"

"No."

Then he pointed to Non'gae.

"Yes."

The General continued in Korean, "She is beautiful."

Non'gae, with her recherché charm lowered her long eyelashes, looked down and away, feigning embarrassment, and said, "Thank you," with characteristic Oriental mummery.

She asked, "Would Mr. Pak like old whiskey or rice wine?"

"Whiskey."

Dr. Houghton poured three ounces of Scotch into a glass which the General drank with polite smacking of the lips. When he placed the glass on the table, he reached over and cupped Miss Chang's left breast.

She withdrew from this unexpected assault.

Dr. Houghton said, "She did not buy them in the PX." But inside he boiled with disgust.

377

General Ku laughed, but the three girls scowled at this typical Korean behavior. With Dr. Houghton they were usually protected from such impolite impulses.

General Ku turned to Dr. Houghton and carefully surveyed his costume. He ventured some remark that Dr. Houghton did not understand but convulsed the girls. He thumped Dr. Houghton on the chest and felt his biceps. He ceased the exploration when he noticed the handle of the forty-five. General Ku then looked at Non'gae, "Black Belt?"

"Yes, first degree Black Belt," she said.

He then asked, "Is it big?"

Non'gae retained complete self-control and replied, "It's indeed big; number one."

Little Miss Kim giggled behind her hand. Miss Chang flushed.

In an attempt to walk on less offensive ground, Dr. Houghton said, "Mr. Pak number one man."

But, as suddenly as he came, General Ku said, "I go."

Dr. Houghton walked him to the gate. The driver asked, "Where does the Honorable General wish to go?"

The General just pointed.

Dr. Houghton saluted.

General Ku saluted and then drove off without further comment.

Non'gae, who had followed them outside, saw the three illuminated stars on the jeep license plate. She said, "Oh, boy! I go monkey house. Why you no say that man General Ku? You a simpleton, Reginald?"

Miss Chang echoed in Korean, "I almost punched him in the nose. Then I spend a long time in the monkey house."

"You know, Non'gae, the General said you're beautiful."

"I knows," she laughed and capered back to the table.

"Now," Dr. Houghton said to Miss Chang in Korean, "besides Colonel Newton and General Ku, who are smart men, I want to make love to you."

"It's OK," Non'gae said.

"Good idea," Miss Chang answered in English, but she immediately changed the subject. She imitated Non'gae with identical un-Korean haughtiness. "It is big. Number one."

At this mimicry, they all laughed, recalling that Non'gae had actually said this to General Ku. The laughter echoed in the surrounding hills for many minutes.

.   .   .

378

After days of inner turmoil, Dr. Houghton crossed his Rubicon and stepped onto the helicopter to Seoul. He told Non'gae that he had to go to Seoul on military business which was true and would be back the next day, on Sunday, also true. He brought his overnight bag and a one cubic foot metal box with the false top. As the noisy Huey flew down to Seoul, he one more time reviewed the rationale for taking the jadeite amaranth field carving. This carving was stolen by the Japanese from China; it was not Korean property; no one sees it, it is not appreciated; by Korean standards, if the Abbot did not protect it, it was "fair game;" and General Lee had made an arrangement with the Abbot. Moreover, Dr. Houghton had already paid for it and General Lee said the Abbot "swindled him." Thus the carving was really his property. If he could safely snatch it and be gone, he would do so. But he would not take excessive risks *and* Miss Hu would not know. He thought of Sargeant Clooney – who from the grave of Arlington National Cemetery was helping him. Clooney the master jewel thief would applaud his effort.

He completed his business quickly in Seoul, finishing his paperwork before being sent back to the States. He also briefly saw General Samet who congratulated him on his Hap Gi Do Black Belt. General Samet made an appointment with him the morning of the day he would finally leave. He said, "I want to spend more time with you. I have some personal issues I want to discuss with you and I hope to have good news. Goodbye, Doc."

A pleased Dr. Houghton said, "Goodbye, General."

General Samet's driver dropped him off at Kimpo, the main airport in South Korea. Like so much of South Korea, the airport was dusty and smelled. He boarded a military cargo plane to Taegu. At Taegu airport he changed into black wool slacks and a royal blue shirt. He grabbed a taxi to the Golden Happiness Chinese Restraurant. He arrived promptly at five.

With a silent deep bow, the maitre d' escorted him to a small private back room, opened the door-window and signaled him to enter. He saw Miss Hu seated on the floor in front of the low table. She wore a tight royal blue silk skirt; colorless nylons and a white silk tuxedo blouse. He said, "Are you Miss Hu?" He now spoke almost always in Korean as did she. No more degrading GI macaronic English.

She smiled, showing off her perfect white teeth framed by her Cupid's bow scarlet lips. "Yes I am Miss Hu, but later tonight I will join the company of Celestial Angels, Yes?"

Dr. Houghton experienced the emotions of the sixth grade Reginald when he saw a pretty woman: confusion, lust, longing. He was aghast at her appearance. What a change from the sick Miss Hu of two months ago. He was indeed ready to meet Celestial Angels.

She said, "Do I look good? Many people do not recognize me. You did this to me." She stood and slowly turned around. He noted her straight, shapely long legs.

Finally he said, "You should have been a queen."

She said, "Yes, I made my hair in the royal tradition. Do you like the top braid?"

"Your hair is so rich, so thick. You are no longer anemic."

She said, "As you requested, I did not eat kimchi or garlic for three days." She breathed on him from across the table; wintergreen."

He said, "I smelled the osmanthus perfume the minute I came in."

Almost immediately, a boy brought in the Mongolian barbecue equipment. A server bowed deeply and entered, lit the charcoal and started cooking the thin strips of beef over the open flame. Dr. Houghton offered Miss Hu some of the Scotch whiskey from his flask.

She said, "No thank you, Honorable Captain. I drink on my job every night. Tonight I want a clear head." After a time Miss Hu excused the server.

Dr. Houghton could not wait any longer. "What have you to tell me?"

She spoke slowly in the most polite Korean fashion as if talking to an Emperor. "Congratulations Honorable Captain, you will be promoted soon to Honorable Major."

Dr. Houghton was as surprised at this news as at her recaptured resplendent beauty. "How in the world do you know?"

She laughed and said, "I know." She glowed with the mystery.

"Tell me please." He was begging.

"You know General Dr. Kim."

"Of course."

"He has a Kisaeng that he supports in an apartment in Chun Chon. I know her very well. She told me that General Kim wrote a letter for you and the promotion just came through from the Pentagon."

Dr. Houghton's first thought was his reflexive Puritanism: Dr. Kim, the family man, what a hypocrite! But that was too harsh. With women like Miss Hu, who could resist? Then he tried to suppress a few renegade tears that involuntarily appeared, but he could not stop them. He was not intoxicated. He had only drunk two ounces of Scotch. Could she be correct? That is probably what General Samet wanted to tell him in a few days – the good news.

He said, "Thank you for the great news. Tonight I will walk on the ceiling."

She smiled broadly although she did not understand walking on the ceiling. He was not a spider. But she knew she had judged him correctly.

He could not contain himself. He had decided to do it later, only after he heard the Celestial Angels sing. But why not do it now? He knew he should not keep it. He didn't earn it. Why not give it to someone who could really benefit? After all it was just a colored stone. So he took the three caret ruby out and passed it to Miss Hu.

She looked at it, stunned. Kisaeng knew jewels. She immediately scratched a glass with it. She said, "It is hard." The expression in Korean-Chinese referred more to people than stones and had strong sexual overtones.

Dr. Houghton understood the pun and laughed. "It is very hard, a perfect ruby." He had looked up the spectral lines in Seoul. He also found the orange Padparadscha sapphire was real and even more valuable in Korea. Of course he would give the sapphire to Non'gae. God bless him; Clooney was a very discriminating jewel thief.

She said, "I would have to work ten years and save every won I earned to have this much money. With my meager savings and this, I can now be an independent woman. Thank you so much, Honorable Major. Miss Han was correct about you. You have saved my body and now my future." She placed the ruby pendent around her neck.

He responded, "You do not know if Miss Han was correct. You have not yet heard the Celestial Angels sing!"

She smiled, winked and said, "Let's go," an expression the business ladies used.

The mini-taxi let them off at villa 202 at the Inn of the Amaranth Flowers.

He said, "Why don't you take a long bath while I go out and stretch my legs. They have a nice bathroom here. Take your time; then I will take a shower and we will search for the Celestials together." He winked.

After she entered the bathroom he put on his dark sneakers and picked up the locked metal box, which he had told her contained papers. He walked quickly over to the Golden Buddhist monastery. It was almost nine and quite dark although there was a moon sliver. He gingerly walked up the back steps of the monastery; the door opened easily. He listened and heard a cat meow. Then he heard nothing for about a minute. As he tip-toed across the dark corridor, he heard the monks begin soft chanting for the Amida, the Pure Land Buddha, from the Great Hall. He pushed the unlocked backroom door open carefully, went in and then closed it. He waited a minute. Using his low intensity flashlight, he slowly snipped through an arm of the cheap lock and opened the middle cabinet. He painstakingly picked the carving out of its box and placed it in his. It fit perfectly. When he heard someone pass down the corridor, he held his breath. When it was quiet again, he closed the cabinet door, repositioned the severed lock, and opened the door. After a short wait, he looked both ways and gently closed the door which squeaked a little this time. As quickly as possible, he tip-toed back across the corridor and out the back door. He felt a cat rub against his leg as he passed but that was all. It was that easy.

In ten minutes he was back in the villa. He locked the metal case, and put it and his sneakers in the closet. Miss Hu emerged from the bathroom a few minutes later. He said, behaving casually, "There are moon flowers on a trellis out there. Let's go look."

She slipped into a white shift-dress.

Hand in hand they walked in the small garden, admiring the flat white moon flowers. He said, "They are huge, over six inches in diameter." In those few minutes, Dr. Houghton calmed down from his successful snatch.

She said, "Let's go inside." She kissed him gently, under a riot of fragrant moonflowers. She also said, "Many men have tried to sleep with me since I became healthy. I now seem to attract even very rich men. Several offered me the moon and the stars." She pointed at them in the sky. "I rejected them all. I decided to wait for you, tonight. I will make you very happy."

He said, "One more minute, please!" He sniffed her. She smelled of osmanthus; then, like a big bee, he sniffed the moon flowers, a few scrawny roses and the Angel's trumpet flowers. He was intoxicated with the various fragrances around the villa. On the way in, he said, "There is something else here?"

"You are right; Jasmine, over there."

As Dr. Houghton showered he guessed that no one in the monastery would look at the amaranth carving for months or even years. When he first saw it, the carving was covered with a decade or more of grime and dust. He and the carving would be gone in days. Moreover, no one at the Inn knew he was here. Miss Hu had checked in and paid in cash. She had no idea what he had done. Finally he had a Bill of Sale with all five objects on it, signed and chopped by the careless Abbot Kim. Thank you General Lee.

That night, Dr. Houghton discovered another first. Miss Hu was a true "double." The professional soldiers were correct; there was such a thing. Not only did she achieve status orgasmus with its attendant plateau, repeated barrel spasms, palpable uterine contractions and loud hissing and whoosing sexual suction sounds but she was also a magic lady, better even than Non'gae and presumably like Miss Judy. Moreover, Miss Galt and the Miss Hans were also correct about angels. Both Dr. Houghton and Miss Hu definitely saw and heard Celestial Angels that night. When he was finally able to speak, he mumbled, "My angels had big wings."

Miss Hu said, "That is silly. Celestial Angels, Chinese Apsarases, do not have wings. They fly without wings; that is why they are Celestials. If they had wings, they would be birds. You have a jadeite carving of a Celestial Angel. Does she have wings? "

"No."

"Also Celestial Angels are Shape-Shifters; did you see that?"

"I will look more closely next time."

At four in the morning, the indefatigable Miss Hu was reciting and explaining Li Po's Chinese poetry about love, longing and abandonment. She knew the poems by heart. She had the same enthusiasm for Chinese poetry that his father had for Italian opera.

He said, "How did you learn this? You were an orphan and did not go to college?" Dr. Houghton remembered what Sergeant Song said when he first met Miss Hu; that she was very smart and very accomplished in Chinese and Chinese poetry and literature. Coming from a prize winner in Chinese poetry, this was quite a recommendation.

Miss Hu said, "The Kisaeng House operator let me go to middle and high school if I did my work. In middle school, I read a story translated into Korean by a Russian Jew called 'You Can Not Know Too Much.' I believed it. The operator also thought knowledge of Chinese poetry and persiflage would be good for the business. He was correct. I am now the number one girl. Do you know the Jewish story?"

"I think so."

"I studied very hard with a little help from an old Yangban scholar. I have a tremendous memory and can see the pages in my mind. I even cleaned Sergeant Song's clock!"

"What does that mean?"

"I knew more characters than him; more than 60,000, and more poems. I still study characters one hour every day."

Dr. Houghton wanted to weep. Here he was a Harvard high honors graduate in chemistry; in one year with a lot of work he only learned 250. "You also learned dance, singing and music. You are very accomplished."

"Yes, I am."

"Just one more poem; it is very late." He was now an emotional and physical wreck; the poems were very sad, and he was very tired.

She recited and then translated another poem into simple Korean. Then she decided to test him - the Hap Gi Do Black Belt, the Foreign Tiger. She said, "Once more, please."

Dr. Houghton then made a fortunate mistake. He said to himself, I am leaving this modern Xanadu in a few days, ultimately for the Brigham, a kind of modern Hades. He saw the image of Reginald as Sisyphus, with his medical stone, pushing it up the hill endlessly. Moreover, he might never again make love to a true double. Furthermore, she yielded a dividend; the nonpareil poetry of Li Po with tuition-free professorial level exposition and commentary. He said, "Give me thirty minutes."

She laughed and said, "You Black Belt," and pawed like a tiger.

Dr. Houghton went to the bathroom and took a pill, the one that his friend Henry had given him. It was Spanish Flies. Henry had tried it with "good results." Dr. Houghton decided to try it this once although he knew it was a urinary irritant as well as an aphrodisiac. In thirty minutes he did have a mild burning sensation when he urinated. But he was soon again ready for love.

She apparently was also affected because the next morning she too was extremely swollen. At six, she mumbled in Chinese, "You are a real tiger, not a paper tiger."

Dr. Houghton did not think he could make the check-out time of eleven or the flight back to Seoul at one. He lay in bed while she went for coffee and, he hoped, a buttered role with strawberry jam and not a bowl of rice. When he urinated, it still burned; he also saw his member was very swollen and discolored but he did not panic.

Back in bed alone he decided Schopenhauer was right and wrong. Schopenhauer was wrong about women; he was totally wrong. But he was right about how to spend your time. Schopenhauer liked the arts, especially music, because it put us in touch with the world as Will. Dr. Houghton also liked music and poetry but even more his jadeite carvings which captured both the artist's skill and reality in a resplendent stone. Moreover, Schopenhauer, like the Buddhists down the road in the Golden Monastery, saw the world as full of suffering. Schopenhauer also admired compassion. However, in the modern world of chemistry and biology, people like Dr. Houghton, unlike Schopenhauer, could actually do something meaningful about suffering. At that moment Dr. Houghton decided once and for all he would become a Professor of Medicine. He would do medical research, teach the students and care for patients. Schopenhauer and his father would be proud of him. The life of pleasure was great fun but, in the end, led no place except to extreme exhaustion and a damaged member.

He said, "God bless you," when Miss Hu brought in coffee and buttered rolls. He almost collapsed when she said, "Once, again, Honorable Major."

He decided to bluff. When he went to grab her, she said, "No. No. I am too swollen."

He pawed like a tiger.

She made several meows.

Later she thanked him profusely for the ruby and the Celestials. She said, "As I told you, I am forever in your debt. I will do anything for you; anything. When can I see you again?"

He gave her his address in the US and promised to see her in May 1970 just before he started his senior residency. He would return to Korea once more for a visit. He still had eight months of easy army duty in Fort Ord in California. Finally he said, "I want to see you in two days in Chun Chon at the Red Door Tea House at six."

As he flew back to Chun Chon, he compared himself to the big four: Shiva, the sexual Zeus, the great god Pan and of course Priapus. But he knew he cheated. He was also quite weak for the party tonight. In the future, he should not fritter his strength; he *must* use his talents in chemistry, medicine and science to accomplish something. He could never compete with the Koreans in Hap Gi Do, Chinese poetry or Korean literature; or for that matter sexual performance. He was already past his peak.

As he reflected more on the Buddhists, he thought they were on the right track with emphasis on compassion in the year 500 BC. But now they just talked and prayed, most often for their own spiritual elevation. In the monastery, he again heard them wasting time last night. They were just "sponges" to quote his father. But unlike the monks, he could actually do something for the sick and downtrodden - cure infections and infestations, stop seizures and the rest; and there was so much more to be done. He must put all his power into medicine and science. He was now certain of his decision. But as the day wore on and he felt stronger he concluded that he should not carry this too far; after all, he did have this wonderful functional middle leg. He should not let it rust.

The Deputy insisted on Beautiful Flower's presence for Dr. Houghton's going away party. She had reservations but came. She dressed, walked and looked like a Korean princess in Western silk clothes. She gleamed and her glorious black hair shined in the overhead light.

Dr. Houghton drank too much gin and tonic. Within ten minutes, his protoplasm was saturated with the juniper juice. Almost as quickly, the others were equally intoxicated except Beautiful Flower, who did not enjoy alcohol and merely watched the Americans.

But she clearly gloried in the attention and numerous compliments. Her cheeks were red, and not from rouge. From Colonel Bennet to the still monkish Lieutenant Humbert, she collected winks and propositions; but on the solemn oath of the Deputy to bring her to America in return for a single kiss, she would not yield.

Had Dr. Houghton been an egotist, he might have resented Beautiful Flower as the cynosure. But he gloried in her beauty, which was obvious to all, and in her poise. During the cocktail hour, Colonel Newton stood beside her for a few minutes. He insinuated his huge arm around her and his hand covered her right breast lightly.

She did not recoil. She knew his Mary Lee was flat chested - poor Colonel Newton.

Colonel Newton, as if the feel of her flesh was decisive, whispered, "Doctor, you should marry this girl." His face contorted; it was an effort for him to say this.

Dr. Houghton knew that Colonel Newton was the textbook example of lechery and hypocrisy. With Miss Mary Lee, Colonel Newton achieved joys he never found in America. But marriage to a foreigner of any status, an alien, really horrified Colonel Newton until today. "You're crazy if you do not marry her, Doc," he repeated.

Before the dinner, Colonel Bennet offered his speech. The men surrounded the Colonel and Dr. Houghton in a three quarter circle. Beautiful Flower and Captain Chang, the only Koreans present, sat on tall chairs at the bar.

The Colonel stood directly under one of the yellow overhead lights. A strange glow covered him and reflected off his bald head. He began swaying back and forth in his cowboy boots. His speech was slurred. "Doc Houghton's a tiger. No question about it. We're proud of him with his Black Belt and his extra-army activities, and there sits one ..." The Colonel paused and pointed to Beautiful

386

Flower; he now rolled back and forth on his toes and heels, as if some invisible wind blew on him. "On the compound, Doc has been superb with the civic action, the Korean sick call."

Someone said, "Amen."

The Colonel scowled, "I remember he even told the Inspector General that Colonel Bennet never drinks to excess." At this fond memory, he doubled over in laughter, splashing his scotch over the floor. He shook the spillage off his right hand after transferring the glass to his left. All this was done with the slow, careful-as-possible ineptness of an intoxicated man.

Dr. Houghton interrupted and said, "I said on duty."

In his Texas slur, ignoring Dr. Houghton's response, Colonel Bennet continued, "But it was his advisory effort that I remember most; unit after unit, Dr. Houghton had been there before me, particularly up around the DMZ. But, after all, that was his job and he did it well. The Koreans really appreciated it."

Everone applauded.

The Colonel continued, "Doctor, it's been a pleasure, a real pleasure, and I present you with your plate with best wishes and good luck. Unfortunately, you are the last of the medical advisors here; soon they plan to close down the entire detachment."

Dr. Houghton accepted the heavy brass plate with his name, rank, K-MAG, United States Army, Korea and the date inscribed in the middle. He said, "I'd like to say a few words," and pulled out a roll of toilet paper with some black Chinese characters on a few sheets. "In Korea, this is more valuable than gold; that is what it says here."

Non'gae held her nose. Others booed or laughed.

After the raucousness died down, he said, "I was happy to participate in defending freedom's frontier, but I am still not sure if this is just propaganda. Do you know Mike?"

Mike did not respond and no one laughed. He needed to skate off the thin ice.

"But seriously, I've enjoyed the advisory work. I feel the civic action program was worthwhile. We patched up a lot of Koreans who would otherwise be in a box. Sergeant Morse and I saved and improved the lives of many Koreans who would have received no attention whatsoever. President Kennedy commented that 'life is often unfair' and that is surely true in Korea.

"In the village, I made many friends, two of whom are here tonight, Miss Pak and Captain Chang. Not only have they been best friends - indeed, I hold hands with both of them - but they have taught me a lot. Miss Pak has taught me so much – aside of the

Korean language. For her kindness and love, I owe her a deep debt which I will never be able to repay fully."

Non'gae wiped away a tear while everone applauded politely, turning toward her.

"But almost equally enjoyable and instructive have been the Americans with whom I worked. Over there sits the pristine pure Major Mike as Miss Kim calls him."

Mike screamed, "Slander, Doc. I am a Light Colonel. That's slander, or is it libel? I always get those mixed up." Mike was very drunk, saddened by Dr. Houghton's immanent departure.

"Mike, as we all know, is a nuclear bomber pilot, an excellent one, who for the past year has warmed jeep seats. I first met Mike during the counter infiltrator operations. He took me to Japan and Hong Kong. But all jokes aside, I'd trust Mike in a nuclear-armed S.A.C. bomber any day, but with one reservation, that he is the co-pilot. We want to keep the world intact."

At this, Mike guffawed.

"Over there," he continued, "I see Captain Chang who has been a gentleman and a dear friend. He has shown me that Koreans can be smart, honest and true. But most of all I envy Captain Chang his wife who is a charming and beautiful woman."

Captain Chang smiled.

"Next, I see Colonel Newton, two Colonel Newtons, the devil and the saint; one of whom I should shoot for putting his hand on my girl. From Colonel Newton I've learned about leadership, women, and sex. I'll never forget Colonel Newton's aphorisms; for example, the one he learned in basic that has guided him to the exalted rank of full Colonel. I quote: 'If you have a buddy who is fine and true, screw that man before he screws you.'"

The Americans all burst out laughing and applauding. Captain Chang and Beautiful Flower did not.

"Of course, Colonel Newton's appetites are legendary. He told my village housegirl that he eats small women for breakfast. She still shakes at the mention of his name. Even after he leaves, I'm sure his spirit will be seen walking the back alleys of the village for years, looking for small girls to eat."

"Nice talk, Doc," Colonel Newton said.

"Seriously though, I've learned a great deal about the Army, the techniques of advising, and certain hard facts of life from Colonel Newton. And, Colonel Newton taught me the equivalent of a course in grand strategy as well as tactics. I owe him a debt for his patient instruction. I now know how to win, by fair means or foul. But, there is one important request I've denied him. I hope he bears no ill feeling."

Colonel Newton answered, "No hard feeling, although it still hurts. Miss Chang is the *real* thing."

Dr. Houghton tensed slightly as the laughter died down. "The Deputy has been kind to me. I won't tell his wife that he tired to corrupt my Miss Pak tonight. He and I have made several trips together to visit the hospitals and medical units in his Corps. He was full of good ideas and suggestions, and he helped me with the implementation of several important programs.

The Deputy smiled and mouthed, "Thank you."

"Of course, I'll never forget Lieutenant Humbert who loved the tube more than women. He'll never look back at Korea with a palpitating nostalgia, nor will Jeff our superconscientious wire man. If Jeff could find the man who stole his wire, he'd kill him on the spot. I know who it was."

Jeff implored, "Who Doc?"

Dr. Houghton did not reply. In fact, he had used some of Jeff's wire for his village house phone.

"Finally, I turn to Colonel Bennet. The Colonel has treated me like a son. He's given me liberties and bent regulations so that I could pursue my activities. I will be eternally grateful. But there is one achievement the Colonel did not mention of which I am very proud; it is our successful VD program - only two cases in the last eight months. With all the loose penises around, I consider this my greatest triumph."

Everyone laughed, hooted and applauded.

"Who got VD? I demand to know!"

"You know I can't tell you, Colonel."

"In summary, I wish to thank you all, before I fall down, for your good-humored support and camaraderie."

Everyone applauded.

The Deputy placed his arm around Dr. Houghton. "Why don't you and Miss Pak join the Colonel and me for dinner?"

"We'd be honored."

The meal was only a vague spinning memory to Dr. Houghton except he did remember the fillet mignon steak was excellent. The following day, without absolute certainty, he recollected that the drunken Deputy mumbled Colonel Bennet had put him on the five percent list for promotion to major. This was now old news since the blessed Miss Hu had informed him the promotion actually went through.

But Dr. Houghton would always remember that Beautiful Flower was the only woman to dine at the Colonel's table in thirteen months. He would always remember her as the almond-eyed beauty who downed her chicken with polite gusto. She used the fork, knife and spoons with consummate skill.

The next day the army packers came. He had his Bill of Sale for the jadeite pieces- all five – signed with the Abbot's chop. He was worried but ready.

Sargeant Smith said, "Captain, we are only interested in your not bringing drugs, guns, bombs, explosives, ammo or women in your home baggage. We will carefully pack your baggage in wooden crates which will arrive within two weeks of your arrival back home. Any questions?"

"No, sounds good to me; actually I do have one question. Do Customs look at my baggage at the port of entry? "

"No, I am Customs."

Dr. Houghton's heartburn immediately cleared. He had packed the jadeite pieces in layers of silk in cardboard boxes inside metal cases. They would soon be on their way to America.

Three nights before leaving, Dr. Houghton prepared for his adoption of little Miss Kim. He explained his proposal to ex-Sergeant Song who had come from Seoul for a brief visit. Dr. Houghton said, "I hope we can arrange a marriage for dispensary Corporal Heme and a nice cherry girl I know, Miss Kim. As you know, Corporal Heme is an orphan. I know in Korean society that without a family, he has few rights. He has a bleak future with absolutely no connections. Like everyone else, Corporal Heme has great respect for you. He still refers to you as Honorable Sergeant Song. Soon he will be discharged. I hope you can find him a good job with your many connections."

"There will be no problem," Sergeant Song replied.

Dr. Houghton said, "Good. This girl, little Miss Kim, I would like you to meet. If you agree that she is suitable, I'll adopt her as my daughter and provide her with enough for a wedding and dowry."

Sergeant Song, after visiting Miss Kim, replied, "I've talked with her. I have also spoken with Corporal Heme. He says that if you and I think she is OK, and she is a cherry girl, then he is happy."

"Corporal Heme," Dr. Houghton called.

Corporal Heme walked in and bowed too deeply to Sergeant Song.

Dr. Houghton was now quite fluent in Korean. He said, "How many times have I told you that Sergeant Song is not the Son of Heaven!"

"Yes, Sir," Corporal Heme smiled. "I am grateful to Captain Houghton for finding me a wife and now a job. I'm only an orphan boy. Without your help, I many worry about my destiny. After Army, I would be in big trouble." He switched into English. "Now all things very OK. Inner feeling very good."

"Excellent," Dr. Houghton said. "Tonight at eight o'clock, I want you to come to my house in the village."

That night, when Miss Kim arrived, she immediately sat on Dr. Houghton's cross-legged knees; she had the image of Dr. Houghton as steel in physical strength. After all she knew every nook and cranny of his body.

"Come here," Non'gae commanded. She placed the finishing touch on Miss Kim's eyes, cheeks, lips and coiffured hair. Miss Kim was starting her finest hour.

Dr. Houghton explained in Korean, "I've decided to adopt you as my daughter."

"Why?"

"Non'gae and I want you to be happy."

"OK," Miss Kim replied. She knew what was going to happen. She turned to Non'gae. "Now I'll have to call you new mother, rather than elder sister."

Dr. Houghton continued, "Now that you are my daughter, I have decided to marry you off."

"Ha! Ha! Ha!" Miss Kim giggled. She politely put her hand over her mouth.

Dr. Houghton observed little Miss Kim's expression transform from pretended skepticism through wonder to joy. Her eyes glistened as they filled with tears.

Non'gae stopped her. "Do not cry now, you will spoil your makeup."

At the appointed time, Corporal Heme arrived in a borrowed suit and tie. They all drank rice wine and laughed. Little Miss Kim dared not even glance at Corporal Heme.

Dr. Houghton wearied of his role as matchmaker after a short time. He asked "OK?"

Corporal Heme answered happily, "OK."

"OK, Miss Kim?"

She bowed which he interpreted was an affirmative reply.

Corporal Heme returned to the detachment. Then Dr. Houghton presented Miss Kim with a large stack of Korean money and two pieces of green jade jewelry. He hoped the money would not go through her hands like a colander. Non'gae promised to counsel her in thrift.

Dr. Houghton wished to be alone with Non'gae, so he walked little Miss Kim to the bus for the final time. They said nothing, but she held his hand tightly. They sat on the flat stones at the side of the dark road.

As the bus approached, she seized the initiative. Unlike her usual self and with near flirtation, she said, "Thank you very much. I am very happy." She kissed him on the lips like a woman. "Soon I too will walk on the ceiling."

His eyes expressed surprise.

Miss Kim, about to be a married woman, asked, "Was that good?"

"Terrific," he said and kissed her again.

As the bus stopped, he helped her on. "Good luck," he said in traditional Chinese. Through the window, she waved the lateral happy good-bye of children to Americans. He waved back. There was a momentary view of "his" little Miss Kim with tears in her eyes. As he walked back, he knew he would sorely miss her magic palms and knuckles and toes. They so often soothed his battered body. He also knew he could trust her with his secret.

Dr. Houghton arrived at the Red Door Tea House to say goodbye to Miss Hu. She had inadvertently helped him with a key life decision and unknowingly with the recovery of his jadeite carving from the Abbott. As he inhaled her osmanthus perfume, he said, "You look wonderful, Miss Hu." He skipped the usual polite greetings. He knew it would be hard to leave this nonpareil woman; a Chinese poetry scholar/poetess and a double.

She wore the ruby pendant around her neck and a décolleté white silk blouse revealing the cleavage of her taut generous bosom. She said, "Thank you (most polite form). I have new news for you."

He said, "I love your ruby; it becomes you, but I love your bosom more." He thought she blushed but wasn't sure. "What is the news?"

"I quit the Kisaeng House. I paid all my debts and am moving to Seoul to open a dress and perfume shop boutique. Two of my friends will help me as sales assistants; I will be the buyer and manager. "

"That is wonderful."

"May I show you some of the perfumes we will sell, honorable Major Houghton?"

"Yes, please."

"I have five essences here - osmanthus which you know well, jasmine, rose, jujube and moon flower." She rubbed one sample after another on his arm to smell. "Honorable Reginald, you know the Fragrant Concubine of Emperor Qianlong wore jujube flower perfume? You know the story?"

"I do."

When she mentioned the fragrant concubine, Dr. Houghton was overcome with lust; he was re-enraptured by Miss Hu.

She put a little osmanthus perfume on her upper exposed bosom and said, "Smell."

As he leaned over to smell her bosom, Dr. Houghton, now dizzy, thought he should leave the West and come to live in Korea with this woman. To hell with all his other plans! He noted she had even enchanted his taut scrotum. He imagined his testosterone was off the scale. He was frantic and just about to speak - to propose a new plan - when he remembered his predecessors, Dr. Barnes, crapulous and sexually debauched, and the tuxedoed Dr. Tierney in the whorehouse. Was he as crazy as those two? No, he was not. He also recalled what General Samet said. He heard his mother say he *must* stick to his plan to become a Professor of Medicine and jadeite collector *in America*. She said that Miss Hu would fade - sooner rather than later. Miss Hu was not an Amaranth. But would he rue this day forever - the road not taken? He took three deep breaths and said nothing.

She looked at him carefully, wondering what he was thinking; then she continued, "I owe my good fortune to you. I love you; you saved me, Honorable Major Houghton."

As he calmed down, Dr. Houghton thought that she also owed Sergeant Clooney. Every time he reminisced about Clooney, he thought of Presidents Kennedy and Johnson. He wanted to spit on the floor. These two imbeciles killed so many for this now clearly ill-conceived and unnecessary Vietnam War.

She continued in the most polite Korean, "Please promise you will write me frequently and see me this May in Seoul. Also, I am making you a silent partner in my business. I will send you something every year you don't visit. Finally, when you visit me in May I will teach you a Taoist arcanum, a secret very few know."

"What?"

"I will teach you how to prolong your pleasure as long as you desire."

"I have heard of that; is it possible?"

"Over two thousand years ago, the Chinese Taoists learned how but it is very secret and difficult, but will not be hard for you, my tiger."

Dr. Houghton laughed at the word play. He saw her now, he thought realistically, as a healthy resplendent double, a Chinese poetry scholar/poetess and a nonpareil enchantress, full of modern and ancient secrets. He looked at her carefully; to imprint her face and being in his mind. Finally, he stood and kissed her passionately.

She wiped a few tears from his face with her smooth silk handkerchief. She said, "I will see you in May, Major Houghton."

He tried hard to think of something witty to say and finally said, "I will see you in May, Ruby Hu."

She laughed and waved goodbye.

After returning from his painful goodbye with Miss Hu, as he emerged from the shower in the Q, he answered the persistent phone. A crackling barely audible Sergeant Morse said, "Miss Hu wants you to call her. You remember her. She just called." Sergeant Morse did not know of his subsequent close relations with Miss Hu.

Almost a miracle, he reached her at the number she gave on the first try. He spoke in Korean, "Hello, Miss Hu, I miss you already."

She sounded distressed, weepy. She said, "I have a sick sister. I just found out she is being tortured by a bad person and his evil wife. I am sorry I did not tell you about her before. I want you to help me, help us. I have no one to turn too. I have a plan. Please come tomorrow night to the Red Door Tea House, I beg you. Bring your gun and wear your fatigues. It should only take an hour. I beg you."

Dr. Houghton was uncertain what to answer. In three days he would be gone. He was very reluctant to embroil himself in an interpersonal Korean conflict. He said, "Why didn't you tell me this before?"

Miss Hu said, "As I told you, I just received a note from her. She is desperate; she is coughing up blood. They are putting out cigarettes on her."

"I will see you tomorrow night at the Red Door Tea House and we will see what to do."

The next evening, Miss Hu told him that her mother delivered her younger sister, Moon Flower, the year after she was born. She was brought up in a Christian orphanage, married a very bad man and was divorced. Recently, in desperation she became the concubine of a rich evil person who was abusing her. He was putting out cigarettes on her bottom. His wife was doing even worse things to her. She was being held captive by them.

"Why doesn't she just leave?"

"You are too simple, Honorable Major." She grasped his hand.

"Why?"

"She has debts to this man. Also he has body guards."

"What kind of man is he?"

"He runs an empire of business ladies and prostitutes on the hill outside Camp Page in Chun Chon. He is rich."

"Why does he keep your sister if she is sick?"

"She is very beautiful and like me." Miss Hu blushed, "You know."

"A double?"

"Yes. Will you help?"

"What can I do?"

Miss Hu outlined her plan - a quick snatch of her sister and her sister's debt contract. Miss Hu would then take her to Seoul and safety.

Dr. Houghton liked the plan; he thought of the James Bond movies. But he was sure he should not do this. This was as crazy as when he and Sean had planted the potassium sulfide in Miss Burtis' heating duct and stank up the class room. It was unnecessary and dangerous too. He was going to be a professor of medicine, not James Bond. He said, "I do not think I can do this."

Wiping her tear-filled eyes, she said, as the table-candle flickered in unseen winds, "She is sick. She coughs up blood. You are a Doctor." She grasped his hand tightly.

He hesitated. She thought she had him. "Remember, I showed you Celestial Angels-without wings." She beamed her best mirror-practiced enchanting smile. "I have so much more to teach you, skills no one else possesses. You will never regret this!"

"Let me tell my driver to wait."

In silence, they walked ten minutes up the narrow back alleys of "prostitutes' hill" to the captor's house. As they walked along, he saw shadowy girls. They didn't approach him since he was with a girl. He heard music blaring from the hooches and bars. From his medical work he well knew the degradation and sickness inside. He remembered several finished business ladies, toothless emaciated hags. There was not just venereal disease here including the ravages of pelvic inflammatory disease and untreated tertiary syphilis but also TB, parasites and most discouraging, terrible mental illness-depression, violence, and suicide. This place reminded him of the various descriptions of Hell. Theseus, Hercules and Orpheus had descended into Greek Hell. It wasn't so bad. The Buddhists and Christians had their Hells. But at least the victims had committed evil deeds, more or less, and were being punished. He greatly enjoyed Dante's and Michelangelo's visions of Hell, especially the lower reaches. In recent years Marx and then Marcuse had described the Hell of the modern factory. He knew they captured a lot of truth after working in his great-uncle's factory. Sartre correctly evoked the Hell of being with boring people, forever. And of course Camus won a Nobel Prize as he dissected Sisyphus' thoughts as he rolled the stone up the hill endlessly. But this Hell outside Camp Page was worse. These women were humped and screwed until they fell apart from disease or age. Then they were discarded. There was no escape since they were outcasts.

Teary-eyed, Dr. Houghton could not imagine being violated day after day in every orifice by vigorous faceless men. Sometimes these poor girls did not even have lubricant. Why didn't Korean society do something? He had asked the Governor who agreed; he was doing something - the taxi driver initiative - but this was not enough. Dr. Houghton had also done his best. Now Miss Hu was asking him to rescue one more victim.

As they walked through the unlocked Captor's gate, a man emerged from the large house. He said, "What do you want?"

Miss Hu said, "I want to see my sister."

The bodyguard said in impolite Korean, as if speaking to a dog, "Get out."

She said, "You dog."

He pulled out a knife, "Get out." He made a treatening gesture at Dr. Houghton.

Dr. Houghton pointed behind the man who hesitated. In that instant, Dr. Houghton kicked him first in one shin, then the other. He felt the bodyguard's right shin bone smush. The man howled, dropped the knife and fell to the ground. Miss Hu picked up the knife. She said, "If you move or shout I will cut off your balls. Understand?"

At that moment Mr. and Mrs. Kim emerged from the house. They looked at the body guard on the ground. "What do you want?"

"Moon Flower; we want Moon Flower, now!"

"She's not here."

Dr. Houghton pulled out his forty five. "Do not lie." He told them to go into the house and lie on the floor. He asked Miss Hu to accompany the wife and find Moon Flower. In a few minutes Moon Flower and the wife emerged.

Dr. Houghton said, "Hello. We have come to rescue you." He saw she was the image of her older sister but clearly pale and sick. He said, "Before we proceed, I need to see what they did. Lower your pants!" Dr. Houghton had promised himself he would seek evidence before proceeding any further.

Miss Hu whispered to her sister and she stepped to the side and complied.

396

Dr. Houghton was shocked. She had at least ten cigarette burns on her bottom. On a hunch, he said, "Turn around."

"They burned her vulva, too," he said in English. "In Hell, where would Dante or the Buddhist's place these people?" In Korean he said, "Who did it?"

Moon Flower pointed at the husband and wife with a Shakespearean flourish.

Miss Hu said to Mr. Kim, "Where are the debt papers of Moon Flower? Give them to us and we will leave." The husband didn't move. Miss Hu then stood over him and said, "Turn over and lower your pants." He refused. Dr. Houghton placed the forty five on his forhead.

Mr. Kim said, "I will find you at Camp Page."

Dr. Houghton cocked the forty five and said, "Over!"

Mr. Kim turned over and lowered his pants.

Miss Hu lit a cigarette and then put it out on Mr. Kim's bottom. He screamed.

She said, "Shut up.and get the papers, you dog."

Under the cover of Dr. Houghton's forty five, Mr. Kim took a stack of papers out of a cabinet; he pulled out Moon Flowers debt paper. Miss Hu said, "Lie down, all three of you. Take off all your clothes!"

The Kims and bodyguard complied.

Miss Hu then placed the entire stack of papers in a cloth carrying bag. She said, "If you make no further trouble, in seven days, after destroying Moon Flower's debt paper, we will return all the rest of these papers. If more trouble, we will destroy them - all."

Mr. Kim said, "You will ruin me - without the papers." But after realizing he was defeated, he said, "I will wait for the papers."

Miss Hu went into the kitchen and brought out three glasses of water. As pre- arranged with Dr. Houghton, she gave four Seconal tablets each to the naked Kims and bodyguard, and made certain they swallowed them. She said, "You will sleep very well tonight." The she said to Mrs. Kim, "Turn over." She lit a cigarette and placed her hand on Mrs. Kim's lower back. Her intention was clear.

In anticipation, Mrs. Kim screamed.

Dr. Houghton said, "Miss Hu, no. That's enough. We have what we want. Let's go."

Moon Flower went to her room, packed a few items and in thirty minutes they left the sleeping Kims and bodyguard. In retrospect, Dr. Houghton always wondered where the household help was that night. He must ask Miss Hu.

Outside they walked over to the waiting jeep which took them back to Miss Hu's room. Miss Hu said that she was packed. That night Miss Hu and her sister planned to take the bus and disappear into Seoul. At this point, Moon Flower had a paroxysm of coughing and brought up a little blood.

When Dr. Houghton saw the blood, he wrote out a letter to Dr. Horace Howard at Eighth Army in Seoul asking him to diagnose and treat Moon Flower. He guessed she had TB. He also told Miss Hu he would call Dr. Howard in the morning. Horace was a classmate at Yale. Finally, he said, "I insist you take a taxi to Seoul. Here is a hundred US. Promise me."

"I promise."

"Now I must go." They walked outside. Dr. Houghton said, "I am glad I was able to assist you, Miss Hu. You have helped me enormously and I have now partially repaid my debt."

She said, "I have so much more to offer you. I can teach you many things. Remember I will do anything for you." She smiled like the enigmatic enchantress Circe in the famous Dossi painting.

"What will you teach me? Be specific!"

"I will teach you about art, poetry, nature and most of all, physical and spiritual love. After all, we Kisaeng have been practicing these arts for two thousand years. I will not lie to you and claim we have the elixir of immortality. Rather I can teach you, Honorable Major, worthwhile knowledge and pleasurable skills."

He grasped her, kissed her for a long time and finally let her go. He inhaled deeply her osmanthus perfume, a fragrance that would always remind him of her. "Goodbye. I will see you in May. I can hardly wait. Please send me a telegram when I arrive back in the States in three days. I want to know that you and your sister are OK. " He walked toward his jeep, turned and waved goodbye.

She smiled and called, "Goodbye until May." As he walked away, a solitary tear slowly rolled down her cheek. She thought that if she had one more weekend with him she could have captured him forever. She almost had him yesterday with her perfumes. But, alas, it was not to be. She remembered only a few English poems but she did know the Korean translation of Maud Muller, by John Greenleaf Whittier. She wept at the last line: The saddest words of tongue or pen are these; it might have been.

The last two days before leaving for Seoul he asked Non'gae to postpone all serious thoughts and conversations until they arrived at Seoul. He was busy in the detachment finishing his work; he wanted to devote his thoughts to her completely during their Seoul idyll. They enjoyed their last village time together in a hazy, unreal world surrounded by the proverbial thousand flowers; Chinese primroses, poppies, wild roses, carnations, white dahlias, and flowers of unknown names. Silently moving among these "sisters," Beautiful Flower brought delicious refreshments; Swiss cheese, fresh Japanese Fuji apples and juicy Korean pears.

Dr. Houghton liked Beautiful Flower but he he loved Yi Non'gae even more.

The final evening, on his way to the village, he succumbed to an irresistible impulse to say good-bye to Miss Judy whom he had not seen since she asked him to sleep with her.

He knocked on her door, "May I come in, Miss Judy?"

She looked down with uncharacteristic sadness, a sorrow that crushed him.

"I am sorry I did not come to visit but I came to say good-bye. You helped me and the Korean indigent people in the clinic a lot. I want to thank you. You also helped me with Major Norman. That was a close call!"

She was silent. She continued to look down.

"I know you exposed your inner feelings to me and – I am sorry."

He reached over and took her warm hand, an error, for he felt her passionate nature pulse and flow into him. "I must go. Good-bye, Miss Judy."

She finally looked at him. Her eyes were red, choked with tears. Did he, like the Koreans, consider her an outcast? "Why, Doc, why you no come?"

He could only say, "You have my best wishes. You are a really good person." At this, tears flowed freely over her strikingly high cheek bones. "Please answer my letters," he said. He left, not daring to look back at the weeping woman.

As he walked slowly to his village house, the deserted lady fell in beside him. She whispered in polite Korean as he reached the gate, "General Ku came today."

He stopped in mid-stride.

"Why?"

"He wants Beautiful Flower. He told her to come tonight."

"What did she say?"

"She did not answer and he left."

"Thank you for the information." He gave her two dollars.

He entered the house. Non'gae greeted him with a long kiss. "Please sit down," she said.

He said, "Non'gae, you are lovelier each day, and I ...."

399

But she said in English, "Please be quiet. I am sorry. I must go. You see, I many thinks."

He knew why, but he feigned, "Why?"

"General Ku came today. He placed hand on me. He ordered me to come tonight. He thinks you gone." She then switched into Korean. "But I will not yield to him for I love you. So I have packed my jewels, my valuables and money. I must go to Seoul now. The deserted lady and Sugi will watch the house until it is safe for me to return. General Ku cannot leave the Corps area so I will be safe. Tomorrow I will meet you in Seoul at the U.S. Eighth Army main gate at six o'clock. Then we go to hotel."

Against regulations, he drove her to the bus depot in his jeep. He helped her and two big suitcases board the bus to Seoul. He said, "I have a fine gift for you."

She smiled; then she beamed, "Give me now!"

He said, "In Seoul, I will give it to you. You will love it."

She pouted, said "Tomorrow in Seoul" and was gone.

He and Non'gae would decide what to do in the next few days in Seoul.

As he drove back to the detachment, he knew he had made a huge error with General Ku. One must not "show off" certain valuables; it breeds jealously and rapacity. In the fifth century BC, the Athenian Greeks, then the mandarin Chinese and now the Muslims knew this. They never, ever allowed other men into their wives or concubines private quarters. He would not repeat that mistake.

"The sweetest flower that blows,
I give to you as we part.
For you it is a rose
For me it is my heart."
"At Parting," Frederick Peterson

Chapter XXIV
Seoul

In the late-October chill, both General Kim and Dr. Houghton shivered in the back seat of General Kim's poorly heated car. He had insisted on driving Dr. Houghton to Seoul for their final trip together. Dr. Houghton accepted, flattered by his graciousness. As the conversation lapsed, Dr. Houghton observed the empty brown rice paddies, presaging the coming of the brutal Korean winter. He was impressed with the repetitious cycles of the seasons in agricultural Korea. But, like every Westerner, he enjoyed controlling nature. The cold reminded him of his promise. He said, "I'll send you another electric blanket from Japan when I stop there on my way to California."

General Kim replied, "That'll be good."

On observing several old men by the roadside in the traditional costume of those who survived sixty-two years, the Papasons, Dr. Houghton was reminded of his village elders. Two evenings ago, just before dusk, the village Mayor and several select elders had come to his home in the village to say good-bye. They then escorted him and Non'gae in her fancy traditional Korean hanbok to the small village square. The Mayor recited an over-long encomium and presented him with a letter of appreciation for his many good deeds. As required, Dr. Houghton drank a few sips of rice wine, and toasted the Mayor and village elders in polite Korean. They were pleased. He bowed deeply to the entire group and departed with effusive thanks. One farmer, however, follwed him back to his house.

The farmer said, "Honorable Doctor, I have a final request of you."

Dr. Houghton remembered this farmer well. He had successfully treated his wife for tuberculosis of the kidney. He asked, "What do you wish?"

The old man snapped his fingers, and a lovely nine year old girl came forward. The child bowed to Dr. Houghton.

"I want you to take my granddaughter with you to America," the old farmer said. "She is yours."

Dr. Houghton looked at Non'gae.

She said, "This little girl's mother and father died. Grandfather cannot take care of her. What's she going to do? Maybe soon an entertainer; grandfather very sad."

Dr. Houghton observed the exquisite creature. He was momentarily overcome with emotion. He almost said yes. But, he immediately saw a compromise. "What is you name?"

"Proper Etiquette," her name translated.

He said to the farmer, "If she writes me one letter every month, I shall assure her that she never need become an entertainer." Dr. Houghton lived up to his end of the bargain. In fact, he had made a prudent investment. Much later, Proper Etiquette would work for Non'gae in Seoul.

As they passed through Chun Chon on the road to Seoul, General Kim suggested they lunch at his "apartment" before going to Seoul. Dr. Houghton had not been there before. After they sat down, a beautiful Kisaeng appeared. Miss Hu had mentioned her. A maid served them Chinese noodles. He thought General Kim was finally showing off; demonstrating his character and high position. He was a "closet Yangban" after all.

To make small talk, Dr. Houghton said, "winter is around the corner."

The Kisaeng simulated shivering.

"Isn't General Kim a warm boy friend?"

"Yes, he is hot, but on some weekends, he goes to his wife in Seoul, and I'm cold."

"I'll send you an electric blanket." With the talk of electric blankets, she indicated she knew about Miss Han as well as Miss Hu; and that he had given them both electric blankets. There were no secrets in Korea.

General Kim only laughed. He obviously knew this too, all along.

Out of the blue, she lowered her eyes and whispered, "I want to go to America with you. I also want to hear Celestial Angels."

Dr. Houghton looked at General Kim who did not seem to understand the allusion. Dr. Houghton said, not wanting to spill any beans, "If you can climb into my suitcase, you can go."

General Kim laughed, but his laugh was forced. They soon left.

Near Seoul, General Kim queried, "What do you think of her and me?"

"She is very beautiful. You are lucky to have two good women, the Kisaeng and your wife."

"Yes, but if I'm to make Surgeon General of the Army, I must give her up. General Ku insisted."

Dr. Houghton thought what a hypocritical bastard - what a "plick" General Ku was. But he said, "What do you want most?"

"I don't know."

"You're joking, General Kim. I know you want that job."

"No, I really don't know. I've been warned repeatedly to discard her."

"And you haven't?"

"I cannot."

Dr. Houghton was astonished. His judgment of General Kim over one year was wrong. He knew Colonel Kim desired above all his earlier promotion to General Officer with all its power and prestige, and now he thought Kim would kill for promotion to army Surgeon General. And yet, like so many Americans who became attached to their sloe-eyed Korean women, General Kim could not easily discard his Kisaeng.

Beautiful Flower suggested the brand new hilltop Tower Hotel that presented a glittering view of Seoul. Sitting in a chair high above the city, as the wind ever-so- slightly swaying the hotel, Dr. Houghton tried to think rationally about the future. He must decide. That evening Beautiful Flower wished to attend a Chinese regicide movie at Seoul's classiest theatre.

Suddenly, she popped out of the bright western style bath with its glaring florescent lights and long mirror. She adored the room. Moreover, in the revealing mirror with the harsh light, she observed clearly, perhaps for the first time, the true excellence of her complexion. Covered only by a towel, she was a slender hour glass. As requested Dr. Houghton positioned the long, gold jade-tipped hairpins for her. Every black strand was now in its proper place. Then he carefully placed a small unknown white flower above her left ear.

Singing happily, she disappeared into the bathroom. He pondered how her names affected her. Was she Yi Non'gae, the scion of the old Yangban families? Was she the avatar of the patriotic heroine, Non'gae, who pushed the Japanese general to his death? Could he blame the Koreans for these secret longings after centuries of Chinese, then Japanese and now American domination? He did not know. When they visited the memorial and statue of Non'gae, he could not fathom her true inner feelings although he tried. She would also not tell him much about her family.

Or perhaps she was Beautiful Flower after all. Although in high school and her three years in college, she learned Chinese, art, culture and history, and some English, she was an expert in flower botany. Her knowledge of flowers was very broad. He remembered the time when she lectured him about how "smart" flowers are. They always choose the correct sexual partners. She asked him if he knew about pollen tubes.

"Not much," he confessed.

"You dummy! Pollen from stamen goes on top of pistil and starts to burrow down the pistil toward the ovary. Understand? Then, if the pollen is from the same species, pollen sperm goes down the tube and fertilizes egg in ovary."

"Why is flower smart?"

"You don't know! Where have you been? Where did you go to school?"

"Tell me!"

She answered professorily, "Flower smart because, if pollen come from another species, flower blocks pollen tube and sperm can not reach ovary. Flowers are not promiscuous."

"There are millions of species, very similar."

"That is why flowers very smart. They can discriminate." She went on for ten minutes about the biological details of pollen tubes. Then she winked. "I can also discriminate."

That night he made many jokes about his penis being a fancy pollen tube.

She held her nose and said, "Bad funny man - buffoon!"

Later he looked up pollen tubes and she was correct; right up-to-date. He had previously thought of her knowledge as just sciolism but the pollen tube discussion convinved him she had acquired, atypical for Koreans, substantial analytical skill.

As he thought about her, he inexplicably remembered Beautiful Flower most clearly when they visited the amaranth fields near Taegu. He now perceived her as an amaranth, not a rose or lily or poppy. She glowed; she bloomed that day. She was as bright as the red and yellow in the Joseph's Coat amaranth leaves. Suddenly, unexpectedly, he remembered an episode, from his youth. He jumped to his feet, sweating. Something within his mind rejoiced. He walked back and forth with new understanding. He now vividly recalled being kept after school for bad behavior. Miss Morgan, his second grade teacher, made him copy the dictionary. This drove the little boy to his wit's end. He remembered that awful grinding feeling as he copied. Even the recollection angered him. But that day he copied the word amaranth ten times. The definition intrigued him for years, especially the poetic notion of an undying flower, a flower that never wilted. Was there such a flower? Aesop suggested there was. But now in the real world, he had found such a flower, Beautiful Flower, or had he? He knew the jadeite amaranth forest carving was undying, but it was just a representation. General Samet intimated, indeed told him, such things existed in Japan and he was not talking about flowers. He needed to talk with General Samet.

On the other hand, at the movie, Dr. Houghton observed her as Non'gae. She was fascinated with the extreme violence of the Chinese movie. Made in Hong Kong, in wide screen and brilliant colors, the plot was a Kendo tale of a poor young man, excellent with the sword. The young man was adopted by a nobleman to assassinate a Chinese Emperor turned tyrant. The blood the regicide spilled made James Bond appear like a minor ruffian. Yet, Beautiful Flower defended the regicide's every action based on nuanced notions of honor and revenge, not justice or law. A few months before, Dr. Houghton had spent two days in Seoul on emergency duty helping the surgeons deal with the overflow of wounded American and Korean soldiers from Vietnam. He was sickened by the damage that AK-47's and the Vietnamese use of captured M-16 rifles did to the human body. Dr. Houghton was equally repelled by the movie slicings, skinnings, and assorted tortures, never portrayed in American movies, but actually happening in Vietnam.

As they walked the streets of Seoul, he was conscious of the great number of Koreans who paused to look at her. He believed it was her elegant carriage and classic beauty not the gold ornaments and bright silk dress. She now had a high headed, almost arrogant appearance, but there still existed a hint of a proper, underlying passivity.

Dr. Houghton remembered what Lieutenant Ahn told him a year ago. The Koreans could differentiate entertainers from respectable women by subtle cues as well as their overuse of cosmetics. By definition, respectable women never dated Americans. Yet, Beautiful Flower appeared attractive and respectable. This was the paradox. He finally commented, "Everyone stops to look at you."

"I knows," she said and held his arm tightly.

"You have accepted me, Beautiful Flower, even though I'm a hairy barbarian?"

"Yes, you mink," she laughed at her own joke.

He thought she accepted him without reservations. She did not accept the ancient Korean attitudes about racial purity or the rest of the ethnocentric bigotry.

In the hotel, she once again demonstrated that she was a sexual treasure. He still wondered if this arcanum could be taught. He made a final effort, including verbal coaxing, to solve the mystery. In the end, he looked under the bed and in the bathroom.

"Magics," she giggled. "You don't know. You doctor? Ha! My mother same - before she died."

After a few restful minutes, she quietly said, "Old Korean custom, stick gold pin through testicle to make man work, OK?" She produced a long gold needle.

He immediately pinioned her arms. He did not need the needle. He said, "My pollen tube works."

Dr.Houghton awoke to find Beautiful Flower replaced by a note on her pillow. She wrote, "I am not here. I'm gone for two hours to beauty house." A sketch of a smiling Korean female followed.

He rose and looked at his image in the full length mirror. He almost did not recognize the reflection. He did not see the frazzled, worn out resident who deplaned in Korea over one year ago. The image now was of muscle and sinew, with a thirty-three inch waist and a forty-four inch chest, really a stranger. Even the deep vertical furrow on his forehead was smoothed over. He knew his cholesterol, formerly elevated, was now normal. His fatty blood no longer corroded his vessels with atheromatous sludge. And the objects of previous barbs by Miss Galt and Marsha, his thin spindly calves, had developed into muscular bulges. Dr. Hougthon took a small leap and watched the muscles in his legs quiver and contract. The transformation was striking. How long would it last?

Beautiful Flower bounced into the room, fresh from the beauty house. The alteration in her over the nine months was equally sriking. There were the physical improvements from the correction of her severe anemia. Her cheeks were now naturally reddish without rouge. There was marked accretion in her bosom. Her legs were now straight. Dr. Houghton also thought that the healthy sex contributed greatly to this transformation, but Miss Galt slugged him once when he made such an observation.

But even more noticeable was her new confidence and independence of spirit, a realistic haughtiness, a causal swing of a pocketbook when in occidental dress, or smiling, down-looking twinkling eyes in a Korean traditional dress.

The two afternoons at the ancient Korean palaces in Seoul were as he had anticipated. The buildings were said to be almost exact copies of those in China. They walked through these shabby dusty relics and unkempt gardens, where the Korean Emperors strolled with their favorites. The contrast with the meticulously cared-for Japanese temples and arranged gardens was striking.

The first buildings were the "courts" where the Korean emperors made critical decisions on the advice of the unctuous minister of the right or the cruel minister of the left. Then they saw the pavilions where the Emperor's concubines lived.

He said, "If they want me to, I'll be glad to rule."

Beautiful Flower laughed, "Funny man."

"Let's go in there." Dr. Houghton pointed to the pavilion which the final King of Korea had erected for his favorite concubine. Although not permitted, they removed their shoes and entered. This pavilion was quite distant from the palace proper. The muffled din of the undisciplined Seoul traffic reverberated inside the pavilion.

They ensconced themselves on a bench in a nook, unseen by the passers-by. They gazed at a decaying picture of the final favorite, whom on a careless inspection, he might mistake for Beautiful Flower.

Beautiful Flower made it easy, almost painless. She said, as she rotated a long stemmed red carnation in her fingers, "I know you don't take me Stateside. For a long time I hoped you would marry me. After all, I am Yi Non'gae and Magic Lady." She smiled mysteriously. "But, I don't think I would be happy in America. Toooo different!"

Dr. Houghton did not breathe until she continued.

"My plan is to have a dress shop when you go. Maybe I'll sell gold, jade and other stuffs too. In the bank, I have enough money. I move to Seoul now. General Ku will never catch me in Seoul. In three months, I will open a dress shop." She looked at him for a response.

He grinned, "Can you hold your breath?"

"Why?"

"I wish to give you your present, a Padparadscha sapphire. Do you know what that is?"

"I do but you funny man. Only Queen of Siam and Empress of Ceylon have such a jewel."

He passed her the jewel box he bought in Seoul. She opened it and looked. She didn't say anything. Instead, she opened her purse, took out a perfume bottle and scratched the glass with the sapphire. "It is very hard."

"It is real. It is worth twenty years of salary for you in the Teahouse or more."

She jumped on him and smothered him with hot kisses. She wept.

He passed her his handkerchief. He said. "Please sit down. They will see us in here. I do not want to go to the monkey house."

She smiled.

"I think your plan is a good idea," he said. Yet he was saddened that he wouldn't figure in her future.

She continued, "Of course, I want you most, but I know you are an American soldier man. I am very grateful to you. When you came, I had nothing. Only two dresses; sometimes I was too sick to eat. Now, all this!" She pointed at the sapphire and her new dress. "My condition, my kibun is very good. Soon I hope to open dress shop."

"Soon," he inmitated her, "you'll be a very rich woman. Then many Korean men will want to marry you."

She was annoyed. "Many times, I told you, I no marry Korean man. No can do."

To stop this too cruel persiflage, his error, he said, "In May, I'll come here on leave."

"No lie?" she said, grasping his hand. Again she showered kisses on him and then studied the sapphire much more carefully. "Where did you buy this?"

"Don't ask." He thought of Sergeant Clooney. Gazing into her glowing, hopeful eyes, he said, "Yes, I intend to return for two weeks in May."

She held up her right little finger. He clasped hers in his indicating a solemn promise.

Beautiful Flower quieted. She had expected only a lingering kiss and a sad good-bye. Now she was suddenly a rich woman with her sapphire; she was gloriously happy.

He asked her to stand and placed the sapphire pendant around her neck. He said, "But you must promise me a nice present as soon as you make money in your dress shop." He raised his little finger, and she confirmed the solemn promise. This gesture, he knew, would diminish her debt and thus lighten her burden.

She said, "I want to see it." She pulled out her purse mirror and studied the sapphire around her neck. With a smile, she said in polite Korean, "A Beautiful Flower waits for you across the sea."

"I will never forget you. I'll come in May."

He also made another decision at that moment. Henceforth he decided he would reward as best he could anyone who helped him, taught him, or loved him - like he had now done for Miss Hu and Beautiful Flower. He would never again make the mistake he made with Miss Han.

Dr. Houghton met his friend, ex-Sergeant Song, at the University. Beautiful Flower did not wish to come. Walking through Seoul National University, Song said he would obtain his doctorate in January. He waxed sentimental. He talked extensively about Miss Han and the dangerous times on the Korean east coast when the infiltrators came. As they walked along, Dr. Houghton saw Miss Han's image in her many different moods, smiling, singing and even pouting. Her final "do not forget my face" always hurt him.

Dr. Houghton smiled and tried to change the subject. "I found out why everyone calls you 'Honorable.'"

"Why?" Song asked.

"Your father was a leader in the resistance against the Japanese. And you won the international poetry contest. You are a national hero. Why didn't you tell me?"

He replied, "I knew you would find out."

Just before they parted, Dr. Houghton asked, "I want you to tell me what Miss Pak's past contains."

Song did not answer.

"I wish you were a Sergeant so I could order you. Do you know? Is it ....?"

"It is not sexual immorality as you think. In Korea it is far worse. But you would not understand."

"Well ... tell me."

He did not respond; he only looked at the ground.

That day, Dr. Houghton gave up the futile effort. Four months later, however, in a warm bed in Fort Ord near San Francisco, he woke in the middle of the night. He finally thought he understood why Sergeant Song liked Miss Han so much and disliked Yi Non'gae. He knew the facts all along but somehow could not position them in the proper perspective. What might he have done, if he had resolved his solitary doubt about Yi Non'gae sooner? While in Korea, he could not see that there was nothing in her past. Sergeant Song disliked her for her relationship with him, a barbarian - an outsider. While it was permissible for Miss Han as a Kisaeng to keep company with Dr. Houghton, it was not for Yi Non'gae, a scion of the Yangban. Song yielded entirely to the traditional belief that as a respectable Korean girl, she should not associate with a foreigner.

Why did Song think this - a very smart man? Dr. Houghton knew this type of thinking exists everywhere. It is the basis of class, clans, tribalism and even the idea of social engineering. He also thought it had to do with the Korean tendency to learn facts, not critical thinking. The Korean children were indoctrinated while very young with notions of Korean superiority, racial purity and "Juche" - not being "pushed around" by foreigners. All this led to slogans and nationalistic propaganda, even among the Korean intelligentsia. The social constructs of Korea were frequently opposite those of America; all men were not created equal.

Or, did Sergeant Song have intimations of what General Samet told him his last day in Seoul? Dr. Houghton shuddered at that thought.

His final day in Korea, after his early morning visit with General Samet, Beautiful Flower insisted they visit the Taoist Temple near the hotel. Although full of unanswered questions, Dr. Houghton went. He didn't know whether he should confront her with General Samet's account or say nothing, but he decided to wait until he knew more. Why would General Samet lie?

As they walked to the Temple, he mentioned that he had seen the great Taoist Temple in Hong Kong with Mike, an enormous "high." He also told her he was very curious to see the Seoul Temple. An hour later, as they strolled around and through this decrepit Taoist Temple he listened to Beautiful Flower's clear exposition of Taoism, although she could not explain one Chinese black-ink brush painting of an adept and a high flying black bird. Could the adept talk to birds? Almost in a trance as she talked, he "saw" the various nature gods and mysterious spirits in clouds of swirling incense.

All this he thoroughly understood since he had originally studied Taoist ideas at Harvard College. He grasped the notion that there is a spirit in all things emanating from the Tao, and that change is constant, like water flowing downhill, and you must "go with the flow." Yet he also knew the Taoists indefatigably tried to modify nature as Miss Hu would teach him; in fact, the Taoist adepts spent years, even decades, looking for the Elixir of Immortality. Although a Taoist sympathizer since college, Reg would be smarter than the Taoist adepts; he would use science and medicine. Someday as a professor of medicine he *would* pursue the Elixir. He and his fellow professors might succeed at least partially, unlike the Taoist adepts who failed abysmally and, in the process, poisoned themselves with mercury and other hopeless substances.

But finally, it was beyond time to go. Back in the hotel, he put on his uniform, a soldier again. "Now Beautiful Flower, you must not insist upon coming to the airport. When I go, I want you to go to your friend's house. It will be easier for us that way."

"As you say," she replied. The uniform appeared to break her spirit, with its harsh green ugliness. It signified the end. A thin stream of sorrow poured down her red cheeks.

"I *must* go, Beautiful Flower," he said, unsure of what to do except to wipe her cheeks. But after a few seconds of extreme vacillation, he resisted a strong impulse to ask her questions about spying. "I'll come back in May. Take care; do what you think is best." These words did not retard her tears, but his solitary tear finally did.

On seeing it, she suddenly smiled with glowing hope.

At that moment, he almost asked her to come to America with him. But he needed more time to decide what to do. He must understand the truth about her. "I'll bet you're thirsty now," he said, after a final kiss.

She said, "Funny man to the end."

At the Military Airport, Dr. Houghton waited. Suddenly, he was terrified. His heart thumped and skipped. His stomach knotted in a painful spasm. The Military Police gradually walked toward him. He couldn't believe they knew about Lieutenant Ahn resting on the bottom of the river *or* the humanitarian abduction of Moon Flower *or* the justifiable snatch of the jadeite amaranth carving, now in its wood crate on the way to America. As the MP's approached, he nearly collapsed but they by-passed him and cornered a sergeant. Dr. Houghton had to sit down before he fell down.

When he glanced up, he saw Miss Hu standing in front of him against the bright sunny background. She wore a short amaranth-colored skirt and a white silk blouse with Clooney's ruby pendant. She also had a large visitor's pass around her neck. He asked her in Korean, "How did you you sneak in?"

She smiled broadly, "Magics."

When he looked at her more carefully, enveloped by the sunbeams from the high airport windows, he was reminded of representations of the Buddha or Mary or Apollo with their golden haloes. She looked like an old master's vision of the Sublime. He had found it!

She said, "I didn't sneak in. After all, I know General Kim and General Lee! After all, I was the best Kisaeng in Chun Chon and you helped me." She smiled in triumph. "Don't go; stay with me in Seoul, just for a few more days."

"Are you and Moon Flower alright?"

"Yes. Very fine so far. Stay with me, please."

He knew he could. There were two days of flexibility in his army orders. He grasped her, before she disappeared like a modern

411

Euridice, and kissed her. He was ready to follow her although his knees were weak. Moreover, he thought of his father's general advice to "Make hay while the sun shines." But he hesitated when he thought of Sergeant Clooney – reminded by Miss Hu's sparkling ruby. An unmarried Sergeant Clooney, who employed two business ladies to satisfy his prodigious lust, repeatedly told him not to marry until he was "old. Be a rolling stone until then." At that moment, he heard Clooney singing his favorite song - "I married a girl who had no hips at all - no hips at all; no hips at all. I married a girl who had no hips at all." Dr. Houghton banished this irrelevant melody from his mind. Why did it appear anyhow?

Dr. Houghton realized he was confronted by Miss Hu's cornucopia of temptations, not least her doublehood. He asked himself once more - why should I resist? After all, he too was a trove of diverse lusts and aching longings for both her unblemished body and delicious mind. He was ready to burst like a ripe pomegranate. She really was awesome. Why not go with her now? But again he hesitated. He wondered if he was just rebounding from General Samet's revelations about Non'gae.

Miss Hu did not realize she had him. Erroneously, she interpreted his prolonged hesitation as a "No Go." Since she did not want to lose face, lose her dignity, she unexpectedly said, "I will see you in May." She blew him a kiss, winked and quickly walked toward the Exit. At the Exit, she turned, smiled and waved. In a trice she was gone. As she departed, looking forward to May, she knew she would catch him then – finally and totally. At long last she could satisfy her bottomless lust for Reg Houghton, her Hap Gi Do physician, a superior man.

When she turned to walk away, he said, "See you in May. Write me in California." As she walked on, smiling, straight backed, chest out, head held high, he noted the lingering soft notes of her osmanthus perfume and the scrouping sound of her nylons rubbing against her inner thighs, a froufrou sound that made his brimming lust overflow. Yet he did not move or scream - "Come Back"- but instead only smiled and waved goodbye. But he had immediate second thoughts. Must he wait until May to see her nonpareil flawless skin and her bosom, a wonder that required no skyhooks; must he wait until May to listen to her translations of Chinese love poetry? When he decided to chase her, it was too late.

A few minutes later, still shaken by the close call with the MP's and Miss Hu's unexpected appearance and her sudden departure, he ambled toward the portable stairway to board the old Boeing 707. A desultory glance at the high observation tower revealed Beautiful Flower dressed in white, holding a long-stemmed

412

red flower. She waved. Above the din of the Great Bird's black jet exhausts, he was certain he heard a plaintive "Good-bye, Reginald."

Pleased at her presence, he waved vigorously from the top step and then entered the dark interior. After thirteen months, he was on his way home.

"The more I see of other countries,
the more I love my own."
Mme. De Steel

Epilogue

With substantial effort, the fully loaded Great Silver Sea Bird rose above the cinereous clouds over Korea. Dr. Houghton had one final glance at Beautiful Flower before he flew away. As he settled into the flight, he still marveled at these flying technological marvels, regrettably now bringing war to the East. Maybe someday, they would bring irenic trade, democracy, equality, freedom, law, and good health instead. We should be building factories in Vietnam, he thought, not bombing it back to the Stone Age. Even so, he was glad he had served in the army in Korea; he learned a lot. At Harvard, he obtained general knowledge and specific information about chemistry; at Yale about biology, medicine and pathology; and at the Brigham about practical medicine. In the army he learned about the real world and a different culture. Not everyone thinks like they do at Harvard. Veritas is not the world's priority. He also learned that Harvard "wise" men are sometimes wrong, disastrously wrong; Vietnam the example. But most importantly he learned about himself. He now knew what he wanted or what he needed to investigate; in the army he had a group of superb teachers - General Samet, Colonels Bennet and Newton, Major Mike, and Sergeants Morse, Song and Clooney. Of course he learned a lot from the Miss Hans and Hu, Non'gae and even Miss Galt in Texas during "basic." They taught him among other things that celestial angels, Chinese apsarases, do not have wings. Just before he left, he wrote another note to Miss Han in Hong Kong. He asked her to inform him immediately if any fine jadeite carvings become available.

He was very proud of his accomplishments. But these were all mainly unfinished. He needed more Hap Gi Do training, just as he was becoming proficient. He knew he would never feel the power of three, four or five white lines coursing across his Black Belt, rather than just one. Neither magic nor money, but only time and persistence could add real lines.

His study of the Korean language was now finished. He could speak and read quite well using polite forms. But the rapid, familiar slangy talk sometimes eluded him as did the nuances and subtleties of Korean novels.

He greatly enjoyed his civic action program. He learned a lot and helped hundreds, perhaps a thousand Korean patients. This was really raw medicine. But unfortunately when he left, the clinic disappeared. This was the problem with "do-gooder"efforts. He realized that the dominant Christian notions of Faith, Hope and Charity of missionary work were greatly inferior to the ancient Greek paideia of Wisdom, Justice, Courage and Moderation. With these, you could build permanence and excellence. You could "do, build and accomplish," not just give, hope and pray.

The jadeite collecting went splendidly. He had seven glorious pieces. He felt like dancing on the ceiling of the airplane when he thought of them. His mother and father pointed out he had made good use of his Harvard education – especially his knowledge of oriental art and chemistry. Moreover, they adored the first two jadeite carvings from Hong Kong; his father "loved" the spirit of longevity, and his mother the basket of fruits. In fact, they would come to visit him in San Francisco when the other five carvings from the Golden Buddhist Monastery arrived in his baggage. They would hand carry them back to Massachusetts. He joked that they wanted to see these Forbidden City carvings more than him. He also told them he would build a magnificent collection, an idea they applauded. He was certain the collection would be very valuable. However, when he was old, near the end, he would give the collection to Harvard or Yale in return for a named professorship: the Reginald Houghton Professor of Oriental Art.

His father told him his trust was doing very well; in two years, when he was thirty, it would be his. He was certain the Korean girls never had any idea about this.

In Korea, he had worked very hard on his clinical medicine. For several hours every day he had read medicine. He also saw a large number of interesting and challenging patients in the civic action clinic. He was more than ready for his senior residency, his final year as a student. He thought he would be a terrific senior. Who else could expatiate for an hour on the natural history of human lung flukes?

But he was unsure what to do about the Hong Kong Miss Han, Miss Hu or Non'gae. Miss Han was easiest. He would visit her in Hong Kong in May to purchase more jadeite carvings. In terms of cui bono – who benefits – they both would. He would obtain quality jadeite art and she would further her sales career.

The now ex- Kisaeng Miss Hu was more difficult but he would also see her in May, in Seoul. He promised. Moreover she in turn vowed to teach him Taoist Arcana and other important lessons. He believed she could. He wanted to learn. But as he remembered their rescue of Moon Flower, he thought: What would General Samet say? Would he say Dr. Houghton showed courage and wise use of his new Hap Gi Do and Korean language skills, or quixotic recklessness? Or was he just Miss Hu's puppet?

In one matter, though, Miss Hu had spoiled him. She confirmed the whispers he had first heard as a Harvard student and then from the Sergeant Major and other experienced soldiers. As a double, she showed him that sexual relations could actually be sublime. Even more ironic, she had more to teach him. On the other hand, he was now certain that once you experienced sexual sublimity, by comparison, even excellent relations could only be a disappointment. Hence, butterflying from woman to woman, like Jack Kennedy, made little sense. His problem would be: Where could he find an acceptable wife with such characteristics? Was General Samet correct in his advice that morning?

Finally he continued to wonder what was inside Miss Hu's "soul." Was he correct that she was a human treasure like the historical Buddha? He remembered the greatest miracle of all, the Miracle of the Double at Sravasti, where the Buddha convinced the doubters. From a seated position, the Buddha, duplicating himself, raised his body high in the air, emitting flames from his shoulders and water from his feet. Images of this miracle were all over Korea and Thailand. Were both Miss Hu and the Buddha really exceptional humans, two kinds of doubles? *Or* could she be an Old Testament Lilith *or* a New Testament Jezebel *or* wicked like Silvia in Ford Madox Ford's Parade's End - a brilliant novel he had read twice while in Korea. He doubted it. Or was she some place in between? Would he ever know? Was it even a good question? Do people have an essence, or are Hume, the existentialists and Buddhists correct? In the end he thought he should study her and her biology and find out the answers. It would be fun.

But Non'gae was the most difficult problem. Who was she really: Non'gae or Beautiful Flower or possibly a Spy? He needed to digest what General Samet told him that morning and then decide what to do. He was still reeling from the disclosures.

After he finished reviewing his accomplishments, he reviewed the failures. He deeply regretted the suicide of Miss Han. He should have done more. However, after what General Samet told him that morning about Lieutanant Ahn, he felt little guilt about Ahn.

Gradually as the tedious hours passed, his thoughts become disorganized and autonomous. He dozed off and on. Perhaps, if like most of the other Americans, he had wiled the time away in Korea drinking heavily, discontent, oblivious, and waiting, he would have been happier now. But he would have no accomplishments, no joyous memories to haunt him and no enchanted future to beckon. There would only be a vague feeling of an uncomfortable dislike for the bowing deceit of the yellow man. But, he discarded these thoughts as stupid and fatuous.

Suddenly, he felt a smashing Hap Gi Do heel hit him in mid-chest. He could not breathe. After a full minute, he managed a little breath, then a little more, then relief and finally laughter. He briefly awoke. Then he asked the Universe, "Why did Ahn fall forward? The Hap Gi Do guys never do." After this question, he noticed he was sweaty and uncomfortable. Suddenly, Miss Judy appeared. "Docs, why didn't you ever make love to me? Am I too old or too ugly? Men say I am number one Korean lover. Why Docs? But, let me dance for you." To the juke box music in the NCO Club, a stunning Miss Judy and a black Sergeant Morse danced - the entertainer and natural. They were nonpareil. They were both in the wrong business. Next he smelled osmanthus flowers and then glimpsed a smiling, beckoning Miss Hu wearing Clooney's ruby. A few minutes later, he held Non'gae's hand when she sat down beside him on the plane. She wore her Padparadscha sapphire and everyone turned to gaze at her. When he finally awoke, she too was gone.

After a seemingly endless bumpy ride over the Pacific, he gobbled a bland army sandwich and a delicious cold coke. Then he reviewed his 7 AM meeting with General Samet that morning. Reg was still astonished at his ignorance, humbled by his naivete.

"Good morning General."

"Please, sit. I don't have much time but I wanted to talk to you. First, the good news; congratulations! You will be Major Houghton when you arrive in Califonia. It is very unusual to be promoted after only one year but I thought you deserved it. We promoted you because of you excellence as an advisor, your superb monthly reports, and your helpful civic action program. We had no trouble in your area because of the good will you generated. Also you performed well in combat when you shot the infiltrator. Finally the Koreans, the Army Chief of Staff, Lieutenant General Lee and Dr. Kim liked you and wrote strong letters as did Colonels Bennet and Newton. I also admired your Hap Gi Do exhibition and success. You, my lad, have balls of steel - to put up with the Hap Gi Do training. You should be very proud; you succeeded where so many others have failed."

"Thank you for the kind words and the promotion. I hope I can help you someday. I am in your debt."

"We will come to that. Now the bad news; Yi Non'gae is a spy or, should I say, traffics with spies"

"What?"

"You know she has family, an older brother, in North Korea. We discussed this. We have been reading her mail and her connection to Lieutenant Ahn, a definite spy."

"I did not know she had a brother. She never told me. She mentioned relatives."

"Anyhow, she sent him letters via Japan. He recruited her playing on familial, Confucian loyalty; Lieutanant Ahn also tried to work with her but without success."

"What was in the letters?"

"She openly talked about you and in microdots rejected most of her brother's requests. She said you had no access to anything important. We were able to find her one time key-pad code in your house in Tae Bat."

"You were in my house?"

"Yes; last week, the only time. She left the key in a botany book and we found it. Do you want to see a blow-up of her last microdot? Here it is."

"It's just numbers. How did she make them? What did she say about me? I need to know. Will you arrest her? Will the Koreans arrest her?"

"No. She committed no clear crime. In fact she apparently rejected spying. She will now live in Seoul as you know; she is no longer even remotely a concern."

"What did she say about me? I really want to know." His heart was racing.

"If you really want to know," he paused, a very pregnant pause, "she said in her last microdot, and I quote, Dr. Houghton is a 'nice simpleton, a medical magician, a Hap Gi Do Black Belt, and a handsome person with a beautiful body.'"

"A simpleton? That really hurts."

"She also repeated that you did not know and did not have access to any important secrets, especially about our tactical nuclear weapons or nuclear personnel." General Samet paused, "Now the other player is Lieutenant Ahn. We and the Koreans have been watching him for months but he seems to have disappeared. We tried to find out his contacts unsuccessfully. But you should know that, although he was in a safe once, he obtained nothing of any value. The Koreans think he may have gone North."

Dr. Houghton tried to retain his poker face.

"We also know he unsuccessfully tried to blackmail Yi Non'gae into helping him with his objectives. That's it. Any questions?"

"Yes," he said; he had to change the subject. He was flabbergasted and needed to digest what he just heard. "I want to ask you about the Four Perfections you mentioned some months ago. The sergeants also gave me similar advice."

"A Chinese amah and Chinese food is a softball. Dr. Houghton, you can not continue to eat 12 ounce sirloin steaks any more. They will kill you. You will understand that as you grow older. You need to change your diet. I did, and look at how lean and muscular I am. Also you will find the enchantment of sex decreases with time, especially after thirty. You should never marry for sex, even a rare double."

Dr. Houghton wondered if General Samet knew about Miss Hu. How could he? Could he read minds? But he said, "How about a double that is expert in Chinese poetry, dance, song and music?"

"You mean a Kisaeng?"

Did he know of Miss Hu? Had he talked to General Kim who probably knew?

General Samet continued, "Second, no question - you must live in an American house in America. Agree?"

"I agree."

"By the way, have you decided on your future?"

"Yes, I want to be a professor of medicine. I am interested in endocrinology, the human sexual response, and hormonal life extension."

"Wonderful choice!" General Samet laughed and then said, "By the way, I have some personal medical issues I would like to discuss with you. I rotate back to the states next month and I will see you at Fort Ord. As you may have guessed I no longer believe in the Vietnam effort. I am leaving the army after my next rotation; I also need to earn more money. I have smart children who want to attend Yale and Princeton - expensive as hell."

"I know."

"Where were we? Three, German culture - Kant, Nietzsche, Schopenhauer, Mozart, Bach, Beethoven, Freud, Plank, Einstein; is there any question?

"No, although I am personally quite interested in Oriental culture and art, especially from Japan and China."

"Finally, you need a high class Japanese wife; the fourth and most important Perfection. But they are very hard to find and meet. They are like rare Alexandrites or Padparadscha sapphires."

419

A suddenly panicky Dr. Houghton felt he was on a high escarpment, like the historical Non'gae and the Japanese general Keyamura Rokusuke. Did General Samet know about Clooney and the jewels? Had Non'gae or Miss Hu blabbered? Would Samet throw him over? Still barely in control, he said, "You sound like the Sergeant Major."

General Samet continued, "The Japanese women are properly brought up. They are not like the Christians who think sex is dirty and all the rest of the other neurotic nonsense. They support their husbands; they want everything done right; they are artistic with flower arranging and other skills; they are scrupulouslessly clean and neat; they run the house and know how to bring up children; and most importantly they have stable, everlasting souls. The Sergeant Major is correct."

Dr. Houghton decompressed as General Samet talked; he guessed, "Did you find one, General?"

General Samet, who had a doctorate in structural engineering, said, "Yes; her name is Me Ho, Beautiful Mind. I found her when she was a Japanese graduate student at Stanford. As we say, she is perdurable."

At that point the General's adjutant interrupted. "General, it's time."

As he was leaving, Dr. Houghton asked one final question, a last try, "Do you think there are such women in Korea - with a perdurable soul; with a good soul? Or are they all Business Ladies or worse; Lilith's or Jezebel's or Sylvia's?"

General Samet's expression was not encouraging, but he only said, "Sylvia, Parade's End, Ford Madox Ford; right?"

In a total daze Dr. Houghton staggered off the Great Silver Bird at Travis Air Force Base in California after thirteen months in Korea. No one noticed as he bent down and touched the runway.

A Sergeant Clark met him in the terminal. He said, "Congratulations Major." He removed Dr. Houghton's silver captain's bars and pinned on his major's golden oak leaves. He said, "Major, the commander of Fort Ord wishes to see you now. You must be a VIP. I will drive you, Sir." When they arrived at Headquarters, he said, "I will wait here, Major. Good luck, Sir. As you may know, there have been serious problems here."

After a brief wait, General Smith escorted Dr. Houghton into his sparse office. He said, "Let me immediately come to the point. I spoke to your supervisors at the Brigham and General Samet. They all agreed you are a superb physician, hard working and a talented administrator. Samet said, and I quote, you are a 'medical

420

magician.' I also heard you earned a Black Belt in Hap Gi Do. I myself never made it beyond a red belt. My compliments to you, Major; you are clearly an accomplished officer."

"Thank you."

"I need your help here at Ord. I have a tough assignment for you. I want you to be in charge of all ID - infectious disease - here. We have had several disasters here including deaths; Congress is investigating whether there is widespread incompetence. As you know, we send many thousands of young recruits to Vietnam each year and there is a lot of infectious disease here. I spoke to Colonel Hewitt, our senior medical officer, and he supports your appointment."

"But I am not trained in ID, General."

"I want you to do it. Our board-certified ID folks have been a disaster. I want someone new, smart and accomplished. I want you to review the situation with fresh eyes and come up with a plan in the next few days. I am giving you total authority."

"I will do it, General, but my interest is in endocrinology."

"Samet told me you are interested in sexual function endocrinology and you want to be a professor of medicine, yes?"

"Very much!"

"When I was the military liaison in India last year, there was also a great deal of interest in sex. The Indians are maniacally interested in fertility, erections and pheromones. Do you know Shiva, the Destroyer of Worlds?"

"Yes, you are going to mention the lingams all over the place in India, I know."

General Smith roared with laughter. He said, "So you can read minds too. They really are all over the place, these phallic symbols; they worship them both as apotropaic objects and fertility symbols."

"Many Americans do, too, especially in the Army."

General Smith, no longer the dour Commander, said, "Houghton, some night soon we must have a drink together. I could use a little advice about......"

"Erections?"

"Houghton, I think this is the start of a beautiful, how should I say it, relationship."

"I hope so."

As Dr. Houghton was leaving, General Smith said, "One secret. When I was in India I bought a solid gold ithyphallic lingam. I bought it as an investment in gold. But I admit I touch it each night for...... Don't tell." General Smith grinned.

"Mum is the word."

A suddenly severe General Smith said, "Good luck with your new assignment, Major. Remember, I want to see you and your plan in 48 hours,"

After Dr. Houghton left, he wondered why he was selected; should he accept General Smith's explanation at face value. Even if true, his new role greatly bothered him. He would now become an important cog in the vast war machine spewing out recruits for the disaster in Vietnam. This horror reminded him of his pre-college work in his uncle's factory running a machine which threw out wrapped straws. Which was worse? The former was immoral and the later mind-withering, brick-wrinkling. But now he must do his best to serve the interests of the recruit-patients. They were innocents. It was too late to object. His only consolation was his mother's apothegm, "All things pass."

When he reentered the car, Sergeant Clark said, "I already took your baggage to your quarters. He continued, "I also picked up you mail. You have three special delivery letters and a telegram from Korea."

Major Houghton opened the telegram first. It said in Korean, "Major Houghton, All well in Korea. I will write details. See you in May when you will see wingless angels. I will also reward you with other joys and lasting knowledge. Love, Hu." He laughed at the "lasting" pun and then breathed a deep sigh, like an overdistended bladder suddenly decompressing. He and Miss Hu had done it, had safely snatched Moon Flower from her Hell. In May, however, he wondered what arcana Miss Hu would teach him. Would he really see wingless celestial angels? Could he wait that long?

He was now absolutely certain Miss Hu was not a Lilith, a Silvia or New Testament Jezebel. She was nothing like these Western demons. But was she one of Mara's daughters, a sister of Lust, who attempted to ensnare the Buddha?

Then he opened the first letter. It was from Marsha. She was divorcing her husband. She and her son must see him. She still loved him. He *must* contact her immediately on his return. But he did not like the demanding tone of the letter and decided to ignore it.

The second letter was from Miss Galt. She said she still loved her "lovely" husband but she couln't sleep well after Reg went to Korea. She MUST see him SOON for just one more tryst; to see the angels again. She admitted she promised him in Texas that she would come no more, a terrible pun, but she was coming to California soon. She would let him know when. He MUST see her. If he didn't, she would throw herself off the Golden Gate Bridge. Major Houghton thought this was a real problem; he did not want another Miss Han but on the other hand he was not a sex toy. Perhaps he would send *her* a sex toy. But he immediately rejected that as a bad idea.

The final letter was from President Nixon. It began with the words, "By order of the President of the United States....." He was now a Major.

As they drove along the coast highway on the way to his new quarters at Ford Ord, he observed the fantastic view of the cerulean Pacific Ocean. Although tired from the trip, he felt very confident. He knew he would succeed; he had a fine plan, perfect health and plenteous resources. He would be a professor of medicine, although he was in reality a closet Taoist. Like the Taoists he would seek the Elixir of Immortality but in an orderly scientific fashion where a partial success was possible, perhaps even probable, for those smart, strong and rich enough. Fortunately, he also had the unconditional and unwavering support of his mother and father. Wait until they saw his new jadeite carvings and his Black Belt! But he would not tell them about Taoism or his search for the Elixir.

That night, he dreamed of a systematic search for a wife. He sought a double; a smart lasting beauty. If he found such a woman, he knew how to immortalize her. He would find a Hong Kong jadeite sculptor to capture her peak loveliness in natural translucent jadeite from Burma - with correctly colored hair, eyes and lips. It would be exceedingly expensive but, with his trust money, he could do it. He would have an undying sculpture - colored and fabulous – unlike marble which slowly decays. His wife's image would glow with jadeite's resplendent hues. With careful planning and sufficient patience, he could, in one important sense, even outdo the greatest sculptors of all time, Michelangelo and the the ancient Greek Praxiteles. Both Michelangelo and Praxiteles used either white Parian or off-white Carerra marble, *not* jadeite. In fact, Praxiteles' statues of his favorite model Phryne no longer exist, and some of Michelangelo's are decaying in the Italian smog.

But somehow, thoughts of everlasting jadeite statues of the perfect wife, whether from America or, as General Samet suggested, Japan, seemed premature. So he slipped back into dreamy thoughts and memories of a real double, the highly intelligent, self-taught Chinese scholar/poetess, and teacher of Taoist arcana - the sublime Miss Hu. He would see her in May. Reg would first take her to the Taoist Temple in Seoul to see the haunting image of the ancient Taoist adept pointing at a bird. Was the adept communicating with the bird? Reg thought that Miss Hu would know what it meant. Beautiful Flower did not. Next he would take Miss Hu to see his favorite Buddhist image, a transcendent representation of the ascending Buddha, the Miracle of the Double at Sravasti in the Seoul National Museum. Afterwards, he would dine with Miss Hu and then, with her expert help, *learn* new things and finally *see* angels without wings.

THE END

Post-End Addendum

On June 20, 2010, a previously healthy Professor Houghton dropped dead. His widow Hiroko Houghton had the seven jadeite carvings Dr. Houghton bought in Hong Kong and Korea in 1969 appraised as worth six million dollars. Hiroko Houghton used the money to endow the Reginald Houghton Professor of Oriental Studies at Harvard and the Reginald Houghton Professor of Endocrine Chemistry at Yale as per Reginald's wishes.

Although Hiroko Houghton never heard of or saw Yi Non'gae or the Kisaeng Miss Hu, three months after Reginald's death she received the following letter from Korea.

"House of Amaranth Flowers   September 20, 2010
Seoul, Korea

Dear Mrs. Houghton,

I want to express sincerest condolences on the death of Reginald. I have known him since 1969 when I helped Captain Houghton obtain the jadeite carvings. I am so much pleased they valued so much and you bought two professorships in his honorable name.

With all good wishes.

Sincerely,

Madam Hu"

Reynold Spector, M.D. is a retired senior executive and currently a Professor of Medicine. He is the author of two hundred scientific papers, a text book, and two novels, *Who Killed Apollo and Julian Augustus?* (2006), and *She Smiled on Constantinople* (2008). He resides in Colts Neck, New Jersey.